double
identity

double identity

A Novel by

Mayer Bendet

with

Hallie Cantor

Published by bp, Inc. Brooklyn, New York

DOUBLE IDENTITY

FIRST EDITION
First Impression — MARCH 1989

Published by
bp, Inc.
705 Foster Avenue
Brooklyn, New York 11230

ISBN 0—932351—22—0

Typography by bp, Inc.
Printed in the U.S.A.

Table of Contents

Chapter 1

The Terror

Midnight. Most of Boro Park lay asleep; the streets were dark and silent in the soft mid-winter night. On occasion a passing car was heard purring down the empty avenues.

In contrast, the Shapiro residence, nestled among the small homes and shops, echoed with noises: feverish cries in one room, the rustle of a boy turning nervously in bed in another.

Shimshon had been asleep until now. But as the sounds filtered through from the adjacent room, he lay restless and alert in bed. Unconsciously, he hugged the covers closer. Apprehensively, he listened. The grandfather clock in the hall struck twelve chimes.

"No! Stop!"

The voice, in a muffled Yiddish-Polish-English, grew more fervent. Shimshon opened his eyes, then shut them again, as if hoping in this way to obliterate the sound. In vain. The voice continued, finally dwindling down into a mournful murmur.

At last Shimshon opened his eyes again, allowing them to adjust gradually to the enveloping darkness. The blinds were a soft white, through which slivers of light penetrated from the nearby street lamp, creating a ghostly sheen off the photographs in the room. The closet, partially open, revealed clothing hung together in a huddled mass.

Shimshon clutched the covers, his eyes and ears now open wide, his heart pounding rapidly. Oh, please go back to sleep, Tati, he thought. Please, not tonight. Not again.

But the voice returned, this time pleading. "No! I can't do it. Please!"

Shimshon trembled. It was strange, in a way, to hear his father speaking Yiddish. His English, after thirty years of American citizenship, was excellent. However, there were occasions when he lapsed into the old dialect — while speaking with elderly Jews or with his friends from Poland.

Friends from Poland. A conversation had taken place the other day between Rabbi Yehuda Shapiro and a long-time friend, Mordechai Silverman. Shimshon happened to be nearby — trying not to listen, but his ears inquisitively catching snatches anyway. He saw the lines on his father's face crinkle and deepen, as if in pain — and somehow the boy saw, etched there, something ominous.

And now here, in the quiet night, he lay awake, sharing in his father's agony. It was as if they shared thoughts.

After an interminable period, the boy pushed back the covers and leaned forward, feet touching the floor. He washed his hands and went over to the window sill. He peered out from behind the blinds.

Outside, the tree branches rustled slightly in the breeze. A light was on in the house across the street. Shimshon knew the neighbor. Another friend of Ta's, he thought. Maybe he's also awake right now.

Shimshon tried to focus on the distant hum of a passing train, tried to black out any sound from his house. But it was not to be.

"Murderers! Leave me alone!"

This time, the intensity propelled Shimshon into the center of the room. He looked about anxiously, and in his semi-awake state, it occurred to him. Robbers in the house! They must be attacking Tati!

Quickly, Shimshon rushed into the other room. A passing car drowned out the hesitant creaking of the door, which finally gave way as Shimshon rushed in and shouted, "Ta, are you all right?"

But his father did not hear him. Moaning, he lay in bed. Though relieved not to find robbers, Shimshon remained in the room and watched the figure writhing under the covers. Silently, he approached him.

The cries, still punctuated with Yiddish expressions, died down. Shimshon sat at the foot of the bed. He took sad note of the oversized room — a painful reminder that there had once been another bed there. And he remembered his mother. She, too, had experienced nightmares.

The crying had at last metamorphosed into whimpers, and as the grandfather clock struck one, into silence. The hulking figure turned over in bed and breathed evenly.

Shimshon lingered a few more minutes, warily. When it seemed that his father was finally at rest, he sighed with relief and returned to his room.

Snuggling under his covers, he hoped he could pass the morning's Mishnah test despite his interrupted sleep. His thoughts returned to his father. If Ta only knew that it had been like this for quite some time. What does he dream about? Ima? The last time I saw him this way was when . . . maybe someone passed away. Someone I don't know about? Or did something else happen to Ta?

Something pretty terrible, Shimshon mused. I must speak to

him. I just can't wait anymore. Something's been on his mind. . . .

Shimshon felt the bed shake.

"Shimshon, wake up."

The boy opened his eyes. His father's face was a blur.

"Shimshon. You overslept."

"Huh? What time is it?"

"Eight. Hurry up. You'll be late for school."

"Can you drive me?"

His father sighed. "All right. But be ready *fast.* I have to be in the city by ten."

Shimshon rolled out of bed groggily. His father opened the blinds, allowing a flood of sunlight into the room. Shimshon squinted.

"Try not to make this a habit, Shimshon, okay?" Rabbi Shapiro prodded gently.

Shimshon caught his father's face as the latter turned to leave. For a moment there was — at least in Shimshon's imagination — a haunted look, a sadness. But it was a quick glimpse. Rabbi Shapiro was hastily out the door.

As Shimshon dressed slowly, he glanced around the room, which seemed to have undergone an almost unreal change in the interval between dark and dawn. The photographs on the wall, now recognizably of *tzaddikim,* Torah giants, smiled at him with protective reassurance. The closet was a cluttered hodgepodge of suits, jackets, and jeans; a pair of loafers stuck out, as if ready to walk away. On the shelf lay Shimshon's sets of Torah and Talmud; on the desk, his baseball glove, schoolbooks, prayer book, and Hebrew-English dictionary. While reciting his morning blessings, he added a mental note of thanks for getting through another taxing night.

The boy went downstairs. His father was not back yet from the synagogue, and Shimshon tried to calculate the time he had left for breakfast. Gathering his belongings, he playfully fingered the *tefillin* his father had given him for his twelfth birthday. Although he would not begin wearing them for another nine months, his father had wanted him to have the old pair now. Rabbi Shapiro had promised him a brand new set of his own, made in Israel, for his bar mitzvah. Shimshon smiled, knowing he would make his father proud, and he resolved not to oversleep in the future. A year from now he could not get away with praying late. He would have to *daven* with a *minyan*.

Thoughts of his bar mitzvah made him especially excited whenever he was in his father's *shul*. He felt increasingly at home there among the worshipers, many of them his father's friends from Poland.

Friends from Poland. Again Shimshon's mind returned to the previous night, and his father's dreams. He realized that now was the opportunity, with his father taking him to school, to discuss the matter.

Just then, the front door opened. Rabbi Shapiro put down his *tefillin* bag and stood by the door, car keys in hand. "Ready, Shimshon?"

The boy nodded and grabbed his school bag. He hurried out the door and into the bright blue Pontiac. He waited while his father circled the car and entered from the driver's side.

Not until they were along Eighteenth Avenue did the rabbi notice his son fidgeting. "Why are you so nervous, Shimshon?" he asked.

Shimshon looked away, feeling awkward. "I have a test today."

"In what?"

"Mishnah."

"I'm sure you'll do just fine."

Silence. The boy watched the rest of Boro Park waking up. Housewives with baby carriages straggled by. Men in dark-colored business suits were seen leaving the various synagogues.

His father turned left onto Sixtieth Street and said, "I had a talk yesterday with Mordechai Silverman."

Shimshon turned his head. "What did he want, Ta?"

"Well . . . this might be premature, mind you, but . . ."

"Yes?" the boy asked anxiously.

"We might have the opportunity to be away for Pesach."

"Oh." Shimshon's face fell.

"Mordechai's cousin Gedalia invited us."

"Yeah, that's nice," Shimshon answered flatly.

His father looked at him, surprised. "You sound disappointed, Shimshon. I thought you liked Monsey."

"Oh, why, yes."

"You told me yourself you wanted to go to high school there. Am I correct?"

"Yeah."

"Well, aren't you excited to spend Pesach there?"

"Well, yeah . . . it's just that . . ." Shimshon squirmed, brushing his right hand through his hair. "I kind of liked it here last Pesach."

His father shook his head uncomprehendingly. "I should think most boys would be glad for the opportunity to be out of New York," he remarked. "And you, especially. It would be a healthy change. You've been through so much here."

"I guess you're right," Shimshon said, sighing.

"Anyway," his father continued, "it's not definite. Gedalia's daughter is expecting around that time, and he might end up in Cleveland for Pesach, especially if there's a *bris*. His first grandchild."

"Well, that's exciting," Shimshon responded brightly.

"Especially for Gedalia." His father was silent. Then he added, "He has little family left."

The car was slowed by Ocean Parkway traffic. From the distance Shimshon saw the yeshiva building. "You can drop me off here, Ta," he said. "With this traffic, I may as well walk."

"It's clearing. Just hang on. Save your energy for the test." With steady hands his father guided the car through the traffic. Shimshon took the opportunity to study his father's features. A sad face — youthful, though in late middle age, framed by a trimmed beard once dark brown but now lightly shot through with gray. Shimshon loved to compare the resemblance between his father and himself. Though he was pale, like his mother, his blond hair was turning dark, like his father's, and his face was acquiring the same pensiveness. Occasionally Shimshon searched in the mirror for other similarities.

What a contrast — noted the boy — between the man behind the wheel and the man underneath the covers. It was as if there were two people existing in a single body, and one of them was an imposter. Shimshon honestly did not know at this point who the real Yehuda Shapiro was.

His father kept his eyes ahead. Other than a certain tiredness, there was nothing — no reminder whatsoever of what he had gone through last night.

Suddenly aware that his son was watching him, the rabbi asked, "Is something the matter, Shimshon?"

"No, no," Shimshon answered quickly.

"You were looking at me rather strangely. Are you all right?"

"I'm fine," Shimshon replied, looking away.

His father glanced at him quickly and said, "Sometimes . . . we're just not ourselves."

Shimshon withdrew. It just wasn't the time to talk. Not yet.

At last the Pontiac pulled up in front of the yeshiva building. Another boy Shimshon's age was racing up the front steps. "Hey, Zev, wait up!" he called. Grabbing his bag, he turned to his father and said, "Bye, Ta."

"Take care, Shimmy," answered the rabbi. "Good luck on the test."

"Thanks."

Shimshon hurried up the walkway. Zev Trotz was waiting at the entrance.

"I'm glad I'm not the only one who's late," said Shimshon breathlessly.

"You could have at least given me a ride to school," Zev remarked, laughing, as they walked together through the hallway. A passing rabbi eyed them sternly.

"So why are you late?" Shimshon asked.

"My brother-in-law called this morning," Zev explained. "Chani had a baby."

"Wow, hey, mazel tov!" Shimshon exclaimed. "Boy or girl?"

"Boy," his friend answered proudly. "Another nephew."

"Mazel tov," Shimshon repeated. "That's really super. So the *bris* is Tuesday?"

"Yeah," answered Zev, "but it'll be in Far Rockaway. And why are *you* late?"

Shimshon was silent. He wished he could be somebody's uncle

and use that as an excuse. He sighed. "Overslept." Then he added jokingly, as they neared the classroom, "Must have thought of you."

The class was well into *shacharis*, the morning prayer. The principal, Rabbi Sender Fein, frowned as he saw the latecomers slink in the back door. Smiling apologetically, they took out their *siddurim.*

Somehow, Shimshon sensed that his prayers were not being said with the proper concentration. He just seemed unable to focus his thoughts on them — and part of the reason had to do with Zev, although he couldn't quite fathom why. It was just that sometimes he envied his friend, with eight brothers and sisters, while he, Shimshon, was an only son. Of course it made him feel special in a way, knowing how much his father loved him. For this reason, it also made him deeply attuned to his father's moods, as if the two of them were sharing a burden. When his father was happy, Shimshon was happy — in fact, ecstatic. When his father was sad — as he had often been lately — Shimshon was deeply distraught. And now, having been kept up half the night because of his father, he felt this bond more strongly than ever.

The congratulations to Zev kept Rabbi Fein from staying angry too long with the boys. Shimshon was glad to have been let in on the good news before anyone else.

At recess, Shimshon's mind began to wander back. He had been born late in his parents' lives. They had wanted children desperately — not only so that they might fulfill the commandment to bear children, but to rebuild their shattered lives. Having offspring was an affirmation that Hitler had failed. But somehow, childbearing didn't come easily to Faige Sarah Shapiro. One child, a girl, had died in infancy. It seemed as if G-d was still testing them, even after everything they had undergone. Finally, in 1972, they went to see a famous rebbe for a blessing. A year later, Shimshon was born. He was named after his maternal grandfather, who had perished in Auschwitz. The rest of Shimshon's family was small. His aunt — his father's sister, Tzvia Rochel, who survived Bergen-Belsen — was now in Israel; his father's brother, Chaim Yosef, who had spent part of the war in a cellar, now lived in Baltimore. These relatives, who had managed to marry and produce a large number of children, were now themselves grandparents. Their offspring and grandchildren were all named after deceased brothers, sisters, aunts, uncles, cousins, nieces, nephews, and whatever else. Shimshon, the "miracle baby," remained the sole representative of Yehuda and Faige Sarah Shapiro.

Shimshon's birth, though a source of great joy, was a cause of physical strain for his mother. Already past forty years of age, she had been weakened by her experiences. Shimshon remembered her as chronically sad and tired, holding him weakly in her thin arms and whispering to him. They never discussed the Holocaust in front of him — she and his father. The past was taboo. But at night the boy often heard the sobbing in the other room.

Later on, she had become sick. That, too, was never discussed in the open. The disease was a blur to him — and at the tender age of eight, he probably could not understand. Nevertheless, watching his mother deteriorate, he knew that something was terribly wrong. In two years' time she grew too sick and listless to even hold him — leaving him instead with Mrs. Friedman, the housekeeper. When she wasn't in bed, she dragged herself around the house, mumbling to herself and sometimes even crying.

His father was the only one, besides himself, to sit *shivah;* none of her own family was left after the war. Mrs. Friedman cooked for them while Shimshon's friends from the yeshiva came to visit.

Over the past two years, the other boys had treated him with special kindness. Shimshon didn't mind feeling different from them — he always had, anyway. Nevertheless, he made friends easily. He was immediately drawn to the stocky, wisecracking Zev — who, in turn, took the motherless boy under his wing, inviting him frequently for Shabbos, and even during the week. Shimshon, in turn, helped Zev with his schoolwork, for his friend was not a good studier. Shimshon made a mental note to buy Chani a baby gift.

Though he got along well with his friends, Shimshon preferred being with his father. Even before his mother was sick, the two of them, father and son, had clung to one another; certainly now they needed each other even more. To Rabbi Shapiro, Shimshon was more than a son. The boy was a survivor, just like himself — each had suffered in his own right.

In time they grew even more protective of one another. Whenever Shimshon was late getting home from school or his friends' houses, his father worried. Whenever his father was late, Shimshon was petrified. He tried to imagine what it would be like to be an orphan, in the world by himself. He had often had nightmares of his own — terrifying dreams of being hunted, dreams that jolted him awake in a cold sweat. To awake one day and actually find himself abandoned was even more frightening.

"Anything wrong, Shimshon?"

Shimshon looked up from the playground bench. Zev was standing there, basketball in hand.

"Don't you want to play?" he asked.

"Don't really feel like it," Shimshon answered evasively. "I'll sit this game out. Still kind of tired from last night."

Zev nodded sympathetically. He understood Shimshon well enough. "Okay," he said. "Maybe later you can help me study for the test."

"Sure."

During lunch he reviewed the Mishnayos with Zev, and both passed the exams — Shimshon with flying colors. Immediately he forgot his sadness — especially when his rebbe congratulated him. Rabbi Fein added that he might be able to represent their class at the upcoming Pirchei Agudas Yisrael convention.

Shimshon enjoyed the rest of the day. Before lunch, school had seemed to drag like a wet cloth. Now he found that he could even sit through English. By six-thirty, when the school bell rang, the class groaned in relief and Shimshon grabbed his books.

The school bus was rowdy. While Zev was still receiving congratulations on the birth of his new nephew, Shimshon sat by the window, dreamily watching the passing trees, and wondering how to approach his father. Should he be direct, or simply wait till the next night and wake him during a nightmare? By the time the bus pulled up in front of his block, he decided that dinner would be the best time for a talk.

Shimshon hurried up the steps, keys in hand, and opened the door.

"Hi, Ta," he called.

No answer. The boy looked around. In the kitchen he heard the sound of dishes. There was a place setting for one.

Mrs. Friedman did not bother to turn around until Shimshon asked, "Where's my father?"

"He called an hour ago to say that he would be home late," she explained in a heavy East European accent.

Shimshon was crestfallen. "But he's not supposed to be late."

"Sometimes he just is, Shimshon. These things happen."

"Did he say why he would be late?"

"No," answered the housekeeper with a trace of annoyance. "Look, Shimshon, don't make a big deal out of it, all right? Sometimes people have to be away. That's life. That's part of being an adult. I made you a nice supper. Why don't you sit down and eat? Later you can go see Zev. Besides, maybe he'll get home early after all. You know that sometimes his schedule changes at a moment's notice."

Sulking, the boy sat down. Just then the phone rang. He ran to answer it.

It was his father. "Uh . . . Shimshon?" he said. "Did Mrs. Friedman give you the message?"

"Yes," answered the boy.

"Sorry I can't be there right now, but I'm stuck here for the moment."

His tone of voice worried Shimshon.

"Where are you?" his son asked.

"At a friend's home. Not far at all from the house."

"What happened?"

"Nothing . . . nothing," answered his father, with Mrs. Friedman's trace of annoyance. "Just some business matters. How was the test?"

"It went great! My rebbe thinks I can be in the Pirchei convention."

"That's exciting!" said his father. "I knew you'd do all right. I couldn't see why you were so nervous. Listen . . . I don't know when I'll be home, so don't count on me tonight for help with Mishnayos. Think you can manage?"

"Yeah," he answered.

"Fine. I'll be home as early as I can. And I'm really sorry."

"Sure. Bye, Ta." Sullenly, Shimshon put down the receiver.

Shimshon ate the food off the heaping plate that Mrs. Friedman had prepared for him. Over and over the memories of the previous night danced in his head. Somehow, they seemed connected to the phone voice — the same tightness and agitation. The vagueness over why Tati was late. The secretiveness, the fear — like a child being locked in a box, with those on the outside trying to hide it from the neighbors. Then Shimshon grunted. Just imagining things. Probably Ta was having problems with work. Maybe that was making him so upset.

Shimshon realized that he was being more protective toward his father than his father was toward him. The two of them, Rabbi Shapiro and Mrs. Friedman, had practically raised him. For this reason the rabbi was rarely home late. And whenever he was, there was an upfront, logical explanation. It wasn't like him to be secretive.

Still, Shimshon was angry at his father for not being home. Rabbi Shapiro was always there for him, as if on special command. The empty house, with its gaping rooms, bothered him. And after Mrs. Friedman left, Shimshon felt even more desolate. Silently he finished his dinner and washed the dishes.

Sitting on the sofa, he casually practiced the *Haftarah* reading for his bar mitzvah. His Torah portion was *Parshas Yisro*. In his speech, his *drasha*, he would talk about the Ten Commandments. He thought of the obligation to honor one's parents — and its impact hit hard.

At times like this, after dinner, Rabbi Shapiro would sit and learn with him. Taking a Gemara, he would listen to Shimshon recite the Aramaic passages. Often he interrupted with commentary — or even with just an interesting, related story about his years spent studying in Bnei Brak, where he had received *semicha*, rabbinic ordination. He had attended a *kollel*, a yeshiva for married men, and had been recognized as the best student among his group. Those were relatively happy years for the Shapiros, after their tragic existence in Poland. They didn't meet and marry till after the war, when the rabbi was studying in Jerusalem and Faige Sarah was a teacher in an elementary school. By the time Shimshon was born, they had moved to Brooklyn, where his father had his own *shul*. During the week, Rabbi Shapiro ran a successful export business. In the growing Boro Park community, he was highly respected for his Torah study as well as his philanthropy; his home became a meeting place for Torah giants, rebbes, and simple Jews alike. Rabbi Shapiro was always on the go — to Torah lectures, conferences, appointments. Somehow, though, he always found time for his son.

Often, besides being a tutor, Rabbi Shapiro was a counselor to Shimshon — giving the boy comfort and advice. Counselor, friend, surrogate mother, or just a crutch — he was everything tied up in one package. No wonder the boy missed him terribly when he was away.

Nine o'clock. Shimshon fingered the pages of his book nervously. He remembered that he had a history quiz, and more Mishnayos to learn. He wondered: Should he wait for his father, or go ahead and study? Was he still in Boro Park, or did he have to go back to the office? Should he call his father at work? He reached for the phone, then pulled back. No, his father might be angry at Shimshon for disturbing him — or for not trusting him.

Shimshon asked himself: Why shouldn't he trust his father? Why *did* Shimshon want to call? To "check up" on him? Why should he doubt his father?

And besides, his father was probably elsewhere. He might be on his way home now. Or, he might have gone to yet another place — a friend, or business acquaintance. Rabbi Shapiro himself never knew what his schedule might be. He often gave *shiurim*, Torah lectures, sometimes on very short notice.

It was 10:30 when Shimshon finally got to bed. He listened for the sound of the Pontiac in the driveway. He tried desperately to assure himself that all was well. Tati is on the way home, he thought. He's safe. Most likely he had to meet with clients. Or students. Or friends. Friends from Poland. Everything is all right.

At 12:07, Shimshon was awakened by a roaring motor under his window. He jumped out of bed in a flash and peeked through the blinds.

His father was leaving the driver's seat. His face, illuminated under the street lamp, had the reflective look of a person lost in a distant world. He walked up the driveway, holding his briefcase.

Shimshon raced down the stairs. His father was startled. "Shimshon," he asked, "why aren't you asleep?"

"I heard you coming, Ta," replied the boy. "I woke up. You had me so worried. I was afraid you wouldn't come home."

"Nothing is wrong," said his father, a mixture of surprise and annoyance registering in his voice. "That mind of yours, Shimshon. I told you I would be late. Now go to sleep. I'm not driving you to school tomorrow, so you'd better get up on time."

"Abba, you're *never* home this late," Shimshon argued. "Never. I don't think you were working the whole time. Where were you?"

"I don't think that's any of your business, Shimshon," his father answered crossly. "I happen to be very busy — that's all. Do I ask you where you spend *your* day? Now, please. Go to bed. It's late."

Morosely, Shimshon turned to leave. Halfway up the stairs he stopped and faced his father. "Ta?" he said.

Rabbi Shapiro was putting away his coat. "What is it *now*, Shimshon?"

"Did something happen lately?"

The rabbi snapped, "Shimshon, I am not in the mood for this. Please. Go to sleep."

Timidly, Shimshon continued. "Ta, do you know why I overslept this morning?"

"Why?"

"Last night I woke up around this time." After a pause, he said, "I heard you crying in your sleep."

His father paled.

Shimshon continued. "Not just crying. Screaming; saying things in Yiddish. I couldn't understand everything, but I heard things like, 'Murderers, leave me alone.' You were tossing and turning. I . . . I went to your room and watched you. I didn't know whether to wake you or not. You seemed so scared."

Nervously, the rabbi answered, "So I had a bad dream. It happens to all of us. And I'm sorry I woke you. We'll both sleep better tonight."

Shimshon swallowed. "Ta," he said, "this wasn't the first time. Uh . . . last week, twice. And many times before. I never wanted to say anything before. But I couldn't help wondering . . . was it about the war?"

Trembling, his father asked, "Why the war, Shimshon?"

" 'Cause Ima used to talk in her sleep too. And she used to cry, just like you do. I never could get her to talk about it. But sometimes your friends told me stories — like Mordechai Silverman. And I know you were talking to him a lot yesterday." Shimshon crouched by the banister. "Ta, it *was* about the war, wasn't it?"

His father took a deep breath. Averting his face, he pushed back the tears. Then he studied his son, who was staring innocently at him. The boy had grown taller over the last few months. A year from now he would be a man, according to Jewish law. He was so much like a man already. The rabbi remembered his own bar mitzvah, in Warsaw — a makeshift ceremony, with a few friends brave enough to come. Shimshon had grown up quickly, just like him. There was a lot he had to know. A lot he was learning on his own.

With a deep sigh, the rabbi said, "I think we need to talk, Shimshon."

Chapter 2

The Survivor

Ignoring the lateness of the hour, the rabbi motioned his son to the living room. Shimshon seated himself on the brown leather couch, while his father sat facing him, on a red wing chair. The rabbi's eyes, moist with tears, appeared deep in thought, probing the dark corridor of memories.

"Shimshon," he began carefully, "tell me what you know about the war."

The boy fidgeted. He didn't like being tested. "Well . . . the Germans killed a lot of Jews . . . six million, right? And the Jews were put in concentration camps and gas chambers. That's what we learned in school."

"What does the word 'Holocaust' mean to you?"

The boy swallowed. He didn't expect to have to give over his knowledge of something which had always seemed hazy to him.

Finally he mumbled, "I think Hashem was angry at the Jews."

"Do you think He was angry at your mother and me?"

The boy was shocked, speechless. He couldn't conceive of his parents misbehaving in any way.

"Do you think we did something wrong?" his father persisted.

Bewildered, the boy thought for a moment, then answered, "Well, He had to be angry at the Jews for a reason. I mean . . .

why else did so many of them have to die?"

Rabbi Shapiro trembled with indignation. He had to remind himself that Shimshon was just a boy. Nevertheless, his son had given a stock explanation for history's most horrendous act. He must have learned that in school, too.

"That's it?"

"Well, that's what I've heard."

"When I was your age, Shimshon," he said, "I watched a sister die of typhus in the Warsaw Ghetto. She was six-years-old. I still wonder why she had to die — a child of six! What could she have possibly done to deserve death? And later, when my parents were dragged off to the trains, never to be seen again, I wondered the same thing. My father, who never missed a *minyan* — and my mother, who gave her own food to others even when she herself was starving. Deep down I knew they had not done anything wrong. Can you understand now what the Holocaust was?"

"Sort of . . ." the boy trailed off, confused and irritated. He knew what his father was driving at, but somehow he just couldn't verbalize it. The idea of people being killed in mass numbers, for no apparent reason, just didn't make sense. There *had* to be a reason — we just didn't see it. Shimshon knew that G-d punished the wicked. That was all. No one ever bothered to explain to him why righteous people had to die also.

"Shimshon, you can't understand what the Holocaust was! You can't because I can't, and I was there! It is impossible to explain the unexplainable. But I'll try to at least give you a taste of what happened."

Shimshon began to fidget.

Rabbi Shapiro took a deep breath. "Do you know what it's like to be hunted and killed just for being Jewish?"

"No," whispered the boy.

"I do," answered the rabbi solemnly. "And your mother. We were there."

Rabbi Shapiro continued. "Both of us — your mother and I — were forced to watch our loved ones die off, one by one. I was luckier than she, at least. I have some family left."

"Yes," Shimshon answered. Three, from a family of ten.

"I met your mother later, after the war," continued the rabbi.

"I know," Shimshon answered. His mother, Faige Sarah — orphaned, and all alone — had befriended an Orthodox couple in a displaced persons camp, and clung to them. The couple, who had lost all of their six children, treated her like a daughter. The three of them attempted to enter Palestine illegally once, in early 1947, and were forced back by British patrol boats. The second time, six months later, they succeeded. Crawling their way through the Lebanese hills, in mud and intense heat, sleeping in open trenches, they finally made it to Jerusalem. Faige Sarah, then seventeen, suffered her second bout with typhus — the first time had been in the Lodz Ghetto. Even when she was young, sickness was her constant nemesis. During the War of Independence, she had lived through more fighting, as well as food shortages.

Yehuda Shapiro had already made it to Palestine — in June 1946. When the Red Army came to Auschwitz a year-and-a-half earlier, he had weighed eighty pounds, and lay delirious in the infirmary. Under the care of Russian doctors, he painfully convalesced and remained in the camp, smart enough to know that the Poles still hated the Jews. Later, after being reunited with the surviving members of his family — Chaim Yosef and Tzvia Rochel — he was able to make his way vertically through the

European continent, arriving in Turkey. From there he sailed to Palestine in a fishing boat.

The first thing he and Chaim Yosef wanted to do, once their feet touched the Holy Land, was to find the nearest yeshiva. They were determined to make up for the six lost years — to inundate themselves with study, to immerse themselves once again in the waters of the Torah. Perhaps these waters would help heal the scars. In the yeshiva, they met other survivors — all with the same thirst, and the same faith, that had sustained the brothers during those terrible years. All had the same fervor, the same intensity for learning and for restoring its citadels, so violently uprooted in Europe.

After the War of Independence, in which Yehuda Shapiro was a gun runner, he returned to his beloved yeshiva, nestled in the Meah She'arim section of Jerusalem. A year later, he met his wife.

This much Shimshon knew about his parents. They had always enjoyed telling him about their life in Israel and their involvement in the Torah communities there. However, their lives before 1945 remained vague to him. They seldom divulged anything to Shimshon — and even when they did, it was never directly. But Shimshon had been around them long enough to sense that they were inexorably different from the adults he knew who had not suffered in Europe.

Though socially active, his mother and father clung to each other, one never going to an affair or event without the other. Their social clique consisted of fellow survivors, most of them from Poland. It was easy to understand what had brought them together: the ordeal of living with stress for so many years. Ima's eyes — how could Shimshon forget? He always wondered: Why did Ima look so sad? And Ta was often so moody. And their friends — Shimshon noticed how they, too, all looked tense, even afraid. Us against them. It was obvious that they not only shared the same experiences, but the same world. These people had all spent years living with awful memories.

"Your mother was never well after that," Rabbi Shapiro explained. "Neither in Israel, nor here. The years of living with fear, hunger, and sickness never left her. The joy in her life was when you were born. But she didn't live to see you grow up."

He sobbed silently. He was crying not only for the loss of his wife, but for his generation — and a communal loss of normality and happiness.

At last he continued. "We tried to shelter you," he said. "We didn't want to upset you. We thought we were doing you a favor. We felt you were too young to know. Too young to understand. Even now I know I can't really make you feel what happened."

"Ta," asked Shimshon, "how bad *was* it?"

"Try to imagine waking up every morning wondering if you'll be alive at the end of the day. Or watching your family and friends scrambling to hide from the latest round-up. Or living on a crust of bread for three days. Then you'll begin to understand what we experienced."

After a moment of silence, he went on. "I once saw a baby snatched out of her mother's arms by a soldier. He smashed her head with a rifle butt."

Shimshon looked away in disgust.

"I *saw* it, Shimshon!" his father exclaimed. "You don't believe me? What if I told you I was made to stand in the freezing rain, wearing only a cotton shirt? Or that your mother hid in a rat-infested bunker for two weeks? Those were everyday occurrences, Shimshon — like your going to school in the morning. Does that answer your question, Shimshon?"

Shimshon was silent. Now he understood why he couldn't be told. There was no calm, casual way. He had been thankfully shielded from their nightmares. And his parents had six years' worth.

"In a world like that, Shimshon," his father said, "it's ridiculous to wonder what it was you did wrong. The whole world was wrong. But it was also frightening and painful — completely unreal and insane. Trying to explain why Hashem made it happen is impossible. Yes, Hashem had a reason. Yes, the Jews of Germany had become very assimilated, and that certainly had something to do with it. But to truly understand the Holocaust in concrete terms — as it relates to my family, my friends, and to the millions who were killed — there is no way to understand.

"So what are we left with? I can tell you what happened. We were fighting — fighting to stay alive, fighting to get an extra soup ration — too busy fighting to stop and understand such things. All I understood was that I was cold and hungry all the time . . . and that everyone around me was being wiped out. One lived for the moment. And if you were lucky to get by one more day, you were a survivor."

The grandfather clock struck one, but neither of them noticed. Rabbi Shapiro leaned back, as if after a long, strenuous battle. He had exhausted his strength, but not his anger. "Perhaps it would be useless to explain everything, Shimshon. The world forgets, the younger ones don't know. . . . *Ach!* No one can ever understand what it was like."

"But Ta," Shimshon argued, "you were saved. That was a miracle."

His father sighed. "Yes, I was saved. And I know that there was

30

a reason for it. I imagine every Yehuda Shapiro feels the same way. Ask any one of us, Shimshon, and he'll tell you: we're 'different' on the inside, we're 'special.' Because we survived such an experience. The physical torture is gone, but the mental torture lives on. And I'm not just speaking of the memories.

"Boro Park alone is full of survivors. Most of us have successfully rebuilt our lives here. Homes, fortunes . . . Hashem rewarded many of us. We fought to keep our lives; once free, we strove to rebuild them. You see me — comfortable, honored, financially well off. Rebbes, people arriving from Israel to collect money, even politicians come to me for advice and financial support. And I give generously to them. It makes me proud to support such causes; many of us give fervently of ourselves. Forty years ago I didn't even think I'd be alive today, let alone successful. I'm grateful. And in staying proudly Jewish, I feel as though I'm paying back a debt to the Jewish world that we lost. My friends, also. Most of them have done well, and outwardly appear normal. But there's always a reminder of where we were . . . what we have to do . . . and why Hashem kept us alive. By remaining committed Jews, we are striking the largest blow we can at the Nazi idea."

He pulled up his sleeve. There, near the elbow, was the blue tattoo.

"This, Shimshon, is our reminder. A reminder that can never be erased. A sort of 'club membership,' so to speak. And in fact, we meet periodically . . . a group of us."

"Your friends?" asked Shimshon.

"Yes. Many of them I knew even before the war — in Poland. A few came from elsewhere. But we all ended up in the same places. And we meet to discuss those places, and to make sure that

31

they are never duplicated here. We feel that we are alive simply to prevent another Holocaust from occurring."

"Do you really think it can happen again, Ta?" Shimshon asked. "Here in America?"

His father eyed him keenly. "And why don't you think it could happen again?" he asked.

"Well . . . you are always telling me how lucky I am to be American," Shimshon answered. This love for America had been drilled into him early. His father always strove to remain politically aware. On Shabbos, his synagogue's policy was to say a prayer for the government. And while everyone dutifully joined in, he prayed with special fervor. Shimshon's parents had never stopped talking about America — its Constitution, and its protection of citizens' rights. Any crackpot group, any threat from foreign powers, any kind of criticism alarmed them. With the exception of Israel, they believed America to be the best place in the world for Jews.

Shimshon thought of himself growing up in New York. He was born and raised in Boro Park, and spent most of his time here. To him, the whole world was Jewish. He went to Jewish schools, shopped at Jewish stores, played with Jewish friends, read Jewish books. Somehow, even though he loved the United States, being American was secondary. It was certainly a part of him, but it was something taken for granted.

Yes, this was the "Land of Opportunity." Yes, he was free to practice his religion — but it wasn't something he thought about day and night. He never had to appreciate it. He was neither taunted nor threatened by non-Jews — at least not in the same way as his father had been in Poland.

Only when he ventured out of Brooklyn was he reminded —

and with great reluctance — that he was living in the diaspora. But he had little to do with it. To Shimshon, ninety-nine percent of the United States was a desert, the sprinkled Jewish communities filling in the other one percent. Anti-Semitism seemed something distant, something unreal. "It can't happen here." This was a phrase the boy had heard many times from others. He simply could not see how.

His father said, "And we're lucky that in America we can help keep the world safe for Jews. Safe for you and your friends. Because people like myself, Mordechai Silverman, and others do what we can to keep it that way. We meet periodically — not only to remind ourselves of the past and the necessity to avoid its reoccurrence, but also to track down Nazi criminals and bring them to justice. Justice, Shimshon — that's what every survivor craves. We research files, reports — even other survivors — for news of ex-Nazis on the loose. And there are quite a few left, Shimshon — even here in America. Do you know how many slipped through here *legally*, because they were needed by the U.S. Government? And how they've been allowed to get away with what they did? Yes, it can happen here — if we are not careful."

His father's voice rose. "And as long as those people are loose, we'll continue to work together."

Then he lowered his voice and said, "That's where I was tonight."

Shimshon blinked. "With your friends, Ta?"

His father nodded. "You are not aware of what is happening now in New York. A few men have been sighted . . . some very 'special' men."

"Special?" Shimshon asked.

His father nodded again. "They are not only ex-Nazis, but they were once very prominent men in the SS."

Shimshon leaned forward, excited. "Storm troopers, right?"

"Yes. My friends recognized them immediately — in a passing car. And they're running freely here. They were seen in midtown Manhattan twice, a week ago."

"Uh huh," Shimshon said. He remembered. Twice last week his father had been screaming in his sleep.

"Yesterday, Mordechai saw an important Nazi in a passing car — right here in Boro Park."

Trembling, Shimshon thought of the phone call the previous day . . . and the look on his father's face. Was the decision to ship him off to Monsey for Pesach a reaction? A way of protecting him? They did not want him to get involved. Perhaps his father felt that both their lives were in danger.

"We had an emergency meeting tonight," his father continued. "We discussed what measures are to be taken."

"The men in the car," Shimshon said. "Who were they?"

"I'll tell you about one of them. This man, Shimshon, I had the pleasure of meeting at Auschwitz." He pulled back his other sleeve to reveal a faded, pink scar near his wrist. "Lighted cigarette. When you see Gedalia in Monsey, he can show you the scar near his forehead. He was beaten unconscious with a cane and left for dead in a ditch. I pulled him out when I realized he was still breathing."

Shimshon whistled in disbelief. Trying to visualize the greatest evil was tough.

"Who was he?" he repeated.

"A man obsessed with killing Jews. Even long after the German defeat. I suppose," his father added with a wry laugh, "you might call him a survivor, also. He outfoxed them all — victims, Allies, everyone. And he remains just as committed to his cause as we are to ours. Only he has far greater manpower and resources than we do. And even greater respectability."

"I don't understand, Ta."

Outside a passing motor was heard. Both of them stopped to listen. They felt a certain relief as the sound faded away.

"This man, Shimshon, was one of the many who escaped undergoing the Nuremberg trials. Since then, he has done very well for himself — they all did."

"They?"

"Him and his pack. They work with scientists, generals, world leaders — remarkable, really, their contribution to modern technology. They're the ones who help design weapons and put them into the hands of terrorists the world over. And they operate with international protection."

"But how can they get away with it?" Shimshon asked, incredulous.

"There are plenty of countries interested enough in their services to let bygones be bygones. Even ours. Plenty who need German technology, German science.

"Amazing, the German mind," he mused darkly. "They live very well in those countries — thanks to us."

"Thanks to us?" Shimshon asked. "Jews?"

"Yes," his father answered flatly. "With the money they stole from us."

"How much did they steal?" Shimshon asked. It was fantastic — a network of bandits who could still terrorize the world, and at the expense of those who suffered the most from them. The victims, burned or buried in countless graves, remained the source of their power and obsession. Hadn't he been taught that evil people — *resha'im* — were punished and destroyed? How could the Nazis still be allowed to live? It just didn't make sense. Even more senseless was the idea that the war was, after a fashion, still going on.

To Shimshon, the Holocaust was history. Chalk up another tragedy for the Jews. But they had triumphed over evil. The Holocaust was finished, over. The Germans were defeated. Now Jews had their own state, their rebirth. They had G-d's special protection. But here his father was insisting that someday a new nation could arise from this gang of Nazis, and a new Holocaust as well. It was just too much.

"They stole billions of dollars. We don't know the precise amount, but it is enough that they wield considerable power."

The boy shook his head. "Ta," he said, "I know you've been through a lot, and I can see how it really bothers you. But I think you worry too much. It won't happen again. It *can't*. Besides, by now these Nazis are old men. They'll die soon."

"And their generation," his father sighed. "And the Jews will be the first to forget. Until the same thing happens again . . . only differently, this time."

As a sort of afterthought, Rabbi Shapiro asked, "Why do you think we celebrate Purim?"

Shimshon paused. It occurred to him that the holiday was not too far away. Then he answered, "To show how Hashem destroys the enemies of the Jews." He seemed pleased with his answer. "And He'll destroy them again."

"But possibly at the expense of Jewish lives as well," his father answered mournfully. "On Purim, at least, no Jews were killed. Why do we have to study the past? To guard the future. And that is why we must not forget."

"And that's why you lose sleep? Worrying that we might forget?"

His father sighed, frustrated that his son could minimalize his fears, even after everything that had just been told to him.

"Shimshon," he explained, "when you've lived through my experiences, you can never forget. In public I hide the past. I can suppress it and go about my everyday business. But I think of the Holocaust at least once a day. Of some act of brutality, or some relative who perished, or some friend screaming. I am haunted, Shimshon. At night, especially. Then, when I'm asleep, that part of my brain takes over. Sometimes I feel as though there are two people inside me, like Yaakov and Esav — each fighting for control. Only, both are Yehuda Shapiro. I was in the war, Shimshon — a war against the Jews. And I am still at war. I have the need to fight the battles for my people. And I will not be at peace until I win."

The clock struck two. Shimshon yawned.

"I think it's way past somebody's bedtime," the rabbi said. He was once again the doting father. He sighed. "Well, looks like I'll have to drive you to school again tomorrow."

The boy grinned sheepishly. He rose.

" 'Night, Ta. I didn't mean to be so nosy."

"No, no, son. Our talk was long overdue. I see now that all this was disturbing you."

"At least now I know certain things."

"Are you satisfied?"

"Sort of." The boy stretched. "Sorry for keeping you up."

His father smiled. "Good night, son. Sleep well."

"No, *you* sleep well, Ta. Please. Maybe now that you've talked about it we can both sleep better."

"I'm sure one of us will sleep better."

Chapter 3

One Friday Night

The weeks passed, as 1984 slid into early March. There were no more late night discussions — only a desire of both father and son to go about their everyday lives.

However, it was impossible to pretend that nothing was wrong. In a way it was a relief for both that Shimshon knew what his father was going through; the night they had talked had broken the bubble of silence, and at last allowed the tears to flow freely. Though talking to his son did alleviate some of the tension, Rabbi Shapiro nevertheless continued to groan and quiver in bed. He would make a joke of it. In the morning, when he saw his son sleepy-eyed, he would ask, embarrassed, "Did something keep you up again?"

Often the rabbi invited Shimshon to sleep in his room. There, the boy's peaceful, innocent breathing put his father's mind to rest. Also, it enabled Shimshon to understand his father's world.

Shimshon learned that his father had had these dreams from the start. Long before Shimshon was born, long before the Shapiros came to the United States, in 1955 — these dreams had occurred even before the Russians came and liberated Auschwitz, ten years earlier. It was as if the rabbi still mentally spent part of his life behind barbed wire.

Shimshon's mother had been helpless to stop the nightmares. She had suffered her own share, which were later mingled with thoughts of illness and death. She had always been haggard and weak, even before she became sick. Nevertheless, casting aside her own problems, she had tried to comfort her husband and fight off his horde of visions. Though husband and wife had separate experiences during the war, they were united, even before they had ever met, through mutual suffering and woe. Only a survivor could really understand another survivor. They knew they were fighting a common enemy — those who hate the Jews.

Moreover, they were not just waging the battle at night. During the day, Faige Sarah was very active in her husband's work. In fact, they had organized the Holocaust survivors' group together. Together they had attended the meetings — read the same reports, the same files on Nazi criminals. She had been just as obsessed with justice as he. And the rabbi, in her presence, felt strong, able to express his stream of consciousness. Now, with her gone, the floodgate of memories had again burst open, with nothing to help hold back the torrent.

The sight of his father, alone and vulnerable like a ship lost at sea, touched Shimshon deeply. He knew he could not take his mother's place; yet he yearned to help his father — to share in his battles and burdens. He began to develop an interest in his father's work.

The more Shimshon tried to understand his father, the more intense his fascination with the Holocaust became. Beforehand, his knowledge of the subject was scanty. It was confined mainly to stories in a children's magazine and elsewhere — usually of the exertion displayed and sacrifices made by concentration camp prisoners to perform G-d's commandments, even in the worst circumstances. Whether they made Chanukah menorahs out of potatoes and matchsticks, or prayed *Kol Nidre* on Yom Kippur in the barracks, the lesson was always the same: G-d is with the Jews everywhere, to test their faith. This ordeal is only a test.

Certainly it was their faith that kept these people alive. G-d *was* testing them. In a place like Auschwitz, it was easy to think that He had abandoned them. But why was it, Shimshon wondered, that G-d seemed to be with certain people more than with others? Naively, he asked his father. But the rabbi only looked away darkly. The boy didn't realize how this question touched a raw nerve among many survivors: Why did *I* survive the war while others didn't? Obviously, there had to be a reason. Only G-d knew. Many survivors shared a sort of collective guilt for having been spared.

In some ways the aftermath was even worse than the trauma itself. After the war, the Rabbi Shapiros of the world gave special thanks for having endured such horror. And then they went on with their lives, under a guise of normalcy. But how normal was it, really? After seeing his father and mother, Shimshon wondered: How *do* these people live? Did they all react the same way? It seemed so schizophrenic — his father's friends, anyway. In every respect, they readjusted to the outside world very well. They quickly adapted to their new country, made their place in the Jewish community, and seemed to have overcome everything. In the stories that the boy had read, the past was always described in a detached, though melodramatic, way. It was over — terrible, yes, but over. But, for Rabbi Shapiro, the past was not over. It was still very tangible — and very much alive inside him.

After reading survivors' memoirs of the Holocaust, Shimshon came to know just how strong and vivid, how lasting and lingering, the images were — even after forty years. Helpless men, women, and children led to the gas chambers; countless Jews beaten and slaughtered; chassidim dragged by their beards through the streets. Shimshon pored over the grainy wartime photographs. That era must have truly been unmatched for horror in the human experience.

Shimshon remembered his own feelings when his mother died. There was pain, loneliness, isolation. Being "different" from everyone else. "Why me?" he often asked. "Why did Hashem choose me to go through this?" Depression, anger. Resenting those who seemed to lead problem-free lives. His nightmares that some day he himself might be taken away. Fortunately, it was a passing phase; as Shimshon grew older, the wounds healed, and he became more tolerant, if not accepting, of death. But try to multiply it by a thousand deaths and a million *yahrzeits* — a life of endless *shivah,* a perpetual mourning for lost family, friends, relatives; a life of lingering sadness. Try to imagine what it was like to watch everyone around you disappear — knowing that it was permanent, that they were never coming back. Try to imagine what it was like to watch others be helplessly swept away before history.

Shimshon made frequent trips to the public library, saturating himself with Holocaust literature. It was not only an effort to understand that period, but also to make his father's words more clear: *Can you understand now what the Holocaust was?*

Most of the books, written for adults, were difficult for a twelve-year-old — even a smart boy like Shimshon. Nevertheless, he was able to garner much of the facts. He read about the rise of Hitler, who promised Germany a glowing future, *Judenrein* — free of Jews. His maniacal dreams were to become, for twelve years' time, an unspeakable reality.

Shimshon read of the first years, 1933-38, of the growing harassment of the German Jews — their loss of prestige and civil rights, the disintegration of their communities, the boycotting and looting of their shops and businesses — and their own reaction: emigration for some, pensive waiting for others. Some, like Rabbi Shapiro's friend Jonah Wasserman, got out in time. Others, however, waited too long. Even much later, on the way to the concentration camp Theresienstadt, they believed that Germany would, once again, be a comfortable place for Jews.

Austria and Czechoslovakia, annexed in 1938, were worse. The Austrians, especially, welcomed the German "liberators" and took pride in humiliating the Jews. People young and old — doctors, lawyers, businessmen, housewives — were seized and publicly forced to wash the streets. It was from Austria where many of the Nazis, including Hitler himself, had sprung — and that was a "distinction" in which the Austrians themselves took pride.

The climax of German hatred was Kristallnacht — November 9, 1938 — when over 600 synagogues throughout Germany were destroyed. Streets were covered with the broken glass of shattered windows belonging to Jewish shops and edifices. Thousands of Jews were branded political prisoners, vermin, enemies of the state, and were imprisoned in concentration camps.

Back then, it would have been difficult, if not impossible, to believe that things could only get worse. But everything until then, as horrible as it was, had only been a prelude. The real horror came in 1939.

World War II was Hitler's war against the Jews. Before that, Germany had at least operated with a certain restraint. But now that nation went completely berserk, overrunning her helpless neighbors, and destroying everything in her way — especially everything Jewish. It was no accident that the European countries which suffered the most were those with the largest Jewish populations. Poland, Russia, Lithuania, Hungary — all fell like severed heads under the swoop of the Nazi sword. Hitler was more obsessed with defeating Jews than he was with killing Americans, Britons, or Russians.

Indeed, all of Eastern Europe, where Rabbi Shapiro and his friends were born, became a systematic killing ground for Jews. So efficient were the SS death squads, the *Einsatzgruppen,* that the lands of Poland and the Ukraine were made fertile with soaked Jewish blood.

Later — beginning in 1941 — came the death camps. Auschwitz, Treblinka, Maidanek, Belzec, Sobibor — their names danced on the map like a macabre puppet show.

The men who commanded these camps and death squads were themselves fanatics. Most of them, like Hitler, had come from either criminal or mediocre backgrounds. Yet, somehow they had succeeded in being in the right place at the right time — Germany in the 1930's — and in becoming masters over millions of conquered, helpless people. And thus grew their lust for power — this same lust that caused Rabbi Shapiro's fear of another Holocaust.

It wasn't just the yesterdays that kept his father up at night. It was knowing that the Holocaust really could happen again. There were plenty of men around, such as these escaped Nazis, who were jealous enough of the Jews to consider them a threat. After going through one trauma, Rabbi Shapiro was particularly eager to avoid a terrifying repeat. To him, among every group of gentiles could be found a potential Nazi. He was not being paranoid; he had simply seen enough hatred by non-Jews to know their terrifying potential.

Rabbi Shapiro knew about, and told Shimshon of, the thousands of non-Jews who, at the risk of life and limb, had assisted Jews on the run from the Nazis. But despite those great people, the Nazis had destroyed one-third of the world's Jewish population. No, this was not paranoia on his part. Rabbi Shapiro was merely assessing the reality that had occurred.

The Nazis were defeated. And it was enticing to forget that such devastation had been visited upon the Jews. But Shimshon learned that the Jews must never forget, that they must never become smug or secure about themselves.

Rabbi Shapiro, moved by his son's curiosity, opened up little by little. Soon he was freely discussing wartime experiences and atrocities — his own and his friends'. Shimshon listened intently.

Once, during dinner, Rabbi Shapiro described an *aktion* — a raid and roundup — that had taken place in the Warsaw Ghetto.

"It was in June 1942. We lived on Niskia Street. I was on my way back from the night shift in the Brushmaker's District, and I saw them: SS, *Polizei*. . . and Ukrainians. The Ukrainians were even worse than the Germans, Shimshon."

"Worse?!" Shimshon exclaimed in wonder. He had forgotten that the Germans had received plenty of outside help in annihilating the Jews.

"Oh, why, yes, Shimshon. In fact, I remember in the ghetto how they . . ." His father trailed off in silence.

"How they what, Ta?" Shimshon asked.

But his father didn't answer. He stared ahead, a distant look of disgust on his face. Shimshon realized that his father was again in that other world.

Quickly shaking his head, his father continued. "From the distance I saw everything . . . armored cars, soldiers. People were being dragged outside, half-dressed, screaming. One man I'll never forget. Before the war he had been a textile manufacturer. Now his head was cracked open by a truncheon; blood gushed out like water from a garden hose. He was thrown to the ground and raked with bullets; his body was a bloody pulp. Children were tossed into the wagons like rag dolls.

"The surrounding streets were deserted. Nobody dared venture out. I was standing there, quite visible, when suddenly I saw him. A Ukrainian guard. Worse, he saw me. He lifted his rifle and took careful aim. I thought I was done for."

"What did you do, Ta?" Shimshon asked, wide-eyed.

"Suddenly, a hand grabbed me — quite forcefully, I might add. My arm was bruised for a week afterward. It pulled me through a doorway just as the bullet went whizzing past. I felt myself being dragged down a dark staircase. The smell was overpowering — the mustiest, dankest mildew you can imagine. Before I knew what was happening, I found myself in a bunker which was perhaps the size of your bedroom.

"I turned around to see the owner of the hand. My cousin, Nachum Mendelssohn." He smiled weakly. "I'll never forget him — thin as a stick, but his eyes — how intensely they shone. Like coral. Seated — or rather, crouched — around him were at least a dozen other people: Nachum's family. Mordechai Silverman was also there. Mice scampered overhead. We stayed down there for two days. Almost no food or water. The air was filthy. Finally, the deportations stopped — for awhile."

The rabbi choked. "I went home. But my parents were gone. And five brothers and sisters. Chaim Yosef and Tzvia Rochel had been hiding in another bunker, with my oldest brother, Yaakov. We later moved in with my uncle, on Mila Street."

Silently the two ate their dinner. After a few minutes, however, Yehuda Shapiro continued. "Nachum and Yaakov later died in the uprising. By then I was in Dachau. I didn't find out what had happened to them until afterwards, when I came to Auschwitz — in June 1944. There I met Nachum's brother, David, who told me."

"So they died fighting," Shimshon interjected.

"Yes," answered his father, wiping away a tear. He added, "David was later killed too."

"But not the same way," Shimshon said wryly.

His father looked at him. "What are you trying to say, Shimshon?" he demanded.

"Ta," Shimshon asked, with a certain hurt, "why didn't *you* fight back?"

The rabbi dropped his fork. It made a loud angry clang. He looked away, bristling with hurt and indignation. It wasn't till later that Shimshon understood why he had reacted this way. It was a plight of the Holocaust survivor: the world's assumption that only those with the guns were heroes.

The rabbi could read the next question in Shimshon's eyes. How did you stay alive, Ta? Obviously, he had to have been either a coward or some kind of criminal — as if he had survived at somebody else's expense. And Rabbi Shapiro waited for the other questions: Ta, were you ever a *kapo* — a collaborator? Did you serve on the *Judenrat* council? Did you work with underworld types? Were you a smuggler? The answer to all of these, fortunately, was no. But the question Shimshon had asked, accompanied by a look of disillusionment — to that his father could not reply.

In Shimshon's mind, "fighting back" meant the Warsaw Ghetto revolt. It meant people like Mordechai Anielewicz, who led the *ZOB,* a pitiful, ragged band of Zionists, against a superior German army for over forty days. It meant his uncle Yaakov, whom the boy had never met, brandishing a machine gun in one hand and a Molotov cocktail in another, the words "Down with the Nazi enemy" on his lips. Together with his comrades he jumped from a burning building, perishing in the smoldering ruins. A soldier's death, in flames — that was the way to go. The rest "died like sheep."

The rabbi brooded over this cliche when he was alone. Most likely, Shimshon was disappointed in him. Rabbi Shapiro knew how his son idolized him. And now, probably, Shimshon felt that his father had let him down. Rabbi Shapiro had not lived up to the image Shimshon had possessed of someone in proud battle against the Nazis. Yet here he was, Rabbi Shapiro, successful after so many years of hardship, a man who had fought to reestablish his place in a world which had wished him dead. Never did he forget how he had struggled during the war — both in the ghetto and in the camps.

Rabbi Shapiro remembered his own father, Mayer. Little did Shimshon know that at one time Rabbi Shapiro was angry at his own father for being a victim. Young Yehuda Shapiro had also wondered why *his* tati just stepped onto the train. And at night, Yehuda Shapiro still called for him, heartrendingly. Somehow, his father had seemed to go without a fight.

But did Shimshon also know that a coward could hold a gun

just as easily as a hero? The Germans were stronger only because they were the ones who had the guns. It was frightfully easy to terrorize a civilian population. Even the non-Jews were made submissive. Usually, the Germans sapped their victims of strength and morale before finishing them off.

But this they couldn't do to Mayer Shapiro. This quiet man had conducted Torah classes, and even supervised ritual slaughter, in secrecy, and he marched off to the *Umshlagplatz* in his prayer shawl — his *tallis* — and *tefillin,* singing *Ani Ma'amin.* But somehow, to the boy, all that was meaningless. It did not occur to Shimshon that to hide in a cellar, to smuggle food, to pray secretly, to sing and dance clandestinely with the Torah, even to stay alive one more day — these, too, constituted "fighting back." But by now Shimshon's mind was filled with gory tales he had devoured of German savagery and Jewish passivity. The Warsaw Ghetto, Treblinka, and Sobibor revolts were all that mattered. The rest was pathetic.

"Can you imagine, Zev?" he asked one day on the way home from school. "So many Jews in Europe, and they couldn't get together and fight. If we were there — boy! Bet we would have killed s-o-o-o many Nazis."

Zev listened patiently to his friend. But he knew even less about the Holocaust than Shimshon. His own parents were born in Brooklyn, not Poland. Most of his family had come here before the war.

"Yeah," he murmured at last. "Too bad we weren't there."

With the upcoming Purim holiday, Shimshon's imagination ran wild. While packing *mishlo'ach manos* kits, food packages to send to their friends, he imagined he was smuggling secret packages to *ZOB* fighters in Warsaw. When Haman's name was mentioned at the Megillah reading and he waved his noisemaker, he pretended he was firing a machine gun at every evil person who had ever shot down a member of the Jewish people. He even wanted to dress up as a partisan, but his father said no. Mrs. Friedman had already made a nice costume for him — of an Arab.

No sooner was Purim over than Shimshon checked his calendar for Pesach. He loved the holiday, with all its ritual and preparation. It was a great way — the only way, really — that his father could get him to clean up his room. Now he attacked it with a vengeance. Here again he let himself go in his imagination. With a vacuum cleaner he blasted to smithereens the enemy leaven — *chametz*.

Rabbi Shapiro was still unsure whether or not they would be in Monsey for Pesach. Shimshon still longed to remain at home. He really preferred to be in Boro Park — he loved it here this time of year. In the streets he felt the joy of the holiday shoppers — running home, in panic and excitement, hugging close the boxes of matzoh and other groceries.

Their home, too, took on a different appearance. Quite busy even during the year, now it was swamped with callers — anyone who needed monetary help. No person was ever turned away. Shimshon helped Mrs. Friedman in the kitchen with the cleaning. He remembered his mother, who had weakly managed to prepare the special foods for the Seder. Shimshon thought, with sadness, that this Pesach would be the second without her. At such moments, he would wonder if perhaps it might not be such a bad idea after all to go away for Pesach.

It was Friday, three weeks before Pesach. Shimshon was

putting on his Shabbos suit when the phone rang. It was Reb Zelig, the sexton — *shamash* — of Rabbi Shapiro's synagogue.

"Is your father home?" he asked. His accent was very strong, like Mrs. Friedman's.

"No. Not yet."

"Would you take a message for me?"

"Sure."

"Tell him," said the man, "that we have a visitor here from Yerushalayim. I think he's someone your father would like to meet. His name is Avraham Shulman. A very interesting man, a great Torah scholar — a *gaon.* I think you'll be impressed. He should be in *shul* tonight. Perhaps he'll honor us by speaking tomorrow."

"Wow, sounds great," Shimshon said.

"You'll be sure to tell him, won't you?" asked Reb Zelig.

"You bet."

"I knew I could count on you. Good Shabbos," said the man.

"Good Shabbos," Shimshon replied happily, and put down the receiver.

Minutes later the Pontiac was heard pulling up in the driveway. Still buttoning his sleeves, Shimshon ran outside.

The rabbi's face brightened with interest as he heard the news. Shimshon, too, was glad; maybe this man would take his father's mind off everything else that had been happening lately.

When at last the siren echoed through Boro Park, letting everyone know that Shabbos was here, father and son put on their ties. As they left the house, kissing the *mezuzah*, Shimshon tingled inwardly. He loved sunset on Friday eve. He and his father walked, bodies erect, down the avenue, which was filled with men in a somber parade of hats and coats. Even the air felt different —

heavy and serious, whispering with holiness.

The synagogue was several blocks down, nestled among stately apartment houses, like a child hiding among adults. Father and son were the first to arrive. Taking a large, heavy volume from the cluttered bookcase, the rabbi opened to a page and began studying Gemara with his son. Shimshon strained to follow along. He always tried to emulate his father, so permeated in wisdom. But now he was too excited about the visitor who, Zelig had promised, would be someone special. Though in the past Shimshon had met great Torah scholars, he was by now almost bar mitzvah, a very impressionable age. For that reason this occasion would be even more extraordinary.

Soon other men streamed in. Shimshon counted. He knew them all. Mordechai Silverman walked in. He had the shy, quiet, intense face of an intellectual. Hard to believe that this was the same man who had thrown a grenade at an SS officer. Mordechai went to each person, politely shaking hands and murmuring "Good Shabbos."

Zev walked in with his father. Soon *minchah* would begin. The conversation revolved around weekly events and good tidings. Somebody was a grandfather again.

Reb Zelig walked in. And behind him walked the one who was the tenth man.

All heads turned. The tall, slender frame remained by the doorway, hesitant — as if knowing that he was the night's attraction and developing a sudden case of stagefright. Though his body, cloaked in black, was obscured by the darkening sky, his face, framed by whitening hair and thick earlocks, shone under his chassidic hat — his *shtreimel*. His blue eyes glistened behind a pair of spectacles, and when he turned the lenses glowed, as if fusing with the light. His aura was awesome.

"Friends, this is Avraham Shulman," Reb Zelig announced, smiling. "A guest from Yerushalayim."

There were a few nods and "*Shalom aleichem*"s. Silently, the newcomer nodded.

Reb Zelig turned to him and said, "We are honored to have you here, Rav Shulman."

The man remained standing, wordless.

"Please, it's getting late," the sexton continued. Behind him entered other worshipers, who glanced at the guest with curiosity and surprise. Reb Zelig hurried over to Rabbi Shapiro, clearing his throat. "Let's begin."

"*Hodu Lashem ki tov* . . ." sang Yehuda Shapiro, the melody wafting through the room.

Immediately the *shul* hummed with prayer. Shimshon hurried to get the new man a prayer book. Absently, Avraham Shulman turned to the proper page, but his lips were already moving of their own accord. Humbly, Shimshon retreated.

Minchah began. Shimshon couldn't help looking over his shoulder. Quietly, Avraham Shulman stood, not really reading from the *siddur,* lips tangled in prayer.

After *minchah,* the men momentarily dispersed. Some sat down in the front, expecting a brief lecture. Others were hoping to hear something from Avraham Shulman.

However, Shulman stepped outside into the night air. There he stood, watching the darkening sky and waiting to greet the coming night. Yehuda Shapiro eyed him keenly and left the lectern. Shimshon followed behind.

The man was either talking to himself — rethinking some topic in Talmud — or mouthing Psalms. With languid eyes, he watched the father and son approach him cautiously.

The rabbi spoke in Hebrew. "I'm Rabbi Yehuda Shapiro. Welcome to my synagogue. This is my son, Shimshon."

Slowly Shulman extended his hand. "Good Shabbos," he whispered.

Shimshon grabbed the man's hand, shaking it excitedly. "Good Shabbos," he said loudly.

"It's a pleasure and an honor to meet you, Rav Shulman," said the rabbi.

"Thank you," answered the man, bowing slightly. "I am also honored."

"I hear you are from Jerusalem."

"Yes," answered the man. "The Holy City."

Rabbi Shapiro looked at him strangely. "Your accent . . . I'm trying to place it," he said. "Were you born in Israel?"

"No," answered Shulman solemnly. "I was born in Germany. I came to Israel after the war."

The rabbi's brow wrinkled in disturbed thought. Then he continued, carefully, "I was born in Warsaw. And you? What city?"

"Berlin," answered the man softly.

"Oh, you must have known my relatives. The Goldbergs? They came to Berlin after the First World War." Then, with a knowing sigh, Rabbi Shapiro added, "Unfortunately, they didn't survive the second."

"I'm sorry," Shulman answered nervously. "I did not know them."

The rabbi continued to watch him. Now Shimshon grew uneasy.

"And where were you during the war?" the rabbi asked.

"Oh . . . I was in many places," answered Shulman evasively. His fingers danced nervously against his leg. "I don't think you would want to know of them."

"The camps?"

"No!" The man looked at the rabbi in fright, like a thief caught by his accuser. "No. I was fortunate not to have to know those places. I escaped." His eyes widened till they became even more luminous. "G-d guided me out of Europe."

He averted his face to avoid the scrutinizing gaze of Rabbi Shapiro. Both father and son were surprised at the outburst. Evidently this man contained many dark, painful secrets. Rabbi Shapiro knew what it was like to have to reveal secrets with great reluctance. He did not wish to pry into the man's past. Nevertheless, this man's behavior was enough to leave anyone intrigued.

"And where in Jerusalem do you live?"

"Kiryat Yovel," answered Shulman quickly. He brushed past Rabbi Shapiro. "Excuse me." Quietly he returned to his seat and reopened his *siddur*. Father and son were left standing in amazement.

Rabbi Shapiro was attempting to figure out this serene, kindly man who had suddenly turned into a nervous misanthrope. A real chameleon, the rabbi thought. He was amazed by an even stranger transformation. Arms crossed, as if caressing himself, Avraham Shulman began chanting the Song of Songs, *Shir HaShirim,* his whole body swaying rhythmically. Eyes half drawn, head thrown back, he shook and rocked, scarcely noticing the crowd of spectators. His lips were raised to the ceiling, kissing the air and clearly forming each word.

It was an impressive performance. Shimshon giggled,

fascinated, as if he were watching a Purim play. Rabbi Shapiro kept his eyes on the man. His stare had a haunted and frightening tone.

"Yehuda," came the voice of Reb Zelig, startling him. "It's time."

Quickly going to the lectern, the rabbi chanted the Shabbos liturgy. Shimshon, seated perpendicular to the lectern, followed along in a boyish voice.

His father looked distressed. Instead of being immensely joyful at the arrival of Shabbos, he looked as if, for some reason or other, he was ashamed to let her in. His face, etched in fear, seemed fixed on something which had apparently intruded.

"Mizmor shir leyom hashabbos," he continued mournfully. Too late. Shabbos was here already.

Ma'ariv, the evening service, followed. Finishing with *Aleinu* and *Kaddish,* the rabbi retreated from the lectern, as if grateful at last to be finished. By now Shimshon was nervous. His father never acted this way on Shabbos. Even during *shivah* he had faithfully suspended the laws of mourning on Shabbos. He never allowed himself to be sad on this day. Always, he was a new person.

But the person here this Friday evening seemed a troubled man, cloaked in sadness. "I think about the Holocaust at least once a day," he had told Shimshon. "But never on Shabbos."

While Zelig made the usual announcements, Rabbi Shapiro kept his eyes fixed on the guest, who put down the *siddur* and swiftly turned to the doorway. Before Shimshon could run outside to see, the figure had vanished into the dark, silent night.

Lingering by the lectern, Rabbi Shapiro mumbled "Good Shabbos" absent-mindedly to the congregants. Soon the little synagogue was empty, save for the Shapiros and Zelig. Zelig was to join them for the meal.

"I'll be just a few minutes, Yehuda," he said, hurrying into the storage room.

"We'll wait here," answered Rabbi Shapiro.

He watched the door, as if waiting for the intruder to reappear. He had completely forgotten his son, who crept up softly behind him.

"Strange," murmured the rabbi. "He almost hurried out."

"Ta," Shimshon began, "who *was* that man?"

"An old man from Yerushalayim. A chassid, a Torah scholar, perhaps. That's how he appears." Then the rabbi's face darkened. "But I know that I've seen him before. I can't remember where."

"You think that's why he hurried out?" Shimshon asked. "He didn't want to see you? Or you to see him? He must have known that you recognized him."

"Oh, of that I'm sure," answered his father grimly.

"Maybe," suggested the boy, "he didn't like being asked all those questions. What do you think it was that made him so upset?"

"Most likely his past."

"Do you think he's lying?" Shimshon asked.

Rabbi Shapiro finally turned to his son. His face seemed laced with bitterness. "I don't know," he said. "But I'm positive I've seen him before."

Zelig returned. That was the signal the Shapiros were waiting for. Hastily they grabbed their coats. Stopping at the door, the rabbi looked outside. The night was stark black, the air was vitally crisp, and the crystalline stars winked at them. Turning the corner, they could see chassidim walking softly home.

The rabbi looked around him fearfully, as if wondering whether or not it was really safe to go home. What lay in store?

"There is some inner feeling, Shimshon . . . a whispering from the soul — I don't know . . . but I think we're in for some difficult times ahead."

Chapter 4

Oneg Shabbos

The Shabbos table, carefully arranged, glowed, as if on fire, against the melting flame of the candlelight. The three of them — Rabbi Shapiro, Shimshon, and Zelig — sat alone. The house, which usually brimmed with guests on Friday night, seemed empty. Shimshon was the one in charge of serving — a task his mother had once done. Quietly, he placed the gefilte fish platter, and awaited *Kiddush.*

Slowly raising the silver goblet, Rabbi Shapiro chanted the benedictions. His hand visibly shook, causing the wine to slosh back and forth, spilling onto his fingers, staining them purple. His voice wavered, and his eyes, pondering the lights, seemed to be searching for something in the flames. At last he finished and drank. Zelig quietly made his own *Kiddush,* and Shimshon followed.

After they had washed their hands, the rabbi made the blessing over the challah. Quietly the three began their meal. Shimshon watched the candles burn away in an air heavy with seriousness. It was difficult to believe that just recently Purim had been so festive. Now the house was steeped in sadness.

Most of the conversation was dominated by Rabbi Shapiro and Zelig. In Yiddish peppered with Hebrew they exchanged views on

Torah topics and weekly events. Occasionally Zelig mentioned Avraham Shulman; the rabbi either remained silent or changed the subject. In between singing Shabbos songs and making trips to the kitchen, Shimshon tried to follow the conversation, his ears and mind ever alert to the changing mood. He grew more worried. His father was singing off-key.

Dinner ended early, and Shimshon brought in tea for the men. Having said grace already, he took a Chumash and went into the living room.

His ears perked when he heard Zelig tell his father, "Perhaps we'll hear an interesting *shiur* tomorrow."

"I'll have one prepared," the rabbi said icily.

Zelig looked at the rabbi in surprise. He, no less than Shimshon, expected the honor to go to the newcomer. But Rabbi Shapiro had clearly indicated that this time was going to be an exception. Quietly, he recited grace. Shortly after, the timer went off, leaving the dining room in semi-darkness, the Shabbos candles providing the only light.

After Zelig was ushered out the door, the rabbi wordlessly removed a Talmud volume from the shelf and retired to the kitchen. But though his eyes remained fixed on the printed page, they did not move.

Shimshon was accustomed to studying on Friday night with his father, but he was too puzzled to feel slighted. When he saw his father sitting, haggard and pale, in the kitchen light, he sensed that this was not the right time.

Eleven o'clock. Shimshon felt his eyes growing heavy with weariness. Returning the Chumash to the shelf, he turned and called out, " 'Night, Ta. Good Shabbos."

But his father didn't hear him. His eyes were still fixed on the

Talmud. Sadness seemed to emanate from him like a lingering scent. The candles in the dining room flickered angrily and died.

Quietly, Shimshon went upstairs to his room.

Midnight. The screaming was right on schedule. This time, though, it seemed to penetrate the very walls.

Shimshon burst into his father's room. Rabbi Shapiro was sitting up, rigid; the cry *"Juden, 'Raus"* echoed in the room.

"It's him! I knew it! It's him!" he cried. His shivering body was covered with perspiration. "It's all coming back to me now."

"What is?" Shimshon asked, though he already had an idea.

But Rabbi Shapiro didn't hear. His face, contorted in terror, was staring at something straight ahead. His breathing grew more labored, as he watched a figure materialize, with shocking concreteness, into something powerful.

"Hans Schmidt," he murmured, as if the words were an incantation.

"Oh, no," was the only response Shimshon could muster.

Hans Schmidt. The very name was the essence of cruelty — the man who left the rabbi's pillow soaked with tears night after night. He had mentioned this man to his son many times. Hans Schmidt was only one man among many to cross young Yehuda Shapiro's path. But he was the one who would forever be tattooed on the rabbi's heart. It was Hans Schmidt who had initiated Yehuda into the terrifying world of the concentration camps.

After the last *Aktion,* in August 1942, the Warsaw Ghetto was left depleted, both physically and morally. Yehuda, by then a ragged boy of thirteen, was left to fend for himself and his siblings. In desperation, he joined a pack of smugglers. Day after day he made his way through the sewers, never quite getting used to the slimy, fetid waters. In October he was caught by Polish guards. As he was beaten, he broke away and escaped, fleeing into a bombed-out building site. A sudden air raid alert prevented the guards from flushing him out. Hiding in a garbage bin, he waited till midnight before attempting to return to the ghetto.

He never made it back. Noticing additional SS recruits, he realized it just wasn't safe to try. He sadly realized that he might have seen his family — what was left of it — for the last time. His only hope lay in leaving Warsaw completely — finding refuge in the hostile woods, and placing himself under the tender mercies of peasants. It was an act of desperation. But it was the only way left. All of Eastern Europe lay clenched in Germany's grip, with every citizen on the prowl for runaway Jews. In this wasteland, Yehuda had no right to live.

After many nights in ditches, groves, and fields, he finally arrived at a train depot near the Czech border. Lacking money and false papers, he tried to hide under a car and get a free ride into the Slovakian Protectorate. The conductor saw him, protruding under the siding. The man was drunk, and thought of the bottle of vodka promised to every Pole who found a runaway Jew. Before Yehuda could slide out from underneath, he was surrounded by fifteen men with dogs. He was taken to a prison cell, originally built to accommodate four men, now filled with twenty — most of them Jewish. Throughout the night they took turns sitting and standing. Two died in the interim. In the morning they were taken out and packed into a truck, which transported them to the nearest cattle car.

The train ride was the first in a series of transfers and deportations which wound through Germany and Poland like a snake, finally ending up in Auschwitz. But Yehuda Shapiro had to be prepared for this final destination. Perhaps Hashem planned it that way; once he was broken in, he could adjust more easily to his new environment. Perhaps that was why he was sent to Malberg, a small labor camp northeast of Munich. Perhaps that was why he met Hans Schmidt.

Hans Schmidt, *Sturmbannfuhrer* of Malberg, was one of the heads of the "children's camp." Smiling, whip in hand, he waited at the siding while the boy was separated from the adults and thrust into the crowd of youngsters.

"Welcome to Malberg," he recited in a sweet, almost angelic voice. "Your Fatherland needs you for awhile. You will help to build a new Germany. The world will never forget you . . . *The world will never forget . . .*"

These words echoed in the rabbi's mind like a tape recorder gone insanely out of control. "The same voice," he whispered. "Tonight, when Shulman recited *Shir HaShirim* . . ."

Shimshon immediately got the point. "No, Ta!" he cried sharply. "You're wrong!"

"How could I be wrong, Shimshon?" his father demanded defensively.

"But Ta," the boy repeated pleadingly, "you *are.* That man is not Hans Schmidt. There is no way he can be Hans Schmidt. That man is Avraham Shulman, from Yerushalayim."

"And I tell you, Shimshon, that I'm right. Everything about that man . . . his face, his features . . . tells me that Avraham Shulman is Hans Schmidt."

"What was he like, Ta?"

"Like every commander," answered the rabbi, his face expressing a look of revulsion. "Cold. Arrogant. Proud of himself and the Master Race. He saw every Jew as a piece of garbage."

"But Ta, this man is a Jew. A chassid. What you're saying

doesn't make sense!" Shimshon cried, his eyes filled with tears. Shimshon did not know why this upset him so, but it did. He loved his father more than anyone in the world, and seeing him express these thoughts was disquieting. Was his father losing his mind? Shimshon vividly remembered the face of Avraham Shulman. Serene, intense. His penetrating eyes shone with purity, not evil. His manner, his movement . . . Avraham Shulman lived for holiness. Every fiber of his being, every act of his was to elevate the world — not to drag it down into a slimy pit. How could anyone compare this man to an SS officer? Just because Hans Schmidt was cultured, like many of his kind? It was like comparing poison ivy to a rose. Any refinement Schmidt had was just a veneer. Underneath his trim, tailor-made uniform lay a demon. Underneath the neat and clean gabardine of Avraham Shulman lay a saint. But Shimshon knew that right now he could not argue with his father. Something about Shulman had triggered off a powerful association. Shimshon wondered just how much and how dangerously reality was becoming confused with illusion.

The rabbi jumped out of bed and paced the room, muttering to himself — frightening the boy even further.

"I must let them know immediately . . . it was *hashgachah pratis* that he came to my *shul*, of all the ones in Boro Park."

"Do you think anyone else recognized him?" asked Shimshon. Since he couldn't reason with Tati, at least he could play along with him.

But his father didn't hear. He was still engrossed in his own thoughts — a completely different person. Shimshon knew it was impossible now to calm him down. At least he was awake and out of bed. The dreams would stop for the meantime. Shimshon could now get some rest himself.

"'Night, Ta," Shimshon said, turning toward the door. "Good Shabbos."

Shimshon slipped back under his own covers. His father was still mumbling in the other room.

Six a.m. Shimshon awoke. As the rays of light tickled his eyes open, he yawned, stretched, and recited *Modeh Ani.* He quickly rose and washed his hands. He dressed and went downstairs.

His father was sitting in the living room, preparing the day's lecture. Quietly the rabbi scanned through his bookcase, finally removing a Talmud volume. Then he looked at his son. Rabbi Shapiro's eyes were red from lack of sleep.

Shimshon sat beside him, glancing at the geometric blocks of print fluttering in the sunlight. Pointing his finger to the appropriate passage, the rabbi softly chanted the words. The boy followed along quietly, occasionally glancing out the window. The tree branches moved gracefully in the cool wind, as if swaying to the tune of Torah study. For a moment Shimshon let himself forget the events of the night. If his father couldn't, at least Shimshon wished to pretend that right now, on Shabbos, the world was at peace.

Seven o'clock. A few men were already at the *shul,* waiting for Rabbi Shapiro. Some, still groggy, were helping themselves to coffee, courtesy of Zelig.

When Rabbi Shapiro entered, they stood, and turned toward him reverently, as if they had been awaiting a prominent dignitary. Calmly, the rabbi took his seat near the lectern and immediately began discussing the Tosafos commentary on a topic in Tractate Bava Metzia. Shimshon sat directly in front of him. He tried not to wave to Zev, who walked in with his father.

Rabbi Shapiro's entire visage transformed magically. If he had been up all night, by the time he was well into his exposition it no longer showed. His mind, ever alert when it came to Torah study, thrived on it and gained new vitality, no matter how overcrowded it was with other thoughts. His eyes, no longer red, widened each time he explained a certain topic, integrating the various disputes and tying them up into a neat little package.

His audience, by now more than enough for a quorum, listened, nodding profoundly after each major point of argument. Shimshon was able to pick up only a little bit more than the rudimentary concepts. He looked forward to the time when, as it was with his father, Talmudic wisdom would be in much easier grasp. Already, their time together studying was paying off.

Eight o'clock. At the sound of approaching footsteps, the boy suddenly stiffened. He was cold — only partly because of the draft, which penetrated the room when Avraham Shulman opened the door.

The man remained standing in the back. With his tall figure framed by the doorway, he looked almost like an English lord in a country painting.

He did not utter a sound. He stroked the long white beard that cascaded over his shiny clean gabardine. His prayer shawl hung nonchalantly over his broad shoulders, like a tapestry over a solid block of wood. His blue eyes rested thoughtfully on Rabbi Shapiro.

Shimshon tried to keep his eyes on his father. But suddenly the chair felt cold and hard, like granite. He tried several positions, but ended up each time feeling more uncomfortable. His heart pounded wildly.

Rabbi Shapiro, meanwhile, continued his lecture, placidly unaware of the intruder. When his eyes finally met Shulman's, he stopped, cut short as if with a dagger. He quickly looked away and continued to speak, his voice now at a higher pitch.

But he couldn't go on. Pausing in the middle of a topic, the rabbi tried to retrieve his lost thoughts. Suddenly he felt like an old man who was wearing his glasses on his head and complaining that he couldn't find them. The men around him looked bewildered.

From far in the back came a voice in a soft German accent. *"Selicha,* Rabbi."

All heads turned. With great reluctance, Rabbi Shapiro cleared his throat. "Yes?" he asked in Hebrew.

"I would like to comment on a particular commentator that you mentioned."

"What about it?" Rabbi Shapiro asked curtly.

"If the rabbi would permit me, I feel that there is a point regarding the Tosafos that needs clarification."

Surprised, and slightly offended, Rabbi Shapiro asked, "Did I make an error?"

"That is correct," Shulman answered apologetically.

Showdown. Gritting his teeth, Rabbi Shapiro replied, "Perhaps, then, you should explain it . . . Rav Shulman."

Removing a Talmud volume from the bookcase, the man walked lightly down the aisle, his eyes high and straight ahead. The congregants slowly rose. Facing the rabbi, keeping only his back visible to the audience, the man opened the text to the appropriate section and began to read.

As he spoke, his voice was subdued at first, then resonant and wonderfully intoxicating. Melifluously he explained the Aramaic passages, not pausing even to catch his breath. The Torah language poured forth from him. His voice, controlled, rose in pitch as he demonstrated the fallacy in Rabbi Shapiro's interpretation, shooting it down like a hunted sparrow. He then introduced his own stream of thought; it flowed and broke into countless different linear streams, converging, like a *mikvah,* at a final resting place, from where they had originally sprung.

The men watched in amazement. Shimshon, especially, felt as if an ancient *Tanna,* Talmudic sage, from his history book had elegantly dropped by to visit. Shulman's erudition made Rabbi Shapiro's seem like the bar mitzvah speech Shimshon was painfully preparing at home. To hear Shulman was to truly hear a Torah giant speak.

After he had finished, there were a few overawed congratulations from the congregants. Rabbi Shapiro eyed his victor steadily.

Politely, Avraham Shulman said, "And that, I feel, is Tosafos's main thrust. I hope the rabbi will forgive my interruption. My intention was not to embarrass him, only to defend and elucidate what I feel is the position of Tosafos."

Placing the Gemara volume near a table, he glided to the back. For some reason, Shimshon had expected him to click his heels. However, quickly reviewing the impressive show that had just taken place, he tried to imagine Torah wisdom coming from — what? A Nazi criminal? That can't be! That just can't be! No Nazi, no matter how much an expert in "Racial Studies," could ever know Gemara the way Shulman did. If only his father could see it that way.

But his father was seeing the guest differently. As the older man spoke, Rabbi Shapiro remained transfixed, his face twisting into recollective horror. The polished prose that swept his son off his feet bothered Rabbi Shapiro further, as he remembered: Hans Schmidt had spoken, quite eloquently, to the child prisoners as well.

Avraham Shulman wrapped his prayer shawl protectively around himself. The man swayed as he chanted the morning benedictions, like a giant butterfly under the fluttering fringes. The sunlight now streamed in from the open window, turning his once yellow hair into a violent shade of gold.

Quietly, Rabbi Shapiro put aside the Gemara. The men, still mesmerized by the confrontation, now rose from their seats, reminding one another of the time by which one is required to recite the *Shma,* and went to get *siddurim.*

Shacharis went by smoothly. Some of the men huddled near Shulman, hoping to sample some of his holiness. Even the handful of women who were there pointed through the partition and commented on the imposing visitor.

Rav Shulman continued praying, apparently oblivious to his growing clique of admirers. Only once in awhile his half-closed eyes opened wide, and he cast a penetrating gaze at someone nearby, like a king bestowing favor on his subjects. Most of the time, however, he casually tossed his head as the prayers flowed from him. In the *shemoneh esrei,* while others rocked like the pendulum in a metronome, he bowed and stood with erect posture. Only his eyes remained downward, to show servitude to the true King.

When the Torah was brought out and escorted to the lectern, he recited the accompanying prayer with gusto and fire. Naturally, Shimshon, along with everyone else, expected him to receive an *aliyah.*

When the *kohen* was called, one of Rabbi Shapiro's friends came forward. Well, Shulman's not a *kohen,* thought Shimshon. He's not a *levi,* either, Shimshon concluded, after the second man's name was called.

As the subsequent *aliyos* were called, Shimshon tried to avoid counting. Nevertheless, he could not hide his surprise when others were called instead. Avraham Shulman's name was not mentioned. Even Zelig waited, expecting the man to be called up. But finally he, too, looked at the rabbi, perplexed. Certainly someone like Rav Shulman deserved this honor.

Rabbi Shapiro kept his face toward the lectern, and stayed as far away as possible from the person seated in the back. A look of satisfaction crossed his face. Perhaps even cruelty? Shimshon wondered.

Avraham Shulman kept his eyes fixed on the Chumash before him. His face, ever serene and placid, betrayed neither disappointment nor hurt.

Only after the seventh man was called did he raise his slender hand and say, timidly, "*Selicha.*"

Rabbi Shapiro turned and faced his opponent. "Yes?" he asked, as if addressing a child.

"I have a request."

The congregation hushed.

"What is it?" Rabbi Shapiro demanded.

Shulman replied, "I would like to say *bircas hagomel* and a *mi sheberach.*" His voice was laced with poignancy.

The men looked at Shulman, then at Rabbi Shapiro. The air, in spite of the open window, was heavy with hostility. The seventh man remained standing awkwardly in the middle.

Rabbi Shapiro nodded. With a certain grace, Shulman

approached the lectern and recited the appropriate prayer. The congregational response resounded through the synagogue — even Rabbi Shapiro responded, albeit grudgingly. Then, reciting the *mi sheberach,* the man called out the name Chava Rivkah bas Breinda, every syllable echoing funereally through the sanctuary. Sighing, he then retreated, his eyes filmy with tears.

During *musaf,* the additional service, Shulman was almost inaudible. Only his lips moved, causing his beard to rustle. After *Aleinu* he took out a Book of Psalms, ignoring the others who remained for the last recitation of *Kaddish.* At last he put the book away. Keeping his face down in gloomy self-absorption, he moved in a slow, military gait toward the door. Hand raised to the *mezuzah,* he exhaled a deep sigh and departed, like a defeated general taking leave of his army.

Shimshon watched him go. He continued watching the door, as if to feel the lingering presence, expecting the man to return.

At last he hurried to his father. "Ta," he asked accusingly, "why didn't you give him an *aliyah?*"

Rabbi Shapiro was busy collecting the *siddurim.* At first he didn't seem to hear his son. But finally he answered, with uncertainty, "I just couldn't."

Shimshon searched his father's face for signs of any remorse. Other than a certain confusion, there was no trace of regret whatsoever.

"Are you having doubts about him?"

Rabbi Shapiro again hesitated, reflecting over the question as if he were about to render a halachic decision. "No," he finally answered.

Lunch was livelier than the previous evening had been, with a young *kollel* couple and Zelig in attendance. Shimshon and the wife served. Shimshon was asked to speak about the Torah portion of the week. Blushing, he recited something he had learned in school that week. He took advantage of the moment when his father was talking to the guests, and he whispered to Zelig, "Where is Avraham Shulman having his lunch?"

With a shrug, Zelig answered, "He must have arranged to eat somewhere else, Shimshon."

Sure, Shimshon thought sullenly. He was scared away by Tati. Who can blame him, really?

But . . . strange, Shimshon thought. Shulman was not afraid to be in *shul* today. If he really were afraid of Ta, then why would he dare show his face again there? Only if he knew that whatever Ta thought wasn't true. Perhaps it was to prove Tati wrong? Perhaps he was trying to show how silly it was to even suspect him. After all, if he really were guilty, would he freely turn up in *shul,* knowing that Tati recognized him?

"Shimshon, why aren't you singing?" his father asked.

Quickly the boy began: "*Yom zeh mechubad mikol yamim . . .*"

Avraham Shulman. Hans Schmidt. Which of the two did others see? Perhaps it was Shimshon, and not his father, who was being played for a sap. Perhaps there was something in Shulman that Shimshon couldn't see . . . something only an adult might know. Something revealing, that his father could detect. Telltale mannerisms, phrases. After all, his father could not rid himself of the past. It crept in at certain moments, often the wrong times, invading his thoughts and speech. Shimshon could tell when it was happening. He knew his father. Shouldn't it be the same with Avraham Shulman? Even an actor would eventually have to give away some of his real personality. Somewhere, there had to be a trace of his inner being. But alas, Shimshon didn't know Hans Schmidt at all, so he had no real yardstick.

All afternoon Shimshon pondered this strange new man. If he really was a Nazi, then he was brilliant. Only a genius could pull it off this well — especially when it came to delivering a Gemara *shiur* for religious, learned men.

He could not pay attention to his own *Haftarah* reading, which he was practicing that Shabbos afternoon.

"Shimshon, you're not even listening to what you're saying," said his father, irritated.

"Sorry, Ta," Shimshon said, managing a grin. "Guess I'm just not with it today."

Five-thirty. The paling sky mournfully broadcast the news that Shabbos would be departing very soon. Quickly Shimshon and his father threw on their coats and walked out into the quiet streets.

Shimshon stood at the synagogue corner, looking for any sign of Shulman. The avenue, striped by the elongated shadows of trees and telephone poles, was filled with figures dressed in black and fur, on their way to or from *minchah*. However, even though they looked alike, Shulman would somehow stand out among them all.

"Are you coming inside, Shimshon?" his father asked sternly at the *shul* entrance.

"Yeah, Ta," the boy answered, embarrassed, and scurried in.

Abruptly the rabbi began the service, though there was barely a *minyan*. Everyone, surprised, hurried to find a *siddur*, looking at the rabbi as if to ask: Why the rush? Rabbi Shapiro chanted rapidly, as if he were competing in a race.

While the Torah was being removed, Shimshon turned around,

a look mixed with worry and hope plastered on his face. Still no Avraham Shulman. Afterwards came *shemoneh esrei*. To combat his disappointment, Shimshon helped Zelig set up for the *seudah shlishis*, the third meal.

The tables were set up as a rectangle and tablecloths were quickly placed. One by one the dishes were brought out — salad, cole slaw, tuna fish, challah. Some of the men had left to join their families. The rest quickly lined up, single file, at the sink.

Shimshon lingered by the door.

"Nervous today, Shimshon?" asked somebody.

Shimshon turned. Mordechai Silverman faced him, smiling.

"Oh, just waiting for somebody," the boy answered.

Then he saw his father. The look on Tati's face suggested that he wash — quickly. Sorrowfully, he took a last, lingering look outside the door. The sky was now a darkening gray, the sun hovering indecisively between the buildings.

Each man piled a portion of food on his plate. Rabbi Shapiro was chatting with Silverman. In a few minutes, he would begin his last Torah lecture of the day.

Then they all felt it. The chill enveloping the room, the rustle of a long black cloak. The same spectral figure, his towering frame dominating the doorway, the blond-white beard poised over the chest. His right hand rose slowly, aiming for the *mezuzah*. He pressed his fingers to his lips.

"Good Shabbos," he whispered.

The men, seated at the tables, watched him silently. No one was more silent than Rabbi Shapiro. Zelig hurried for a chair, placing it next to Shimshon. The boy smiled in delight.

Shulman almost floated to the sink. Cupping his hands drenched with water, he raised them to his massive chest and pronounced the benediction. Taking his seat by Shimshon, he held the challah as if handling a precious stone; after the blessing, he daintily broke off a piece and dipped it in salt. Placing a napkin on his lap, Shulman carefully ate the bread over it. Hardly a crumb fell.

Rabbi Shapiro glared at him. His own food remained untouched. Finally he announced, "I'm afraid my *drashos* do not measure up to half the wisdom of our guest, sitting here with us, who was able to correct me this morning. Rav Shulman, since you impressed us so much with your erudition, perhaps you would like to share with us a little Torah this afternoon?"

Shimshon was surprised. Was his father trying to trap the man? Or was he himself feeling intimidated because of that morning? Or was he envious — expecting anything he said to be shot away by Shulman's rapid-fire delivery?

Shulman, slowly and deliberately, continued eating. Not until his plate was completely clean, fork resting primly, did he begin to speak.

This time the subject was the weekly portion. He delivered his discourse with prose calculated enough to appear spontaneous. First the simple explanation, then the accompanying exposition, with oratory that was positively exquisite. Weaving in Talmudic and Midrashic legends, along with the thoughts of various commentators, he was able to make several ideas collide with spiritual force. Every turn of speech, every movement of the hand seemed rehearsed, yet natural, simultaneously.

But the wisdom! No, it wasn't just his logic and analytical thought; it was the fire that emanated from him, giving them life. Shulman was not just advancing new insights on the portion; he was forming his views into something concrete and identifiable, like a sculptor delicately carving a fine piece of marble.

The audience gaped. The food remained uneaten. Even Rabbi Shapiro seemed impressed, with certain reservations. After Shulman had finally finished, he said, *"Yasher ko'ach!"* in reluctant acknowledgment.

After grace, the men rushed to put on their jackets.

Shulman stayed for *ma'ariv.* He even lingered after *havdalah,* cheerfully wishing the congregants a good week and turning down several invitations for *melaveh malkah,* the Saturday night repast. Rabbi Shapiro looked away and went into the kitchen with Zelig, who was putting away the leftovers.

Elegantly Shulman slipped into his coat. Shimshon approached him shyly. "Your *drasha,* sir — why, it was great!" he exclaimed.

Avraham Shulman noticed the boy and a vague smile crossed his lips. "Thank you, Shimshon," he answered sweetly.

The boy was glad Shulman had remembered his name. "Are you a rebbe?" he asked.

The man chuckled. "No."

"A rav?"

Again Shulman chuckled, flattered. "Why, no. In fact, *I* have rebbes. In Kiryat Yovel there are many whose knowledge far exceeds mine." He spoke English fluently.

"What's it like there?" asked the boy.

Shulman smiled vaguely, sensing that he was not going to escape this conversation easily. Actually, though, he did not really feel the need to leave. Young people had always been his weakness. He sat down squarely so he could face the boy directly.

Then, slowly and quite accurately, he described the little streets and stone houses of the Jerusalem district. He also described the place where he studied, Kollel Ohr Menuchah, which was nestled in a quaint storefront. Shimshon listened, breathing expansively and feeling infused with new life. Just hearing about Jerusalem brought back memories of last year's summer vacation. His father had sent him there for a change of scenery. At home he had brooded too much. Now, he realized how much he longed to go back.

"Do you know my aunt's family?" Shimshon asked eagerly. "Menachem and Tzvia Rochel Leventhal. I don't think they live too far from you. Anyway, she came there with my father and uncle after the war."

Immediately, the man's voice tightened. "I don't know her. Or her family."

"I think my father's foster parents live there. He met them in Auschwitz, and—"

"I don't know anyone there," the man answered testily, "except the *kollel* families."

"Oh," Shimshon said weakly.

Silence. Shimshon grew as nervous as Rav Shulman. Then he asked, timidly, "May I ask why you're in New York?"

With a deep, pitiful sigh, the man answered, "My daughter is very sick." As if on cue, his eyes welled up with tears, his face appropriately downcast.

"Chava Rivkah?" Shimshon asked, remembering the *mi sheberach* Shulman had made.

"Yes," Shulman answered.

"I'm sorry," Shimshon said, his faced clouded with thought. Oh, so he has a daughter. Shimshon wanted to ask him if she was also staying in Boro Park. But there was something in Shulman's voice — either the sorrow or the defensiveness — that held him back. "I hope she gets well quickly," he finally said.

"Thank you," answered the man.

Awkwardly, Shimshon hung out his hand, as if unsure what to do with it. Shulman shook it forcefully. His own hand seemed powerfully strong and athletic, and for a moment Shimshon feared being caught in its strong, pulsating grip. Quietly, Shulman turned and walked away.

Shimshon watched him vanish into the darkness. Suddenly he felt in his heart a strange attraction. In spite of this man's aloofness, there was something about him that seemed commanding; he had an aura of destiny about him. At the same time, Shimshon genuinely felt sorry for him. Avraham Shulman was neither a saint nor a Nazi — only a sad, elderly man appealing to G-d to spare his daughter's life.

He did not hear his father approach him, followed by Zelig.

"Coming, Shimshon?" the rabbi asked.

Shimshon turned around, startled. "Yeah . . . sure, Ta. Whenever you're ready."

Rabbi Shapiro exchanged glances with Zelig. Shimshon frowned.

As they were putting on their coats, Shimshon asked, "Ta?"

"What is it, Shimmy?"

"Ta, what do you think now of Avraham Shulman?"

The rabbi paused. He seemed calmer than before, yet the mention of the man's name seemed to jab him. "I don't know," he answered.

"After hearing him speak today," Shimshon said, "don't you agree that he's a good man?"

"I think," his father replied after a pause, "that he's a clever man."

"He's brilliant!" Shimshon exclaimed. "Ta . . . he's a genius. A *gaon*, just as Zelig said. He's wonderful. I want to be just like him some day."

His father looked at him sharply. "Shimshon," he said, "do you remember my once telling you not to judge a book by its cover?"

"I know, Ta," Shimshon answered, annoyed. "I know what you're saying."

"But it's not getting through to you, Shimshon."

They stopped at the door. Rabbi Shapiro turned and faced his son. "Not everyone can be Avraham Shulman," he announced solemnly. "I will admit . . . he's unique. I have never met anyone like him. He is unique . . . yes. But wonderful . . . no. I have spent a lifetime wondering why Hashem put people like him on this earth."

Chapter 5

Making Plans

Ten o'clock. The remains of the *melaveh malkah* had been cleared away. Rabbi Shapiro felt strangely relaxed. His eyes, watery and contemplative, were focused intensely on some inner reflection.

Upstairs, Shimshon was getting undressed. His mind was preparing for the week ahead. He tried to remember the topics for the next day's quiz. But his mind was still programed on the previous day's events. He processed the different happenings, and produced enormous emotional feedback.

Timing was crucial. He did not know how long Avraham Shulman intended to stay in Boro Park — if he had not already been intimidated enough to pack his bags. Remembering the look on his father's face the last time Shulman appeared, Shimshon couldn't tell which person it really was who had filled the *shul* with the awesome presence. Each, in his own way, was a powerful reminder of something terrible that had long ago taken place. Each, in his own way, was obsessed with the past, and connected it to something terrible that was now occurring. There was no telling what might happen next. Who would be the one to act — Avraham Shulman, or Yehuda Shapiro? Shulman was no fool. He knew to stay out of range — long enough, at least, to make the next move. Perhaps even now Shulman was sitting down at his own *melaveh malkah* — a diabolical one — thinking up some fiendish Nazi plot.

Shimshon shook his head frantically in disbelief, like a computer gone haywire from illogic. It was just too crazy. No, it was more than crazy — it was ridiculous! He laughed to himself . . . a Nazi at a *melaveh malkah*. But he stopped himself. He realized he was accusing Shulman of something — or of being something — about which Shimshon knew very little. True, this man was secretive about his past. But remembering how he spoke during *seudah shlishis* at *shul* that afternoon, Shimshon just could not imagine this man, a religious Jew, as anything but a Jew. How could a Nazi even think like a Jew? A being he hated for its very essence?

Of course, there was no reason that a Nazi couldn't be intelligent. Cunning was the word. The Nazis had to be in order to have ruled half of Europe. And a gentile could study Judaism. But Shimshon remembered the glowing light in Shulman's eyes whenever the latter spoke about the Torah. No non-Jew could ever feel that way.

The more he was convinced that Shulman could never have been a Nazi, the more he wondered if Shulman might have been a *kapo,* or some other Jew his father recognized — someone who had long ago collaborated with the Germans in order to survive. Maybe he was just too ashamed of his past to discuss it. Now that he had repented, he only desired to be left alone.

Still, it was upsetting to think that Shulman could have been a coward or conniver. He just didn't seem like that kind of person. There was something heroic about him . . . as if he were fighting a private battle. He was even a role model of sorts. Shimshon realized that he was truly growing infatuated with this man. He liked him — he didn't know why, he just did. And he could tell that Shulman liked him as well. Shulman seemed happy the last time he saw Shimshon in *shul,* and was glad to sit next to him. Shimshon sensed that this man liked children. He seemed drawn to them — and they to him. It was as if he had a certain power over them. And he certainly had a presence. But — Shimshon trembled at the thought — Hans Schmidt had run a children's camp.

Shimshon, by now, was thoroughly confused and distressed. On the one hand, he loathed to think of Shulman as a villain, but on the other, he hated to consider that his father was wrong. It was as if each person were tugging at him, trying to win him over to his side. But in order to prove Shulman guilty or innocent of any crime, he had to first learn who the man really was.

In his pajamas, the boy hurried to his desk and took out a small white envelope. Carefully, he wrote the address:

Yishmael Leventhal
Kiryat Yovel 48
Jerusalem, ISRAEL

Part one accomplished. Addressing the envelope was the easy part. Writing the letter would be more difficult. Shimshon never had the patience for letters. Besides, remembering his cousin's broken English, he wanted to write in Hebrew. Using his tattered dictionary, he carefully guided his pen leftward across the page, forcibly simplifying his thoughts. A shame his father couldn't help him with this.

An hour later, the letter was finally composed:

Dear Yishmael,
Hi! It's a long time since I've written. How are you?

I need your help. I want to know a little bit about a man named Avraham Shulman. He says he lives in your neighborhood, but Ta thinks he's from somewhere else. Have you ever heard of him? If so, please tell me what you know about him.

How is Aunt Tzvia Rochel? We're fine here, thank G-d. What are your plans for Pesach? We might be in Monsey. I don't know yet. I really wish we could stay in Boro Park.

Please tell Uncle Menachem I said hello. Maybe I'll see you again next year.

Love, Shimshon

The boy read and reread the letter. Satisfied at last, he folded it into the envelope, his hands noticeably trembling.

Tiptoeing down the stairs, he saw his father nodding off silently on the living room sofa. At the sound of the boy's footsteps, the rabbi shook himself awake.

"Still up, Shimshon?" he asked.

The boy grinned. "Got any stamps, Ta?"

"They're in the drawer in my desk."

The boy went quietly to the desk, which was in the den. Turning, he looked to see his father staring ahead; he appeared tranquil. Shimshon felt an overwhelming urge to sit with him for awhile. The boy went over to the couch and plopped himself down.

The rabbi looked at his son and smiled wearily. "This is getting to be a habit, you know — my driving you to school."

"I know, Ta."

"So why aren't you in bed?"

"I'm in my pajamas, Ta."

The rabbi was silent. A strange smile crossed his face. He felt at rest. The worries, terrors, obligations — everything had momentarily vanished. From a house nearby he heard a *melaveh malkah* celebration.

He continued to watch Shimshon wordlessly. He said with a wink, "Why don't you make us some hot chocolate?"

Bouncing off his chair, Shimshon abruptly turned to the kitchen, like a private responding to his sergeant. He smiled as he stirred the milk, watching the chocolate swirl and finally dissolve into a creamy brown layer. That's how his father liked to drink it. Thick and rich. Perhaps, over chocolate, his father would tell him more stories.

Another two days went by before Shimshon finally remembered the letter. Till then it had lain patiently in his pocket, waiting to be mailed. But somehow, a school function and an impromptu baseball game did a lot to divert a boy's attention. Not until Wednesday, as he ran his hands through his pockets searching for *chametz*, did he feel the envelope. He dropped it into the corner mailbox that very evening.

Returning home, he saw his father at the desk, the phone pressed close to his mouth. Shimshon frowned. He did not like the look on his father's face. The latter had not even heard his son enter the house.

Not until he had put down the receiver did Rabbi Shapiro look up and notice his son standing motionless in the archway. Shimshon's eyes rested on his father with knowing concern.

"Uh, Shimshon, looks like we're going to be here for Pesach," he said.

The boy stared wordlessly.

"Well, I should think you'd be pleased," his father replied somewhat indignantly. "You kept saying how you wanted to stay here. We have a definite change of plan."

Still Shimshon didn't answer. His father turned away angrily. "You confuse me sometimes, Shimshon. If you don't want to communicate with me, please go upstairs."

Quietly withdrawing, Shimshon went to his room and threw himself on the bed, resting his hands behind his head and keeping his eyes fixed on the ceiling.

So Gedalia Silverman's daughter had a boy and he had to go to Cleveland for Pesach. Or was there another reason? Tati had not said why they were staying in Boro Park. Shimshon sensed his father was hiding something from him. Something important. Something that was upsetting him. If only his father could have seen his own face right now . . . the tension, the struggle to keep control, the awful waiting. And Ta will start dreaming again . . . just like last night.

Shimshon was relieved that he had finally mailed the letter. He was irked at having waited four days. It would mean four days longer to receive an answer — assuming, of course, that his cousin wrote on time. And with the outrageously slow mail to and from Israel, who knew how long it would take? Strange, Shimshon thought. No sooner had he mailed the letter regarding background information on Shulman than the phone call to his father had come. They really needed the information from Israel quickly.

Shimshon shuddered, only partly from fear. He enjoyed letting his imagination run wild. He even found this cat-and-mouse game with Shulman a bit exciting. During the time it took to send a letter to Israel and get one back, Shulman could act swiftly. He might be planning this very minute to bring harm to the Shapiro residence. Or, at the very least, Shulman might be leaving town. He might be going back to Israel, or no, better still, South America, where all the Nazis were supposed to be hiding. They were there, in their mansions and fancy cars, surrounded by guards and vicious dogs. Probably Shulman had a mansion of his own somewhere.

But then Shimshon thought of Shulman's daughter, Chava Rivkah. Remembering how the old man's eyes had welled up at the mention of her name, Shimshon wondered if she was real — and if she truly was sick. She seemed to be. Like Shulman's knowledge, the *mi sheberach* had seemed real enough. She was part of his reason for being in the States — or so he said. And if so, Shulman wouldn't be in too big a hurry to leave.

Of course, how real were Shulman's tears? Perhaps he had just made the whole story up, to fool everybody. Yet he had looked so sad.

That's it, Shimshon thought, bouncing off the bed. He had to see this man again. There was no other way. He had to confront him, challenge him, strip away the mask. There would be no more contradictions, no more hiding. Avraham Shulman would show his true self.

Actually, Shimshon knew his true reason for going to Shulman: he simply wished to see the man again. It wasn't even his aura of mystery . . . it was more the way he had spoken about Torah, nearly burning Shimshon away with his fire. The boy longed to hear more of his wisdom.

Throwing on his jacket, Shimshon looked at the clock. Seven o'clock. Good, he thought, still early enough. He prayed that Shulman was still in town. Somehow, the boy sensed that he was.

This man was not the kind to leave a place without finishing his work.

At the top of the stairs, Shimshon stopped. It occurred to him: he had absolutely no idea where Shulman lived. The only person who might know was Zelig, but Shimshon knew it was unwise to call Zelig, who was most likely communicating with his father on this matter. Shimshon wondered if everyone in the *shul* was just as suspicious as Rabbi Shapiro. Leaning against the balcony, Shimshon watched his father, who was mumbling on the phone in Yiddish. In one hand, he pressed the receiver close; in the other, he was writing something down on a small slip of paper.

His father put down the receiver and moved toward the kitchen. Shimshon raced down the stairs and hurried to the desk.

On a little slip of paper an address and phone number were etched in ink:

2001 Justin Road
555-8679

There was no name. But, somehow, Shimshon knew. He's there, waiting for me. The boy memorized the address and phone number, repeating them constantly.

Justin Road. Wasn't that off the old subway tracks? He vaguely remembered having passed by it once on his bike. It was the kind of place he would rather forget. Nevertheless, he calculated how far it was from his house.

Just then his father walked in. "You're not staying for dinner, Shimshon?" he asked, noticing the boy in his jacket.

"No, Ta," Shimshon explained. "Gotta go somewhere. Gotta see a friend of mine."

"And when are you going to clean for Pesach?"

"Later tonight, Ta."

His father continued to eye him suspiciously. "Who are you going to visit?" he asked.

"A friend," Shimshon answered hastily, and bolted out the door.

He felt guilty about lying to his father. But then, he thought, Avraham Shulman *was* a friend . . . sort of. And besides, maybe now it was Shimshon's turn to keep a secret from his father.

The nocturnal wind rustled through the blackening neighborhood, causing the shadows of the trees to dance under the street lights. In the sky, dark streaks of clouds were slowly drifting into a silent mass. Shimshon hugged his coat tighter, and felt a growing chill.

As he passed by a phone booth, he wondered if perhaps he should let Shulman know ahead of time that he was coming. It was certainly proper. But then it might be best to just drop in on the man and catch him off guard. That way, Shimshon could see him exactly as he was. There would be no facade.

Racing down the avenue, Shimshon felt expansive with pride and adventure. He was delighted with his cleverness and his ability to make adult decisions. He was feeling more and more like his father. In fact, he couldn't help seeing himself as some kind of hero. Even more than that — he felt like a secret agent, one with a special mission to perform to help save his people . . . his and Hashem's. Boy, Shulman will be impressed, he thought. And Ta.

But other, more disturbing thoughts began to creep in. It occurred to Shimshon that this trip could also be dangerous. Shulman might not like visitors . . . especially considering how he guarded his privacy. Shimshon's steps faltered, and he stopped, hesitating, wondering if perhaps he should just be a good boy — go home, and stick to spy novels instead. Besides, there was no telling what a Nazi might do. Shulman might kill him, or lock him up, or hold him hostage. In fact, Shulman didn't even have to be a Nazi; any crazy man was capable of doing those things.

Shimshon froze. He was already well down the avenue, but he felt tempted to turn around and run back to his father. His little secret agent game was over. He was playing with a dangerous fire, which threatened to consume him and those he loved.

Besides, Shimshon thought, what if this wasn't Shulman's address? It could very well be someone else's . . . a friend of Ta. And how would this person like it if Shimshon showed up at his door, unannounced and uninvited?

The more Shimshon pondered the matter, the more he was convinced that he would be doing the right thing by turning back. But it was too late. His feet were transporting him without the least resistance, as if following orders from somewhere else. Shimshon realized that he no longer had control over his movements. He was being led to Justin Road. And he knew that he would find Shulman there.

He felt his trepidation growing by leaps and bounds as he left the safety of Boro Park.

Heading left, he heard the loud hiss of a slithering subway train. By now his home was a distant memory. Shimshon, following the tracks, turned sharply right, and searched for the tiny side street, where he remembered seeing a small leather factory. He grew nervous as he noticed a street sign obscured by a dismal clump of trees. He grew even more nervous as he turned and entered a wide cul-de-sac, which was just beyond a scrapyard. Above, the parallel tracks circled the factory, winding and abruptly ending by the distant industrial buildings. Off to their side began, as if in afterthought, a narrow stretch of pavement, ending after several hundred yards with a billboard just waiting to collapse. Justin Road.

Approaching the block, Shimshon finally rested. Again repeating the address, he looked ahead in bewilderment.

In the distance, past a vacant, trash-laden lot, he saw a medium-sized apartment complex. It was a painfully delapidated four-story structure, surrounded by scattered huts, like an ancient mausoleum in a deserted graveyard. It might have once been modern, even elegant, but that era had long ago passed, and it had succumbed to decay. It was flanked on both sides by high embankments and tall, shriveled trees, which writhed in the wind like snakes. Two pale street lamps cast a haunting, wretched yellow tint on the streaked glass entrance. The painted numbers, indicating the address, were faded, but the outline remained: 2001 Justin Road.

"Carlos! Ven aca!"

Nervously, Shimshon turned to see a group of children yelling on a wooden porch of a nearby house. One boy was running to his mother, a corpulent woman who was standing in an open doorway; behind her flickered the bluish glow of an old TV set. Shimshon retreated as he saw, off to the right, a group of teenagers sitting around a parked car, laughing. One of them, standing among empty beer cans, had a radio turned up to a deafening volume. It was a bit unnerving, although Shimshon did not understand why it should frighten him. They were not harming anybody. Still, he felt a tinge of fear. He was further shaken by a pack of scruffy stray dogs which scampered across the potholed street. Ignoring Shimshon, they wandered off into the vacant lot.

Taking a deep breath, he moved his legs, which now felt like lead, but nevertheless carried him to the entrance. He was no longer their master. The stench of garbage was overpowering. Shimshon was grateful that he had skipped dinner. Already he was thoroughly nauseated, and he doubted that he could have held anything down. Finally, he entered through the glass doors.

The mailboxes were two symmetrical rows of dented metal doors. The last had the name Shulman marked above it in fresh ink: Apartment 4D; the highest story.

The elevator, its doors dented so that it looked like a giant mailbox, was out of order. Shimshon was actually relieved; it eliminated the decision of whether or not to place himself under its tender mercies. The last thing he needed was to be trapped inside, unable to call for help. In the stairwell, at least, he could escape if necessary.

When he opened the door, however, he recoiled as he was confronted by the malodorous stairwell. The corridor was filthy; the iron steps were smeared with soot. The walls displayed an interesting array of graffiti. Clutching his nose, Shimshon began the ascent.

All the way up, Shimshon glanced about fearfully, expecting to find one of the street people he had seen in old alleyways. There were so many of them, too; they were usually seen shuffling around in their tattered garments, mumbling furiously at the world and chain-smoking cigarettes. Though they looked menacing, most of them seemed as afraid of Shimshon as he was of them. Shimshon was always amazed at how anyone could fall to such a level. These people reminded him somehow of the pictures he had seen of concentration camp survivors — living symbols of degeneration and despair. Of course, his father had always explained that these people couldn't really help themselves. No one in his right mind chose to be sick and poor.

But he couldn't imagine Shulman living this way — unless, of course, Shulman was insane. Perhaps he was too embarrassed to tell anyone where he lived; it could also explain why he was so secretive about himself. Probably he had lived in even worse places. Maybe he needed financial help.

The last flight of stairs was cleaner — in fact refined compared to the rest of the building. Probably, Shimshon guessed, no one ever got up this far but the tenants. The others were too drunk to make it past the first floor.

Nevertheless, the floor was in sorry condition. Chunks of plaster were strewn on the carpet in crumbly heaps, their shapes matching the holes in the walls. The doors were painted a sickening brown.

Anxiously Shimshon paused by each door and studied the number: 4A, 4B — he counted, his heart pounding rapidly. At the end of the hall was 4D.

Shaking, Shimshon stopped, gasping for breath. He knew he was afraid — there was no use hiding it. It wasn't just because of this neighborhood. It was because of this person he was about to meet — a person willing to live in this dirty, foul place. Already Shimshon had an idea what kind of man Avraham Shulman was.

He stood before the door. My last chance to get away, he thought. Looking up, he noticed a *mezuzah.* With a certain relief, he raised his hands and pressed his fingers to it.

Suddenly, he stiffened. Through the door he heard voices. There were several, actually, but two seemed to predominate: one cold and authoritative, the other meditative but argumentative. The language trickling through sounded like Yiddish.

After several seconds, Shimshon knocked.

Instantly, the voices hushed. He could hear footsteps getting nearer, and then the door abruptly opened.

Shimshon backed away. Instead of a tall, lithe man dressed in chassidic black, a squat, stocky man, with a balding pate, eyes as hard as stone, and a mouth to match glared at him. There was a fierce-looking moustache spread over his face In his youth this man might have been a boxer or wrestler.

"What do you want?" he growled.

"I . . . I . . ."

"Well?"

Shimshon croaked, "Is Avraham Shulman here?"

The man did not answer. Instead, he surveyed this pale boy in the plaid yarmulke, whose brown eyes were wide with fright and who was now cringing in the hallway.

"He can't come to the door right now," he barked.

"Who is it, Heinz?" asked a voice approaching from behind.

Avraham Shulman gasped. "Shimshon! What are you doing here?"

Shulman was standing erect. His white, creaseless shirt was carefully tucked inside his pants, and his long *tzitzis* flowed down his sides. The black yarmulke was perched squarely on the back of his head. "I am shocked," he said.

Shimshon turned the color of salt. "I wanted to surprise you with a visit, Rav Shulman," he stammered.

With a flick of the hand, Shulman sent Heinz away. He himself remained by the door.

Blushing, Shimshon continued, "You were so interesting in *shul* . . . I loved to hear you talk about Yerushalayim. And I wanted to know . . . how's your daughter?"

Avraham Shulman kept his gaze steadfastly on the boy. His eyes, so luminous, seemed like two crystal daggers, ready to slice into Shimshon's flesh at a whim. Then, from steely hazel, they changed to deep sapphire blue.

His face twitched. "You should have phoned me first, Shimshon," he said.

Now Shimshon really wished that he had. Confused, he peeked inside. The apartment was dark, but a hanging lamp cast enough light to allow him a glimpse. In the living room he discerned four men dressed in dark business suits. They were scowling like a pack of trolls at this young intruder. Even from a distance they exuded power.

Shimshon felt himself sinking into the floor. "I'm sorry," he whispered.

"I am also shocked that you would walk to this area at night," Shulman continued sternly. "A young boy like you. I don't know whether you are brave or foolish." Then he added, "I can't imagine your father would let you come here alone."

"He doesn't know I'm here," Shimshon replied. He was shivering.

"Then you are even more foolish." He added, more gently, "I would love to talk with you, but unfortunately I am preoccupied tonight with some very important business. Why don't you come some other time?"

"All right," Shimshon answered. He felt humiliated.

"And during the day," Shulman added.

"Yes, sir."

"And Shimshon . . . one other thing . . ."

"Yes?"

"Please call first," Shulman commanded.

"Yes, I will," Shimshon answered. "Good night."

"Good night." Shulman closed the door.

Shimshon lingered by the door, his mind still disoriented, as if he had seen something wildly out of place. Inside the apartment, all was silent. Perhaps they were waiting for him to leave. But Shimshon had little desire to eavesdrop. And even if he had, he knew he would not have understood what they were saying. He backed away slowly, then trotted, and finally broke off into a run.

He hurried down the putrid staircase, grateful not to find a derelict waiting for him. He had already had enough excitement for the evening. All he wanted to do was to flee this haunted house and blot out its memories. After he made it to the bottom, he paused to catch his breath, as well as his wits.

The encounter with Shulman left him feeling even more bewildered. But looking around this squalid place, he still could not make any connection to Shulman. The man was here, in all his glory. It did not make sense what he was doing here. And Shimshon didn't dare ask. He had come to the wrong place at the wrong time.

Or was it the right place at the right time? Inside, 4D seemed like another world. There was something there that Shimshon was not supposed to see. Those men — were they businessmen? And what kind of business? Was Shulman himself one of them? Of that Shimshon was not sure. Was Avraham Shulman a religious Jew? Of this Shimshon was certain.

But one question aroused the most curiosity in Shimshon: Was Avraham Shulman a Nazi? Shimshon compared the man who stood in a half-condemned building off of Justin Road and the man at the lectern in a *shul* off Eighteenth Avenue. Outwardly, they were one and the same. Nevertheless, Shulman seemed to have two personalities tied in one bundle — quiet and intense on the one hand, powerful and forbidding on the other. Both aspects were integrated into the man's life. And he had been defensive when Shimshon tried to see him in a more personal light. Still, Shimshon thought as he gazed out the glass doors, Shulman didn't seem at all like a Nazi. Even when angry, he had spoken to Shimshon kindly.

Yet who said all Nazis were outwardly cruel? It seemed to Shimshon — after reading all the Holocaust literature he had recently consumed — as if there were two kinds: the vicious SS guard and the quiet, intellectual bureaucrat. Maybe Shulman — Schmidt? — was the second type. But could somebody that passive have run a concentration camp?

Then Shimshon was aware of something else: tonight he had seen Shulman without his long black coat. The man possessed a powerful build. He might have been an athlete in his younger days. He probably had the physical prowess needed to run a camp.

Shimshon's mind raced with questions. Why did Shulman choose to live in such a dump? Was this all he could afford? Surely a businessman could splurge on better accommodations — especially if he were entertaining clients. Why, Shimshon's father, himself a businessman, would never think of meeting in a dump like this. Maybe Shulman wasn't a very good businessman.

Further, why rent a place among non-Jews when a Jewish neighborhood was nearby? Also, those men in Shulman's apartment — especially Heinz — didn't seem Jewish.

As the boy stood in the hallway, he heard the loud clamor of footsteps descending the stairs. He also heard a masculine roar in the same language that had come from 4D. Quickly he pushed open the glass door and hurried out.

Outside, the street sounds had died down. The children were

gone. There was no sign of the dogs, either. Teenage laughter echoed from down the block.

Shimshon was tempted to run. But as if commanded by an inner voice, he remained riveted to the ground. Noticing a forlorn group of trees opposite the building, he darted across the street and flattened himself against a trunk.

From this vantage point he was able to observe the front of 2001 Justin Road. Four men exited the building. Standing and facing the curb, their figures were illuminated, ghost-like, under the lamps. Though their features were blurred, their faces were unquestionably elderly and European. Each of them wore a three-piece business suit, clean and sharply creased. The tallest one pulled out from his vest a gold pocket watch and glanced at it with a certain diffidence. Shimshon looked at his own watch. Eight-thirty sharp.

Suddenly a limousine, its sleek blackness gleaming even in the dark night, hummed down the street and pulled abruptly to a halt. The teenage gang turned to stare at this magnificent vehicle, as if it were a movie prop that had wandered into the wrong set.

Shimshon, too, stared in amazement. Out of the front seat stepped a chauffeur, as impeccably dressed as the men in their three-piece suits. He circled the car, opening the doors, then waited stiffly.

Deftly the men entered. The tallest, the one with the gold watch, was the last one to go in. He remained under the lamppost, waiting. The light shone on his features, making them more distinct, enabling Shimshon to see him more clearly. His lean face appeared almost as youthful as Shulman's. His white hair was streaked with remnants of blond. From his other breast pocket he removed a silver cigarette case. Lighting a cigarette, he momentarily leaned his slender frame against the lamppost and blew gray circles into the air. He looked off in the direction of Boro Park, and a very sardonic-seeming smile crossed his face. He smiled, half in triumph, half in mockery. His mouth twisted satanically, baring a row of even white teeth.

Shimshon continued to watch this man in utter fascination. The man's bearing seemed even more aristocratic than Shulman's. But somehow it was a different kind of royalty — like a crown prince of darkness, or a robber baron. If he commanded respect, it was neither because of character nor due to achievement, but through fear. Also, unlike Shulman, he didn't seem at all out of place in this wasteland.

So absorbed was Shimshon that he completely forgot a basic for aspiring detectives: get the license plate number. By the time it occurred to him to do so, it was too late; the limousine, gliding into reverse, entered the cul-de-sac and vanished into the darkness. Only the smell of gas lingered.

Shimshon continued to watch the building. From not too far away he heard the morbid hum of trains. He became aware that it was late and that by now his father was, with good reason, getting worried. Shimshon had not told him where he was going. And he could not tell him now, either –- not until he had learned more about Shulman, and possibly the men who were with him tonight.

The boy turned and headed home, forgetting his fear of the neighborhood. He was too busy brooding over his failures. He was angry for not being able to talk to Shulman. He was angry for not being able to understand what Shulman and those men were saying. But mostly, he was angry for not getting the license plate number.

Some detective you are, Shimshon, he chided himself on the way home. He had been so proud of his ability to plan ahead. And now, he had missed the most crucial piece of information. The license plate number could have led to very useful data.

Still, Shimshon mused, as he turned right and walked up Eighteenth Avenue, the evening was not a total loss. He felt that he had gained a little insight into the private world of Avraham Shulman — a world of secrecy and suspicion, which was slowly becoming part of Shimshon's own world.

As Shimshon approached the familiar streets, he breathed a sigh of relief, as if he had just escaped from dangerous clutches. Never before had he looked forward to seeing his father as he did now.

By the time he made it past Fiftieth Street, it had begun to rain. Covering his head tightly with his jacket, Shimshon felt the cool drops splatter. Through the window of one building he heard the singsong of Torah study. Here, among Jews, he felt safe.

When he arrived, breathlessly, at the front door, he saw his father seated at his desk, with an open briefcase and various documents.

Glancing at the boy, the rabbi said, "You had me worried, Shimshon." He looked at his watch disapprovingly, as if to make his point.

Shyly, Shimshon hung up his coat.

"So much in a rush," the rabbi said, shaking his head. "Was it such an emergency?"

Shimshon nodded. "I didn't stay too long, Ta — *honest.*"

"Then what did you do all this time?"

"Oh . . . I walked. And thought about a lot of things."

"I hope you thought about your Pesach cleaning—"

"Yeah, Ta, I know."

"And your homework?"

"I know, Ta, I'll do it."

"It's an effort to keep after you. But maybe now you'll settle down and concentrate on more important things."

Shimshon murmured dreamily. "I did, Ta."

Chapter 6

Fateful Encounter

The following Friday was unseasonably warm, and the air from the cloudless skies wafted through the silent streets, filtering into the crowded *shul*. Rabbi Shapiro and Shimshon took their places, and *minchah* began. As usual, the latecomers made noise coming in, disturbing those who had arrived on time.

After the sky had gradually turned dusky gray, and the *shul* had sufficiently swelled with congregants, *Kabbalas Shabbos,* the prayer which welcomes the Sabbath, began. In a clear voice, Rabbi Shapiro began singing *Lecha Dodi,* carefully annunciating each word, his face radiantly announcing the arrival of Shabbos. There could be no doubt that Rabbi Shapiro looked forward to Shabbos the way a husband looks forward to seeing his wife after having been away an entire week.

Shimshon, too, had looked forward to greeting a long-lost visitor, but his voice trailed along weakly in disappointment, as he realized that what he was waiting for simply would not materialize. He sat at the back of the sanctuary, hoping to see Avraham Shulman arrive, but as the sky filled with stars, he was nowhere to be seen. In vain, Shimshon tried to lift his sagging spirits, but in the end he could barely concentrate on *ma'ariv.*

During the meal, however, he brightened. Here, his attention was piqued by a guest — a friend of his father named Jonah Wasserman, from Washington Heights. This Shabbos he was in Boro Park to attend his grandson's *bris.*

Jonah Wasserman, born in Frankfurt, Germany, had emigrated with his family in 1939 — first to England (he was fifteen at the time), and then to the United States, in 1952. He had readily picked up English, speaking it even more fluently than Rabbi Shapiro. His accent, which Shimshon always enjoyed hearing, rang British even after all these years, with faint German undertones.

Jonah Wasserman, the son of a clothing manufacturer, had become one himself, eventually building up a moderately successful chain of retail stores throughout the East Coast. Like Yehuda Shapiro, he had left Europe in fear and poverty — the Nazis brutally stripping his family of everything before allowing them to leave. However, unlike Yehuda Shapiro, his immediate family had left their former land intact. His seven brothers and sisters had settled throughout the world, transplanting their lives and beginning newer, happier stories. Jonah himself had married in England, later bringing to the United States his wife and son, who now had a son of his own.

At the table, Wasserman exuded a jovial and relaxed feeling. He seemed very much a proud patriarch. Other than a middle-aged paunch, he carried no burdens with him. Like Rabbi Shapiro, he had become a successful businessman and community member. There were no bitter tears, no nightmares, no traumas, no horror stories. He had happily severed ties with the European continent the moment his feet touched British soil. Of course, he had left Germany at the right time. Here again he differed from Rabbi Shapiro. They were two halves who made a whole: Jonah Wasserman, who experienced the beginnings of Nazism — during the years before 1939 — and was spared the climax; and Yehuda Shapiro, who picked up where Jonah left off and felt a far more devastating impact.

Shimshon had met this friend of his father many times before, but always at a respectful distance. Of course, what would a small boy have to do with him, anyway? Nevertheless, Shimshon had always liked this big, warmhearted man with the deep booming voice. Previously, Shimshon would never have thought to ask Wasserman about his past — and neither would Jonah Wasserman himself have considered discussing it. Only tonight, during dessert, as the latter was calmly sipping tea, did Shimshon speak up.

"Mr. Wasserman," he said, "what was it like living in Germany back then?"

The eyes on the man's jowly face widened at the mention of the words "back then." From the kitchen, Yehuda Shapiro flung a very disapproving glance.

Jonah Wasserman put down his cup and, like any good businessman, waited thoughtfully before answering. "Well . . . 'back then' was over forty years ago, Shimshon. A lot happens to a person in such a time span. A lot. Helps me to forget about all those times 'back then.' Also," he added with a wink, "I'll let you in on a secret. I'm a little older than I used to be. It's sometimes difficult to remember everything. After awhile, things get hazy."

"So you don't remember anything at all," Shimshon replied, crestfallen.

Amused, Jonah Wasserman looked at him, sensing that somehow this boy had hoped to hear something juicy. "No, actually I do." Wasserman's voice rose. "There are, in fact, certain things that to this day stand out in my mind."

"Like what?" Shimshon asked.

"Oh . . . like the Brownshirts throwing stones at my father's store. And seeing signs painted over it . . . filthy, insulting things." Jonah Wasserman's eyes glazed. "A knock on the door late at night was enough to make anyone cold with terror."

"Why?"

Wasserman's eyes narrowed. "Gestapo. They usually came at night. Some of my father's friends were taken away . . . and never returned."

With a sigh, Wasserman continued. "I was just a boy, Shimshon. It's difficult for a boy to grow up and have to see that. To be confronted every day with ridicule and violence. Why, I clearly remember — must have been in '34 or '35 — being taken by my parents to *cheder* as the Hitler *Jugend* — Hitler Youth, that is — jeered at us in the streets."

"What did you do?" asked Shimshon incredulously.

"Nothing. Basically, we tried to ignore them. What else could we do? They were stronger than us. And they didn't want us in Germany anymore. By the time our synagogue was destroyed — in 1938 — my family finally took the hint. Through relatives in London, we got emigration visas."

After a sigh, Wasserman continued drinking his tea. His expression indicated that the tea was no longer steaming, but he sipped it anyway.

Shimshon asked, "Did you ever once try to fight back?"

Jonah Wasserman remained in meditative silence, as if he were about to make a profound decision. Fingering the teacup, he finally answered, "To ignore them . . . and to continue being Jewish . . . seem defiant, don't they?"

To Shimshon, somehow they didn't. He was tempted to argue, but another glance from his father held him back. Lately, his father had been speaking harshly with him. Shimshon was wasting his time reading, Rabbi Shapiro complained, instead of cleaning for Pesach. His room and closets were still in disarray, as Shimshon had never got around to working on them the night he had gone out to see his "friend."

Rabbi Shapiro was growing agitated at his son's obsession with the Holocaust. My fault, he reflected sadly; had he not kept his son awake nights, this might never have happened. But by now, he was worried that the books Shimshon was devouring were actually feeding certain fantasies. And Rabbi Shapiro had additional cause for concern. Shimshon had become terribly fond of Avraham Shulman.

When during *shacharis* the next day the rabbi saw his son again watching the door, he frowned. Shimshon, noticing his father's disapproval, slunk into his seat and kept his eyes steadfast on his *siddur.* By the time of the Torah reading he had resigned himself to the fact that Shulman would not show up.

During *seudah shlishis,* after *minchah,* Shimshon tried to keep his mind on his father's *drasha* and his face toward the table. But by the time *havdalah* was made he approached Zelig and asked pleadingly where Shulman had gone.

Zelig was evasive. "He didn't speak with me at all, Shimshon. Maybe he's away."

"Yeah," the boy answered sullenly. "We scared him away."

"That's enough, Shimshon," his father interjected sharply. "It's best that he isn't here. I don't think it's a good idea for you to be around him."

The boy argued, "But Ta—"

"Shimshon, I don't want to have to repeat myself," his father said angrily. Clutching his son firmly by the shoulders, the rabbi knelt. "Shimshon, listen to me. Avraham Shulman is a strange man, and dangerous. You don't know him. Please. He knows you're my son, and he might try to use that to his advantage."

"He likes me," Shimshon insisted, fighting tears.

"Don't take that at face value, Shimshon. He knows how to lie to children."

The boy stared at his father in shock.

"You still think he's a Nazi?" he asked, hurt.

"What do *you* think?" the rabbi retorted.

The father answered his own question. "I think he's a liar. He is not to be trusted. And I want to protect you from his kind."

Morosely, Shimshon followed his father home. He had never questioned his father's authority. But somehow he just could not accept what he had heard this evening.

He himself could not understand his attachment to Avraham Shulman. But this man's absence had left the *shul* — and Shimshon — feeling desolate, like a deserted isle. Perhaps it was his scholarship, which peeled away the delicate layers of Torah like a rare fruit. Or perhaps, as Rabbi Shapiro implied, it was a dark side . . . his amazing ability to deceptively dazzle his audience with his sense of command and power.

During the week, using the yeshiva pay phone, Shimshon repeatedly dialed Shulman's number. No answer. Many times during the daytime, as well as into the evening (from a friend's house), he persisted. Still no answer. Shimshon was frantic. Perhaps Rav Shulman really had gone away, he thought. Perhaps he was aware of Tati's suspicions. If he did leave for that reason — out of fear of being discovered — then Tati was correct.

Shimshon was tempted to just drop in on Shulman as he had done previously, but he remembered the old man's insistence on being notified ahead of time. Either Shulman was formal, or he liked to be prepared.

By the following Shabbos, Shimshon's frustration had given way to despair. Again he sat alone in the back of the *shul.* Again, Shimshon recited his prayers without enthusiasm; the old man's departure had left a gaping void.

His father simply refused to discuss Shulman. It was amazing. This man, Avraham Shulman, was the one responsible for the nightmares and terror; and yet, now Rabbi Shapiro regarded the man as if he were hardly worth spitting at. But then, perhaps ignoring him was the best way. If Avraham Shulman represented something to Yehuda Shapiro, then regarding him as a mere annoyance rather than a threat meant refusing to be intimidated. Treating Shulman with contemptful silence did perhaps make sense. As Jonah Wasserman had suggested, continuing to live one's regular life constituted an act of defiance.

By the end of Shabbos, Shimshon was seriously considering the possibility that his father was really right. Just forget about Shulman. Eventually his interest would dissipate, and Shulman would become a vague memory. Along with everything of his past.

Shimshon turned his focus instead on Pesach and its preparations. He knew he would have to overcome a slow start, especially if he wanted to get back into his father's good graces. He had lost enough time. Carefully, the boy sat down and made a list of the remaining rooms to clean, things to buy, errands to run, laws of Pesach to review. Buy lots of aluminum foil, he thought. Get a haircut.

After school, Shimshon would wind his way among the crowds of people in the various stores, open late for the pre-Pesach rush. After standing in line for what seemed like hours, he would return home, groceries in hand. Then he would help Mrs. Friedman around the house.

The yeshiva ended classes several days before Passover. Shimshon was thankful for this extra time. It was early Tuesday afternoon when Shimshon came home with an arm load of shopping bags and found the mail left on the dining room table by Mrs. Friedman. On top of the small bundle lay an airmail envelope with a colorful Israeli stamp. Shimshon quickly put down his coat and tore open the envelope. The letter was in Hebrew.

Dear Shimmy,

It was great to hear from you again. Everything here is fine. Mom says hello.

Everyone here knows Avraham Shulman. He lives two blocks away, in one of the kollel *buildings. His son Shmueli is in my class. My father sometimes prays at Ohr Menuchah.*

Sometimes on the way to school I see Avraham Shulman on a bench, learning. He has a lot of guests — somehow he fits them all into his tiny place. His wife, Breinda, cooks for the yeshiva. She is always doing good things, such as visiting the sick people in the area; she was the one who sent food to Mom after she had Devorah.

They told me Rav Shulman was away again. I

didn't know he went to Boro Park this time. He travels a lot — I think to raise money. He does all kinds of work for the yeshiva; he's the sexton there. His whole family does a lot of kindness. He's really a nice man, and supposedly brilliant. He likes talking to me and my friends a lot.

Have a happy Pesach. Please say hi to Uncle Yehuda for me.

Yishmael

Shimshon scrutinized the letter as carefully as if he were reviewing a page of Gemara. Absently, he remained in the doorway, reading the contents again and again.

So Avraham Shulman *did* exist. And according to Yishmael, he was a Talmud scholar who feared G-d. His Torah study was no game. But somehow Shimshon knew that already. From his cousin's description, Shulman almost sounded like a Jerusalem beggar — one of the quaint, eccentric characters with inner secrets and a certain folk wisdom. Shimshon smiled as he visualized Shulman in tattered garments, sitting on the cobblestone steps, collection box in hand, reciting Psalms. Certainly that image was far more believable than the one of a Nazi in a starched uniform, standing at a train station, holding a whip and quoting *Mein Kampf.*

Yet, poring over the letter's contents, it occurred to Shimshon that something was missing. His cousin had said nothing about the daughter's illness. Of Shulman's children, Yishmael only mentioned a son, Shmueli. Yishmael did not bother to mention — what was her name? — Chava Rivkah. Did Yishmael know that Shulman had a daughter? Strange that he wouldn't, Shimshon thought. She was the reason that Shulman had come to Boro Park. Or perhaps Shulman, for whatever reason, never told anyone about her.

In fact, Yishmael had been vague about Shulman's absence. He assumed that Shulman was away raising money for the *kollel* — something Shulman apparently did often. According to Yishmael, Shulman often traveled abroad — especially "lately." But had he traveled much in the past? And how often? Were there other reasons for traveling?

And — Shimshon argued further — why so many trips? If his business was legitimate, why didn't he do it all at once? Then the answer, obviously: the yeshiva must want it that way. But it seemed strange that such an impoverished *kollel* could afford to send someone away this often — unless there was no other way.

But remembering the men Shimshon had seen, it seemed more plausible to him that, yes, Shulman *was* meeting with businessmen to raise money. Still, why would he meet with them in that filthy place on Justin Road? Unless he was trying to elicit sympathy. Come and see how impoverished Torah scholars live, folks. That might be further proof that Shulman was raising money for the *kollel* — if that was the only kind of place the *kollel* could afford for him. Most likely — since Yishmael called Shulman's place "tiny" — the place Shimshon had seen on Justin Road was luxurious compared to how Shulman was living in Israel.

However, the idea of Shulman — an intense, scholarly recluse — being a fund-raiser seemed almost as farfetched as the thought of his being a Nazi. Shimshon thought, in contrast, of the well-dressed, cultured Jonah Wasserman. Now Wasserman struck one as a man who was involved in financial affairs. Not Shulman.

Still, Shulman himself seemed authoritative. And he didn't lack refinement. Also, if Shulman was able to associate with such wealthy, professional-looking men like the ones Shimshon had seen that night, it indicated that he possessed a measure of financial importance. But wouldn't it be odd that someone who had been in a sheltered, quiet *kollel* all these years suddenly decided to enter the aggressive and competitive world of fund-raising? However — Shimshon argued — knowing Shulman's mind, why should it be surprising? Shulman was — Shimshon's father implied — shrewd and calculating. Whether by personality or by acquisition, he had the skills needed to succeed in business: decisiveness, analytical judgment, secrecy, the ability to size up the immediate situation. His sharp, penetrating mind, undoubtedly refined through years of Torah study, was probably well suited for business. His Torah lectures were warehouses of seemingly contradictory, yet related, ideas complementing one another and merging into one solid block of thoughts.

Shulman was definitely a man of ideas. But he was, at the same time, pragmatic. He probably knew when to act. Also, he had other inner resources — tremendous charisma, as well as physical strength. Who knows? With his fertile mind and ability to bring ideas down to a concrete form, he could go very far in business. He was extraordinary. Why not a financial wizard as well? Shulman was the kind of man who could succeed at most anything in life.

Knowing Shulman's scholarship and refinement, Shimshon felt ashamed that he had questioned the man's character. The letter from Yishmael confirmed it. Here was a man who was committed to Torah, and used his intellectual gifts to help Torah institutions. As for Shulman's family, Yishmael had not mentioned Shulman's daughter because he simply did not know that Chava Rivkah was sick. Shulman never bothered to discuss it. Why should Yishmael know? Certainly a humble man like Shulman would not want to bring up the subject of disease. Besides, Shulman would never be that intimate with Yishmael, who was of a completely different generation. Moreover, Yishmael's parents were not part of the *kollel;* Yishmael's father only prayed there from time to time. And knowing how secretive Shulman was, Shimshon guessed that he was probably reluctant to give out much personal information. Still, Shimshon mused with a certain trepidation, he did enjoy talking to children there . . .

The more Shimshon pondered, the more it made sense that a man of such talent and strength, who could easily attract businessmen to his causes, would naturally be asked to travel for fund-raising purposes. And probably too, because he was modest, he had chosen to live in such a place as 2001 Justin Road. A Torah scholar knew not to waste his money on worldly pleasures. Also, like many businessmen, Shulman was naturally frugal. He would think of ways to save money on himself.

But remembering how those men he had seen with Shulman had looked — dressed to a tee, with a limousine for transportation — Shimshon could not help connecting them to the sordidness of that place. And his thoughts began to take on an ominous bent. Somehow, the men seemed to be the reason Shulman chose to meet — no, *had* to meet — in an isolated place, far away from Jewish Boro Park. They did not look Jewish. That beefy man, Heinz, was definitely not Jewish — Shimshon could tell that much. They would not feel comfortable in Boro Park. Or welcome.

In fact, how could a real *kollel* man deal with these people at all? And why would he rely on non-Jews to support a *kollel?* Or was it for something else? Something for which they had to avoid being seen?

The more Shimshon thought about it, the more the evidence indicated that Shulman was not an upstanding individual. Shulman was secretive — even to people in Israel. No one seemed to know the nature of his travels — or even that his daughter was sick. And here he was — in a run-down area, with odd-looking foreigners, lying and avoiding people. He was hiding something. Tati was right. Avraham Shulman was a Nazi.

Shimshon felt a pang of guilt for judging too much based on cloudy, circumstantial evidence. He knew that according to the Jewish way of looking at things he could not rely on such evidence. There was really nothing conclusive — and the boy felt ashamed for possibly misreading Shulman's motives. True, he was secretive. His reasons for traveling were strange — and those men he met with were also strange. But that was hardly enough to prove that this old man was a Nazi.

Yet his father remained convinced that Shulman was. Or, at the very least, a liar. About what was Shulman lying? Shimshon groped desperately in his memory. Had Shulman done or said anything really odd? Nothing — except his defensiveness about his past.

But was the man's defensiveness a cover-up? Could he possibly be either lying or trying desperately to hide something? Something awesome? Something that was keeping Shimshon's father awake at nights? Could there possibly be another person lurking in the shadows — another past, another life? Or was there a strange power waiting to take control? Or which Shulman was already controlling? And using to manipulate others?

Not until Shimshon felt the draft through his legs did he realize that he had been standing in the open doorway for over a half hour. Quickly putting away the Pesach groceries, he hurried upstairs.

Removing a pad of paper and pen from his newly cleaned room, he attempted to gather his rambling, contradictory thoughts and place them methodically into organized form. Listing all he had seen and heard from Shulman, his father, and his cousin, Shimshon attempted to sketch a definite portrait of this enigmatic person. But to Shimshon's dismay, the picture remained fuzzy and distorted by his own recurrent thoughts. He imagined a two-headed creature — one pure and benevolent and smiling in genuine warmth, the other hard and cold, its mouth twisted in a devilish sneer. The image was alarming, if not ludicrous. Shimshon, try as he might, could not imagine these two people, opposites of one another, coexisting, becoming one and the same.

At last the questions were put down in systematic order, their meanings inextricably linked:

Where was Avraham Shulman during the Holocaust? Just knowing of the man's activities would truly shed light on any Nazi involvement. He had already stated that he was German-born. His accent was German — and probably the language he had spoken to those men was German. He might still keep in contact with Nazis, even if for nostalgic reasons. There were many around who were loyal to the philosophy and who actively participated in wartime activities. Years later, they simply felt that they had acted out of patriotism.

Thinking about Avraham Shulman's past brought the boy to his second question: If he *is* a Nazi, why does everyone think he is a Torah scholar? And — more maddening — he *is*. To everyone, that is, except Yehuda Shapiro. The boy's father, though he acknowledged that Shulman was smart, remained neither impressed nor swayed by the man's Torah intelligence. To Yehuda Shapiro, everything about Shulman was a lie. He would probably be even more convinced of it had he seen those four men.

But then — third question — what was the reason for this disguise? Assuming that Rabbi Shapiro was correct, of course. If the disguise was necessary in order to conduct his secret business, then — question four — what *was* his business? What *was* Shulman's reason for his frequent trips? And what was his relationship to these men? — question five. For some reason, the man under the street lamp came most vividly to mind. He seemed to convey some terrifying force. Also, he seemed like the one behind any dirty business. And would that even be the reason — question six — for meeting in such a run-down place? And the reason that Shulman needed to remain out of sight?

Reviewing the list of questions, Shimshon again realized, to his chagrin, that they were quite possibly based on one massive, ridiculous lie. He was still assuming — and fighting it in his own mind — that Shulman was a Nazi.

But if he really was a Jew — and his learning authentic — then why was he so evasive about his past? This question — number seven — jabbed at Shimshon like a razor blade. What was his past (number eight)? Could it be that Shulman had survived the camps, but in a devious way (number nine)? After all, his mind was calculating enough. Perhaps he had been a *kapo,* or an informer. Shimshon had read about such survivors. Possibly — perhaps the most painful thought — Shulman was not a Nazi at all. Perhaps he was no more than a common criminal — a Jewish one, but a criminal nonetheless.

Shimshon wondered if he might have stepped into some underworld ring — some web of intrigue and general evil. If so, then he had to find an answer to question ten: Who in New York could help him solve this mystery? So far, Shimshon had been forced to keep his detective work a secret. He had to; he could not let his father know — not yet, anyway. Perhaps later, after Shulman's identity had been finally revealed, he would make his father proud. Or possibly infuriated. But as it was now, the boy had no one to turn to — not even Zev, who probably thought by now his friend was crazy. And Shimshon lacked the money to hire professional help.

Sadly, Shimshon realized that this affair could be handled by him and him alone. Logically, too, it was up to him to finish what he had started. For the final question, number eleven, Shimshon drew an enormous question mark: What was *he* to do?

The boy put down his pen and sighed. Somehow these cloak-and-dagger escapades were not for him. Perhaps he should just drop the whole thing and stick to reading spy novels instead. However, with question eleven in mind, he recalled that he had once heard his father remark that a leader always follows through. Shimshon felt that he had to do this to prove something — he didn't quite know what — to his father.

It took awhile, but question eleven attained an answer. Shimshon hit upon a plan of action.

He looked at his watch. Four o'clock. Leaving his room, he leaned over the banister to see if his father might have read his mind and decided to leave Manhattan early this afternoon. No. Good, he thought. With a little luck, Tati might be giving a lecture on the laws of Pesach tonight.

Quickly, Shimshon went to the phone and dialed.

It rang twice. A voice answered softly. "Hello?"

Shimshon was speechless. Having been disappointed so often in his wish to see Shulman again, he somehow had nothing to say.

After another curious "Hello?" the voice suddenly grew tense. "Who is this?" he demanded.

"Hi . . . uh . . . is this Rav Shulman?" Shimshon choked.

Silence. "Shimshon?"

"Yes . . . it's me," answered the boy, more relaxed.

The voice over the phone was also relaxed. "How are you, *mein Kind?*"

"Baruch Hashem, fine. I called to find out how you're doing," Shimshon continued.

Shulman chuckled, with disarming openness. "I wondered when you were going to call. Was I too harsh with you that evening?"

The boy breathed a sigh of relief. *He's in a good mood.* Shimshon cautiously answered, "Oh, no. I must have embarrassed *you* — dropping in, not calling first. I'm really sorry about that."

"Oh, don't worry about it."

"I hope I didn't interrupt anything important," the boy hinted.

"Nonsense."

"Would it be all right . . . if I came over?"

"When?"

"Like . . . now?"

Silence. "Does your father know?"

Shimshon swallowed. "He isn't home."

"You may come."

117

Click went the phone.

Immediately grabbing his coat, Shimshon hurried into the busy street. Around him, busy holiday shoppers glanced curiously at this young boy brushing past them through the bustling avenue.

Shimshon did indeed feel light with grace and energy. It was as if he were filled, after a lull, with new enthusiasm. Inwardly, he felt immense relief that Avraham Shulman was still in New York. Now was Shimshon's chance to meet him one-on-one and speak to this most private of men.

The day was bright and crisp, an indication that these early days of April would bring much more into the world than just a vibrant spring. The few trees in Boro Park were already budding, bringing forth new life. Shimshon found himself actually enjoying the walk. Even as he left the Jewish section, and the familiar names melted away into a blur, he felt more fascinated than afraid. He had no trouble remembering the directions. In the distance he saw the deep shadows of the old subway tracks. He would be there soon.

Somehow, during the day, the neighborhood where Shulman lived looked different. Spacious, lined with ancient shrubbery, it seemed far less forbidding than in the dark. It was as if the demons only came out at night, leaving the normal, living people alone during the day to do what they had to do. Or perhaps, too, because it was just a nice spring day — the sun bouncing off the abandoned cars, and hitting the old aluminum cans that littered the yards and alleyways. In the distance, the pale smoke rose lightly from factory chimneys. Shimshon turned left, approaching a row of cottages by the cul-de-sac. Around him, ragged children wheeled by on squeaky bicycles and tricycles. Shimshon whistled. Just knowing that Shulman would be alone made him less afraid.

It would be one on one.

Besides, Shimshon felt more sure of his mission. This time he was not going to Shulman partly out of simple curiosity. He was going for his father's sake — as well as his own. He felt that he would be in for something big.

The awful smells, however, hit him as soon as he turned the corner onto Justin Road. And at the sight of the building, hovering there on the rusty soil, his knees began to feel weak and jelly-like. Not even the sunlight was powerful enough to eliminate the overwhelming darkness of 2001 Justin Road. The small cluster of youths dancing to the blaring music reminded Shimshon further that he was about to enter unfamiliar territory. He understood too well why Shulman had wanted him to come only during the daytime. Remembering Shulman's query — "Does your father know?" — filled the boy with additional trepidation. It occurred to him now that perhaps they should have met in a more public place — and in a different area. Shimshon whispered a prayer.

Arriving at the streaked glass door, Shimshon automatically by-passed the elevator and opened the staircase entrance; he clutched his nose. Ignoring the graffiti, he raced upstairs.

The fourth floor had changed little. The plaster had not yet been cleared away, and by now the crumbly heaps had become imbedded in the old, threadbare carpet. Down the corridor Shimshon went. He knocked on 4D.

His heart pounded. The faint footsteps grew heavier.

"Who is it?" asked the voice softly.

"It's Shimshon."

Click went the top lock. Then the middle. And the third. At last the door opened.

"Shalom aleichem," Shulman whispered.

The man stood stiffly in the doorway, his tall figure framed by the doorposts in muted majesty. From somewhere inside a thin, yellow light cast a pallor on his already pale face, circling his hair and producing a fluffy halo. In his neatly pressed slacks and vest he remained standing, in a slightly military posture, until at last he extended his hand to Shimshon.

"Aleichem shalom," answered the boy in awe.

"Come in, please," said the man, with a sweep of the wrist.

Shimshon entered. Shulman gently shut the door and led the boy into the living room.

Shimshon looked around. The dwelling looked like an ancient motel room — which, in fact, it might have been. The vinyl furniture, shag carpet, cottage cheese ceiling, and gaudy landscape painting looked vintage 1960 — an era that had existed and faded long before Shimshon was born. The pale green curtains were tightly drawn, blocking out quite effectively the infiltrating sunlight.

Apartment 4D was poorly lit, and had the potential to appear truly dismal. However, the little place was redeemed by its orderliness. Everything — the furnishings, the stack of thick paper plates, the plastic cutlery, the hot plate, the papers — was neat, and arranged with geometric, almost obsessive, precision. The carpet and furnishings, though shabby, were spotless. A partially open door revealed the bedroom, which looked as tidy as everything else; the bedspread was exactly three inches off the floor, and the long black cloak hung over a hook.

I wish I could be as neat as this, Shimshon mused. This man must have worked awfully hard to rid himself of his *chametz.*

Shulman steered the boy to one of the cheap dinette set chairs.

It was difficult to get comfortable in the chair due to its cheap construction, but Shimshon tried to hide his discomfort. Shulman then scurried to the refrigerator. Though at least thirty years old, the refrigerator looked practically new after being just as meticulously cleaned as everything else. Its interior, systematically arranged, looked very much like a miniature world.

In the door stood only a handful of jars containing processed foods — juices and condiments. The shelves and bins were neatly filled with fresh fruits and vegetables.

"Hmm . . . let me see what I can offer you . . ." mused the man.

"Oh, really, I'm not hungry," Shimshon protested. He was feeling awkward, like a little boy visiting an old, doting relative.

Shulman didn't seem to hear. Opening one of the cupboards, he pondered its contents. Shimshon noticed over a dozen cans of sardines, stacked one on top of another.

Soon the man returned with a jar of apple juice and a package of coffee cake. The boy declined the cake, but helped himself to the juice.

Shulman looked disappointed. "Perhaps I can offer you some fruit, instead?"

"Oh, no, thank you," Shimshon replied, embarrassed by the formality. "I had a late lunch. Besides, I don't want to get your place all dirty."

Nervously, he raised the plastic cup to his lips. Shulman watched, waiting to say "Amen" to the blessing.

Shimshon said, "I hope I'm not troubling you."

"Nonsense," Shulman replied, laughing warmly. "In fact, your company is giving me the greatest pleasure. And you're allowing me the opportunity to do the *mitzvah* of *hachnasas orchim*. It's not something I've had time for these days."

This last statement, ending in a sigh, puzzled Shimshon.

"You usually don't get guests?" he asked, remembering his cousin's letter.

"Not here," Shulman answered, a trace of sadness in his voice. "I'm afraid I have not been able to entertain. In Kiryat Yovel, my home was filled with visitors. But now . . ." he motioned with his hand around the depressing place, and his voice lowered, ". . . I am far away from home."

"Yes, you are far away," Shimshon answered evasively. Far away from Jews, he thought. Far away from your world. Anyone willing to come here would be risking his health.

Shimshon continued, "I waited for you in *shul* last week . . . but you didn't show up and I got worried."

"Worried? Whatever for, Shimshon?"

"I thought you left — went back to Israel . . . or somewhere else."

Avraham Shulman began fingering his *tzitzis*. "Why did you think I left, Shimshon?"

The boy played with his paper cup. "Because . . . you weren't in *shul*."

Stalemate. Shimshon poured himself another cup of apple juice. He asked, offhandedly, "How is your daughter?"

The host bit his lip. Instantly tears welled in his eyes.

"I'm sorry," Shimshon replied. "I guess you'd rather not discuss it."

"Thank you," the man whispered.

Shimshon glanced around; his eyes wandered over the surroundings in a desperate search for a conversation piece. On his right, in a makeshift bookcase, lay little rows of holy books, alphabetically arranged and standing stiffly upright, like toy soldiers. Shimshon scanned the familiar titles . . . *Mishnah Berurah, Igros Moshe, Chayei Adam* . . . an impressive display of Jewish scholarship. Shimshon wondered what else Shulman had brought with him. No doubt these *sefarim* were used in frequent moments of study — and were as indispensable to Avraham Shulman as a compass is to a sailor.

Shulman, noticing the boy's admiration, apologetically remarked that the rest of his library was in Israel. "Most of these I obtained here in New York," he explained. "I felt it was simply cheaper than to send over volumes upon volumes."

He must plan to be here awhile, Shimshon thought. His eyes rested on a very old book, tucked away at the far end of the bookcase. Among the other, handsomer volumes, it could have easily been overlooked. In fact, Shimshon was surprised to have noticed it. Removing it from the shelf, Shimshon fingered the almost threadbare jacket and opened the cover.

He saw that the pages were nearly translucent. On the first, in Gothic lettering, the title read *Deutsches-Hebraisches Woerterbuch.* On the inside of the jacket was some faded writing, and at the bottom of the message was a signature, inscribed with great flourish: *M. Sternfeld.*

"Is this a dictionary?" Shimshon asked curiously.

At the sight of the tattered book, Shulman nodded quickly. "My father-in-law's," he choked. "Please . . . put it back. That book is quite precious to me."

Casually, Shimshon slipped the book in between the other volumes. Shulman, however, intervened, and asked that it be put in its original place, at the very end of the shelf. Evidently, the little library had been arranged methodically, and with loving care.

Shimshon avoided handling the other books; if an old dictionary was that precious to Shulman, how much more so was the rest of the collection.

Shimshon waved his hand toward the library. "This is where you get your *divrei Torah,* right?" he asked. "I guess that's why I missed you so much. There was something special about your *drashos* . . . and not just the way you spoke. You know the *mefarshim* so well. I never met anyone like you."

Under the full beard of Shulman lay a thin-lipped smile. "You are quite young," he answered. "Just wait. In due time you'll either meet far worthier people than me . . . or you will in fact become one yourself. Of that I have no doubt." Then, as an afterthought, he added, "When I was your age I did not receive your kind of education."

Shimshon was shocked. This man seemed educated from the cradle. To hear such an admission was astonishing. Yet, remembering the story of Rabbi Akiva — who began his Jewish education at the age of forty — Shimshon realized that it really was possible for someone to get a late start in life . . . especially if part of his life had been spent in Germany. Probably he would be even more motivated later to deepen his Jewish roots. And someone like Shulman, who seemed endowed with a special soul, would have a natural thirst for knowledge.

"Ta — uh, people — always tell me how I'm lucky to have a Jewish education," Shimshon said. "They said it was different back then. What was it like?"

Shulman was by now playing with his *tzitzis.* His crystalline eyes were as still as rocks, and as blue as the sky. Thoughtfully he answered, "It was a difficult time . . . and a frightening one for young people. You should thank G-d every day that you and your friends don't have that problem today."

Shulman asked, "How old are you?"

"Twelve," the boy answered.

"My goodness," Shulman declared, "you're almost a young man. And tell me, please . . . when will you be bar mitzvah?"

"Oh, not till Shevat next year."

"You're lucky to have a bar mitzvah," replied Shulman sadly.

By this remark Shimshon assumed that this man had never had one, for reasons best left unsaid. Shimshon mentally compared him to his own father, Yehuda Shapiro, who had turned thirteen in 1942. But, Shimshon wondered, how old was Shulman then? Shimshon could not even guess how old he was now. Fifty? Sixty? Like many of his genre, Avraham Shulman seemed ageless. Most likely he was older than he really appeared. But his learning was a life force that gave him the glow of eternal youthfulness — a phenomenon that came from far beyond the material world. His face had scarcely a wrinkle. His whitening beard made him look more like an albino than like someone ancient. This old/young man's vague remarks about his past made him mysterious. Shimshon felt as if he were talking to a ghost.

Suddenly the boy's face brightened. "Would you like to hear my bar mitzvah speech?" he asked, excited.

Shulman's eyes sparkled, making his face shine even brighter. "I would certainly love to hear *divrei Torah* from you, Shimshon."

"It still needs work, a lot of work. I've got a lot to go on it. I hope I remember everything."

"I'm sure you'll do fine, Shimshon."

"Well . . . maybe you could correct me on the Yiddish."

"With pleasure, Shimshon," said the man.

Shimshon cleared his throat and made a brief introduction, determined to play the eager schoolboy to the hilt. In spite of himself, however, he really was eager; he sincerely wished to hear Shulman's opinion. As he spoke, in Yiddish, on the portion of Yisro, he stammered, stumbling on a number of passages and giggling nervously at others. Somewhere in the middle, while explaining the Ten Commandments, he faltered and broke off the topic in mid-sentence, leaving his participle to dangle helplessly in a chasm of lost thought. Truly embarrassed, he groped for the appropriate verse.

Shulman remained placid and statue-like, his lustrous eyes resting thoughtfully on the boy and slowly closing. Shimshon continued hesitantly, wondering if the man was transplanted somewhere in a spiritual realm, or just bored. When the boy finished, he waited for either approval or critique.

Silence.

"Need more practice, don't I?" he asked shyly.

Still no answer. The man before him kept his eyes closed. Oh, no, I really did put him to sleep, Shimshon thought. He waited to hear a snore. Nothing. Then he felt a trifle indignant. "I wasn't *that* bad," he said defensively.

Suddenly the eyes opened wide. They shone an even fiercer blue — startling the boy — like two flames that had been kindled from dry candle wicks. The face that had rested serenely now tensed with scholarship, and Shulman's eyes suddenly squinted, crinkling his smooth temples.

"Your speech, Shimshon . . . it moved me so deeply that I had to reflect awhile on its meaning."

Shimshon smiled sheepishly. "You really liked it?"

"Why, Shimshon," said the man, "it was beautiful."

The boy blushed. "I thought I kind of botched it up."

Sternly Shulman replied, "You must not speak like that, Shimshon. You have no right to denigrate yourself. It is Hashem's will that you delve into the Torah and understand it. Torah study is His gift — and an obligation for every Jew. When you apply yourself with great effort, the knowledge will come, with Hashem's help. Already I see that you have great enthusiasm for your learning. And you are still quite young. When you are older, and stronger in wisdom, as well as self-confidence, you will feel far less intimidated. You must never forget your achievements, Shimshon. Though you still have far to go, I can see a bright road for you. You are the future . . . the future of our people."

"Really?" Shimshon asked. This speech left him feeling mesmerized and transformed; he was palpitating with strange new energy. He felt an incredible urge to devour an entire library of Torah books — for the sake of Avraham Shulman. So convincing was this man — so much his words exuded authority and self-assurance — that one wanted to place himself totally under him in blind obedience. Most likely Shulman had spoken this way even when he was thirteen.

"However," continued the man, his face tightening with even greater intensity, "there is a certain subject within the Ramban on the first verse . . . *Vayishma Yisro kohen* . . . which I feel needs greater clarification."

"Really?" Shimshon repeated, still in a daze.

Shulman nodded. He immediately lapsed into a medley of verses and commentaries, words tinkling on his lips like crystal on a chandelier, intricately linked, interwoven in a dazzling spiral of complex form. These words, lightly mixed with a faint mid-European accent and East European inflection, were truly gems, for every syllable that Shulman spoke contained precious sparks and matched the holiness in his eyes' reflection.

He spoke, becoming oblivious to Shimshon; he spoke as if addressing the angels swirling around him in rapt submission, having come down from the fiery firmament above to lay at his feet. The dingy room became alive and transformed into a supernal realm, the walls reverberating with the resonant, sensual grace of Shulman's prose.

Strangely enough, Shulman did not seem in love with his rhetoric. Not that he was detached — rather, it all came naturally to him, and he toyed with it. The gift of speech was his for the asking: the cadence and rhythms in his voice were something to be tossed playfully toward the captive listener. Sometimes Shulman spoke like an actor delivering a soliloquy, other times as if he were a wise father addressing a son. But it was not only the speech. What wisdom! The Torah knowledge within him was so connected to him, like an additional limb, that he treated it as such: something noticed, nourished, loved. This vital limb would cause him great pain — even death — if severed.

His thoughts were clear, as well as his words. But even more amazing was his ability to channel the cluttered storehouse of wisdom into vast and visible compartments. Like a shepherd dancing from one hilltop to the next, Shulman followed idea after idea on the Ten Commandments, never stumbling or stopping in confusion. As he spoke, his voice remained ever-controlled, imbued with growing power. He finally receded into quiet conclusion.

Having finished, he leaned back, feeling a twinge of victory and satisfaction. He looked at Shimshon coyly, as if to say, "*Nu?*"

Shimshon did not respond. His eyes were too wide to blink, and his jaw had dropped to somewhere around his chest.

"Perhaps I'm the one out of practice," joked the man.

Shimshon gasped. "Are you a *rosh yeshiva*?"

Shulman shook his head.

"A rebbe, then?"

"No."

"Not even a rav?"

Shulman smiled. "I am the smallest of *talmidei chachamim*."

"That's amazing!" the boy exclaimed. "I . . . I never heard anyone like you. You're a genius! I can't believe there are others who know more than you."

"Shimshon, what do our Sages say? 'We are like midgets sitting on the shoulders of giants.' All that I have ever acquired is from others. I am their student, just like they are the students of others. I bring honor to my rebbes, but can I be completely like them? Never! Like Yehoshua, who learned from Moshe Rabbeinu, I am the moon, who receives her light from the sun. My 'radiance,' so to speak, is borrowed, and dependent on others."

Shimshon was spellbound. "But you can guide others less learned than you. You could be a leader."

Shulman smiled darkly. For a moment his features were clouded. Then he said, in a sonorous tone, "There are times in one's life when one chooses to be the leader and take charge, as you say. At other times he must learn to follow orders. When to do which? The secret lies in the ability to recognize the truth. Know the truth, Shimshon . . . know what you're striving for . . . know the truth in others and rely on them for strength. Then you gain the power to make your own decisions. And once you know that your decisions are based on truth, then you'll believe more in your ability to do the right thing."

Watching Shimshon's eyes glaze, Shulman halted. He remembered that he was addressing a twelve-year-old. Over a child it was easy to hold sway.

Changing the subject, he explained, offhandedly, that he only studied part time in his *kollel.* The demands of his schedule left little time for regular study.

"Why only part time?" Shimshon asked.

Shulman explained that as a fund-raiser for the *kollel* and other institutions he was constantly traveling in Israel, and often being sent to the diaspora — America, Canada, France, South Africa. He had done the whole circuit, representing the *kollel* and being a guest speaker at many a business meeting and yeshiva dinner. The end of a whirlwind tour made him long to return to the simple life.

Because of his gift for language and speech, the *kollel* selected him for this task. He had virtually become a walking public relations firm for the institutions he represented. Shulman spoke of his *kollel,* Ohr Menuchah, as if he were describing one of his children. He spoke earnestly of its students and their families — all committed fervently to Torah study, regardless of the sacrifices which had to be made. It took tremendous strength on his part to keep the *kollel* financially afloat; in fact, this burden rested on his shoulders alone. But he did not mind. He knew that G-d had never given him a task that he could not handle. And he had of late been successful. His reason for choosing to live in this apartment was solely an economic one. Every dollar was precious; walking a mile to the synagogue was far preferable to paying a higher rent. In the past, just as in the present, life had been a constant struggle to raise funds.

"Yeah, I know how it is," Shimshon remarked. His yeshiva had the same problem.

Of the money he raised, Shulman continued, he kept very little for himself — only enough to keep his family fed and to be able to have guests. Fortunately, his family made few demands. His wife, Breinda, helped out in whatever way she could, by cooking for the *kollel* and the local *cheder*. She was also active in community work.

Shimshon longed to comment on the *mitzvah* she had done for his aunt Tzvia Rochel after the latter had had a difficult pregnancy. But he didn't dare tell Shulman of the letter he had written to his cousin.

For the most part, Shulman continued, his family was content to live in poverty. A life style committed to Torah and *mitzvos* was something priceless — this Shimshon, as well as Shulman, understood fully. The boy hoped some day to be able to study in a *kollel*.

Shulman mentioned how he especially looked forward to coming home this time, as this trip had been his longest and most difficult. He not only needed to raise money for the *kollel,* but for his daughter's operation as well, and, in fact, had placed appeals in several Jewish-American newspapers. Shimshon pointed out that his yeshiva had often tried to raise money for the sick in Israel. Shimshon had been active in this sort of fund-raising. Perhaps Shulman's daughter would receive something from it as well.

Shulman smiled tearfully. "May G-d grant you much *hatzlachah*," he said.

"Amen," answered Shimshon. "And I hope He gives a *refuah sheleimah* to your daughter."

"Amen," replied the man.

"Do you have any other children? Besides your daughter?"

"Why, yes," Shulman answered brightly. "I have six all

together. Three are still at home. In fact, I have grandchildren, too."

"Really?" Shimshon said. He felt strangely excited. He could imagine this man with an entire legacy of Torah scholars. "Do you have any pictures?"

With childlike enthusiasm, the old man bounced off his seat and hurried to a small desk. Opening a drawer, he took out a small packet of pictures, clutching it like a bag of pearls. He held the photographs before Shimshon, like any proud grandfather, explaining each one.

"This is my eldest girl, Miriam, with her husband — they're in Bnei Brak — and their two boys. That's my oldest son, Chanoch, and two of his girls. And Yeshayah, my third. He was named after my wife's grandfather. Yeshayah got married last year."

"Mazel tov," said Shimshon.

"Thank you. My daughter-in-law is due any day," Shulman added.

Momentarily forgetting the pictures, Shulman was absorbed in some gloomy reflection. Then he continued. "These are the children who still live with me."

Shimshon looked down at a photograph of two adolescent boys, both with reddish-blond hair and pale blue eyes, giggling and posing for the camera. One looked about Shimshon's age.

"That's Shmueli," Shulman said, pointing. "He just had his bar mitzvah. And the older one is Yerachmiel."

There was one picture left.

"This is my wife, Breinda. And with her is my other daughter . . . my youngest, Chava Rivkah."

Shimshon looked at the faded color print. The face of the girl, framed in reddish-blonde braids, was wan, but smiling, and she looked at the camera with great seriousness. Assuming that the picture was taken recently (though with the cheap print it was hard to tell), she appeared to be Shimshon's age. Her mother, though facing the camera, was turned partially to her daughter, her arms resting tenderly on the latter's thin shoulders. She, too, was smiling, but it was easy to tell that she was trying to hide great sorrow. Like her husband, she had a youthful countenance which could neither be concealed nor crushed by the cruelties of life. And there was something in the woman's face which painfully reminded Shimshon of his own mother. Was it the moodiness? Or the hidden fears? It would be safe to guess that Breinda Shulman, like her husband, was a person of secrets.

The daughter, Chava Rivkah, seemed to have inherited this moodiness — though from which parent it was unclear. Before the camera she appeared stoic, like her father. But there was a pathetic frailty emanating from mother as well as daughter. It was this sickliness which reminded Shimshon most of his own mother. And it occurred to Shimshon that Chava Rivkah's parents had had her late in life too.

"She's the one who's sick?" Shimshon asked.

Biting his lip, Shulman nodded.

Shimshon dared not ask what kind of illness it was. He had already used up his quota of questions for the day. He felt sad and ashamed — sad because the old man had sacrificed so much, ashamed because of his own inquisitiveness and suspicions. Shulman cared little about his own needs, and instead placed others' first — the Torah and its institutions, and now his daughter. These were integral to his life; in fact, they were his *very* life.

Shimshon felt remorse for having questioned this man's

character. Now everything made sense — the business meetings, this run-down location, the secrecy. Like a hidden *tzaddik* — which no doubt he was — this man was quietly going his own way, helping the world with his special gifts. Lacking interest in either personal or monetary rewards, he simply felt that the Torah was his mission — to study it, and preserve it for future generations. Certainly, after being through so much, it meant so much more to him than it could to most others. Though Shimshon was satisfied at last to have his questions answered, he was not at all proud of having been devious.

Shimshon looked at his watch. "It's late," he said.

Gathering the pictures, Shulman placed them neatly in the drawer. Shimshon quickly threw on his coat and zipped it.

"It sure was great talking to you, Rav Shulman," he said, beaming.

Smiling, Shulman extended his hand. He took Shimson's and clasped it in a firm, athletic grip.

"It was my pleasure," he replied, bowing slightly. "Please come again, Shimshon. As long as I am here. And any time you would like to practice your bar mitzvah speech, I am available."

"Thanks," said the boy, laughing, "but I already have a coach. My father helps me."

Shulman was silent. His eyes scanned the boy up and down, as if comparing him to something and sorting it out among recent and distant memories.

"Your father," he said pensively, "is an extraordinary man. A man of great learning and refinement. And incredible strength. He reminds me so much . . . of someone I once knew." His voice trailed off.

Shimshon watched intently. Here was his chance.

He swallowed. "Rav Shulman . . ."

"Yes?"

The boy turned toward the door. He took a deep breath and then faced Shulman. "My father looked at you strangely . . . that Shabbos in *shul*. I hope he didn't make you too uncomfortable. 'Cause I wondered if that was why you weren't in *shul* after that."

Shulman's fingers began to dance against his leg.

"If that was the reason, I'm sorry," Shimshon continued. "But you see . . . he's a Holocaust survivor. And I don't know if you know what it's like to live through that . . . but he gets upset sometimes, you know? Sometimes he gets ticked off by something. I guess he gets easily reminded about the concentration camps. And when he saw you, that's what happened." Shimshon lowered his head. "So I really do apologize. Honest."

His leg now shaking, Shulman replied, "Nonsense. I wasn't frightened away."

"But you didn't come back, so I wondered—"

"The reason I didn't come back, Shimshon, was because I had found a closer *shul*. That is all."

"Oh . . . all right," Shimshon answered uncertainly.

Quietly, Shulman opened the door. Shimshon was about to leave, but stopped.

"But there is something between you and my father, and it made you upset," the boy argued. "I know. I was there."

Shulman tried to chuckle. "That mind of yours, Shimshon. Are you always this inquisitive?"

"Sometimes," the boy answered. "Tati always says I ask too many questions. Maybe that's why I wanted to know more about you. And your past."

Shulman's eyes glistened. "My past is no one's business, Shimshon — no one's. I absolutely refuse to discuss it with anyone."

"Why?" Shimshon demanded. "What are you hiding?"

Shulman twitched. "What?"

"Why won't you say anything about what happened during the war?" Shimshon's voice was accusative, and almost pleading. "My father said you reminded him of somebody else — no, no . . . he said you *were* somebody else. A war criminal." Looking away, Shimshon whispered, "He said your name is really Hans Schmidt."

Shimshon looked at him. There were tears in his eyes. "Is it true? Were you ever a Nazi?"

The face of Avraham Shulman turned a fiery red, and his eyes bulged in anger and disbelief. His strong hands clenched, livid, and his body went rigid. His beard bristled, and through it words escaped, in scornful hyperventilation.

"How dare you!" he hissed.

Shimshon backed away towards the door.

"How dare you!" Shulman repeated. "You have more than insulted me. You have injured me with your vile talk. Why, this is worse than *lashon hara*. This is the blackest of lies — you have mercilessly killed me."

Shimshon cringed. He felt as if he were standing before Heinz.

"Is this what you came here for — to deceive and to mock me?!" The man continued to shout, waving his arms over his head. "Get out!"

Shimshon's hand, trembling, groped for the doorknob, and he fumbled, turning it and practically falling out. The tall, quaking figure emerged in the threshold.

"And don't ever come back!" he shouted, slamming the door so loudly that the walls vibrated with anger. Some of the neighbors opened their own doors in curiosity.

Shimshon hurriedly stumbled down the musty corridor and the smelly flight of stairs, his eyes blinded with tears. Not until he landed safely at the bottom of the stairs did he break down and cry.

He had to stay here and have his cry. He could not let his father see him this way. He owed it to himself to vent out his sorrow before returning home. Also, he felt in dire need of cleansing — for shaming a Torah scholar, believing the evil talk about him, and harboring malevolent thoughts. The list of sins was endless. Most of all, he had disobeyed his father, who had told him not to get involved in the first place. And now, Shimshon was forced to have serious doubts about his father's credibility. It was a double shame he was forced to live with.

But pressing his hands back against the gushing tears, Shimshon couldn't help putting some of the blame on his father. After all, it was he who had first told his son that Avraham Shulman was a Nazi named Hans Schmidt. Shimshon could not believe it. He knew it was untrue. If only he could tell Shulman now how sorry he was — and that he had risked coming here, to this dangerous place, to defend him, not accuse him. He had admired this man from the start, and wanted desperately to prove his father wrong. And now, because he wanted to know the truth, he had shamed all three — Avraham Shulman, himself, and, most importantly, his father.

Great going, Shimmy, he muttered to himself. You really got carried away this time.

A young couple, looking like part of the building, stared at this red-eyed boy with the skullcap who was sitting penitentially by the open staircase. Shimshon ignored them. He knew he was still in need of a good sulk.

Thinking about his father, Shimshon realized that he cared more about him than he did about himself. Yet now he had made Tati look, in Shulman's eyes, like either a liar or some paranoid fanatic. And after Shulman had called Yehuda Shapiro "a man of learning and incredible strength." Shimshon realized that not only had he questioned Shulman's reputation, but he had damaged his father's as well.

Finally wiping the vestige of tears from his eyes, Shimshon opened the dirty door and headed out into the breezy twilight. Outside, the sun had nearly vanished, leaving just a thumbnail orange behind the tufts of clouds. The moon was timidly venturing out from behind a clump of trees. Now the neighborhood was taking on its latent character, as the surrounding soil became deathly white, the concrete embankment to the right shimmering eerily under the solitary street lights.

Miserably, he headed home. On their own accord, his feet carried him past the scarred buildings of Justin Road. In the distance the young people gathered, children of the night, laughing, their radio tuned to a solid roar.

By the time Shimshon turned left onto Sixtieth Street, he decided that he simply had to speak to his father. Perhaps that would have been best all along, rather than this silly, sloppy, beyond-amateurish detective work — playing games behind everyone's back, poking his nose into everyone's business. His father had been open with him — most of the time, anyway. Now it was Shimshon's turn to be frank. He had to tell him everything that had happened, all he had done. At least Avraham Shulman would be wrong in one respect: he could not call Shimshon deceptive. Perhaps later he might even forgive the boy and his father; certainly, if he were truly a religious Jew, as he appeared to be, he would be able to forgive. Most important, he would forget the past.

Forget the past, Shimshon thought. That's all he longed to do right now — forget everything.

Seven o'clock. Shimshon finally reached the safety and comfort of his house. Looks like I'll have to have my dinner cold, he thought. But he wasn't hungry. It wasn't a lack of food that gnawed at his innards right now — only an aching, painful guilt. Right now, Shimshon cared little about anything else. He noticed with only mild surprise that his father's car was not in the driveway. He's probably doing something far more important than what I've ever done, Shimshon told himself.

Mournfully, he went straight to his room, flung himself on the bed, and waited.

Chapter 7

The Meeting

The crowd at Gregg's Happy Hour was practically spilling over onto Eighty-fourth Street and Lexington Avenue. The crowd was varied. There were young up-and-coming professionals, faces flushed from the joy of a stock market killing or some other financial coup. There were middle-aged couples, fashionably dressed and excited as they contemplated their evening out. There were local residents, irked to be elbowed out of their favorite watering hole. Finally, there were outcasts, simply desiring to belong somewhere. Everyone was at Gregg's to take delight in the watered-down screwdrivers and scotch. Above the bar, its pale blue screen hardly noticed, the TV set blared. The decor was an odd cross between a Swiss chalet and an antique shop; turn-of-the-century paraphernalia hung on the oak-paneled walls alongside old hunting rifles and trophies. A Tyrolian hat rested on top of a giant moosehead. In one corner, a little bird chirped seven times from a cuckoo clock. Glasses tinkled, voices roared; the air was a stale combination of cigarette smoke and *hors d'oeuvres.*

At the far end of the lounge, overlooking Eighty-third and Park, were the booths, linked side by side, like a broken bracelet. Groups and couples huddled in the darkness, their forms a mass of shadows illuminated occasionally by a flickering match.

In the corner farthest from the door, four men were seated: three with cocktail in hand, one with a beer. Each wore a three-piece suit, pinstriped and creaseless; they were an older version of the stockbrokers by the bar. Indeed, there was little besides age to distinguish them externally from anyone else. With the exception of Heinz, who was born at the end of the war, these men were all over fifty. Their language was not English, but that mattered little in a city teeming with foreigners.

Casually, one of them sipped his drink and contorted his face. "*Ach,* these Americans . . ." he said wryly. "I never could understand their taste for this sort of thing. They still have not learned the art of drinking."

The one sitting next to him smiled. Older than the others, he rested his thin face almost effeminately against one hand; his features were obscured by a sickening gray haze of cigarette smoke coming from the thin Winston in his other hand. He seemed to be fascinated with any quirk of human behavior.

Heinz lustily raised his beer mug, as if to taunt his companion. "I never go near that kind of thing," he laughed, pointing to the cocktail.

Another companion, seated next to Heinz, probably cared little, if at all, about the American phenomenon called "cocktails." His own glass lay full, the ice cubes already dissolving into molten rectangles. Short and wiry, he watched the entrance intensely, his watery eyes scanning the incoming shapes of bodies. At last, in desperation, he turned to the man with the Winston. "He isn't coming. I knew it."

"Fritz, calm down. Please. You're making us all nervous," the other replied.

"I still feel you've made a very foolish mistake, Ludwig."

Ludwig slowly exhaled another puff of smoke and rolled his eyes in mild annoyance. "We've discussed this before, Fritz. Please — must I repeat myself again?"

"But I don't know if he's to be trusted," the short man insisted. He now fingered the swizzle stick nervously, needing something to occupy his hands. His speech was clipped, and his accent sounded more Spanish than German.

"Nonsense," answered Ludwig soothingly, as if trying to calm a child. "Nonsense. Groundless rumors."

Fritz was now waving his hands dramatically. "But why did he leave the Fatherland?"

Ludwig now leaned back, his body arched against the hard, unyielding vinyl. "He is a man of foresight . . . tremendous foresight. And wisdom." Ludwig was completely calm. His eyes, a fierce, icy blue, made a panoramic sweep of the lounge before him, as if surveying an Alpine valley. He glanced at his watch nonchalantly.

Fritz shook his head doubtfully. "I don't know, Ludwig. I still think he's a strange one. He is not one of us."

Ludwig smiled again, displaying his even teeth. He had to remind himself that certain people were to be addressed in a certain manner. And — a more painful thought — after all these years, he was forced to reside among persons of lower intelligence. "Once a man like him has been with us, he is branded for life. Believe me, Fritz, he is one of us."

Fritz was silent. He sipped his watery drink meditatively and glanced at his watch. "He's late, too."

"Only five minutes. Fritz, calm down — *please*," Ludwig pleaded. He crushed his cigarette. "You must believe me . . . I know him better than you do. He will not let us down."

Ludwig sighed. His manicured hand slowly reached for his brandy, and he fingered the glass meditatively before at last raising it to his mouth. He did not know why, but at times — usually when he drank — he felt like an astronaut, condemned to live on a planet full of inferior life. He still winced at the thought of making Fritz his peer. In the old days, a man like Fritz would have been his chauffeur. But the old order was temporarily suspended.

Suddenly he put down his glass. His steely-blue eyes were fixed on the entrance ahead. The others turned and put down their drinks. Ludwig smiled.

Even in the hazy, sordid darkness, the one they were waiting for was difficult to miss. For as he glided past, all heads turned. Like an invading angel, his face shone under the white-blond hair and earlocks, forcing all those present to stare, against their will. Yet his long black cloak merged into the surrounding darkness, as if to suggest that deep down he was at one with this environment. Bodies continued to fall by the wayside as he floated past. His eyes, obscured by his flashing spectacles, remained focused on the lighted wax bowls, like a slow-sailing ship guided by red flares. So intent was he on the four men in the distance that he was completely oblivious to the stares and remarks of the patrons. His solemn dignity seemed to negate any intimidation.

Halting before the four men, he raised his hand slightly in an awkward salute. "Heil!" he whispered.

The others merely nodded, but a disapproving glance from Ludwig indicated that this man had just done something inappropriate and dangerous. "Herr Schmidt," he hissed, "you really must be more careful. I suggest you refrain from anything that might give us away. Our business here is too important to permit any slips of the tongue."

The other wilted. "I apologize," he answered, embarrassed. Somehow, a frown from Ludwig affected him more than derision from strangers.

Fritz moved aside and motioned him to sit beside him. Concealing a certain distaste, the man in chassidic garb strategically positioned himself a good foot from Fritz.

Though he had made an impressive entrance, this man, once seated here among his companions, was a different person. His rigid posture went slack as he glanced about him — like a fallen angel suddenly realizing where he had landed, and needing a way to escape. In extreme discomfort he surveyed the cavernous lounge.

A waitress walked over to take his order.

"Just water, please," he said.

Ludgwig ordered another brandy.

The fourth man, seated on Ludwig's right, lit a match. He shared more in common with Ludwig than just the same brand of cigarettes. Like Ludwig, he was tall and slender, with blond-white hair. He observed through limpid eyes this newcomer, enjoying the performance of Schmidt, who seemed to have awkwardly dropped in, like a little corporal parachuted behind enemy lines. He offered the latter a Marlboro as a sort of goodwill gesture.

"No, thank you, Kurt," the man answered.

Kurt offered one to Ludwig and lit it for him. Ludwig slowly inhaled and blew a cloud of smoke into the air, letting it float, halo-like, behind his head. He smiled inwardly, enjoying the scene — a chassidic Jew sitting here among a crowd that looked like something out of a magazine. How uncultured, this race. He meant both Americans and Jews.

Wryly, he said, "I must commend you, Hans, on your

appearance. Your manner is most convincing."

Tense with anger, the man called Hans kept his face down and mumbled, "I didn't wish to meet here."

"You had in mind, perhaps, a kosher restaurant?"

The others laughed.

"No," Hans answered curtly. "But we could have met someplace a bit more neutral. And secluded. Of course I feel out of place here. Don't you realize how dangerous it is for someone like me to be seen here?"

"Why, Hans," Ludwig answered condescendingly, "forgive me. Please. I did not expect to find your friends here."

Again the others laughed.

"That's not what I meant," Hans mumbled.

"Well, then, what *do* you mean?" asked Ludwig in mock wonder.

"You wouldn't understand," Hans answered with a frustrated look. No, it was not the risk of being seen by men from Boro Park that worried him. It was some greater fear, connected with the kind of men who came from places remote from his environment. If these men only knew how much he hated being here. "If I am most convincing, as you said, then you must understand why I do not feel comfortable here. Don't you realize that you are giving away my cover?"

The joviality dissipated.

Ludwig frowned. "Very well. Next time I shall be more cautious in selecting a meeting place. Besides, we won't have to meet this way much longer." His eyes narrowed. "The closer we are to our target, the better."

"When were you last there?" asked Hans.

"This afternoon."

"And you know specifically where it is?"

"Not yet. We only know its general environs. But our sources tell us that we are very close. Soon we'll have it, and our project will be on its way."

"*Amen,*" said Hans, using the Hebrew pronunciation.

Ludwig smiled. "I don't understand the Jew-language, Hans. I know you have to stay in character, but please explain."

"I said 'Amen,' " Hans clarified. It was funny to translate the language into German, of all languages. However, his German was neither peasant-like, thick and drawled, like Heinz's, nor metallic, like Kurt's Hamburg dialect. Rather, it had a soft, lilting sound, like an ancient liturgy. Though he never could rid himself completely of his own Berlin accent, he had, of late, developed a sing-song inflection.

Of course, most of the men had their accents diluted to a certain degree. Fritz's Austrian pronunciation was oddly accompanied by an Argentinian lilt, and integrated with Spanish colloquialisms. Kurt was often heard humming Brazilian pop tunes. Even Heinz, the youngest, born in Munich in 1944 but whisked out of Germany, spoke a Bavarian that only vaguely evoked the accent of his parents, who had taken up residence in Caracas. Only Ludwig retained a distinct Prussian accent, as monotonous and military as a marching jackboot.

"The faster we reach our goals and are well out of here, the better off we are," Hans continued.

Ludwig threw him a searching look. "You are strangely tense, Hans. What is wrong?"

For the first time Hans looked at Ludwig directly. His face registered a look of intense pain. "You don't realize how dangerous it is for me to be here. I cannot emphasize this enough."

"Did I not say, Hans, that in the future we shall meet somewhere else?"

"I mean here in New York!" the other hissed. "This city spells danger for Hans Schmidt!"

Ludwig was puzzled. "But this is not your first time here, Hans. Why should it be particularly dangerous now?"

"Because this time something has happened." The man in the chassidic cloak closed his eyes and breathed heavily. "I have been recognized by one of the Jews in Boro Park."

Ludwig and Kurt exchanged knowing glances. Theirs was the look of predators closing in for the kill, only to find that there was a hunter standing over them, shotgun in hand. For years they had felt satisfied, having managed to elude their pursuers and at the same time eliminating everything and everyone that stood in their way. But mixed in with the smugness was the terror, the paranoia, the unspoken fear among Nazis of being discovered. How well they all knew the feeling. Fritz had changed residences eight times in his thirty-some-year exile.

Nor did the hiding end with their move to South America. Though they had successfully slipped, like a pack of rats, past the Allied War Crimes Commission, they had paid the price: a life of perpetual fear, running, and hiding. Ludwig Dietrich, whose very presence in the old days made men tremble and subservient, himself became a terrified child whenever he was in public and heard a Middle-Eastern accent several yards away. The haunted, darting looks: Is this man standing near me an Israeli? And the next question: Does anyone recognize me? Once, in an elevator, Ludwig found himself standing next to an elderly Jewish couple. The old man, waving his tattooed arm over his head, shouted something to his wife in Yiddish, while his other hand pointed to

Ludwig. The Nazi did not wait to reach the ground floor. Quickly pushing all the buttons to slow the elevator's descent, he got off at the next stop and — all of sixty years old at the time — ran down the remaining twelve flights of stairs.

Each day he and his friends would scan the German-language periodicals for news of any captured war criminals, all of whom were old comrades. The greatest aspiration was to die of old age, though they certainly had not accorded the same courtesy to their millions of victims. Inwardly each person knew he was living on borrowed time. It could be — five years? Ten? Twenty? Like Cain, they were condemned to the life of a fugitive, forever fleeing justice, forever running to different places. Days were filled with outward normality and everyday life, as these men later remarried and established families and businesses in their adoptive countries. During the nights, however, the fantasies emerged, of being trapped and hunted down — or worse, of meeting face to face both captors and victims alike. All it took was the familiar face of a former prisoner — though they had all looked alike back then — to trigger the powerful memories and emotions.

Not surprisingly, then, Ludwig was visibly shaken, and he asked, "Are you certain that he recognized you?"

"Positive."

"He knew you?"

"*Ja.*"

"What did you do?" asked Fritz.

"I went to a different synagogue to pray. I hoped to avoid recognition."

"It was foolish to go somewhere else at all," Fritz snorted. "Who knows? You might have been recognized by another Jew." He shook his head in contempt and, turning to Ludwig, said, "I told you he's strange, Ludwig. He's played this little role of his to the hilt and totally endangered our operation — if not our lives."

"Herr Loehmann," answered Hans with hostile courtesy, "I assure you that I found a synagogue where I knew nobody."

Hans turned away in disgust. How he had loathed, from the depths of his soul, this slimy little man with the beady little eyes and the small upturned nose. The man, Fritz Loehmann, looked exactly like the Austrian janitor's son that he was. Whenever Hans felt in need of a good laugh, all he had to do was remember Fritz in the officer's training camp. How he got there still remained one of life's mysteries. Even then, he was fawning and subservient toward *Oberfuhrer* Ludwig Dietrich, eager to take orders and saddle himself with all the paperwork. "Lackey Fritz," everyone sneered behind his back. However, the loyalty paid off well. Later, when transferred to the Gestapo, he took his new responsibilities quite seriously. With great zeal he applied himself to his clerical duties, recording in triplicate the names of all the prominent Reich Jews who were forced to emigrate, as well as their financial holdings. The energy he displayed for robbing these Jews was surpassed only by his sadism toward prisoners in Gestapo cells. Such enthusiasm was a credit to his methodology, if not his intelligence. It was to earn him a special place later in Adolf Eichmann's heart.

As usual, it was Dietrich who put him in his place. "Your comments are unnecessary, Fritz. However . . . I do wonder, Hans, why you would take your behavior to the extreme. It would appear strange to me . . . since you had verbally expressed your fear of being seen in the wrong places. Why is it necessary for you to frequent a synagogue? Certainly that should be just as dangerous as a cocktail lounge."

"Herr Dietrich," Schmidt began sonorously, "do you honestly believe that by remaining secluded and detached from all things Jewish I could avoid suspicion? Or that no one would notice me? Certainly not. I shall explain my reasoning little by little.

"First of all, it is impossible for anyone here to avoid contact with Jews. There are so many of them in New York. And frankly, I am no less safe walking in Boro Park dressed like this than you are walking in Manhattan in your impeccable European style of clothing. Has that, Herr Dietrich, ever helped you to avoid recognition by someone from Malberg?"

Dietrich winced at the mention of the camp.

"And actually, I might be safer than you. For in Boro Park, I fit in. After all, only a fraction of New York's Jews are Holocaust survivors. The fact that I met one of them is providential. We obviously had to meet for some reason. Perhaps it is to remind us of how unsafe we still are.

"But the fact is, Herr Dietrich, that most of the Jews there not only fail to recognize me. In fact, when they see me in this garb, they respect me for my piety. They trust me, and see that I follow the Bible. Observance encompasses everything — my dress, my prayers, my diet — everything. Judaism is a complete life style. These *mitzvos* — commandments — are not only a link between a Jew and G-d, but between one Jew and another. And only a fellow Jew could understand their importance. To you these practices are all clownish and barbaric; but to a Jew, they are the mark of integrity, as well as G-d's goodness. Only in a G-d-fearing Jew would other Jews put their complete faith and trust.

"Certainly, then, I would have aroused even greater suspicion had I chosen to avoid contact with other Jews. By not coming to the synagogue, by shunning everyone, I would be even more quickly recognized as Hans Schmidt. And worse," Schmidt concluded with a sigh, "Avraham Shulman might be labeled a fraud."

He finished his soliloquy, feeling victorious. The others were in silent awe of his logic. Heinz grunted, baboon-like, and grinned in his master's direction.

Ludwig Dietrich eyed the man cynically. Yes, he's definitely Hans Schmidt. They didn't call him "Jew-lover" at Hoffbaden for nothing.

"Well done," he finally said. "Your performance is superb. I suppose that is why you were one of my most talented pupils, Hans."

Hans was silent. The years at Hoffbaden, the SS training school, under the tutelage of Ludwig Dietrich, returned to him in dark, hazy undertones.

"I see you have gone to great lengths to cultivate your image," Ludwig continued. Then he darkened. "Let us hope, however, that you have not gone too far."

"Do not worry," Hans asserted.

"But someone *did* recognize you," said Fritz.

"And I've been able to prove him wrong," Hans countered.

"How?" asked Fritz.

"I know his son." Hans trailed off sadly at the thought of his last meeting with Shimshon.

"Hans," Heinz interjected, "that boy who came to your place that night and interrupted us. He was standing at the door. Is he the one?"

"Yes."

"How did he get to you?" asked Kurt.

"He is part of our problem," Hans replied. "He strongly

believes his father . . . and *in* his father, as well."

"Who is his father?" asked Ludwig.

"His name," Hans murmured, "is Rabbi Yehuda Shapiro."

"Yehuda Shapiro," mumbled Ludwig Dietrich, as his slender hand brushed across his neatly-trimmed hair in morbid recollection. For some reason, the name struck an inconsonant chord, and he tried to sort it out from among the debris of tortured, vanished lives. Where had he met the man? The name was familiar.

And then, a smile curled satanically across his face. Yes, it all came back now. In April 1943. Yes, he was there — they both were, at Malberg. Of course, on different sides of the machine gun. An emaciated guttersnipe — it was difficult to determine his age. He was ragged and filthy like the rest of them — but what eyes! How they burned deep brownish-black with raging fire. This boy had been assigned quarry duty — moving away rubble from the anti-aircraft ditch. He had stupidly tripped and knocked over a cartwheel of stones, spilling its contents into the ditch. Typical of the Jews — so lazy and careless when it came to honest labor. And the quota had to be met! Before the next Allied bombing. Dietrich had decided, in the face of his own irritation, to give the wretch a lesson. He stuck a lighted cigarette into the latter's arm, and had him flogged. Dietrich had been tempted to draw out his Mauser and simply finish him off. Had he known what was to be, he would have. But there was something in the boy's eyes that held him back. Even as the boy was dragged away, a bloody mess, he stared at the officer with such intense hatred that Dietrich, in spite of his position, trembled. He ordered the boy sent back to the barracks. This young Yehuda Shapiro did not realize how fortunate he had been. He had got off easy. He could have ended up in someone's bathroom, adorning a soap dish.

Later on, Yehuda Shapiro was transferred to Dachau. Dietrich had heard this later. So much for the past. But the name also evoked more recent memories. Word had got around in Buenos Aires and elsewhere about a group of survivors in Boro Park, Brooklyn, which was dedicated to hunting down Dietrich and his friends. The name Yehuda Shapiro had come up in conjunction with this group. The memories gushed out of Dietrich, like pus from an open sore. He cursed himself for not having fired his pistol back then. It certainly was — what did Schmidt call it? — providential that he had to spar with the man whose life he had graciously spared. No gratitude for the kindness he had bestowed upon the Jew! Wasn't it just like Shapiro to forget — so typical of these people.

It was Heinz who spoke again — gruffly. "I remember the boy's name. From you, Hans. It was Shimshon — right?"

"Yes," answered Hans softly.

"But didn't you say that you were able to prove Yehuda Shapiro wrong?" argued Fritz. "And through his son? How was that so? Especially if you say that he believes his father so strongly?"

Hans swallowed. "Yesterday afternoon . . . the boy came to see me."

"Really?" Ludwig's eyes widened momentarily, in a flicker of interest.

"Yes." Schmidt quickly added, "He wanted to recite his bar mitzvah speech to me. Very well done, I must say. He's a clever lad." Hans looked down wistfully at his glass of water. It remained on the table, untouched.

"Continue. What happened then?"

"When the boy accused me of being Hans Schmidt, I called him a liar. Worse than that . . . I scolded him and ordered him out of the house. I told him never to come back."

"Do you really think he believes you?" asked Fritz.

"I don't know," answered Hans. "I hope so. He admires Avraham Shulman."

"Yes, apparently," Ludwig commented. He studied his drink.

"And I'd hate to have him think," Hans continued soberly, "that I am not what he believes."

"Why, this is most distressing news," said Kurt. "You must avoid this boy at all costs."

"No," whispered Hans. "You mustn't worry about Shimshon. Please." He saw the look on Dietrich's face. "He won't bother us anymore." He looked away in trepidation. Who knows what they might do to the boy.

"I should think not." Ludwig Dietrich glanced at his watch. Nine o'clock. He summoned the waitress and asked for the check. "But soon, gentlemen, we won't have to worry about this anymore. Soon we'll be close to the gold. Once it's in our hands, we'll no longer have to be bothered at all by little Jewish boys."

"What am I to do now?" asked Hans.

"Await further orders," Ludwig commanded, rising from the table. The other three followed suit. "You'll hear from me next week."

"Very good," answered Hans. "I am at your service."

Putting on his black hat, Hans shook hands with each of them and bowed slightly. He felt relieved to revert to his old role again. Politely excusing himself, he stepped back into the mass of bodies and inched his way past the bar to the entrance.

Kurt leaned over the vinyl couch and looked out the window.

Through the tinted glass he watched impassively as the figure disappeared into the neon lights of the nocturnal city.

Slowly, Ludwig Dietrich lit another cigarette.

Kurt addressed him. "So?" he asked Ludwig, taking another Marlboro. "What do you think? Is he still loyal?"

Ludwig smiled sardonically. Through half-closed eyes, he answered, "He is still of service to our cause."

The "cause" was a forty-year-old obsession, dating back to the glory days of the Third Reich. The year was 1942. Germany was not only the epitome of evil, but at her evil zenith. Most of Europe had succumbed to her conquest, and millions of people had been sacrificed to her systematic terror and extermination. Millions more had yet to die.

And yet, the inevitable occurred. When the enemies of the Jews are enjoying their greatest moment, G-d activates the plan for their ultimate downfall. So it was with Germany. By November 1942, the Wehrmacht, now fighting on a host of fronts and battling the United States as well as the European allies and the Soviet Union, had overextended itself. By the end of that year, it had suffered staggering casualties — and begun an irreversible decline.

But so obsessed was Hitler with his Final Solution and his war against the Jews that he ignored reality. It was only a question of time before Germany would be exhausted and overrun. To Hitler, that mattered little. Nothing was of consequence except the total annihilation of the Jewish people. And nothing — repeated Allied bombings, civilian revolts, critical manpower shortages in the German factories and armed forces — could stop the murder machine. Like an ulcer, that machine began devouring itself, as Germany not only maintained her path of destruction, but eventually consumed her own citizens as well. Hitler, literally till the end of his life, did not compromise on his obsession to rid the world of all Jews.

The result was that he rid the world of Nazis — or so it seemed. The major ones, at any rate. They, as well as many of the lesser lights, were brought to Nuremberg and tried and hanged, or given prison sentences, for "crimes against humanity." It was a painful lip service paid to the millions that might have been saved a lot sooner.

But there were plenty of these men left who, unlike Hitler, had the foresight to predict defeat. Unlike their Fuhrer, they were grounded enough in reality — having heard of or experienced the disasters at Stalingrad or El Alamein — to privately plan their own escape ahead of time. Even as early as 1941, after Germany declared war on Russia, they somehow sensed that Germany's victories were only an illusion. It was merely a question of time before she would lie devastated under the Russian onslaught. However, some day she would reemerge as an economic power, thanks to the noble German work ethic, and pick up the pieces of her plan for world conquest.

A new leader would be needed for this Fourth Reich. Wealth and capital would be needed as well, and these men began stashing away gold, silver, precious stones, and other commodities. It was not a difficult task; the Reichsbank overflowed with Jewish gold in much the same way that the ancient Nile overflowed with Jewish blood. How fitting and ironic, these men thought, that these Jews, whose international conspiracy had begun the war, and whose annihilation was contributing to the German defeat, would be used to help rebuild the Reich.

The gold was melted down, and the valuables were hidden, to be shipped clandestinely out of Europe. But where? The United States was ultimately the best choice. Isolated, safe from attack, and with a stable economy, it was the country that the Nazis rightly predicted would become the dominant world power. However, their plans were thwarted in December 1941 when America entered the war, officially becoming an enemy.

Nevertheless, the Nazis instinctively felt that America was the right place to deposit their gold. But how to find a way? The answer: have the gold shipped through Switzerland, a neutral country; from there it would be sent into the United States. But a messenger would be needed — one who could supervise and prepare everything for the German conquest. Moreover, such a messenger would have to be pragmatic in business and efficiently organized.

Such a person was found in a short, middle-aged man named Joachim Schwimmer. Before 1933, Schwimmer, a Jew, had been a banker and realtor of distinction. He was known for his amazing acumen in buying up buildings nobody wanted and then developing them, thereby increasing their property value. By 1942, he and his immediate family, like most of the Jews who were still left in Berlin, had been reduced to virtual poverty. Schwimmer, who had financed many a Bauhaus architect during the Weimar Republic, still could not believe that his beloved homeland was capable of such deportment. Even as he watched his father, a World War I veteran, being transported to Theresienstadt, the "model" concentration camp, he assumed that this was all just one big mistake.

He fearfully went to Gestapo headquarters and pleaded for his father's life. Sitting behind the desk was none other than Fritz

Loehmann himself. He reviewed Schwimmer's background, and a sinister smile crossed his face. Quietly, he dialed RSHA headquarters — the Reich Security Main Office.

Ludwig Dietrich smiled with delight as he heard Loehmann's suggestion. (For this Loehmann received a promotion later by Eichmann's office.) Secretly, these men met with Schwimmer and worked out a plan. In exchange for his family's visas to Stockholm, Schwimmer would leave Germany with his wife for Switzerland. From there, they would emigrate to the United States. Schwimmer could simply appeal to the World Jewish Congress, which would arrange for his entry. Fortunately, too, Schwimmer had a friend in New York who would be willing to sponsor him, else he would not be accepted as an immigrant. Once in the United States, Schimmer would be in charge of receiving the gold. His expertise in real estate would come in handy. His family would be held hostage in Theresienstadt until the plan was effected.

Eagerly, Schwimmer cooperated — not only to save his family's life, but even to show, in a way, that his loyalty to Germany was still intact and that this Nazi business was all an unfortunate mistake.

The plan went brilliantly. Schwimmer aroused enough international sympathy to earn himself and his wife a permanent resident card. Residency quickly squared away, he settled down in Washington Heights, the "Frankfurt on the Hudson," a community teeming with fellow Germans, where he was quickly liked and accepted. He found it a pleasure to again utilize his business expertise. With dollars smuggled in by Nazi agents, he purchased a fine Manhattan apartment complex, quickly establishing himself as a well-to-do banker and importer.

With more smuggled dollars, he acquired additional property. Soon the money generated more money, and by February 1944, eighteen months after his arrival, he had amassed a considerable fortune in real estate. In the meantime, he kept in touch sporadically with his family, who sent interesting postcards with funny messages.

The problem remained, however, of bringing the gold, undetected, to the United States. This was finally accomplished by packing gold dust into charming little Swiss dolls. Thousands of these dolls were imported to the United States to entertain little girls whose fathers were away at war.

Having purchased an old warehouse in the Bowery, Schwimmer was there to receive the goods. The gold was then extracted, as it is from teeth (whence some of it originally came), and melted down again into bricks. These bricks were built into the structures of several prominent New York City buildings. By January 1945, the buildings were completed.

Inside the structures of these buildings were hidden fabulous sums of jewelry, currency, and art treasures — all hand-picked with great taste by the most cultured thieves in all of Europe. Their value was enough to finance any government. Noticing the influx of masterpieces, Schwimmer commented that some day he would build a museum.

However, he did not live to see it come to pass. In February 1945, he collapsed and died, in his office, of a heart attack. Perhaps it was just as well; he didn't have to live to find out that his entire family had been deported from Theresienstadt and perished at Auschwitz some six months earlier.

Roughly twelve years after its establishment, the Third Reich was crumbling fast under the weight of Russian tanks and

American bombers. Their hands still soaked with blood, the Nazis packed their bags and tried to get out before they met the drivers of the tanks and planes. Railway passage was booked for Switzerland, Spain, Portugal; boats to Argentina, Brazil — they headed anywhere that would provide haven for them.

Frantically, they tried to contact Schwimmer's widow and obtain blueprints of the buildings where the gold had been implanted. However, the Americans, invading southern Germany, had divided it in half, and closed off access to Switzerland, the neutral location from which they could make contact with the States.

By the time they did reach Schwimmer's widow — in April 1945, as the Third Reich was croaking its last inside a Berlin bunker — they were in for a shock. A grieved Frau Schwimmer, who had known nothing of her late husband's activities, had quietly sold off the properties. She had never liked New York; she longed to settle down and retire in the countryside, and this she did in Hunter, a quaint town upstate which reminded her of the Rhineland. Much later, the money she had received for the buildings was donated to Jewish charities, in memory of her loved ones.

She outlived her husband by only four years. She died in 1949, in Hunter. The loss of her family had done much to hasten her own demise.

There were no surviving children or relatives, no other heirs to the Schwimmer legacy. There was no one who came to reclaim the old fortune — what was left of it. The buildings lay nestled within the teeming, expanding metropolis of New York.

But the treasures were there — along with the costly structures surrounding them. That the Nazis knew. And their obsession to find those treasures was still there. How to locate them was one problem. *When* to find them was a different matter. In the confusion of the postwar population shifts and reconstruction, the Nazis were nowhere near ready to reemerge, like a Jack-in-the-Box, and begin their diabolical work. For this they would have to wait. Their plans to build the Fourth Reich would of necessity be shelved. There were more important things to do.

For the next thirty years or so, this gang of criminals stealthily burrowed underground. Like an undetected carcinoma, the Nazis planned their work in secret — maintaining and reviving old friendships in different places, calculating the time and manner of their eventual reemergence, making contacts in important places. In short, they strengthened themselves.

Through German diligence and ingenuity, as befitting the Master Race, they reestablished themselves — under new names and nationalities. They were warmly welcomed by the developing nations for their expertise in business, science, and technology. Like snakes, these men quickly shed their old uniforms and put on new, professional garments. Together, as modern-day industrialists, bankers, and scientists, they looked down upon the inferior peoples whose lands they graciously exploited — Paraguay, Uruguay, Bolivia, and others — and quickly established German supremacy.

While waiting to make their big move, they pleasantly filled their days with international terrorist activities. They trained some of the finest Palestine Liberation Organization people to emerge from the refugee camps. They were everywhere — aiding terrorists, bombing subways and buses, plotting assassinations and military coups.

In time, the Nazis felt certain growing pains. They were becoming weary of Brazilian jungles and subtropical climes. Quietly they expanded, along the way recruiting neo-Nazi organizations, criminals, psychopaths, and general drifters — an array of misfits looking for a way to vent their rage on the world.

There were also men from the old school, like Ludwig Dietrich. The son of a Prussian officer — poised, handsome, gifted in playing the violin and writing poetry — he eloquently lamented the collapse of the Third Reich, but deplored how such peanuts as Heinz, who couldn't appreciate Schiller and Goethe, had elbowed their way into the new Reich apparatus. With his charisma, Dietrich made his way into the upper echelons of developing Third World governments. There he was able to hire men for secret research, in much the same way he had done at both RSHA and the Hoffbaden SS training center. Files, dossiers on fellow criminals as well as "enemies" of the Reich — all were compiled in exquisite detail, meticulously recorded just as they were in 1933 — only now, on computer.

Over years of exhaustive research, Dietrich and his men located twelve of the buildings in which Schwimmer was involved. They were scattered all over New York City — most in Manhattan, some in the other four boroughs. A majority of these buildings were owned or inhabited by Jews — many of whom, like Schwimmer, were refugees from Europe.

Thus the Nazis waited in their mansions and estates, wallowing in hatred and frustration and looking forward to the time when they could complete what they had left unfinished the last time: the ridding of the world, once and for all, of the kind of people who lived in these buildings.

The men first tried to send American gentiles, respectable-looking businessmen, to speak with these Jews. But the businessmen were turned away.

Dietrich realized that someone was needed who really knew these people. Someone, he felt, who could understand them, their religion, their psyche — someone who shared their background. They needed to find a Jew, more, a survivor, who would help them, but finding someone who was both a Jew and a Holocaust survivor, yet was actually willing to collaborate with Nazis, was next to impossible; the *Judenrat* was gone for good.

However, much to Dietrich's surprise, they found a much better specimen for the task. And he was truly amazing, as Kurt had promised. *Sturmbannfuhrer* Hans Schmidt, who had worked with Kurt at the Malberg labor camp, and who had mysteriously fled Germany, was the person for Dietrich and his crusade.

Dietrich had met Hans Schmidt long ago — first at Hoffbaden officer's training camp, and later through his friend *Oberfuhrer* Erich Lederer. Shortly before he was hanged, Lederer had smuggled out, from his British prison cell, a coded message to Dietrich: *Hans Schmidt is the one.* Hans, who had worked under Lederer at Malberg concentration camp, had displayed an extraordinary rapport with the Jews; he had simultaneously earned their trust while leaving them to their fate. There was a rumor that he had been in love with a Jewish girl, but it had quickly been disproven. She had later been disposed of, anyway.

Like Dietrich, Hans had been able, either through cold logic or a premonition, to predict Germany's eventual defeat. Or so it was assumed. He had acted independently of the others. He had made his own escape. In 1943, he left Germany — determined, he told Kurt, to return later and make his mark on the world. Spoken like a true Nazi, said Dietrich. Beforehand, even as early as 1938, Dietrich had had certain doubts about this man.

And indeed, Schmidt did reemerge. Only this time, he was no longer Hans Schmidt. Or a Nazi. He was Avraham Shulman, an Orthodox Jew living in a Jerusalem suburb. There he amazingly adapted to the ways of those around him. He seemed to fit in wonderfully; in fact, so internalized was the Jewish life that he himself had to be reminded that once upon a time he had actually been somebody else — and that he and that somebody else were one and the same.

It was Avraham Shulman who contacted Dietrich — through Kurt Zerner, a former *Untersturmbannfuhrer,* and a classmate at Weissgarten academy — while in Buenos Aires. Introducing himself over the pay phone as Hans Schmidt, he whispered an urgent plea in German: "Don't be shocked when you see me."

A meeting was arranged at the Hotel Castillar, in downtown Buenos Aires. When Dietrich beheld Avraham Shulman, formerly Hans Schmidt — the latter's tall, lithe figure wrapped in black, his crystalline eyes shining with acquired wisdom, his bold countenance framed in whitening hair, beard, and earlocks, and his entire fibre exuding a sense of destiny — the older Nazi rubbed his delicate hands together, and said to himself, *danke schoen,* Erich. You always were a faithful friend. Hans Schmidt *is* the one. For truly he is a gift to the world — a man with a double life, and a double identity. He is truly the chosen one. He will lead us all to the gold.

Chapter 8

The Investigation

Rabbi Shapiro was berating his son. "Did I permit you to see Avraham Shulman? Didn't I tell you to keep away from that man? Why did you disobey me?"

It was nine p.m. on the day after Shimshon had been thrown out of Shulman's apartment, and exactly one hour after Shimshon had finally approached his father, shamefaced, and told him what had happened the previous night.

His father listened, first patiently, then with growing horror, as he realized not only where his son **had** gone, but what had brought him there. Soon his shock gave way to anger. And now, here he was — Yehuda Shapiro, a man normally slow to anger — standing over his son, who was cowering on the living room sofa.

At that same hour, Avraham Shulman had just taken leave of his companions in the Upper East Side lounge.

"Don't you know how dangerous it was to do such a thing, Shimshon?" he shouted. "Trusting this person . . . naively going there, behind my back, to see him . . . and all by yourself, in such a neighborhood. How could you?"

Shimshon remained helplessly quiet, too defenseless in his guilt to argue with his father. He now regretted ever striking up the nerve to tell his father of his conversation with Shulman. Stern reprimand, yes; rage, no.

Though Shimshon knew he could not argue the fact that he had acted contrary to his father's wishes, he found himself desiring to defend Shulman, who was not here to speak in his own behalf. Yes, Shimshon had disobeyed his father; yes, he had explicitly been told not to get involved with Shulman. But it was, he felt, for a greater cause — to bridge a misunderstanding. In vain, Shimshon had described this man's learning and spirituality, and how Shulman had even complimented Yehuda Shapiro. But all this made no impression whatsoever.

Then a disturbing thought came to Shimshon's mind. Remembering that his father had written down Shulman's address on a piece of paper, and that he was now scolding Shimshon for going to "such a neighborhood," Shimshon wondered — had his father been there? When? Last week? Last night? It would have been long after Shimshon had left Justin Road. His father hadn't gotten home till *very* late. Shimshon had waited for him until midnight before he finally fell asleep.

At last the rabbi sighed, and sagged into the armchair. His face, drained of angry intensity, was now strangely sad and haggard. Shimshon had rarely seen his father this way before. The boy felt doubly ashamed, as he now realized how much his father had been affected by his action.

"You don't know how much you have upset me, Shimshon. I am very disappointed in you."

The boy squirmed. "Ta, I'm . . . sorry — I really am," he managed to say. There were tears in his eyes. "I felt like . . . I was trying to help you. I didn't mean to do anything sneaky. It's just that . . . I don't know . . . I just *had* to see him — and find out who he was."

Shimshon looked away in distress and confusion. He honestly could not explain the power Avraham Shulman had over him. "I didn't mean to hurt you. Or him. Honest. And I thought by talking to him I could get to know him better. And maybe find out if he really was who you said."

His father looked at him squarely. "What did you expect him to say, Shimmy?" This time his voice was firm, but more gentle. "That yes, he *is* a Nazi? Did you honestly expect him to admit that? Here in Brooklyn? And then what? What might have happened to you, a Jewish boy and *my* son, alone with him? You were lucky he reacted the way he did. Even had you not said anything at all to him, it was dangerous to be there. Moreover, what you said was foolish. Because only a fool states the obvious. And now he knows just a bit more about me. You've shown our hand to him."

Shimshon gasped. He had done worse than humiliate or disobey his father; he had actually endangered his father's life.

"Ta," the boy asked fearfully, "it's not just Shulman's being a Nazi that bothers you, huh? You think . . . he wants to do something really bad to you? To us?"

The look on Yehuda Shapiro's face reminded Shimshon of many nights past, filled with screaming and writhing in bed. It was enough to see his father's eyes, the irises pulsating darkly in the light, to know what hidden terrors he harbored.

An emergency meeting was called for the next evening at a home in Flatbush. The cars were parked several blocks away, with survivors weaving in and out of streets and avenues to avoid being followed. Finally, they met and argued, mainly in Yiddish, over what to do. The curtains in the house were tightly drawn.

For the first time, Yehuda Shapiro brought his son to such a meeting. The boy sat bewildered, as if he had been dragged to a bridge game. Only here there wasn't a group of gossiping women — just bickering grown men. There were over two dozen of them — most his father's age, a few older. Each was tense and haunted; each had his own private tale and his own ghosts from the past. Shimshon recognized some of the men from his father's *shul* or business. He knew their stories vaguely.

There was Menachem Glazer, his father's accountant, who had been smuggled to Palestine via Hungary. There was also Itzhak Rifkin, who had spent two years at Auschwitz, and at war's end weighed seventy-five pounds. They had been brought together by a collective past, and collective memories. But now it was something else that kept them perpetually united: it was men like Hans Schmidt, alias Avraḥam Shulman — it was a continuous fight against evil.

The mention of the man's name was a catalyst for the introduction of other names, which were repeated in an emotional frenzy over the course of the evening. Suggestions were tossed back and forth — mainly about having Shulman arrested and tried. Some, like Baruch Minkowitz, who had been a partisan, simply wanted him killed.

"I say hire a hit man and finish him off!" he boomed. A big, barrel-chested man in his late fifties, he exuded fierce strength, like the big furry bears of the forests where he had spent his youth. He looked like he could kill a Nazi with his bare hands — and he could.

"Don't you think that's a little unfair?" replied Menachem Glazer. "After all, we owe him the courtesy of a trial."

Baruch grunted. "Fair? You want to be fair? Were those

animals fair to my parents when they shot them down in an open pit? Fair? They should all burn." He spat in contempt.

"Well, it's certainly not practical," answered Menachem, as banally as if he were discussing a tax cut. "Someone like Hans Schmidt could lead us to other men in hiding. It would be foolish to have him killed." Then he added, in prudent afterthought, "Not yet, anyway."

"Ha! Listen to *him!*" Baruch the Fighter again roared, pointing to Glazer as if the latter were some oddity that had wandered into the meeting by time warp. "He thinks he's still living in Warsaw. Do you actually think Shulman will help us? He'll stay loyal to his friends, no matter what. He'll never betray them — or the cause. Not even to save his own neck."

They argued further, each raising his voice and gesticulating wildly — each shouting down the others, and asking others to take sides. Some proposed ways to bring the former SS officer to justice. The meeting finally climaxed into noisy confusion. Shimshon continued to sit and watch quietly, in fascination. So did his father. Each marveled at how oddly grown men could act sometimes. His father, more so, was intrigued at this sight of adults acting like children. He was reminded, somewhat bitterly, of the Warsaw Ghetto. There too, arguing was the favorite pastime among the helpless residents — even as they were being taken away. It was all one could do in the face of disaster, when hysteria took the place of decisive action.

At last he raised his hands. "Gentlemen," he pronounced firmly. The voices hushed. "Your suggestions concerning this man are not based on logic. First of all, we're dealing with the powerful force behind this man. Extremely powerful. By acting carelessly, we may end up with a bigger problem on our hands."

"Such as?" said Baruch.

"Such as dealing with the men he is in league with. Bringing immediate retribution to Hans Schmidt might bring immediate harm to ourselves and those we love."

"Is there evidence that Schmidt is planning something against us now?" asked Itzhak Rifkin.

"Yes."

Now all voices were morbidly still, as Rabbi Shapiro spoke, anger in his voice. "Certain men have been sighted again — together — in New York. They were seen passing by some apartment complexes in the Bronx and Staten Island. They have been recognized by many survivors."

"Was Schmidt with them?"

"No. But there is certainly reason to believe that he is in contact with them. Hans Schmidt knows that I have recognized him. Which places *me* in grave danger."

The group was completely silent. Shimshon felt a sting of guilt, knowing that he was partly the cause of all this.

The rabbi continued. "As I speak to you now, they could very well be plotting their next move. Most likely I am their first target. Or my son."

Shimshon trembled.

"Or that criminal Schmidt could be out of town by now," growled Baruch.

"I doubt it," the rabbi retorted.

"How do you know?"

"Moshe Kaplan and I drove by his place yesterday evening, around eight. We spoke to some people who saw a man fitting his description leave the building around five o'clock."

Shimshon gasped. He realized that he had been correct; his

father had, all along, done his own legwork. So that was why he had told Shimshon to butt out. Shimshon wondered: How many other times had Tati gone there?

"They said he headed toward the subway station," the rabbi continued. "We spoke to the token clerk, and she said that he went in the direction of Manhattan."

"She's sure it was him?" Glazer asked carefully.

"Positive. He spoke to her for a couple of minutes, so she was able to place him. I think it's very ironic that a beast like him would take the time to be nice to a token clerk. But we all know that the Nazis were quite schizophrenic in their behavior."

"And he always goes to Manhattan?" asked Rifkin. "On the F-train?"

"Most of the time — when he's on the F-train. Sometimes he stays on till Queens. His movements, though, have not been regular. In fact, he moves at very strange hours."

"He might have gotten off and taken a train to Williamsburg," Glazer suggested.

"No. If he had, Reuven would have seen him."

Reuven Fox, a furrier who was also an Auschwitz survivor, lived in Williamsburg. He sat quietly in the back, and nodded to show agreement with and support of Rabbi Shapiro.

"But so far," the rabbi continued, "he has not been there — not even to visit. As far as Jewish areas go, he mainly stays in Boro Park. And when he isn't in Boro Park, he's usually in Manhattan."

"Is there ever anyone with him?" asked Itzhak Rifkin. "Or has he met with anyone there?"

"No. Not whenever we saw him. He was always by himself. I'm inclined to believe that Schmidt is a lone wolf." The rabbi was silent. "I have sighted him at times on my way to work; he is most frequently in the midtown area. His movement has not been regular enough for us to find a definite pattern. He has also on occasion appeared in other areas — the Lower East Side, mainly. Also once in Rego Park. However, all at different times of the day."

"And you haven't noticed any unusual behavior?" asked Menachem Glazer.

"No. Depending, of course, on what you consider unusual. Mostly he walks around and stares at buildings. I really can't say much else at this point. But I do know that he is here — in New York. And it's up to us to find out the reason."

The room was now filled with the strange silence of stalemate.

Timidly, Shimshon cleared his throat. "Ta," he said, "*I* saw Shulman — I mean Schmidt — with some men. The first time I was there, in his apartment."

"The *first* time?" His father frowned.

The boy cringed guiltily. "I went there once before. I saw four men in his living room."

Rabbi Shapiro's face had a stunned look pasted on it. "What did they look like?"

Shimshon described them. He told them the name of the fat man, Heinz, and about the limousine that had picked them up afterwards. Listening to him, his father frowned, and he looked at Menachem Glazer. The boy explained apologetically that he had neglected to take down the license plate number.

"Perhaps," Menachem suggested, "we should have Shulman followed."

"But we *have*," the rabbi retorted. "Reuven and Moshe have seen to that. And they can't seem to find a clue as to the true nature of his activity."

"I have a suggestion," said Menachem. "We should have him photographed."

"You mean . . . hire an investigator?" said Rabbi Shapiro.

"Yes."

An enthusiastic murmur of approval rippled through the group. Even Baruch responded positively. "Why didn't we think of it sooner?" he said.

Rabbi Shapiro said, "I am still opposed to hiring professional help. Not yet. To do so would only bring unwanted publicity and send Schmidt back underground."

"But the way we're doing it now — this sloppy, amateurish tailing — will most likely produce the same result," Glazer replied. "Face it, Yehuda. I think at this point professional help is not only preferred, but necessary."

Itzhak Rifkin brightened. "I know somebody who could help us," he said.

"Who?"

"My nephew Jack."

"Your nephew?" the rabbi asked.

"Yes. He was the one who got the photos for the Richardson trial — you know, the one that was in all the papers."

"That was a divorce case, Yitzy." Rabbi Shapiro smiled slightly.

"It doesn't matter," Rifkin argued, a trifle indignant. "He caught the guy, didn't he? Thanks to Jack, that lawyer showed up Alex Richardson before all of New York — and got his wife a good settlement, too. Why, that Richardson had a track record you wouldn't believe—"

"You're sure Jack can keep a secret?" Rabbi Shaprio interrupted hastily. "Can he be trusted to be discreet?"

"You have my word."

"I have one other concern," the rabbi said hesitantly. "Nowadays a divorce is far more understandable than what we're trying to do. Do you think Jack would be sympathetic? Also, would he feel comfortable working with us? I'm getting the sense that he's not religious."

Sheepishly, Rifkin replied, "I think it's time Jack had a Jewish education."

Jack Rifkin, born in Long Island, had always referred to his paternal uncle as either "a little strange — he was in the war, you know," or "one of those Orthodox guys — doesn't answer the phone on Saturdays." When his secretary informed him that his Uncle Yitzy was on the phone, he groaned, took a deep breath, and counted to ten before picking up the receiver. When he heard his uncle's description of a chassidic-looking man who was supposed to be a Nazi, Jack's eyes widened a fraction of an inch. Well, it happened at last — he said to himself — Uncle Yitzy finally went off the deep end. He was always raving about the Holocaust; it got to him worse than I thought. Or it must be that crazy ghetto, Williamsburg. Thank G-d Dad got out of there when he did.

Nevertheless, Jack Rifkin went to Flatbush and bought a cheap satin yarmulke, the kind handed out to him at the synagogue when he went there, three times a year — on the High Holidays. The next day he waited behind a garbage bin on Justin Road as the figure shrouded in black left the run-down building, rounded the cul-de-sac, and headed up the street, the wind billowing through his gabardine, in the direction of Boro Park. Jack, in the meantime, clutched his yarmulke, which was not designed for constant wear, much less windy days.

Much of that day was spent in Boro Park. Jack Rifkin, whose specialty was divorce cases, had flown to places such as Las Vegas and Miami to track down errant husbands or wives. Now, in spite of his initial discomfort, he somewhat enjoyed being in the somehow more exotic clime of Boro Park, and mingling with people who reminded him of his grandfather. While watching Shulman shop for matzoh and wine across the street, he munched on a falafel sandwich. The only difficulty was changing into different disguises. Somewhere on Thirteenth Avenue the satin yarmulke was taken off, and in its place went a beautiful, embroidered work which made him look like a doorman from Casablanca. While Shulman was examining *haggados* in a bookstore, Jack slipped into a phone booth near a Chinese restaurant, *a la* Superman, and emerged wearing a black hat, coat, and fake beard courtesy of a costume store two blocks from his office. Inside the black coat was a small cut, through which peeped a Nikon.

During the week, donning ever more elaborate disguises, he followed Shulman on the F-train into Manhattan. Once they went all the way to Queens. On Sunday, two days before Passover, he presented Rabbi Shapiro with an interesting set of prints.

The rabbi scanned them on Sunday afternoon in the living room, with Shimshon peering over his shoulder. Rifkin sat awkwardly on the sofa, wearing the satin yarmulke out of respect. He stared at the bookcase full of Hebrew volumes and felt nervous among such intense, overt Jewishness. He felt that he had swallowed an overdose of it during the week — as well as enough falafel to last a lifetime.

The prints, the majority taken in Boro Park and Manhattan, were mostly in black and white, and positively artistic; in fact, they would have been ideal for a photo essay on "Chassidim in the Modern World." In some of the pictures, Shulman was gazing soulfully ahead at some unseen object. In others, his blue eyes, gray in the photographs, were filled with melancholy. In one intriguing print, his figure was silhouetted by a noonday sun against a diamond shop on Forty-seventh Street in Manhattan, as if to hint symbolically at his "dark side." In fact, Shulman looked as if he had some kind of special relationship with the sun. In a particularly stunning pose, his profile blocked the blades of light, which bounced off his large head and sprouted rays, angelically, behind his back. This was clearly a man made to be photographed, a man whose charisma made nature itself point to his uniqueness.

Shimshon was fascinated. He hadn't expected Shulman to be so photogenic. The boy remembered how he and his friends had to line up, giggling, for school pictures, and how the pictures usually ended up looking "really stupid." But seeing these, of Shulman, made Shimshon — himself a budding photographer — realize the awesome power of a camera. How regal Shulman looked! Seeing them also made Shimshon realize what had attracted him to the man in the first place. The latter's being radiated the natural charisma of a leader — a true leader, one with depth and strength of character, not a flashiness that quickly expired either under pressure or next year's trend.

One picture, more than all the rest, caught Shimshon's eye, and seemed to convey the Avraham Shulman he had met in the synagogue and at home. Shulman was standing at a traffic light, in what looked like a deserted area not far from Justin Road.

Conspicuous in his black coat and hat, surrounded by a gaudy crowd in bright, immodestly-cut clothes, he seemed strangely sad and weary. The bag he held, bulging with goods, seemed symbolic in a way — suggesting, perhaps, that its carrier was alone against the world, and shouldering its burdens.

Rabbi Shapiro had a different reaction. He studied each picture coldly, like an agent perusing an actor's publicity stills. Occasionally he nodded, as if to confirm some inner thought.

Finally, he asked the investigator, "Do you remember which day of the week each was taken?"

Jack smiled. "Hey, you're insulting a professional," he replied. "I wrote down the exact time and place that each shot was snapped. Look." He extracted from his pocket a small notebook, with names and dates scribbled on the pages. "I'll show you. This one, at Forty-seventh Street, was on Friday at three in the afternoon. And this one, which your son seems to like, was also taken Friday afternoon — around five o'clock."

"Were any taken on Shabbos?" the rabbi asked.

Again Rifkin smiled. "Don't worry, Rabbi," he said. "You think I'd bring the wrath of G-d and Uncle Yitzy on me? For years he's been trying to drag me to synagogue. Out for my soul. He insisted that I not take any pictures of Shulman on Shabbos.

" 'But Uncle Yitzy,' I argued, 'you claim to be dealing with a man who really isn't Jewish. That means he may very well be doing the things you are interested in finding out about on Saturday.'

" 'Manage what you can, Yaakov,' " Jack quoted his uncle, mimicking the Yiddish accent, " 'but don't do it on Shabbos.' So, I planned ahead . . . I had my associate, Alan Hopkins, help me out. He's not Jewish, so he hung around Shulman till right before sunset on Friday. He was very helpful."

Jack pointed to several pictures. "These were taken Friday afternoon around candle-lighting time. I had gone home," he said.

Father and son looked down. Shulman was walking past an old junkyard, clutching his chassidic hat both against the wind and against certain people who might find the fur a costly temptation. His friend the sun was slowly bidding him goodbye in the distance.

"That was the last one taken until last night," Jack explained. "I drove past his place around nine p.m., but he wasn't back yet."

"*I* saw him," replied Rabbi Shapiro. Shapiro had walked by a synagogue off Seventeenth Avenue and Forty-third Street. In the distance he had seen Shulman talking intensely with a young chassid.

Jack laughed. "Brother, can you imagine this guy in German uniform?"

Rabbi Shapiro looked at him with a trace of contempt. "You don't think he's a Nazi?" he asked.

"Sure, Rabbi, just like *Hogan's Heroes*," the investigator guffawed. He inhaled, lowered his voice, and growled, "*I know nuu-tink! Nuuuuuu-tink!*"

Shimshon looked at him uncomprehendingly. Then he brightened. "TV, right?" he asked. He smiled.

Jack stopped himself short, looking around the room and realizing that, among the Hebrew books and Jewish ritual objects, nary a television set lay in sight. He remembered, in embarrassment, that this was not his usual audience — and that the show had gone off the air, anyway, before Shimshon was born. Still, it did occasionally pop up in syndication, especially late at night. Too bad, he thought. His Sergeant Shultz imitation had been the hit at many a backyard barbecue.

He cleared his throat and quickly continued. "The most recent shot was taken early this morning, as he was leaving for somewhere. He had a bag under his arm."

"Probably a *tallis* bag," the rabbi mumbled.

"A what?"

"A prayer shawl," the rabbi said, smiling. "Did you at any time see him with anybody?"

Jack frowned. "No, Rabbi. He was always alone. But don't say I didn't try. I followed him everywhere."

"Was there any particular area that Shulman frequented?"

"Actually, yes," Jack answered. He again took out his notebook. "Sunday, 4:30 p.m., Monday, 2:45 p.m., Tuesday, six p.m., Wednesday, 10:20 a.m. . . . in fact, he was seen every day in the vicinity of Thirty-eighth Street and Seventh Avenue."

Rabbi Shapiro stared at Rifkin alertly. "In Manhattan?" he asked.

"Yes. Are you very familiar with the area, Rabbi?"

"Yes, I am. I work near Forty-third and Eighth."

"Then you would know, more than I, Rabbi, if there is anything there of interest to Avraham Shulman."

"Not that I know of," answered the rabbi distantly. He groped for a mental picture of the area. "I vaguely recall a German restaurant near Thirty-sixth and Seventh."

"The Lorelei?"

"Yes," answered the rabbi eagerly. "Was he ever there?"

"No," replied Rifkin. "I did see him pass by it once or twice. However, it was always on the way to somewhere else. I had the impression that he was looking for something — in one of the buildings. But I never saw him stop there or go inside the restaurant. I wondered about it, and made a mental note of the place. After all, if he's what you say he is, then it would seem logical for him to go there. I went inside to speak with the owners. They gave me some rather strange looks. But they said they never saw anyone like this man in their restaurant."

"It would seem just as logical, Mr. Rifkin, for him to avoid that kind of place."

"I have given you everything there is, Rabbi Shapiro," Rifkin said. "I'm sorry I cannot give you anything more. I checked with the Israeli embassy . . . the West German and East German consulates . . . everything. But apparently there's nothing new I have on the background of Avraham Shulman or Hans Schmidt that you don't already seem to know."

"You've done more than enough for us, Mr. Rifkin," said Rabbi Shapiro, rising. "You will be paid well."

"Listen," said Rifkin, "don't bother. If it means this much to you and our people, consider it a *mitzvah* from me. Probably doesn't mean much from a guy who doesn't even keep kosher. I always had a hard time taking Uncle Yitzy seriously. But after meeting you . . . well . . . I've changed my mind somewhat."

The two shook hands.

"May I keep the photographs?" asked the rabbi.

"Of course. I have the negatives. Also, I'll leave this folder with you; it has all the information I could find on this man. Give me a call if there's anything else. You have my card."

Rifkin patted Shimshon on the head, and put on his coat. The rabbi followed him to the door.

Rifkin was halfway out when Rabbi Shapiro stopped him. "Thank you for all your help. And you're wrong. Whether or not you keep kosher, you've done a great service for your people. G-d looks at each of a man's deeds separately, and He is certainly proud of you today. Happy Passover."

"Happy Passover to *you*," said the man, and was gone.

The rabbi stood in the doorway and watched Rifkin's Audi pull away toward the late afternoon sun. When he returned to the living room, he saw Shimshon still staring at the photos.

Frowning, the rabbi gathered them carefully into a manila envelope, and grabbed his car keys. Shimshon followed.

Parking his car off of Sixteenth and Fifty-fifth, the rabbi hurriedly passed a yeshiva and stopped at a camera store. Behind the glass door a CLOSED sign was dangling. Rabbi Shapiro knocked.

In the darkened interior, a short, rotund man Rabbi Shapiro's age became visible. Seeing the rabbi, he nodded, and quickly unlocked the door.

Hastily leading father and son through the hallways, he steered them into the darkroom. There, the little man extracted the contents of the manila envelope and held them near the flourescent light.

"*Nu*?" asked Rabbi Shapiro. "What do you think, Mosh?"

Moshe Kaplan squinted under the lamps. He was holding the picture of Shulman by the traffic light.

"With this one there shouldn't be any difficulty."

"Think I could get it by Chol HaMoed?"

"Well, according to *halacha* I can't develop on Chol HaMoed. I'm always closed for the entire Pesach."

"I'm well aware of the *halacha*! But every day we lose is another day that Shulman might get away. In this circumstance, you are allowed to develop film on Chol HaMoed."

"Well, if that's the case, it should not be a problem."

The rabbi then removed a picture from another envelope.

Shimshon's eyes widened in shock. A semi-profile of a young German officer, his eyes turned intently toward the camera in a vague, thin-lipped smile, seemed to be staring in boyish defiance. Shimshon was further shocked when the rabbi held the close-up of Avraham Shulman next to the sepia-toned portrait, circa 1940, of Hans Schmidt. Possibly the only thing these two faces had in common, besides their seriousness, was a shine — the German's, of fleeting youth; the Jew's, of ageless Torah wisdom. But possibly there was more.

"Good *yom tov*," said Rabbi Shapiro to Moshe Kaplan, "and good luck."

"Thanks."

Passover was an immensely welcome break; indeed, a true feeling of freedom engulfed the Shapiros. Shimshon, after a taxing month, relished the festival of liberation — to rejoice in G-d's redemption of His people, and the downfall of His enemies.

"*Shefoch chamascha,* Pour out Thy wrath," sang Rabbi Shapiro, dressed in white and surrounded by his friends and their wives. All of them were there — a legacy of survivors, here tonight to remember G-d's redemption of the Jewish people, and the horrors perpetrated against the Jews as well. Like Rabbi Shapiro, they had come out of the Holocaust whole — bitter, broken, but accepting of G-d's will. And though they had to struggle to rebuild their lives, never did they cease affirming their commitment as Jews. It was a covenant made many Passovers ago with their forefather Avraham — that the Jews would survive, no matter the stumbling blocks. The Nazis were merely one link on a seemingly endless chain of persecutors. There might be more. But eventually, Shimshon knew, the enemies of the Jewish people ended up the same way.

Somewhere else in Boro Park, someone else was observing the festival of Jewish freedom. Avraham Shulman had taken quite a liking to a nice young man he had met in the synagogue on Shabbos HaGaddol, the Sabbath before Passover, and was delighted to get an invitation — not only for the *sedarim*, but for all the meals. It turned out that this man had just moved to Boro Park a year earlier from Williamsburg, after his marriage, to study in a *kollel*. His wife, who had just had a baby, was delighted to have such a distinguished guest to honor their Passover table. Shulman, in turn, flattered by their flurry of attention, considered it an honor to be invited to their home. The reciprocity worked out well for both parties.

Holding a goblet and dressed in white, like his adversary several blocks away, Shulman also recited the fateful verse: "Pour out Thy wrath," trembling and wondering for whom the wrath was intended this year.

Shimshon turned down an offer to go to the Great Adventure amusement park on Chol HaMoed with Zev and the gang. He wanted to stick around to watch the results of the photo technician's work.

On the first day of Chol HaMoed, he went with his father back to Moshe Kaplan's store.

In the back room, Moshe held up the results. Shimshon looked, and his eyes opened even wider than before.

The photo, softened and grainy due to airbrushing, looked slightly out of focus. The surroundings — traffic light, people, garbage — had been whited out into oblivion, so that Shulman looked eerily like a figure frozen in a sandblast. Nevertheless, after the round black hat was removed, the beard and earlocks were technologically trimmed away, and the wrinkles were magically flattened, the rest remained vivid. A German hat and uniform were superimposed on top of the blond hair and broad frame of Avraham Shulman. Then Rabbi Shapiro held it against the 1940 photo.

It was there. Unbelievable, but there. The resemblance was too real. In his youth, the gentle blue eyes of the chassid had transformed to a hard icy blue; the benevolent smile had become a sneer.

"Hans Schmidt," whispered the rabbi.

His son had gone numb. It was like finding out that one's favorite uncle, or the kindly old man who lived down the lane, was the greatest child-murderer ever to walk the earth.

The Forty-first Precinct was situated near a group of grayish municipal buildings off East Third Street and Ditmas Avenue. A row of blue-and-white vehicles were parked diagonally against the granite structure, and outside the entrance a forlorn-looking group of people was waiting under the roof, watching the pounding rain.

Rabbi Shapiro turned his blue Pontiac into the big driveway, looking through the splattered windshield for a spot adjacent to the relative safety of a police car. In the front seat, between him and Shimshon, lay the manila envelope.

Shimshon stared wistfully out the window, watching the bleak, chilly grayness of the cloudy sky. Too bad it hadn't rained yesterday, he thought with a sigh. He wouldn't have felt so bad about missing the trip to Great Adventure.

Inside the building it was an even bleaker gray. The waiting room was miserably lit by flourescent lights. The walls were slabs of chipping plaster, which reminded Shimshon vaguely of Shulman's apartment house. The people sitting on the slatted benches were drenched with a combination of different liquids — rain, beer, vomit, blood. Drunks looking for a place to sleep it off; drab housewives in old raincoats, complaining that their homes had been ransacked or their purses snatched; teenage gang members picked up for fighting; bruised and beaten men waiting near their own muggers — all watched half cynically, half curiously, this tall, silent Jew in a neat black hat and coat, and his son.

A black woman, scarcely out of her teens, was loudly popping gum by her desk and typing. At the sight of Rabbi Shapiro and his son, she curtly told them to take a number: thirty-two.

"Number twelve!" called an officer from an open door.

The rabbi soberly took the seat vacated by number twelve. Shimshon sat beside him, huddling protectively close.

Rabbi Shapiro took out a small Talmud volume. Shimshon looked about the room, trying to read the different people.

A woman in an old corduroy jacket and skirt was brooding on the edge of a bench on Shimshon's right. Next to her was another woman, in her sixties, clutching her poodle for dear life, and staring fearfully at the hulking, menacing youth on her left with the headphones.

A man with a five o'clock shadow, torn trenchcoat, greasy hair, and filth-encrusted fingernails was mumbling to himself on the floor. Occasionally he darted hateful glances at the humanity around him and vehemently spewed words not in a normal person's range of vocabulary. He snarled at Shimshon for no apparent reason. The boy quickly turned his head the other way and studied the interesting mug shots of criminals on the bulletin board instead. He tried to visualize Avraham Shulman's picture up there among bank robbers and arsonists.

Suddenly an enormous woman waddled in through the door. She was abnormally obese; one chin held another in place, as she moved her jowls meditatively in search of a place to sit. At last she did find a place — an entire bench, for both herself and her two equally enormous shopping bags. She plopped herself down comfortably.

Then she opened her mouth and began singing. Rabbi Shapiro looked up, startled.

"Oh, they took away my checks . . ." Something about a welfare agency; an improvised ballad of her and her enemies.

The girl typing at the desk looked at her and smiled. "They threw you out again, Rosie, huh?" she said patronizingly.

The woman nodded and went on singing, her glazed eyes staring straight ahead. Her voice was sweet and resonant. Most likely she had received her musical training in a church choir.

The secretary explained to Shimshon. "She did that last week on the subway. A little hard on the audience, though — they were trapped in a B-train over the bridge. But she gave quite a show."

At last number thirty-two was called. Rabbi Shapiro carefully pocketed the little Talmud volume and went into a dingy cubicle past the secretary's desk. Shimshon followed.

Sgt. Tim Hogan sat frowning, the remains of a ham sandwich resting to his side. He was a large, burly man, and his belly bulged through a sweat-stained shirt, causing one button to stay open. He stank of stale Camels, and extracted another one from his pocket. He called to a passing secretary for a cup of strong black coffee.

Rabbi Shapiro recoiled at the acrid cigarette smoke, as he sat facing the officer. The latter, in turn, studied the rabbi through bored, half-closed eyes. He allowed Rabbi Shapiro to do the talking, all the while stifling a yawn and thinking about the fight he had had the previous night with his wife. They had been up till three.

Rabbi Shapiro calmly explained the story of Hans Schmidt, Nazi turned Jew, and how he was currently residing nearby, on Justin Road.

Hogan's fat eyes widened. "Justin Road?" he asked.

The rabbi's eyes widened in turn. "Yes. The name is familiar?"

"Yeah. That near Loma Drive?"

"Yes." The rabbi was growing more hopeful.

"Yesterday a postman was mugged there."

"Oh." The rabbi's face fell.

"Yeah. He was punched real bad by some punk who needed money for a fix."

"I'm very sorry to hear that," answered the rabbi flatly. He had a feeling that a crazed drug addict who attacked a lone mailman was going to take precedence over an evil genius who had been a party to the murder of millions.

The rabbi, feigning interest, asked, "Did they catch the man?"

"Yeah. He was shooting up in a warehouse off of Sixtieth and Nineteenth."

"Thank G-d," the rabbi answered. "Perhaps, then, you'll be able to help me bring Hans Schmidt to justice."

Gruffly the sergeant answered, "I'm sorry, Rabbi Shapiro, but we simply have no grounds to arrest this man you're looking for."

The rabbi was stunned. "What?"

The sergeant continued. "Rabbi Shapiro, we get on the average ten calls a day from people who claim they sighted some criminal.

Often their testimony is based on an emotional reaction triggered by something — usually something they saw on TV."

"I do not watch television," the rabbi answered coldly. "What I saw is based on real life."

"But not on conclusive evidence." The sergeant sighed, and put out his cigarette in the already overloaded ashtray. "As for your evidence — a cleverly retouched photograph? Heck, I see stuff like that all the time. Don't prove that this man was a Nazi forty years ago. It's very easy to distort features.

"Besides," he added, leaning his giant frame against the back of the swivel chair, "tracking down ex-Nazis is not within the realm of the New York Police Department. We have no jurisdiction. This is a federal matter."

"I thought you are supposed to track down criminals!" exclaimed the rabbi indignantly.

"Criminals who committed their acts in New York City, Rabbi Shapiro."

"But this man is dangerous," the rabbi insisted. "He is responsible for the loss of countless lives, and may constitute a threat to other lives."

"Hey, Sally, get me another coffee, will you? And this time — make it strong. I want it as black as shoe polish."

"I'm talking to you, Sergeant."

Tim Hogan lit another Camel. He needed this today like a hole in the head. First his wife was complaining that he was never home for her. She, holed up in her little Bronx duplex, didn't know what it was like to be out on the street for twenty hours straight, looking for a local nut with a sawed-off shotgun. Or how it was to face some junkie who slices you up with a razor blade so badly that the only thing holding you together is forty stitches.

And now here, sitting before him, looking like he's dressed for the opera, was this holier-than-thou rabbi, still beating his breast and crying for a bunch of his kind killed how many years ago. If he only knew how tired everyone was of hearing about it.

Over his file cabinet hung a little sign: *Tact is the ability to tell someone to go take a hike and make him feel good about it.* Well, here goes, he thought.

"Rabbi Shapiro," he began, pointing to the waiting room, "do you see those people out there waiting? Each and every one of them has a similar complaint. I don't mean about some criminal. I mean against us, against the system. It's our duty to track criminals down, to bring them to justice. When an assailant gets away, it's *us* they blame — not the friends who usually helped him escape."

He held up a thick folder. "See this? Here are reports taken down just over the last two days. I got a guy who thinks he's some kind of god . . . walking around, carving up people as part of his religious practice. Here's a woman who kept her five-year-old son in a cage for two years. And here's a kid who just beat an old woman to death — not for money, but for fun. As a minor, he'll get off lightly. And this little folder is only a fraction of the cases that come in daily to NYPD. We deal with so many, Rabbi Shapiro, and it's an achievement if we can put even a twentieth of these people into jail. Think of it, Rabbi: countless numbers of our citizens are victims, and we just can't help them. There are just too many. Do you think that's fair?"

"I never thought life was fair, Sergeant Hogan," he answered.

The sergeant's voice was milder. "Look, if you present me with solid evidence that this man endangers citizens of New York City, I can help you. So far you haven't done so. So I suggest you try the federal agencies. They are involved in this kind of work. They have the experience, as well as the resources. And they have jurisdiction." Then the sergeant added, sincerely, "I really am sorry, Rabbi — and I'm sorry to be a grouch. It's just that I got too much on my back right now. It's a jungle out there — and I have other animals to fight than Nazis. Try the Justice Department. Maybe they can help you. Good luck."

Clutching the envelope tightly, the rabbi exited the cubicle, his son close behind. This place was suddenly making him feel claustrophobic. They hurried past the rows of desks.

Near the entrance, Rosie was singing another ballad. A bum, evidently a music critic, scowled at her. A wild-looking man burst in the door, raving that his welfare check was gone and that the communists had taken it to finance an underground missile base. He growled at the angry rabbi brushing swiftly past him, bolting through the entrance doors and, ignoring the rain, heading in the direction of the Pontiac. Shimshon looked back at the police station. Noticing the motley assortment of people in there, he felt strangely relieved not to have to bring Shulman to this kind of place. Somehow, he didn't belong here.

The headaches really began after Passover. No sooner was the aluminum foil torn away from the sinks and the special cutlery stored than the phone calls were made to the state and federal agencies. Rabbi Shapiro was grateful for the relative rest and relaxation the last two days of Passover had given him. He had not realized what lay in store.

He began an odyssey of checking every listing in the phone book for anything remotely of service to his cause. With one agency, he waited two weeks for an appointment. It was canceled at the last minute. Many times Rabbi Shapiro called the

Department of Immigration, the FBI, or the CIA. The calls were either unreturned, or simply cut off, leaving the phone to ring mockingly in the rabbi's ear. Calendar pages waited to be filled with appointment times. Day after day they remained blank.

Rabbi Shapiro contacted various embassy offices. The reaction from most of them was courteous but cold — even, to his surprise, from the Israeli embassy. The ambassador politely shook hands with the rabbi and explained that his government was already involved in this kind of work in its own office in Tel Aviv. Though Rabbi Shapiro's help was appreciated, it was hardly needed. In vain, the rabbi tried to explain that a Nazi was living in Boro Park, and that he, Rabbi Shapiro, could lead the authorities to him, but the ambassador quickly bustled him away with the assurance that it had already been taken care of. Certainly, he said, as if addressing a mental patient, if Avraham Shulman were who the rabbi claimed, then he would have been caught long ago by the Shin Bet.

The West German embassy gave him a similar answer. He was told that West Germany had already given plenty of assistance, including reparations, to the Jewish people. They even offered to increase the rabbi's reparations money. The rabbi, who loathed even being with these people, stormed out.

The rabbi sent letters to offices in Albany and Washington — the War Crimes Commission, the Department of Justice, INTERPOL. He would grow excited upon receiving a prompt letter, only to open the envelope and find: "*Your request has been received, and a reply is forthcoming.*" Somehow the rabbi knew not to hold his breath.

Three weeks after Passover, the rabbi was sitting dejectedly on the sofa, another form letter on the coffee table. Shimshon, having finished his homework, made his father a cup of hot chocolate.

"It's amazing," groaned the man. "Absolutely amazing. It's as if the whole world is suddenly oblivious to history. No one wants to remember. They no longer feel sympathy. But worse than that, Shimmy — they don't want to help us."

"You can't give up, Ta," answered the boy, handing him the steaming mug of hot chocolate. "Don't lose hope."

"Hope?" answered his father bitterly. "Yes . . . hope." He knew the saying: *A Jew lives on hope.* It was hope that sustained the Warsaw Ghetto. The deportations will stop. Just a few thousand people, that's all. Things will return to normal soon. Just wait and see. The lives that were spent and wasted hoping and waiting for deliverance. A Jew could also die on hope.

It was close to Lag B'Omer when Rabbi Shapiro received a call from the War Crimes Division. To his surprise and delight, he was invited to meet with its director, a Mr. Frank Porter, in Washington.

A meeting was arranged for Monday, the day after Lag B'Omer. Rabbi Shapiro thought it a good opportunity for Shimshon to come along and see the nation's capital.

Of course, Shimshon didn't have to be asked twice. Rising promptly at six a.m., he washed, dressed, and went to *shul.* After eating a quick breakfast, he ran out and waited for his father by the car.

They passed quickly through the different states — New Jersey, Delaware, and Maryland — watching the endless suburban and industrial landscapes.

They reached the capital by noon and, after lunch, took a little sightseeing drive around the famous buildings. As the rabbi pointed out and explained each one, Shimshon was awed by the nation's immense power.

"Bet they could stop the Nazis," he said.

"If they wanted to," answered his father with a sigh, remembering the nation's indifference toward Jews during the Roosevelt era.

At three o'clock they arrived at an immense, ultra-modern complex, a maze of buildings about a mile from the White House. Entering the lobby of the building where they had the appointment, they felt themselves engulfed by its vastness and power. After being cleared through security, they passed through a long corridor leading to an elevator, which deposited them on the fourteenth floor. From there they went through a labyrinth of doors and offices. At last, they came to one with a small metal sign: War Crimes Division.

The office, much to their surprise, was quite small, with a narrow table and several easy chairs in the waiting room. The rabbi took out his Talmud volume, while Shimshon entertained himself by reading one of the popular magazines on the rack.

At last a tall man opened the door. "Rabbi Shapiro?" he asked.

The rabbi looked up. The man was waiting.

"I'm Frank Porter."

Quickly, father and son rose. The rabbi shook hands with the man, who led them into his office.

Frank Porter, a rugged, square-jawed man in late middle age, pulled out the chair from behind his desk. Suddenly noticing the boy, he sensed the latter's awe of him.

"Who is this young man?" he asked.

"My son, Shimshon."

"Pleased to meet you," he said, grabbing Shimshon's hand. It was a hearty, vigorous shake, coming from a handsome, robust man of athletic build. Mostly likely this man had been on some varsity team. Shimshon looked around. Sure enough, behind Porter were old photographs of a younger, slimmer version of himself in helmet and football gear. Apparently, he had changed little since then. He still looked fit, like a Greek statue.

After the usual amenities, Frank Porter took the manila envelope from Rabbi Shapiro. Putting on a pair of horn-rimmed glasses, he pored meditatively over the folder's contents. Shimshon was surprised that such a powerful-looking man would need reading glasses. And such funny glasses, too; now he looked like a nearsighted Greek statue.

Finally, the agent cleared his throat. "Rabbi Shapiro," he said, "this accusation you are making is highly peculiar. According to you, this elderly man of whom you speak, a Mr. Abraham Shulman, is actually a former Nazi SS officer."

"That is correct," answered the rabbi.

"Rabbi Shapiro," said Frank Porter, "are you willing and able to verify your claim?"

"Yes, of course," answered the rabbi.

"In the face of conflicting evidence?"

"What?"

"As incredible as it may sound, Rabbi Shapiro, the Allied War Crimes Commission did its legwork long ago on this man."

Frank Porter removed a well-worn folder from a drawer and spilled its contents onto the desk. He held up one sheet of paper for the rabbi and his son to read.

NAME: Schmidt, Hans Johann.

DATE OF BIRTH: June 2, 1918.

Double Identity

PLACE OF BIRTH: Berlin, Germany.

FAMILY: Parents Franz and Marianne (*nee* Obermeister), married 1913, sister Lotte (1914-21).

RELIGION: Lutheran.

EDUCATION: Elementary school, Berlin, 1924-31, Weissgarten Academy, Heidelberg, 1930-36, Hitler Youth Director, 1934-36. Hoffbaden SS Training Institute, 1936-1938. Municipal swimming and archery champion, 1936.

BACKGROUND: Mother cleaning lady and housekeeper. Father World War One veteran, textile worker, caretaker, physician's assistant, director of Berlin Medical Clinic (later bomb shelter), Berlin Civilian Defense Corps. Both parents died in Berlin, 1945.

MILITARY RECORD: After graduating Hoffbaden Institute with rank of Untersturmfuhrer (Amer. equiv.: 2nd Lieutenant), Schmidt was stationed in Austria, and later Slovakia, in 1938. In 1939, now Obersturmfuhrer (1st Lieutenant), he was sent to SS Panzer division, in France. In 1940, promoted to Haupsturmfuhrer (Captain), he was slightly wounded in Belgium, and returned to Germany. He was twice decorated for extraordinary bravery in battle; in 1940, he crossed enemy fire to rescue two of his comrades. After again being promoted, to Sturmbannfuhrer (Major), in 1940, Schmidt was sent to Malberg concentration camp, where, under leadership of Oberfuhrer (Colonel) Erich Lederer, he was initially commander of the children's division. In January 1943, after liquidation of the children's camp, he was transferred to the women's division, where he remained until his disappearance in May of that year.

Described by survivors as aloof and even ethereal, Schmidt was responsible for the division of labor within Malberg concentration camp. He would greet the waiting prisoners on the platform, deliver a "welcoming" speech, and direct them to the barracks. Most of the prisoners, some as young as six years of age, were consigned to labor in a quarry, digging and transporting heavy stones. Of the 15,000 prisoners sent to Malberg, fewer than 400 survived. Malberg, a small labor camp located in southeast Germany, was essentially a transfer point for most of the prisoners on the way to Mauthausen, Dachau, or one of the other major extermination camps in the east. Therefore, most of the survivors were located in the camps already mentioned. Malberg itself was abandoned in March 1945, its remaining prisoners liquidated in a death march away from the approaching Allied army. Erich Lederer was caught near the Danish border by British troops, and tried and hanged in 1946. According to Lederer, Schmidt had fled Germany in 1943, and in 1945 was heard from in Argentina. According to the captured SS men who remembered Schmidt, he was diligent in his work, though shy and secretive. In fact, his standoffishness made him unpopular among his fellow soldiers. His reasons for prematurely leaving Malberg were unclear, as he never openly expressed dissatisfaction or disillusionment with his work; it is surmised that he had sensed impending German defeat and, given the opportunity, chose to flee Germany ahead of time.

Hans Schmidt was later seen living in Paraguay under the name Manuel Scharfmann. There he lived with a small German community, and according to the local residents owned a small magazine and tobacco store. He was described as a loner — a quiet, intense man. Again the word "standoffish" appears in several testimonies.

When word of his whereabouts reached Israeli intelligence in 1973, he fled Paraguay. He was last reported in Honduras, where he has become a recluse and an invalid, suffering from a heart ailment.

At the last paragraph, Rabbi Shapiro went white with amazement and fury.

"That's a lie!" he roared.

Frank Porter leaned back, his horn-rimmed eyes resting calmly. "I wish I could contradict this evidence, Rabbi," he answered. "But it has been verified by the appropriate sources. Here it is, an extensive biography of this man — his background, activities, and notoriety. Much of it was received from both the War Crimes Commission and organizations like the Simon Wiesenthal Center. I believe it is sufficient for our division."

"Mr. Porter," the rabbi argued, "I, too, have extensive background on this man. It is based on testimony from survivors of Malberg — myself included. I was sent there after my arrest. If you perhaps have time to look over what I have compiled —"

"Rabbi Shapiro, there is no need for that. So far, you have shown us nothing conclusive."

"But I have a photograph," the rabbi argued. He extracted the retouched photo from his folder and held it up.

Frank Porter smiled. The naivete of some people always

touched him. It never ceased to amaze him — how their imaginations ran wild.

"Rabbi Shapiro," he chided, "are you telling me that a cleverly retouched photograph is proof of this man's identity?"

"No," the rabbi countered, "but when it is combined with other evidence, it certainly can be more conclusive. At least it's worth another investigation. I don't understand your reluctance to have this man arrested and brought to trial."

"Rabbi Shapiro, this man, Mr. Shulman, came into this country legally, on an Israeli passport. To arrest him would require the cooperation of that government, as well as ours. Before we even consider going through all that, Rabbi, we would have to have you leave your folder here for further review and reference."

"How long might that take?" the rabbi demanded.

"Weeks, probably — maybe months. We're dreadfully backlogged now, Rabbi."

"But this man could disappear."

"Rabbi Shapiro. You simply must understand that we have no immediate time for this."

"But your job is to track down Nazi war criminals!"

"It's simply this, Rabbi Shapiro," Frank Porter began. Like Sergeant Hogan, he had learned very early the art of tact — though with Porter, it came more naturally. "In this wonderful land of ours, we are controlled by a tight bureaucracy. I myself have bosses — dozens of them. And they have bosses as well. It's all one pyramid, Rabbi Shapiro, ending with the man in the White House. Yes, I handle war crimes cases, but we have a priority list, and a limited budget. The Justice Department as a whole has other cases it must worry about first. In fact, to put it bluntly, we are besieged. And unfortunately, too, too often our bureaucracy is understaffed and overworked; therefore, we don't have all the time in the world for every case. If you wish, I can show you a ten-inch file, dating back to 1970, of unsolved cases."

"No, thank you," answered the rabbi glumly. He was feeling a touch of *deja vu,* brought on by his similar conversation with Sergeant Hogan.

"A pity you don't. Some of our claims involve Nazis who were spotted in this country. Some of these men are no longer Nazis. They actually work for the U.S. Government, for our national interest, and are therefore under government protection — which makes it difficult for men like me to bring them to justice. Reporting them is actually contrary to our national interest. Others, in the interim of our investigation process, have simply died of old age or, like Hans Schmidt, moved away to relative obscurity."

"He did not move away."

"In the meantime," Frank Porter continued, not bothering to respond to the rabbi, "I can show you other files, equally thick, of terrorists, extremist groups, international drug rings, Mafia bosses — all kinds of interesting cases — which currently take up the bulk of our time. Now, you are certainly aware that we have been vigorously pursuing many cases concerning alleged Nazi war criminals. The government has woken up to this problem in the last ten years or so. But the case you are presenting is simply too farfetched. If we had the time, we would pursue every single lead and every single complaint. But in the overall picture, there is a priority system — among cases concerning Nazis in particular, and among all cases concerning criminals in general. Priority is given to those situations which may affect national security. I doubt if precious time could be wasted right now on an old man being subjected to a claim as amazing as yours — that he is a Nazi masquerading as a Jew."

Rabbi Shapiro could scarcely contain his anger. After all the U.S. had not done to prevent the Holocaust, how could Porter dare talk to him in this fashion? How well the rabbi remembered his own experience in the refugee camps after the war. It was bad enough when the Russians found him at Auschwitz, emaciated and devitalized. But he was not dehumanized! He was still a man, with emotions seething within. Nevertheless, he was regarded as some kind of helpless child, an unfortunate pawn in history. At Auschwitz, he was #307864. Now, he was refugee #407896. Your family and culture were wiped out? How awful. Now on to the next catastrophe. Even the best-meaning people could not completely comprehend the silent rage inside the survivors. And now the rabbi felt helpless against an overwhelming bureaucracy.

"Mr. Porter," the rabbi began, "while I was in the Warsaw Ghetto, shoveling gravel for a crust of bread, I waited eagerly for the American liberators. After 1941, that was the subject on everyone's lips . . . 'when the Americans come, we'll be free.' And later in Dachau, and then in Auschwitz. I assumed back then that as soon as the outside world knew what was going on in Europe the killings would stop. The Americans would come and save us.

"But I was wrong. They didn't come. Nobody. No planes, no tanks, nothing — not even diplomats. In the meantime, people were being gassed at the rate of ten thousand a day. We sent secret messages to the outside, pleading with the world to come to our aid and to avenge the millions murdered. Somehow, the victimization of Jews was considered a side thing, an unfortunate footnote to World War II.

"Well, Mr. Porter, you're wrong. It was not. It was, unbelievably, Hitler's obsession from the start — the very reason for the war. Do you know that even during Germany's military decline the deportations didn't stop? That in fact they speeded up? And do you know that the Allies, when they were clearly winning the war, did nothing to bomb the railways or camps? Their attitude was silence. And after forty years, it still hasn't changed. No one cared then, and no one cares now. Somehow, again we've been pushed to the back page of history. There's no longer any room for us in your file cabinet or data entry base. Our grievance has been minimized and priority given to other groups — dope peddlers, the lunatic fringe, gangsters.

"But what if I told you, Mr. Porter, that a Nazi was all that plus more? To you, this man, Avraham Shulman, is at most some kind of kook — if you believe at all that he exists. Or worse, you may think that *I* am some kind of kook. But if you would take the time to read my files, you might believe otherwise. Because, Mr. Porter, this man is just as dangerous as any terrorist. He is the source of all impurity — the one behind all these terrorists, gangsters, thieves, and whatever else comes out of the woodwork to turn up, in triplicate, on your desk. You know the Nazis have their hands in all sorts of illegitimate activities. I can also assure you, sir, that his stay in New York has a purpose — a deadly one — one against the entire Jewish race, one against mankind. He is not a sick old man in Honduras, as your 'evidence' attests. He is here, very much alive and well, with others of his kind — and plotting something against people like me.

"So I'll end with this, Mr. Porter. Your people misjudged the situation once before. By negating the atrocities forty years ago, by calling them fabrications and hysteria, you allowed six million people to be destroyed. How do you think Hitler was able to get away with all that he did? It wasn't just his gang of murderers. It was people like you, who sat back and did nothing. And he knew that the world would be indifferent. Now, by discounting men like me, by accusing us of overreacting, you're allowing history to repeat itself. And unless you've lived through that part of history, you won't understand why people like me react as we do."

Frank Porter let the papers in his hand fall silently to his desk. "Is that all, Rabbi Shapiro?"

The rabbi rose majestically. His son followed suit.

"Yes," he answered. "That's all . . . for now."

"Then you shall hear from me once we have this evidence corroborated," said the man. "I assure you that we shall give this our fullest attention."

"Yes, I'm sure. I'll be waiting," answered the rabbi. "Come, Shimshon."

"Ta, you were great!" the boy exclaimed when they had exited the office. "You really gave it to Mr. Porter."

"There is still a lot of work left to be done, Shimmy," countered his father. "Without Frank Porter."

The rabbi stared straight ahead, his teary eyes still stinging from the encounter. He did not know why Porter upset him so. As he had told Tim Hogan, he had learned not to expect anything from life. Moreover, he had learned, after years in this work, to expect this very kind of reaction. He just had not expected to find it in a man whose very task it was to fight Nazism. Indifference, mixed with contempt and impatience. The rabbi should have been desensitized by now. After all these years, was he still naive enough to expect help from the government? Why was he trying

to work through legal channels? If, after all his experiences, he still
had a ghetto mentality, then he certainly was deserving of ridicule.

The rabbi and his son returned in silence to the car and headed
toward the Baltimore Post Road. Somewhere in New Jersey, they
would stop for *minchah*. The seven o'clock sun was a gentle
yellow-orange, like a giant citrus fruit floating serenely in the sky
and watching the blue Pontiac disappear. The rabbi bid an ironic
farewell to the nation's capital, now ending its busy workday and
eager to forget, until tomorrow, the world's problems. It simply
had more important things to do than tend to someone like Hans
Schmidt.

There was nowhere else to turn. No other recourse, really. The
rabbi had spent the last three weeks butting his head against
bureaucratic walls. And now this — a five-hour drive for a half-
hour of rebuff. In the meantime, Schmidt could possibly have one
foot out the door — leaving the country, while laughing over his
shoulder at him, Rabbi Shapiro. Schmidt most likely had enough
experience, direct or indirect, with federal agencies and whatever
else to know their ineffectuality — as well as their complacency.
He was most likely laughing right now at all his enemies.

His enemies. The rabbi's eyes glistened with renewed hatred
when he thought of all those who stood in his way. There were
those, men just like Schmidt, ready to help the Nazi actively —
instead of passively, like the government agencies. There was a
power in back of Schmidt — an awesome power that had to be
reckoned with. Rabbi Shapiro knew that Schmidt was not alone.

However, there was a power far greater than any Nazi, or any
Washington bureaucrat, that would never let evil triumph. The
rabbi knew that he was not completely alone. It wasn't just the
help of his son, or his fellow survivors. He knew that he had

Heavenly power on his side — a power that could deal with a hundred Hans Schmidts, and a thousand more of his friends.

But it was up to Rabbi Shapiro to harness this power, to lay the plans, to stop the machinations of this cunning man. The whole thing lay on his shoulders — his and Avraham Shulman's. It was he and Avraham Shulman — the two of them in their own battle.

Yehuda Shapiro tried to calculate what he had to do, and how much time he had left.

Chapter 9

The Deal

Ten a.m. The phone rang.

Avraham Shulman counted eight rings before he raised the receiver snappily and stiffly held it to his ear, as if in salute.

The voice, in German, was cool and authoritative. "We found it."

Avraham Shulman nodded to himself. "Give me the address."

"It's 225 West Thirty-seventh Street."

Shulman nodded again. "Midtown."

"*Ja.* Between Seventh and Eighth Avenues. There's a kosher restaurant on the ground floor — the only one in that area. That's fortunate for you, Herr Schmidt."

Shulman winced. "Why?"

"The owner of the restaurant is a religious Jew, Aaron Zimmerman. He's the one you'll have to contend with. Speak to him, Schmidt. You should have no problem at all talking to such a man."

Ludwig Dietrich's tone, sly and insinuating, trailed off into demonic laughter. He seemed to enjoy these jibes at Shulman; strangely enough, Shulman, though bothered by them, was flattered at the same time. If he had become that convincing in his role, then he liked to think that he had accomplished his goal.

Shulman asked, "What should I tell this Zimmerman?"

"Simply that you wish to buy the building. Make a substantial offer. But first, explain to him what it's for. This man is no fool; he'll want to know the reason for buying it. He himself deals in real estate."

"How do I explain it?" asked Hans.

"Simple. Tell him you wish to turn the building into a co-op."

Again Shulman nodded. He understood. The city had become a breeding ground for young up-and-coming professionals. Thousands of them were swarming to the great city in search of success and good times. In turn, the city had become a minting facility for those with enough foresight and savvy to know a trend when they saw one. Buildings were being acquired with the speed of light and being converted equally quickly into living quarters for these hip, high-living young adults. These buildings, in turn, became lucrative investments for those who catered to these adults' ceaseless needs.

One thirty p.m. The mid-May sun bounced off the surrounding steel and glass, momentarily blinding Avraham Shulman as he exited Penn Station onto Thirty-third Street. Somehow the brightness seemed more intense in Manhattan than anywhere else, he thought. But it was a different kind of light — an irritating glare that was created by a hodgepodge of neon signs, flourescent office lighting, and traffic lamps; it was worlds away from the silently shimmering radiance of the inside of a synagogue. He paused and scrutinized the narrow blocks of buildings. A derelict approached him, asking for change. Shulman quickly removed a few coins from his pocket and placed them in the man's palm.

At last, his blue eyes focused on the street signs. Heading

northwest, Shulman kept his eyes on the building numbers, till at last they rested on the sign by a ground-floor entrance: *Empire Glatt Kosher Delicatessen.* The building was, as Shulman expected, one of the older structures along the street: twelve stories, painted rust-brown, with protruding fire escapes, flanked by modern high-rises. Somehow the block reminded Shulman of the working-class tenements of his youth in Berlin. Indeed, it was a quaint, if not stubborn, reminder of a less hostile era. The restaurant, occupying the right half of the ground floor, was obscured by wide tinted glass. He entered.

The inside was noisy, filled with the lunch time crowd. Plates of cold cuts and sandwiches passed by, and a whiff of steaming chicken soup drifted into Shulman's nostrils, making him hungry even though he had already eaten. No one stopped to stare at the tall, black-garbed man standing silently by the cash register. Men dressed like that were commonplace here.

The head waiter casually looked Shulman's way. "One, sir?" he asked.

"I would like to speak with Mr. Aaron Zimmerman."

The waiter was startled. "I'm afraid he's busy right now. Perhaps if you come back later—"

"Please tell him it is urgent. I cannot wait."

The waiter eyed this man keenly, feeling some hostility for having to argue. However, there was something in the man's presence — either his unwavering form, or his majestically shining eyes — that compelled the waiter to brush past the busboys toward the cash register.

He returned, accompanied by a stocky, rotund man with black heavy-set eyes, a rounded black beard, and a stomach to match. The well-fed Aaron Zimmerman looked like he enjoyed his work in more ways than one. With a mixture of detachment and condescension he surveyed this angelic-looking man, and introduced himself. Then he asked what the latter wanted.

Quickly introducing himself, Shulman said, "What I have to say to you I must say in private . . . away from here. May we go into your office?"

The man's eyes widened. He was somewhat amazed and slightly bemused by this chassid's impetuousness. He led Shulman through the maze of tables toward the exit. In the corridor left of the exit was a small staircase, which led up to a black door. Shulman silently followed the man inside.

The office was cluttered with receipts, bills, and other papers that indicated that Aaron Zimmerman sold more than pastrami. Seating his plump torso behind the desk, Zimmerman quickly explained that he was a part-time realtor for the building's owner, Emmanuel Perlow, who was now retired and living in Miami. In return, Zimmerman was able to run his restaurant with a seventy-five percent rent reduction. In addition, he managed the building, as well as Perlow's other holdings.

"I've been here over thirty years," Zimmerman explained. As he spoke he stared out the window, which faced an alleyway. "Since I left Brownsville. That was when Manny bought this building. One of his first, actually. For that reason, I think, he has held onto it — sentimental attachment. Since then, property values have skyrocketed. I watched the other places on the block either change ownership or be demolished one by one. Somehow, we held on. Somehow, we survived. Survival . . ." He brooded. "One thing I've learned in life, the hard way, is that nothing stays. Nothing is permanent. You have to learn to roll with the punches."

"Yes," Shulman said quietly.

"Thanks to Manny, I was spared the headache of paying rent. He let me open my restaurant. In return, he receives a part of the profit. One hand washes the other, you might say. He and I go back a long way. We came from the same town in Hungary. We helped each other then; we help each other now."

His sleeve, slightly rolled, revealed part of a blue tattoo. Shulman stiffened, but said nothing.

"Anyway, I am his principal agent. I do all the dealings for him. I keep in touch, let him know what's happening."

"How long has Mr. Perlow lived in Miami?"

"Four years. But he makes enough trips to New York during the year to make him a resident."

"Then it shouldn't be a problem at all to contact him for me."

Zimmerman leaned back and said expansively, "Of course. But may I ask what the reason is?"

"Certainly," answered Shulman placidly. "It concerns real estate."

Zimmerman smiled, amused at this man's ways. "What shall I say to him?"

"Please tell him," answered Shulman slowly, "that I wish to purchase this building."

Zimmerman sucked in his breath and clutched the armrest. His eyes first seemed ready to pounce out of their sockets, then narrowed. "Did I hear you right, Mr. Shulman?"

"Shall I repeat myself?"

"You said . . . you wish to purchase this building?"

"That is correct."

Zimmerman's pudgy hands fell to his sides. He felt as deflated as a punctured tire. "Mr. Shulman," he asked, "are you serious?"

"Deadly."

The agent gulped and leaned forward. "I'm afraid this building is not for sale, Mr. Shulman."

"Please tell Mr. Perlow that I am able to make a generous offer."

"I don't think you heard me, Mr. Shulman. I said, this building is not for sale. Moreover, I doubt that Mr. Perlow is even remotely interested in selling. The building is completely his; mortgage, taxes — everything is paid up. It is too much of an investment for him to sell. Or for me." He took to this threat on his nearly rent-free restaurant like an animal defending its territory. "If you'd like, there are other properties for consideration."

"Mr. Zimmerman, the other properties are of no concern to me."

Zimmerman studied this man. Shulman sat upright in the metal chair, never taking his eyes off Zimmerman. The agent was nearly tempted to throw this man out the door. Yet something in the latter's voice, which was soothing, yet commanding, prevented him. Zimmerman felt intrigued enough to press for information. "Why specifically this building?" he asked.

"I find its location most suitable, as well as profitable, for young people," Shulman explained evenly. "Young, affluent people. People willing to pay for the privilege of living here in New York. People who want all the conveniences, and who are willing to do anything — willing to pay the price — to have them within easy reach." He smiled.

Zimmerman frowned. Something in this little speech disturbed him — perhaps its formality, which seemed cold and strangely un-Jewish. It even seemed morbid. There was something in this man's corpse-like blue eyes that chilled him, reminding him of something; he couldn't quite place it. Zimmerman decided that although the man looked like he had spent his entire life in a *shtetl* this was a facade, just like the fake iron doors that tried to shelter the ghetto Jews from the outside world. The man had obviously been somewhere else.

"I could suggest some other buildings with similarly advantageous locations," Zimmerman said uneasily.

"Tell Mr. Perlow," continued Shulman, "that I am offering seven million dollars. And to you — an eighty percent rent reduction. Plus one hundred thousand dollars. Cash. As a brokerage fee."

Zimmerman gasped. His wide eyes, which had narrowed in suspicion, suddenly gleamed.

"Mr. Shulman, I . . . I—"

"Two hundred."

With trembling hands, Zimmerman seized a pencil. Not taking his eyes off the steady gaze of Shulman, he scribbled some figures on the desk.

Seven million. The building was not worth more than five-and-a-half million. This was unreal. A million-five-hundred-thousand-dollar profit for Manny. And two hundred for him. He still had Sima and Sharna to marry off. And for years Yehudis had been nagging him about moving to Monsey.

Shulman sat, quietly waiting. Give him a few more minutes to think it over, he thought. Let him feel as if he's in control.

Putting down the pencil at last, Zimmerman drew in his breath meditatively. "I think," he finally answered, "that Mr. Perlow can be reasonable."

"You have four hours to call him," Shulman said. He rose to his full height, gazing coldly at Zimmerman, as if this agent were either a menial servant or of a subhuman species. Certain people needed to know their place.

"I shall call Manny at once," stammered Zimmerman.

Immediately he dialed, then hung up. He explained apologetically to Shulman that the line was busy. Shulman appeared patient. Putting on his coat, he told Zimmerman that he would be back.

Shulman decided to amuse himself with a brisk walk around the block. To survey the territory, he explained. Get to know the property better. Zimmerman promised to reach Perlow in the interim.

Several hours had elapsed by the time Shulman returned. Zimmerman, perspiring heavily, mumbled that Perlow had finally been reached. He mumbled to Shulman about a bad connection.

"A hurricane or something. Anyway, it looks like it's set."

"And the price is acceptable?"

"He's flying in tomorrow to discuss it with you."

"Splendid. I shall be most cooperative. With him . . . and with you." Shulman quietly shook hands with Zimmerman and turned to leave, his blond earlocks bouncing against his sallow cheeks. Stopping at the door, he turned, facing Zimmerman, his metallic eyes narrowing on the agent, as if closing in on a target.

"Oh, and Mr. Zimmerman," he whispered, "I *always* keep my promises."

Shulman returned home, grateful at last to be away from Manhattan. He intensely disliked the city — particularly the midtown area, with its noise and mass of humanity. In Boro Park, he felt less vulnerable to the elements. Here, he could sit and await orders. Here, too, he could think.

Nine o'clock. The phone rang. Right on time.

"Perlow is meeting me tomorrow, at two o'clock."

"Splendid." Dietrich's voice was as melifluous as bourbon drained from a flask. "I trust you had to bargain with this Zimmerman, Schmidt."

"I offered him two hundred thousand dollars instead of one," answered Schmidt, "and he responded affirmatively. Other than that, he said nothing about the price of the building itself. Seven million is fine."

"No doubt Perlow will haggle. It's in their blood. Give him whatever he wants. What we have invested there is worth several times whatever we have to pay."

At precisely two o'clock the next day, Shulman appeared at Empire Glatt Kosher Delicatessen, a slender white envelope tucked under his coat. A knowing nod from the waiter sent him upstairs.

Emmanuel Perlow was a short man with gray balding hair and eyes that squinted cantankerously at the world from behind a pair of spectacles. He shook hands with Shulman and spoke rapidly in Yiddish — complaining, mostly, of the hurricane, which had aggravated his ulcer, and about this sudden trip which Zimmerman said he had to take. He had managed to get a flight, although his doctor had told him to stay off his feet due to his bad back.

Perlow forgot his health problems very quickly when he saw a check for seven million dollars waving in front of him. As Dietrich had predicted, Perlow snapped that he wanted another million; to his surprise, Shulman calmly drew out a small checkbook, and with exquisite European penmanship wrote out another draft. Zimmerman stood, waiting and watching impassively.

In a tiny, almost child-like scrawl, Perlow signed away 225 West Thirty-seventh Street. The transaction was carried out solemnly, as if it were a religious rite, and the building was transferred to the full power of its new master.

Emmanuel Perlow stayed long enough to chat briefly with the new owner, before returning to the airport to catch a five o'clock plane. The New York air, he complained, was bad for his lungs. While waiting for the taxi, he promised to contact his lawyers about the rest of the details.

After he had left, Shulman, flushed with victory, pocketed the deed in his long gabardine and sat down in Zimmerman's chair. He was amazed, knowing that he had truly done what no other mortal had managed to achieve: the purchase of a Manhattan building in less than twenty-four hours. It amazed him even more to know that the building was now completely his, to put to whatever use he desired.

Extracting from his gabardine the envelope, he promptly handed it to Zimmerman. The agent grabbed it and practically tore it apart. He examined its contents: four hundred five-hundred-dollar bills.

"Thank you, Rav Shulman," he answered in a daze. "I am truly overwhelmed. It was a pleasure doing business with you."

"I knew that this venture would be profitable for us both," answered the other. He added softly, "Providing, of course, that one is cooperative."

He informed the agent curtly that he would retain the latter's services.

"How may I help you now?" asked Zimmerman.

"I want a public parking lot constructed underneath the building," answered Shulman, as nonchalantly as if he were asking a tailor to sew an extra button in his coat.

Zimmerman recoiled, the benevolent smile fading from his face into a frown of bewilderment. By now he had believed himself to be unfazed by this man's idiosyncrasies; but he should have known, he chided himself, not to be too sure. This man, Shulman, was so unpredictable. There was no telling what he would do next — or what he was capable of doing.

"I'm afraid that isn't feasible," answered Zimmerman shakily.

"Why not?"

"Well, a parking lot would be a violation of the Manhattan building code. A potential fire hazard. The building is quite old. It is not easy to demolish the foundation. Besides, I'm not sure that the offices which rent from us would be supportive."

"And why not? Don't the people who work here have automobiles? Right now their employees probably spend precious time looking for a parking lot with space."

"No," answered Zimmerman. He felt angry for having to argue. "Many of them do not. They will not want the rent increase."

Shulman had been ready for this. Slowly, as if explaining a fine point in the Talmud, he proceeded. "I can't see how the tenants would oppose such a project. If they realize how much it will benefit them, they will support me one hundred percent. Firstly, it conforms to my plans to eventually turn this building into a co-op. The owners of the businesses located in the building will have first rights to acquire apartments. I'm sure they'll be happy with that. They will want to be able to park their cars in their building. Meanwhile, they will have parking for themselves and their employees. As for the building code, I have already had that thoroughly researched. There is no violation for anything that is considered an improvement."

"The zoning laws are stringent, Mr. Shulman. A public parking lot — anything for profit might not be considered an improvement."

"Which is why I am allowing the tenants free parking — with no rent increase. Mr. Zimmerman" — Shulman's voice softened — "I *always* keep my promises. I have already spoken to the district managers to obtain a variance in order to build."

Zimmerman's eyes widened. Apparently this man had done his leg work. Zimmerman wondered who it was on the local board who had spoken to Shulman. Rita Kraus? Shawn Ferguson? Zimmerman knew them all. He himself had lined many a pocket to obtain variances for Perlow and himself. But never so quickly. But then, this man, Shulman, seemed like one for ruthless efficiency.

Shulman concluded, "All the safety laws will be observed, Mr. Zimmerman."

"But will it interfere with the tenants' movement?" asked Zimmerman weakly. He felt himself yielding to one armed with too much legal and verbal ammunition. "The noise of the construction will disturb them."

"It will be done as quietly as possible," Shulman answered. He cooed gently, as if soothing a worried wife. "You must have faith, Mr. Zimmerman, that Hashem will help us to succeed in our work. Faith, Mr. Zimmerman . . . that is what the world needs. I will allow nothing to interrupt my work. Any offices which disapprove of my plans may drop their lease and leave. I shall offer them paid moving expenses and will pay, for six months, any rent increase they receive in their new locations."

Zimmerman sat back in his chair, defeated. This new boss of his had it figured out at all angles, as in a chess game. Every loophole was known, every strategy was calculated, every obstacle was overcome and combined into a skillful masterwork of calculation. Shulman was more than a fighter; he was a hunter — one who knew the movements of his adversaries and turned them to his advantage, to close in on the kill.

After Shulman left, Zimmerman sighed and leaned back against his swivel chair. He was not a fighter, like Shulman; just a follower. He dialed the building superintendent.

When the local district board members examined the building, prodding and poking the ceilings and beams, they discovered the faulty construction in some of the walls, indicating that they had not been solidly built. Following them around the structure, Shulman trembled inwardly, knowing how correct these men were. If they only knew what lay concealed behind these walls, Shulman would receive a different kind of warrant.

The board members, having finished examining the building, informed Shulman that acquiring the variance would take time. They pointed out the faulty beams, as well as some other violations.

Shulman assured them that the beams would be quickly fixed, and the other problems resolved as well. With this promise, he was given a temporary permit to commence building.

The plan would work according to schedule. Shulman could now hire a crew to start digging. Once the workers reached the foundation, they would suddenly be ordered to stop, for lack of funds to continue. When more money was obtained they could continue — much later. Without the money to continue, Shulman could stall for time — enough time to enable him to bring in his own men and uncover the gold mine that lay waiting amid the shambles.

Afterwards, Shulman thought wistfully, he could return home. Home, he sighed. From the subway that carried him over the Manhattan Bridge he gazed with contempt at the Manhattan skyline behind him. Home was a universe away from this greed and connivance. He closed his eyes wearily, thinking of the land that awaited him, the land where he was accepted for being himself. A land where there was no one to condemn him. There, he did not have to hide.

Though he had grown to like Boro Park, to him it remained a temporary home. Lately — perhaps because, at sixty-six, he was finally feeling his age — he had pondered, more than ever, half a lifetime of constant lies and concealment. It was a strenuous and never-ending game, played a hundred times in a hundred different places. Evidently, however, some power or merit — he did not know whose — was behind him. He had managed never to be caught.

But, he mused, he was fooling himself. Though healthy, vigorous, and youthful looking, he knew it was only a question of time before he would have to give an account and reckoning of his actions. If not to a human court, then to a celestial one. Everyone ends up the same way . . . an expression he himself had used regarding so many others.

Shulman thought of his extraordinary life, and of what he had accomplished. He had certainly done much. But he did not know how much more he had to do. He had the feeling, more so than ever, that his past would catch up with him. Indeed, it was catching up now.

He thought of Yehuda Shapiro, whose synagogue, out of

hundreds in Boro Park, Shulman had had the misfortune to pick. If only Shapiro knew how much Shulman admired him. Here was a man who, years after the Holocaust had taken place and those involved were fading, was able, as if by radar, to pinpoint Shulman's kind from afar. Obviously, some power was behind Shapiro as well, watching over him. And it had brought the two of them together.

Amazing, Shulman thought. The ability of a survivor to remember. Like a sixth sense. Even after so many years, it remained an obsession, no, a Divine mission, for these men never to let the world forget. And besides his own experience and fervor, Yehuda Shapiro had his natural talents to aid him in his work, just as Shulman's abilities aided him in his. Shapiro was just as much a superman as Shulman. Probably, too, like Shulman, Shapiro had never intended to be a fighter. He would have been happy to sit back quietly in Boro Park, studying, and running a *shul* and a business. However, like it or not, destiny was thrust upon him. He had gone through an ordeal in history. For Yehuda Shapiro, the war was not over . . . yet. It couldn't be. And it was up to him to take command. Men like him were ready to take on a whole battalion of Nazis.

Well, Shulman mused to himself, you've finally met your match. Perhaps Yehuda Shapiro came into your life for a reason. It just might be time to let the world know about Avraham Shulman. After priding yourself on never being caught, you may have to face up to it that this time you just might not get away.

Actually, there *was* another time that Shulman was nearly caught. It had happened three years ago, in Buenos Aires, where he was sharing the *mikvah* with a number of other men one Friday afternoon. His fault, actually; in retrospect, Shulman realized that he had not been careful. He had stupidly dropped his guard — and since then, had made very sure that it would not happen again.

While immersing himself, he had raised his arms to allow the water to purify his body. Enjoying the water's soothing warmth, and directing his attention on the coming Sabbath, he had, for the moment, completely forgotten about the SS symbol tattooed under his arm. Though it had been surgically removed long ago, its snake-like twin-lightning shape remained imprinted in his flesh like a birthmark — the mark of Cain, a symbol of terrible significance to those who had suffered. A few of them were there in the *mikvah* with him.

He was spotted by one of the bathers, who quickly alerted the others, pointing him out. When Shulman became aware that he had an audience, he froze in terror. The scene was almost comical: Avraham Shulman, standing there naked and dripping wet, surrounded by a bunch of equally naked and dripping wet men, all watching him, like a pack of animals defensively circling a predator. He hurriedly grabbed his towel and ran out the door.

Shulman was lucky to have slipped away. But that event marked a mournful turning point for him. Somehow, he sensed that it would be less and less easy for him in the future. It was a question of time before he was discovered. And he did not know how much time he had left.

While studying the old blueprints of the building, Shulman was amazed at Schwimmer's wisdom. This man had probably never realized how much he had aided the Nazis. Schwimmer had been known, in Weimar days, for taking something drab and transforming it into something desirable. He had a gift for detecting properties of little worth, buildings which no one wanted, and recognizing their potential. Outwardly, the building at 225 West Thirty-seventh Street was cheerfully old-fashioned — just the kind that would appeal to nostalgia buffs. But inside, its structure was not only old, it was crumbling. Little wonder a variance was needed. But the building would be a cinch to take apart.

The choice of building was certainly fortunate for Shulman. It would be easy to accomplish his work. The gold would be removed in no time, and with its current value running high, there would be no shortage of buyers.

As for him . . . Shulman knew he would have to move quickly. And shrewdly. There were too many men around depending on him . . . and who believed in him. He could not let them down. In the end, they would triumph. Despite Yehuda Shapiro.

Chapter 10

Attack and Counterattack

The crowd of journalists was frantic with activity. Cameras whirred; microphones were thrust forward as tapes reeled. One newscaster, standing by an open van, spoke intently before a camera.

"This is Mark Burns, WNOD news, in Boro Park, Brooklyn."

The small crowd that had gathered near the Shapiro home — little boys with thick earlocks, men in black coats, bewigged or kerchiefed women — stared curiously at the vast media apparatus that now stood, like a spaceship with its adjunct materiel, on the Shapiro front lawn. In return, the crew looked around curiously at this strange world where an ex-Nazi had supposedly landed. Some of the cameramen eagerly filmed a pair of chassidim who happened to walk by.

Yehuda Shapiro stood in the driveway, bewildered by the crowd of reporters now surrounding him and avidly taking notes, like students attending a college lecture. The rabbi, acutely aware that he had been thrust onto center stage, spoke nervously into a microphone.

"Louder!" barked the cameraman.

Shimshon, standing beside his father, was staring, fascinated, at himself in a TV monitor, and fighting the urge to make funny faces. A microphone was thrust under his nose and he was asked, "What do you think of your father's work?"

The boy squirmed. "It's pretty neat, I guess."

He giggled and looked away, waving to his friend Zev, who stood behind the camera crew. In the distance a group of Shimshon's classmates had gathered.

A reporter asked, "Rabbi Shapiro, how were you able to recognize Hans Schmidt?"

The rabbi answered, "His physical presence . . . his eyes, especially. That is what remains embedded in my memory of an SS man. The eyes. Cold, steely. That no one can ever forget. Of course, his voice . . . and his accent as well. It did not sound at all Jewish."

"But that doesn't sound like very convincing evidence," said another reporter.

"I know that, sir," answered the rabbi, a trace of contempt in his voice. "That is why I asked this man where he was from. He reacted in such a strange way that my suspicions were confirmed. I know he is a Nazi!"

"How did he react to your inquiries?" asked another.

"Vague. Defensive. Especially when I asked where he had been during the war."

"And that alone made you believe that this man was an SS officer?" pressed another. "Besides a physical resemblance?"

"Well, no . . ."

The rabbi's voice trailed off. He sensed he would have a difficult time explaining to these people that the ability to recognize a Nazi transcended steely eyes. Standing here, among the crowd of gaping reporters, he began to feel queasy with discomfort, and he wished that he had never heeded Menachem

Glazer's suggestion in the first place. The latter's desire to contact the press was not so much farfetched as it was dangerous. Right now the skepticism engraved on these people's faces was awesome.

An immaculately groomed woman asked him, "Rabbi Shapiro, you've talked about a photograph which you allege proves Shulman is actually a Nazi. Do you feel that a photograph is conclusive evidence of physical resemblance — especially as it was retouched?"

"I feel it serves its purpose," the rabbi answered, choosing his words carefully. "But a photograph by itself cannot convey the words of a thousand witnesses."

"Rabbi, why would a certain desire to guard one's privacy appear strange?"

"Rabbi, why in your opinion would a Nazi choose to dress up as an Orthodox Jew?"

"Rabbi, do you know much about this man's present activities?"

"Rabbi, in your opinion, has the War Crimes Division of the Justice Department been effective in tracing these criminals?"

The rabbi recoiled, besieged by a flood of questions he could not answer — not because he did not know how, but because they would require explanations too lengthy to encapsulate in a one-minute interview slot. Some reporters went back to their vans. One of them slurped down a cup of coffee brought by one of the crew, spilling some of the contents onto the grass. A gofer pushed his way through the crowd with a steaming box of kosher pizza.

Yehuda Shapiro longed to be far away from this spectacle — perhaps in more dignified territories like his *shul* or office — but he knew that at this point there was no turning back.

Two days earlier, again due to Menachem Glazer's advice, he had met with the editor of the *New York Star*. He had been against it, but reluctantly acquiesced, under group pressure. Besides, the editor's father was supposedly a friend of Itzhak Rifkin. Submitting the retouched photo of Shulman, as well as documents on his Nazi past, the rabbi pleaded and argued with the editor, hoping to awaken in him the proverbial journalist's compassion. Alas, Rabbi Shapiro, who had very little to do with newspapers — or at least sensationalist ones like the *New York Star* — was sadly out of touch with the times. These days, cynicism, not social conscience, was the name of the game, and a Nazi posing as a Jew had become something of a laughing matter.

The editor, himself a Jew, listened quietly, all the while chewing his pen thoughtfully — a habit he had picked up since he quit smoking — and studying the photographs that the rabbi had given him. He wondered if Shapiro was a bit touched by all that had happened to him. Maybe all survivors were this way. No one in his immediate family had been in Europe during the war, so that period had never been discussed at home. He did have a distant relative who had died in Bergen-Belsen, but that was the extent of his contact.

Nevertheless, the editor did feel enough of a Jew, as well as a journalist, to want to help the rabbi. He was glad that there were those who still cried out for justice. Besides, a catchy story like this would certainly increase newsstand sales, and maybe even get the paper out of the red. He assigned a newsman who had previously covered sports to write up an article for the next day's edition.

And indeed, it did appear the next day. "Orthodox Jew Is Ex-Nazi," the headline screamed — generating, sure enough, an all-time record for sales. Some people bought the paper out of outrage, some out of curiosity, others out of mild surprise that there were still any Nazis left. Still others bought it in surprise that, even were there any Nazis left, there were still people around who cared to make an issue of them. Others bought it simply for fun; given the paper's propensity toward sensationalism, they were eager to read the latest oddity.

The article, set in large type, was long, running into a second page, adjacent to a photo spread on people who had communicated with the dead. Along with pictures of Hans Schmidt, circa 1940, and the present-day Avraham Shulman, there were survivors' testimonials of Malberg, where Schmidt was *Sturmbannfuhrer.* "Man of iron will," ran a sub-headline; "Enigmatic and cunning," ran another. Also mentioned were names of men from Boro Park, friends of Rabbi Shapiro.

An Orthodox Jew has been accused of being a former SS officer who ran a Nazi concentration camp 40 years ago.

Abraham Shulman, 66, described by many as a quiet, scholarly man, has been living on the outskirts of Boro Park, Brooklyn, for the past three months. A resident of Jerusalem for nearly thirty years, he claims to be in the United States to raise money both for his yeshiva (a place of Jewish learning) and for his daughter Chava Rivkah, diagnosed as having leukemia. A new, experimental chemotherapy treatment is currently being arranged for her at Hadassah Medical Center in Jerusalem.

Shulman was recognized by Rabbi Yehuda Shapiro, 55, who runs a small synagogue, Tifereth Yaakov, in Boro Park. It was there that Shulman appeared one Friday night, when the Jewish Sabbath begins, and was immediately identified by the rabbi. Rabbi Shapiro, who had been in Malberg concentration camp, distinctly remembered its commander, Hans Schmidt, who ran the children's division. Struck by the similarity of the physical features and mannerisms between the two, Shapiro alerted a group of Holocaust survivors, who, like him, are involved in the hunt and investigation of ex-Nazis.

"To bring Hans Schmidt to justice," the rabbi says, "would be one of the world's biggest achievements. It would be a cry of victory for the fallen victims of the Jewish people, as well as the living, who have suffered and can never, ever forget."

Mr. Shulman has not yet been either arrested or questioned for comment. It has been reported, however, by an acquaintance of his in Boro Park, another religious Jew, that Shulman considers this accusation "a gross and outrageous lie," as well as an insult.

The article went on to describe the Boro Park area, "home of a predominantly chassidic community — ultra-Orthodox Jews adhering to the strictest commandments of the Torah." There was a picture of Thirteenth Avenue on a Friday afternoon, filled with "busy shoppers, many originally from Eastern Europe, preparing for the Sabbath." Rabbi Shapiro, glancing at the photo caption, marveled cynically at the quaint portrayal of his people's tribal rites.

At last he angrily threw the paper down. Beside him sat Zelig and Shimshon, watching sympathetically.

"What did CBS say?" asked Zelig.

"They're coming tomorrow," the rabbi answered.

"Well, that's splendid," the sexton said.

"Or idiotic," the rabbi snapped.

Zelig sighed. Over the years — ten, to be exact — he had worked alongside the rabbi, forever amazed at the latter's reserves of strength and commitment. But he sensed that his friend was now coming to the end of his rope, a rope very long, and very much frayed from frustration and despair — a rope ready to break apart in the face of public cynicism. It was sad, if not sickening, to know that there was more than one enemy to deal with.

"This article is revolting," the rabbi continued.

Zelig was puzzled. "Why, what's wrong with it?" he asked.

"Its point of view," the rabbi explained, distressed. "Its layout — everything. No dignity, no depth — I don't feel this was our best choice of newspaper. Even if the editor *is* a friend of Yitzy's."

"I thought the editor was most helpful, Yehuda."

"I spoke with him, Zelig. I saw the look on his face. The same as the reporters. They think our accusation is strange. They think *we're* strange. Their attitude—"

"Yehuda, *please.* I think it will succeed in arousing public interest. Or at least intimidate Schmidt. Time will tell."

"Time is our enemy, Zelig. There is no telling how much longer Schmidt will remain here. And now . . . with all this publicity . . ." The rabbi sighed in disgust. Sitting down, he rested his forehead meditatively against his hand. "We just might be getting publicity we don't really need. Unfortunately, I went to the *Star,* because my arm was twisted. But I guess I'm to blame also. What could I do, actually? I didn't know where else to go. After what happened in Washington . . ."

The rabbi was gloomy. "I'm afraid this paper may not be helping us in the end. If anything, it might make us look like a bunch of pathetic, hysterical men. Will anyone believe us, Zelig?"

"They will, they will," clucked the little man enthusiastically. "You must have faith, Yehuda. This is a popular newspaper. People will read the article. There will be other articles in other newspapers. We've got the whole media interested in this case. We can't stop now. They'll finish the job for us — they'll make Schmidt look like the criminal he is."

The rabbi shook his head in disagreement. "They'll make us look ridiculous."

"But it is focusing attention on Schmidt," Zelig argued. "The man's days are numbered!"

"He'll leave the country before he's ever caught. All our plans will go to waste. Knowing Schmidt, he'll do another one of his disappearing acts — all the while clearing his name. He's done it before." The rabbi's eyes were now moist.

"He won't get away with it this time," Shimshon piped up.

Rabbi Shapiro turned to his son. For some reason, he smiled. It wasn't just the boy's reaction — so spontaneous, so sincere — that touched him. It was the boy's earnestness to share in his father's work; the rabbi knew that Shimshon believed him at last.

Rabbi Shapiro remembered his own first encounter with Schmidt. Standing there in filthy rags among tired, emaciated children, young Yehuda felt defiant. Like Shimshon, he was fascinated by this man. Schmidt exuded a certain presence, a luster, like a shiny new coin. But by then Yehuda had been around enough evil men to recognize their veneer of falsehood. Thus he stood there, in line for roll call, burning with hatred and the desire to avenge the deaths of so many children. Such memories sustained his search for justice; in turn, his search for justice sustained the memories.

Unfortunately, however, he had to contend with people who had no memories to go by, and who, like Shimshon, were easily taken in by outward appearances. Schmidt, in his long black cloak and long white beard, looked so pious, so "Jewish" — how could anyone suspect him? His disguise, like bulletproof armor, shielded him well from public attack. Moreover, the rabbi knew that Schmidt had another ally on his side besides mass ignorance: mass apathy, a far more insidious ally.

Shimshon, though quite young, was nevertheless the son of a Holocaust survivor. In him were implanted the memories and nightmares of his parents. He needed no newspaper article to feel rage. He had experienced it directly, from his father, every night since the nightmares began. But beyond Shimshon's generation it was useless. In another twenty-five years, or less, the Holocaust would be a different world, the memories hazy and unclear, like an old black-and-white picture of one's greatgrandmother.

Yehuda Shapiro sighed. Perhaps Zelig was right. The press, no matter how silly or patronizing it could be, was at least needed right now to keep Schmidt in the spotlight and the unaware public stimulated for a few days.

Thanks to the newspaper article, Rabbi Yehuda Shapiro became the current media darling, a "spokesman on the Holocaust." The following days were filled with countless TV interviews. On one news show, after a dog food commercial, the rabbi, his eyes squinting under the hard glare of the studio lights, spoke with an anchorman about his camp experiences. The segment was followed by comments from "prominent Jews," as well as other survivors.

At another station, the rabbi sat, somewhat uncomfortably, with other rabbis, some with dubious ordination, commenting on the atrocities. He was later asked to appear on a talk show, but he flatly refused when he heard he was to be preceded by dancing chimpanzees.

Shavuos arrived, and the rabbi lay down after the evening meal to rest for a few minutes before heading to *shul* to study Torah all night, in accordance with the custom on the holiday. He was terribly relieved not to have to face any cameras for the next couple of days. He hoped that he hadn't looked too ridiculous on TV.

However, he couldn't help wondering: Had he accomplished anything, or had he publicly made a fool of himself? Somewhere out there, were there any people who were in some way affected? Anyone willing to listen to him before switching channels?

Immediately after Shavuos the rabbi met with a reporter from the prestigious *New York World.*

Simultaneously, in a small hotel room overlooking the Hudson, four concerned men met to discuss the latest events.

Ludwig Dietrich, lighting what was to be the first of many cigarettes, spoke. "It appears that our plans have been somewhat thwarted. We can't keep digging the site with all the suspicion that's focused on Schmidt. It will attract too much attention to the building, and that's the last thing we want."

Kurt whistled under his breath. He wondered if it weren't too late to catch that midnight plane to Rio.

"But the demolition is already underway," argued Fritz. "What a time for this to happen!"

Dietrich ignored Fritz. "The most pressing matter for us to discuss is, of course, what Schmidt will now do. You don't expect Schmidt to remain in the States, do you?"

"Yes," came a voice from the entrance.

All heads turned. The spectral figure of the newcomer was framed in the doorway.

"Hans, when did you get here?" asked Dietrich, frowning with mistrust.

"What difference does it make?" the man retorted casually, standing at the door with his arms crossed. "Long enough to hear your comments. But it seems that I missed nothing of substance, Herr Dietrich. Therefore" — he sauntered into the room — "if you will permit me to make a suggestion . . ."

"Such as?"

"That we continue digging."

The other three men looked at one another incredulously. But Ludwig Dietrich kept his hard eyes on Schmidt; they conveyed a mixture of dismay, fascination, and, most of all, hatred.

"He's utterly mad," said Fritz, to no one in particular.

"And what do you think that will accomplish, Hans?" asked Dietrich.

"Elimination of suspicion," answered Schmidt abruptly.

"Kindly explain."

"When people see me going about my routine, they will wonder how I could possibly be a Nazi. It will leave doubts as to the sanity of Yehuda Shapiro."

Dietrich, silenced by the cold logic, pondered his next words. "I would be concerned about your physical safety in Boro Park as long as Shapiro is there to persecute you."

"I say, why don't we just finish him off?" growled Fritz. "That Jew is a grave danger to all of us."

"No!" cried Hans.

The others stared.

Hans quickly explained. "Killing him — or his son — would only prove him correct in the public eye. It will make the public more suspicious. That in turn will undermine our actions more than any harmful publicity would ever do. Wouldn't you agree that were we to undermine his credibility it would divert the public's attention from us to him? Already he is being questioned. Already people are tired of hearing about the Holocaust. And a Jew being accused of being a Nazi — they're having difficulty taking that seriously. By my challenging him openly, insisting on my innocence, I will make his accusations appear to be the ravings of a lunatic — a man completely traumatized by his experiences."

"But isn't he already believed, Hans?" argued Dietrich. "Our sources say that he is a respected rabbi and businessman, and a well-liked member of the Boro Park community. He has many friends. He is considered quite sane. Moreover, it is his word against a stranger's."

"A stranger who is learned and observant," countered Schmidt. And he quickly muttered, "If I may flatter myself so."

Dietrich slowly exhaled a cloud of smoke and grinned, revealing his set of teeth, perfect except for their yellowish tint, the bane of smokers. This was an indication that he was not quite ready to yield. "That mind of yours, Schmidt. So quick with an answer. Sometimes, however, I think you believe too much in yourself."

Taking a deep breath, Schmidt answered, "I have confidence in my abilities, Herr Dietrich. And I will achieve what I must, with G-d's help."

Dietrich smiled. "Your language is amusing, Hans. You really have taken over your role *so* convincingly." He darkened. "Or has your role taken over you?"

Schmidt replied, "I have spent many years working on myself. I can never let down my guard. I must talk as if I were an Orthodox Jew. Otherwise, I might make a mistake at a crucial time."

"But Schmidt," said Dietrich, his eyes burning behind the smoky air, turning black, "You don't feel that you might be *too* convincing? And I refer not only to your demeanor."

"Then to what, Herr Dietrich?"

"I refer to your believing too much in your own strength. It is easy to become blinded to one's own pitfalls. Perhaps it might be best for you to disappear for awhile. Return later, after the publicity dies down. At the moment there's no telling what this Shapiro might try to do."

"I *must* take the risk, Herr Dietrich," Hans pleaded. "I *must* challenge Yehuda Shapiro openly. I must face my opponents."

Schmidt was still standing defiantly erect, facing the opponents who were now staring at him skeptically. For a moment, he felt as if he were standing again in front of Aaron Zimmerman — or better yet, in front of children. Then, just as now, he was determined to win in argument.

"Shapiro wouldn't dare harm me physically once he feels he lacks public support. It would only make *me* appear as the wronged one."

Fritz snorted and looked away. "We'll all suffer because of this man," he said.

"Which one? Are you referring to Shapiro, or to Shulman?" asked Dietrich, eliciting smiles from the rest.

Schmidt bristled, but forced himself to be still.

"Hans," Dietrich continued, "you do realize, don't you, how embarrassing this whole matter has become to us. We must admit that you've become, for the moment, quite a lucrative subject for the media. Already your apartment is being watched, and people are being questioned. It is unsafe for you to remain in Boro Park. And," he added glumly, "no doubt you were followed on your way here."

For a moment Schmidt felt himself being knifed by hostile glances. He answered stiffly, "I made quite certain that I would not be followed. I swear to you that no one saw me come here."

"Not even Shapiro?" asked Kurt.

"No one," Schmidt repeated.

"Or to Empire?" asked Fritz anxiously.

Schmidt glared at the man, feeling as if he had just eaten an enormous, wormy apple. "I assure you, Herr Loehmann, that I have been most careful. Besides, the safest way to deal with the press would be to confront them. Go head to head with them.

Answer their questions. Call it all a joke."

"Yes, it *is* amusing, isn't it? Terribly droll," Kurt said wryly, turning his back and going over to the window.

"Yes. In fact, it *is*," Shulman asserted, to the man's back. "Think of it, Kurt — can you imagine someone looking at me and believing the Jew Shapiro? I will dismiss the accusations forcefully. More than that — I will aggressively challenge Shapiro, accusing him of defamation of character. They have such flimsy evidence — a retouched photograph?" Hans chuckled pleasantly. "Under the circumstances . . . why, it is very, very easy to be a Nazi nowadays."

"Or a Jew, it appears." countered Ludwig.

Schmidt slumped, as if punched in the stomach. Until now he had tolerated Dietrich's mordant humor, but this time the man had gone too far — by hinting at something particularly vicious regarding Avraham Shulman and his illusoriness. Schmidt knew that Dietrich was fascinated by him . . . both as a Jew and as a Nazi. And Dietrich detected in Schmidt's ability to pose as a sworn enemy of the Nazis a certain weakness for the Jewish people. For this reason, try as he might, Schmidt was inevitably ill at ease with the former general. Ever the realist, Dietrich was not fooled by appearances. He had seen enough hypocrisy in Berlin; he had been part of it. Therefore, he was not particularly kind and forgiving to those by whom he felt betrayed, and Hans trembled inwardly at the stories of how those people ended up. Because of this, Hans was not trying to win the argument for the thrill, but because his life might be at stake. It was crucial that Dietrich clearly know whose side he was on.

"Trust me, Herr Dietrich," replied Hans softly. "You must trust me. I have impressed far greater men than you have ever imagined. You don't have to question my loyalty to my people."

"All right, Schmidt, you win."

"What are you saying, Ludwig?" cried Fritz in disbelief.

"Simple. Hans — oh, forgive me . . . *Avraham.* I must get used to his new name. He will carry on as if nothing has happened."

"But how will they possibly let him?" asked Fritz, turning to Dietrich and waving his hands excitedly. "Do you realize how many people he'll have to fight if he starts on such a project? It will quickly get publicity, and that's the last thing we want now. Besides, even that agent of his, Zimmerman, is a Jew. Do you think he will allow himself to work for a Nazi?"

"I will deal with Zimmerman appropriately," countered Hans. "He will leave us alone."

"You don't feel he'll interrupt the digging?" asked Kurt.

"Nonsense. Trust me," said Schmidt soothingly. "I will be able to continue my work. Nothing will interfere."

He smiled weakly in an effort to put the men at ease. But Fritz was unimpressed. "He's fooling himself. He'll destroy us all."

Schmidt waited for a quick nod from Dietrich, to signify final agreement.

Dietrich raised his hands. "Gentlemen," he said, "I am embarrassed now to think of our outburst. Why, we have behaved quite shamefully — very much like little boys; afraid of Jews. Certainly we are more powerful than they. It is best to follow Schmidt's advice and continue our digging. Schmidt, you win. The project is yours. If you feel you can either ignore or eliminate the obstacles, then by all means continue. But remember this" — his voice lowered ominously — "the responsibility rests solely on you."

Schmidt allowed himself one last jibe. "It always has. I've never been one to run away from it."

Dietrich smiled slightly. Touche.

"If you fail," he added, "you can expect our just reaction."

"And if I succeed?"

"The gold is ours. And you'll have a share in it."

"Excellent." Schmidt smiled broadly. He felt as if he had overcome the most powerful obstacle — convincing these men that they were not in danger.

Dietrich rose. The other men followed.

"Well," Dietrich said, "I'm for a late lunch. Anyone else?"

The other men nodded in agreement.

"Anyone for the Lorelei again? A pity you can't join us, Hans." The others snickered. "Well, *bis spaeter.*"

Schmidt bowed. "And so, I shall await further orders, no?" He turned to leave.

"Schmidt—"

Schmidt turned around. "Yes?"

Dietrich, flanked on both sides by his men, glowered at him. "Remember who you are. And who your enemies are. *Bitte.* Your life right now hangs in the balance."

"Which is why this mission is most crucial to me," Schmidt replied. "I have put much into it. Its outcome is my own outcome."

Between thin lips Dietrich smiled. "Always so quick with an answer. Whatever role you've played out now, I know only one thing: you're not the young Hans Schmidt who sat there shy and stammering in my office in Berlin. It's hard to remember you that way. Seeing how you've changed. But," he added, sighing, "we've all had to, I suppose. *Auf Wiedersehen.*"

After saluting, Shulman made his exit. He pressed the elevator button for the fifth floor and walked down the rest of the way, then carefully took a detour through the emergency exit. He walked through the alleyway until he had made his way several buildings down. Continuing to avoid the street, he finally emerged five blocks away from the building where they had met. There he hailed a taxi. Then another. Then another. The drivers usually responded with an interesting vocabulary when asked to make sharp, sudden turns. Finally, he was deposited at a subway station. From there he took three different trains and three different flights of stairs before finally taking the B.

By the time he emerged into the open air outside Penn Station, Shulman was panting and clutching his chest.

"Hey, mister, you all right?" asked a pedestrian.

"Yes . . . it's nothing," he gasped. "I'm just exhausted, that's all."

It occurred to Shulman that he had been lucky not to be recognized, given the recent TV exposure. Then again, who would bother to notice him? Old Jewish men tended to look alike.

On the subway he had seen a tattered copy of the day's paper, discarded and left on a seat. There was no photo of him. However, there was a small editorial entitled: "The Nazis Among Us." In it, his name was mentioned.

The Schmidt-Shulman case reveals a frightful, hidden fact: there are countless Nazis who eluded the Allied War Crimes Commission and nestled, like parasitic insects, within the mainstream of modern society. It also reveals the openness of our society, which has allowed these people to once again become full-fledged members — ironically, right within the company of the very people whom the Nazis sought to destroy. The fact that a Nazi is able to hide, disguised and undetected, within the heart of this nation, is appalling. Still, many Jewish people, traditionally concerned with justice, have, after years of Holocaust awareness and indictment of its perpetrators, themselves chosen to forget.

Articles like this sent his heart palpitating. He remembered the time in the *mikvah* in Buenos Aires, and the SS mark imbedded in his arm, along with the German accent he had tried desperately to eradicate, but used on occasion to his advantage. He wondered if perhaps by remaining here he truly was placing himself in great danger.

When Shulman finally arrived at 225 West Thirty-seventh Street, he quickly made his way to his makeshift office, a former storeroom directly above the restaurant. He was grateful to find his papers still intact, not destroyed or vengefully left in disarray by Zimmerman. Yesterday, the agent had stormed into his office, snarling at him and calling him a "Nazi beast." Shulman had managed to hold him at bay by curtly informing him that the stories were a lie, and that he planned to take Yehuda Shapiro to a Jewish court of law, a *beis din*. Lastly, he threatened to have Empire shut down in order to expand the parking lot. Zimmerman slunk out, growling all the while that henceforth he would no longer be in Shulman's service. He would not allow himself to be accused of complicity.

Shulman opened the drawers of a rickety desk and rummaged through its contents. The blueprints were carefully rolled and hidden inside a false bottom. He sighed with relief. Everything was still there. Zimmerman hadn't touched anything, even out of curiosity.

Sitting down, Shulman pondered his next plan of attack. It was agreed: he was to continue his work as if nothing were happening. Just pretend nothing was wrong. Pretend again he was in Germany, growing up in Nazified Berlin, where atrocity was blithely covered up under a cloak of the most routine, mundane events. Even in the town of Malberg, located outside the camp, every citizen got on with his life, blocking out the sounds and smells, and had a prepared excuse in order to justify himself with the curious — most notably American soldiers. This building demolition was basically a reenactment of the same mentality. Only this time, instead of the Final Solution, it was a real estate development. The noise, the demolition, were all routine. The tenants couldn't possibly know what was going on.

However, Shulman wondered how long he could hide from the world. As Dietrich had said, right now his life hung in the balance. The world was on Yehuda Shapiro's side because of the public's fascination with evil — particularly the Nazis, who were evil incarnate. It was difficult to estimate just how much exposure Shulman had already received. But, though not a journalist, he knew one thing: overexposure eventually brings apathy. The public might at least become desensitized to his particular problem.

In the meantime, how was he to keep the horde of journalists and others at bay? Dietrich, of course, would be able to block some of the stories at their source. He always knew whom to pay off. But once a story got the ear of journalists . . . well, Shulman knew one thing about journalists: they could not be threatened. Threatening them only intensified their desire to track down their story. Shulman also knew that the only way to fight a disease was to increase the resistance to it. If he was on center stage, then there was no way left but to remain there and play out his role for all it was worth.

And play it he did — with the skill to rival any Broadway actor. He knew to be passive at first. He remained in Boro Park, albeit at a distance from Yehuda Shapiro. He was surprised at how he could still remain inconspicuous among all the bearded, elderly men on Thirteenth Avenue. When occasionally recognized and confronted by a pedestrian or journalist, he would freeze, expand his chest like a penguin, and reply with the greatest indignation, "The story is complete nonsense — slander. Only a fool wouldn't see how amateurishly the photographs have been retouched."

Invariably a crowd would gather, and Shulman, straightening his posture even more, would speak defiantly, freely answering questions about his background as well as his current life as a *kollel* fund-raiser. He explained that yes, he was German by birth, but had left Europe long before the war, long before Hitler, to study Torah in the Holy Land. He had no other connection with Germany; he had not set foot on German soil in nearly fifty years. He had been reluctant to discuss his past only because of his understandable distaste for his former land.

To one roving reporter who stopped by his apartment, Shulman showed pictures of his family and explained, apologetically, how dire circumstance forced him to live in such a squalid place. But how could he possibly allow himself the luxury of a better domicile, knowing that so many *kollel* families depended on money from abroad?

Soon Shulman, timing his instincts, became aggressive. He lamented to the press, and any sympathetic listener, how he had been vilified. In a very short time, just as he had calculated, public opinion turned. He was not only exonerated, but was lionized as well. Avraham Shulman became a star — not only a man wrongly accused, but possibly a saint — one whose contribution to the world was cruelly being undermined by misguided, paranoid Nazi-hunters. By month's end the transformation was complete: Avraham Shulman was a full-fledged hero.

Articles soon cropped up about Avraham Shulman the pious

Jew, studying Talmud in Jerusalem and acting as *kollel* caretaker and fund-raiser. Testimonials from Shulman's wife, who was also from Germany and was a Holocaust survivor herself, appeared, as well as letters from various deans of yeshivos. After awhile, even the Jewish newspapers gave way. One paper began printing Shulman's Torah novellae, to demonstrate his pure and penetrating mind. Alongside photos of Chava Rivkah Shulman, smiling stoically from a hospital bed, an intravenous unit attached to her arm, were photos of her brothers and sisters, themselves either yeshiva students or married to yeshiva students. Long letters were submitted from impoverished Jerusalem couples, praising the Shulmans and describing in fervent detail the family's untiring work and self-sacrifice. Ethical pronouncements were soon made, under stern titles such as "The Sin of *Lashon Hara*" and "Honoring Our Torah Scholars." Letters came from people who mentioned how the Shulmans had helped them on the rocky road back to Judaism. Even the Israeli government issued a vociferous two-page proclamation in support of Avraham Shulman.

An editorial appeared in the Sunday *New York World.* It was entitled "Have They Gone Too Far?" It contained a searing critique of the Nazi-hunters:

> It appears that a gang of old men, pitifully beating their chests and howling empty war cries at imaginary villains, has finally been forced to admit defeat. The Schmidt/Shulman case has been a gross embarrassment as well as a moral failure for those who are obsessed with revenge, whatever the cost. Perhaps it is time for men like Rabbi Yehuda Shapiro, though noble their intent may be, to reevaluate their methods of investigation and grounds for accusation.

Polls were conducted with citizens who had followed the Schmidt/Shulman case. Over sixty percent interviewed reported that they were "tired of hearing about the Holocaust." A whopping eighty percent felt that Shulman was completely innocent, and that the real Hans Schmidt was still on the loose. Another article soon appeared, in a prominent magazine, entitled "Time to Lay It to Rest":

> Over the years, the issue of the Holocaust has degenerated into rampant sensationalism. The tone has become one of ghoulish fascination with anything connected to Nazis. Those still haunted enough by it can capitalize on the public's hunger to believe any testimony, no matter how groundless. Isn't it time, perhaps, to bury once and for all these grotesque memories, the rampant wailing, and the subsequent ruthless exploitation of that era?

Rabbi Shapiro followed the articles that appeared, first with amazement, then with contempt, at last with growing despair. Whether he was too angry to be depressed or too depressed to be angry mattered little. He knew only one thing: Shulman, a.k.a. Schmidt, had triumphed. This ugly man had not only cleared his name, but was now a hero in the eyes of many. And he had also succeeded in making Rabbi Yehuda Shapiro look like the biggest fool in New York City.

When the rabbi came across an article in a psychology magazine on certain "post-traumatic pathologies" evinced by Holocaust survivors, he vehemently threw the magazine across the living room. Shimshon and Zelig, sitting in the room, looked on in shock.

Since only his son and Zelig were there, he felt he could allow himself the liberty of venting his rage and feeling of impotence. Shutting his eyes and taking deep breaths, the rabbi fought desperately to keep control. "I am helpless," he muttered. Noticing his son, who was watching him sympathetically, he said aloud, "Shimshon, I feel there's nothing we can do."

"Ta," his son answered weakly, "Hashem will help us."

The rabbi sighed. "Shimshon, Hashem will help us, but we first have to find a way to help ourselves. We're not supposed to sit around and wait for a miracle to occur. But I just don't know what Hashem wants me to do. Meanwhile, everyone thinks I'm *meshuge.*"

"Yehuda," Zelig said, "perhaps you're reacting a bit prematurely. Why, these articles are completely ridiculous—"

"Ridiculous?!" the rabbi interrupted, shouting. "Are you aware of the looks and the comments I've been getting on the street, at work, in *shul?* They're all laughing at me, Zelig. They think *I'm* ridiculous. That I'm fighting phantoms, that I'm obsessed, neurotic, even psychotic. Schmidt has them believing completely in him; even some of our own men are doubting us now."

Zelig looked away in meditative silence. "The man is amazing. I've never seen anyone like him. Of course, I did not have direct contact like you." Zelig had been at Bergen-Belsen. "Obviously some diabolical power is backing him."

"The man is manipulative," the rabbi said. "Of that I am certain. He always knows what to say, how to act. He holds sway over emotions — he did so even in the camps. The man was an actor, a consummate actor. If I may give enemies of the Jews certain credit, he must be commended for his skill at manipulating an entire nation."

With a sigh, the rabbi glanced again at the periodicals sprawled over the carpet. His eyes rested on the print, but refused to read its venomous letters. They remained black shapes and figures, without real meaning or impact. Nothing in writing could ever convey an experience that consumed all of one's physical and emotional being. He clenched his fists, feeling the silent rage and helplessness of a man who knew that he was virtually alone against the world. And remembering the blase professionalism of the camera crews, the silly superficiality of the anchormen, the leering curiosity of the audience, the intellectual hostility of the critics, he began to wonder just exactly who his real enemies were.

Suddenly, the articles ceased. Within a week, no mention of Hans Schmidt/Avraham Shulman was to be found. One by one, the headlines about "Nazi turned Jew" were gone, to be replaced with the latest local subway murder. It seemed the story, which had saturated the media so thoroughly, had now dried up and run its course.

Desperately Yehuda Shapiro scanned the magazines, both religious and secular, for any news on the case. Nothing. Shulman had completely vanished from the pages of print, just as he had vanished forty years ago from Europe — and as casually as a neighbor who had lived quietly down the street for many years and then simply packed his bags. The problem was, Shulman had not moved away. He was still in Boro Park, a mile away from Shapiro. During this whole time of accusation and pursuit, he had remained quietly on Justin Road, going about his business. Yehuda Shapiro knew that by Shulman's defying the press, by his continuing to pose as a Jew, he was simply waiting till the public grew tired of its fascination with Nazis. Ever the chameleon, Schmidt was wearing the disguise of a pious old man, whom it would be downright embarrassing to harass. Just sit back, and let human nature do the rest.

Rabbi Shapiro spoke to people who owned television sets, inquiring if Shulman, or other Nazis, had in any way made the news. The people shook their heads. In an age of instant celebrity, and instant celebrity turnover, Avraham Shulman, a.k.a. Hans Schmidt, had become old news.

The survivors' meeting was smaller than usual. This time, they gathered in the den of a one-bedroom apartment rather than in a spacious living room. Those who were there debated and quarreled as vehemently as before. However, noticing the number of absent persons, Rabbi Shapiro was dismayed. Avraham Shulman had succeeded, with far bleaker repercussions than the rabbi had imagined.

Again he brought Shimshon to the meeting. The boy sat silently, weary after some strenuous ballplaying that afternoon. Where last time he had been fascinated by these men, for some reason now he felt irritated, just wishing the whole thing would be over and they could decide already what to do. Though he hated to tell his father, he, too, was getting tired of hearing about the Holocaust. Even the books he had read were starting to lose their effect, and for the first time since his mother died the boy was longing intensely for a normal life.

Menachem Glazer and Baruch were at it again, leveling their rage not only at the press, but at the world at large.

"Murderers, all of them!" Baruch growled. "No one believed us then; no one believes us now. Didn't I tell you we were wasting our time? Why doesn't anyone listen to me? What was I doing — talking to myself? Didn't I say we should just find Shulman and finish him off?"

"Baruch," Glazer countered, "didn't you read the papers? Even the Israelis are behind Shulman. We can't touch him."

"Yes," mumbled Yehuda Shapiro to himself. He looked at the floor in disturbed thought. He added gloomily, "Strange, isn't it? I used to think we could rely on Israel to help us."

"He has them all fooled — that's why!" Baruch Minkowitz boomed. "Just like everyone else. They were all swept off their feet because he knew a little Gemara. That's all."

"He seems to have impressed a number of our people as well," Shapiro answered soberly, sweeping his hand across the half-empty room.

The men sank into morbid silence. Just seeing that Shulman had thinned out the ranks made it painfully clear what kind of person they were dealing with.

The rabbi broke the silence. "Well, gentlemen, it looks as if we're back to square one. It's up to us to deal with this ourselves. We can expect no help. We are alone — more than we realize. We are now devoid of support, of strategy, of funds. Only G-d is with us. Thanks to Schmidt, everyone else has either written us off or laughed us off."

The men continued their gloomy silence. At last Itzhak Rifkin, seated near the door, stirred. "I can understand," he said, "how Shulman might have deluded the press. But I wonder how he was able to *silence* them — and so effectively, too."

"Obviously, he has people behind him," the rabbi answered. "Men of power — who know how to use it."

"Against men who fear Schmidt and his kind," Baruch snorted. "Plenty of them, too — cowards, all of them. Afraid to make waves then — afraid now."

"They're afraid for their *lives,* Baruch," the rabbi countered. He added thoughtfully, "I can't blame them, really. It's not easy to get involved these days. I'm afraid heroes are at a premium."

"Heroes and martyrs," Glazer said gloomily. "But there's no shortage of villains."

"But *is* Shulman the real villain?"

The men turned. Shimshon, up till now, had remained respectfully quiet, drifting into his own fantasy world of cops and robbers, good guys and bad guys. Not till his father's mention of a power behind Schmidt did the boy shake himself alert, and it occurred to him: he had seen, more than anyone else, enough of the bad guys to know that Schmidt was not acting alone.

"Ta," he suggested timidly, "remember those four men I mentioned? That time I went to Schmidt's apartment?"

His father stared intently.

The boy went on. "Maybe . . . they're the ones who are backing Schmidt. And maybe they were the ones who talked to the press — you know, like, kept them quiet or something."

His father hurried to Shimshon and stood before him. "Shimmy, do you still remember what they looked like? You would still know them if you saw them?"

"Sort of . . ." Shimshon said, hating to admit that some of the memories, unlike his father's, were fading.

"Schmidt's accomplices," Glazer murmured.

The rabbi said, "Our task now, it seems, would be to track them down."

"Perhaps the men in league with Schmidt return often to his apartment," Glazer suggested. "If the boy were to go back there and watch—"

"No!" the rabbi roared. "I didn't want him there the first time. I cannot willingly expose Shimshon to that kind of danger."

Glazer backed off. "Sorry. You're right. Besides, that time Shimmy was there might have just been a fluke. If these men are wise, they won't go back to Justin Road."

"But they have to meet somewhere," said Rifkin.

Shimshon ventured, "If you could find them . . . I think I could point them out to you."

"Finding four men in all of New York," the rabbi snorted,

turning away in disgust and facing the window. Outside, the Flatbush community was morosely still. "How can we possibly know where to find them?"

"We do," volunteered a man from the back.

The men turned. Moshe Kaplan had been sitting quietly. However, unlike Shimshon, he had not been daydreaming about cops and robbers. The little photographer had learned much about his craft back in the days when he had made fake documents for Warsaw Ghetto couriers. His eyes had developed an acute sense and perception of detail. A photographer knew how to perceive things that others didn't see.

"I reviewed some of the photographs Yitzy's nephew made. He had mentioned Schmidt wandering around Thirty-seventh and Seventh. A few photographs especially caught my attention."

He removed from his coat a photograph and held it up for the others to see: Shulman buying flowers at a stand off Seventh Avenue. Moshe pointed to the background. Faintly in the distance was a sign: *Empire Glatt Kosher Delicatessen.*

"This restaurant appears in a number of the pictures, from different angles. If you look closely, it seems that in most of them Schmidt is looking at it. I wonder if Mr. Rifkin was aware of this when he took the pictures. I have the feeling he was, though it may have been just a coincidence. Though I *am* surprised, after seeing the picture, that Rifkin wouldn't stop to have a look inside the place himself."

Itzhak Rifkin shrugged. He considered the remark a blow to his nephew's professionalism. "Maybe he did, Mosh. And he found nothing there. What's the big deal about that restaurant? There are many buildings which appear in more than one picture."

"Wait. I didn't finish telling you—"

Rabbi Shapiro interrupted anxiously. "I eat there quite often."

"Lately?"

The rabbi frowned. "No. The last time, I think, was before Pesach. I never saw Shulman there, though." He added, with a slight laugh, "And I somehow doubt you'll find his friends there."

"Not his friends," answered Moshe. "But there might be plenty of reason for Shulman to be there. Perhaps he started coming there *after* Pesach. After we had these pictures taken. Maybe the pictures just show him surveying it."

"Do you think Schmidt eats there now?" asked the rabbi. "And what if?"

"I'm not talking about eating, Yehuda."

The rabbi's eyes narrowed. "You mean there are other reasons for being at Empire?"

"Possibly."

"What *does* he do there?"

"That would be easy to find out," Glazer interjected. "Simply ask the owner."

Moshe smiled sickeningly, like a mortician offering condolences. "No, he doesn't eat there, Yehuda. He never goes inside the restaurant. And he only started going to the building recently — which is why neither we nor Rifkin could possibly have known about it sooner. I spoke to Aharon Zimmerman. He used to be a client of mine — I did his kids' weddings. I asked the kinds of questions you're asking now. And he told me a few things about Shulman."

Moshe lowered his voice. "Gentlemen, Shulman *is* the owner."

To a man, the others had shocked looks on their faces. All lapsed into silence. It was a silence based on the grim realization that Shulman had, in a sense, moved away from Boro Park. He was waiting for them at 225 West Thirty-seventh Street, in Manhattan.

Chapter 11

The Antagonist

Mid-June. The synagogue Tifereth Yaakov was crowded, like many are at this time of year, due to an *aufruf*, the celebration of a groom's upcoming wedding. Even in the women's section, which was normally half-empty, seats were difficult to find. The groom, Binyamin, stood nervously during the Torah-reading alongside his father, Menachem Glazer. It was a touching scene: father and eldest son fulfilling a vow the elder Glazer had defiantly made — in Warsaw days — to perpetuate his lineage.

Shimshon, as well as a number of his classmates who had come this Shabbos for the occasion, were standing eagerly, bags of candy ready to throw at "Bennie," their former camp counselor, in accordance with the custom. When Bennie's *aliyah* to the Torah concluded, the youngsters had their fun; of course, no one minded, even Rabbi Shapiro himself, who got pelted with a lollipop or two. Casually, he brushed them away. Binyamin tried to remain straight-faced, especially when Dov, his youngest brother, took careful aim at the former's hat and — whack! — bounced it off his shoulders, sending it rolling across the aisle. Finally, after several "mazel tovs," the young man shook hands with the rabbi and sat down.

As the rabbi stood with the Torah-reader, Arthur Braverman,

examining a possible defect in the scroll, Shimshon retreated to the back, knowing that it wasn't every week he had the chance to be with so many of his friends at once on Shabbos. Usually, they prayed with their fathers elsewhere. But Binyamin, as well as his father, was well liked, and his upcoming marriage to a girl from Chicago had brought a welcome change of mood to Tifereth Yaakov. The wedding was on Tuesday in the girl's hometown, so many New Yorkers would miss it — part of the reason for such a large turnout for the *aufruf.*

While waiting for Rabbi Shapiro to determine the status of the Torah scroll, Shimshon's friend Jonathan broke the tedium by grabbing a large handful of candies that were strewn on the ground, creeping up on Zev, and stuffing them down the latter's shirt. Zev promptly turned around, bent down, scooped up a handful himself, and took careful aim at Jonathan. He missed, and the candies landed on some of the other boys. A free-for-all ensued; Shimshon giggled, while his father turned away, frowning. The boys slunk further in the back, away from the men, and entertained themselves with a hunt for the candies that were dropping intermittently from Zev's shirt.

Shimshon stood near the entrance. Though initially enjoying the fun, he underwent a sudden and disturbing change of mood. Dazed and apprehensive, he kept watch near the door, wondering if it was the heat of the late spring sun flowing through the windows that made him feel strangely vulnerable. He did not know why, but he had a premonition that someone was due for an appearance. He sensed it. And he wondered if his father did as well.

He sadly understood that Binyamin's wedding was a welcome change for another reason — a reason that was not openly acknowledged. For quite awhile, even before Shavous, many people had avoided coming to his father's *shul*. Outwardly, there were plenty of "legitimate" excuses — a closer synagogue, an affair somewhere else — but the boy, no less than his father, knew. The same friends who were now goofing off and showering him with leftover candy had been looking at him sympathetically just two days ago, wondering how the boy could have a father who was now considered . . . well, in a word, cracked. Twice Shimshon had come home from school that week with his clothing torn and bloodied, after getting into a fight with some of the tougher boys. Sobbing, he had told his father about the insulting remarks levied at himself and Rabbi Shapiro. Swallowing hard and fighting back his own tears, the man helped clean the blood off his son.

Today, on Shabbos, the synagogue was airy with the relaxation of tension. It was finally agreed that the Torah scroll needed fixing. It was put away, and Binyamin prepared to chant the *Haftarah*, the reading from Prophets which occurs after the Torah is read. However, just then the light that had been coming through the open door and bouncing off Shimshon's blond hair was momentarily blocked by the entrance of something. Then the synagogue darkened.

Shimshon turned, wondering why the sunlight had suddenly disappeared. Then, slowly, he backed away.

The form, immobile, towered in the entrance. That Shulman arrived so late during the service seemed more surprising than the fact that he had dared show his face at all. He stood calmly, his thin hands resting on his beard, his luminescent eyes gazing ahead.

At last he took a seat near the door. Taking a Book of Psalms as well as a Chumash, he turned to a page of the latter and began moving his lips rapidly. The absence of a prayer book made Shimshon wonder if Shulman had gone elsewhere to pray first and intentionally come here afterward — though for whatever purpose the boy could only guess. Somehow, he doubted that this man was a friend of the groom.

Hurrying to the group of boys, Shimshon poked Zev, who was still shaking candies out of his shirt.

"What is it, Shimmy?" he asked.

Shimshon pointed, and his friend followed the direction of the hand. When Zev's eyes rested on Shulman, he froze.

"That's him," Shimshon whispered.

Zev studied the old man, his face registering wonderment and fascination. Twice that week he had also come home from school bruised and bloodied, in defense of his friend; now, he wished to see just exactly what it was he was defending. While Shimshon was busy tapping his other friends, pointing to the old man and saying, "That's Schmidt . . . the Nazi," Zev's face changed from disgust to skepticism. Initially the boy had been tempted to hit Shulman with a candy or two — the next best thing to stoning an enemy of the Jews — but something about the man made him hesitate. Though not as bright as Shimshon, Zev felt he instinctively knew the difference between good and evil. For some reason, he was having difficulty imagining this tall, bearded man as an enemy of the Jews.

The men were still facing forward, absorbed in the lilting melody of the *Haftarah* passages that were being read. Not until the reader had finished and the synagogue was deathly quiet did the boyish voice echo through the sanctuary. "You Nazi!"

All heads turned. Some women peered through the curtain. Rabbi Shapiro frowned.

Slowly, Shimshon advanced toward the old man, much to everyone's surprise — much to his own, as well. A finger pointing accusingly, Shimshon continued to shout: "Get out of here, you — you pig, you murderer! A *shul* is no place for you."

"Shimshon!" cried a voice from behind the curtain. It was Mrs. Friedman.

Shimshon didn't hear. Something from within had blocked out all interference, allowing the boy to direct all his reserves of hatred on this alien. No one standing there, wide-eyed and wide-mouthed, dared scold the boy for what would normally have been considered an appalling lack of respect toward an elder. They were spellbound.

Not until the man quietly closed the Chumash and put it aside did he bother looking at Shimshon. His eyes, so lustrously blue, became teary with sadness.

He sighed. "Shimshon, you're wrong. You are completely mistaken about me."

"You liar!" the boy shrieked. Still no one restrained him. "You're full of baloney! You're Hans Schmidt, and you belong behind bars — in a cage, like an animal. That's what you are — an animal."

"*Mein Kind*, you must—"

"And that beard of yours will be shaved off, just like you shaved the beards of Jews!"

Suddenly a pair of hands grabbed Shimshon roughly by the shoulders and pulled him away. Still snarling, Shimshon shook himself free and again advanced toward Shulman.

"Shimshon!" his father finally uttered, hurrying to the boy's side and trying to pull him away.

The synagogue was now filled with murmuring. It was not

every day that the congregants saw a boy not even bar mitzvah age openly insult an old man. In the front, Binyamin stood, bewildered, with his father.

"We'll get you in the end," the boy mumbled viciously. "You're not getting away with anything."

He cut himself short in terror — too late. He could read into Shulman's eyes, which had momentarily widened with shock, then narrowed and darkened with suspicion, that the man wondered what was meant by "we."

The boy then yelled, "Get out of here!"

The rabbi, at last holding his son tightly, curtly tossed a comment Shulman's way. "I'm afraid I'll have to ask you to leave, sir."

"Why?" Shulman asked, his voice full of hurt.

The rabbi continued to hold his squirming son and answered, "You know very well, Mr. Schmidt. There is no room here for people like you."

Clutching a chair, his knuckles white with tension, Shulman argued, "If, my dear Rabbi Shapiro, it is your habit to forcibly prevent fellow Jews from fulfilling the *mitzvah* of *davening*, then I am surprised you are allowed to run this *shul*."

"And if people like you succeeded in what you tried to do, there wouldn't be any *shuls* left in the world. Please go." The rabbi fought to keep his voice steady; it was important, at all costs, not to lose control. Nevertheless, he hissed, "How dare you come here? How can you possibly show your face? You're an animal — you and anyone associated with you. Out!"

Rising to his full height, Shulman towered threateningly over the rabbi and his son, practically shielding the light overhead. This was no longer an old man, but rather an ancient warrior, who now eyed his opponent keenly in an effort to square off with him in battle.

"Sir, I will say to you what I said to your son. Your accusations are completely false. I am a true Jew — just like the others here — and have my right to *daven* like anyone else." His voice rumbled loudly from the very depths of his being, to make certain that everyone could hear him. "My right . . . *no one* can take from me — certainly not because of some pathetic mental image you have of someone who resembles me."

He continued, with a certain haughtiness, "Ask me what you wish. Make all your accusations. I can quote the Mishnah, Gemara — all the *poskim.* You have no proof of guilt on my part. If anything" — he raised his head higher — "I hold *you* guilty, Rabbi, of publicly shaming a fellow Jew. A basic prohibition, no? One every child has learned — certainly a boy your son's age. But I wonder if his father has truly set an example."

The rabbi trembled, livid.

Wagging a finger sternly, Shulman continued. "Embarrassing a Jew is akin to spilling blood. Do you understand, Rabbi? And to think that you accuse *me* of it. Furthermore, Rabbi" — he waved his hand across the room in a panoramic sweep — "you have deprived your congregation of their right to *daven*, by interrupting the service.

"However," he concluded, "I forgive you for what you have done to me. My only wish is that in the future you will not shame other Jews."

Benevolently, he declared, "I forgive you completely, Rabbi Shapiro, for what you have done." He flashed him a smile — a smile sweet with victory.

It took every ounce of strength Rabbi Shapiro possessed — he pressed his hands to his temples in order to hold back the mounting fury — to keep the walls of the synagogue from trembling with him down to the very foundations. The absurdity of this was so great that he was even tempted to laugh: a man who was trying to undermine Rabbi Shapiro had just eloquently sermonized about the sin of embarrassing a "fellow Jew." Feeling the eyes of the congregation and guests, and hearing the whispering behind his back, he had to remind himself where he was, and how he had to present himself — especially at a time like this.

Everyone waited in terrified suspense for something to pierce the stillness. Even the toddlers were silent.

Suddenly, a voice boomed out, "Excuse me, Rabbi Shapiro."

All heads turned. A man in a quilted satin gabardine and a *shtreimel*, a chassidic hat, advanced slowly, interrupting the showdown.

Shimshon knew this man at once. Rabbi Shlomo Bernstein, who normally prayed with his chassidim in a large synagogue down the street, was here, like everyone else, in Binyamin's honor. He was a corpulent man, with muscles bulging under the gabardine, fiery dark eyes, slightly pockmarked olive skin, and hair still streaked with black, though he was well into his sixties. In the little *shul* of Tifereth Yaakov, he stood out like an enormous fish in a tiny pond. His presence dominated the congregation, as if he, rather than the groom, were the guest of honor.

Rabbi Bernstein was a Holocaust survivor, just like Rabbi Shapiro — for two years a guest at Auschwitz, after being dragged out of a Warsaw bunker, where he had been studying Torah secretly with a group of fellow chassidim. The timing, ironically, was perfect: they had just completed half of the Talmud, which

Bernstein could practically recite in his sleep. A child prodigy, he had later learned virtually all of the Talmud by heart, as well as parts of Shulchan Aruch — the Code of Jewish Law — and countless Biblical passages. His power of memorization was not only phenomenal, but quite handy at Auschwitz, where he often had been forced to stand in the freezing weather for hours. The mental acuity kept his mind off his numbed feet — though he nevertheless had to have two toes amputated. He also suffered a permanent limp. In Auschwitz, as well as in the Warsaw Ghetto, he had held secret prayer and study groups; his faith and wisdom had kept many alive, even through the most sadistic of tortures. Once, during a particularly savage beating by a *kapo*, young Shlomo rattled off pages and pages of Mishnah, while his emaciated pupils, one of whom was Binyamin's father, looked on in amazement. Little did they know that their rebbe had survived several other beatings in just that fashion.

After liberation, though sick with dysentery and weighing but eighty-five pounds, he had found and gathered remnants of his chassidim within the camp. In 1947, they made illegal entry into Palestine. Later, in the United States, he and his group reestablished themselves. By then, Shlomo Bernstein had regained his full weight — 200 pounds — and his strength, till he resembled a bull in a *shtreimel*. By then, his mind had become a virtual encyclopedia of Talmudic knowledge, bursting with spiritual energy which was barely confined within his powerful frame.

Hobbling toward Yehuda Shapiro, he called the younger man aside. Though Rabbi Shapiro's senior by only ten years, Shlomo Bernstein regarded the rabbi, and probably everyone else in the world, as a son. Rabbi Shapiro had a special place in Rabbi

Bernstein's heart; both were from Warsaw and both had lived on the same block in the ghetto. Shlomo Bernstein had watched his entire family carried away screaming, yet he reacted with an even stronger acceptance of G-d's will. This undying faith elicited from Rabbi Shapiro the deepest respect for this man; the rabbi was always receptive to the former's counsel and advice.

Shulman, noticing the chassid, smiled and said, "Good Shabbos, Rav Bernstein. *Shalom aleichem.*"

"*Aleichem shalom,*" the man answered, and turned to a very amazed Rabbi Shapiro.

Although he tried to whisper, Rabbi Bernstein's deep, booming voice was naturally resonant, and Shimshon, standing just a few feet away, caught many bits and pieces, spoken in fervent Yiddish.

"I have spoken to Rav Shulman many times . . . discussed many matters of *halacha* . . . a *gaon,* a genius . . . true, but I cannot understand how this man could be — or possibly could have been — a Nazi . . . what? . . . yes, Yehuda, I know; physical disguise is only superficial. But could a Nazi possess such Talmudic knowledge? It just can't be."

Turning to the congregation, he said, "Please, my friends, it is already quite late. Reb Yehuda, certainly you should have the *davening* continue." Quietly going to Shulman, who had been reciting Psalms the whole time, he said politely, "Rav Shulman, I ask that for the sake of peace you go elsewhere. I'm afraid that your presence, whether or not it should be this way, has upset our rabbi."

Slowly, Shulman shut the Psalms book and placed it squarely on a lectern. He then rested the Chumash on top. He spoke casually, as if nothing had occurred. "Rav Bernstein, I should very much like to discuss more matters of *halacha* with you later this afternoon." His head held high, he turned and faced the packed hall. "Good Shabbos," he announced, and swept out the door with the air of an offended king.

Musaf was soon recited, with Rav Bernstein leading the prayer. Rabbi Shapiro stood behind him, still quaking with anger. Near the door, Shimshon kept his face averted from his friends. During the silent prayer, the boy kept his face down in his *siddur,* his tears splashing the pages.

Though he tried hard to concentrate on the prayers before him, his mind inevitably turned to the man who had walked in and disrupted the service. Why did he have to come here? Hadn't he done enough? No doubt he now felt even more victorious — after having his piety sanctioned by Rabbi Bernstein. Perhaps that was why Shulman came; he knew in advance that Rabbi Bernstein would be here, and that he would defend him.

The boy had detected a smile on Shulman's face even before Rabbi Bernstein had spoken with his father. It was right after Shulman had delivered his sermon to the captivated audience. Ta was right: Shulman, or rather, Schmidt, was a pro when it came to public speaking. He knew well how to manipulate, and to humiliate as well. Accusing his father of all those things — when he had most likely done far worse in his life. Spilling blood, indeed! Schmidt had virtually plunged a dagger deep into his father's heart.

Schmidt had accomplished what he had set out to do. Behind the curtain, Shimshon heard female whispers: "Is he always like that, Mrs. Friedman?" "What a pity his son has to live with that." "Didn't you read the papers?" "If I were Shulman, I'd sue." Morosely, the boy moved away.

Even worse were the comments from his friends. Shimshon

saw them pointing to his father, whispering. Zev approached Shimshon and said weakly, "Don't worry, Shimmy. I'm behind you one-hundred percent." He wasn't very convincing.

Shimshon in turn smiled weakly, saying, "Thanks, Zev," and inwardly decided that he was also tired of hearing about the Holocaust.

Lunch was held privately, with only father and son present. In the past many a guest would have vied for the honor of eating at Rabbi Yehuda Shapiro's table. Quietly, his son served him the first course.

"Why don't you sing for me, Shimmy?" his father asked after finishing his fish.

The boy shook his head sadly. "Not today, Ta. I just don't feel like it."

"I don't either, Shimmy," his father murmured, staring mournfully at the blackened stubs of candlestick wax.

During the long afternoon, Shimshon stayed home. Usually at this time of year he enjoyed having much of the day to play in the alleyways and back yards with his friends, or simply to take a long walk. Today, however, he was content to hide in his room, his eyes resting listlessly on a Chumash. Not until his room turned pale did the boy look outside the window. Observing the setting sun, he quickly went downstairs, where his father was already waiting, jacket in hand.

This week, in honor of Binyamin, the synagogue was in for a treat. Rabbi Bernstein had offered to enliven the third meal with a lengthy discourse on the weekly Torah portion. Among the remains of tuna salad he spoke, with dramatic flair, surrounded not only by the members of Rabbi Shapiro's *minyan,* but by a number of parishioners from his own synagogue as well. Though he had asked them to stay there, the idea of missing a Shabbos with their beloved rebbe was inconceivable.

With intricate perfection, Rabbi Bernstein spoke; the audience was spellbound. However, Rabbi Bernstein was forced to stop, somewhat indignantly, when he noticed that all heads were slowly turning away from him toward the direction of the door. Someone had arrived.

Avraham Shulman stood in the back, musing over a volume of Talmud, as if waiting for a bus. He did not approach the table. This time he knew he would have to wait until dark. Silently, Talmud volume in hand, he withdrew and waited in the women's section.

Trembling, Shimshon looked away. He tried to face Rabbi Bernstein, who continued to address his audience. Rabbi Shapiro rose and retreated to the back room with Zelig, not reemerging until grace was to be said. As if in a hypnotic trance, the others alternately watched Rabbi Bernstein and the steadily darkening sky. In the dimly lit area behind the curtain the figure of Shulman became faintly silhouetted.

Ma'ariv and *havdalah* were concluded hastily, with most of the men leaving afterwards to join their families. Shulman had prayed quietly, staying in the women's section. He waited for Rabbi Bernstein to approach him and steer him behind the partition. Shimshon, waiting for his father, tiptoed over to the curtain — all the while feeling guilty, but just not being able to help himself.

The language was far more complicated than the Hebrew and Yiddish he had picked up in school and at home. The boy knew that the topics being discussed were on a level far beyond that of a twelve-year-old. Occasionally phrases which Shimshon was just being exposed to in school — Aramaic terms, passages from the Mishnah and other holy works — were bounced to and fro, as if in a tennis tournament. It was difficult to guess who was more learned than whom. Bernstein's rumbling voice was answered by Shulman's quiet lilt, like a whispering wind after a thunderstorm.

When Shimshon saw his father approach him, frowning, he backed away. Silently, he followed his father home. Only Zelig remained behind, keys in hand.

Outside it had begun to rain. Shimshon lowered his head and felt the warm drops hit the back of his neck like bullets. He looked up at his father. Rabbi Shapiro walked solemnly ahead, as if at a funeral, completely oblivious to the sudden storm. The rain danced frantically off his hat and coat, but at last, having nowhere else to go, it fell, defeated, to the pavement.

Well into the night Shimshon lay awake in bed, listening to the cries in the next room. They had of late grown more intense, often echoing into the living room below. At three a.m., Shimshon opened his eyes wide and stared at the ceiling, the memory of Shabbos morning circling his head in a mocking dance.

He tried not to think of Shulman smiling, leaving his enemy to look like a fool. Instead, the boy thought of his father's words, which were spat at Shulman: *You're an animal — you and anyone associated with you.*

Shimshon shot up. Slyly, other words crept into his head.

Is Schmidt the real villain?

Obviously, he has people backing him, his father had said. *Men of power. And who know how to use it.*

Slowly he reviewed the rest of the conversation that had taken place at the survivors' meeting.

The words came easily. *Ta, remember those four men I*

mentioned? That time I went to Schmidt's apartment?

Shimshon sprang out of bed. By now completely oblivious to the cries in the other room, he sat at his desk, in the dark, and pensively rested his chin on his hands.

Maybe . . . they were the ones behind Schmidt. And they were the ones who talked to the press — you know, like, kept them quiet or something.

Shimshon groped to remember an old saying — what was it? Oh, yes: *You can tell a man by the company he keeps.*

With this, he decided he had found a solution. Find the friends of Hans Schmidt and discover whether they are Nazis or not.

Coming up with the idea was somewhat easier than carrying it out. Right now the boy had absolutely no idea where to go about finding those men — assuming, of course, that they really were Nazis. Besides, even were they nice enough to show up for the boy, his father's words dinned into his ears: *I cannot willingly expose Shimshon to that kind of danger.* Knowing the pain his father was in now, Shimshon dared not disobey him and act on his own.

Disgruntled, the boy returned to his bed. He was going to lose sleep again because of his overactive mind — and with finals coming up too. He turned over in bed, hoping to fall asleep.

But the thoughts came back. Until now the only photographs taken of Schmidt were when he was by himself — never with anyone else. There was as yet no physical evidence of the men Shimshon had seen with Schmidt that night at the old apartment house. If there could be some way of showing the world Hans Schmidt together with his friends, then Shimshon's father might be believed.

Shimshon sighed, pondering where and how he could find such

an opportunity. If only a multitude of pictures existed of Schmidt with Nazi officers. Better still — of Avraham Shulman, in his chassidic outfit, alongside them, just like that night when Shimshon had dropped by unexpectedly.

Shimshon was expressly forbidden to go back to Justin Road. He somehow doubted, anyway, that Shulman would want to see him, although he had claimed to "completely forgive" the boy's father. If only Shimshon could find him somewhere else.

The boy allowed his mind to drift off to sleep.

Mostly he walks around. And stares at buildings.

Shimshon grew restless again.

Every day he was seen in the vicinity of Thirty-eighth and seventh, Jack Rifkin had said.

In Manhattan? his father had asked.

Shimshon turned onto his right side.

A few photographs caught my attention, especially.

He removed from his coat a photograph, and held it up for the others to see: Shulman buying flowers from a stand off of Seventh Avenue. Moshe pointed to the background. Faintly in the distance was a sign: Empire Glatt Kosher Delicatessen.

I wonder if Mr. Rifkin was aware of this place when he took the picture, Moshe Kaplan had said. *I have the feeling, though, it was just a coincidence. Though I am surprised, after seeing the picture, that he wouldn't stop to have a look inside the place himself.*

Shimshon opened his eyes wide and sprang out of bed again. The address burst forth from his brain: 225 West Thirty-seventh Street.

There! Of course! He had to go there! What he wanted was there — in that restaurant. He had to go there himself, and find those men with Shulman.

Remembering Moshe Kaplan, who had often kidded with Shimshon, telling the boy how he could take pictures of his own bar mitzvah celebration, Shimshon thought of the talent he was starting to display for photography. Ever since his father had given him a camera for his last birthday, Shimshon had taken to the hobby with great enthusiasm; he had even converted a small basement closet into a darkroom. Well, here was his chance to get more practice!

Shimshon soured as he slunk back into bed. He was endangering his father again. He would be endangering his own life, too, should he fall into the hands of those people. In two weeks school would be out. Perhaps then, before getting sent off to camp, he might have time to go to Manhattan. However, a lot could happen in two weeks. Shulman or his friends might be gone by then.

Shimshon whistled under his breath. If Shulman owned the building, then he obviously was not in a hurry to get away. Somehow, though, timing seemed crucial. With the controversy about Shulman still fresh in people's minds, this trip was just too urgent to be put off for any length of time.

Moshe Kaplan had mentioned construction work going on in the building. A parking lot or something. Obviously, Sunday would not be a good day to go; without the construction crew there, Schmidt and his friends might not bother to come. It would have to be during the week. Thinking of each day and the projects of his that were due, Shimshon decided that the only good day to go would be Tuesday.

The thought of the "tons of Mishnayos" he had to learn made Shimshon hate to lose a day of school. He also disliked being dishonest. In addition, he remembered his father's recurrent warning that he was too young to act alone against Nazis. But finally Shimshon reasoned that there really was no other way.

At last drifting off to sleep, Shimshon realized how he had changed in the past three months. He was becoming a better spy than ever.

Tuesday morning, six-thirty. Shimshon rose, bleary-eyed, and quickly got dressed. He knew it was important to carry out his usual routine. His father must not know.

But as luck had it, his father was waiting downstairs for him.

"Need a ride to school today, Shimmy?" he asked, a smile on his face. "I have to be in Flatbush this morning, so I can take you."

The boy was startled. "Oh, thanks, Ta, but I . . . I don't really need a ride. I feel like taking the bus." Then he asked quickly, "You're not going at all into Manhattan today, are you?"

The smile faded. "Not till later this afternoon. Why?"

"Just asking." The boy went into the kitchen, turned, and stammered, "It just seemed kind of weird, you know — your not going in the morning. I got sort of used to it."

His father shook his head uncomprehendingly. Taking his *tallis* bag in hand, he said sternly, "I'll be back."

At eight o'clock, when Rabbi Shapiro returned from *minyan*, Shimshon hugged his school bag, feeling it to make sure the zoom lens was not poking out between the zipper. Standing outside the door a few feet away from his father, looking nervously into the sunny, open air, he loudly announced, "What a beautiful day. I think I'll walk to school instead."

"Are you sure you don't want a ride, Shimmy?"

"I'm positive. Bye, Tati."

He marched down the driveway, whistling, turned right when

he reached the sidewalk, and headed left onto Eighteenth Avenue. Then he bolted. In the distance was the F-train.

He found a seat in a subway car near the back and placed his book bag on the seat next to him, his hand resting protectively on top. Not until the train left did Shimshon become aware that his heart was pounding furiously, and that his breath was coming in short, excited gasps. He realized it was not fear he was feeling, but guilt — intense guilt for once again disobeying his father. If he had luck, he would not be in Manhattan for too long. Maybe what he needed to see would be there waiting, and the whole thing would be done in a snap — a snapshot, that is.

Shimshon looked out the window. At least the sun was pretty. And it *was* nice outside — too nice to be in school. Cottony tufts of clouds drifted through the pastel blue air, wrapping themselves around the Manhattan skyline. It was supposed to be warm today. Shimshon hoped he would get enough light to be able to take good pictures.

Shimshon exited the subway at Penn Station and found himself in a cavernous world, his senses brutally assaulted by garish neon light. Though outside there was broad, sunny daylight, inside it was a land of perpetual night. Noise, filth, soot — the elements engulfed him, carrying him away along with the jostling crowds of people that were deposited from a variety of subway trains. Derelicts greeted him at the escalators; in the distance he heard the wailing saxophone of a jazz musician, who was standing in the dank corridor, a few coins strewn in his saxophone case. The boy hugged his school bag closer, not sure if he was protecting it, or the other way around.

When he arrived outside at last, he stood and squinted,

bewildered, at the intersection. It was nine o'clock, the time when half of Manhattan was sitting down at a desk, starting the day. Tires screeched, cars honked angrily, drivers and pedestrians cursed each other vehemently. "Getchur paper," cried a vendor, who was besieged by hurrying businesspersons. A giant radio with a man attached to it brushed by Shimshon; the speakers blared a pounding, repetitive rhythm.

Shimshon did not know why, but he had the urge then and there to cry. He felt as if he were five again, lost at the Lag B'Omer carnival. Only after a lonely search through the different games and rides did he find his parents. They scolded him and told him never to go wandering around by himself again. Even then, Shimshon had always seemed to get into trouble.

By the time he had walked two blocks, to Thirty-sixth Street, he felt better. Here, the noise was far less intense, and the sidewalks were far less crowded. The traffic had cleared, and with it the honking. Nevertheless, Shimshon looked forward to getting out of Manhattan as soon as possible. And to think his father came here every day.

Shimshon froze in terror when he saw a man in a round black hat and a gabardine heading his way. He looked around frantically in search of a hiding place, as the figure came closer. However, the man simply brushed past Shimshon, quietly turned right at the intersection, and headed east, toward Sixth and Thirty-seventh. As Shimshon studied the man's features, realizing that he was at least a head shorter than Shulman, the boy breathed a sigh a relief. In the distance, he saw another chassid — tall, thin, and majestic-looking — however, with black hair, instead of golden-white.

Shimshon headed toward Eighth and Thirty-seventh. Though

it was only half-past nine, he was already perspiring from the bright spring sun hovering overhead. Stopping at a Korean grocery, he bought himself a bottle of Coke and, stuffing it into his book bag, continued west.

The sign appeared in the distance: *Empire Glatt Kosher Delicatessen.* Shimshon's eyes widened in surprise. Was *this* the place Shulman had bought? The restaurant was underneath a drab old building, which someone had tried to spruce up a bit by painting brown. Somehow, Shimshon just couldn't imagine Shulman as the owner of either this building or the restaurant. Certainly not Hans Schmidt, the Nazi — unless this place reminded him of home. Had Berlin been full of drab old buildings? Wasn't it a center of spectacular architecture?

The boy scanned the surrounding area, which contained a few old factory warehouses; the rest were modern high-rises. Alongside of him a small row of cars was waiting, with the drivers honking their horns. In the distance, adjacent to Empire, a construction crew directed the inching traffic.

The air, heavy with exhaust fumes and noise, made Shimshon dizzy, and he turned to find a place to sit. Spotting a bench in front of a high-rise, the boy opened his book bag and examined its contents. There, keeping his notebook warm, was the camera. With loving care the boy extracted the photographic equipment, removed the lens cap, and attached the zoom lens to the mount. He tried to remember his photography lessons. Set exposure time, aperture. The film cartridge — where was it?

Suddenly his heart pounded, as he saw in the distance a tall, gabardined figure framed in whitening yellow hair, holding a briefcase.

Looking around frantically, Shimshon noticed, diagonally

across the street, an alleyway and loading dock. Grabbing his bag and his camera, he ran and hid behind a bunch of boxes, one piled on top of the other, and peered into the street.

Avraham Shulman, looking straight ahead, marched briskly down Thirty-seventh Street. Before entering the restaurant, he paused to talk to a workman in the construction crew. The workman pointed to something on the debris-filled sidewalk, and Shulman nodded soberly.

Quickly, Shimshon raised his camera. Click.

"Hey, what're ya doin' here?"

Shimshon turned around and gasped. Before him a big, very burly man stood frowning. He was wearing a sweat-stained T-shirt, and had his hairy arms crossed over his chest. Behind him stood a man who was thinner, but no less angry.

"Well? What're ya doin' here?" the big man repeated.

The boy backed away: "I . . . I . . ."

"Don't you know it's dangerous to be here? This is a loading zone, kid. You might get hurt. A boy like you should be in school, anyways."

Shimshon brightened. "This is a project I'm doing for school," he said eagerly. "For my photography class. I'm taking pictures of buildings in Manhattan."

The man frowned. "That old building don't seem too special. Looks more to me like you're takin' pictures of things that ain't your business. I'll tell you what. I'll give you the benefit of the doubt. But please do your project somewheres else. We ain't got the insurance to cover your gettin' hurt."

The boy nodded quickly and grabbed his bag. He looked across the street, and noticed with relief that Shulman had just entered Empire.

The boy scampered past the pile of boxes to an alleyway next to the 234 building. He found two large garbage bins and secured himself squarely in between them, ignoring the sickening smell that emanated from the bins and the flies it attracted. Shimshon was generally pleased with the location; he had enough shade, provided by the adjacent wall, to keep him both cool and hidden, yet he was at enough of an angle to catch the sunlight against 225 West Thirty-seventh Street. There was even a place for him to sit down — a rickety, discarded chair, with one of its arms missing.

Nevertheless, the boy found himself standing throughout much of the day. Though Shulman rarely appeared, the boy waited, taking intermittent shots of the building and its environs. A well-dressed woman left the building and hailed a taxi. A professional-looking man left five minutes later. A rotund man with a black beard and a skullcap exited the restaurant to talk with the construction crew. Then he went back inside. A very young couple, both with spiked hair, exited together, laughing at some private joke. So it went, as the minutes turned into hours.

Click went the camera each time. Shimshon was grateful he had remembered to bring a small notebook, now resting under his Chumash. Each time a picture was taken, he wrote down the time of day, as well as other observations which he made partly for fun, partly out of a sense that they might prove significant. He couldn't help feeling a tinge of pride — just like a genuine sleuth. If he succeeded, he thought happily, his father would be really proud. And boy would he be surprised.

By four o'clock, however, he was starting to feel tired and uncomfortable. His skullcap offered little protection against the sun. He was on his third bottle of Coke, and it was nearly drained. Shimshon was now feeling the effect on his bladder, and he squirmed and crossed his legs. He was angry at himself for forgetting to pack lunch along with his detective equipment. In his growing hunger he looked at the restaurant longingly. Nevertheless, his feet remained stubbornly implanted in the pavement, desperate for that moment of evidence which he could bring to his father. The boy hated to admit that he might have just wasted his time. He prayed for something to happen.

At exactly 4:30, his prayers were answered. A black limousine appeared in the distance, near Eighth Avenue, and waited. Just then, the figure of Shulman appeared outside the restaurant. Looking back and forth, he nodded in the direction of the limousine and walked ahead.

Shimshon waited by the bins, confused. Should he follow Shulman, or wait? Would it be possible to photograph the limousine from this far? Not likely, he thought — not even with the zoom lens. The boy waited till Shulman was a good half block away before he inched his way out from between the bins and followed.

To the boy's surprise, the limousine pulled away from the curb and glided down the street. Shulman continued ahead; Shimshon remained behind. Soon the limousine turned right and disappeared. Shimshon watched as Shulman turned right, heading toward Thirty-eighth.

On Forty-second, Shulman turned right again, and walked to the end of the block, where the limousine was waiting. Shimshon, turning the corner, froze, then dove into another loading dock and another set of boxes.

This time the boy looked behind him to make sure there were no angry men standing nearby. Then he took out his camera and note pad.

Shulman bent over, his back to Shimshon, and faced the limousine. He listened more than spoke. Shimshon's view of the door was blocked. He quickly wrote down the license plate number. He did not remember if this was the same limousine he had seen that night on Justin Road, but he hoped it would matter little. Through the tinted glass it was disappointingly impossible for Shimshon to identify the passengers; however, four shapes besides the driver were visible. Click went the camera, Shimshon deciding that a rear view picture of Shulman was better than none at all.

He was about to put his camera down when suddenly Shulman walked away, leaving the passenger — the one who had been speaking — exposed through the rolled down window. Shimshon gasped. He recognized this man at once. He seemed to be calling to Shulman, who turned around and again approached the vehicle. This time he stood by the chauffeur, instead of at the passenger door. Shulman listened, smiled, and, raising his hand, held his index finger and thumb together — "O.K."

O.K.! Shimshon brightened, barely containing his excitement. Here goes. Click, click went the camera. Click again. Thank you, Mr. Schmidt. Click. And whoever you are, mister, in the car.

One of the other men leaned out and frowned at Shulman. Shimshon again gasped, his hands shaking as he pressed the shutter. Click. How fat Heinz looked next to the thin man.

Suddenly Heinz looked past Shulman and pointed sharply in Shimshon's direction. All heads turned. The boy, horrified, quickly ducked into the loading dock. He hurried to an elevator and frantically pushed the buttons. After an interminable thirty seconds, the doors opened.

Shimshon recoiled, as he came face to face with a burly man, who was evidently the foreman of the crew which was working there.

"Hey! What are you doing here?" asked the foreman.

Shimshon bolted. Finding the bright red *Exit* sign, he pushed open the door and found himself in a maze of alleyways. His eyes filled with tears as he tried to steer himself. He turned right, into an open doorway, and found himself inside a garage. Noticing a ramp, he turned and headed upwards, toward a distant elevator. The place was dangerously dark and fetid with stale grease; twice Shimshon nearly slipped, and he tore his new shirt on a protruding wire grate.

At last he reached an elevator. With trembling fingers he pressed the button, and waited.

In the distance he heard the footsteps growing ominously closer, echoing through the tunnel-like garage as if they were jackboots. Shimshon did not dare wait for the elevator. Noticing an adjacent staircase, he pushed open the door and hurried through the corridor, his heart pounding.

Directly above him, he saw rectangular rows and rows of stairs, each ascending, crisscrossing, and overlapping the others, like a giant, three-dimensional Lego set. He zoomed up the first flight of stairs and pushed the door wide open.

"Shimshon!"

The boy screamed in terror, and then opened his eyes in disbelief.

The blue Pontiac was idling in traffic. Through the window the face of Rabbi Yehuda Shapiro was filled with amazement.

Sobbing, the boy ran to the car and opened its back door. Once he was safely inside he collapsed on the seat, the telltale contents of his book bag spilling out onto the floor.

His father looked at him and shook his head knowingly. A strange smile crossed his face.

Chapter 12

In Righteous Anger

Rabbi Shapiro remained silent during the drive home. As the traffic slowed to a crawl and then a halt over the Brooklyn Bridge, he listened to his son quietly sob and at last drift into sleep. The boy's arms, rendered bright red by the sun, were enough to indicate that he had not spent the day indoors.

By the time the Pontiac rolled down Eighteenth Avenue and turned sharply into the driveway, Shimshon was squirming into wakefulness. He sat up in a daze, his feet resting against the camera, which had rolled under the seat. He rubbed his eyes and gathered his things into the book bag.

Exiting the car, the boy hurried to the sidewalk and looked around, expecting to see either the limousine go by or Shulman and his friends jump out from under a bush.

"Hello!"

The boy gasped and turned.

A friend of his waved cheerfully from down the street. "Shimmy, hi! Where were you today?"

Shimshon sighed with relief. By the entrance stood his father, waiting. Still wavering with nervousness and uncertainty, the boy turned and headed inside, feeling a new kind of terror. All right, now I'm going to get it, he thought.

But to his surprise, his father did not explode. Calmly putting away his coat, he directed his son into the living room. Apprehensively, the boy took a seat.

"All right, let's hear it, Shimmy," his father began, sitting down in the armchair and facing his son. "I want to know why you weren't in school."

"Promise not to get *too* mad?" the boy asked timidly.

"I promise."

The boy swallowed. "I went to the building site today."

His father nodded, unblinking. "Schmidt's?"

He nodded.

His father replied, "And can you tell me, please, how you ended up running out of my building like a madman?"

The boy's eyes widened. "You work there?"

The rabbi shook his head in dismay. "You know very well I work there, Shimmy. Sixth and Forty-third. You've been there so many times before."

The boy began to giggle hysterically. "I got so scared . . . I didn't know where I was going . . . I sort of ran inside a bunch of buildings. That's how I found you."

"Ran? Buildings?" His father frowned. "What were you doing there, Shimmy?"

Suddenly the giggling stopped, and Shimshon swallowed again. "I went to see where Avraham Schmidt — I mean Hans Shulman — I mean — well, you know." The boy lowered his head. "Ta, I wanted to take a picture of him."

"You mean spy on him."

"I thought . . . maybe if I got a picture of him and his friends people would believe you." He bit his lip and sniffed. "I'm sorry, Ta. I know I shouldn't have gone there — or missed school. I

279

guess I should've minded my own business. But I was only trying to help." At last he broke down and cried.

Rabbi Shapiro tapped the armrest meditatively. He had anticipated some kind of blow-up on his part — and justifiably so — but the combination of late spring heat and the sight of his son, frightened and upset, had left him devoid of steam. He looked out the window, watched the paling sky, and made a mental note that it was time soon for *minchah.*

Sternly, but not ungently, he said, "Sometimes . . . we all get the urge to be a hero. But it's not like in the movies, Shimmy. Somebody just doesn't come in and magically save the world. Often people get hurt. Innocent people. Young people like you. Being some kind of secret agent is not at all glamorous. And not always fruitful. Did you gain anything by it, Shimmy?"

The boy brightened. "Ta, I *did* get some pictures you might like — of Schmidt's friends. I saw a limousine. And inside there were four men — the men I saw that night in Schmidt's apartment."

His father leaned forward. "Are you sure it was them?"

"Positive. At least two of them." Wiping his eyes, the boy chattered eagerly. "I used the camera you gave me for my birthday. I waited all day outside the restaurant, and I got a bunch of shots. Hope they come out."

"I hope so too," his father murmured, quickly rising from the chair and heading toward the closet for his jacket. "Come with me, Shimmy. And bring your camera."

The boy stared, crestfallen. "Ta, they're *my* pictures. *I* took them. Why can't *I* develop them?"

Smiling, his father approached him and bent down. "Shimmy," he said, "I know you like to do your own camera work. I don't doubt that you have the ability. I remember when you won the contest. I am very proud of you. But right now I need a professional — and Moshe, besides being a close friend and colleague, has been doing this kind of work for years. Right now I can rely on him more to do the kind of job I need. His participation is most crucial."

Shimshon nodded in agreement. Just seeing that his father wasn't mad anymore made him grateful, and he was smart enough not to argue. Immediately grabbing his camera, he darted out the door.

The car pulled up on Sixteenth Avenue directly in front of the photography store. Rabbi Shapiro rapped loudly on the darkened store window. He waited a few seconds and then rapped again.

The little figure of Moshe Kaplan became visible. He nodded and quickly opened the door.

The rabbi quickly handed his friend the cartridge. "Mosh, how soon can you develop this?"

"How soon do you need it?"

"Yesterday."

"As good as done. Whose are these?"

"Shimmy's."

Moshe Kaplan smiled broadly at the boy. "Shimmy, well . . . I'm sure I'll be in for a surprise."

"He went through a lot to get them. I explained to him how I needed a pro to finish the job. If possible, I want blow-ups of all the people, as well as any other pertinent details."

"Trust me, Yehuda. Have I ever let you down?"

"Thanks, we'll be next door, in the yeshiva. See you in awhile."

In the yeshiva, as the men gathered for *minchah,* Shimshon spotted Zev, who was standing with his father. The boys quickly retreated to one of the bookcases.

"How come you weren't in school?" his friend whispered.

"I'll explain later. What did I miss?" Shimshon asked.

"Just a dumb quiz. And Calev fell down the stairs."

"*Again?*"

The boys searched for *siddurim* among the other holy books strewn on the tables.

After *minchah*, the rabbi and his son lingered on long enough for *ma'ariv,* long enough for Moshe Kaplan to wash the prints in the developer tray. When father and son at last exited the little yeshiva, they were confronted with an intense evening sky dotted with pulsating white constellations. The air was invitingly warm, perfect for a walk. Instead, however, they knocked on Moshe's door.

"Beautiful," said the photographer, as he steered the pair through the cluttered back room, like a museum tour guide. "Better than any wedding photographer. Shimmy, you definitely have a profession waiting for you."

Shimshon smiled modestly at the compliment, though being the world's greatest photographer no longer interested him. He had stopped to admire a handsome telescope perched on a tripod, and was now busy imagining himself as the world's greatest astronomer.

Rabbi Shapiro remained oblivious to the equipment which had transported his son into a delightfully different world. He was more concerned with the photographs — which might reveal those who had transported him to a place far more hellish than one who had not been there could imagine.

Along the darkroom walls, prints large and small were hanging to dry. "These have just been rinsed," Moshe explained, pointing to some that were dripping wet. "That's the last of them."

When Shimshon entered the compact cubicle and found himself surrounded by a panorama of colored and black-and-white faces, he stared, fascinated, his fantasies of astronomy fading.

As usual, Shulman was photogenic, dazzling. In a few photographs he stood with his eyes directed intently toward something. However, the darkroom light cast a devilishly red glow over the man's face, as with the other photographs, eerily distorting the features.

Moshe pointed to a heavy-set man and explained, "That's Aharon Zimmerman. He's the manager of Empire."

"A survivor?" asked the rabbi.

"Yes."

The rabbi frowned. "Why does he work for this man? Does he know that Schmidt is a Nazi?"

Moshe sighed. "I asked him, Yehuda. He believed us, at first. But now, thanks to Avraham Shulman and his great PR, Aharon believes him, like everyone else does. In fact, he defends Shulman vehemently. Calls him a 'saint,' a 'man much misunderstood.' Evidently, Shulman's been good to him. Gives him a large rent reduction."

"In New York that's enough to make any man a saint."

Moshe laughed. His nasal laughter conveyed a man who was gifted with a warm sense of humor; even in the most intense of situations — of which he had had plenty — he had the ability to remain jolly. "Interestingly, Schmidt won't eat in the restaurant — or any, for that manner. He never trusts the *kashrus*. Not eating in your own restaurant, I think, convinced Zimmerman more than anything else of his employer's spiritual purity."

Rabbi Shapiro smiled sardonically. "Someone ought to tell him that Hitler was a vegetarian."

Again Moshe laughed. "As usual, my dear rabbi, your ability for ironic observation leaves me in stitches. If only Schmidt could hear you now."

"If he's such a saint, I'm sure he can."

With a slight tug, the little photographer pulled a new set of prints off the line on which they had been drying. "I think these would be of interest to you in particular, Yehuda. You might remember this man quite well."

Instantly the humor dissipated, and the rabbi's smile faded. "I'm not sure I want to, Mosh."

Gravely, Moshe answered, "I must compliment your son, Yehuda, on his initiative. Shimmy, you're a finer detective than we thought. We should have had him working with us long ago."

The boy turned crimson in the red light.

"Shimmy," said Moshe, "since you took the pictures, why don't you show us, please, which people you saw that night on Justin Road."

Slowly, Shimshon raised his hand. He pointed to an exceptionally large photo. The limousine window surrounding the pictured man was framed concentrically by the car's chrome.

The man's face, through which leered a pair of soulless black eyes, was overshadowed on his right by a black coat, presumably Shulman's. His left side, however, remained quite visible. His thin lips curled openly, as if to laugh. But at what? The world? Here, in the camera shop, the levity had long ago subsided. Baring his teeth, this man seemed prepared to bite — which he had been known to do on several occasions. In Malberg, as well as other places, he was known for an exceptionally sick and whimsical sense of humor. All this immediately crossed the mind of Rabbi Shapiro.

"Oh, no," he whispered.

Moshe, standing behind him, nodded in grim remembrance. Long ago, a special gassing had been done in this man's honor — and Moshe's sister Henia had been one of the participants.

"Why should it surprise us that he's still alive?" he asked, fighting to control his trembling.

"Strange . . ." Rabbi Shapiro murmured, in a tone of voice that echoed his nighttime cries. "They told me he had died. In Uruguay. Of course, they also said that Schmidt was sick and living in Honduras. I should have known, actually. That kind of man doesn't die easily."

"Ta," Shimshon asked timidly, "who is that man?"

His father answered softly, "His name, Shimshon, is Ludwig Dietrich."

The boy stared intently at the photo and ventured, "He's someone important, right?"

His father smiled. Silently unrolling his sleeve, he displayed the cigarette burn. Shimshon remembered.

"*He* was the one?"

His father nodded.

The boy whistled fearfully. "He's the one you told me about? An important Nazi in New York? He was seen by friends of yours?"

His father nodded again. "When Mordechai Silverman told me of the man he had seen, I just couldn't believe it. Wasn't he dead and buried? After all these years I can still be naive." He sighed in utter dejection.

Shimshon realized that he himself was trembling. He did not

know why, but he felt like crying. He should have been happy that he had successfully exposed the secret side of Avraham Shulman, but somehow he did not feel at all like a hero. Instead, he felt like an intruder — a ghoul who had crept into a graveyard of hidden deeds and thoughts, and dug up something rotten and ugly to show the world. Previously, because Shulman had been photographed alone, there was enough room left open for doubt — and hope — as to his true character. Now these photographs confirmed it. Shulman was in league with Amalek. The boy was truly saddened.

Moshe studied another photograph. Pointing to someone next to Dietrich, he asked, "Who is this man?"

"I have no idea," answered the rabbi.

"That's Heinz," Shimshon piped.

Moshe turned to Rabbi Shapiro. "What do you think, Yehuda?"

The rabbi shrugged. "Probably a bodyguard. Nothing more. Couldn't possibly be a mastermind. But hardly less dangerous."

"You don't think this Heinz was seen by Mordechai as well?" asked Moshe.

"Probably. But Heinz wouldn't be worth noticing. It was Dietrich who caught his attention."

"When was that?"

"Three months ago." The rabbi lapsed into silence. Three months ago the seeds of treachery had just been planted. Shimshon had still been quietly attending school, and the rabbi had considered sending him to Monsey for Passover to be out of range. Then life was still free of torturing doubts. But it was too late for that. Three months ago was already ancient history.

"Menachem Glazer described a man much shorter than either

of these two," Moshe said, growing agitated. "Perhaps that is why we weren't able to confirm until now that it was Dietrich. Glazer's report differed from Silverman's."

"Apparently Menachem was thinking of someone else," the rabbi commented.

"There are other men with Dietrich. There *have* to be."

"Shimmy said he saw four."

"Shimmy," Moshe said, turning anxiously to Shimshon. "You said Schmidt called Heinz by name. Do you remember him identifying anyone else?"

"No," Shimshon answered vaguely. "I don't think so."

"*Please*," implored the man, shaking the boy emphatically. "You must remember. Were there any other names mentioned?"

"That guy Dietrich seemed like the leader . . . I couldn't get the other names . . ."

"Were any of them short?"

"Kind of . . ." Shimshon desperately focused his mind on the four men he had seen that night entering the limousine, trying to remember what they looked like. Suddenly, his face brightened. "Mr. Kaplan, I wrote down the license plate number of the limousine in the pictures."

Moshe turned to the rabbi. "Mordechai said he saw Dietrich in a limousine."

"Think it's the same one, Mosh?"

"We'll find out. Shimmy, you're a better detective than I thought."

"Thanks," the boy answered, feeling dazed and overwhelmed.

"We'll track down the plate and the company," Moshe continued eagerly, as if he were the twelve-year-old instead of Shimshon. "It might give us a clue as to where they went."

Rabbi Shapiro looked away pensively. "I would be more interested to find out where they are now — and what they're doing in New York."

"The limousine company might know. They might give us a hotel address."

"Where did Mordechai see him?"

"Queens, I think. He was on his way back from a *bris* in Rego Park. He saw them approach a limousine parked outside an apartment building."

The rabbi leaned forward, in sudden interest. "What is the address?"

Moshe squinted, deep in thought. "I think it was something Wetherole Street."

"Was it 278-10?"

"Why, yes," Moshe answered, amazed. "How did you know?"

"Because Schimdt was spotted there."

The face of Yehuda Shapiro was lost in reflective calculation. "Jack Rifkin wrote down the names of several areas where Schmidt was seen. He said that Schmidt seemed to be wandering and looking around, as if he were trying to find something."

"What do you think it is, Yehuda?"

"I don't know. But he stopped by certain buildings and looked at them intently. Then he walked away."

"Was he looking to buy other property?"

"Possibly."

"Do you think Schmidt owns these other buildings? Or Dietrich?"

"It would most likely be in Schmidt's name — Shulman's, that is. It would certainly be easy to find out. We could contact the superintendents."

"And if the limousine service gave us the names of these places, we might find a pattern, Yehuda! That's a great idea!" Moshe wheeled around, beaming. "We might be able to track them down."

"And catch them," Shimshon interjected. "Especially Schmidt." The boy giggled with delight. "Ta, I guess it was worth it for me to go there today. Even if I had to risk my life. Heinz really gave me quite a scare when he chased me."

The rabbi turned, a look of horror on his face. "He did what?!"

Shimshon sank in painful remembrance. He reluctantly described how Heinz had spotted him from afar with the camera and, along with the others, sent him running helter skelter.

The rabbi sank into the vinyl stool. "Oh, no. Shimmy, tell me you weren't seen by them today."

The boy answered nervously, "I . . . I'm afraid so, Ta. That's why I ran into your building . . . remember?"

Gloomily, the rabbi said, "Then they know they're being watched. You might say that we are all marked. None of us is safe. We're all in this. Now it's a question of who gets whom. Shimmy, you might have put your life in more serious danger than you realize."

The boy froze in shock. "But . . . they wouldn't hurt me," he said. "A kid?" His eyes leaked tears of terror.

His father and the photographer remained silent. Shimshon tried desperately to blot out the fact that Hans Schmidt had once run a children's camp — and that a million-and-a-half people even younger than Shimshon had died in such places, at the hands of such people.

"I think if they had wanted to harm the boy they would have done it a long time ago, Yehuda," Moshe finally suggested. "After all, they knew Shimshon had seen them previously. Up until now he has been left alone. In fact, I often have had the feeling that Shimshon has been given extra protection from above."

"Before, I imagine, they were afraid," answered the rabbi. "They were able to remain underground. Harming Shimshon would have exposed them. And he wasn't sure of their identity. Now, they may feel there's no choice. My son has been a nuisance to Schmidt and his friends. Thanks to him, they've already been exposed — and identified. Shimshon has seen too much. He knows too much. He would be completely counterproductive to their plans. Also, before it was *me* they were after, not him. Now these men have a double reason to go after him — to keep him out of their affairs, and to get back at me. Schmidt knows that if he destroys my son he'll destroy me. And the public is in Schmidt's corner."

"Yehuda, not in front of Shimshon!"

"I want him to hear this. Let him realize the kind of beast we are fighting!"

"But these pictures will shed new light," Moshe argued. "They'll stir public pressure against Schmidt. Then he'll back off. He won't touch your son."

"I don't think the pictures alone would turn the tide. They'll make it look like an accident. Schmidt will appear blameless."

Shimshon, in a corner, was cringing with fear.

"We'll put them behind bars. We'll send these pictures everywhere . . . the commissions, the Justice Department. We'll have demonstrations — mass picketing in front of federal buildings."

The rabbi laughed bitterly. "Demonstrations. A bunch of old men carrying placards."

"It's worked before," Moshe cried passionately. "Think of Soviet Jewry, Yehuda. Now that we have evidence of who he's involved with, they'll listen to us."

"And while I'm running around in circles again trying to convince people, Dietrich will have us followed. He'll come around . . . to school, to camp . . . a gun in his hand, aimed at my son! Right now, I can no longer even be concerned with bringing these men to justice." The rabbi sat down wearily. "I just want them to leave Shimmy alone. He's all I have left." His shoulders shook in silent dread.

Shimshon looked sadly at Moshe, then at his father. "Ta, tonight can I sleep at Zev's house?" he asked shakily. "Maybe I'll be safe there. I told him all about those men. He knows what's going on."

His father asked keenly, "Who else did you tell, Shimshon?"

The boy squirmed in embarrassment. He had never been one to keep secrets. "Oh . . . just a few friends."

"Who've told 'just a few' of their friends, no doubt. I didn't want anyone to know, Shimmy — neither about those men, nor about our meetings. I don't want anyone to know what took place tonight. I hope you didn't tell your friends where you were going today. Next thing you know we'll have half the school outside the building site, watching Shulman." He added bitterly, "That's all we need."

"That's it!" cried Shimshon, spinning around his father and nearly knocking the telescope off its tripod.

"What?" his father asked flatly.

"What you said before! A demonstration! That's what we need! Only . . . have kids out there in front of the restaurant — my friends; and your friends also."

The rabbi looked at his son intently. "Are you serious, Shimmy?"

"See you on the six o'clock news," Moshe said sarcastically, putting away the photographs.

"You know, Mosh, I think he might have something there," the rabbi said, rising.

"And why that instead of 'old men'? Or the press? Hasn't Shimmy been exposed to enough danger?"

"You don't understand, Mosh. The press will be far more sympathetic to children. Especially in light of Schmidt's past. If we bring the Schmidt case out into the open — show mass support — Schmidt and his men will be frightened away. And it will get the public interested again. Not to mention protect my son."

Moshe shook his head doubtfully. "I don't know, Yehuda. It sounds dangerous. There's no telling what Schmidt might do in retaliation. It's bad enough having Shimshon's life in danger. I hate the thought of getting an entire group of kids involved."

"But don't you see, Mosh?" The rabbi grabbed his friend's arm forcefully. "They won't touch a large group of children. They *can't.* Besides, the only way to combat these men is to make a show of force. And there is safety in numbers. At this point, if we try to act secretly, they'll react secretly. We must fight Schmidt openly."

"This might make Schmidt move back underground. And leave you and your son sitting ducks."

"I disagree that we would be in danger. A demonstration like this might put pressure on the public to reexamine the Schmidt case. Especially with the evidence of the photographs. And if it either intimidates or humiliates Schmidt enough, I think Shimmy would be safe from harm. If we shine so much light on Schmidt that he cannot be invisible, I think we'll be buying ourselves time."

"My friends would want to help out," Shimshòn exclaimed. Watching his father made his own excitement grow. "Zev, and Calev, and Jonathan, and the rest."

"Will they believe you, Shimmy?" his father asked with a sudden trace of sadness. He remembered the time he had spent in the bathroom cleaning the blood off his son.

"They will now, Ta. After what I saw. We can get half of Boro Park and Flatbush there. There must be a couple of hundred of us at school. Me and my friends—"

"My friends and I," the rabbi corrected.

"My friends and I could arrange transportation — charter buses or something — and they can take us after school to the building." He gesticulated wildly. "The kids can start shouting against this Nazi creep. And they'll hold up signs. It'll attract reporters — they'll listen to kids."

"You know, it just might work," his father said, smiling at him. "Shimshon, that's quite an idea! Sometimes that mind of yours . . ."

Moshe also smiled at the boy. "You'll go a long way, kid. And I don't mean in photography."

"Then it's agreed," the rabbi said. "We'll contact all the schools in the general New York area. We'll set a date to be there."

"It must be soon," Moshe added. "Very soon. Thursday, if possible."

"Yes. There's no telling when Schmidt will act. Or how long Shimmy can stay out of danger."

"I don't mean that, Yehuda. I'm thinking about how long the schools will still be open. Before the kids go off to camp. My oldest son's already leaving next week, because they want the counselors there ahead of time."

"Oh, you're right." The rabbi frowned. "Then that leaves us twenty-four hours to make all the necessary phone calls. Shimmy, do you think you can spread the word around?"

"Can I!" The boy jumped up and down excitedly. "I'll make sure that all my friends come and that they bring their families too."

His father turned to Moshe. "Call as many limousine services as possible. Give them that license plate number. Find out if there's a correlation between its destinations and the different buildings. Who knows? This might be the first of many demonstrations."

Moshe said quietly, "I have a better suggestion, Yehuda. *You* call them . . . and *I'll* call the yeshiva principals."

"Do you think you can persuade them, Mosh?"

Moshe grinned. "I've done half their weddings. They still owe me. Amazing, isn't it — how money talks."

Rabbi Shapiro, remembering the lambasting he had recently undergone by the public, suddenly became somber. "We have the evidence of the photographs. But how will we bring it before the public? To the people who've been following this case, I'm a laughing stock!"

Moshe patted the rabbi on his right shoulder. "Yehuda, leave it to me."

Sure enough, within several hours, lampposts throughout Boro Park and Flatbush had been covered with xeroxes of the pictures Shimshon had taken. And just as quickly, public opinion turned. Many people recognized the Nazi butchers depicted in the photos. They became filled with fury at the man who had demonstrated the gall to masquerade as a Jew, when he was no more than a Nazi beast.

As for the yeshivos, they had never been so cooperative, and Moshe Kaplan never so convincing. By the end of the day, the various principals agreed to postpone some finals and allow the students to take off half of Thursday in order to participate in the demonstration.

Accordingly, Thursday afternoon, some 2,000 youths descended upon midtown Manhattan. Some came by bus, others by subway or car. The day was pleasantly bright and sunny; every cloud in the sky had been eliminated for this occasion. Many of the students, their spirits already heightened by the imminent end of school, were rejoicing in the weather and the chance to be outdoors, anticipating summer's approach and the exhilaration it always brought. Toddlers clutched the hands of their older brothers and sisters; some of the bigger students had signs slung over their shoulders.

Shimshon and his father were waiting outside the restaurant, standing on a "podium" — a number of boards resting on top of bricks and boxes. In his hand Shimshon held his father's megaphone. Together with Zev, who had gotten a ride in with them, they watched the avenue swell with young people.

"Is he here?" Zev asked Shimshon.

"Who?"

"Shulman."

"You mean Schmidt. I think so. A friend of Ta saw him leave this morning for Manhattan."

Zev surveyed the swelling population and whistled. "Will you look at this crowd, Shimmy? Wow. I haven't seen this many people since the Pirchei rally."

"Yeah," Shimshon said, "looks like half of Boro Park came."

"Half of New York. They must have come from all over — some of them. Check it out, Shimmy. They all have banners identifying them. There's our yeshiva there . . . I see Bobov . . . Ger . . . Lubavitch. There's Bais Yaakov. And B.Y.A. There's Flatbush. And Shulamis. And Prospect Park. Hey, they even brought the older guys in. I see my brother's friends. Why, there's my cousin!" Zev yelled, "Hey, Shraga! Hi!"

"Shhh!" Shimshon hissed. "This is supposed to be serious."

"Well, I *am* serious," his friend protested. "Didn't I help you make all those calls last night? I really heard it from Dad for tying up the phone."

"You can talk to Shraga later. You have to help me."

Zev shrugged, and turned away so that he was facing the restaurant. Through the tinted glass he saw human shapes. "They're looking at us, Shimmy."

"Who?"

"The people inside the restaurant. They're wondering what's going on."

"Good! Maybe they'll join us."

To the right Rabbi Shapiro was arguing with Aharon Zimmerman.

"We have a right to gather here, Mr. Zimmerman," the rabbi asserted firmly, his arms folded. "It's in the Constitution." His words, in Yiddish, were partly drowned out by the sound of helicopters circling overhead. "We know our rights. And we have a permit to use a megaphone. But I assure you that our demonstration will be peaceful. There will be no violence."

Zimmerman wrung his hands pleadingly. "You don't understand the damage you are about to cause. Please. I beg you to call off all these children. They should not be involved in this."

"Mr. Zimmerman, do you have any children?"

"Yes, I have five. In fact, I have grandchildren."

"Then you certainly should be sympathetic to us. Especially as a survivor. You must know the damage and devastation that people their age went through — and be determined that it will never happen again." He added passionately, "I am surprised that you can still defend the likes of Schmidt."

"Rabbi Shapiro," countered the man earnestly, "I assure you that I have given quite generously to the memorial institutions." He raised his arm to display the blue tattoo. "I wear this proudly on my arm — and in my heart. It is not my intention to cover up the truth. I am not blinded by greed or impure motives. I do not associate with evil people. I just wish to avoid situations with damaging consequences. What you are doing is dangerous to us all."

"Your attempt to silence us is far more dangerous, Mr. Zimmerman. You are trying to still the rage of an entire people. There were men like you in the ghettos and camps. If you still feel, after all these years, that by being quiet trouble will disappear, then you haven't learned a thing from the Holocaust."

Zimmerman sighed. He scanned the length and breadth of Thirty-seventh Street, now jam-packed, and knew that he would not have his way. He had never been one to argue. He couldn't argue with Shulman; all the more so with an angry rabbi and hordes of screaming kids. Perhaps Shulman had met his match.

"As you wish," he finally said. "I won't interfere. I only ask that you not harass my customers."

"I assure you, Mr. Zimmerman, that everything will be done according to the law."

The restaurateur turned to the construction crew, sadly dismissing them with a wave of the hand, and retreated inside.

"Shulman is here," Moshe Kaplan panted, coming up to Rabbi Shapiro. A camera hung around his neck.

"Yes. I was told he's been here since eight this morning. *'Tzaddikim'* get up early, you know. But he hasn't graced us with his presence. Not yet, anyway. He's stayed inside his office so far."

"Does he know about this?"

"I'm sure he's been informed."

Moshe smiled. "Once we get the kids to start yelling, that will drive him out . . . like a rat from a ship."

The rabbi smiled in return. The picture ironically came to his mind of a pied piper, whose melody in the past had held so much sway over young people. Now this man had the chance once again to be before such an audience.

"I have a report on the limousine," said the rabbi, still watching the crowd.

Moshe's eyes widened in interest. "Yes?"

"Three of the locations matched Schmidt's. They also listed the Lorelei."

"What's that?"

"A German restaurant a quarter-of-a-mile from here. They stopped there a lot to eat. Incidentally, the limousine was leased under the name Diego Lopez."

"Do you think that's the name Dietrich uses?"

"Certainly sounds like it. I should think the gentleman would have enough sense to pick a name which didn't merely transpose his initials. And to think I gave these people credit for pragmatism."

"What name did he use in Uruguay?"

"Gunther Hartmann." The rabbi added bitterly, "Deceased in 1979."

Shimshon came running up to his father. "Ta," he said breathlessly, "I think everyone's here. I see a bunch of your friends."

Moshe turned to the rabbi. "Glazer was on the phone till three in the morning."

"Wonderful. Leave it to Menachem to get things done."

"Ta," Shimshon asked, "what should I do now?"

The rabbi scanned the scene. Around him, tens of feet above, heads poked out of windows like pegs. He had hoped that one of them might be Shulman's, and he sighed in growing disappointment. He would hate to see the demonstration end up being ineffectual.

Suddenly he brightened with inspiration. "Well, Shimmy," he said slowly, "since this is your idea, I'm going to let you take over. I'll watch. Take the megaphone. You know what to do."

The boy gasped. "Me?"

"Yes."

"You want *me* to lead them?"

"Of course. You're a big boy."

"I . . . I don't think I can, Ta. I'm too nervous."

"About what?"

"I don't know," the boy answered vaguely. He stared in the direction of the building, and the thought of Shulman lurking inside made his stomach turn queasy with nausea. "I guess I'm too shy."

"Shy? You? I hardly think so. You can do it, Shimshon. Shulman's still inside the building. We have to get him out. It's up to you. Do you remember the Pirchei rally?"

"Yes," the boy answered, trembling.

"Well, if you shout the same way you led the cheers there, I think it might work. Zev can join in."

With immense trepidation, Shimshon turned to the street. The crowd was already beginning to stir restlessly, ready to burst. Something had to happen, or they would leave.

The boy took a deep breath. "All right. Here goes."

With a certain majesty, the boy advanced toward the center of the podium. When Zev, who was waving to acquaintances, saw the look in his friend's eye, he backed away and motioned to the crowd to be silent.

Shimshon gazed across the crowd, and the initial terror which had engulfed and silenced him slowly, strangely dissipated, giving way to a growing sense of power and strength.

Holding the megaphone close to his lips, he hollered, "Listen up, everybody. Quiet, please."

They continued to murmur.

"I want it *quiet!*"

The crowd hushed. From the distance was heard the honking of cars caught in traffic on Seventh Avenue.

The boy swallowed. Feeling over two thousand pairs of eyes on him, he suddenly felt the stage fright returning and debated whether to call his father over. At last he drew in another breath, and continued to speak over the megaphone. "Uh . . . you all know why we're here today . . . and I . . . I want to thank you all for coming." He stared helplessly at Zev. His friend winked in encouragement. Shimshon continued, "Uh . . . we have to let this guy Schmidt know he's not getting away with anything. Right?"

Immediately the crowd roared. Shimshon smiled, dazed, and

again raised the megaphone.

"We have to see this guy behind bars, right?"

The crowd cheered.

In growing elation the boy turned around and faced the building, in which lurked Shulman. In the distance he saw his father, surrounded by reporters, smiling. Nearby, Menachem Glazer and his father's other friends were standing, mouthing their approval.

Shimshon again turned and faced the crowd. "We won't let another Holocaust happen, right?"

"*No!*" the children shouted.

"We have to remember the six million that were killed!" Shimshon cried. "And many of them were kids like us. Babies, even. They were killed by people like Hans Schmidt. He's here, in this building. We have to let him know what we think of him." The boy paused. "So I want you all to call out after me: 'Nazi murderer!' "

"Nazi murderer!" the crowd responded in unison.

"Get out of America!"

"Get out of America!"

"Never again!"

"Never again!" This time some of the adults were joining in as well.

The last cry, as if on special command, finally penetrated the concrete walls, echoing through the hallways. In his office, Avraham Shulman, who had been inside all day and who until now had been carefully scribbling figures, pen in one hand and calculator in the other, looked up. Accustomed as he was to the rat-a-tat of the jackhammer, it suddenly occurred to him that it was strangely quiet — until the cry of *Never again!* pierced his ears, producing an expression on his face, first of recognition, then of dread. He put down his instruments, went across the hallway, and looked curiously out the window.

"Oh, no," he groaned.

His blue eyes bulged. In horror they swept across a sea of faces, mostly children's and adolescents', which were choking the entire block and spilling over onto Seventh and Eighth Avenues. Girls in dresses, boys in skullcaps of all varieties, with earlocks long and short, adults — some in long black coats and hats, others in suits, yet others in jeans and T-shirts, and even mothers with babies — all were staring his way in loathing and contempt. Signs were being held up high. Some were crudely painted, with childish misspellings. Some signs were carried by those who were too young to even understand their meaning. On one there was an old photograph of him in Nazi uniform, next to one of Ludwig Dietrich. Another showed a picture of a globe surrounded by barbed wire, with the message under it: "The Nazis plan to take over the world."

Suddenly, someone pointed up. The crowd slowly focused its attention on him. The protesters became frenzied. Raising their signs even higher, they merged their voices until all one heard was a violent crescendo. Below on his right Shulman saw the face of Rabbi Yehuda Shapiro sneering victoriously at him. In the center stood Shimshon, waving the megaphone like a baton and looking up over his shoulder toward the window. A bigger boy stood at his side, snarling. A row of police cars had pulled up near the intersection, forcing the crowd to split, Red Sea-like, and press in further against the podium.

Shulman, in horror, looked away. The sight of the thin, brown-haired figure of Shimshon conducting this strange orchestra was frightening. Yet, in a way Shulman felt fascinated by and even proud of Shimshon, who, standing authoritatively before the masses, seemed so much a leader. Shulman guessed, from the median age of the crowd, that this entire demonstration was Shimshon's idea, and he almost wished he could come down and compliment the boy on his ingenuity. Though frightened by the display, Shulman couldn't help but make certain comparisons with himself. If only you could be one of us, Shimshon, he thought. If only you could be one of us.

Nevertheless, Shulman backed away from the window and hurried to his desk. Trembling, he dialed.

After quite a few rings, Shulman grew anxious. At last came an accented voice. "Empire."

"Where is Aharon Zimmerman?"

"Oh, why, Mr. Shulman," responded the voice. "It's good you all right."

"Who is this?"

"Mario. Everyone leave. They go out through back. Where are you?"

"Upstairs. What is happening?"

"Children make big demonstration." The busboy said with a laugh, "They think Nazi here."

"Let me speak to Mr. Zimmerman."

"He no here, Mr. Shulman."

"Did he leave?"

"Yes. I lock up."

"Did he go home?" Shulman demanded.

"He no say, Mr. Shulman."

"I'll speak to him later."

"Can I go home, Mr. Shulman?"

"Yes, you may."

"Thank you. Goodbye."

"Goodbye," Shulman answered, slowly putting down the receiver.

In utter weariness, he rested his forehead against his hands. He felt his temples pulsating.

If only Shimshon could know, he thought. He must be told. It can no longer be put off. He, Shulman, should have done it long ago. He had been content to leave Shimshon dangling in suspense and pursuing his amateur detective work. He had even found it amusing to see the boy stand in the alleyway with the camera. But he had miscalculated the length of time he could wait. Also, he had miscalculated the determination of the boy's father — as well as the boy's devotion to his father. Before, Shulman thought it had been dangerous. But he had never expected it to go this far. Now it was up to him to put a stop to this lunacy. It had gone beyond all bounds.

Shulman sighed, as he pondered the risks of getting the boy deeply involved in something dangerously beyond the latter's realm. Shulman had already overexerted himself to keep the boy out of harm's way — even after Heinz had spotted him. But at this point there was no choice. Shimshon, no less than his father, was marked. He was already more deeply involved than he could possibly be aware.

Shulman felt somewhat better at having reached a solution at last. He reached for the phone and began to dial.

Chapter 13

Heroes

The West Side apartment was located on a secluded street, opposite a massive construction site. Its large windows, overlooking the Hudson River eleven stories down, would have luxuriously received the late afternoon light, if not for the drawn curtains, which left the interior in furtive darkness. Every light had been left off, save in the living room, where a solitary lamp rested on a rickety end table. Occasionally the window was opened, very cautiously, in order to let out some of the cigarette smoke, which left the living room permeated with a thick gray haze.

Even with the lights on there was very little worth noticing about the apartment. What scant furniture existed was a melancholy mismatch of pieces, suggesting that either its inhabitants had just moved in, or that the decorator simply didn't care. Where a Louis XIV cabinet may have reclined or a Monet painting might have hung now stood bare walls, glaring in their whiteness. On the ceiling dangled a chandelier, with half its crystal missing and four of its branches chipped. In place of an enticing velvet sofa stood three folding chairs, where three men sat, conversing in agitated whispers.

On the floor, where a Persian rug could have lain, were strewn well-filled ash trays and empty Coke cans. After a while one of the men went to the kitchen, opened the ancient refrigerator door, and poked his head inside.

"*Ach!* Out of soda," he growled. He slammed the door shut and, going over to the air conditioner, kicked it in disgust.

He was a big man — stocky, around thirty, with curly black hair and an olive complexion made even more dark by the fierce Mediterranean sun. His sleeves, soaked in sweat, were rolled up, revealing his hairy arms, and his massive chest was barely concealed under the partly unbuttoned shirt.

He returned to the living room, where the two others were still in fervent debate. One man seemed to do most of the talking; the other listened, and watched.

The man speaking passionately, in a foreign tongue, waved his thin hands wildly, and at one point began pacing the room. Facing the floor, his short body slightly bent, he conveyed the image of a bird scanning the ground in search of a worm or an insect. His audience of two smiled, and the hairy man thoughtfully moved the chair away so the speaker wouldn't trip over it.

The latter paused, in the middle of his ravings, to cast a look in the direction of his subordinates, as if waiting for a response. He sensed they were as fascinated with his rhetoric as he was. In the three years of their existence as a team, the antics of their leader had never ceased to amaze his two younger colleagues. Though physically taller and stronger than he — they would have been even were he their age — they were deferrent, afraid that his powerful mental acuity, pulsating from his irises like an overcircuited computer, would suddenly lash out and strike them. In the stuffy apartment, which was sweltering because the air conditioner was in poor shape, the sweat oozed out of his balding top and dribbled into the whitening remains of his hair.

As the man spoke of the need for justice, he turned his head back and forth — facing them, then facing the wall. His tongue, which, even after forty years, was still with his native accent, now tripped over his rapid-fire speech, unable to keep up with his train of ideas.

He was cut short by the telephone's ringing. The two others jumped. The hairy man went to answer it.

"No! Wait two more rings," the older man commanded.

The subordinate paused tensely. After two more rings, he picked up the receiver. "Hello?" he barked. He listened for a moment, then turned to the older man. "Here," he said gruffly, handing him the receiver and turning away.

The young men watched as their leader listened intensely over the phone.

"Yes," he began tersely. "What? . . . Are you kidding?" His facial expression changed, along with his tone of voice, from initial impatience to amazement to solemnity. "It's a risk," he calculated doubtfully, "but I agree . . . we may have no choice. If you're willing to chance it . . . do what you can. Good luck."

After he hung up the phone, he gave an exaggerated shrug and sighed. "A snag in our plans. Not important, really — happens all the time."

The hairy man eyed him keenly. "Shulman?" he growled.

The leader nodded.

The hairy man looked away in dismay. "I'd be afraid to ask what went wrong this time." His voice, in contrast to his leader's high-pitched tone, was quite low and masculine.

"Nothing," the smaller man cooed, like a father calming his worried child. "I assure you, Raffi, that everything is still under control."

"He was supposed to have gotten back to us hours ago," Raffi argued. "Instead, we've had to stay here and bake our brains out."

"I could call out for more Coke," his companion offered weakly.

"Also food. I'm starving," Raffi replied.

"We all are." His companion turned to the older man. "You know, he's right, Naftali. We seem to have hit so many stone walls. If it's not one thing, it's something else. First the rabbi, then the press . . ."

"All that was taken care of," Naftali countered hastily.

"And you still believe that he'll do the job?"

"He always has. He has never let us down." Naftali again raised his hands. "Remember Eberhardt?"

"That was awhile ago," replied Raffi.

"So what? He got him, didn't he? He helped us then."

"With great reluctance," answered Raffi's companion sourly. "This time we had to practically drag him out of Kiryat Yovel. He didn't want to leave his holy books."

The last words, in reference to religion, were spoken with such contempt that Naftali Hertz eyed his subordinate cynically. He knew how Aryeh Kessler, third-generation pioneer, felt about bearded old men.

"I might have been in Kiryat Yovel myself," Naftali soberly announced. "But because of Ludwig Dietrich, I'm not."

The origins of Naftali Hertz could be traced to Cracow, Poland, where his family had migrated from Germany and dwelt for nearly four hundred years. The Hertz family had settled comfortably in a city renowned for its Torah scholars, and there established a mini-dynasty of its own of chassidim and community leaders. There Naftali's father, Azriel Hertz, married at eighteen and by middle age had sired nine children. While building up his garment business, he spent two hours a day in the local *beis midrash,* all the while longing for the day that he could devote all his energies to Talmud study.

Naftali, born in 1921, was a sickly child — small, with piercing brown eyes, and an expression that was wise, like an old man's. He was aptly named after his grandfather, a Torah scholar who as a youth was also sickly, and who might thus possibly intercede on behalf of the frail infant. His parents fretted over him constantly, doubting if the tiny boy would survive. Nevertheless, he grew — in years, if not in height — and became a special joy to his father, who saw in the youngster an intensely analytical mind, so suited to the study of Jewish works.

By the time the boy was eight, he had already become well-versed in Chumash. He could conjure up, quite accurately, a mental map of the Land of Israel in the different historical periods just by reading the Biblical passages. He took prophetic delight at mapping ancient military strategies, and even devised a few of his own. When, the following year, he began studying Mishnah, he displayed an amazing ability for analysis and memorization, and he was praised in front of his father.

"An *illuy* — a budding genius," his rebbe said, his face radiant. "Just like his grandfather."

"G-d willing, he'll rear many Torah scholars," Azriel Hertz replied.

The boy's bar mitzvah speech, delivered in front of prominent rabbis, left them so impressed that they persuaded his father to have him placed in one of Cracow's leading yeshivos, rather than at a small place out of town. Naftali, though he had hoped to see the world a little bit, nevertheless looked forward to years of further study and great discussions with great men. He would make his parents proud.

The next five years were filled with drills, review, and memorization. The boy felt the wisdom rapidly sinking in, as water saturates thirsty roots, until his mind was ready to overflow and burst. Three-quarters of the day was spent studying Talmud, the rest on the Shulchan Aruch and its commentaries. Naftali enjoyed the different disciplines. He specialized in anticipating the Talmud's give and take. He even compiled a notebook of his own thoughts, which the *rosh yeshiva* suggested be published.

The adolescent spent many evenings with the family of the *rosh yeshiva,* who treated the young man like a son. Naftali ate his meals there, often studying afterwards with the pious, older scholar until late in the evening. The rebbetzin tried in vain to fatten the boy with her cooking, but Naftali remained small and rather frail. In compensation, his fervent mind kept his pint-sized body battery-charged.

In the mornings, after services, the boy studied with his father, who would come from the other side of town just to be with his son. Watching his son argue about the Talmud with his study partner made Azriel Hertz euphoric; he was even more elated when Naftali announced his plans for a rabbinic career. Sometimes, in the afternoon, when he needed a break, Naftali dropped in on his father's factory for a visit and a friendly chat. He often joked with his brother Simcha, who was a year younger and worked there. Simcha, who admittedly lacked a mind for intensive Torah study, displayed his mother's talent with a needle and thread; he even taught his older brother how to sew, much to the latter's amusement. Naftali didn't realize how handy this skill would come in later in his life.

Naftali loved his charmed life. Most of all, he loved the yeshiva. The yeshiva building was old, but the walls were thick — able to block out the trauma and turmoil of recent events, both in Poland and elsewhere. During these years, places like Auschwitz and Treblinka and Belzec were still obscure towns on a map, and no one could ever think of them otherwise — least of all young Naftali, who by 1939 had mastered much of the Talmud. The horror stories, to be sure, had reached Cracow — brought by refugees, Polish Jews who had been expelled from Germany. Nevertheless, Germany remained a distant world, even after Austria and Czechoslovakia had been gobbled up — and even after the latest German indignation over Danzig and the "Polish corridor," and Hitler's talk of all-out war. After all, Britain and France were backing Poland, weren't they? How could Hitler ever dare make good on such threats? By August 1939, Naftali Hertz's biggest concern was deciding on a proper marriage partner from among the opportunities being presented him by several matchmakers.

The boy's world was shattered the following month, when Hitler actually followed through on his threats and declared war on Poland. Cracow itself was spared much of the relentless bombing and harassment that Warsaw and other cities suffered. Nevertheless, the large Jewish population of Cracow was not spared the terror that lay ahead.

Naftali was in the *beis midrash* that morning in November 1939, as usual, with his father, when the SS men invaded the yeshiva. Savagely kicking down the door, the soldiers stormed the place, overturning books and furniture, shooting at random, and making their way into the main hall. The *rosh yeshiva*, a scion of great rabbis, looked up, bewildered, from his Talmud volume, just before the top of his head was blown away. In no time the yeshiva walls were splattered with blood and brains. In raucous laughter the soldiers approached the ark and threw its doors wide open. When Naftali's father rushed to the ark in an effort to defend the Torah scrolls from desecration, he was struck through the heart by a bullet, and he immediately slumped over, dead.

His son, in the meantime, had been dragged out of his chair and thrown into the street, where a group of frightened Jewish men were already rounded up and waiting. Some of them had been beaten; others had had their beards set on fire. Still others were forced to entertain the delighted crowd of onlookers with humiliating acts. Amidst the tumult, Naftali tore his cloak in mourning, though parts of his coat had already been ripped by SS guards.

At age eighteen Naftali Hertz found himself the head of the family. He and his mother, brothers, and sisters were shipped to the newly-formed ghetto in the Government General. This was the place he was to call home for the next two years. This was also where he was to lose all innocence.

The boy quit the yeshiva, forever closing the doors on formal academia. With his brother Simcha he went to work at one of the factories, sorting and mending German uniforms. From nine in the morning till nine at night he toiled at a sewing machine, and for his efforts was given a ration of soup made with straw.

Through a fellow worker Naftali came in contact with the budding underground, a group of young, mainly secular Jews who had been discontented even in prewar times. The underground was an extension of the various prewar factions.

Naftali, who in the past hardly knew the name of the Polish president — and cared not a wit — was bewildered by the vast array of political differences, and sickened by the bickering that went on within these groups because of their differences. There were Zionists, Labor Zionists, Religious Zionists, Communists, Socialists — people of every creed, each with its own ideas and its own vision of utopia. Valiantly, they spoke of the temporariness of the German occupation and the glorious future that awaited Poland (or Palestine, depending on whichever ideology).

Naftali, though naive when it came to politics, knew enough about utopia to be certain these groups did not have the answer. Nevertheless, he listened patiently to the exchange of ideas, finding somehow pathetic the references to "freedom for all mankind." In light of Poland's history of anti-Semitism, he wondered if "all mankind" included Jews. Seeing the growing dejection and degeneration in the ghetto made him ponder, even more despairingly, if there might even be enough Jews left in Poland after the war. One by one, he watched his family members die — and the greater his feelings of rage, the greater his desire for revenge against German barbarism became. He had hoped to see the underground unite militarily, and rather than speak of the future concentrate instead on the present — killing every Nazi who walked the earth. Only then, he thought, would there be "freedom for all mankind."

Naftali and Simcha were working in the uniform factory one day in February 1942 when a Gestapo officer burst into the hall and invalidated all work permits. Naftali and the other laborers were swiftly herded into the outer courtyard and were marched off to the *Umshlagplatz,* where the trains were already waiting.

The train station was a writhing mass of filth and hysteria.

Mothers clutched their babies, old men prayed, children wept as their parents argued desperately with the officers. Naftali spotted his mother, who staggered and fell as she was being pushed into one of the cars along with Naftali's sisters. When Simcha, instead of surrendering his valuables, spat in the requisitioning officer's face, he was answered with a bullet between the eyes. His body was thrown against a wall, next to the suicides. Naftali, standing nearby, watching his brother's life be brutally terminated, could not weep. It was as if he had already delivered his quota of tears, along with his quota of uniforms. In the pandemonium, he felt himself being swept along to the platform.

The cattle car they were shoved into was crowded beyond belief. Standing (for there was no room to sit), huddled together compactly, bodies pressed, these remnants of Polish Jewry swayed mournfully with the passing train, as if in prayer. Amid the moaning and weeping, some of them softly chanted *Ani Ma'amin*. The stench of the unwashed passengers — many of them already dead — permeated the entire car, and a few fainted standing up.

Pressed against the window, Naftali watched the snow-covered Polish countryside, dotted with animal tracks. Skeletal trees danced by him and an occasional fox or rabbit darted across the landscape.

The powdery snow turned light silver in the late afternoon sun, and through the frosty glass Naftali's eyes followed a row of pines, which formed a jagged pattern in the hilly skyline. In spite of the cold which seeped in, Naftali welcomed the draft, which filtered through his flimsy corduroy jacket, offering relief from the body heat around him.

A draft! Naftali's eyes turned upward and caught sight of the window above. Its top latch seemed to be loose. Struggling to free his arms, which were pinned to his sides by the adjacent bodies, he raised them to the latch, prying it and lowering it slowly, slowly . . . till it was open a good ten inches. The sudden blast of frost elicited groans of relief from the passengers.

He studied the speed of the passing landscape, calculated the distance between him and the hostile ground below, and determined his chances of surviving the impact. He studied the width of the open window, then his own thin frame, and finally decided that he had to try. What did he have to lose? If he succeeded, he might live a lot longer; if not, he would just die a little sooner.

Mumbling a prayer, he lifted his thin frame and inched his way out of the sweating flesh. For the first time in his life he was grateful for being undersized. When his foot rested on the head of a corpse, he grimaced; nevertheless, he continued making his way to the window.

At last poking his head out of the window, he felt the icy wind whip his face and he looked down. The racing tracks made him dizzy, and he momentarily reeled, paling. Then he noticed a sharp bend ahead in the tracks near a hill. He could already feel the train slowing down. He wriggled himself out of the window, extending his legs over the side of the frame, still clutching the bars. Then he waited.

Tensely, he turned his head backward. And he choked. There, just a few cars behind, a machine gun with a smiling SS guard behind it was aimed ever so carefully in his direction. At that moment, however, the train decelerated even more as it rounded the bend. Naftali pushed himself out the window. The bullet whizzed by and grazed his sunken cheek as he hurled himself rapidly down the snowy incline, tumbling and rolling over rocks and small tree stumps. Falling, falling . . . hitting patches of ice and stone, finally landing in a muddy ditch. He rested, completely oblivious to the pain and cold, absorbing the fact that he was alive . . . and free.

His eyes shut tight, he thanked G-d for giving him another chance at life. At last he opened them and the darkening winter sky above was revealed before him, imbuing him with a blessed, inner peace.

However, when he tried to raise himself, he winced, and felt his body go limp. He could not stand up. He noticed that the trail he was making in the snow, which shone dully in the dwindling sunlight, was stained with patches of red. Remembering the SS man who had seen him on the train roof, he worried that he was now easy prey for the soldiers who would eventually come.

Naftali forced himself to stand. The fact that he was able to do so made him guess that nothing was broken; the thick, recent snow had broken his fall. Nevertheless, he had suffered a number of cuts and bruises, which made any kind of rapid movement impossible. Moreover, the frost, which till now had been ignored, began to make its presence felt as it crept through his wet garments, infiltrating his bones, chilling him with the reminder that he was no longer behind the somewhat protective warmth of ghetto walls. Naftali shivered, but only partly due to the cold.

He gazed at his surroundings. A clump of pine trees nearby, shrouded in snow, hovered over the fields. Everything lay in waiting for him. Noticing tracks imbedded in the ground, Naftali bent over, with difficulty, and examined them more closely.

Footprints. Several. Men's boots, with adjacent paw prints. Naftali assumed that the area was routinely patrolled — most likely as a hiding place for partisans, and travelers like himself, courtesy of cattle cars. He wondered if others who attempted the same escape as he had survived not only the daredevil stunt but also the hostile elements, both natural and man-made. But he knew he couldn't spend too much time dwelling on the question. A small wind rustled, and sent minuscule snowflakes dancing over his face. Stumbling over branches and twigs, he wandered off in search of a village.

The bullet landed near his knee, ricocheting off a mound of rocks.

"Halt da! Komm hier!" echoed a hoarse cry, accompanied by canine barking.

Naftali dropped to the ground — just in time for a volley of rifle shots to riddle the nearby trees.

"Was siehst du da?"

"Jude."

The last word, uttered in hate, sent Naftali ducking into another hedge of trees, which opened onto a snowy ravine. Down he rolled, landing in another patch of mud. When he at last dove under a protruding rock — praying all the while not to meet a bear — he crouched, and from above heard a group of guttural voices echoing.

Too dazed to fully listen, he nevertheless caught enough German passages:

"Must have been an animal . . ."

"No, definitely a Jew . . ."

"Same thing."

"We hit him; look at all the blood . . ."

"Think he's from the trains?"

"Probably. He'll die out here anyway; it's snowing again.

We've done what we can. Let's go."

A dog whined.

"Come on, Effie."

The scrunching of jackboots faded away. In the distance a motor roared, and a set of brakes screeched. But he could not be certain they had truly left. Perhaps they were trying to draw him out. So all through the night he waited, never venturing to come up from under the rock, convinced that the soldiers were still waiting above, rifles pointed, laughing, anticipating their fun. He watched snowflakes fluttering down and felt a slight wind rustling through the trees. Towards dawn his eyes gradually closed. He sprawled under the rock, and his body, by now wracked with pain, sagged into tortured sleep.

In a dream he saw himself fleeing through the forest again — only this time the hills were verdant with spring, and the air was misty but warm. In the distance he saw a man in a prayer shawl beckoning to him; his hands were raised either in prayerful plea or joyous salutation. When Naftali, bouncing lightly on his feet as if carried by the wind, came closer, he recognized the man at once.

Tati, it's been so long.

I know, son.

Tati, I can't hold out much longer.

You must.

Why?

We need you. Your mother is here.

And Simcha?

Yes. Everybody . . . we're all here.

Can I join you?

No. We need you. The men are waiting.

Tati!

His father's form dissipated, with a crackling sound, like flames, which seemed to engulf him. He disappeared, but the noise grew louder, like a snapping branch — then another, then another.

When Naftali awoke, his eyes, caked shut with tears, reluctantly opened to witness the daylight. With great anguish he rolled over on his side, suppressing a sharp cry of pain, and propped himself up. Suddenly he noticed, near the rock, a pair of legs in shabby boots.

Crawling out from under the rock, Naftali counted additional numbers of legs. Eight. He looked up to see five men standing, sawed-off shotguns in hand, wearing faded uniforms. Five pairs of eyes rested on him, laden with hostile suspicion.

"Jew, what are you doing here?!" one of them demanded in Polish, pointing a gun.

Naftali's jaw dropped. He trembled as he studied the man behind the weapon. The latter's grizzled face was framed by a three-day stubble, and his matted blond hair hung limply over eyes which were as hard as crystal.

Naftali cringed. "I . . . I jumped off the train."

"Liar!" the man shouted. "You're here to spy!"

"No! I swear it!" Naftali cried passionately, then winced in pain. He groaned helplessly and retreated.

The grizzled man raised his gun higher.

"No! Wait!"

Heads turned to a slender young man with tousled blond hair, and gray eyes to match the cloudiness of the day. A rifle was slung casually over his shoulder, and a soldier's cap was cocked to one side. His clothes were trim and neat, along with his person, and compared to the grizzled man, he looked like a British lord on a safari.

The others parted, allowing him through. Silently he approached the ragged, bloody figure.

"How long have you been here?" he politely asked.

"Since last night."

"And how did you jump from the train?"

Naftali stared, taken aback by such a strange question, surprised that it made any difference. Nevertheless, he answered, "Through an open window. When the train rounded the bend." He added, stammering, "I hung onto the ledge and waited. I . . . I . . . I must have fallen not even a kilometer from here. I rolled down a hill, and landed here."

As he spoke, describing how he had heard a German patrol, he kept his eyes on the young man. Neither scowling at Naftali nor cutting him short, the man instead waited patiently for the latter to finish; afterwards, he turned to the others.

"He's telling the truth," he announced.

"How can you believe him?" exclaimed a squat, dirty man, speaking in a peasant drawl.

"Simple. I picked up word yesterday from one of our sentries that a man was seen jumping out the train window in proximity to our base." The young man turned to Naftali. "You're quite lucky, you know. Lucky for us all. The new snowfall wiped away your tracks. You left quite a trail."

His Polish, lilting and rhythmic, rolled off his tongue in urbane cadences. Momentarily forgetting his pain, Naftali stared, fascinated by this man. The perfect gentleman, he thought. Of course, so were many of the Nazis.

"It's a bigger miracle that you survived," the man continued casually, "and from the looks of you, in one piece. Isn't that right, Victor?"

He turned to the man standing at his left — a distinguished-looking man in early middle-age. Victor glanced at Naftali with a certain condescension, then nodded quickly and smiled. Something about Victor touched a familiar chord in Naftali, and he found himself smiling back.

"So far," the young man continued matter-of-factly, "I've seen three of them jump off, but they didn't end up like you. Usually we find them after a few days, not far from the tracks, looking quite a mess. We have to draw lots to bury them. We're afraid the bodies will attract more patrols."

Naftali grunted in disgust.

"Amazing, actually, that you're alive. It's especially difficult for somebody your size to take such a leap."

Naftali winced with insult. Then he answered, "Maybe it was *because* of my size."

The man laughed. "You *are* amazing. Somebody up there likes you."

"Yes," Naftali answered dreamily.

"What is your name?" the man asked.

"Naftali."

"Only one name?"

"Naftali Hertz."

"Andrei here. Andrei Smollar." He bowed slightly. "And this is Victor Parkowski. And Roman Kecik. I wouldn't bother introducing those men there, since they apparently can't show even a little courtesy."

The peasant and the grizzled man turned and growled.

"But I shall, anyway. The man who first greeted you is Pytor Bielasiak. And the other is Antek."

"Antek what?" Naftali shyly asked.

"We haven't decided." Andrei laughed gaily. The peasant continued to look away in open belligerence, then turned, mumbling, to Pytor. Andrei frowned. "Your manners, Antek. Really."

At the sight of these men, Naftali went numb with fear, feeling even more indebted to this Andrei for saving his life. He turned to speak, but as he twisted he suddenly doubled over in pain, and had to clutch the rock for support.

Victor ran to his side. "Sit down and breathe slowly," he commanded, in a voice both authoritative and scholarly.

Andrei quietly watched the scene. He said sadly, "Perhaps I was wrong about your condition. You're obviously in worse pain than I thought. I haven't the foggiest idea what to do with you."

"Why don't you roll him up and put him in your knapsack?" Antek barked. Pytor guffawed.

Ignoring them, Naftali managed to rise gallantly to full height — five feet three inches. Though his face was contorted in agony, he gasped, "I ran away from the train . . . and the camps . . . to fight the Nazis. For two years I've longed to find men like you. I wish to be part of your group." Clutching his side, he nearly collapsed to the ground, and held onto Victor.

"I say finish him off!" barked Antek. "We don't need his kind. He'll have us all killed."

"Put him out of his misery, at least," said Pytor. "He's suffering."

"He's young and strong," Victor argued. "I don't detect anything seriously wrong. Just some trauma. I can get him back into shape." His dark eyes shone with urgency.

Andrei smiled slightly. "So you feel he might, uh . . . be of use to us?"

322

"Positive," the little man answered. "He might cook for us . . . or carry our supplies."

"I want to fight," Naftali pleaded hoarsely.

"Do you really believe he can be trusted?" asked Roman.

"He has a fighting spirit. Unusual for a Jew," Andrei mused.

"All Jews stink!" roared Antek, running his finger across his neck. "He'll run away, just like the rest."

"Antek, you're acting most improperly," Andrei scolded. "Personally, I think we should give the lad a chance. What do you say?"

Antek growled.

"Well, no one can say that I'm not democratic," Andrei continued. "That's what we're fighting for, right? Shall we take a vote? Come on, let's see a show of hands. All in favor of keeping him on, raise your hand."

Instantly three hands went up — Andrei's, Victor's, and Roman's, the last somewhat hesitantly.

"Well," Andrei said, "looks like majority rules. Congratulations, Naftali. You've been saved. After you're looked over and cleaned up a bit, you'll have the honor of working with us. Victor will take you back. He's a doctor. Come on."

Painfully, Naftali began to follow. Suddenly, Andrei stopped and turned.

"But bear this in mind, my friend," he said, his voice stern and menacing. "We expect complete loyalty. One wrong move and you'll wish you had stayed on the train. Do I make myself clear?"

"Yes."

With Victor's arm around his waist, Naftali was half dragged through a row of trees, deeper and deeper into the evergreen hills. Passive, he let his legs follow along, his side throbbing and his mind, struggling to stay alert, weakened with massive fatigue. The other partisans walked ahead, talking, and occasionally Naftali saw Antek turn to scowl. By the time they came to a clearing, Naftali, nearly unconscious due to the shooting pains in his side, was able to discern a number of tents and a group of ragged men.

"We're here. You'll be safe," a voice whispered to him in Yiddish, and that was the last thing Naftali heard before he fainted.

When Naftali awoke, he was lying on a cot, wrapped snugly in blankets, with bottles of drugs at his side. There was even, strangely enough, a decanter of cologne. Across the tent he recognized Victor, who was boiling instruments while humming a popular prewar melody. Noticing his patient was awake, Victor walked over and lifted the sheet.

Naftali tried to rise, but Victor held him down. "No, don't get up," he said. "You must stay off your feet."

His voice! The language! Naftali realized that this man was the one who had spoken in Yiddish.

"You're Jewish!" he exclaimed.

"Ssshh!" Victor hissed, and then answered in Polish, "You must address me in Polish . . . at all times. Understand?"

Naftali nodded.

"You're not in the ghetto anymore."

"Obviously."

Naftali leaned back as the man uncovered the blanket and examined him.

"How am I?" Naftali asked.

"You'll live. A fractured rib . . . some nasty cuts and scratches. Other than that . . . nothing *too* serious. You're lucky you didn't hemorrhage. You're quite resilient, I must say. My dear man, you will be bedridden for quite awhile."

Naftali leaned back and whistled. "Will I play the violin?"

"Probably. Why?"

"I never played before."

Victor chuckled. "I thought you wanted to fight."

Naftali winced as Victor poked him. "I took one look at Antek and I wondered just who exactly my enemies were."

"Now you know why I speak Polish."

Naftali's smile faded. "How long have you been with these people?"

"A year. I left Warsaw and joined."

"The ghetto?"

"No. I wasn't too far away, though. I had fake identity papers and lived on the Aryan side. I left my wife Sonya in the basement of our former housekeeper's building. Sonya looks more Aryan than myself. I think she'll manage. She sends me messages from time to time."

"Why did you leave her?"

"I felt I was endangering her life, as well as my own." He stopped, and stared analytically under the sheet. "I'd better change your dressing."

Naftali felt the removal of bandages as the man skillfully worked.

"Anyway," Victor continued, "twice I was stopped on the street by men who recognized me and threatened to turn me in for a gram of lard. I think I'm worth more than that. It got to the point where I spent half my money on bribes. I decided to leave Warsaw and take my chance in the woods — with a different set of animals."

He lowered the sheet and pointed to a bottle. "If the pain gets too intense, I'll give you some morphine, though I'd rather avoid it if possible."

"How did you get the drugs?" Naftali asked incredulously.

"Before the war I was a pharmacist. I stored these in my basement."

"And the cologne?"

Victor smiled. "Living on the Aryan side does have its advantages, you know. A going-away present from my wife. She felt I had to smell nice in uniform. Comes in handy for sterilizing wounds and instruments."

"Did you use it on me?"

"Of course. Rest assured, my boy, that you're now the most fragrant soldier in the woods."

"Do you have soap?"

"As a matter of fact, yes. Along with gauze and other items. In Warsaw I did a brisk business selling these items — both in the ghetto and on the Aryan side."

"And you're also a doctor?"

"I studied medicine long ago. The medical board, however, wouldn't pass me because they had already filled their Jewish quota, so I became a pharmacist instead. Fortunately, I remembered enough from my anatomy and science classes to perform rudimentary first aid and operations. I treated some of the most prominent people — including Andrei. I saved his life, once — pulled a bullet out of him. In return, he allowed me to join his group."

"How did you meet him in the first place?" Naftali asked as Victor organized his bottles.

"His father was a friend of mine. A very fine man — a scientist

and writer. We went to school together. When the Germans came
to Warsaw, he was one of the first men they rounded up and shot.
They also went after Andrei . . . shot him and left him for dead.
But he was alive, and he came to me. Later I came to him. Andrei
was wanted by the Germans in his own right."

"Why?"

"Even before the war he had been something of a politician. At
Warsaw University, where he was a law student, he led protests
on behalf of the workers. He later joined the Socialist party and
became one of its most prominent members. Naturally, he has
worked with a lot of Jews. He has an open mind."

"He knows you're Jewish?"

"Yes. He's the *only* one — not even Roman knows. I changed
my name; long ago I was Velvel Pinchowitz. But please. I'm
telling you all this because I like you. You must call me Victor."

"I saw how Andrei looked at me," Naftali murmured in
contempt, remembering Andrei's words: *He has a fighting spirit.
Unusual for a Jew.*

"Don't forget, he has to be a certain way in front of the men.
How do you think he was able to win over the workers? But he
really is quite a decent fellow."

Naftali bitterly shook his head. "They're all the same to me."

"Shhh!" the doctor hissed. "Remember. He saved your life.
You must be grateful. And I warn you: Andrei is dead serious
when he speaks of complete loyalty. I've seen him shoot traitors
and deserters. He is not vicious, but he is fervently committed to
his work. He hates the Germans as much as you do. He virtually
started this group from scratch. And he keeps in touch with the
Home Army. Do you know he was one of the few in favor of
arming the Jewish underground? The rest were either against it or

indifferent. He is the only one I know who has acknowledged the Jewish contribution to the war. You mustn't be narrow-minded, Naftali. You're not in some *shtetl* anymore. If you are to work with us you must change your way of thinking."

Naftali lapsed into probing silence. He believed he knew a lot about the ways of the world. Yet somehow Andrei and Victor, both full of enlightenment, made him feel as boorish and ignorant as Antek.

"I'd better get you something to eat."

After Victor left, Naftali leaned back, probing the canvas ceiling and contemplating events. Forty-eight hours earlier, he was packed along with the other sardines in a train, awaiting certain death. Only yesterday, he had been threatened twice — first by a German patrol, which left him for dead, then by Polish partisans, who didn't care to see a Jew alive. Also, he was injured and in severe pain. Now he was lying in bed, nursing his wounds — and not only being granted the chance to live, but the chance to avenge his family's death as well. Naftali's heart expanded with feelings of destiny, and as he remembered his family being dragged helplessly onto the trains, his mind clouded with rage and hatred. He determined to make good on his desire for vengeance.

Victor returned with a steaming bowl of soup. He smiled as he watched Naftali make a blessing. "Which yeshiva were you attending?"

"How do you know I was in a yeshiva?"

"Let's just say it's my intuition. You don't quite look like the type to be climbing trees in the forest. I know a yeshiva *bochur* when I see one. Let me guess: before the war you were learning, right? And somehow Hitler disrupted your plans to be a great rabbi."

Naftali put down the spoon. A tear trickled down the corner of his eye as he thought of the world he had left behind — a world violently uprooted over two years ago.

Quickly Victor wiped away the tear with the bedsheet. "Oh, forgive me . . . please. I didn't mean to sound irreverent."

"No, no," Naftali answered softly. "It's just . . . I was thinking of my father. He was in my dream last night. He had wanted me to be a great scholar. And I was on my way to making him proud. He was killed defending the Torah."

Victor was silent. "I'm sure you're making him proud now, Naftali. You're surviving. And you, too, are defending the Torah. You must live for him and his memory."

Naftali sniffed. "As soon as I'm out of this bed, I want to lay my hands on every German skunk and strangle him."

"Antek's good at that," Victor said.

Naftali smiled weakly. "I hate to think what he might have done to me."

The men laughed. Naftali studied Victor's features — his manicured hands, and his salt-and-pepper hair, fashionably brushed. Like Andrei, Victor kept his uniform, as well as his person, immaculate. He even wore a pocket watch — an ironic reminder of his own past. His baritone laugh exuded the warmth of a man imbued with worldly charm, who felt more at home in a lecture hall or cafe than in the rustic hills. No wonder he was drawn to Andrei, whose level of sophistication was close to his own, and who shared the same uprooted world. How we've all been misplaced, Naftali thought.

"You were never in yeshiva, were you?" Naftali asked rhetorically.

Victor shook his head. "No. Gymnasium. In Warsaw. Later I

went to Warsaw University. I'm sorry to say that my family was one of those not inclined towards Judaism. Reminded them of the *shtetl.* I only know Yiddish because of my patients. My father believed fervently in the brotherhood of man. I admire you, Naftali. You didn't lose your faith. I did. I watched my ideals fade away."

Naftali looked away in sadness. He truly felt sorry for this man — and not just because of the war.

Andrei came to visit Naftali that afternoon. Formally knocking at the tent, he exchanged a few words with Victor, then sauntered over to the patient. Naftali was slowly awakening from a nap when through groggy eyes he saw the leader bending over and smiling at him.

Naftali guessed Andrei to be in his late twenties. His face, which once might have been silken smooth, was creased with incipient worry lines. His gray eyes were focused on the patient, betraying a sharpness and calculation that came with combat leadership.

Andrei remained wordless and went away, but each day he returned to visit and to talk with Victor. One day he brought winter clothes and a pair of warm, albeit shabby, boots. Under the pharmacist-cum-medic's care, Naftali convalesced rapidly. The cuts and bruises healed, and so did the rib, although it took slightly longer to mend. The shooting pains disappeared — with minimal drugs — and soon Naftali was able to get out of bed without Victor's aid. The latter, however, still had to help Naftali walk and dress himself.

The weather prevented Naftali from practicing to walk outside the camp. Moreover, he was afraid of being seen too freely by the other partisans, who still had not quite accepted this little Jew in their midst. Remaining as much as possible near the tent, he could be near Victor in case he needed help, and at the same time remain inconspicuous. In the morning, however, he was able to take walks around the camp perimeters, first with a cane, then without one. He exercised privately, bending his legs and flexing his muscles.

By the end of a fortnight, Naftali was diagnosed as able-bodied and ready to work. He anticipated tossing live grenades at German soldiers and convoys. To his disappointment, however, he was assigned instead the lowly task of rifle bearer. Naftali had desired sweet revenge as soon as possible, and accepted with difficulty Victor's argument that he was too inexperienced to fight. However, he knew he was not in a position to argue. It wasn't just the rationale of Victor's words; it was also the hatred of Antek and others of his ilk. Hearing the word "Christ-killer" said behind his back, Naftali wondered where this hatred ended or began. It seemed that the Nazis were only a symptom of an age-old disease. Whenever Naftali walked within range of Antek and his friends, one of whom once pointed his rifle not so jokingly at Naftali and laughed, he trembled. If not for Andrei, he would have been killed long ago.

Naftali, like Victor, felt himself drawn to Andrei, albeit for different reasons. The young Pole was a natural fighter — cunning and agile; at the same time, he was a diplomat, earning everyone's friendship, and in turn their loyalty. Never was he haughty or patronizing, like many leaders. He didn't drink as frequently as the other men; in fact, he avoided most alcohol, while the other men often got wildly intoxicated after battle. The man got by on several hours sleep; the rest of his long day and longer nights were spent planning strategies and raising morale.

At day's end he was often seen with Victor, discussing art or politics. Neither subject was familiar to Naftali, and he resented feeling excluded. The more he felt ignored, the more he felt irritated, and in his growing frustration Naftali finally asked Andrei to allow him a chance for combat.

Andrei looked at him skeptically. "A lad like you . . . I don't know."

"I'm not a 'lad,' I'm twenty-one!" Naftali snapped. "I'm not much younger than you."

"How old do I look?" Andrei asked softly.

"I don't know . . . twenty-eight, maybe?"

"I'm thirty-two. Not exactly old enough to be your father, but old enough to tell you a few things. Like to stay out of trouble. You might get hurt."

"But how do you know I can't fight when you haven't given me the chance?"

"Because I've seen too many of your kind."

"Because I'm a Jew, right?"

"No." With a trace of annoyance, Andrei explained, "I don't mean *that*, Naftali. I mean your personality. You're too cocky. A soldier must be able to follow orders, not just his own instincts. The moment I saw you pulled out from under the rock, I sensed the spirit in you. You're too reckless. You're too bent on killing anything that speaks German to calm down and plan a course of action. Killing a solitary German isn't going to help us win the war, Naftali."

"No, but it'll avenge my family's death!" Naftali cried.

"They killed my wife and children," Andrei retorted, "but I realize that there's nothing immediate I can do. To undermine the German military machine takes time and strength — not impetuousness. So far, I've seen over ten men with your type of nature needlessly killed. Some of them Jews, like you." His eyes narrowed. "They came here fresh from the ghettos and camps, too green to know either the forest or the ways of war. Not all of them were killed by Germans. I'm sure Victor explained."

"Yes," Naftali answered glumly.

"Both Victor and I have tried to keep you out of the way of the other men. As far as they're concerned, you're a nuisance and a bad luck charm. I've lost so many of them, as it is." Andrei sighed. "Besides Victor, only Antek and a few others are left of the original thirty or so who joined me. They weren't any more experienced than the others. Just lucky — so far. I can't guarantee the same for you."

"I don't ask for a guarantee. When on the train I thought I was a dead man. Whether or not I live through the war is in G-d's hands. I only ask for the chance to fight. I promise I won't let you down." Naftali stated, his eyes pleading with the leader.

Andrei sighed. "All right. You win. Meet me here tomorrow at dawn."

Naftali slept hardly a wink that night. Early the next day, he appeared for his first lesson in loading and shooting a rifle. Then, every morning the two secretly slipped away for target practice. Holding the sawed-off shotgun awkwardly in his hands, as gingerly as if it were a newborn infant, Naftali shot bottles off a tree stump.

Soon he discovered something else about Andrei: the latter was very adept at boosting confidence. By speaking encouragingly to Naftali, by showing him the correct way to position and aim, the young man's ability, as well as personality, transformed and blossomed. Soon Naftali graduated from sawed-off shotguns to

Mausers and Messerschmidts, taken from the soldiers Andrei had killed. And in no time Naftali was taking part in operations — first in small-scale activities such as raiding local villages for food, then in more ambitious, military operations, such as derailing trains and blowing up German armories.

Andrei discovered something about Naftali: this shy, scholarly runt displayed a calculating mind not only to match his own, but far surpassing it. Naftali was able to plan certain strategies, spot at a glance an opponent's weakness, and make quick, accurate judgments on the amount of men or time needed for a certain operation. There were times when Naftali took the initiative, with Andrei at his side, nodding in agreement. Naftali was able to calculate the length and width of the forest, and its proximity to strategic areas. In time he began to receive left-handed compliments from his comrades: "Not bad for a Jew," and an uneasy respect. Gradually the young Jew's leadership qualities began to emerge — and Andrei's admiration, as well. A friendship developed between the two. So great was the bond that Andrei failed to notice Antek's growing resentment and jealousy.

After one particular victory, in April 1943, when the partisans had just grenaded a munitions factory, they were laughing and dancing wildly in the woods, passing swigs of vodka. Victor, besides being a pharmacist and doctor, was a fine violinist. He gaily played a polka on the instrument, accompanied by Pytor on the accordion. Toasts were made to one another, and Andrei raised the bottle toward Naftali, the organizer of the operation.

The only one not celebrating was Antek. He stood sullenly off to the side, scowling and muttering to himself. Andrei eyed him uneasily, then approached him and placed his arm around him in a friendly embrace. "Antek, my friend," he said magnanimously, "what's wrong? Why won't you help celebrate our victory?"

Antek growled, then turned away. Andrei frowned. "What's with you, Antek? I'm shocked. But I'm sorry if we've been neglecting you. After all, a lot of the credit goes to you. Why, if not for your courage and skill we would never have blown up the watchtower. Isn't that right, men?" He turned to the others, who nodded eagerly. Only Naftali frowned.

The next day, after an anxious sleep, Naftali awoke and dressed hurriedly. He tried to get up before the others in order to pray in the woods. Hurrying past the tents, he noticed one in disarray and peeked inside.

Everything had been cleaned out: clothing, weapons — all signs of habitation had been eliminated. When Naftali looked up, he caught sight of a squat figure panting and puffing through the trees.

"Hey, you!" he shouted.

Rushing through the woods, Naftali raised his pistol and fired. He missed, and the bullet echoed through the trees, waking the other partisans. Half-dressed, pistols in hand, they rushed out of the tents, and in a garble of voices demanded to know what had happened.

Andrei, too, rushed out of his tent. "What is it? Germans?" he demanded.

"Antek's gone," Naftali whispered.

Most of the men did not know why Antek had deserted, but both Andrei and Naftali knew that their location was now compromised. Within hours, the band of partisans dismantled and packed its tents; the men forlornly trudged through the muddy fields.

The spring day was invitingly crisp and clear, the ground a symphony of rich earth tones dotted with tiny patches of brownish snow. Above them the blue sky was crisscrossed by overhanging pines. The hills opened onto a rolling golden pasture, flecked with peasants reaping an unusually large wheat harvest. For the first time in over a year, Naftali was aware of how stunningly beautiful the Polish countryside was. However, looks were deceiving. He was also aware of the discrepancy between the land's physical loveliness and the moral ugliness that it had bred. This land, he knew, could never be his; it never had been. Its crops were abundant this year in fields made fertile with Jewish blood. The Jews had made their final contribution to a land which had so viciously rejected them. Everyone else in the little group, including Victor, spoke of the future, of a "free Poland." Yes, Naftali joked bitterly to himself — free of Jews.

At night, alone in his tent, he had often wept in grief, the memories of his family appearing before him, standing in deathly silence. Naftali certainly was worldly. But not in the way Victor would have dreamed. Naftali had lost all illusions of "culture" and "international brotherhood." He and he alone fought simply for revenge. A dead German was at least something tangible. A hate-free homeland was only an illusion.

Toward evening, as the setting sun gave the countryside a rust hue, the partisans encamped near a cornfield. Through binoculars, Naftali surveyed a group of cottages, and, adjacent to them, armored vehicles and barracks.

Andrei stood next to him, also with binoculars. "Wait here till dark," he said. "Then we'll make our way through the field."

Naftali shook his head emphatically. "I don't think we're safe," he argued. "In the fields we're too easily spotted."

"But the corn is long. It'll hide us."

"The peasants can spot us easily. They know the land. I think we should move on."

"Nonsense," Andrei replied. "They won't come around at night. I know them better than you do. Besides, we're low on food, as well as guns. With this raid we'll be amply supplied. A simple operation, and we'll be off. I insist we stay here."

An hour after dark, the men unpacked their arms. Slinging their rifles over their shoulders, they prepared to sneak through the field. Summoning a fourteen-year-old boy, himself a runaway peasant and the youngest in the group, Andrei commanded him to cut through the stalks of corn. The others would follow from behind.

Nodding eagerly, the boy crouched and scampered, catlike, through the stalks. Soon, their leaves shimmering in the moonlight, the stalks quivered with human movement. The men silently crept through the ripening fields.

The fields opened up to a broad pasture, just east of the village. The boy had just arrived at a large patch of bare ground when his foot touched something round which was imbedded in the soil. By the time they all heard the ticking sound, it was too late to cry out in warning. The soil erupted and the boy's body was violently torn to bits.

The others recoiled in horror and quickly retreated. A few staggered, and tripped and fell, landing on the mine field. Their torsos shattered and scattered in the ensuing explosions.

By the time the rest returned to the other end of the field, they were greeted with machine guns and helmeted soldiers poised behind them.

"*Polnische Schweine!*" yelled a sergeant.

"Run!" shouted Naftali, as he fired his pistol squarely at the sergeant, killing him. He then broke off at full speed.

The band of partisans frantically dispersed. Victor and Naftali raced behind Andrei, turning occasionally to fire. Victor yelped in pain and clutched his side, dropping his pistol. He staggered and slowed down. Naftali stopped. Meanwhile, Andrei continued running ahead.

Quickly dragging the older man to the end of the fields, Naftali pulled him into a gully. He pushed Victor against an earthy wall and stuffed a handkerchief into the moaning pharmacist's mouth, so that he would have something on which to bite down. Then, furtively poking his head upward, he withdrew his binoculars.

"Oh, Andrei . . . no!" he moaned.

From the distance he saw the partisan leader racing up a rocky hill southwest of the village. Bullets flew angrily at the latter's feet, bouncing off the crags and boulders, coming closer. When Andrei reached the very top, he froze, suspended, writhed violently, then dropped his gun, his clean uniform bursting into crimson. In agony, he turned around, and Naftali gasped at the sight of him. The leader opened his mouth to cry, either in pain or in rage, then at last tumbled forward, over the crest, and disappeared.

Stunned, Naftali sank back into the refuge of the gully. In his grief he lay his head in the mossy earth, which was as soothing as a mother's caress. For the first time in over three years he wept. The tears dribbled softly down his cheeks. When he finally raised his head, he remembered Victor, whose moaning by now had dwindled to a whimper. The handkerchief, which had dropped from his mouth, rested on a shirt drenched in blood. Dirty, his face streaked with tears, Naftali crawled to him.

Victor smiled weakly at Naftali. "*Nu,* Andrei's dead?"

Naftali nodded.

A tear trickled down Victor's glazed eye. "Always had to be in the forefront. I don't think he mentally ever left Warsaw." He sighed. "Oh well. I hope our G-d has room for him up there."

"Hashem will reward him."

"I wonder what my reward might be. I stopped facing east thirty years ago, after my bar mitzvah. But things were different then. I didn't expect all this to happen." He sighed again. "No one did, I suppose."

"I'll take you to a village," said Naftali passionately. "In fact, I know a little first aid — perhaps I could treat you, if you tell me how—"

Victor shook his head. "No. Forget it, son. I'm gone. Just pray for me. Please. And I'll give you a little piece of advice, assuming you survive this war — and I think you will."

"Why do you think so?"

"I saw it from the start. The look in your eye . . . your mind . . . the way you acted in camp . . . so eager, so quick with ideas. You've got a mission, my son. You must live. Did anyone ever tell you that you're special?"

"Once," Naftali answered vaguely, the memory of his rebbe a distant dream dancing around his mind. Then he quickly asked, "What is the advice?"

"After this is over . . . get out . . . of Poland. This is . . . no place for you. Go to . . . Palestine."

"I didn't know you were a Zionist."

It was becoming progressively harder for Victor to talk. "I became . . . one five minutes ago. If anyone had . . . suggested the possibility . . . to me five years ago, I would have laughed . . . in his face. Now I would give . . . anything to get there myself. Perhaps . . . my wife . . . will. Or my son. He left to join . . . the Soviets. And if you're smart, you'll . . . do the same. Try to get in . . . touch with the Red . . . Army. But remember. All that . . . is temporary. Forget about Poland. Your . . . real home is in Palestine."

Throughout the night Naftali remained with the dying Victor, cradling him and helping him to recite *Shma* and *Viduy*, the prayer of confession. When the morning sun swept over the silent fields, he crept out of the gully and surveyed the area. In the distance a flock of crows cawed, their echoing cries emphasizing the muted vastness of the land. It was difficult to believe that the previous night massive carnage had taken place. In the distance, Naftali perceived a small brook, flowing between a clump of trees. He brought the corpse over and performed the cleansing rites. Then he dug a deep hole near a stone and buried the pharmacist. With a piece of charcoal, he etched words into the stone and placed it above the mound of earth: *Velvel Pinchowitz, died 22.4.43, Chol HaMoed Pesach, 5703.*

He was alone. There were no trains, no soldiers, no ghettos, no camps, no loved ones. Everything had been either destroyed or abandoned.

This time, however, he was not the cringing, half-starved, half-frozen waif that had been extracted from the snow. So he could not consider himself completely alone. Nature had become his friend; over the past fourteen months, the forests and hills had become his allies. It was the forest where he ran after an attack or explosion, the river where he swam when being chased, the ditches where he ducked a volley of rifle shots. He knew how to identify a bird call and differentiate it from a signal; he knew how to start a fire, read a compass or map, locate and trap wild animals, hunt and kill.

But despite his acquired skills, he relied mostly on his mind, refined by the prewar learning exercises in Talmud and Shulchan Aruch. He felt that much more could be accomplished through mental acuity and discipline than with physical strength. And though the partisan life had hardened him, made him stronger and more rugged, he still remained short and nervous, looking for all the world like the rebbetzin's pampered yeshiva boy that he was. He could never stop thinking, even before the war; now, under such precarious circumstances, he had trained himself to automatically think ahead — to plan the next step, to plot all the angles.

After the makeshift funeral, Naftali sat on a stump and rested. With Victor's real son absent, Naftali felt he owed Victor the courtesy of vicariously sitting *shivah* — for a man who had not only helped save his life, but who had in a way been a father to him. He wondered where Andrei had been buried — if he had been.

Naftali also wondered about the ambush: Who had been behind it? Antek, perhaps? Had he alerted the Germans of their activity? Had the entire village collaborated? Naftali felt a pang of guilt, knowing that Antek had deserted partly because of him. If it were true about Antek — that he had gone to the Germans — then Naftali was partly the cause of the ambush. He certainly hadn't expected Antek's resentment of him to go this far.

Soon the thoughts of grief gave way to gnawing guilt, then to seething anger, then to a desire for revenge. In his thirst for vengeance, Naftali pondered the different methods of counterattack available to him.

Suddenly, the bushes rustled. Naftali jumped off the stump and drew out his Mauser.

"Who's there?" he demanded.

The figure emerged.

Naftali gasped. "Roman."

The Pole grinned sheepishly. His bloodstained uniform was torn and caked with dirt, a wild mockery of his soldier's status. Hesitantly the two of them stood, watching each other.

Finally, Naftali asked, "Who's left?"

"Me and four of the others," Roman answered.

"Pytor?"

"Gone."

"Where are the others?"

"About a kilometer from here. On the other side."

"What are they doing?"

"Waiting."

"Waiting for what?"

Roman shrugged. Suddenly, his body shook convulsively, and he burst into tears. Naftali approached him.

"Everything happened so quickly," Roman sobbed. "I tried to help Andrei—"

"It's no one's fault," Naftali said, grasping his arm. "But thank G-d we're alive. And now it's up to us."

Three nights later, Naftali and the five surviving men circled the little village, through the outer forest — this time carefully avoiding the deadly cornfield. Coming within sight of the cottages, they ducked behind a cattle trough, waiting till the last of the inhabitants had gone to sleep, till all the cottages were dark. Then they dispersed and scampered across the village square.

Carefully surveying the German post, Naftali timed the change of guard. Ten p.m. Naftali crept behind a cottage. Scrutinizing the movements of the watchtower guard, he waited as the latter lit a cigarette, turned away, and tilted the searchlight toward the vacant farmland. Ten-thirty. With a soft whistle, he called to his friends, who slithered in between the cottages.

Eleven p.m. At the eastern end of the village they gathered behind a tanning shed. Huddled close, they waited again for the searchlight.

Midnight. The bungalow lay on the southeast corner. Dimly lit by a solitary light bulb, it was smoky and noisy with the laughter of men, relaxing around a card table and merrily braying in German. Along the walls were ranged a dozen or so bunks, where some of the men lay asleep.

With a flick of his finger, Naftali signaled the men, who tiptoed behind him, inching their way around the barracks towards the entrance. With a whisper — "One, two, three" — the wild-looking yeshiva boy leapt full view into the barracks.

"For the Fatherland," he shouted, pointing his gun.

The soldiers bolted from their seats, overturning the card table and its contents. In confusion, beer mugs crashed to the floor, and the cries of the men were soon drowned out in the roar of machine gun fire. Then all was silent.

But not for long. The sirens wailed, and the band of partisans bolted. Nearly slipping on a puddle of blood, Naftali scrambled for the exit, firing blindly.

Outside, a convoy of SS men dismounted and opened fire. A partisan was sprayed with bullets while Naftali advanced and threw a grenade. With a boom, the convoy shook violently, releasing pieces of men everywhere. Naftali threw another grenade, wiping out any surviving Nazis.

343

"Naftali! Here, quick!" called Roman from the direction of the watchtower. Standing by a peasant's hut, he waved frantically.

The shot pierced Roman's brain, as he stared in sad surprise in the direction of the bullet. Then he sank to the ground, lifeless. From the hut window, his hand gripped over the smoking gun, Antek grinned.

Turning casually toward Naftali, the peasant's smile faded and was replaced by a mouth open wide in shock and recognition. His eyes bulged in terror as the bullet from Naftali flew right between them. The man's big body slumped, then fell backward. Inside, a woman screamed.

The other villagers watched in horror from their windows. One stood outside his door, swinging an ax at a partisan, knocking the latter down lethally; he became a bloody heap. After Naftali fired, the villager instantly collapsed, falling over the corpse of the partisan. Hurling himself over a fence, Naftali darted through the open pasture and raced into the night.

Running, running, staggering over rocks and roots, skinning his knee, panting and groaning . . . not until he was deep into the company of trees did Naftali Hertz at last lie exhausted on the mossy soil.

When his breathing had evened, he began to laugh hysterically. It occurred to him that tonight was the seventh day of Passover, when the Jews were finally taken out of danger from the Egyptians, who drowned in the Red Sea. Somewhere people were rejoicing.

By Succos, Naftali Hertz had a price on his head. Alone or with a group of men, he had destroyed several German bases and blown up a munitions factory. Always adept at choosing the right targets, he knew when and how to strike, seldom missing, always managing to elude his pursuers.

By January 1944, Naftali Hertz was commanding his own team of former Polish and Russian soldiers, armed with a mass acquisition of German materiel. Additional supplies were often dropped from Russian planes. In time, this nucleus of men developed into a full-fledged army, the majority of recruits Jews — refugees not only from the camps and ghettos, but from other partisan armies as well.

In fact, Naftali was amazed at the number of Jews who were active in the underground. From the Balkans to the Ukraine, many of them had performed the most dangerous types of sabotage. Some had gained prominence in previous partisan or resistance groups; most, like Victor, had changed their names in order to work unharassed. They urged Naftali himself to use a Polish name, for safety's sake, but the man refused.

"I'm not a Pole; I'm a Jew!" he declared. "I am not intimidated by those who hate me. I am fighting for the Jewish people. Their deaths will be avenged millions of times over."

Naftali Hertz became known far and wide not only as a good fighter, but as a good leader as well — one whose fiery mind gained the admiration of those near him, and whose wisdom, tempered with kindness, endeared him to those he met. He had a feel for a person's weaknesses and strengths, and assigned respective tasks. He encouraged potential; in turn, the partisans gave him loyalty. Other groups were often plagued with internal bickering and resentments. Not so with Naftali Hertz's regiment. Like Aaron the High Priest, he was concerned with the welfare of each person, going out of his way to reconcile differences. The loss of a fighter was like the loss of a son, and Naftali mourned every casualty. The small army became a unified, cohesive force under his firm leadership.

Not only soldiers, but families too, joined the unit. Making their way into the woods, they contacted the band and set up kitchens, hospitals, even schools. Women cooked and cleaned, but quite a few of them became just as active and effective in combat as the men. Naftali knew them all. Concerned with their safety, he knew how to remain one step ahead of the German army. His group never stayed in one place in the forest long enough to be spotted by enemy planes or tanks. He was a brilliant organizer, planning carefully the attack or counterattack, incurring minimal losses.

His name was whispered by enemy officers and soldiers with dread and hatred. Patrols were sent, bombs were dropped, but somehow Naftali Hertz managed to dodge them all. In fact, his ability to use the Nazis' cunning to his advantage earned him a reputation as a manipulator and tactician. Often he based his own method of attack on theirs. He knew, for example, that the Germans were more potent in groups than in guerrilla warfare, so he sent tiny, disciplined groups of men to different areas to confuse and undermine them. In one daring raid, he slipped into the enemy camp disguised as an SS officer and freed a contingent of Jewish slave laborers. The majority fled with him into the forest, where they joined up with his group.

Almost every strategy of his was successful, and each served to refine his technique. On several occasions, in fulfillment of Victor's wish, he approached and befriended Soviet generals, who offered him a position in their own army. But Naftali refused. He could not see himself serving a country whose ideals were so opposite his own. He did, however, agree to intercept messages between enemy bases, and offered his well-equipped little army as a buffer between the mightier German and Russian troops. So adept was he in rooting out the enemy that he was awarded a Red Army medal, an honor rarely accorded partisans.

At war's end he was heralded by many, though never publicly acknowledged, as a hero truly on a par with Churchill and Eisenhower. He was even allowed to march through Red Square during a massive victory parade.

However, the mind of Naftali Hertz was not on the Allied victory. It drifted sadly away to a faraway time in a faraway yeshiva, in Cracow. But the yeshiva was gone forever — and anyone connected with it too. Though the city of Cracow, spared the bombing, remained lovely, it was still ugly, even after the war — ugly with Polish hate. Naftali had heard enough of the new pogroms to know that Jews were not welcome back there.

Marching through Moscow, oblivious to the cheering crowds, he pondered the way events had turned out. Had he never taken that chance and jumped from the train in February 1942, he would have long ago met with physical death. Now, staying in Russia meant a slow spiritual death. Hearing stories from his own men, as well as from those in the Red Army, he sensed that deep down Stalin and Hitler were essentially one and the same. The words of Victor Parkowski, *ne* Velvel Pinchowitz, rang ever more loudly: *Your real home is in Palestine.*

Making his way out of Russia was no small feat. No sooner were the guns of battle silenced than the Cold War gloomily set in, and emigration from Eastern Europe became tantamount to escape. Once again, Naftali became a fugitive. Hiding in forests and ravaged villages, towns of rubble and wastelands of filth, migrating from one dismal postwar city to the next, he at last arrived in Vienna, a city of displaced persons. Contacting the office in charge of refugees, he became one of the thousands of surviving Jews searching for their past.

But his past was over. His family and friends were gone — every one of them. The train from which he had fatefully escaped had unloaded all its passengers at Auschwitz. His mother, his sisters, his friends — all had long ago become statistics. So Naftali found company among the masses of huddled survivors like himself, orphaned in history and haunted by memories. Just as in the forest, he was not alone.

Through one last guileful effort he managed to slip into the American army base. Getting a job as a janitor at the base, he rented a small apartment which was located near a row of bombed-out buildings. After years of tension, a delayed reaction set in, as Naftali Hertz sunk deeper and deeper into depression. Day after day he sulked, wandering aimlessly around the base and the streets of Vienna, mumbling to himself, so that passers-by stared and thought him crazy.

The life of Naftali Hertz might have ended this way, had he not taken a wrong turn one day in the downtown section of Vienna.

It was there, in October 1946, that Naftali happened to meet a former neighbor of his from Cracow. This man, who had had the good sense to emigrate to Palestine with his family several years before the war, was now working in the newly restored Zionist office on Vienna's main street. He noticed through the window a little Jew in a shabby suit, standing befuddled, his face crinkled, scrutinizing.

Curious, the man opened the door. "Excuse me," he asked. "Aren't you Naftali Hertz?"

Naftali stared bewildered at this tanned, robust man, so out of place in postwar Europe. "Yes?"

"Don't you remember me?" the other man said in Yiddish. "You always dropped by on Purim for some of my mother's *hamantashen*; you swore up and down that it was the best in all of Cracow."

Naftali stared at him intently. Then, for the first time in a long while, his face beamed. "Michah! Michah Gorovitz! *Shalom aleichem!* It's great to see you!" They embraced.

"*Aleichem shalom.* The pleasure is mine," answered Michah. He studied Naftali intently. "Thank G-d you're alive."

"Yes, thank G-d," Naftali agreed, sighing, "but I've been through a lot."

"Yes, I know. We've all heard about you."

Naftali narrowed his eyes. " 'We?' "

"Come inside. Please."

Naftali was ushered into a tiny office, half of it taken up by Michah's desk, which was almost buried under papers and official-looking documents. In the far corner there was just enough space, squared off as if enshrined, for a photograph of a woman with two small children. Naftali stared at them, fascinated, as if he were observing life on a distant planet.

"That's Daniella, my wife," he explained. "We met five years ago on a kibbutz. As you can see, we've been busy. That's my son, Amir. And Sharon, my daughter."

"Yes," Naftali murmured, his eyes welling with tears.

Michah watched him knowingly. "They're all gone, right?"

Naftali nodded. He sobbed quietly. Michah, silently watching, handed him a handkerchief.

"I lost all my relatives," Michah said softly. "My parents — they live in Haifa now — took it really hard. At least now I'm starting a family of my own. My brother, also. And I wish the same to you. That would be the best revenge against the murderers."

"I already had my share of revenge," Naftali sniffed, wiping his eyes. "I was a partisan."

"Yes, I know," Michah replied. "I told you. We heard all about you."

"Really?"

"Yes. From some of our 'customers.' "

"Customers?"

"People wanting to get into Palestine. Fast. Zionists who sprang up overnight. People with nowhere to go. People who lived very well before the war and were fooled into thinking that Berlin or Warsaw or Budapest could be a suitable replacement for Jerusalem." He lowered his voice. "People who see the establishment of a Jewish land, and the restoration of the Jewish people, as the ultimate revenge."

"And where exactly do *I* come in?" Naftali asked coolly.

"We need you, Naftali. We need you for our work. Someone with your expertise and experience in military matters. You wouldn't believe how famous you are. We've heard quite flattering stories about you. From the way people talk, you'd think they were describing a chassidic rebbe."

"Hardly," Naftali answered with a slight laugh. "I lived with chassidic rebbes, yes. I was just a *bochur* breaking my teeth over Tosafos. If anyone had asked me ten years ago how I was going to spend the rest of my life, I would have told him I was going to be a tailor, and a practicing rabbi on the side. Or the other way around. Ten years ago I used to run from the tough Polish boys on the block. Me, a partisan? I wonder if even a rebbe could have foreseen that. I think it is unbelievable!"

"Often we turn out differently than what we expected, or hoped," Michah said. He began playing thoughtfully with an eraser. "I never thought I'd wind up here. Ten years ago I couldn't wait to get out of Europe. I was happy on the kibbutz. All I wanted was to stay in Palestine. Sometimes, however, we're given a certain mission, and we simply have to go out and do it. Even if we would rather be doing something else. You, out of six million, were picked for a reason. Are you going to say that out of mere coincidence you were wandering by here? Can you really tell me that you would turn your back, after all these years, and simply choose to go your own way? You can't forget — you know that as well as I. Once you've been through such a thing, you never will."

The lecture left Michah feeling drained, and Naftali as well. Quietly, the former leaned back, allowing the flavor of his rhetoric to permeate the little man sitting across from him.

"It's up to you, Naftali," he finally said. "We need you. Please help us."

Naftali, not one to sit still even in normal times, was stirring restlessly in his chair. His mind, atrophied after so many months of inactivity, once again became fervent with decisiveness and destiny. The words of Victor echoed through his mind from the grave: *Did anyone ever tell you that you're special?* Special, special. The partisans cheered: *Naftali Hertz will lead us all to victory.* His father's cry before the bullet ran him through. His mother and sisters being pushed into the waiting trains. His brother spitting hatefully into the eye of the German guard. And the dream, that lonely winter night in the Polish woods: *You must live; the men are waiting.* Was his need for revenge satiated at last? Or did the voices — six million of them — still cry out to him?

"Yes," Naftali announced forcefully, his eyes glazed in a mixture of new hope and old desolation. "I am ready."

Michah Gorovitz smiled.

Chapter 14

In Endless Battle

Naftali was fortunate, in more ways than he ever realized, to have met Michah Gorovitz. The husky Zionist opened up a variety of doors, each one enabling Naftali to renew and develop his unique talents.

Naftali was eternally grateful that G-d had pulled him out of the abyss of obscurity and set him on a new course, with a new role in history. Most importantly, Naftali had a completely new attitude. Before, he was a ghetto orphan, seeking revenge for indignities committed against him and his family. Now, at twenty-six, he was a more mature Naftali Hertz. Having felt that one task had already been completed, he changed, and so did his perspective. He saw himself shouldering the responsibility for an entire people.

The European Jews had become a nation of survivors. From the camps, forests, cellars they came — each with his own tale, his mind an inner gallery of horror. Many longed to flee the graveyard that now covered Europe, and to find more hospitable, permanent sanctuary in Palestine. It was up to Naftali Hertz, former king of the partisans, to help these people make their way home. At the same time, Naftali Hertz would make his own way in the world.

In January 1947, after his initial encounter with Michah

Gorovitz, he was introduced to Colonel Francis Holmes, head of the American army base in Vienna. The colonel, a tall, robust man who had acquired his physique by spending years on a Minnesota farm, was surprised to learn of "Tali the janitor's" past. Of course, the colonel mused to his wife, why should it surprise him? From the moment he had met the little man, shuffling around the boiler rooms and latrines, he sensed that this was someone with many secrets.

Naftali — who bought a new suit for the occasion — met Holmes in the colonel's office on a Wednesday afternoon. The meeting lasted four hours. The colonel spent half the time listening, enthralled, through an interpreter to Naftali's war stories. He was able to come up with more than a few of his own. The colonel had fought in a number of major battles, seen firsthand the concentration camps, and even testified at Nuremberg, but never in his wartime life had he experienced the lessons Naftali Hertz had gained in inhumanity.

Naftali was sent to Munich, where he was given a position at American intelligence tracing and documenting lists of ex-Nazis. Naftali, whose clockwork mind was suited to anything systematic, found this task a refreshing change from the blood and dirt of the wilderness. Physically, too, he seemed less incongruent behind a desk than a tree.

Nevertheless, he had trouble sitting still. He felt distressed; he did not know why. He frequently left his desk to take walks around the grounds or drink the watery, ersatz coffee at the canteen. The walks allowed him glimpses of postwar Germany. Frozen, miserable. The sight of refugees was most disturbing — many of them Germans fleeing Russian-occupied territory. He had no sympathy for them, knowing of the compliance and affiliation with the Nazis in earlier times by many of them. He was irked to be on German soil, and to see the faces of the people who had caused him so much grief appalled him, though these people themselves, walled up in rubble, now groveled in abject defeat and humiliation. He wondered: Just how repentant were they, really? Was it only because they had lost the war? Many of them claimed ignorance, even outrage, at the atrocities. But was it only because they were now eager to win over the Americans?

Seeing the names of major war criminals on the dossiers and realizing how many of them still roamed free made him even more bitter and restless. Not only were a large number still loose, but — Naftali began to suspect — many were actually being helped by the Allies. Naftali had successfully caught a few Nazis, most of whom had tried to escape into Switzerland, and had turned them over to the authorities. However, he had also heard of the "Rat Line" and other secret passageways out of Europe — aid to former Nazis, courtesy of the Allies and the Vatican. The schemes involved bribery, false passports, new names and positions. The assisted were Nazis with either wealth or influence whose expertise was needed by various governments and whose past could thus be charitably overlooked.

Naftali wondered about some of the people who worked in other offices in his building. One, a Bavarian who had once boasted to him of helping "a Jewish friend" during the war, was often seen after work with a group of his friends sneaking off to a bar and reminiscing about wartime battles. Another, an American, complained how the "dirty Jewish refugees" were a nuisance.

Naftali felt nauseated by the hypocrisy around him. He had hoped for justice and revenge for his people, through this work.

However, he sadly realized how the world could no longer be neatly divided into good guys and bad guys. Before, revenge against German atrocities meant simple sabotage against an army base or troop; now, working with the Allied victors, and seeing their own laxness, as well as cynicism, toward de-Nazification, Naftali realized that justice and revenge for the Jews would encompass more — much more. He would have to take on the whole world.

Naftali met with Michah Gorovitz late in May. His reason for meeting the Zionist was twofold: first, to supply him with names of uncaptured Nazis — a list Naftali had meticulously copied and given to Jewish agents. Second, Naftali simply longed to see an old face. Gorovitz had cured him once before of his depression; now, in his deepening frustration, Naftali longed to be uplifted once more.

Gorovitz was delighted at the outward change in Naftali. From a little oddball, the latter had grown sophisticated in his thinking, and his manner was more professional. Instead of broken phrases, he now spoke a fluent English. Dressed in a new suit which he had purchased from the American PX, he had descended the train at the Vienna station and embraced Gorovitz in utter joy.

Nevertheless, Naftali was identifiably moody. Over lunch he voiced his grievances to Gorovitz, barely noticing the lovely spring outdoors.

"They're all in the same league," he grumbled. "Nobody cares about us; nobody is doing anything to help us. Our brothers are rotting in displacement camps, and all they get is a bunch of do-good ambassadors. Meanwhile, the Nazi murderers get money and travel expenses."

Gorovitz listened carefully, and one of his enigmatic smiles crossed his face. "You *can* do something, Naftali. I once said we needed you. What did you think I meant?"

Naftali put down his fork and stared uncomprehendingly. "So what do you want me to do? Go back to the woods?"

"No," Gorovitz said, laughing, "of course not. Maybe that's the problem with you, Naftali. You're still mentally there. Sorry to say, my friend, but you live in the past. We're in a different time and a different world. We must adopt a different plan of action."

"But your assessment of me is based on the past. On what I did as a partisan and a refugee. And to be very honest, your accolades are no longer of any interest to me. The past doesn't concern me. It's the present I'm worried about, and the future — if, G-d forbid, this kind of human animal should ever again take control. Right now I have the urge to get even with every one of them."

"Splendid!" Gorovitz said, beaming. "Then you're ready to help in our work."

"What kind of work?" Naftali asked carefully.

"With the DP's."

Naftali blinked. "You mean . . . entry into Palestine."

"Yes."

"But what does that have to do with Nazis?"

"Don't you see, Naftali? You will be helping to establish a Jewish homeland. Once our people are rightfully reinstated in Palestine, we'll be able to deal with the Nazis on an international basis. And this whole *aliyah* business will certainly raise your fighting spirit."

Naftali looked away doubtfully. "Leading a band of men through the forest is one thing, Michah. Do you really expect me to take boatloads of people past the British?"

"Do you want my honest answer?"

"All right, let's hear it."

"I have complete faith in you, Naftali. If you could outmaneuver hardened troops, I think you can handle the British."

"And the Arabs?"

"I think they'll be even less of a problem." Michah tried a joke. "One look at you and they'll run like crazy."

"But I don't know my way around the desert at all," Naftali argued. Then he remembered the Biblical maps of his boyhood. "Not too well, anyway. And I won't have the trees to shelter me. Also, as far as combat is concerned, I'm a little out of practice, sitting behind a desk. As you said, Michah, it's a different world. I'm sadly out of touch. I can't do it alone."

"You'll have professional help — friends of mine, people I have wanted you to meet for quite a long time. You'll be oriented very quickly into their ways. You won't be alone this time, I assure you."

Naftali gazed philosophically at the avenue, which long ago had been filled with elegant pedestrians and shoppers. He reflected on his life and mused, "I don't think I was ever alone . . . totally. The times I was living on my wits I felt the hand of G-d helping me. Other times, I was just lucky to have met the right people. I hope this time my luck won't run out."

His American army days over, Naftali Hertz found himself once again a fugitive. He was forced to go underground. Once again he was at war — this time with the British, the very people who had been his allies during the war. Now they were his enemies.

Naftali left his job and Munich, the birthplace of Nazism, and made his way to Cyprus. The sight of the Jewish refugees languishing under British guard doubled his anger and his craving for justice. With a false American passport, and official-looking papers which he had smuggled out from his former job, he was given entry into Palestine.

At last reaching the Holy Land, Naftali allowed himself the brief luxury of playing tourist, as he wept at the Western Wall and other holy sites. The spirituality assailed his senses — a sad reminder of the religious milieu from which he had been tragically wrenched. He had horribly lapsed in all his practices. He still tried to maintain a semblance of religiosity, but the war had taken its toll. Shabbos had become Saturday, and the prayers he had once uttered every day were now said only on rare occasion. And to think he had once wanted to be a rabbi. Somehow, life didn't happen quite as he had planned.

Naftali made a decision. Just like his father had longed to spend the rest of his days studying Talmud after his business was established, so did Naftali Hertz resolve to spend the rest of *his* days, once peace and justice were established, immersing himself once again in the yeshiva world and proper Torah observance.

But life for Naftali did not turn out that way. He was never through with his fight for peace and justice. Initially, Naftali worked with the Irgun, training, and in turn being trained by, hardened desert soldiers. He practiced his new skills on the British, bombing different bases and outposts and leading small bands of frightened, desperate people across the Palestine borders. In the same way that the forest had been his friend, he in a short time adapted quickly to the desert — with its slimy swamps, endless heat, and vast sands. Instead of hostile Polish peasantry, he now had to confront murderous Arab gangs, who "welcomed" what they called the "Jewish infidels."

As in wartime Europe, Naftali Hertz soon had a price on his head. He skillfully defied the British blockade, bringing Jews into Palestine. He was there waiting in boats and trucks, in different towns and different climates. Instead of a mental map created out of Biblical stories sketched in a childish imagination, he painted a realistic landscape of the Land of Israel and its inhabitants, with an adult's attention to strategic details, right down to the last hill. To him a certain area was not just an ancient battleground in the Book of Joshua; it was also a hiding place for stolen machine guns, or a route for smuggling children. Every technique he had acquired and perfected over the war years for Jewish survival was now utilized and exploited for Jewish continuity.

Though still bitter over past injustices, Naftali found satisfaction in helping his fellow Jews. He felt grateful that his wartime experiences, though he had never craved them, had trained him well for this work, and were now contributing to the creation of a Jewish state. Originally a lukewarm Zionist at best, he grew to love the land and all that it represented. Whenever he found himself walking through a town or kibbutz, hearing the laughter of young people, he offered thanks to G-d for restoring the pride buried deep within the Jewish soul.

In the War of Independence, Naftali Hertz was in the forefront, leading his band of outnumbered men against the Arab multitudes and pushing back the latter in many decisive battles. After the Battle of Jerusalem, however, he wept at the loss of the Old City and for a long time considered himself a failure. Only another visit from Michah Gorovitz consoled him.

Michah himself had fought bravely for the establishment of

Israel, and danced at the announcement of the truce in 1949. A grenade had cost him two fingers and an eye; nevertheless, he remained irrepressibly cheerful as he stopped by the "residence" of Naftali Hertz — a one-room flat located in Haifa.

Naftali was pacing like an animal in a cage — which in fact the place resembled, with its bachelor's dirt and disorder. He was chain-smoking and muttering to himself. When Michah opened the door, he recoiled at the stench of tobacco and gasped in Hebrew, "Since when did you take up smoking?"

"What difference does it make?" Naftali snapped, keeping his face toward the floor. When he looked up and saw Michah's eyepatch, he exclaimed, "Why, you look just like Moshe Dayan!"

"I told you to be prepared for a surprise. Wait. I didn't show you this." He raised his left hand.

Naftali stammered, "I . . . I'm very sorry, Michah."

"Don't be. It's not your fault."

"But the loss of Jerusalem is. The thought of our holy city going to the enemy pains me to no end," Naftali responded sadly.

"So that's why I see you carrying on like a *meshugene*?" Michah grasped Naftali by the shoulders, steering him toward the door. "First of all, we're getting out of this place. Are you hungry?"

"Sort of," Naftali answered vaguely.

"Good. We're going to my parents' house for a good Jewish dinner. Probably your first home-cooked meal in quite a long time, *nu*? Then we're going to get down to business. And please don't smoke there. My mother has asthma."

Dinner was delightfully traditional, as Michah had promised. Michah's sister, Naomi, served the group and — under her brother's prodding — chatted with Naftali. Naftali had remembered Naomi vaguely from Cracow days. A bookworm and a loner, she had been at age eleven a thin girl with long black braids, whose skin was pale from life indoors. Now, thirteen years later, she had benefited and blossomed in a new life style, in a new land. She had grown quite beautiful. But she retained the shyness of her girlhood. She hurriedly put the dishes away and remained in the kitchen with her mother.

After dessert, Michah let Naftali rush to the porch for a cigarette, as he himself pulled out two patio chairs. Naftali sat down, for the first time in many years feeling contented.

"A shame it's not Purim," he remarked. "I'd ask your mother for some of her *hamantashen.* The rest of her meal has been so wonderful that it brings back memories. Pleasant memories, for a change. I had nearly forgotten what Jewish food in a Jewish home tastes like. It's been ten years."

"Still think about Poland?" Michah asked.

"I can never forget," Naftali answered. "I didn't come here the same way as you, Michah. The war brought me here — through you, of course. It's as simple as that. If not for the war, I would have been in a little Polish *shtetl* somewhere."

"A tailor's shop," Michah added. "Isn't that what you said?"

"You remember our conversation," Naftali answered. "More than I do."

"I remember other things," Michah continued softly.

"Such as?"

"Such as our conversation over lunch in Vienna. And your disgust and shock over the Nazis. Are you still interested in seeing those men brought to justice?"

Naftali shot up. "Are you serious, Michah?"

"Deadly serious. I know some people who might be of use to

you. And vice-versa. Now that you've helped the Jewish state, it's time for you to do the 'real work.' The work you've been waiting to do the past ten years. The long work ahead."

Naftali sat down again, his mind racing. His chance at last to pursue his real mission! A mission to which he could give total commitment. Looking at the man sitting next to him, one man among many who had studded his life, Naftali felt his heart expanding with love and gratitude. If not for this man, Naftali might have still been a half-crazed janitor.

"Michah," he whispered, "you've been so helpful to me. I don't know how I can ever repay you for your kindness."

"Well . . ." Michah sucked in his breath in mock meditation. "I can think of something."

"What?" Naftali asked eagerly.

"Maybe you can ask my sister out on a date."

Shortly after his marriage, Naftali Hertz embarked on a strange new life. He was lucky to have found a wife supportive of his work; Naomi never complained, never questioned him, even during weeks-long intervals of absence. Quietly, in their little Tel Aviv apartment, she cooked, cleaned, and tended their two children, Gad and Aviva. Naftali felt doubly blessed — first, for having the perfect wife, and second, for being able to experience once more the joys of family life. It was, just like the Jewish state, a rebirth.

Again thanks to his brother-in-law Michah, Naftali was introduced to people who could help him in his work. And again Naftali was fortunate. These people shared Naftali's obsession with revenge and justice. Through them Naftali became immersed in the world of the Holocaust avenger.

In 1950, Naftali became part of a newly-created elite division of the Mossad which dealt specifically with the location and extradition — or murder — of Nazis, most of whom lived very comfortably in foreign lands. Rising rapidly through the ranks, Naftali was frequently sent overseas on "good-will missions."

Naftali never forgot his first major assignment — tracking down a former SS colonel who had supervised the destruction of a Jewish town, and who after the war had fled to Bolivia. Naftali prided himself on having planned the entire strategy alone. Disguising himself as an Israeli tourist, the thirty-year-old arrived in La Paz and traced the man to a seemingly impenetrable mansion just outside the capital.

In retrospect, the job seemed so easy that Naftali felt he had simply had beginner's luck. He became the crazy janitor again, mumbling to himself — only this time in Spanish, instead of Yiddish. (He was later to master Portuguese and Arabic, as well.) Finding out the name of the man's favorite restaurant, he took a job there mopping floors.

He looked so comical, tripping over his bucket and sloshing his oversized trousers, that the colonel, flanked by former soldiers, was not irritated at this tramp who was disturbing his meal. So amused was he that he failed to notice that inside the mop was a pistol, which Naftali extracted ever so quietly. Standing at the exit, he aimed, fired, and disappeared into the horrified crowd.

Beginner's luck, Naftali thought. Definitely so. Later assignments, however, were neither so lucky nor so simple — especially once word got around about Naftali Hertz. Twice Naftali was operated on for the removal of bullets — bullets which just missed vital organs. Twice he was stabbed, and he had a long abdominal scar, courtesy of someone's bodyguard. He crawled through jungles, over barbed wire, on jagged cliffs, past high-tech security — even in forests, as in the old days. He lost a number of his men over the years. Just as in the old days, when he mourned for a fallen partisan, he now mourned, sitting *shivah* upon the death of an agent.

The two men Naftali worked with in 1984, Rafael Tzioni and Aryeh Kessler, were recent recruits. Previously with an anti-terrorist unit, they were successful enough to be considered for promotion. Both Raffi, as he was called, and Aryeh had heard of Naftali Hertz. Everyone had. "A man totally dedicated," was one description often given. "Ruthless," "obsessed," "maniacal," were some others. Even now, at sixty-plus, the man had lost little of his energies. As head of the division, he was not only an authority figure, but a mentor — one who worked with the men personally. He trained them and gave them advice based on his wartime experiences.

With Raffi and Aryeh, however, Naftali sadly sensed that he was just not getting through. These men, the youngest he had ever worked with, were card-carrying *sabras*. They did not come from ravaged European towns and villages; they were born after the 1948 war and grew up on developing kibbutzim and settlements. Their parents, too, came from kibbutzim and settlements. The Holocaust was a subject that remained respectful but remote. To these young men, a Nazi was simply a blond image from the past. The current pressures facing Israel from her neighbors as well as other hostile nations were far more relevant than the crimes against the Jewish people done forty-some-odd years ago. Though Raffi and Aryeh had heard all the horror stories — after all, they had learned about the Holocaust in school — Naftali's enthusiasm failed to rub off on them. At least the little man's mannerisms kept them entertained.

Naftali, in turn, was distressed by his men's professional detachment. Remembering how his war stories had once kept many people not only spellbound but indignant, he longed for the early days of Israel, when memories of the Holocaust were still recent and effective — not only as a rallying point for justice, but also as a means of raising money and support for the new state.

Naftali remembered his first trip to America, in 1952, when he was sent on the lecture circuit. Stepping off the boat with his wife at New York Harbor and encountering the great number of Jews in the city, he was so much reminded of Cracow that he had to fight the urge to burst into tears. The nineteenth-century buildings further enhanced Manhattan's European character, sinking Naftali deeper into memories. When he spoke before his audiences, his voice quivered with emotion as he talked of his boyhood and violent entrance into adulthood.

The same thing happened wherever he went — Chicago, Detroit, Denver, Los Angeles. The audiences, usually women in mink and men in suit and tie, were able to go numb enough with shock to take out their check books for the desired donation. The concentration camp footage or stories from returning GI's were still vivid enough to make people cry out in anger. Touring the country, Naftali was impressed with the American Jewish communities. Sons of paupers and peddlers were now doctors, lawyers, professors, and businessmen. A few were Holocaust survivors themselves. It might be easy to scoff at the growing materialism that he saw. However, Naftali detected the saving grace: no matter what his level of observance or financial status in life, each Jew had that special connection to his people which surfaced in the face of communal tragedy.

Tragedy, Naftali thought. Perhaps it takes a tragedy to unite the Jews, to arouse them from apathy. Nowadays, sons of those doctors, lawyers, professors, and businessmen had turned their backs on the past, as well as on their own heritage. The audiences were dwindling; the memories were growing dimmer. Apathy was the enemy of the Jews — deadlier and more encompassing than any Nazi. It wasn't just apathy to the past that bothered Naftali. It was the blithe disregard for the present as well. Neo-Nazi and other paramilitary organizations held little excitement for the younger Jews; they were caricatures on TV. Nobody could really take them seriously.

Except Naftali Hertz. While working with Raffi and Aryeh he made a terrifying discovery. Their first assignment together, over a year ago, had been the capture of Conrad Eberhardt, the former *Oberfuhrer* of a concentration camp near the Austrian border. Eberhardt had been a particularly elusive prize to catch — a sugar cane baron living in an estate on the outskirts of Sao Paulo, Brazil. The capture had taken two years of planning, and involved several near-misses. Finally, the criminal was lured outside his manor and escorted back to West Germany.

The trial covered several pages of prominent international newspapers. The verdict, life imprisonment, was a joke; Eberhardt, a man of seventy with a heart ailment, had very little life left in him. However, the arrogance and cruelty remained, reflected in his deep-set eyes, as he strolled regally down the courtroom aisle with a cane, glancing at Naftali Hertz in utter contempt.

Much to the amazement of the prison warden, he later asked to speak with Naftali. The agent, appearing one wintry afternoon in the Berlin building, was ushered inside the little cell.

The old man had badly deteriorated during his several months in prison. His whitening hair now had the appearance of a bleached ball of string, and his face was shriveled with wrinkles, like a mummy's. Accustomed to a more elegant life in a palatial manor, he seemed to crumble with decay, like the faded plaster walls now surrounding him. His sunken eyes, however, remained arrogant — and fixed on Naftali Hertz, who, though only eight years younger, looked like his son in comparison.

Naftali, normally restless, stood still as a post. Never at ease in normal society, he felt completely in control around his enemies. He waited patiently for Eberhardt to speak.

The old man, sitting on his cot, studied his captor at length, with a mixture of admiration and bemusement. Naftali remained immobile.

At last Eberhardt spokě, his voice soft and cultured. "I never really had a good look at you before, Herr Hertz. In the past I never bothered to notice people like you; somehow I thought it beneath my dignity."

Naftali remained wordless, but his feline eyes clouded with loathing.

"But you, of all people, I wish to remember well." With trembling hands the old man took a bottle from his night table and opened it. A large pill fell out, which he popped into his mouth. He grimaced. "My medication," he explained. "Beastly stuff."

"Why did you send for me, Herr Eberhardt?"

"Oh, yes," the Nazi answered distractedly. "You'll have to excuse the ramblings of a dying man. In fact . . . that is the reason that I called you, Hertz. Because I'm dying . . . and I wish to make a confession, if you will."

"Why not to a priest?"

"Somehow I don't feel that a priest would be as effective. Besides, I have, of late, lapsed in some of my religious observances, so I am uncertain of . . . shall we say . . . getting into heaven through any other recourse but talking to you, a Jew."

"I'm not sure I can get you there either, Herr Eberhardt."

The man chuckled. "You're terribly witty, you know. I had heard that about you from some of my people." He coughed from a throat thick with phlegm. "Some of yours, too. In fact . . . that was something I wished to discuss."

"What?"

"Our people."

" 'Our'?"

"The matter is of mutual concern. Of utmost importance." The old man sniffed. "As I said, it is a confession of sorts. Now let me say first that this is not a trap. I have no interest in taking revenge against you. I suppose this imprisonment was long overdue. It is an atonement of sorts. So don't worry — I hold no bitterness toward you."

"I wouldn't worry about it if you did."

"Splendid. Then you'll be most receptive to what I have to say. Actually, it's a sort of revenge against someone else." His eyes narrowed. "Both revenge and atonement." The old man straightened himself on the cot, trying once again to look authoritative. His gray eyes were now staring directly at Hertz. "Go to New York. It's there, waiting for you."

Naftali stirred. "Waiting?"

"Yes, waiting."

"What is it?"

"Something of vital interest to everyone concerned."

"How will I know this . . . thing of 'vital interest'?"

"Once you find him."

"Find whom?"

"My colleague. The one who left me to your tender mercies — and made off with half my assets. To him, I suppose, I was too sick to just finish off. I was dispensable. And he got what he wanted, anyway." The man's face darkened. "I didn't trust him from the start. Always with his head blown up twice his size — sanctimonious snake. All he ever cared about was himself. Wanted it all to himself."

Naftali edged closer to the cot. "Who is this 'colleague' of yours?"

The older man whispered, "Ludwig Dietrich."

Naftali clutched the headboard for support. The name still had greater potency than any lethal drug. "He's in New York?"

"*Jawohl.* He left Buenos Aires awhile ago and headed there. To get what he's after."

Naftali studied this man, observing the ravaged features, and wondering how Dietrich must look. Supposedly he was still quite handsome.

"This little guessing game of yours, Eberhardt, is tedious. And supposing he *is* there, you haven't given me the foggiest clue what it is he's after."

"Dietrich will tell you. Find him."

"Thank you, but I've tried that for years. For some reason, he doesn't seem to want to get in touch with me."

The old man smiled. "I admit that he might be a bit more difficult to track down than I. After all, I was foolish enough to be living out in the open all these years."

"Yes, everyone in Sao Paulo heard of 'Gunther Hartmann.' "

"I'm afraid that Dietrich remains a well-kept secret. He isn't a very public figure."

Naftali nodded. He himself had never met the man — only heard about him. Dietrich's name had been conspicuously absent from the lists of uncaptured war criminals with names such as Josef Mengele and Klaus Barbie. Mention of his name drew a blank among most listeners. Perhaps that was because he had always kept a low profile, even in Third Reich days. However, he was certainly no less dangerous than the others — perhaps even more, for that very reason.

"Find him," Eberhardt whispered, "and you'll find the gold."

Naftali looked up. "Gold?"

"Yes," the old man whispered.

Naftali stared in meditative silence, and slowly his eyes widened in dreadful knowledge. He angrily banged the cell door, hissing, "You thief. German animal. You know where it is. We won't need Dietrich to get it out of you."

Eberhardt paled. "I swear to you, I can't lead you to the gold. I don't know exactly where it is. Dietrich does — it was his obsession. I only know *of* it. We all did. Dietrich never told me the details; he didn't trust me. If he knew I was telling you now, he would kill me."

"Guards!" Naftali cried, and then he froze. He turned and smiled defiantly at the man. "I get it. This is Dietrich's idea, right? To taunt me."

The old man shook his head. He clutched his chest and gasped convulsively. "The gold is there. And Dietrich is there. In New York. Find Dietrich and you'll find the gold. That is all I know."

His whitening face twisted in agony. He lay down, wheezing. His eyes rolled.

Naftali watched him anxiously, then shouted down the halls again. "Guards!"

The Nazi trembled and lay still, his jaw open. By the time the guards rushed in, they found Naftali kneeling at the old man's side, holding the latter's withered wrist in his fingers and feeling the pulse. At last he let the lifeless arm drop.

Conrad Eberhardt had been poisoned.

Six a.m. Frankfurt International Airport was quiet , as it was the off-season. The TWA terminal was mostly filled with stern-faced businessmen and older tourists in elegant attire.

Naftali Hertz fidgeted in his seat, his little hand clutching an endless series of cigarettes. After all these years, how he still hated being in Germany! Looking around the room, noticing the tell-tale signs of affluence among these people, he thought bitterly how he had spent a lifetime in pursuit of their relatives. How many of them had got away, only to return, even more powerful and more respectable? How many of them now carried briefcases, and drove sleek Mercedes Benz automobiles? He was grateful not to be flying Lufthansa, though it offered an earlier flight. He hated to patronize the German airline.

"*Achtung!*" came the voice on the loudspeaker — a word which sent chills through him to this day. "Flight 578 for Tel Aviv now boarding at Gate 17."

Clutching his flight bag, Naftali advanced to the gateway, ticket in hand. Not until the plane had taken off and the patchwork German countryside faded away into Swiss Alps did he sigh with relief.

So he had been at Eberhardt's deathbed. How touching. Naftali had to admit that he made a lousy priest. Besides, no one in this world could ever forgive the man.

However, Naftali wasn't sure what to make of his last words. *Find Dietrich and you'll find the gold.* Obviously, the meeting was a trap. But for what?

Yet the gold did exist. Naftali had known about it for years — and about the looted treasures that had never been recovered, that lay hidden, waiting to be used by the right people. This was what Eberhardt had meant. But of the gold's exact location, the Nazi had claimed ignorance.

It's there, waiting for you. Eberhardt had simply told him to find Dietrich — a not-so-simple task. And now Hertz had to call upon another colleague of Eberhardt's — a man who, as far as the world believed, was living in Honduras.

Hans Schmidt.

Chapter 15

Hide-and-Go-Seek

Five o'clock. The demonstration had swelled to a thundering mass. Not only yeshiva and seminary students, but survivors, their family and relatives, sympathizers, curious onlookers — all had gathered around the old building to vent their rage, collectively as well as vicariously, against a man they did not know personally, but who represented an era that many had experienced.

Near the construction site stood a stooped, elderly man, waving a sign that read, *My father, my mother, my wife, my children, my brothers — Is it my turn?* A boy, about six-years-old, with shaven head and thick earlocks, struggled to hold up a sign twice his size, reading, *Ware will your next concintrashun camp be?*

Although throwing things was forbidden, someone threw an egg at the restaurant. It splattered against the glass, and the yolk slithered down in yellow streaks and at last merged into a blob with random pieces of shell. Another egg, apparently intended for Shulman himself, missed and flew inside an open window adjacent to his. A tenant appeared, yelling and angrily shaking his fist.

On the podium stood Shimshon, his face radiantly triumphant. Tiptoeing on a milk crate, he surveyed the screaming crowd before him, cheering them on.

He raised the megaphone to his lips. "Murderers!"

"Murderers!" the crowd chorused.

"Pig!"

"Pig!"

Shimshon paused, his mind suddenly blank, groping to continue.

Zev tapped him. "How about 'Remember our dead.' "

"Remember our dead!" Shimshon shouted, and he turned to Zev. "You know, that sounds funny."

Zev shrugged.

A man boarded the podium, microphone in hand, followed by a small crew with TV cameras. Shimshon watched in awe as the apparatus approached him. The man behind the microphone asked, "Shimshon, why don't you say a few words to our viewers?"

Bewildered, the boy turned back to the crowd, which had grown even more frenzied. "Go for it, Shimmy!" Zev urged. In the foreground, a group of kids chanted rhythmically, "Shimmy, Shimmy, *Shim-mee!"*

"What should I say?" Shimmy stammered, studying the reporter's impeccable hair wave. He giggled nervously at the thought of his image being transmitted via satellite all over the world — especially since up until recently much of his own world had barely extended beyond Flatbush. In confusion, he looked at his father, who was also being interviewed, by a woman in a pin-striped suit.

The man answered, "Why don't you tell us about your reasons for this demonstration?"

With boyish candor, Shimshon mumbled how he had lost most of his relatives in the Holocaust, and how important it was for people not to forget. Pointing to his father, he explained how he had recognized Hans Schmidt, alias Avraham Shulman, and wanted to see him brought to justice. As he spoke, he watched the journalists who had lined up near the camera jot down his words in shorthand. In the distance Shimshon heard a familiar voice. He turned to see a man speaking before a van in a smooth, professional voice: "This is Mark Burns, WNOD News, on Thirty-seventh Street."

"Excuse me. Are you Shimshon?"

The speech was slow and careful, in a strange accent — Spanish, perhaps; Shimshon did not know. He turned, puzzled, with a certain trepidation, and was even more surprised.

Standing near him was a Korean man of about twenty — medium height, slim, with straight black hair and a slight moustache. He was dressed in jeans and a work apron over a cotton T-shirt. In his hand he held several folded slips of paper.

"He asked me to give them to you one at a time," he explained. He handed the first to Shimshon.

The outside of the slip was numbered: #1. Puzzled, the boy opened it, and instantly his legs went numb. He began to sway uncertainly.

Slowly turn toward the building and face me. Then quickly look away, please.

Shimshon turned. On the third floor the face of Avraham Shulman stood watching, erect and silent.

The Oriental waited before handing him another slip of paper — #2. Trembling, Shimshon opened and read.

Splendid. Now perhaps we can meet? Alone?

The boy shook his head violently as he clutched the slips. Zev watched him and frowned.

The youth handed Shimshon the final piece of paper.

"I'm not sure I want to read it," Shimshon said. But he opened it. This time the message was in block letters.

I WON'T TOUCH YOU.

"Shimmy, are you all right?" Zev asked, hurrying to his side. "You look pale."

"I'm all right," Shimshon answered weakly. He turned to the Korean. "Are you going back to him?"

The boy shook his head. "I don't even know him. He sent me here; I work at a grocery store."

" 'He'?"

The grocery boy shrugged. "Some man came in — bought a bunch of Cokes and took me here. He took me around the back, by the fire escape, where an old man gave me the notes for you."

"What did the guy who bought the Cokes look like?" Shimshon asked.

The boy shrugged. "Young . . . thirty, maybe? Kind of dark; spoke English funny. I think he was Italian."

Shimshon and Zev looked at each other quizzically.

"Sure doesn't sound like Dietrich," Shimshon replied.

"Maybe it is," Zev countered. "Not all Germans are blond, you know. Or maybe it's a bodyguard."

"That was Heinz. He wasn't dark. Or Italian."

"Then who do you think it could have been?"

"Well . . ." Shimshon pondered the matter uncertainly. "Italy was on Germany's side during the war. We learned that in school. Maybe he has some of them working for him. You know, like

Mussolini's men — 'Fascists,' I think they were called."

Zev gasped. "Maybe it's the Mafia," he whispered.

Shimshon trembled. "Zev, I'm really scared. I didn't think Shulman was a gangster."

"Look, I've got to go back," the Oriental interrupted impatiently. "They need me at work. If you like, I'll take you there. I'll show you where to go."

Zev looked at Shimshon hesitantly. "Maybe you should tell your father first," he offered. But deep down he knew as well as Shimshon what the response would be.

"Are you kidding?!" Shimshon exclaimed. "You think I'd ask permission to see Shulman?"

"But you've got to," Zev argued. "I think your father has gotta know."

"He'll never let me go," retorted Shimshon passionately.

"He would be right. Maybe you shouldn't," Zev said. "*I* wouldn't go there. I don't trust Shulman either."

"But he wants to see me, Zev."

"But do you want to see *him*, Shimmy?"

Shimshon hesitated. His common sense told him to stay away. Otherwise, he would be placing his life in danger. Shulman would hardly be the benevolent old man he had appeared to be in *shul* or on Justin Road. Yet there was some kind of voice beckoning Shimshon — some higher, primal command compelling him from within the building's walls, soothing him with florid prose, inviting him inside to learn even more about this incredible man.

Shimshon looked again in the building's direction. This time Shulman waved.

Shimshon looked again at the message. *I won't touch you.* He could almost hear Shulman's flowing lilt. The voice reassuring, courteous — yet with gentle urgency. He wondered: Could Shulman be lying? Shulman wrote that he wouldn't harm Shimshon. But there really was no telling what he was capable of doing — or what his real intentions might be.

Shimshon turned once more to the grocery boy, who was fidgeting alongside him. "The man who took you here," he said. "Is he still with you?"

"No. He left."

"Was there anyone else with him?"

The youth shrugged. "Nope. No one. He was alone. I'll take you to the fire escape."

Shimshon could feel himself breathing heavily. He turned to his friend and whispered, "Zev, Avraham Shulman wants to see me. I must go." Handing the slips of paper to Zev, he said, "Give these to Ta . . . after I leave. I'll go with this guy. Tell Ta I'll be back soon. I hope."

"You're crazy, Shimmy!" Zev hissed, clutching his friend's arm. "You think Shulman will let you out alive?"

"He said he wouldn't hurt me," Shimshon insisted, prying himself loose.

"And you *believe* him?"

"Yes. I don't think he would try anything here. There are too many witnesses."

"But the two of you will be alone!"

"People will see me leave. Besides, if he's trying to prove he's not a Nazi, then hurting me wouldn't be the way."

"But maybe by now he wouldn't care if he did." Again Zev clutched his friend's arm. Again Shimshon pulled himself away, and began descending the platform. Zev followed. "He may figure he's been caught anyway, and has nothing to lose. He may just want to even the score. He may try to kidnap you." Zev's voice was passionate, terrified. "Shimmy, you're taking a big chance. Don't do it . . . *please.*"

The Korean interrupted. "Oh, I forgot." He extracted from his pocket another slip of paper. "He said to give this to . . . Rabbi Shapiro?"

"My father," Shimshon said.

"After you leave," the grocery boy said. He turned to Zev. "Maybe you'll give it."

"No way," Zev argued, backing off. "I don't want to get in trouble." He gave the other slips to the Oriental. "Here. Take these to him too."

"Please do it," Shimshon said to the grocery boy. "After you take me there. Give them to my father. He's the man standing there in the . . ." He trailed off, bewildered, as he realized that more than half the men were wearing black hats and coats. "Gosh, they all look alike, don't they?" he said to the Oriental. He continued, "My friend here, Zev, will point him out. Zev, wait till after he comes back before you speak to my father." Handing him the megaphone, he ordered, "You'll have to take over."

"Me?" his friend said, stunned.

"Yeah. Good luck."

"Shimmy, I don't know what do!" In horror Zev stared at the crowd, now growing restless.

"It's easy. Just jump up and down. You're bigger than I am. They'll see you. Also, you've got a loud voice; you always like to make noise — no offense."

"And what if your father sees you leave the podium?" Zev argued. "What am I supposed to tell him?"

"I don't know. Tell him . . . tell him I went to get a drink or something. Yeah, that's it."

The crowd murmured curiously as Shimshon scampered off the platform with the grocery boy. Pausing thoughtfully, he turned to Zev and called, "Better yet . . . tell him I had to leave for something important. Important to Jews everywhere. Tell him there's a whole lot at stake."

Carefully keeping out of his father's sight, Shimshon followed the Oriental past the debris of the construction site, toward Seventh Avenue, ignoring the small children who watched him and straggled along.

"Where ya going, Shimmy?" asked one of them.

"I'll be right back," Shimshon answered patronizingly. "I just have to do something. My friend's up there. His name is Zev. You just do what he says, okay?"

"Okay," the child answered cheerfully.

Turning the corner onto Seventh Avenue, the two walked about a hundred yards. They passed a carpet store, and the Oriental stopped. Shimshon noticed a narrow alleyway lined with garbage cans.

Nervously Shimshon clutched his nose and trailed after the Oriental, twice nearly stumbling over potholes and puddles of grease. The sound of the demonstration had receded and then faded out as the two passed between the tall rows of concrete overtowering them. Shimshon turned his head constantly to watch the freight loading docks, gaping black and open at his sides. *He's waiting,* he thought. The darkness, the delapidation, and the stench reminded him alarmingly of the apartment house on Justin Road. By the time the building loomed in view, Shimshon was very nervous.

At the building's midpoint was the fire escape — its rickety, skeletal bars extending vertically, ending just two feet above the pavement. The Oriental stopped and turned.

"He brought me here," he said. "We went up five floors. Then I waited outside till the old man came."

"Five floors?" Shimshon exclaimed. He looked apprehensively at the rusty ladder. "I don't know . . . I'm a little scared."

"It's not hard. I'll help you."

Grasping the metal firmly, the grocery boy climbed the ladder, agile as a monkey. Swinging himself gymnastically over the railing, he leaned over. "Come up," he called.

Trembling, Shimshon grabbed the ladder and rested his feet firmly on the rungs. Keeping his eyes upward, he followed the ascendant horizontal-on-vertical pattern. When he reached the railing of the fifth floor, he clutched the Oriental's hand for dear life and bounced onto the platform. It jiggled slightly.

Grasping the metal again, the grocery boy lifted himself over the railing as if mounting a horse, his feet landing in the rungs as if they were the stirrups of a saddle.

Shimshon gasped. "You're leaving?" he cried.

The grocery boy nodded. "Back to work. Wait here. He'll come soon."

Looking around frantically, Shimshon caught sight of the ground below, and was gripped with dizziness. He cried beseechingly, "Don't leave me up here . . . please!"

"Don't worry. The man will come. Maybe you should knock on the window."

"You'll remember to see my father. Please?"

"Okay. But first I go to . . . Zev?"

"Right. You think you'll remember what he looks like?"

"Big kid, right?"

"Yeah. He'll take you to my father. I told him to wait for you."

"Yeah."

"And please . . . give him the message!"

"Okay."

The grocery boy's wiry frame undulated swiftly down the ladder. When he reached the bottom, he called out, "Good luck."

Shimshon watched him disappear. The form leaped away, like a ballet dancer, past the watching walls of the buildings. The sound of footsteps echoed through the alleyway and gradually faded into the street. Shimshon was left alone — completely alone. Just out of view were masses of people. Here, silence reigned.

Shimshon shut his eyes and tried to imagine himself at age seven, on the giant oak tree in the park. He alone, of everyone there, was able to climb to the highest branch.

Look at me, Ma! he had called.

Shimmy, get down from there. Right now!

The boy opened his eyes wide in terror. He looked up and saw several more sets of staircases, crisscrossing each other like — no! That was somewhere else! He was not far away when they saw him then. They were after him, and he fled inside, to lose himself. He had escaped — to his father. Now, he was here, standing outside — trapped! A sitting duck!

Terrified, Shimshon crouched on the platform. How foolish of me, he thought. Of course Shulman would want to meet me here. He knows I can't get down so easily. *I won't touch you,* he said. No, but he would shoot me. Or have someone else do the work. Here there was no place to go.

A pigeon stopped by and rested on the railing. Through beady eyes it looked curiously at this intruder, then glided across the alley to the opposite building. Shimshon longed for a pair of wings so he could fly away at a moment's notice. Feeling the loose, thin slats under his feet, he advanced toward the window, and his hands groped the sill.

Still trembling, the boy bent over and knocked. No response. He knocked again. He peered through the glass. The room inside was still; there was absolutely no sign of activity, nor were there any lights on. He wondered: Would Shulman come? Did he know Shimshon was here, waiting?

Curiously — as sort of an afterthought — Shimshon juggled the window. To his surprise, it lifted wide open. It was not locked from inside. Of course not! Shimshon thought. He's waiting. He's waiting for me to go inside. However, Shimshon still hesitated, looking at the darkness within, feeling as if he were about to enter a cave with wild animals. Perhaps his father would come. He would come running after the grocery boy spoke to him.

"Hey, you! What are you doing there?"

Oh, no! Not again! He conjured up memories of a burly, sweat-stained man hovering over him, staring angrily and speaking in a vulgar tone of voice.

"Hey, kid! You get off of there!"

But the voice this time was smooth and resonant, coming from two flights above. A young man, thirtyish, slightly muscular, with a chiseled face, stylish hair like the reporter's, and a bright red T-shirt saying *Nautilus Network*, was leaning over the window sill.

Shimshon answered, "I . . . I'm waiting for somebody."

"On the fire escape? Baloney!" the man shouted.

"Who is it, Bill?" A woman, also in a T-shirt, appeared at the window.

"Some punk on the fire escape."

The woman looked down. When she saw Shimshon, she clutched her throat dramatically with her slender hands. "Oh, my goodness," she exclaimed breathily. "What are you doing there?"

"Waiting for somebody," Shimshon answered simply. By now he felt no desire to make up a story.

"That's dangerous!"

"I know," Shimshon answered. He was in no mood to argue, either.

"Why, who would send a boy up a fire escape?" the woman said. "Especially ours — why, it's not a fire escape, it's a fire *hazard.*"

Shimshon glanced about fearfully, and clutched the sill even tighter.

The woman continued to look down in horror. "Get down from there. Right now!"

"You know something — I think he's here to rob somebody," Bill said.

"Oh, no — look, Bill. He's wearing one of those things on his head. Must be one of the kids from out front."

"You Jewish?" asked Bill.

"Let's call Mr. Shulman."

"That's who I'm waiting for," Shimshon chirped.

"You want to harass him some more, right?" Bill spat. "You want to break into his place. I'm calling the police."

"They're right out in front, Bill," his friend said. "Maybe you should go out and ask one of them — why, he's gone. The boy's gone!"

While she was speaking, Shimshon had slipped inside. Hurriedly shutting the window after him, blocking out the conversation — he did not care to hear the rest — he inched inside. At last his feet landed on the hard wooden floor.

The sunless room was empty — devoid of habitation. Four unpainted walls bleakly faced each other. Shimshon glanced ahead and noticed beyond the door a darkened hallway, extending past several other doors. No *mezuzos*. A solitary light bulb was stuck firmly inside a socket on the hallway ceiling. With trembling hands, Shimshon flicked on the switch.

"Shulman?" he called.

His voice reverberated off the pale walls. The walls of 2001 Justin Road also had falling plaster. Shimshon shut his eyes, blocking out the vivid similarities. When he opened them again, they held tears of fright.

"Shulman?" the boy called again.

Slowly, he walked down the hallway, turning the knob of each door, opening it carefully. Each door revealed another empty room.

He finally came to a room that had some furniture — the bathroom. It contained a toilet with cigarette butts floating on top, and an old-fashioned bathtub, resting on top of legs that resembled animal paws. Shimshon hesitantly opened the bathtub curtains. He gasped. There, atop the dusty porcelain, an enormous cockroach peered at him, waving its antennae. Making a face, Shimshon backed away, quickly closing the curtains. He hurriedly left the bathroom.

He made his way into the next room and turned on the light. What he saw made his heart jump.

He was sitting on a stool by a table — the only pieces of furniture in the room.

"Hello, Shimshon," he whispered.

The boy backed away, toward the door.

"No, please . . . don't be afraid," the old man pleaded, as he slowly rose from the table. "I'm so glad you came."

Avraham Shulman stood in the light and opened his coat, revealing his white shirt and black trousers. Holding his coat out at both ends, he looked, especially with his pale skin, like a vampire in a cape. "See? No gun. No weapons. I said I wouldn't harm you. I always keep my word." His voice was caressing and liquid-sweet, like warm syrup over buttered pancakes. He approached Shimshon. "Come. We'll walk out together."

When he tried to hold the boy's arm, the latter backed away in revulsion, as if the man were leprous. Shulman smiled and retreated.

"Still don't trust me, eh? Very well, then. I won't touch you. Walk in front of me. I'll tell you where to go. I'll take you there myself, to our destination. Once we're there, we can talk more freely."

Then, pointing toward the front door, he ordered sternly, "Go."

"He *what?*"

Rabbi Sharpiro stared wide-eyed at Zev, who stood, cringing. Behind Zev, a few feet away, was the Korean.

"He went to see him, Rabbi Shapiro," Zev repeated fearfully.

"And you let him?"

"I . . . I tried to stop him, sir," Zev answered. "But Shimmy was dead set on going. He told me to go to you after he left."

"Why on earth would he *do* such a thing?!" Rabbi Shapiro thundered.

"Shulman asked to see him," Zev answered miserably.

The rabbi, taking a deep breath, scanned the dispersing crowd, then the building, hoping to catch a glimpse of a twelve-year-old boy in one of the windows. Nothing — except more irate tenants. He didn't know what disturbed him more: Shimshon being there alone with Shulman, or his still being magically obedient to the man. It would take more than a demonstration to destroy Shulman's diabolical charisma.

The Korean approached him and said, "Pardon me, Rabbi Shapiro."

The rabbi looked at him. "Yes?"

The grocery boy removed a slip of paper from an apron pocket. "This is from Mr. Shulman. He said to give this to you after your son arrived there."

The rabbi opened the neatly folded paper. The letter, written in English, was made even more chilling by the flowery, European penmanship.

> *My dear Rabbi Shapiro,*
>
> *Please do not be alarmed, and please forgive this slight intrusion. I bear no ill will toward you, in spite of your opinion of me, nor toward your son, in spite of this dreadful demonstration. I have taken the liberty of bringing him along to a meeting of sorts. May I suggest a meeting with you,* alone, *at 56th Street and Columbus Avenue.* Minchah *is at seven o'clock.*
>
> *Yours Truly,*
> *A. Shulman*

Absently folding the paper and stuffing it into his pocket, Rabbi Shapiro dwelt morbidly on the underlined word *alone*. Only the sight of Zev's worried stare brought him back to the world of the living.

The rabbi looked at his watch: five o'clock; two hours to go.

"Zev," he said, "do you think you can get everyone here to leave?"

Zev stared, puzzled. "Leave?"

"Yes. To go home."

"I think so. Why?"

"Well, it's getting quite late. I think they've all been a great help, but the demonstration has pretty much run its course." He turned to the Korean. "Did Shulman tell you anything else?"

"No." The grocery boy turned to leave. "I have to get back to work."

"May I ask how you know Avraham Shulman?"

The Korean shrugged. "I don't. I work part time at a grocery store. A man came in to buy soda and talk with me. He asked if I'd do him a favor. He brought me here."

"He said the man was Italian!" Zev exclaimed.

"He took me to the back of this building," the grocery boy continued, "and we waited for an old man in a long black coat."

The rabbi asked the Korean, "Excuse me, did you say he took you 'to the back?' "

"Yes."

"Where?"

"The back of the building. There's a fire escape."

The rabbi cried, "Take me there at once!"

Shimshon hesitantly walked out, feeling Shulman's presence every step of the way — not more than three feet from him. Shulman remained wordless. Only intermittently he said, "Turn!" or "Go left!" steering the boy through the emergency exit and down five flights of stairs. At each floor, Shulman ordered him to stop, as he himself carefully leaned over the banister, his shiny eyes scrutizing every angle for any possible signs of a waiting, hidden attacker.

Shimshon, watching, longed to explain that he had come alone, as was mutually agreed; he had brought no one with him. But he remained silent. Only once did he shakily ask, "How long will it take — our talk?"

"An hour . . . possibly two. It depends. We're not sure yet what to do with you, really."

This last remark, uttered ever so casually, sent Shimshon trembling with a new wave of panic. By the time they reached the bottom, he was contemplating breaking away, and hoped that by now either his father or the police would be waiting at the staircase. When he opened the exit door, he stared in shock.

A yellow taxi was waiting in the alley; the driver sat at the wheel, looking over Shimshon's shoulder.

"You Bill?" the cabbie asked.

"Yes," answered Shulman.

Shimshon gasped in surprise and comprehension.

Quickly, Shulman opened the taxi door and ushered Shimshon inside. The old man slid in beside him.

"Where to?" asked the driver.

"Three-ten East Sixty-seventh Street. Please hurry."

"No sweat."

Shimshon turned his head toward Shulman in amazement. "Was that guy Bill in on this?" he demanded.

Shulman smiled diplomatically. "It pays to have an actor for one of my tenants," he explained, with a trace of humor. "Especially when he owes me two months' rent. He runs an acting studio in my building. It was a favor of sorts; when Bill and his wife saw you, they let me know you were there."

"Yeah. They musta thought I was crazy!"

"Possibly. I had to talk them out of calling the police to report a crazy young boy on a fire escape. Instead, they called a taxi. Though I would have called one myself anyway. *And* come out to greet you. I was hoping you would have come inside sooner, to avoid the embarrassment of being seen on the fire escape. I had specifically left the window open for you, hoping you would take the hint."

Shimshon's head pounded. Though he was long ago off the fire escape, he suddenly felt dizzy. "Was that a joke?" he demanded.

"What?"

"Getting me on the fire escape. Leaving me there."

"Oh, no, quite the contrary," Shulman answered softly. "But it was a nice way to get you inside the building, don't you think? It certainly was better than my going outside and facing those friends of yours."

"You could've asked me to walk through the entrance."

"In plain sight of your father?"

"So you brought me around to the fire escape to scare the daylights out of me?"

"An indirect result, perhaps, but not the main intention. Actually, I had two. One: to show you that I mean no harm. I could have easily pointed a gun at you there, but I didn't."

"No, but your friends might have!"

"Further proof that you have nothing to fear from me. My friends have orders not to touch you," Shulman answered darkly. "If they did, I would make things most unpleasant for them."

"But leaving me on the fire escape is dangerous. I'm just a kid — remember?"

"Oh, yes. I became aware of it this afternoon."

"I coulda gotten killed! That fire escape must be a hundred years old!"

"So? The people in my building had to use it today, thanks to your blocking the front door. Does that bother you?"

"Well . . ." Shimshon's voice trailed off.

"Some of them are younger than you, others are older than myself. A seventy-year-old man went down the fire escape with his eight-year-old grandson from the ninth floor. They had gone up to buy a suit. So, reason number two: to show *you* what it feels like to be terrified." Shulman again smiled, playing the wise sage. He calmly continued, "Isn't that what you've been trying to do to *me?* Trap me, intimidate me? And on other occasions as well. Up till now I've been very patient with you, Shimshon — though you've endangered many people's lives." Shulman paused, then added ominously, "I can easily put you in far worse situations."

The last remark made Shimshon tremble with fear again; nevertheless, he continued to feel both angry and just plain stupid for the whole charade on the fire escape. Wouldn't it be like Shulman to put him in his place.

Shulman silently studied the rear view mirror. Immediately his expression changed from serenity to worry, though he remained calmly seated. His eyes, however, followed something in motion.

Shimshon watched him with growing concern. He turned around to look, and his eyes widened.

"No, don't," Shulman ordered quickly. "Keep your head forward."

Shimshon caught sight of a blue car behind theirs. "Ta!" he called.

"Silence!" Shulman commanded, grabbing hold of Shimshon's

head and turning it around like a screw. "Don't look back!" He leaned forward and told the driver, "Turn right at the next block."

"Are you crazy?" the man commanded. "I'm in the far left lane."

"Do as I say. I'll make it worth your while — I promise."

The car turned suddenly, swerving through three lanes, cutting off other cars, and triggering a cacophony of screeching brakes down the avenue.

"You stupid idiot!" Shimshon heard someone yell. He clutched the arm rest in terror as the cabbie made the right turn.

"Now — get into the left lane!" Shulman ordered.

"What—"

"Now!"

The taxi tailgated the car in front and swiftly pulled into the left lane. The car behind jerked and turned, nearly colliding with another vehicle.

"Now — turn into this alleyway," Shulman commanded.

"It's awfully tight," the driver argued.

"Just *do it!*"

The taxi jerked at a nearly ninety-degree angle, knocking down a row of garbage cans as if they were dominoes. It crushed a sack of garbage and crawled through the alley, nearly scraping its doors against an embankment on one side and a large building on the other. As it glided behind a restaurant, a couple of busboys, observing the scene, pointed and gesticulated.

The taxi passed behind a small industrial building, and Shulman ordered the driver to halt.

"We'll get out here," he said, tossing the man a fifty-dollar bill for the ten-dollar ride.

The driver stared at the bill in disbelief. "You've got to be kidding. I . . . I can't make change for this."

"Keep it," Shulman said. "Thank you very much."

"Thank *you!*" the driver exclaimed, as Shulman ordered Shimshon out of the car.

Dazed, Shimshon stood in the driveway, vaguely aware that Shulman was clutching his arm in a bony grip. Shimshon struggled to detach himself, remembering Shulman's words: *I won't touch you;* by now he was terrified at what else this horrid man might try to do.

"Let me go," he whimpered.

Shulman remained as rigid as stone. "I will not harm you; I gave you my word. Just do as I say. I warn you." Then, with a certain gentleness, he added, "*Please.* I haven't time now to explain." He looked to his right. "Come on," he said. "This way."

He pulled Shimshon through a back door of what appeared to be a print shop. The workers looked up from their machinery in surprise at the newcomers — an old man whose black coat brushed past the gigantic printing press clutching a boy pale with fright.

"Hey, what are you two doing here?" barked the foreman.

Shimshon tried to turn and explain that they were just passing through, but he was swiftly led out the door, past the front office.

"Hey!" yelled a burly man as the two figures made their exit. But not before Shimshon heard, "Crazy Jews."

Standing outside the shop, they were on a street overlooking a mixture of office buildings and co-op apartments. In the five-second interval that he used to catch his breath, Shimshon glanced at a corner sign. Twenty-third and Madison. He leaned against the wall in a daze. They were nowhere near the address Shulman had given the driver. Shulman, meanwhile, raised his hand stiffly in the air and immediately caught the attention of a passing taxi.

The cab pulled up and Shulman practically shoved the boy inside. He himself slid in quickly.

"Seventy-eight Pike," he ordered.

"Chinatown, right?" the driver said.

"Yes. Please hurry."

Again Shulman studied the rear view mirror, outwardly appearing calm and dignified. His blue eyes coldly scanned Broadway, like a field marshal surveying the battlefield.

"At the next block," he commanded, "make a right."

"But Pike's the other way," the driver argued.

"Do it!"

The driver shrugged. He turned sharply right, eliciting screeching brakes from the other drivers on the avenue.

"Now make a left."

The cabbie moved into the left lane and slowed down as the light turned yellow.

"Now!" Shulman barked.

Like an automatic reflex, the taxi jolted and roared through the intersection as the oncoming cars slammed on their brakes, skidding, missing the taxi's fender by inches. Shimshon, glued to the back seat, felt his stomach churning from both fear and car sickness. He did not know how much longer he could keep down his lunch.

The taxi stopped at Canal Street, in the center of Chinatown. Shulman pulled Shimshon out of the car and flung a large bill at the driver. Still clutching Shimshon's arm, he led him across the street into a subway tunnel.

Reaching into his pocket, Shulman deposited two tokens — Shimshon wondered if he had saved them for this occasion — and dragged the boy through the turnstile. Shimshon tried to break away from the man's iron grip, but to no avail. When the train arrived, Shulman hurried to a deserted car and yanked the boy through the open doors, nearly pulling Shimshon's arm from its socket.

Shimshon again attempted to break free.

Shulman yanked him still. "Enough!" the old man hissed. "If you try to escape, you and your father will die!"

So staggered was Shimshon by his harsh tone of voice that he believed the man, and was silent. A Chinese couple who had come in after them observed them, perplexed.

At the next stop, Shulman again pulled Shimshon from his seat; they rushed up the filthy stairs and emerged outside. They were still in Chinatown, near a street filled with busy shoppers. Quickly Shulman raised his arm, summoning a taxi.

The next driver was from El Salvador.

"Five hundred West Eighty-third Street, *por favor,*" Shulman ordered. He continued, in excellent Spanish, "This is an emergency. I'm a rabbi, on my way to visit a dying man. I urge you to hurry. Go through red lights if you have to — I'll reward you generously. But please get there as quickly as possible."

The driver nodded.

"Thank you and G-d bless you."

Shulman calmly reclined against the seat, and kept his gaze on the rear view mirror. For a man of sixty-six, he seemed completely unperturbed by the wild tour of Manhattan that had just taken place. Not a hair was out of place, and he had not lost his composure. Shimshon, in the meantime, who was pressed against the opposite side of the taxi, as far away from the man as possible, was a disheveled wreck. A sleeve was torn; his yarmulke hung awry; his hair was a mess. He looked like a street kid.

The driver needed no further prodding to drive quickly. He by-passed rush hour traffic by illegally turning at several intersections, at one point riding onto the sidewalk and terrifying a man pushing a baby carriage.

Passing along Riverside Drive, Shimshon kept his face by the window, watching the Hudson and clutching his wrist. Though Shulman had released his grip, the nail marks remained imbedded in the flesh. Boy, was I dumb, Shimshon thought gloomily as the tears rolled down his face — tears of anguish and remorse, for having disobeyed his father for possibly the very last time.

The taxi pulled up at a construction site. Shulman jerkily extracted Shimshon from the taxi and handed the driver a large bill.

"Muchas gracias," he said.

"Muchas gracias," the driver answered. *"Y buena salud a su amigo."*

Shimshon was as white as a ghost by the time he exited the taxi. He staggered over to the wooden walls of the site and waited. Shulman stood on the street, his black coat stark against the still bright sun, and intensely surveyed the area. However, at the sight of something ahead, his expression changed from worry to sober acknowledgment, and he turned to speak to Shimshon. He looked around in a panic. Shimshon was gone.

"Shimshon?" he called. "Shimshon, where are you?"

A few yards away he noticed a body bent over, shaking convulsively. Shimshon had dragged himself behind the construction site, where he was now busy vomiting.

With a sudden gentleness, Shulman pulled the boy up and urged him on, while he himself continued to scan the area anxiously, turning his neck to and fro, like a spectator at a tennis match. With trembling legs the boy followed the man to the corner.

"It's that building there," Shulman said, pointing ahead.

Shimshon's eyes widened. He had expected some drab and neglected place in a depressed neighborhood, like 2001 Justin Road. But 540 West Eighty-third Street was quite a different sight. It was a modern structure, painted gold and white, with symmetrical rows of balconies and glass windows. It overlooked the Hudson on one side, a small garden bordering a row of brownstones on the other. The only thing marring the block was the construction site — a large, half-built foundation of dirt and granite blocks, with a sign off to the side saying: *Future Home of Galaxy Condominiums. Seidler and Nussbaum Realty.*

In front of the 540 building was a broad driveway leading to the entrance; it was lined with trim shrubbery. The doorman was busy escorting a middle-aged couple to a Rolls Royce parked in front of the beige-and-white awning. Just a few paces away a woman stood by a tree, walking a dachshund. At the sight of Shulman's awesome figure, the dog yapped and strained at its leash, which the woman tugged with annoyance. As Shulman, with Shimshon, approached the entrance, the doorman nodded silently and opened the broad glass door.

Once inside the lobby, Shulman paused to make a quick note of a man in a business suit who was sitting on one of the sofas, reading a newspaper. The man looked up curiously, then returned to his paper. With a flick of the hand, Shulman signaled Shimshon to wait by the elevators. Shimshon, surveying the palatial lobby, was in awe; its large chandelier shadowed a scarlet carpet, which was patterned with a black and gold floral pattern. It reminded him of the halls where he had attended many weddings and bar mitzvahs. Through tinted glass he watched the late afternoon sky, and thought that it was the last sunlight he might ever see.

When an elevator full of people appeared, Shimshon was about to enter, but was held back by Shulman. Not until ten minutes had passed, till an empty car gaped open, did he release Shimshon's arm and usher him inside.

After pressing the twelfth-floor button, Shulman turned to the boy and for the first time spoke like the man Shimshon had first met at his father's synagogue. "Please forgive our little ride this afternoon. But you'll soon understand why it was necessary. My intention was certainly not to make you frightened. Or car-sick."

"*You* make me sick — not the taxi," Shimshon snarled.

Shulman stared at the boy in sad surprise, his eyes brimming with tears. "You hurt me, Shimshon."

"Good."

"You can't really mean that."

"I do." The boy mumbled sullenly, "I want my father."

Shulman softly retorted, "Did you think of him when you went to see me? Or all those times you were off in search of adventure? That's what you wanted, wasn't it — adventure? Why didn't you leave me this afternoon?"

"I was afraid," Shimshon murmured. "And I couldn't let go of you. You were holding me pretty tight."

"Really? Was I? Am I really that much stronger than you? You could have simply walked off the subway, or screamed for help. You could have warned the taxi driver, or pedestrians. I didn't have a gun. I'm an old man; I couldn't chase after you. Admit it Shimshon; deep down you were still curious. Forever curious. It's not a bad trait, actually; when used properly, curiosity leads to knowledge. Used improperly, however, it leads to dangerous adventure. But again, that's what you wanted. I thought I'd be willing to oblige a nice little boy like you."

Nice little boy, Shimshon thought. Nice little boys like me are home right now, staying out of trouble.

The elevator landed at the twelfth floor; the doors opened. Shimshon was about to exit, when again he was restrained by Shulman, who pushed several buttons. The doors closed, and the elevator ascended another four flights.

"Just a precaution," he said.

The elevator finally descended, stopping first on each floor. When the doors opened on the eleventh, Shulman, holding the doors, stuck out his golden-white head and looked up and down the corridor. With a flick of the wrist, he summoned Shimshon outside.

They walked through a corridor carpeted in a motif similar to the one in the lobby downstairs, with elegantly curved lamps hanging from velveteen panels. Through one door Shimshon heard a woman's voice: "Horace, please take out the garbage."

Shimshon counted off the apartments: 11D, 11E, 11F. When one door opened, Shulman quickly jerked him back. A woman of about sixty emerged, studied the pair through her glasses, and walked away. Her gaze gave Shimshon a certain incentive to make his appearance neater. He smoothed back his hair and adjusted his yarmulke.

At 11K, they stopped. Shulman knocked four times. Then four times again.

"At five years of age, the study of Scripture," came a voice in perfect Hebrew.

"At ten — the study of Mishnah," Shulman responded, also in

perfect Hebrew. At the mention of the Torah passage, he smiled beatifically.

"At thirteen the mitzvos."

"At fifteen — the study of Gemara."

"At eighteen — marriage."

"At twenty — pursuit of a livelihood."

"At thirty — full strength."

Shimshon knew the rest; Ethics of the Fathers, the end of Chapter Five. Just two weeks ago, before Shavous, he and half the Jewish world had finished reading the entire tractate.

They heard the sound of the door being unlocked. Turning to Shimshon, Shulman announced, his eyes gazing with fearful solemnity, "I do hope, Shimshon, that this meeting will be fruitful. G-d willing, you'll get to know me better — and my situation. We've both, in our own way, taken a terrible chance in coming here."

Chapter 16

Leaders

Six-forty. Yehuda Shapiro, usually the most patient of men, waited with frantic impatience in the driver's seat, fingers tapping the dashboard, as he watched the rush hour traffic in despair. He passed by the street sign: Fiftieth and Seventh. A quarter of a mile left.

A meeting. What kind of meeting did Shulman have in mind? Was it to be where he had cordially "invited" Shimmy? What — the rabbi thought, fighting back the tears — were his chances of ever seeing his son again alive?

He groaned. He had just missed them; he had arrived there just in time to see the taxi careening out of the alley. Had Shimmy seen him? At least he was off the fire escape. The thought of his son standing five floors above the pavement on a decrepit structure had made his father's heart palpitate with fear. Schmidt had always had more than one way to frighten children and adults alike.

He looked at his watch: 6:55. The rabbi turned the corner on Fifty-sixth Street and headed toward Columbus Avenue. Here he was — the Upper West Side. Some of his acquaintances lived here, in the well-kept brownstones on the elegant tree-lined streets. His eyes scanned the street as the car crawled past a group of men moving furniture into an apartment house. One of the men glanced at the rabbi with blasé curiosity, then turned away. Nearby, most of the shops and boutiques were either closed or closing; strolling past them, completing the picture, were young fashionably-dressed couples, ready for their evening out.

Rabbi Shapiro reached the corner of Columbus in time to see an Orthodox Jew in a tan coat and hat hurry into a building. Coming the opposite way, his back to the setting sun, was another young man in similar attire. He too went into the building. Rabbi Shapiro had guessed that the "meeting place" was a synagogue; he vaguely remembered a *shul* in this area which he had used once or twice when he had missed the office *minyan*. Sure enough, when he drove closer he saw a Star of David above the door and a sign under it in Hebrew and Roman letters: *Kehillas Zion*. By the entrance was a schedule in movable block letters: *Weekday minchah: 7:00 p.m.*

The rabbi glanced at his watch: 6:58. He had approximately two minutes left to find a parking place. An impossible feat in Manhattan, he thought to himself. However, he saw just ahead of him a Toyota pulling out, and somehow he managed to fit his Pontiac within the tight perimeters of the space.

Leaving his car, the rabbi froze. There in the distance was a tall, white-haired figure, his long black coat fluttering in the wind like the flag on a pirate ship. Seven o'clock sharp. Leave it to Avraham Shulman to be punctual.

The rabbi hastened his gait and quickly reached the synagogue. He rushed up the steps to the entrance, and opened the door. "Shulman!" he called.

"Yes?" came a voice.

The rabbi looked, and retreated. A young man in a beige jacket and an intricately-woven blue-and-white skullcap stared at Yehuda Shapiro curiously.

"You wished to speak to me?" the man asked.

"Who are you?" the rabbi asked.

"Steve Shulman. Who are *you*?"

"Oh, forgive me," Rabbi Shapiro stammered. "I'm looking for Avraham Shulman."

The man smiled apologetically. "No relation. Never heard of him." He turned away.

The chassid had retreated to the far pews. His back still turned to Rabbi Shapiro, he was wrapping a *gartel* around his waist and fervently reciting the prayers. He seemed not only oblivious to, but out of place among, the other worshipers, who were mostly young men in modern business suits, chatting in American slang among themselves, discussing the grueling day in the boardrooms or on the stock exchange. Most likely, this man, rhythmically bowing and bending to his own chant, could not speak their language on any level.

"Avraham Shulman!" called Rabbi Shapiro again more quietly, approaching the man.

The man did not turn. He continued to pray.

At last Rabbi Shapiro tapped the chassid's shoulder. The latter turned around sharply, and the rabbi backed away in shock and chagrin.

"What do you want? Can't you see I'm busy?" the man snapped in an accent that leaned more toward Budapest than Berlin.

"I'm terribly sorry," the rabbi again stammered, this time in Yiddish. "I thought you were someone else."

In bewilderment, Rabbi Shapiro took a seat a certain distance away. During the service, his eyes quickly scanned the little room, probing the other congregants, watching to see if anyone resembling Shulman — Avraham, not Steve — would walk in. No one. Rabbi Shapiro did not dare leave his place to look around in futile search and possibly embarrass himself a third time. After *Aleinu* and *Kaddish,* he watched the men disperse and the chassid silently unwrap and roll up his *gartel.* Passing by Rabbi Shapiro, the man stopped to glare at him for a moment, then left. No, he's definitely not Avraham Shulman, the rabbi thought ironically.

Soon the hall was silent. Only a few men remained, and they took seats in the front. The evening *shiur,* Rabbi Shapiro supposed. He thought wistfully of his own *shul* in Boro Park, and how he longed to be with his own congregation.

Well, he concluded, this time I'll be on the other side of the pulpit. He quietly took a seat behind a middle-aged man with an English sports cap.

The rabbi entered — a Yechiel Morgenstern, whom Yehuda Shapiro recognized from a recent convention of rabbis. Spotting his colleague in the audience, Rabbi Morgenstern said brightly, "Yehuda! *Shalom aleichem!*"

"*Aleichem shalom,* Yechiel," Rabbi Shapiro answered quietly.

"What brings you to these parts?"

"I'm waiting for someone," the rabbi answered casually. "I was told to meet him here."

"Anyone I know?"

"I doubt it. Mind if I listen in?"

"Not at all!" Rabbi Morgenstern exclaimed. "Perhaps you'll delight us with a few of your own insights. I've never forgotten that wonderful speech you gave."

Feeling more relaxed, Rabbi Shapiro leaned back and listened to a rather simple explanation on a particular Talmudic subject. Occasionally he glanced at the door, then his watch, trying to hide his growing anxiety and mentally inventing a number of excuses for why Avraham Shulman had not appeared. He was frightened away, the rabbi thought. He didn't trust me; he didn't believe I would actually come here alone. Or perhaps he had just been delayed.

The rabbi casually studied the synagogue. It was about the size of his own, though it more resembled a small auditorium than a *beis midrash,* with its rows of connected, folding chairs, and its high ceiling. On a bulletin board, near the exit, were general announcements. *Israeli Concert in Staten Island* ran one ad, in large type. *Bungalow for Sale* ran another. The white sheets of paper were taped strategically along the walls. A small kitchen and a *kiddush* hall ran off to the side, just to the right of the stairs that led to the women's section.

The women's section! Rabbi Shapiro looked up. Behind the tinted glass, he saw a muted figure, sitting rigidly and silently looking his way. The rabbi tensed, his breath coming heavily.

Rabbi Morgenstern, noticing Rabbi Shapiro's demeanor, trailed off. "Is something wrong, Yehuda?" The others turned and looked.

"No, nothing," Rabbi Shapiro answered hastily. "I think I see my friend. Pardon me."

Bowing slightly, he left his seat and hurried past the aisle. The others turned to Rabbi Morgenstern, who continued his lecture. Rabbi Shapiro went in the direction of the kitchen, then turned left and walked up a small flight of stairs. He paused to control his trembling, then opened the door. He stopped, startled.

A young man, close to thirty, with wavy brown hair on which a satin "temple" skullcap rested awkwardly, watched him with the cool, cynical look of a professional. He neither rose from his seat nor offered Rabbi Shapiro a chair. Only when the older man approached him did he say gruffly, "Rabbi Shapiro, *nachon?*"

Rabbi Shapiro nodded.

"Na'im me'od." The stranger did not offer his hand.

"And who are you?" the rabbi asked, bewildered.

"Friend," the other answered in accented English.

"Of Shulman?" the rabbi asked, nodding.

The other shrugged. "I suppose so," he answered casually.

"What does *that* mean?"

"It means, Rabbi, that he was the one who sent me here."

"When did you arrive?"

"A few minutes ago. I waited for you to pray," he answered, with a trace of sarcasm.

The rabbi studied this man's features, probing the latter's intelligent eyes, his prominent cheekbones, his slight curvature of a nose. No, he's definitely not Italian — the accent, anyway. The man's attitude, however, left much to be desired. "Where is Shulman?" he asked in Hebrew. "And my son?"

"Come with me," the man ordered.

"You'll take me to Shulman?" the rabbi asked hopefully.

"I have my orders," the other man answered.

He leaned forward and peered through the partition. Rabbi Morgenstern was debating a point of Jewish law with the man in the English sports cap.

"We can wait here, if you like, for — *ma'ariv,* is it?" he said, turning to Shapiro.

"I can wait till I get home," the rabbi answered swiftly. "I have my own synagogue. Please. Take me to Shulman."

"I suggest you pray here," the man retorted.

The rabbi paused, comprehending. Evidently, this man was not in a rush to bring him to Shulman. He had his orders to wait; the "meeting" was to be delayed.

"Just tell me one thing," the rabbi whispered pleadingly. "Is my son all right?"

"He's fine," the man answered.

Too terse. Rabbi Shapiro was able to detect the evasiveness and he asked, "How did he look?"

"I don't know. I didn't see him."

"You didn't *see* him?!" the rabbi exclaimed.

"No. I left before he came."

"But then how do you know he's all right?!" the rabbi cried, in a tone that caused heads below to turn.

"Shhh!!" the man whispered harshly. "Don't worry. I promise you that you'll see him."

The rabbi fell into a helpless silence. In noticeable pain he studied this man again and asked critically, "You're an Israeli — am I correct?"

The other nodded.

"How can you be involved with the kind of person Shulman is?"

"I am not involved with Avraham Shulman."

"But you work with him, don't you?" the rabbi demanded passionately.

"Not with him."

"But you just called him a friend."

"We're — how shall I say? Acquaintances."

" 'Acquaintances'?"

"Let's just say," the man answered, "that he and I have more in common than you would like to think."

The doorknob turned slowly and at last gave way; the person behind the door remained unseen. Bewildered, Shimshon walked in, still feeling Shulman's presence behind him. The boy crinkled his nose at the hazy stench of tobacco and immediately was overwhelmed by the room's heat.

"Perhaps we might leave the windows open for awhile?" Avraham Shulman suggested, noticing the boy's discomfort.

"All right. But only awhile," answered Naftali Hertz.

His English reminded Shimshon vaguely of his father's friends. The boy studied the little man with the white tufts of hair protruding from his head in all directions. He had the penetrating eyes of an intellectual, but they were gentle. Naftali Hertz in turn studied Shimshon, remaining wordless but all the while smiling.

Shimshon tried to imagine this man in a Nazi uniform, but somehow could not. He seemed more like a misplaced math teacher than a Nazi officer or bureaucrat. For that matter, he didn't look at all German; in fact, he looked . . . why, Jewish! Certainly, he didn't look like Ludwig Dietrich — though admittedly Shimshon had only seen Dietrich from afar.

Shimshon looked at the tall young man with dark hair and complexion. He was greasy with sweat, and stood near the door, peering outside and sipping a Coke. The one who had sent the grocery boy to him. The Italian, Shimshon thought, with a certain awe.

"See anyone, Raffi?" Naftali asked tensely in Hebrew.

Raffi shook his head.

Shimshon was surprised to hear the language of the Jews being spoken in this place. It dawned on him that this man, this

"Italian," Raffi, was of quite a different nationality.

"Please, sit down, Shimshon," Naftali Hertz said cheerfully. "Take a seat . . . anywhere."

The boy looked around, and was struck by the bareness of the room. Where to find a seat? He took a folding chair which was by a garbage bag filled with empty Coke cans and sat down, feeling the paternal gaze of the two elderly men — Shulman, in his chassidic garb, who had retreated to a corner, and this man . . . this . . . Shimshon looked at him questioningly.

"Naftali Hertz," offered the man, reading Shimshon's mind. He extended his hand.

Hesitantly, Shimshon shook it, and was amazed that such a little man had such a strong grip.

"And over there is Rafael Tzioni. We call him Raffi." Naftali pointed to the *sabra,* who nodded casually to Shimshon. "May I call you Shimmy?" asked Naftali.

"My friends do," Shimshon answered softly.

"Yes, I know."

Shimshon's eyes widened. "You do?" he exclaimed.

"Oh, yes. We know everything about you," Naftali answered casually.

Shimshon began to fidget. "You do?" he repeated.

"Oh, yes. In fact, I also know your full name — Shimshon Hirsch Shapiro. I can tell you where and when you were born — Boro Park, 1972. Even the month and the day — February second. Anything else?"

Shimshon, still not quite over the shock of hearing the perfect Hebrew, felt partly intrigued, partly afraid. Even his friends couldn't remember his birthday. This man's mind was like a computer, one with a giant memory storage base. Even the way he recited the data, in clipped, automatic tones, indicated a man charged with energetic knowledge. No wonder he and Avraham Shulman seemed so attracted to each other; they had the same kind of mind, though Shulman's was tempered with calmness. This little man moved about nervously between intermittent puffs on his cigarette, his limbs waving joltingly, like a remote-control toy.

Naftali Hertz lit another cigarette, and threw one to Raffi. With a muscular arm the young man snatched it. Shulman made a face to indicate his displeasure at the smell of tobacco.

Naftali offered Shimshon a Coke. "I make it a rule to learn as much as I can about our subjects," he explained, smiling.

" 'Subjects'?" Shimshon asked warily.

"People we end up getting involved with. Willingly or unwillingly. Expectedly or unexpectedly."

Shimshon felt queasy. Something about these men — Naftali smiling at his desk, Raffi glancing cynically across the room, Shulman smiling enigmatically — made Shimshon feel weirdly sick, and as out of control as if he were forcibly strapped down in a roller-coaster ride.

Naftali continued watching Shimshon, noticing the boy's confusion. He finally continued, "You're a brave lad, Shimmy."

"I am?" Shimshon asked uneasily. The last thing he expected to hear was a compliment.

"Oh, yes," Naftali replied. "We've heard a lot about you. You have no idea how much trouble you've caused us."

Shimshon wasn't sure what surprised him more — what Naftali said, or how he said it. His voice remained pleasant, rather than angry or threatening. It was as if it were the most natural thing in the world to see a twelve-year-old play around with danger. Naftali must have had an amazing life.

"What kind of trouble?" Shimshon asked.

"For openers, alerting Dietrich and his men," Naftali answered, after a quick puff on his cigarette.

"I didn't alert him," Shimshon said defensively. He pointed to Avraham Shulman. "*He* did."

Hertz and Shulman smiled at each other.

"Not quite," Hertz answered.

"Yes, he did," Shimshon insisted. "Don't tell me he didn't. I saw him with those guys." He smiled defiantly. "That's why you brought me here, right? You're just waiting for Dietrich to show up."

"I wouldn't be surprised if he did," Hertz answered calmly. "After your little charade today."

"Whaddya mean 'my little charade'? I'm proud of what we did. And I don't care if Dietrich knows about it."

"I'm sure by now he does. You weren't exactly subtle this afternoon."

Shulman stepped forward. "I was concerned that Dietrich had followed us here," he explained. "I thought I had seen his car tailing the taxis."

Shimshon stared wonderingly at Shulman. "You weren't running from my father?"

Shulman stared back. "Your father was behind us?" he asked.

His tone of surprise sounded all too genuine.

Shimshon turned to Naftali Hertz. "You mean you're not with Dietrich?" he asked, confused.

Naftali stared, offended. "Do *I* look like I'd be in league with *him*?"

"Well—" Shimshon started.

Raffi slammed the door shut. Immediately, Shulman and Hertz rose. Shimshon himself shot up, but Raffi, with a wave of the hand, waved him to sit down and be still.

Raffi was looking through the peephole. The sound of footsteps grew louder. The footsteps paused momentarily outside the door, then another door was opened, diagonally across from theirs. The door shut. Silence. Muffled sounds of conversation, in English, could be heard from across the hall.

Suddenly Raffi whipped out a gun, which sent Shimshon backing against the wall in terror. The man swiftly opened the door. Shimshon curled under the chair and covered his eyes, expecting a bloodbath.

Raffi looked around, up and down the hall. Nothing. Silence. He slowly shut the door and locked the chains. Shimshon hesitantly got up on his feet.

"How many were there?" Shulman asked, visibly nervous.

"Two," Raffi answered gruffly.

"What did they look like?" Shulman asked.

"Nondescript. Medium, dark hair — business suits. They sounded American."

Shulman listened, then shook his head. "That's meaningless," he said. "They may be decoys."

"Was there anything else you noticed?" Naftali asked.

Raffi answered, "One of them seemed to have a limp."

Naftali looked quizzically at Shulman. The latter pondered the description, like a rabbi reflecting on a philosophical question. He shook his head. "No one I know of." He snickered. "Except Goebbels. He had a club foot."

"Where did they go?" Naftali asked Raffi.

"Across the hall, to 11J."

"Very well. We'll trace the occupant."

Shimshon watched the scene in wonder, then distress. The conversation upset him — particularly Shulman's casual mention of one of Germany's most infamous Nazis, as if Goebbels had been a personal acquaintance. Yet here he was, Avraham Shulman, fraternizing with both Naftali Hertz, certainly a Jew, and Rafael Tzioni, who looked like he ate Nazis for dessert. Shimshon felt as if he were being excluded from one big secret — and a maddening one at that.

"Where am I?" he demanded. "What's going on here?" A moment later, he wailed, "Who *are* you people?"

Naftali Hertz and Avraham Shulman exchanged glances. Calmly, Shulman retreated to a chair near the window, and Naftali, pulling up a chair, sat down and faced Shimshon.

"Relax," he said. "We won't hurt you. We promise. We will not hurt a Jewish boy. We are Jews."

"Including *him*?" asked Shimshon, pointing to Shulman.

"Yes. Including him."

Shimshon was stunned. He stared in amazement at Avraham Shulman, who looked modestly downward, stroking his beard.

"But . . . that's crazy," Shimshon asked. "How can he be a Jew?"

"So you're still convinced he's a Nazi," Naftali Hertz said softly.

Shimshon felt like crying. "But he is, isn't he? Hans Schmidt. He knows Dietrich. And *you* know him. What do you all have to do with him?"

"So many questions," Naftali Hertz replied, laughing. I'll try to answer them all in the course of our conversation."

Crushing his cigarette into an overloaded ashtray, Naftali rose and paced the room. Though short, his powerful mental energy seemed to give him extra height, and he filled the room with his presence. Shimshon sensed that this man had difficulty sitting still.

With a smile, Naftali said, "I'll have to explain myself again — this time more clearly. The four of us—"

"*Four?*" Shimshon asked.

"The fourth you'll meet soon. We are all members of the Israeli Secret Service. No doubt you have heard of us?"

Shimshon nodded. "The Mossad or something? You hunt Arabs, right?"

"Yes. Some of us. But some of us also hunt Nazis."

Shimshon stared, dazed, at the carpet, with the knowledge that was slowly dawning.

"We belong to a particular branch called the War Crimes Unit. We are dedicated to seeking out Nazi war criminals and their collaborators."

Shimshon looked at Shulman, who continued sitting, calmly staring across the room, as if waiting for a bus.

"Even Avraham Shulman? Is he also dedicated to hunting down Nazis?" he asked, careful not to use the man's other name.

"Yes, young man," answered Naftali Hertz expansively. "In fact, he's one of the best we've ever had. A man of deep integrity, the most loyal, most energetic, most methodical — in short, a *mentsch.* In all my forty years in this line of work, hunting Nazis, I have never met anyone like Avraham Shulman — anyone with such dedication to our cause. He has been one of my trusted agents for years — and he has helped bring many to justice."

Though Shimshon knew he was naive, he somehow detected the truth in this man's voice. The way Naftali Hertz spoke — throwing his arms wide open, as if to broadcast the news to all four corners of the globe — indicated his joy and excitement about Avraham Shulman. At the same time, Shimshon felt his blood pounding into his temples in shame and confusion.

"Have you ever heard of Conrad Eberhardt?" Naftali suddenly asked.

Shimshon stopped to think. "Yeah. I think we read about him in current events. Didn't he run a concentration camp or something?"

Naftali nodded. "Then you know he was caught recently?"

Shimshon nodded.

"And who do you think helped to capture him?"

Shimshon's eyes widened. *"Him?"* he exclaimed, pointing to Shulman.

Hertz smiled, waiting for the revelation to take effect.

Indeed it did, as Shimshon felt the sudden urge to sink to the floor in deep disgrace. He thought over and over of the painful truth, the jigsaw puzzle that was finally being pieced together. Avraham Shulman was a double agent, working for the Israeli government. Not only was he not a Nazi, but in fact he was a Nazi-hunter. That explained the secretiveness about his past as well as his work. It also explained why the Israelis, along with everyone else, had refused to become involved in this case. And most likely they had been in league with the American government as well — who had helped to give his father the runaround.

Shulman's anger at the accusations, his attempts to counteract them — all were done in hurt and defense, never in vengeance. It occurred — most painfully — to Shimshon: Avraham Shulman had never harmed him, nor even tried, though there had been plenty of reasons and opportunities to do so. If anything, he had retained the deepest respect for both Shapiros. *Your father is an extraordinary man. A man of great learning and refinement.* The way Shulman had behaved in the taxis, and the subway — *You and your father will die!* — he was trying to protect them, save their lives — especially, to keep Shimshon from being harmed by Dietrich. That also confirmed Avraham Shulman's Jewishness — his loyalty to his people. They were *his* people. He cared for them, shared in their joy and sufferings, fought their battles, all at great risk to his life. He would not have harmed Shimshon — not a Jewish boy. He would never, *could* never, malevolently touch a Jewish boy. Instead, he felt an innate duty to protect him. Shulman himself had children—

Children? Now Shimshon wondered — Chava Rivkah. Was she real? Or was it a cover-up? Yet she had been interviewed in the papers. And her mother, Shulman's wife Breinda? — wasn't that her name? Or the *kollel*? Was it all one colossal lie, again invented for the sake of secrecy? What else were they hiding? He remembered another of Shulman's declarations: *Know the truth . . . know what you're striving for . . . know the truth in others and rely on them for strength.*

Through narrowed eyes, Shimshon looked at Naftali Hertz. "How do I know all this is true — that you're really an Israeli agent?"

Hertz shrugged and lit another cigarette. "No problem. Would you like me to call the Israeli embassy for you? Or if you like, I could call Israel direct."

Shimshon was taken aback by the man's casualness.

Hertz continued, "Who would you like to speak to? The President? Prime Minister? Chief Rabbi?"

"Well . . . no," Shimshon muttered, somewhat embarrassed. "I'll skip it. But I'd like to know about Shulman's daughter."

Suddenly Shulman trembled. He bit his lip and looked away.

417

Naftali Hertz explained. "Partly because of her did he agree to take this job — in spite of the dangers. He knows he may not ever see her again. But he hopes that in the merit of doing this his daughter will be cured. Not to mention that we have been paying her hospital bills. A prod of sorts, to secure Shulman's cooperation — though he'd help us anyway. Half the *kollel* is reciting *Tehillim* for her right now."

"Oh, then she *is* real," Shimshon murmured. "And she really is sick." The *kollel* was real too, he thought. He again cringed, thinking that he may have not only deprived Shulman of his livelihood, but of a chance to heal his daughter. Shimshon had placed far too many people's lives in danger.

Shimshon decided he had best change the topic. He said, "I would like to know how you found out so much about me."

Naftali Hertz smiled at Shulman, then at Raffi. "Excuse me," he said, going into the other room, then returning half-a-minute later with two thick folders. "You know quite a lot, but not enough. It's time you learned a little more."

He stood stiffly and held out one folder before the boy, like a royal servant presenting a gift.

Shimshon stared at it hesitantly.

"Please," Naftali Hertz gently urged.

Shimshon took it and uncertainly turned the cover. What he saw made him gasp in astonishment.

On the first page, in computer type, was the name *Rabbi Yehuda Leib Shapiro,* alongside a photograph of his father, apparently taken somewhere in public — most likely by a detective with a secret camera. While his father had hired an investigator to have Shulman traced and photographed, Shulman had apparently done his own investigation.

He turned to the next page.

DATE OF BIRTH: April 1, 1929.
PLACE OF BIRTH: Warsaw, Poland.
PARENTS: Mayer Shapiro, Malka Kaplinsky.

Beginning with his childhood in prewar Europe, the extensive biography encapsulated Shimshon's father's life — including details Shimshon did not know. Pages and pages of business dealings, bank statements, credit card references, income tax returns, lists of properties, photostats of his American naturalization papers and his ordination, a log of his activities beginning in February (when he had first met Avraham Shulman), his synagogue activities, yeshiva sessions, Holocaust work, business appointments. Virtually the man's entire life, a world just as private as Shulman's and just as busy, lay revealed.

Shimshon turned the page, and he choked.

FAIGE SARAH SHAPIRO
DATE OF BIRTH: January 29, 1930.
PLACE OF BIRTH: Lodz, Poland.
PARENTS: Shimshon Hirsch Gottesman, Hinda Baila Kaplan.

There on the page was a picture of his mother, taken right before her illness had irreversibly progressed. Where had they obtained it? Her wig hung stiffly over a pale, sad face, framing it in light brown. Her eyes, which Shimshon had inherited, focused tenderly on something within her view. This was precisely how Shimshon liked to remember her. There was a brief biographical sketch about her — ending morbidly with *DECEASED: July 23, 1982.* It occurred to Shimshon that her *yahrzeit* was not far off.

There were other pages as well, about Rabbi Shapiro's friends, relatives, neighbors, and colleagues — brief sketches, mostly inconsequential; a cast of tens. It was clearly Rabbi Yehuda Leib Shapiro who occupied center stage — and rightfully so. Reading about his father's achievements renewed Shimshon's pride.

There was a blank page after all the sketches, and Shimshon was about to return the folder when Naftali Hertz said eagerly, "Oh, no — go on, go on. Please."

Curious, Shimshon turned to the next page.

SHIMSHON HIRSCH SHAPIRO
DATE OF BIRTH: February 2, 1972.
PLACE OF BIRTH: Brooklyn, New York, USA.

As with his father, there was an extensive biography — though of course much shorter. Not only was there one recent photograph of Shimshon, there were several: Shimshon at school talking to his rebbe; Shimshon after school playing ball with his friends; Shimshon with Zev at a Thirteenth Avenue pizza shop — and Shimshon by himself, outside a Manhattan building, with a camera! While he was hiding so that he could photograph Shulman, somebody had been photographing him!

There was additional information culled from legal and medical records. Trust funds, inheritances. Birth certificate, school records, scholastic awards (much to his pride), report cards (much to his embarrassment). Blood type (O), allergies (none); dental and orthodontic records (three fillings, two back molars removed). There was also a small paragraph on Zev, and a smaller one on Mrs. Friedman.

The boy closed the folder and giggled hysterically, not knowing whether to feel frightened that so much was known about him, or flattered that he would even be considered that important. It seemed fantastic to know that all this time he had been followed

— a pack of secret agents, tapping him on the shoulder, holding guns and shouting, "Shimshon Hirsch Shapiro, this is your life!" Not a bad one, Shimshon reflected. Not bad at all. And to think he could have stupidly ended it by poking his nose into this risky business.

Quietly, he handed it back to Naftali Hertz. "You really know a lot about me," he said.

"Wait — we're not finished," said Naftali, tucking the folder under his arm. "I want to show you more."

"You mean — there's more about me?" Shimshon asked incredulously.

"Not about you. But I think you'll find it just as interesting. Read on . . . please." Naftali Hertz held out another folder, this time less regally.

Quietly, Shimshon took it. He turned to the first page — and his hands shook.

LUDWIG DIETRICH
DATE OF BIRTH: August 2, 1910.
PLACE OF BIRTH: East Prussia.

Shimshon's eyes bulged as he read further:

PARENTS: Father Emil Dietrich, naval officer, mother Margarette Meisner, army colonel's daughter. Sibling: brother Helmut, born 1913, Wehrmacht lieutenant, died in Greece, 1943.

The sketch went on. It was equally impressive — in the opposite way, of course. Accomplishments: Weissgarten Academy, top student, champion swimmer. Favorite subjects: History and Latin. University of Heidelberg, law, captain of fencing team, head of notoriously anti-Semitic student fraternity. Decided instead on military career — a natural decision, it would seem, having grown up in a military environment.

The list of achievements continued. Marriage to Marta Knaut, admiral's daughter, 1931. Four children. Eleven grandchildren; even a greatgrandchild. Shimshon was shocked to learn that six of his descendants occupied prominent positions in certain governments.

The Nazi activities occupied thirty pages, beginning with 1930, when Dietrich joined the Nazi Party. Befriended Himmler, became one of earliest members of SS. By 1933, when Hitler became Chancellor of Germany, Dietrich was already *Sturmbannfuhrer* (major). Throughout the next twelve years he climbed the ranks with the greatest of self-assurance. Participated in 1934 murder of the leading Nazi figure Ernst Roehm during a purge of the SA by the SS. In 1935, became part of Himmler's personal staff. Mingled easily with the upper echelons of society, from which he came. In 1936, worked in RSHA, where evidently he found his niche. He had either planned or carried out countless murders with the Gestapo of "enemies of the Fatherland."

Hans Schmidt was mentioned here. Evidently, Dietrich was the one who had indoctrinated him into the SS, in 1936. Schmidt was in the Waffen SS, the combat division. Dietrich by then had helped initiate the operation of Buchenwald. Later, he assisted in the suppression of Austria, Czechoslovakia, Poland, Hungary — a virtual history of the Third Reich lay glinting from the pages. He was the one behind Hans Schmidt's appointment as head of the Malberg concentration camp, where the commander, *Oberfuhrer* Erich Lederer, was a good friend of Dietrich's (he was later hanged at Nuremberg). Dietrich himself indirectly commanded several camps from behind RSHA office walls. In addition, he was involved with the Race and Resettlement Main Office (a

Frederick "Fritz" Loehmann was mentioned in connection with this), helping to uproot and annihilate Jews, Poles, Gypsies, and other "undesirables." He commanded the murder of millions, ninety-nine percent unseen by him, all of them unpitied. Dietrich remained the hidden enemy — not one who was simply elusive, but one who lurked in unseen corners, ready to reach out and strike.

The Nazi activity did not end in 1945. It continued right up to the present day. In 1945, he fled to Turkey, then to Spain in 1946. In 1947, it was Caracas, La Paz, Bogota; he was a virtual tourist of South America. Final residence: Buenos Aires, Argentina, where he moved in 1970. He was the head of a vast underground neo-Nazi empire living mostly off Jewish-confiscated wealth. The goal: to destroy those responsible for this wealth. There were branches in virtually every major Western country. Here it was — Ludwig Dietrich encapsulated, courtesy of modern-day espionage and global communications.

At the end of the sketch were photographs of Dietrich, taken at different stages of his life. Most noteworthy were those of him in Nazi uniform, during Third Reich days. He looked like a movie star — dapper, handsome, with fashionably slicked-back hair under an officer's cap: standing by a piano in one, holding a cigarette in a long holder in another, his pale eyes staring languidly to his right. There was another of him with his wife, a beautiful woman in a long evening dress. This was obviously the kind of man to succeed in life, any kind of life, one who held the world firmly by the reins, and who luxuriated in his role. Interestingly, however, he seemed to convey a certain modesty mixed in with the arrogance — as if Dietrich, aware of his persona, downplayed it to avoid jealousy and possible treachery from his peers, or

because he simply worked best in the shadows. Unlike many
Nazis, he seemed unimpressed with vulgar displays of wealth, and
his aristocratic trappings were secondary — simply part of the
scenery. He had been brought up in wealth; he was therefore used
to it. He did not need it to feel important. He was already a man of
power, and power was its own reward.

The sketches ended with a recent photograph of Dietrich, taken
in Manhattan — the way Shimshon had seen him. Dressed in a
tailor-made suit, he was well preserved — his chiseled features
still thin, his eyes deep blue and calculating, his skin smooth and
slightly creased, like stretched crepe paper. Staring directly ahead,
he seemed to be smiling at the world, as if to imply that he was
wickedly proud of his achievements and contemptuous of those
who had none to boast of.

Shimshon lingered over the last picture, his mouth twisting into
a sort of grimace. Naftali Hertz, watching him, commented dryly,
"There are other folders. The rest are in Jerusalem. Photographs,
biographies — everything on Dietrich and his friends. This is just
the tip of the iceberg."

Shimshon turned past a blank page and saw the other Nazis. He
recognized them all: Fritz Loehmann (Race and Resettlement
Office), Heinz Neumayer, Kurt Zerner — satellites around
Ludwig Dietrich, the Sun King; each with their own background
and track record, though much less distinguished.

"There's one on Eberhardt," Naftali explained. "But the files
are still being corroborated. He died last year in prison."

"Yeah. A heart attack right? The papers said."

Naftali Hertz did not answer.

Shimshon stopped at a picture taken over forty years ago, with
the following sketch:

Double Identity

JOACHIM SCHWIMMER
DATE OF BIRTH: May 28, 1885.
PLACE OF BIRTH: Frankfurt, Germany.
PARENTS: Max Schwimmer, Maria Lowenbrau.

"Who is this man?" Shimshon asked. "I never saw him before."

"Of course not," Naftali Hertz answered, sipping a Coke. "He died almost thirty years before you were born. But he's part of the reason for our search."

"Search?" Shimshon asked, staring. "You mean for Dietrich?"

"Partly," Hertz answered with a vague smile. "Read on."

Shimshon turned the page. There was mention of Schwimmer's own achievements: his wealth, his prewar philanthropy, his *Mischlinge* ("half-Jewish") status during the war. There were photostats of his and his wife's American naturalization papers, dated 1944, and a picture of his wife at around the same time. The dossier ended with an ominous xerox of a death certificate, dated February 12, 1945.

Shimshon looked at the photograph of the man in middle age. His face seemed to display an intensity of Semitic features — dark hair and eyes close-set, the brows meeting at the bridge of the nose. He looked shrewd, not at all sinister. But, as Shimshon had thoroughly learned, looks could truly be deceiving.

He turned the page. His eyes beheld an aerial montage of New York City with its five boroughs, each on separate pages, followed by more detailed maps of particular neighborhoods and streets.

Shimshon flipped absently through the last pages, which seemed technical and boring — mostly lists of certain addresses, real estate deeds, and documents, some dated as far back as 1944, when Schwimmer first came to the States. There was even a list of objects, running like a millionaire's lost-and-found:

14K Brocaded Necklace, est. $1 million, stolen from K. Dreyfus estate, Brussels
Monet *Two Flowers,* oil on canvas, est. $4 million, stolen from B. Hammerstein, Lyons
Diamond-and-sapphire brooch, est. $780,000, stolen from L. Singerman, Vienna

Shimshon was much more interested when he came to the photographs of certain buildings, including Shulman's complex on Thirty-seventh Street.

Shimshon stopped. The buildings and their addresses reminded him of a conversation from way back.

Mostly he walks around and stares at buildings.

He has also on occasion appeared in other areas — the Lower East Side, mainly. Also once in Rego Park. However, all at different times of the day.

Shimshon excitedly turned the pages backward, fingering the text, while Naftali looked on. The addresses: Wetherole Street — near Rego Park, Queens. Essex Street — the East Side! These were the buildings Avraham Shulman had visited!

Shimshon looked up excitedly, and caught Naftali's stare. They exchanged knowing looks.

"See a connection?" Naftali asked offhandedly.

"There's something in those buildings, right?" Shimshon asked, bug-eyed.

Hertz nodded.

"These things, right?"

Hertz nodded again.

"Wow!" Shimshon exclaimed. "You mean . . . you're trying to get hold of these things?"

"Correct," replied Naftali Hertz.

"Do they belong to Schwimmer?"

"No. The buildings did, though."

Shimshon shook his head thoughtfully. "Also the building Shulman bought?"

Hertz nodded. "Turn the page."

Shimshon did, and his eyes scanned another unfamiliar name.

EMMANUEL PERLOW
DATE OF BIRTH: August 2, 1915.
PLACE OF BIRTH: Budapest, Hungary.

Again there were lists of properties, earnings, achievements. Photographs, both ancient and new, of a life history. Perlow just released from a DP camp in Prague. Perlow's arrival in the United States, in 1948. The most recent, in Kodacolor, were of Perlow in a Hawaiian shirt and shorts, standing on the beach and holding a baby girl, presumably his granddaughter.

"Who is this man?" Shimshon asked.

"The former owner of Shulman's building. He's the one who sold it to Shulman."

"Didn't Zimmerman sell it?"

"He's on the next page. He's Perlow's realtor — and old friend. He was the one who handled the deal. He also manages the restaurant."

Shimshon again felt like sinking to the floor. Now he understood how Zimmerman, a Jew and a Holocaust survivor, could have tolerated Shulman. Most likely he was shown these files. A subtle hint to butt out.

Naftali continued, "And who do you think obtained these documents for us?"

Shimshon began to shake again. "Avraham Shulman?" he asked weakly.

"Yes."

Shimshon kept his eyes desperately downward, not daring to let them meet Shulman's — the man he had connived to publicly expose and disgrace. Instead, it was Shimshon who had ended up the fool. More than that, he was an embarrassment, a thorn in the side, a splinter in the foot, an amateur so excited with his work that he had dangerously interfered with some very serious business.

"Do you understand why it was necessary — all this secrecy?" Naftali Hertz asked.

Shimshon nodded. "Because you don't want Ludwig Dietrich to know."

"Correct. And why do you think we had to accumulate all this information? Because of Avraham's dealings while disguised as a Nazi. Helps us keep in touch, you might say. We have to know whom we're dealing with."

"So you're trying to get hold of this man, Dietrich, in order to get back the wealth?" Shimshon asked. "You want to give it back to the people it belongs to?"

"No," Naftali Hertz answered solemnly. "The people it belonged to are dead. And their loved ones. Where possible, we would give it to their relatives, but there is no way that justice for them can truly be done. Not directly, anyway." He sighed, then added, "The only think we can do is prevent such things from recurring. If this wealth falls into Dietrich's hands, it might."

Shimshon nodded thoughtfully. "So you don't just want to get back this gold. You want to keep it away from Dietrich."

"That is correct."

"But why do you have to deal with him in the first place?"

Naftali Hertz smiled. He knelt before Shimshon and looked at him intently. "Think, Shimmy, think. Who do you think gave us this information about the location of the gold?"

"Why, Shulman, you said. All the information here in these folders."

"And where do you think he got all this information?"

Shimshon paused, then trembled. "D-Dietrich?"

Hertz nodded. "Who do you suppose would want this information besides us?"

"Dietrich," Shimshon whispered.

"Correct, my boy."

"But wouldn't it be easier to just get rid of Dietrich?" Shimshon asked. "The times Shulman has been alone with him, he could have just finished him off."

Hertz got off his knees and stood under the kitchen door, his figure dramatically framed against the doorpost. "It's not all that simple, Shimmy. If you remove the queen bee from the hive, the rest will simply go off in search of another queen. Dietrich is powerful, unique, a man of many gifts. But he is not indispensable. He knows it as well as we do. Even were we to leave him alone, he would eventually die of natural causes. Dietrich is a man of foresight. He possesses as well a certain modesty. He is not concerned with self-aggrandizement. Perhaps in this respect he is unique among his kind. He wishes to leave something to the world, in that he wants it to be a world prepared for the next set of Nazis." He paused for greater effect. "There are plenty of people with him. Through all the years they were waiting patiently. Now they feel the time has come to find this wealth and use it. Their first goal is to destroy the prominent Jews — 'the ones who got away,' they call us. Philanthropists, rabbis — all the Jewish men of power and influence. Including Rabbi Shapiro. His name and mine were thrown about quite freely in their conversations."

Shimshon was shocked. It occurred to him that all the persons under file were men of talent and distinction — his father included. The Nazis could not tolerate them.

Hertz calmly continued: "A venerable ploy — just like the one used in the ghettos. Undermine and eliminate the leadership, then the rest will follow. Of course, to have these men destroyed it would be necessary to obtain as much information about them as possible.

"And believe me, Shimmy, Dietrich has the power to do it — the financial capability. With money he stole from us. That man and his kind have armies behind them — paid armies."

Horrified, Shimshon whispered, "Does my father know of any of this?" His mind turned to his father's recurrent nightmares of being hunted. "Why couldn't you warn him? Or let him in on it? He could have helped you."

Naftali Hertz smiled. "I always knew of your father indirectly," he said, "even before the war. His father knew mine. But Yehuda Shapiro and I never had the pleasure of meeting, even in the best of times. I have always admired him — especially after reading his dossier. He is a fine person, one with many talents and capabilities, one who has used them well and gone far in the world. I hold him in the highest regard."

These words, reminiscent of Shulman's, gave Shimshon a vicarious thrill. He only wished that his father were here to hear them; they might have helped to clear the air, eliminating all the embarrassment. Nevertheless, the question remained: Why hadn't his father been told — especially if he were so admired? Why wouldn't he be included in this work? The kind of work in which he had been involved for years?

"I still think you should have told him," Shimshon declared.

"Your father is being told right now."

The boy sprang up. "Where is he?" He looked around, as if expecting to see his father emerge from behind the walls.

"Relax, Shimmy, he isn't here. You'll meet him soon."

"But where *is* he?"

"In a synagogue on the Upper West Side. My other colleague, Aryeh Kessler, is keeping him company. And telling him a lot about us. We would have told him anyway — just not so soon. I thought I'd spare him the embarrassment of bringing him here and having to confront Avraham Shulman."

"Maybe if he had known about Mr. Shulman sooner all this wouldn't have happened."

Hertz shook his head sadly. "Your father could not be reasoned with. He was too blinded by his emotions and unable to look past his own memories. His goal is to hunt and kill anyone connected with the Holocaust — including Avraham, if we hadn't stopped him."

"How?" Shimshon asked shakily.

"By silencing the press."

Shimshon was stunned. "You mean . . . it wasn't Dietrich who did that?"

"No. Though he would have — only we beat him to it. But he might have done far worse. Had the publicity gone too far, both you and your father might have been eliminated as a threat. And worse, every Holocaust survivor would have come out waving a gun and threatening Shulman, unwittingly bringing death or suffering to three innocent people — and causing our real target, Dietrich, to elude us further. In fact, I'm sure that if your father had had a gun he would have fired point blank at him. I'm sorry to say that the world doesn't operate that way." He looked away bitterly. "I discovered that long ago. I became involved in this work long before your father — while he was still freezing, struggling to survive inside a concentration camp. Nowadays it is no longer sufficient to shoot one person. It is a childish, inane way to take revenge — quick action, but futile in the long run. You aim for something higher. You have to destroy the whole system. Dietrich is a link to the real target we're after. The entire empire behind him." He added acidly, "Though believe me, I would love to kill Dietrich myself."

Shimshon sat, listening, taking in the philosophy and information, putting them together into one concrete block. Yes, it all made sense. However, at the same time, he could not get over the anger of seeing himself humiliated — and his father, partly because of him.

"Why didn't you tell *me,* at least?" he yelled. "If *I* had known, I would never have bothered Shulman. Now what am I going to tell everyone when I see them? Today I looked like one big jerk!"

"Shhh!" Raffi hissed, staring through the door's peephole.

Shimshon didn't hear. He continued, shrilly, "Or my father? You don't think he could be careful? You really think he couldn't understand?" He shouted, "I might be a kid, but he's not! What do you take him for?"

"*Mein Kind,* please," Hertz answered, gesturing with his hands. He studied the boy. Yes, Shimshon would have made quite a partisan. A much younger version of the man who had bolted the train forty years ago. Impetuous; daring. Enough fighting spirit for an entire army. "You don't realize how much you've endangered our plans."

Shimshon was silent. The words were mockingly reminiscent of his father's.

Hertz continued. "Though your work was commendable, Shimmy. I am very impressed. However, I don't know how much has already leaked to the Nazis. They'll do one of two things: go deeper into hiding, or send out even more spies to carry out their work. As it is now, they have spies everywhere. And you wanted to be one, didn't you?" His eyes turned icy hard. "Well, then, my friend, try imagining every person you meet, even a bum on the street, as a potential agent, a potential killer."

Shimshon trembled. He remembered the strange sights, the sounds, the paranoia, Shulman surveying the apartment lobby.

Hertz continued, "You're frightened. Good. How do you think your father feels? The difference is he'll hide his fear when he's with you."

"Not always," Shimshon replied vaguely, remembering the dreams.

"Do you know that Shulman had to talk Dietrich out of having you and your father killed? He told them that it wasn't worthwhile."

"How?" Shimshon whispered.

"By reasoning with them. By explaining that the plans could be carried out without problems. And that any harm to your father would create further suspicion — causing more police and investigators to get involved in this, and stirring up a hornet's nest. Which, in the end, would cause the Nazis to go back underground — and, of course, destroy our own plans. Do you get the point?" These last words were practically spluttered in Shimshon's face, causing the boy to nod quickly.

"Good."

Shimshon remained on the seat, drained and chastened. He finally glanced at Avraham Shulman, who continued to sit

433

wordlessly, his right hand stroking his beard. The boy's shame had given way to overwhelming gratitude to the man who had worked hard not only for his and his father's life, but for the lives of so many other Jews. The boy felt himself growing smaller and smaller, sitting in this room among moral giants.

With tears in his eyes, he rose from his seat and approached Avraham Shulman.

"Rav Shulman," he began, quivering, "I'm really sorry for everything I did — or tried to do. Honest. I . . . I didn't know. Had I known, I would not have done it."

Shulman stared at him intently and broke into a smile. "The Torah says that one should always be slow to anger. I never felt anger toward you, Shimshon. Not in the least. Those times I acted as I did were only the performances of a very good actor, if I do flatter myself. After all, if you did know — if I had made myself that obvious — then I wouldn't be much of an agent, would I?" He smiled under the beard — a smile that was gentle and warm. He extended his hand, and vigorously shook Shimshon's.

Hertz approached the boy. "Shimmy, I think it's time to take you back. Your father's waiting."

Shimshon still kept his eyes fixed on Shulman.

"Shimmy?" Hertz asked uneasily.

The boy didn't answer. He kept his eyes on Shulman and probed the latter's features — the translucent skin, the eyes that dazzled like blue sequins. Then, uncomfortable, he turned away.

Shulman himself, as if to escape Shimshon's scrutiny, looked at Naftali anxiously. "You haven't heard from Aryeh?"

Naftali shook his head. "Wasn't he supposed to call by now?"

"Perhaps there was a delay. I told him I'd drop the boy off at eight. After *ma'ariv.*"

Shulman studied his watch. "There is still time left for *minchah*." He washed his hands, put on his coat, and faced the wall.

They waited in silence while Shulman and Shimshon *davened minchah*. When they had finished, Naftali turned to Raffi. "See anyone out there?" he asked.

Raffi shook his head.

Naftali reached into his wallet and extracted several bills. "Take Shimshon down and summon a taxi."

"What about the car?"

"Too risky. Avraham says it may have been spotted already by Dietrich. I don't want the boy inside."

Shulman said, "Is it safe for them to go home, Naftali?"

"I think so. After today, the last thing Dietrich would want is more publicity. He knows when to stay away."

"Unless you told him not to, Rav Shulman!" Shimshon interjected.

Avraham Shulman turned to Shimshon, and his eyes narrowed darkly. "What are you trying to say, Shimshon?"

The boy backed away, but his eyes stared at the tall man in defiance.

Shulman sternly advanced. "You still don't believe me, do you, Shimshon?" he asked, with a touch of sorrow. "You still think I'm one of them, don't you?" He reached the boy and towered over him. "Well? Don't you?"

Shimshon ran to Naftali Hertz for protection.

Avraham Shulman stood, sober and still. In the dim light, his form threw an elongated shadow along the wall. "I don't understand you, Shimshon. In the past you have tried so hard to believe that I was who I said I was. But now you cannot. Why?"

The boy shook his head in obvious mental agony. "Because there's just one thing I wasn't told. I . . . I have just one question left . . . one thing I just don't understand."

Shulman looked at Naftali Hertz tensely. Then he looked again at the boy. "What is it?" he asked.

The boy looked at the three men — Shulman, Hertz, Raffi. The faces so trusting, so kind, yet at the same time secretive, perhaps inwardly jeering at him and his naivete. He knew that there was still something hidden, something that lay in waiting. He had the urge then and there to burst out in tears.

"Who is Hans Schmidt?!" he wailed.

Naftali and Shulman looked at each other.

"What are you talking about, Shimshon?" Shulman demanded.

Vehemently shaking his head, the boy stamped his feet and cried, "It just doesn't make sense!"

"What doesn't?"

"Why isn't there a file on Hans Schmidt?"

Shulman smiled and turned away.

"Well?" Shimshon yelled at Hertz accusingly. His eyes were wet with tears. "Why isn't there?"

Hertz looked away and answered awkwardly, "He is not important. He is someone who existed long ago."

"You mean he's dead?"

"No."

"*Whaddya mean, then?* He's in Honduras, right?"

"A technicality, Shimshon. To wipe away the trace. From men like your father." Hertz lowered his voice and muttered, "Now you know the real reason that he couldn't be told. He would never listen. To him, all of them were to blame. There was no way possible to get rid of the guilt."

"So Schmidt *is* guilty?"

"Yes," Hertz spat. "Schmidt suffered the crime of being part of Dietrich's race."

"I don't understand." Shimshon stared at Hertz. "What are you trying to tell me? That Hans Schmidt *didn't* run a camp?"

"He did."

"But he isn't guilty of anything bad?"

"That's not what I said. He *was* involved. But in a different way than Dietrich."

"Did he kill anybody?"

Naftali Hertz thought for a moment, then answered evasively, "No."

"How can you tell me he's not a Nazi?!"

"Well, I'm not exactly saying that. He was never exonerated."

"What does that mean?!" Shimshon yelled.

"It means that he is still held responsible for what happened at Marlberg."

"Then why won't he be zonerated?"

"I just explained, Shimmy. Hans Schmidt is not important." Naftali's face twisted. "As far as we are concerned, he no longer exists. He served his purpose. A shell of a man — a pawn to be used and discarded. A dying, senile old man in Central America — hardly worth our time. Not when we are after bigger game, like Dietrich."

Shimshon spun around in rage and frustration, his fists clenched. "Then why does my father insist that that man —" he pointed to Shulman — "is Hans Schmidt? Are they one and the same?"

"I told you, Shimshon," Hertz answered, his voice urgent, "that the man your father saw was a man from the past. Yes, he *did* see Hans Schmidt. But the man you see in front of you now is Avraham Shulman. The other man still exists — but in name only."

Shimshon wildly retorted, "You're giving me crazy answers. You're telling me Schmidt is here. But he's not here."

"In a way, yes."

"But that can't be. He's here. Hans Schmidt is standing right there. My father knew it all along. And you had me and everyone else thinking my father was crazy!" He hissed, "That's what you wanted to do, right? You tried to make him that way — to help Hans Schmidt."

Hertz shook his head wildly. "No, we didn't, Shimshon. We were only trying to protect Avraham Shulman."

"How? By covering him up?"

"No. By getting *rid* of Hans Schmidt."

The boy howled, "But you're *not* rid of him! He's here! And Dietrich knows it; he doesn't seem like the kind of man to be fooled. Would someone explain to me what is going on?"

"Sheket!" Raffi roared.

"No, *you* be quiet," the boy sobbed. He turned to Shulman in desperation. "Tell me, *please. . . .* yes or no. Are you or aren't you Hans Schmidt?"

Shulman did not answer. Instead, he watched the boy in deepest anguish, with the look of one condemned to, one forever haunted by, a present life of secrecy and a past life of pain. At last he turned to the wall. Shimshon watched him in despair, as if sharing the man's inner torment.

Hertz slowly approached the boy and placed his hand on the latter's shoulder. He himself was scarcely a head taller.

"Shimshon," he said, "in all my life I have met many interesting people, each with fascinating experiences and backgrounds. But never have I met anyone with a story so unusual and beautiful as that of Hans Schmidt — a man of courage, a man who did what he felt was right, a man who fought for justice and human dignity.

"For anyone else to give you this information would be a gross injustice. The only person qualified to tell you this valuable life story would be Avraham Shulman. For Avraham Shulman is truly a unique individual."

Watch for the
exciting sequel
to Double Identity

True
Identity

The publisher wishes to thank the following people for their assistance in proofreading and editing Double Identity: Judy Bendet, Annette Bendet, and Shulamit Goldstein.

Other Novels By Mayer Bendet
THE HIGHEST BIDDER

THE HIGHEST BIDDER is the heartwarming story of young yeshiva students willing to risk everything for the chance to rescue Jewish children from a Catholic orphanage. The innocent youth are being robbed of their heritage, and bold steps must be taken to save them.

THE HIGHEST BIDDER describes the operations of the missionaries in the United States and Israel. We meet the Christian agents who will stop at nothing to convert Jewish children. We share the trials and anguish of the yeshiva students as they infiltrate the missionary organization.

THE HIGHEST BIDDER explores the methods used by the missionaries, and describes the vast amount of funds at their disposal. We meet and get to know the innocent victims, who, at the hands of their captors, are brainwashed into accepting a new religion.

The reader is held in suspense by this novel as events move toward a surprising climax.

ISBN 0–932351–02–6

Other Novels By Mayer Bendet
THE ACCUSED (Two Parts)

THE ACCUSED is the stirring saga of a family of orphaned Orthodox Jewish children. Left in the hands of New York City's Child Welfare Agency, the siblings are placed for adoption in different homes.

THE ACCUSED traces the separate lives of each of the children. We are kept spellbound as Rachel, the older sister, attempts to reunite the family.

We meet Mark Find, a man accused of a crime he did not commit. He holds the key that Rachel needs.
THE ACCUSED pits father and son against each other in a gripping courtroom drama, as brother and sister sit on opposing sides of the battle.

The reader forms an emotional bond with the characters while following them through triumph and tragedy.

THE ACCUSED, a two-part novel, dramatizes the all-too-real experiences of those who are separated from family and religion by a merciless bureaucracy.

ISBN 0–932351–03–4

ISBN 0–932351–04–2

Other Novels By Mayer Bendet
OUR MAN IN RUSSIA

OUR MAN IN RUSSIA is the suspense-filled story of a young yeshiva student who is sent behind the Iron Curtain. His undercover mission: to help save the religious underground.

OUR MAN IN RUSSIA documents the growing terror of the Jewish communities in the Soviet Union. The eyes and ears of the KGB are everywhere, but small groups of Orthodox Jews manage to keep their sacred heritage and pass on its holy doctrines to new generations.

The KGB is aware of these activities, but needs to penetrate the underground to gather the information that would incriminate its leaders. The underground members know that if the KGB is not stopped religious Jewish life in Russia will be forever crushed.

OUR MAN IN RUSSIA is a novel about those who are willing to give their lives to protect the eternal values of Judaism.

ISBN 0–932351–01–8

Shabbos Treats That Grew

A Story by **Mayer Bendet**

Written by **Yaffa Leba Gottlieb**
Illustrated by **Miriam Lando**

SHABBOS TREATS THAT GREW is the warm story of a brother and sister who set out to do a small mitzvah, only to find themselves involved in the lives of several Jews in need of their help. Children will delight in this tale, and parents will take pleasure in the character traits that it seeks to promote.

ISBN 0—932351—16—6 (Casebound Edition)
ISBN 0—932351—17—4 (Softcover Edition)
ISBN 0—932351—18—2 (Audio Cassette)

The Farrakhan Phenomenon

The Farrakhan Phenomenon

Race, Reaction, and the Paranoid Style in American Politics

ROBERT SINGH

GEORGETOWN UNIVERSITY PRESS / WASHINGTON, D.C.

Georgetown University Press, Washington, D.C.   20007
© 1997 by Georgetown University Press. All rights reserved.
Printed in the United States of America.
10 9 8 7 6 5 4 3 2 1   1997
THIS VOLUME IS PRINTED ON ACID-FREE OFFSET BOOKPAPER.

Library of Congress Cataloging-in-Publication Data

Singh, Robert.
    The Farrakhan phenomenon :   race, reaction, and the paranoid style
in American politics / Robert Singh.
        p.   cm.
    Includes bibliographical references and index.
    1. Farrakhan, Louis.   2. United States—Race relations.   3. Afro-
Americans—Politics and government.   4. Hate—Political aspects—
United States.   5. United States—Politics and government—1989– .
I. Title.
E185.615S564   1997
305.8′009732—dc21
ISBN 0-87840-657-3 (cloth). —   ISBN 0-87840-658-1 (pbk.)
                                                      97-6103

For my parents

Contents

Preface

In March 1990, upon being asked by the late Professor Aaron Wildavsky for my dominant impressions of America—on only my second visit to the country and my first to Washington, D.C.—I'd tentatively commented upon the feature that had struck me most forcefully: the overarching importance of race to the nation's political and social affairs. Fortunately, for a young British graduate student, the reply elicited the eminent professor's typically gruff approval: "That's right. When people ask me what they should understand about American politics, I tell them race, the first five times." Although I had no way of knowing, then or subsequently, whether Wildavsky actually did offer such repetitive advice to aspiring Americanists, neither academic study nor personal experience since that enjoyable encounter have altered my original view.

The decision to write this book about Louis Farrakhan in part reflected the strongly held conviction that examining the politics of race in America remains a necessary and central—though by no means sufficient—condition of a comprehensive and accurate understanding of politics in the United States today as much as, and probably more than, ever. For as the twentieth century draws to its close, it requires no special critical faculty nor an exceptional gift of intellect to see that the American dilemma of race is little closer to resolution now than at its outset. In over one hundred years, the great progress achieved by black Americans—though remarkable in many respects—has remained manifestly insufficient to bring them fully into the republic's economic and social mainstream. In consequence, of the many emotions invariably occasioned by both public and private discussions of race among American citizens today, that of pessimism is unmistakably widespread. That sentiment, moreover, constitutes an especially conspicuous and resilient exception to the generally optimistic cast of most Americans' speculations upon the future development of their nation.

Compounding that pessimism was most certainly not a motive for composing this treatise, but for some readers it may be an inadvertent and unfortunate result. The monograph originally began life as a much more modest academic paper, whose animating rationale was simply to examine the extent to which it was possible to locate Louis Farrakhan within what the distinguished American political historian, Richard Hofstadter, first identified as the "paranoid style" in American politics. During the course of composing that paper, however, it rapidly became clear not only that the leader of the Nation of Islam (NoI) could indeed be appropriately understood within a framework of authoritarian/paranoid politics in the United States, but also that Farrakhan's meteoric and controversial ascent to national leadership status among African-Americans merited an altogether lengthier, more considered and detailed analytic treatment.

Part of the reason for this extended examination is essentially internal to the Farrakhan phenomenon, residing in the very novelty of the NoI leader's views, leadership style, and ongoing political project. In this relatively narrow but popularly familiar sense, Farrakhan represents an appropriately menacing, divisive, and sharply polarizing political figure for the fin de siècle and, hence, an especially rich and compelling subject for study. Some of the most fascinating and crucial aspects of his recent rise are external to Farrakhan, however; they lie in the varied responses and reactions of other black and nonblack Americans to the NoI's charismatic leader. For few other political figures across American history of any race have elicited the extreme, contradictory, and often virulent reactions that Farrakhan unerringly provokes among a citizenry noted for their tenaciously favoring consensus and moderation over conflict and extremism. Love and hate are deeply emotive terms not readily or widely used in connection with American politics, save perhaps in the more salacious details concerning the ethical lapses of some members of the U.S. Congress. Yet these terms surface with an astonishing regularity in both popular and elite discussions of Farrakhan; the many passions that the Black Muslim arouses are almost palpable, even on paper.

Tempting though it may therefore be to treat Farrakhan in such terms of emotive hyperbole, this monograph eschews such a course. Rather, it is an attempt to consider the Farrakhan phenomenon in an engaged but dispassionate manner, from a physically distant but analytically clear vantage point. At the outset, it must readily be conceded that studying American politics from afar is an odd and sometimes difficult intellectual enterprise. As a long distance observer of African-American politics, in particular, one is constantly reminded of possessing an outsider status, as both a noncitizen and a professional political scientist. If, however, a factor can be said to mitigate the limitations that necessarily accompany this external locus, it is perhaps that the complex dynamics of racial politics in modern America are not inappropriately studied by individuals who have avoided the specifically American version of the scar of race, the universality of which, nonetheless, seems a tragic constant in our contemporary affairs.

The research for the book has drawn extensively upon both published and unpublished secondary data about and by Farrakhan (including his speeches, interviews, and written works), supplemented by a series of background interviews conducted with American politicians, academics, and journalists over the period 1993–96. Although approached several times (in Washington, D.C. and New York City), the NoI proved consistently unwilling to permit either interviews or archival research. The arguments contained herein are therefore made from limited, but sufficient, sources to admit of a comprehensive and accurate analysis of Farrakhan's political beliefs, ascendancy, and significance. The extensive use of secondary data that informs the text is designed both to substantiate my interpretation of the Farrakhan phenomenon (the NoI leader is frequently apt to accuse those whom he deems to be hostile critics of deliberate misinterpretation of his views), and to allow readers the opportunity to follow up those references that time and space have not permitted a full and thorough development of herein. As often as is appropriate, Farrakhan's own words are presented unadorned and unabridged.

Inevitably, substantial intellectual and personal debts are owed to the many individuals and institutions that have assisted in the genesis and evolution of this project, though they are all, of course, absolved of any responsibility for errors of fact or interpretation herein. Most important, the "Oxford Mafia" of Americanists have been tirelessly encouraging and supportive throughout. In particular, the evolution of my thoughts on Farrakhan owes much to Desmond King, a constant source of constructive and pertinent criticism, unceasing professional encouragement, and invaluable scholarly support. Further debts are also owed to my long-established and long-suffering mentors, Nigel Bowles and Byron Shafer, both of whom have maintained with customary equanimity, patience, and great good humor their constant support and outstanding critical skills. My accounts at their banks of expert advice and assistance are now embarrassingly overdrawn, an indebted state for which I continue to crave their forgiveness and ongoing indulgence.

In Ireland, the Department of Political Science at the University of Dublin, Trinity College, provided a very congenial and stimulating intellectual environment in which to work from 1994–96. The refinement and revision of my ideas and arguments benefited considerably from the opportunity to present a research paper on Farrakhan at a departmental seminar in November 1995, as well as from numerous informal discussions. Thanks are especially due to John Gary, Ron Hill, the trinity of Trinity Michaels (Messrs. Gallagher, Laver, and Marsh), John Lyons, and Ben Tonra. Miriam Nestor was also an incomparable source of friendship, encouragement, and administrative assistance. The research for the book was also vitally assisted by grants from the Arts and Social Sciences Benefactions Fund and the Provost's Academic Development Fund, for which I am most grateful.

Invaluable reviews, comments, and advice about particular chapters, specific arguments, and life in general were also generously forthcoming from Martin Conyon, Jon Exten-Wright, Anna-Marie Jatta, Neil Masuda, Louise Owens, Luisa Perrotti, and Lee Roberts. Their continued friendship and humor have afforded the ample sustenance essential to the project's completion. Thanks are also due to Adolph Reed, for initially sparking my critical interest in Farrakhan during my year as an exchange student at Yale University in 1990–91; to Juji Johnson, for introducing me to the practical politics of race in America and for her continued commitment and exceptional faith; and especially, to John Samples of Georgetown University Press, who was a particularly helpful, enthusiastic, and positive publisher. My great thanks go to him and his expert staff at Georgetown for all their professional efforts.

Finally, immense thanks are due to my parents, who have faced, fought, and overcome the ignorance, bigotry, and prejudice of weak and narrow minds in a locus some distance from the United States. It is in grateful recognition of their unceasing love, generosity, and patience that the book is dedicated to them both.

1

The Politics of Organized Hate

Disorganized love is not as effective as organized hate.

Louis Farrakhan, 1994[1]

Supporters and defenders of Minister Louis Farrakhan, leader of the Nation of Islam (NoI), are often apt to draw a simple analogy between the racial problems of the United States of America and a house that is on fire: when a building is burning, they sagely advise the unenlightened, its occupants need not enquire too deeply about the identities of the firemen who have arrived to battle the raging flames. The difficulty here, however, is that when one of those firemen invariably insists upon bringing voluminous quantities of oil instead of water to tackle the blaze, the prospects for its full extinction are decidedly more distant than close at hand. And in the generally smoldering edifice—and sometimes barely latent inferno—that is contemporary race relations in the United States, Louis Farrakhan contributes much gasoline and precious little water to still the ongoing heat.

    Speaking a paranoid language of conspiracies, conversations with the dead, and visitations to spaceships that hover above the Earth waiting to rain down their awesome bombs, Farrakhan is easily the most controversial black American to have achieved a public position of national political influence in the United States since Malcolm X was assassinated a generation ago.[2] The leader of an obscure, unorthodox, and sectarian black separatist organization, Farrakhan has provoked the sharpest and most bitterly protracted exchanges between African-Americans and Jews in the United States in the twentieth century; has won the type of enthusiastic ovations from exceptionally large African-American audiences that elude all other contemporary black political leaders; has alternately embarrassed, antagonized, and condemned prominent national and local black politicians and civil

1

rights activists; has assembled one of the most financially profligate and ethically disreputable black religious organizations in the United States; has elicited admiration and praise from white supremacists and black progressives alike; and has mobilized collective action by African-Americans in the 1990s on an unprecedentedly large scale. In his impressively unerring ability to prompt the most powerfully emotive responses from American citizens of all races, religions, and creeds—and thereby sharply polarize American political opinion—Louis Farrakhan has several demagogic rivals but no contemporary peer.

Farrakhan, political controversy, and mass black popularity have together formed a symbiotic trinity that has gradually but inexorably propelled the Black Muslim minister into the ranks of national African-American political leadership in the 1990s. Unlike most American political figures, Farrakhan's ascendancy has occurred not so much despite, but in large part as a direct result of, his successfully courting national and international controversy. Implicated in the assassination of Malcolm X in 1965, the minister was himself rumored to be the target of such a plot by one of Malcolm's daughters thirty years later. Having nonchalantly described Adolf Hitler as a "wickedly great man" in 1984, Farrakhan was subsequently characterized by the then mayor of New York City as a "Nazi in clerical garb" with "more followers than Hitler," who deserved to "burn in hell."[3] Banned by the British government from even entering the United Kingdom in 1986 on the grounds that his visit "would not be conducive to the public good,"[4] Farrakhan has been enthusiastically received by the brutal authoritarian despots of Iran, Iraq, and Nigeria, and offered a combination of arms, admiration, and generous financial assistance by the Libyan dictator and sponsor of international terrorism, Colonel Mu'ammar Gadhafi. Such deeply discordant national and international reactions together have shaped Farrakhan's steady emergence during the last thirteen years as, simultaneously, the personification of the aspirations and grievances of thousands of African-Americans and the apprehensions and fears of at least as many whites.

For the former, Farrakhan's elegantly clad figure, courageously unbowed demeanor, and fire and brimstone oratory represent a singularly powerful and impeccably heroic symbol of implacable racial defiance to a white America that is apparently distant and hostile—enduringly and increasingly so—to the political, economic, and social interests and aspirations of U.S. blacks. Such a view is itself parasitic upon the multiplicity of negative assessments of the NoI's leader made by many white Americans. For the latter, Farrakhan represents an inglorious blight upon an otherwise dazzling American mosaic. He constitutes a deeply troubling black political figure, whose rhetoric is replete with fear and loathing. Farrakhan's contemporary political locus is thus founded upon an apparently bifurcated emotive apparatus of a frequently professed and unqualified love for his own race, and a more-or-less coded, but equally undiscriminating, hatred of others. For Farrakhan, the content of an individual's character frequently seems effectively determined by the very color of that person's skin, a peculiar, perverse, and pernicious inversion of the Reverend Dr. Martin Luther King Jr.'s inspiring humanitarian dream of the potential racial future of the United States.

The Farrakhan phenomenon, however, is a far more complex political and social entity than either Farrakhan himself or the two explanations most frequently advanced to account for his gradual ascendancy—widespread anti-Semitism and increasing racial bitterness among African-Americans toward whites—in fact allow. Though assuredly apposite, these two factors alone are insufficient to account for Farrakhan's political longevity and recent rise. More than a decade has elapsed since Farrakhan first entered the American national political consciousness in 1984. Despite frequent attempts by many Americans of all races variously to counter his mass black appeal, urge his unequivocal political ostracization by African-American elites, and deny the brute fact of his broad social and political influence among black Americans at large, the NoI's leader has steadfastly refused to disappear from American national politics. Instead, the diffuse public and private efforts of Farrakhan's many critics and political opponents that have sought to achieve his full and enduring exclusion from the ranks of national black political leadership have in part facilitated his increasing inclusion therein.

The roots of the Farrakhan phenomenon are thus evidently deep and resilient. Although political scientists and other critics strongly disagree about both the nature and significance of Farrakhan's current political role, as well as the precise extent of his influence among African-Americans, the NoI's leader has undoubtedly emerged as a national black political figure provoking the starkest, deepest, and most conflicting reactions from American citizens of all races and creeds. For some (especially and overwhelmingly—though not exclusively—among the African-American community), Farrakhan and his besuited, bow-tied Fruit of Islam guards represent beguilingly reassuring and potent political symbols of dignity, responsibility, aspiration, pride, hope, courage, and autonomy. They embody in their outspoken words, fearless deeds, and defiantly independent demeanors the most positive and admirable traits that any human being might aspire toward or strive to emulate.

For others, though, among white Americans in general and Jews in particular, Farrakhan and his militaristic Black Muslim minions more recall brown-shirted fascistic militias, invariably being accorded the type of deep revulsion, fear, and (less commonly) intense ridicule normally reserved for the most outlandish, preposterous, and eccentric of cranks, bigots, and extremists. Far from being worthy of admiration and approbation, they represent much that is most ignoble, mendacious, and poisonous in modern American public life; that threatens ultimately to unravel the delicately sewn and still-frail fabric of American social relations that has for so long been richly embroidered with the painful struggle to achieve lasting racial comity; and that, therefore, merits the most fulsome contempt and unequivocally clear condemnation.

Most politically telling of all, however, few public or private responses to Farrakhan—from either black or white Americans—occupy a neutral, indifferent, or uncertain ground. That this should be the case powerfully reflects the continued centrality and the enduringly controversial character of race in American society and politics at the close of the twentieth century. Expressions of intense interracial conflict in the United States have assumed numerous forms through the republic's checkered history. Attempts to analyze the several painful horns of the "American dilemma" of race that Swedish social scientist Gunnar Myrdal first identified in 1944, however, show that Louis Farrakhan has clearly emerged as one of its sharpest and most vivid contemporary expressions.[5] Where white Americans typically find it at once inexplicable and outrageous that a public figure espousing Farrakhan's beliefs can be taken seriously at all, African-Americans see such incredulous attitudes as complacently ignoring the very real and desperate conditions of much of black America to which Farrakhan so regularly, directly, and forcefully speaks. Just as the racially bifurcated reactions to the O. J. Simpson trial and verdict in October 1995 so starkly revealed, once more, the profound racial gulf that exists at the very heart of modern American social life, so the pronounced dissonance that surrounds black/white evaluations of Farrakhan speaks volumes to the distinct lenses through which the races increasingly view American social, economic, and political affairs in general, and each other in particular.

This book charts such discordant reactions in the context of an exceptionally controversial and compelling case. Its purpose is to explain, as fully and accurately as possible, the nature, causes, and political significance of the Farrakhan phenomenon. Central to its analytic project is a simple, pressing, but as yet unanswered intellectual problem: how has an individual so reviled, repudiated, and reactionary—a man for whom racial hatred is in every sense an abiding article of faith—achieved a social and political impact of substantial consequence among African-Americans at large? In sum, this treatise seeks to analyze how and why such an unabashed leader of organized hate—one both espousing and attracting such intense emotion in kind—has achieved the leadership status he has among an American social group more enduringly the victims than the perpetrators of hatred, prejudice, and bigotry, a minority whose members have more often represented the courageous vanguard in realizing the noble vision of a color-blind society in the United States than bigots succumbing to being blinded by race.

FARRAKHAN AND THE PROMISE OF
RACIAL DISHARMONY IN AMERICAN POLITICS

Although it is often said that the true theater of a demagogue is a democracy, organized hatred has only rarely been the province of American politics. Indeed, to outside observers of the United States especially, one of the most striking features of the American polity has invariably been its apparently stable, consensual, and harmonious character.[6] Compared to the European experience, in particular, American politics is frequently and widely viewed as having been mercifully free from the recurrent threats of tyranny, dictatorship, and totalitarian political regimes that have so often brutally quashed personal liberty and have—intentionally and otherwise—precipitated global wars over the course of the twentieth century. Commitment to the protection of the fundamental civil liberties and rights of individual citizens and minority groups, enshrined in the U.S. Constitution of 1787 and broadly and deeply rooted in American political culture, has survived and prospered for more than two centuries in the United States while struggling—even in the 1990s—to secure a firm and enduring grounding in many European, Asian, and African nations. Although government in general and the federal government in particular have admittedly been familiar targets of widespread and persistent popular political abuse in the United States, rarely has either (with few, though significant, exceptions) been a source of substantial or lasting political oppression to its own citizens—a remarkable political testament to the values and principles bequeathed successive generations of Americans by the founding fathers in the U.S. Constitution.[7]

Moreover, compared to countries in the rest of the world, the citizens of the United States have been remarkably and enduringly unreceptive to either appeals or demands for fundamental change in the nature of their established political, economic, and social arrangements. Although periods of deep social unrest and intense internal political conflict have occurred on many occasions throughout America's history, deriving in part from interpretative conflicts over the values of the American Creed and their distinctive applications to contemporary political problems and social maladies,[8] the liberal democratic consensus underpinning the U.S. polity has ultimately remained robust and fundamentally undisturbed. Thus when discussing revolution in America, we are well accustomed to using the prefix "the" rather than "which," in marked contrast to the revolutions of other regimes.

The primary causes of this systemic phenomenon of pronounced political stability have long been contested by intellectuals: the early achievement of the franchise by the mass of white American males; the geographic security afforded the United States by being bounded by two large oceans; the country's rich abundance of natural resources; the nation's unusual capacity for persistent economic growth; the absence of a feudal past and of fractious conflict over the institution of private property; the extremely limited extent of class consciousness; and the political genius of the design, and subsequent evolution, of the U.S. Constitution.[9] Whatever the various merits and flaws of the principal explanations for its occurrence, however, the empirical fact of the comparative stability of the American political system is clear and undeniable.

When American society is confronted by the abrasive incidence of extremist political figures or social movements, it is therefore not surprising that something appears to be deeply deficient, disturbing, and even malignant about the contemporary body politic. Expressions of political extremism strongly suggest an atypical malfunctioning in the basically centrist, consensual, and moderate nature of American political discourse. Although James Madison certainly envisaged the

United States as a new democratic republic in which conflict rather than consensus would undoubtedly predominate, the bounds of such domestic antagonisms—social, economic, and political alike—were conceived as limited and were constitutionally designed to ensure that they would indeed prove to be so.[10] Thus, the popularity of McCarthyism in the later 1940s and early 1950s; the intense social and political conflicts surrounding the postwar desegregation movement, in both the American South and the North; the prolonged and acute dissension, and sometimes violent domestic disturbances, over American military involvement in the Vietnam War; and the several bloody city riots that broke out from the urban crises of the 1960s, all manifested periods of pronounced and unusually protracted internal dissensus from the historically dominant pattern of domestic politics in the United States. Each has been widely viewed as an essentially aberrant expression of disharmony within the more general environment of a stable American polity whose political development has been fundamentally premised upon an inclusive and broad consensus, and that has been strongly sustained by the achievement of mostly incremental reforms and modest adaptations to changing eras and imperatives (whether domestic or international).

It is, nonetheless, within this context of periodic challenges to the dominant political milieu of American consensus and stability that the Farrakhan phenomenon is most appropriately and clearly located. For since 1984, the name of Louis Farrakhan has become popularly synonymous with notions of an extensive and deep interracial animus and with the existence of a fundamentally disharmonic American polity whose preeminent social division is that of race. To the extent that inscribed upon the names of certain individuals and locations over recent American political history is the controversial legacy of the deep fissures and cleavages in American society based centrally upon race, that of Farrakhan now assumes its full and appropriate historical place alongside those of Bernie Goetz, Howard Beach, Bensonhurst, Tawana Brawley, Crown Heights, Marion Barry, David Duke, Clarence Thomas, Rodney King, Mike Tyson, O. J. Simpson, and Mark Fuhrman as emblematic of the American dilemma, a dilemma no less central to American politics and entrenched in American society in the 1990s than it was during the 1890s.

For sadly, at the twilight of the twentieth century, as much as and, in many ways, more than at its outset, race continues to contribute consistently, powerfully, and divisively to the definition and the sharpening of virtually every social, economic, and political issue in the United States: from unemployment to welfare; from education to crime; and from the family to employment. Despite over thirty years of civil rights legislation and over twenty years of affirmative action policies in both public and private education and employment, black and white Americans in the last decade of the twentieth century remain to a conspicuously striking and alarming degree two separate and mutually suspicious societies, unequal, hostile, and apt to view the same facts and events through diametrically opposed interpretive lenses and emotive prisms. Race, more than any other social division, has been the most persistent and bitter apple of internal domestic discord in America for over 150 years; and it remains demonstrably and disconcertingly so today.[11]

Given the longevity of their deeply troublesome presence, it is hardly surprising that elite and mass responses among the American citizenry to the racial tensions and problems of the United States are far from uniform in character. Thus, for many Americans, both black and white, the reemergence in the 1990s of the starkest indices of racial separation, inequality, and mutual hostility is a tremendously sad, painful, and powerful indictment of what has emerged over recent decades as an unusually recurrent and critically important instance of chronic national failure; this in a nation especially rich in, and justifiably proud of, its long and enviable history of political achievement, social progress, and sustained economic success.

For Farrakhan, however, the obvious and increasing signs of American racial separatism are more a cause for celebration and hope than a depressing stimulus to despair and disillusion. The central problem in contemporary America for the leader of the NoI is not that black and white Americans inhabit two largely separate, suspicious, and increasingly distinct, unequal, and mutually hostile worlds within one nation. Rather, it is that the races in America are not yet set sufficiently apart. Where most American politicians continue to strive bravely for greater social proximity and increasing comity between the races, Farrakhan instead seeks to move them in precisely opposite physical, spiritual, and emotive directions. Where many Americans sincerely wish for the political, social, and economic distance between the races to be irrevocably reduced through increasing integration, Farrakhan desires its substantial and permanent extension through the complete separation of blacks and whites. Where the vast majority of Americans continue to vest enduringly strong faith in the oft-touted virtues of the "American Dream," its inspirational vision of universal and constant individual and collective potential, and the full realization of its inclusive societal appeal, Farrakhan instead emphasizes its multiple vices and failures and evokes the darkest visions of an imminent, violent, and all-encompassing American racial nightmare.

Thus, although Farrakhan bears—in common with all Americans—the "scar of race,"[12] he does so with a particular personal pride and political militancy that, rather than demanding its gradual, surgical removal through further public and private efforts at racial integration or assimilation, champions its rapid and irrevocable elimination through a radical, alternative route: the complete and enduring separation of black and white Americans in the United States.[13] The noble and compelling political and social ideal of a multiracial, pluralist American democracy, so beloved of King and the desegregation movement during the 1950s and 1960s—and still courageously strived for by Jesse Jackson, Colin Powell, John Lewis, and the overwhelming majority of national black political, civic, and religious leaders in the 1990s—is one that the leader of the NoI has manifestly never adhered to and does not currently share. Farrakhan's diagnosis of the American polity's cancerous racial ills is clear and straightforward. Racial integration represents at best a forlorn black American fool's political, economic, and social paradise, at worst a malign and repugnant recipe for a hellish national disaster. Farrakhan's emphatic response to Rodney King's plea after the Los Angeles riots of 1992 for black and white Americans to "get along" is therefore a consistent, vociferous, and unequivocal "no."

At the most fundamental level, then, Louis Farrakhan represents an especially intelligent, shrewd, and articulate African-American advocate of collective black consciousness, black political unity, and separate racial development in modern America. Black power in Minister Farrakhan's view is not a matter of power over white Americans, nor even parity with them; it is power set entirely apart from an oppressive and degenerate white society. Farrakhan's politics are thoroughly informed and infused not by integrative and inclusive racial impulses, but rather by an overwhelming imperative of complete black political, economic, and social disengagement from the majority-white American population. Black independence from white America, not integration with it, is the ultimate political goal for Farrakhan and the organization over which he presides, the tantalizing prize to which he must incessantly draw and keep focused the eyes and attentions of black Americans. Separation of the races is to be effusively celebrated rather than censured, representing a positive societal goal to be zealously encouraged, rather than inhibited, by public policy and private endeavor alike. However illuminating or impaired it may be to his fellow citizens, Farrakhan's vision is therefore one that is most definitely not "deeply rooted in the American Dream"; it stands squarely as an uncompromising and unrelenting challenge to that dream's most commendably uplifting humanitarian aspirations.

In this respect, one of the most acute ironies with which the Farrakhan phenomenon is notably replete resides in the timing of the political ascendancy of the NoI's leader. Manifesting a curious unorthodoxy—even a perversity—that characterizes much of his increasing appeal among African-Americans, Farrakhan's domestic social and political impact has grown in America at precisely the moment that the immense promise of multiracial harmony and interracial cooperation has won new and invigorating political hope abroad, with the dramatic but mostly peaceful revolution in South Africa. Just as the inspirational transformation of South Africa from an apartheid state predicated on keeping the races apart and unequal to a multiracial, pluralist, and liberal democratic regime was being forged, so Farrakhan's strident calls for the achievement of a complete separation of the races in the United States resonated strongly with increasing numbers of American blacks. As national and international political figures, Nelson Mandela and Louis Farrakhan have thus come during the 1990s to represent powerful symbols of national racial futures that point in entirely different directions for the black and nonblack populations of their respective countries: the former striving with immense courage and dignity to lead a long-divided nation decisively away from a deep swamp of historic racial hatred and a ruinously pernicious and discreditable public philosophy of group separatism; the latter enthusiastically encouraging its continued, fulsome, and destructive growth.[14]

As Americans watch Farrakhan prosper upon racial division, antagonism, and animosity, the poignancy of the contrast with South Africa in the 1990s is especially pronounced. W. E. B. Du Bois, the distinguished black American historian and social activist, famously declared in the early years of the 1900s that the main source of prospective national and international social and political conflict in the twentieth century would be centered upon the color line. In several respects, as African-Americans eventually achieved formal civil and political equality with the landmark passage of the Civil Rights Act of 1964 and the Voting Rights Act of 1965, respectively, and as black

African states contemporaneously secured independence from their former colonial rulers and gradually overcame segregation in Rhodesia (and ultimately South Africa), Du Bois's prediction appeared to be realized in the most complete, but at the same time the most positive and liberating, fashion. Progress for black Americans toward their final inclusion as full citizens in the American polity was strongly paralleled outside the United States by the liberation and maturation of Asian and African states attaining national independence.

As the century approaches its close, however, the fundamental features of racial conflict that Du Bois discerned remain substantially in place in the United States and, of course, in the much of the rest of the world. After struggling for such a prolonged period and at such pronounced and grievous cost in human life to achieve equality before the law, the failure of formal, procedural equality to bring about material social and economic improvements in the lives of millions of African-Americans is an extremely vivid and graphic one.[15] For many African-Americans, the bitter and brutal legacies of slavery, segregation, racism, and discrimination that have informed American history have barely been challenged by their collective experiences in the post–civil rights era, just as the legacy of colonial rule has not been erased by the checkered development of African states since independence that has offered so few reasons for enduring optimism about the long-term prospects of black Africa.

Farrakhan, in his unremittingly vehement rejections of integrative ideals and his shrill calls for racial separation, succinctly articulates the sentiments of an increasing number of black—and many nonblack—Americans, for whom the post–civil rights era of race relations in the United States has proven to be a very deep, painful, and persistent disappointment. The once-potent promise of equal treatment before the law has, for many black Americans, been bitterly exposed by the harsh—and in several instances horrific—socioeconomic realities of daily life in America's central cities and rural backwaters in the 1990s as a largely hollow political illusion. King's oft-cited dream of the achievement of a genuinely "beloved community" in the United States has, for many African-Americans, evolved since his tragic assassination as a siren call, an illusive and futile quest for social peace and fraternal cooperation between the races in the face of a growing material nightmare of inter- and intra-racial disharmony, and a rapidly deteriorating and debilitating quality of life for millions of black American citizens nationwide.[16]

Moreover, such disenchantment and disillusion has encompassed many more African-Americans than the disadvantaged and impoverished inhabitants of blighted central cities alone. Even for the rapidly expanded black American middle class, the brutally stark facts of persistent racial prejudice, discrimination, and intermittent conflict in the post–civil rights era remain tenaciously unavoidable. Notwithstanding the day-to-day slights that many African-Americans regularly suffer from authority figures and ordinary citizens alike, the vicious beating of Rodney King by law enforcement officers in Los Angeles in 1992 and the brutal revelations of detective Mark Fuhrman during the O. J. Simpson trial about the prevalence of racial prejudice, discrimination, and coercion in the Los Angeles Police Department in 1995 both issued especially clear and unequivocal national messages to all black Americans: economic affluence and upward social mobility provide substantial, but very much incomplete, protection against still-prevalent patterns of racial prejudice, stereotyping, discrimination, and their many attendant effects. [17] In this sense, Farrakhan's popular black appeal is understandable not only to the deprived and disadvantaged urban African-Americans who form his most eagerly receptive and enthusiastic core political constituency, but also to many socially secure suburban and economically affluent blacks, even if that appeal is encouraged and condoned by relatively few of the latter.

For the foundations of the Farrakhan phenomenon critically encompass the reactions of elite, as well as mass, black Americans. In particular, Farrakhan's current occupation of a wholly distinctive niche in national black American politics reflects powerfully upon the established black American political leadership cadre in the United States more broadly, in terms of both its many achievements and its several purported deficiencies. Farrakhan's rise is, in substantial measure, a direct function of the latter, especially. In the aftermath of the Los Angeles riot of 1992, for example, the apparent lack of effective black American political leadership was one crucial factor often cited by American academics and media commentators to account for the lawlessness of the black youths that took to the city streets soon after the acquittal of the L.A.P.D. officers for beating Rodney King. According to Maulana Karenga, for example:

Those black brothers out there in the street don't listen to the so-called black leaders because they know they aren't leading anyone but themselves. They're simply fed up with preachers and politicians who seem to have no understanding of their situation and of the reasons for their rebellion.[18]

Whether or not one dignifies the riot with the term "rebellion," the horrific scenes of violent brutality transmitted across the nation, so powerfully reminiscent of the 1965 Watts riots in Los Angeles, suggested that little had altered in the intervening twenty-seven years, save perhaps for the rapidity and graphic detail with which sophisticated television outlets such as CNN were now able to reveal to a national and international audience the gravity and violence of an essentially local catastrophe. Both riots, though set almost thirty years apart, were characterized by murders, injuries, extensive damage to private property, and mass confusion adjoined to deep anger on the part of many Americans of all races, not to mention the perplexity of non-Americans that, in the putative land of the free and home of the brave, at a time of relative peace and prosperity, so many of its citizens once again appeared joyfully insistent upon abusing that precious liberty and denying it to their compatriots.

Moreover, as in 1965, the L.A. riots of 1992 offered a parallel in the apparent impotence and ineffectiveness of established local and national black American political leadership in the tumultuous face of mass urban disturbances. The African-Americans among the rioters appeared not only to be intent upon wreaking havoc—whether criminally opportunistic or in violent expression of pent-up frustrations borne of disillusionment with and alienation from the American political and the criminal justice systems—but also to be implacably resistant to the putative authority of community and national black civic and political leaders and their desperate appeals for public order and calm.

Framed by such an explosive context, Minister Louis Farrakhan was the one African-American leader who arose as qualified to address mass black American malcontents and the disaffected. Chicago Alderwoman Dorothy Tillman, for example, stated that:

I can't think of any black leader other than Minister Farrakhan who could command the attention of our angry and frustrated black youth. Not only could Minister Farrakhan get young people's attention, but he also can transform them from a criminal preying on their own neighborhood to a hard-working asset to the neighborhood.[19]

Many other African-Americans concurred with the view that, despite his obviously advancing years, "Louis Farrakhan is probably the only national figure most youths pay any attention to."[20]

While such sentiments were broadly articulated among black commentators, however, they met with especially vehement criticisms from many members of established black American professional and intellectual elites of "the mindlessness of Louis Farrakhan and other spokespersons for what is marketed as 'black self-help'"[21] and the "blind alley" of black capitalism into which Farrakhan was seeking to lead his assembled African-American flock.[22] The veteran civil rights activist and NAACP board member, Julian Bond, scathingly described Farrakhan as "a black Pat Buchanan or David Duke . . . notoriously and unapologetically anti-Semitic, anti-Catholic, anti-white, misogynist, and anti-gay."[23] Rep. Major Owens (D-NY), a Brooklyn-based member of the Congressional Black Caucus, characterized Farrakhan's organization, the NoI, as a "hate-mongering fringe group" that persistently disseminated "dangerous poison."[24] For one leading black American intellectual, Harvard University's Cornel West, the increasing emergence of strong black nationalist sentiments among many African-Americans, younger blacks in particular, that formed the apparent foundation of Farrakhan's growing appeal essentially represented:

> . . . a revolt against this sense of having to "fit in." The variety of black-nationalist ideologies, from the moderate views of Supreme Court Justice Clarence Thomas in his youth to those of Louis Farrakhan today, rest upon a fundamental truth: white America has been historically weak-willed in ensuring racial justice and has continued to resist accepting fully the humanity of blacks.[25]

For the influential African American economist, Glenn Loury, however, Minister Farrakhan constituted simply "the leader of a black fascist sect . . . a hysterical preacher of hate"[26]; while the former Black Panther, Eldridge Cleaver, lambasted Farrakhan as an unadulterated opportunist, a "slimeball, scheming, renegade bandwagoner. . . ."[27]

That a single black American religious activist should elicit such stark, intense, and strongly conflicting reactions from within black communities in the 1990s—flatteringly heralded by some as a uniquely influential and important political authority figure, and harshly excoriated by others as a bigoted black extremist, a marginal social force, and a transparently opportunistic and fraudulent charlatan—is at once striking, unusual, and significant. Few, if any, other African-American public figures have attracted such extreme and contradictory responses since the 1960s. Of post–civil rights era black American public figures, only the nomination of Supreme Court Associate Justice Clarence Thomas provoked an intense political controversy and broad dissensus among African-Americans nationwide on a scale even remotely comparable to Farrakhan.[28] The black reactions to Thomas, however, were in part shaped by contingent factors of essentially transient popular salience. African-American responses to Farrakhan have been much more clearly located in political, economic, and social conditions of a far deeper and more enduring character, and have hence accorded the Farrakhan phenomenon a more pronounced and controversial public salience among black Americans.[29]

When the very forceful and invariably unfavorable responses that the NoI's leader evokes from many nonblack Americans are also considered, Louis Farrakhan assumes a singular political distinction and novelty. The former U.S. Senator and 1996 Republican presidential nominee, Bob Dole, for example, described the NoI minister unequivocally as "a racist and anti-Semite, unhinged by hate."[30] Rep. Peter King (R-NY), one of the NoI's most outspoken national critics, publicly decried Farrakhan during congressional hearings in 1995 as "a racist and a hate monger," and labeled his separatist organization an "empire of hate."[31] Nor was David Broder, the doyen of eminent national American columnists, in isolated critical company when he explicitly identified Farrakhan as "a racist demagogue."[32] Literally scores of white American mass media pundits and editors have repeatedly repudiated Farrakhan in the harshest terms as a "crackpot bigot"; have explicitly denounced his public message as being consistently and graphically "hateful"; have condemned his public discourse as comprising a clear, "unrelenting," and sickeningly offensive diet of rabidly vicious anti-Semitism; and have included Farrakhan among the self-deluded ranks of "America's most demented."[33] According to one representative and succinct summation of such unenamored journalistic views:

> Louis Farrakhan represents a variant of American fascism. His organization is authoritarian, his message dead-end demagoguery and his dope the bracing narcotic of hate.[34]

Few, if any, other contemporary political figures in America, of any race, religion, or creed, attract this type of hostile and unforgiving critical commentary on a scale and with a frequency and passionate intensity even remotely comparable to that of Louis Farrakhan. An exhaustive list of those many Americans who have vigorously repudiated, vilified, and condemned the NoI's leader would assume an almost encyclopedic dimension.

Notwithstanding the many deeply critical interpretations that have been regularly advanced by American media pundits and popular commentators since 1984, however, no systematic academic studies of Farrakhan currently exist. The few American scholars who have offered more or less considered critical interpretations of the Nation of Islam's leader (mostly in op-ed pieces and journal articles) have, moreover, reached strongly conflicting—indeed, contradictory—conclusions about the content of Farrakhan's ideological beliefs, the nature of his evolving political role, and the precise extent of his contemporary political influence among black Americans at large. Like shaking hands with a shadow, accurately identifying Farrakhan's appropriate political locus has thus far seemed an especially elusive and exasperating critical enterprise.

The scholarly dissensus over Farrakhan and his organization is unmistakably marked. In ideological terms, for example, Farrakhan has been identified variously by American social scientists as a "conservative black nationalist,"[35] a "left-wing black nationalist,"[36] and a "proto-fascist."[37] The black American separatist organization that Farrakhan leads has, on the one hand, been included in an international compendium of revolutionary social and political movements[38] while, on the other, a dictionary of radical right-wing organizations around the world also lists the Nation of Islam, but notes, somewhat ambiguously, that the Black Muslim group is "not avowedly right-wing."[39]

Farrakhan's evolving political role and influence among African-Americans at large have also animated competing commentaries and divergent critical assessments. Thus, John White's interpretation of the organization's leader sees Farrakhan as causing the NoI's "fragmentation and decline,"[40] and Nicholas Lemann views Farrakhan, somewhat dismissively, as far "more a popular orator than the leader of an organization."[41] Still others, however, argue convincingly that no analysis of contemporary national black American politics in the

United States can exclude a consideration of the NoI's mercurial leader. Thus, Claudette McFadden-Preston views Farrakhan as having "struck a chord" among many black Americans far more resonant, resilient, and deep than any black or white American religious and political figure since Malcolm X during the 1960s.[42] Clarence Lusane, concurring, argues that Farrakhan "exerts an inordinate amount of stature, visibility, and sway" in current African-American politics.[43] Even some of Farrakhan's strongest critics in the American Academy (such as Henry Louis Gates Jr. and Adolph Reed Jr.) and his most implacable political opponents alike have been noticeably unwilling to dismiss entirely the possibility of the minister's ultimately achieving a disturbingly influential position in national black politics.[44]

That no comprehensive scholarly analysis of the Farrakhan phenomenon yet exists despite the several popular commentaries on his political role, influence, and goals is reflective, in part, of the relatively recent and controversial entry of Farrakhan into the burgeoning ranks of the national black American leadership cadre. As long as Farrakhan remained a largely peripheral and quixotic figure in national African-American politics during the 1980s, his marginal leadership role seemed not to merit systematic and detailed treatment by social scientists. Lack of rigorous academic attention also reflects the very substantial difficulties facing any analyst in researching the head of the Nation of Islam, a highly secretive, exclusionary, and hierarchical race-based organization that remains deeply hostile to outsiders, whatever their national, racial, and ethnic origins. Furthermore, scholarly reluctance to tackle the Farrakhan phenomenon itself reveals the inordinately delicate sensibilities that surround—and, increasingly, help to suppress—informed public discussion of American race relations in general and the NoI's leader in particular. The mutual tolerance, laudable candor and painfully honest reflection that characterize many private discussions of the subject in the United States rarely dignify and enlighten American current public debates. As Nathan Glazer, reflecting succinctly upon the increasing hypersensitivity of the subject in America, once aptly put it, "how can you talk about race when you can't talk about race?"[45]

Thus, for some American critics, inattention to Farrakhan's alleged anti-Semitism, for example, immediately condemns any discussion of the NoI's leader as wholly misplaced, partial, and inadequate; for others, however, any reference to it whatsoever is itself entirely misleading, reductive, and inappropriate. For still others, a focus upon Farrakhan's paranoid style of politics inevitably diminishes the very real significance of the material deprivations of black American communities that exists and that the NoI's leader consistently seeks to address. Yet, for many, no amount of social deprivation, however pronounced and persistent, justifies the promulgation of wild conspiracy theories, defamatory insults, and bigoted and vicious demagoguery on Farrakhan's scale. As many have discovered previously, writing about Farrakhan therefore assumes an almost incendiary quality. It is somewhat akin to lighting a critical fuse to an explosively taboo racial bomb, the existence of which we are all too painfully aware but which most prefer—for the sake of temporary peace, tranquillity, and social comity—studiously to ignore. But such taboos, however powerful, frequently merit exposure, challenge, and, on occasion, explosion, no matter how tenaciously ostrichlike our critical aversion to candid discourse on sensitive matters may have become.

If the obstacles to rational and scholarly inquiry are clearly significant impediments to analysis, they nonetheless do not represent insuperable barriers to a reasonably clear and judicious understanding of Farrakhan's political goals, methods, achievements, and significance. Through careful and informed analysis and suitably balanced judgment, Farrakhan's role and significance not only can be evaluated, but also ought to be assessed at length. This book therefore represents a modest attempt to rectify in part the failure of social scientists to examine the Farrakhan phenomenon in depth, and thereby, it seeks to fill an important void in the scholarly literature of contemporary African-American politics in particular and the politics of race in the United States more broadly. The monograph makes pretensions neither to inside knowledge of the NoI nor to personal interest in advancing a given critical or political goal of either repudiating, endorsing, or defending Farrakhan. Rather, it stands or falls upon its scholarly argument alone, based upon the accumulated evidence as it currently exists. If emotive, rather than (or, in addition to) intellectual, provocation does result, it will be as by-product rather than an intended design, but the treatise was composed with the knowledge that emotive reaction typically accompanies, occasionally eclipses, and frequently transcends rational inquiry into the tragic terrain of race in contemporary America.

FARRAKHAN, RACE, AND REACTION IN AMERICAN POLITICS

The subject of this book is Louis Farrakhan as a political phenomenon. Conversely, it is neither about Farrakhan as a person—issues of his personal qualities, whether saintly, insane, inspired, or otherwise, are not examined herein—nor about the Black Muslim movement in general. In terms of the former, biographies of Farrakhan, of a generally hagiographic and extremely tendentious cast, are already publicly available.[46] Regarding the latter, several studies of a broadly sympathetic character also exist on the Black Muslims in America generally and the Nation of Islam in particular.[47] To the extent that the NoI is a powerfully leader-centric entity, this monograph addresses issues of the wider movement indirectly, insofar as an analysis of Farrakhan must, at least in part, encompass some consideration of his organization as well. It is not, however, upon the organization of the NoI that the main intellectual interest of this study is founded.

Rather, Farrakhan eminently qualifies as a contemporary American sensation by virtue of the peculiar evolution of his political, economic, and social influence among African-Americans in particular, and the treatment accorded him by other political and civic actors in the United States in general, since the early 1980s. Although extensive critical dissensus surrounds the nature of his political role and influence, and especially the sources and significance of the latter, few academics and popular commentators who have seriously observed his development as leader of the NoI contest that Farrakhan has achieved a social and political impact in black American politics of unusual note and undoubted importance. Whatever their distinct assessments of the normative merits and demerits of his recent national rise and the exact reach of his considerable political appeal among African-Americans at large, the brute fact of Farrakhan's current political influence incontestably stands as one of manifest consequence; and one, moreover, that most attentive observers of current American politics find increasingly difficult to deny with either confidence or equanimity.

Farrakhan thus assuredly merits extended critical analysis in terms of his representing a contemporary American political phenomenon of substantial note. The *Oxford English Dictionary* offers a threefold definition of a phenomenon:

> (1) a fact or occurrence that appears or is perceived, esp. one of which the cause is in question (2) a remarkable person or thing

(3) the object of a person's perception; what the senses or the mind notice. [48]

In this triadic definitional sense, the term is indeed strikingly apt in characterizing Louis Farrakhan.

First, Farrakhan's political occurrence or rise has undoubtedly been widely commented upon, such that his presence in current national American politics is difficult—indeed, quite impossible—to ignore. The substantive causes of his current political role and influence are, furthermore, shrouded in some critical confusion and have become the subject of notable academic disagreement.

Second, Farrakhan's personal status as a remarkable individual is self-evident from even the most cursory examination of his political career thus far. Both despised and admired, hated and loved, and repudiated and championed with exceptional intensity by his many opponents and supporters, respectively, Farrakhan constitutes a national African-American political leader who falls fully within Max Weber's traditional definition of "charismatic authority." [49] Even his many avowed critics and adversaries readily concede that Farrakhan is an altogether exceptional character in contemporary American politics.

Third, both scholarly and popular evaluations of Farrakhan frequently occur through observational and critical prisms of decidedly varied hue and distinctive (and sometimes imperfect) design. The elements of Farrakhan's public discourse that are emphasized by analysts and commentators, whether for approbation or censure, are often identified in an extremely selective and partial fashion and evaluated according to demonstrably subjective political tastes, judgments, and overarching goals. [50]

Nonetheless, the Farrakhan phenomenon constitutes significantly more than the mere sum of its component parts. Farrakhan's recent rise to an influential national leadership position in contemporary African-American politics merits rigorous analysis not only in itself, but also because Farrakhan serves as a particularly compelling and remarkably rich embodiment of—and hence an especially powerful and clear window upon—broader developments in recent American politics, and in the politics of race, especially. The analysis of the Farrakhan phenomenon that follows is, hence, neither exclusively nor most importantly about the Black Muslim minister and his ascent to national political leadership status among black Americans. Rather, in order clearly and comprehensively to understand the contemporary Farrakhan phenomenon, it is necessary to locate the NoI's leader within the broader strains of the political environment of post–civil rights era American politics.

This is not, it should be immediately stressed, to seek to diminish the political significance of the particular individual. Individual political actors and entrepreneurs matter a great deal in American politics, as elsewhere, whatever the particular configuration of the broader social forces and societal fissures that necessarily surround and shape their activity. Indeed, an important subtheme of the central argument of this monograph is that, while Farrakhan has undoubtedly capitalized upon—and consistently exploited to substantial effect—conditions that are deeply rooted in the post–1960s structure of black Americans' political, social, and economic development in the United States, it has been his own individual strategic contributions and his particular tactical choices as the leader of the NoI that have powerfully shaped both the direction and the fluctuating pace of his rise to national black American political leadership. Nonetheless, the main analytical significance of the Farrakhan phenomenon resides more in what it reveals about the contours and fissures of contemporary American politics in general than in what it demonstrates about the Nation of Islam or its particular leader per se.

Two broad themes are especially significant in this respect. First and most obvious, Farrakhan reveals and powerfully contributes to the contemporary fissures and divisions in the politics of race in America at the end of the twentieth century. Precisely by virtue of the juxtaposition of Farrakhan's manifest popular appeal among black Americans and the extreme (and predominantly critical and condemnatory) reactions that he invariably elicits from black and, especially, nonblack American elites, the NoI's leader stands squarely upon the racial fault lines of American politics. Farrakhan represents an intensely compelling political figure as the United States continues to grapple with the pressing problem of its inter- and intra-race relations and seeks to define and shape the political meaning and legacy of the 1960s. In this sense, and although their explanations of and solutions to the U.S.'s racial predicament differ markedly, Farrakhan articulates the sentiments shared more broadly among many black (and some nonblack) Americans, at both elite and mass levels: that the landmark achievement of formal black civil and political equality in the mid-1960s was a limited and shallow, if not entirely Pyrrhic, victory for many African-Americans.[51]

To this extent at least the NoI's leader, like his former friend and mentor, Malcolm X, represents a considerably more complex and immeasurably more fascinating political phenomenon than is frequently acknowledged by his many American critics and detractors. Farrakhan certainly does express unyielding hatred, explicitly, frequently, and without apparent regret, remorse, or sufficient reason to seek to atone for that unmistakably clear and consistent animus. Simply to reduce assessments of Farrakhan to being the contemporary arch African-American exemplar of "the hate that hate produced," however, is a grossly inaccurate and misleading oversimplification of both his political base and his substantive national role. Analysis of extremists in general, and of Farrakhan in particular, is assuredly not assisted by "interpretation through diabolism,"[52] eminently susceptible though the NoI's leader undoubtedly is to such a crudely demonic characterization. Precisely by virtue of his currently representing one of the sharpest and most striking horns of Myrdal's American dilemma, the scholarly imperative to grapple dispassionately with both the causes and the broader political significance of the Farrakhan phenomenon is especially great, pressing, and (potentially) intellectually rewarding.

In addition, though, in serving as an especially clear and powerful window upon that racial dilemma as it has manifested itself in America during the 1990s, Farrakhan does so from an unusual political location: as a black American radical right-wing leader. Studies of authoritarian politics in America have conventionally concentrated principally upon the distinctive and heterogeneous fanaticist forces of the extreme white American right-wing.[53] Most detailed examinations of extremism in contemporary racial politics in the United States focus upon the expressions, extent, and manner of the conservative exploitation of race-related concerns among white Americans by avowedly right-wing and populist politicians, political parties, and other organized groups. Thus it is that the Rockwells, Wallaces, Dukes, Helmses, and Buchanans occupy the vast bulk of scholarly attention to modern American right-wing political extremism and authoritarianism.

It is the markedly conservative and overwhelmingly illiberal traditionalist character of Farrakhan's ideological values and beliefs—an unabashed conservatism that is frequently obscured for many observers by his militant black nationalism, anti-Semitic pronouncements, and informal associations with African-American liberals and progressives, such as Jesse Jackson and the Congressional Black Caucus—that casts the Black Muslim leader in a very peculiar, curious, and distinctive contemporary political role. Although the ideological match is imperfect, the parallels between Farrakhan and the radical white right-wing in America, both in their analyses of the current political, economic, and social problems in the United States, and in their political goals and aspirations, are at once several and striking. Farrakhan is perhaps not viewed most appropriately as the bastard black political twin of Louisianan David Duke, the ex-Ku Klux Klan Grand Wizard and Republican party senatorial candidate, but they remain undeniably close relatives in the peculiar dysfunctional extended family of conservative American extremism and political paranoia.

Farrakhan's political rise is also intimately connected to his esoteric brand of theologically based black nationalist conservatism and to the political responses of other U.S. and foreign actors—black and nonblack, secular and religious, at elite and mass levels—to both his individual public pronouncements and his organization's direct action interventions to combat drug use and ameliorate gang violence in many of America's inner-city black communities. An accurate analysis of the Farrakhan phenomenon therefore demands that the Black Muslim leader be assessed in his appropriate political and social context: not as an isolated political figure waging an atomistic and unorthodox course of his own design, but as a religious activist whose political pronouncements, activities, and style are deliberately and precisely calculated to produce strongly outspoken reactions among others which, in turn, contribute further to the consolidation of his own burgeoning political role and influence. Ironically, the responses of some American political elites to the NoI's leader, designed precisely to confront, challenge, and ultimately undermine the Farrakhan phenomenon, frequently serve inadvertently to reinforce its very momentum. Some of Farrakhan's most ardent and implacable American critics thus often end up serving as unwitting accomplices in his unconventional and prophetic national racial project.

The Farrakhan phenomenon, then, is not exclusively about race in contemporary America. It also concerns political reaction in a two-fold sense: first, in ideological terms, as the repressive features of Farrakhan's reactionary worldview are made manifest, despite their being frequently obscured, disregarded, or ignored by both his supporters and critics; and, second, in practical and logistical terms, in the dogged efforts of black and white American elites alike to respond effectively—according to their frequently divergent definitions of effective response—to the Black Muslim leader and his sectarian, separatist organization. It is in large part through the tactical and strategic responses of other political and social elites—both black and white—to Farrakhan that his novel locus and evolving role and influence in current American politics can most appropriately be delineated and profitably assessed.

Consonant with this two-dimensional focus, a dual narrative therefore threads the examination of the Farrakhan phenomenon that follows in this treatise. The peculiarly compelling story of Farrakhan's rise to national political prominence and influence among African-Americans is the first element. As a black political actor of evident—though greatly contested—consequence, Farrakhan merits an extended and thorough examination. In addition, though, the scope and character of the political responses to Farrakhan from other Americans form an integral part of the analysis. For it is in the political responses to the Black Muslim leader—whether hesitant or forceful, condemnatory or laudatory, fearful or encouraging—that many of the deepest racial fault lines of recent American politics can be most clearly identified and, thereby, fruitfully examined.

These twin themes of race and reaction form the underlying core of the entire book. In chapter two, Farrakhan's recent rise to national political leadership status among African-Americans is examined, with particular reference to the two presidential nomination campaigns of the Reverend Jesse Jackson, during 1984 and 1988, and the Million Man March on Washington of October 16, 1995. Farrakhan's ideological and religious beliefs are then outlined and analyzed in chapter three. Therein, the combination of a strident racial separatism (based upon deeply unorthodox theological foundations) with a profoundly conservative economic and social agenda is examined. Prevailing popular notions of Farrakhan's leftist radicalism, and of his status as an effective successor to Malcolm X for black Americans in the 1990s, are also challenged as being at once profoundly misplaced and as ignoring Farrakhan's fundamentally reactionary and repressive worldview.

Chapter four then locates Farrakhan within the broader American tradition of authoritarian political movements and paranoid activists, arguing that Farrakhan is not only a conventional conservative authoritarian populist, but that he also represents the preeminent contemporary African-American exemplar of the paranoid style in American politics. The agents of the alleged conspiracy against black Americans that forms a central political leitmotif of Farrakhan's public discourse are explicitly identified (namely, Jews, the federal government, whites, and African-American accommodationists) and discussed in detail. Although deliberate and premeditated actions against black Americans have undoubtedly occurred over many decades, the impressive scope and passionate intensity of Farrakhan's style of paranoid politics are, at minimum, unusual. In implying an independence of thought and courage of action that his fellow black civic and political leaders do not possess, Farrakhan's brand of political paranoia also contributes strongly to the NoI leader's national self-projection as the autonomous personification of his race's "authentic" collective interests.

Having identified the appropriate political context in which Farrakhan's distinctive ideas and values should be located, the minister's recent popularity and his influence among black Americans at large are explored in chapter five, which draws upon both opinion surveys and secondary accounts to affirm the significant popular appeal of Farrakhan among African-Americans. Consonant with such an affirmation, the chapter also rejects the notion, prevalent among some critical analyses, that the Farrakhan phenomenon is either exclusively or primarily a media creation. Instead, it argues that print and televisual attention has been a necessary, but not sufficient, condition of Farrakhan's recent political ascendancy.

The substantive reasons for the popularity of Farrakhan's distinctive brand of black reactionary and paranoid politics are then examined at length in chapter six, which concentrates upon the Black Muslim minister's exploitation of post–civil rights era interracial differences and intrablack socioeconomic cleavages; the disjunctures between black American elite and mass political opinions; and Farrakhan's antielitist appeals and outsider, "spatial leadership" strategies. In the latter respect, Farrakhan essentially runs for national black American political leadership by running against, and running down, not only whites in the United States but also—both directly and indirectly—black political and civic leaders. Farrakhan's incessant appeals to intraracial unity are, ironically, based upon a political strategy and praxis that is premised fundamentally upon provoking sharp polarization, antagonism, and division among African-Americans themselves, as well as between blacks and whites, in the United States.

In chapter seven, Farrakhan's importance to current black national political leadership is discussed, and his broader significance in contemporary American politics is evaluated. Farrakhan's main political significance lies in the extent to which he vividly demonstrates how far advanced—though still incomplete—the recent incorporation of black American national political leadership into the pluralist American mainstream has become. In this sense, Farrakhan represents, paradoxically, a product and a confirmation of the overarching success, not failure, of traditional black American aspirations to inclusive political empowerment in the United States. In the absence of material improvements in the lives of most African-Americans, however, such inclusion will be insufficient either to remove the fertile ground upon which the Farrakhan phenomenon has thus far depended for its destructive growth or to disturb Farrakhan's hastening of an impending American apartheid.

For both better and worse, Louis Farrakhan is an influential and enthusiastic participant in national black American politics in the 1990s. For political scientists especially, but also for all those interested in the current character of politics in the United States and its evolving racial dimensions, examination of the Black Muslim leader is an integral though insufficient—and at times frustrating, perplexing, and even painful—necessity for a comprehensive and accurate understanding of its contemporary structure and dynamics. However unpalatable, offensive, and eccentric many Americans (and non-Americans) may rightly find Farrakhan's public discourse, lurid rhetoric, and policy prescriptions, simply to demonize and dismiss the NoI's leader as either an aberrant fanatic, an irrelevant lunatic, or an essentially ephemeral and marginal extremist figure is wholly to misinterpret his political salience and mass appeal and, thereby, to lend his own defense more cogency, vigor, and popularity than it otherwise merits. Equally, though, to exaggerate unduly Farrakhan's recent political influence is to ignore the extent to which the NoI's leader thus far remains a still-isolated force in the much broader national black American political leadership cohort and, moreover, confronts many intractable constraints to his achieving an enduring, mainstream national leadership role.

Farrakhan therefore merits careful but disinterested analysis, in the most accurate senses of those terms. Careful, because the nuances and subtleties of his role, influence, and beliefs are often too easily lost amidst the disproportionate attention that is devoted to his more provocative rhetoric and deliberately incendiary public comments; and disinterested, not in terms of diminishing or marginalizing his political and social importance, but in the sense of consistently and dispassionately inquiring as to the purpose and reasons for his actions, their wider public reception, and the political consequences thereof. Without doubt, the Farrakhan phenomenon is of manifest importance to the current and future shape of American race relations in the twentieth and twenty-first centuries, not so much for what Farrakhan himself either says or does, but for what his public discourse and behavior and the reactions to them suggest about the past, present, and future shape of racial politics in America.

NOTES TO CHAPTER 1

1. Quoted in William Gaines and David Jackson, "Profit and Promises," *Chicago Tribune*, 15 March 1995, sec. 1, p. 10.

2. I use the terms "black," "black American" and "African-American" interchangeably throughout the book to refer to people of African descent in the United States. The usage reflects the continued preference of a majority of the social group in question for the appellation "black" or "black American," despite the increasing use of the alternative term. For compelling, though contrasting, discussions of the changes in appellations, see: Ben L. Martin, "From Negro to Black to African American: The Power of Names and Naming," *Political Science Quarterly* 106, no. 1 (1991): 83–107; and Tom W. Smith, "Changing Racial Labels: From 'Colored' to 'Negro' to 'African American'," *Public Opinion Quarterly* 56, no. 4 (1992): 496–515.

3. The remarks were made by Mayor Ed Koch, a noted Jewish target for Farrakhan's public ridicule during the 1980s. See Christopher Thomas, "Black radical taunts US Jews with 'God's oven' gibe," *The (London) Times*, 10 October 1985, p. 7.

4. Farrakhan had been invited by the Hackney Local Council in London, under the control of the Labour Party, and was also due to address the Islamic Council of the United Kingdom. The decision to refuse him entry by then Home Secretary Douglas Hurd, M.P., was made in response to an appeal from Michael Latham, M.P., chairman of the British-Israel Parliamentary Group. See "Black activist barred from Britain," *The (London) Times*, 17 January 1986, p. 2.

5. See Gunnar Myrdal, *An American Dilemma: The Negro Problem and Modern Democracy*, vols. 1 and 2 (New York: Harper and Row, 1944, 1964).

6. Throughout its history, the stability of the regime in the face of pronounced ethnic, racial, religious, and regional heterogeneity has been strongly emphasized by most non-American writers. See, for example: Alexis De Tocqueville, *Democracy in America* (New York: Vintage Books, 1945); and James Bryce, *The American Commonwealth* (New York: Macmillan, 1888).

7. For an extensive and important recent treatment of the extent to which the federal government both legitimated and diffused segregated racial practices in the first half of the twentieth century in the United States, both within and outside the South, see Desmond S. King, *Separate and Unequal: Black Americans and the US Federal Government* (Oxford: Oxford University Press, 1995).

8. The most prominent exponent of this view is Samuel P. Huntington, *American Politics: The Promise of Disharmony* (Cambridge, Mass.: Belknap/ Harvard University Press, 1981). See also the concise discussion of the nexus of stability and conflict in Michael Foley, *American Political Ideas* (Manchester: Manchester University Press, 1991).

9. See the classic "consensus school" accounts: Richard Hofstadter, *The American Political Tradition* (New York: Knopf, 1948); and Louis Hartz, *The Liberal Tradition in America* (New York: Harcourt, Brace, and World, 1955).

10. See Alexander Hamilton, James Madison and John Jay, *The Federalist Papers*, with introduction by Isaac Kramnick (Harmondsworth: Penguin 1987), No. 10.

11. See Andrew Hacker, *Two Nations: Black and White, Separate, Hostile, Unequal* (New York: Ballantine Books, 1992).

12. Paul M. Sniderman and Thomas Piazza, *The Scar of Race* (Cambridge, Mass.: Harvard University Press, 1993). See also Paul M. Sniderman, Philip E. Tetlock, and Edward G. Carmines, eds., *Prejudice, Politics, and the American Dilemma* (Stanford: Stanford University Press, 1993).

13. As chapter three notes in greater detail, Farrakhan's racial separatism has never waned, but it has waxed and wavered over time between advocations of a largely cultural retrenchment by African-Americans (akin to many black nationalists' prescriptions; see William L. Van Deburg, *New Day in Babylon: The Black Power Movement and American Culture, 1965–1975* [Chicago: University of Chicago Press, 1992]) and endorsement of an actual physical separation of the races. On several occasions, the latter has entailed the exodus of black Americans from the United States, most typically with Africa as the proposed destination for their new homeland.

14. Farrakhan's meeting with Mandela in January 1996 attracted widespread international attention. President Mandela's lecturing Farrakhan upon the three foundations of the new South Africa—nonracialism, nonsexism, and freedom of religion—represented a powerful and telling rebuke to the NoI's leader and his prescriptions for America's blacks. See James Bone, "Prophet of Hate," *The London Times (Magazine)*, 3 February 1996, pp. 26–30; and Christopher Munnion, "Farrakhan Tells Whites to Atone for Apartheid," *The Daily London Telegraph*, 29 January 1996, p. 11.

15. On the general shape of post–civil rights black American politics, see: Steven F. Lawson, *In Pursuit of Power* (New York: Columbia University Press, 1985); Hanes Walton, *Invisible Politics: Black Political Behavior* (New York: State University of New York Press, 1985); and Huey L. Perry and Wayne Parent, *Blacks and the American Political System* (Gainesville: University Press of Florida, 1995). Manning Marable provides quasi-Marxist interpretations in *Race, Reform and Rebellion: The Second Reconstruction in Black America,*

1945–1982 (Jackson, Miss.: University of Mississippi Press, 1984) and *Black American Politics: From the Washington Marches to Jesse Jackson* (London: Verso, 1985).

16. See Derrick Bell, *And We Are Not Saved: The Elusive Quest for Racial Justice* (New York: Basic Books, 1979); and James H. Cone, *Martin and Malcolm and America* (London: HarperCollins, 1991).

17. See Robert Gooding-Williams, ed., *Reading Rodney King/Reading Urban Uprising* (New York: Routledge, 1993); and Rochelle Stanfield, "Black Frustration," *National Journal*, 16 May 1992, pp. 1162–66.

18. Cited in Salim Muwakkil, "Leaders Lacking in a Black and White World," in *Inside the L.A. Riots: What Really Happened and Why It Will Happen Again* (New York: Institute for Alternative Journalism, 1992), pp. 106–8, at 107.

19. Muwakkil, "Leaders Lacking," p. 107.

20. Cited in Gooding-Williams, *Reading Rodney King*, pp. 146–47.

21. Jerry G. Watts, "Reflections on the Rodney King Verdict and the Paradoxes of the Black Response," in Gooding-Williams, *Reading Rodney King*, pp. 236–48, at 246.

22. Manning Marable, "In the Business of Prophet Making," *New Statesman*, 13 December 1985, pp. 23–25, at 25.

23. The remarks were made in a memo circulated by Bond to other NAACP board members in the aftermath of the Million Man March. Quoted in Kevin Merida, "Four Months After March, Controversy Follows Farrakhan," *The Washington Post*, 25 February 1996, p. A6.

24. Cited in Michael Wines, "Farrakhan is Bitterly Denounced by House Black Caucus Member," *The New York Times*, 5 February 1994, pp. 1, 7.

25. Cornel West, "Learning to Talk of Race," in Gooding-Williams, *Reading Rodney King*, pp. 255–60, at 257. See also West's collection of essays, *Race Matters* (Boston: Beacon Press, 1993).

26. Quoted in Sylvester Monroe, "The Mirage of Farrakhan," *Time* 144, 30 October 1995, p. 52.

27. Quoted in Henry Louis Gates Jr., "A Reporter at Large: The Charmer," *The New Yorker*, 29 April-6 May 1996, pp. 116–31, at 121.

28. It is mildly ironic that, prior to his confirmation hearings for nomination to the Supreme Court in 1991, Thomas felt compelled to issue public statements repudiating his previous praise for the Nation of Islam's leader. In two speeches in 1983, Thomas praised Farrakhan as "a man I have admired for more than a decade." His statement of July 13, 1991, however, included comments of his unalterable opposition to "anti-Semitism and bigotry of any kind, including . . . Louis Farrakhan." See Robert Pear, "Despite Praising Farrakhan in 1983, Thomas Denies anti-Semitism," *The New York Times*, 13 July 1991, pp. 1, 7.

29. Most notable among the contingent factors conditioning the Thomas furor were his nomination by President George Bush to fill the vacancy created by Thurgood Marshall's retirement, the enthusiastic sponsorship of Senate Republicans, and the allegations of sexual harassment leveled against Thomas—and accorded prime-time network television coverage—by Anita Hill. Though the Thomas nomination animated deep dissensus among black

Americans and spoke directly to many themes of inter- and intra-racial division and tension, the mass salience of the controversy was neither as enduring nor as sharply defined as that surrounding Farrakhan and the NoI. On the Thomas nomination and its associated political controversies, see: Toni Morrisson, ed., *Race-ing Justice, En-Gendering Power: Essays on Anita Hill, Clarence Thomas, and the Construction of Social Reality* (London: Chatto and Windus, 1993); Timothy M. Phelps and Helen Winternitz, *Capitol Games: The Inside Story of Clarence Thomas, Anita Hill, and a Supreme Court Nomination* (New York: HarperPerennial, 1993); and Stephen L. Carter, *The Confirmation Mess: Cleaning Up the Federal Appointments Process* (New York: Basic Books, 1994).

30. Quoted in John Kifner, "With Farrakhan Speaking, a Chorus of G.O.P. Critics Join In," *The New York Times*, 17 October 1995, p. A18.

31. United States House of Representatives, 104th Congress, First Session, Hearing before the Subcommittee on General Oversight and Investigations of the Committee on Banking and Financial Services, March 2, 1995, *Security Contracts Between HUD or HUD Affiliated Entities and Companies Affiliated With the Nation of Islam* (Washington, D.C.: U.S. Government Printing Office, 1995), p. 3.

32. David Broder, "Farrakhan reminder that U.S. still has its own racial problems," *The Atlanta Journal*, 18 September 1985, p. A15.

33. See, respectively: "The Man and the March," editorial, *The New Republic* 208 (1995), p. 9; Andrew Sullivan, "Call to Harm: the Hateful Oratory of Minister Farrakhan," *The New Republic*, 203 (1990), pp. 13–15; Michael C. Kotzin, "Louis Farrakhan's anti-Semitism: A look at the record," *The Christian Century* 111 (1994), pp. 224–25; and Joe Queenan, "America's Most Demented: A Startling Scientific Analysis," *The Washington Post*, 30 May 1993, p. C1. Similar references to Farrakhan's politics of hate can be found in: Bob Herbert, "The Hate Game," *The New York Times*, 9 February 1994, p. A18; and Charles Krauthammer, "The 'Validation' of Louis Farrakhan," *The Washington Post*, 20 October 1995, p. A19.

34. Richard E. Cohen, "At Nuremberg-on-Potomac, A Chanting of Jews, Jews," *International Herald Tribune*, 3 March 1994, p. 7.

35. Manning Marable, *How Capitalism Underdeveloped Black America: Problems in Race, Political Economy and Society* (Boston: South End Press, 1983), p. 84. See also his several references to Farrakhan in the collection of essays, *Beyond Black and White: Transforming African-American Politics* (New York: Verso, 1995).

36. Nicholas Lemann, *The Promised Land: The Great Black Migration and How It Changed America* (London: Macmillan, 1991), p. 289.

37. See the series of articles and op-ed pieces by Adolph Reed Jr.: "The Rise of Louis Farrakhan," *The Nation* 252 (January 21, 1991), pp. 51–52, 54–56; "All for One and None for All," *The Nation* 252 (January 28, 1991), pp. 86–88, 90–92; "Behind the Farrakhan Show," *The Progressive* 58 (April 1994), pp. 16–17; and "Black Leadership in Crisis," *The Progressive* 58 (October 1994), p. 16.

38. See *Revolutionary and Dissident Movements: An International Guide*, 3rd ed. (Harlow: Longman, 1991).

39. C. O. Maolain, *The Radical Right: A World Dictionary* (Harlow, U.K.: Longman, 1987).

40. John White, *Black Leadership in America: From Booker T. Washington to Jesse Jackson*, 2nd ed. (London: Longman, 1990), p. 178.

41. Lemann, *The Promised Land*, p. 302.

42. Claudette McFadden-Preston, "The Rhetoric of Minister Louis Farrakhan: a pluralistic approach" (unpublished Ph.D. thesis, Ohio State University, 1986), p. 162.

43. Clarence Lusane, *African-American Politics at the Crossroads: The Restructuring of Black Leadership and the 1992 Elections* (Boston: South End Press, 1994), p. 29.

44. See, in particular, Reed, "All for One." Reed has been among the most consistent and courageous of Farrakhan's critics and has persistently sought to expose the reactionary features of the NoI leader's beliefs. If some of his interpretations of Farrakhan's political significance are not entirely compelling, much of his analysis of the Black Muslim's mass appeal nonetheless merits close scrutiny.

45. The question was the title of an American politics seminar paper delivered by Glazer at Nuffield College, Oxford, UK, in the summer of 1989. For a related discussion, see the polemic monograph by Arthur M. Schlesinger Jr., *The Disuniting of America: Reflections on a Multicultural Society* (New York: Norton, 1992).

46. See Jabril Muhammad, *Farrakhan, The Traveller* (Phoenix, Ariz.: PHNX SN and Co., 1985); C. Alan Marshall, *The Life and Times of Louis Farrakhan* (New York: Marshall Publications, 1992); and Arthur J. Magida, *Prophet of Rage: A Life of Louis Farrakhan and his Nation* (New York: HarperCollins, 1996).

47. The most useful analyses in an extensive literature on the Black Muslims are: Walter D. Abilla, *The Black Muslims in America: An Introduction to the Theory of Commitment* (Kampala: East African Literature Bureau, 1977); E. U. Essien-Udom, *Black Nationalism: A Search for an Identity in America* (Chicago: University of Chicago Press, 1971); Mattias Gardell, *Countdown to Armageddon: Louis Farrakhan and the Nation of Islam* (London: Hurst, 1996); Martha F. Lee, *The Nation of Islam: An American Millenarian Movement* (Lewiston, N.Y.: E. Mellen Press, 1988); C. Eric Lincoln, *The Black Muslims in America*, 3rd ed. (Grand Rapids, Mich.: Williams B. Eerdmans, 1994); Clifton E. Marsh, *From Black Muslims to Muslims: The Transition from Separatism to Islam, 1930–1980* (London: Scarecrow Press, 1984) and *From Black Muslims to Muslims: The Resurrection, Transformation, and Change of the Lost-found Nation of Islam in America, 1930–1995*, 2nd ed. (Lanham, Md.: Scarecrow Press, 1996); Morroe Berger, "The Black Muslims," *Horizon* 6, no. 1 (1964): 49–65; Leon Douglas Bibb, "A Note on the Black Muslims: They Preach Black to be the Ideal," *Negro History Bulletin* 28, no. 6 (1965): 132–33; H. M. Kaplan, "The Black Muslims and the Negro American's Quest for Communion: A Case Study in the Genesis of Negro Protest Movements," *British Journal of Sociology* 20, no. 2 (1969): 164–76; Joseph M. Kirman, "The Challenge of the Black Muslims," *Social Education* 27, no. 7 (1963): 365–68; James H. Laue, "A Contemporary Revitalization Movement in American Race Relations: The Black Muslims," *Social Forces* 42, no. 3 (1964): 315–23; and Vincent Monteil, "La Religion des Black Muslims," *Esprit* 32, no. 16 (1964): 601–29.

48. R. E. Allen, ed., *The Concise Oxford English Dictionary of Current English*, 8th ed. (Oxford: Clarendon Press, 1990), p. 893.

49. See the collected essays in the volume by Hans Gerth and C. Wright Mills, *From Max Weber: Essays in Sociology* (London: Routledge, 1991).

50. This is perhaps most obviously the case in the pamphlets published by the New York-based Anti-Defamation League of B'Nai B'rith, but it can also be said to characterize the writings of a broad range of academic and popular commentators, such as Richard Cohen, Adolph Reed, Carl Rowan, Cornel West, and Juan Williams. Their assessments of Farrakhan are typically as much polemics against him as examinations of his role, influence, and popular appeal.

51. One of the strongest, though largely unpersuasive, critiques of the integrationist public philosophy of the civil rights movement is Harold Cruse, *Plural But Equal: A Critical Study of Blacks and Minorities in America's Plural Society* (New York: Quill, 1987).

52. Seymour Martin Lipset and Earl Raab, *The Politics of Unreason: Right-Wing Extremism in America, 1790–1977* (Chicago: University of Chicago Press, 1978), p. 484.

53. None of the principal academic studies of right-wing extremism in the United States include discussions of the incidence of the phenomenon among African-Americans. See, for example, Lipset and Raab, *The Politics of Unreason*; Paul Hainsworth, ed., *The Extreme Right in Europe and the USA* (London: Pinter, 1992); Richard Hofstadter, *The Paranoid Style in American Politics* (Chicago: University of Chicago Press, 1979); and Lynne Tower Sargent, ed., *Extremism in America* (New York: New York University Press, 1995).

2

From the Margins to the Mainstream: The Rise of Louis Farrakhan

Louis Farrakhan is a problem.

William A. Henry III, 1994[1]

Although Lou Reed was typically idiosyncratic in including Louis Farrakhan in a rock song, ("Good Evening Mister Waldheim"),[2] the New Yorker was hardly alone in finding in the Nation of Islam (NoI) leader and his followers ample cause for unease, disquiet, and consternation. The Black Muslim minister's rise to a position of national leadership among African-Americans during the 1980s and 1990s has represented a political development that is not only deeply troubling, and even chilling to many white and black Americans, but also extremely difficult for most observers of contemporary American politics to comprehend fully and to explain adequately.

Had Farrakhan's ascendancy occurred as the obvious result of a new issue cleavage arising or a nascent political movement emerging among African-Americans, it would no doubt be more easily explicable. The Farrakhan phenomenon, however, has not arisen as a clear response to some sudden critical event or catastrophic new development among black Americans in which Farrakhan has assumed the leadership of a newly emergent political movement by capitalizing upon a rapidly transformed political situation or an unexpected socioeconomic crisis. The pattern of African-American political, economic, and social development in the post–civil rights era in the United States has been internally differentiated, to be sure, but its overall shape and direction—though profoundly bifurcated by social class and income—has been relatively stable and consistent nonetheless.

Notwithstanding the deep recession of 1982, no sudden lurch or dramatic downturn has occurred in black Americans' collective fortunes since the later 1960s; the pace of socioeconomic change has been steady and gradual rather than precipitous in its nature, scope, and consequences. No functional political equivalent therefore exists for Farrakhan in the 1980s and 1990s comparable to the Montgomery, Alabama, bus boycott for Martin Luther King Jr. and the fledgling civil rights movement in 1955–56.[3]

Furthermore, Farrakhan is neither a new nor an unfamiliar presence in black American communities, having first joined the NoI in 1955, eventually assuming its leadership in 1978. Nor does Farrakhan share the religious convictions of the overwhelming majority of black Americans. It is not simply that Farrakhan is a Muslim, but also that the version of the Islamic faith to which he (and the NoI under his leadership) subscribes is itself extremely unorthodox and adhered to by only a very small minority of the growing Muslim American population in the United States.[4] Although, then, Farrakhan has been very active in African-American public life for several decades, the unconventional "product" that he has offered his compatriots has traditionally attracted very few buyers among black Americans nationwide.

The causes and consequences of Farrakhan's increasing inclusion within the national black political leadership cadre in America have therefore prompted both popular disagreement and substantial academic and critical dissensus. Only in the principal events that have informed Farrakhan's curious but steady political ascendancy has broad critical agreement been reached. It is hence appropriate in this chapter to review the main features of Farrakhan's gradual but inexorable rise to a position of national political leadership among black Americans, before moving on to analyze both the causes and the broader political significance of the Farrakhan phenomenon in contemporary American politics.

Though not an exhaustive list, it is possible to identify four developments as especially influential political landmarks along the Black Muslim's checkered, bumpy, but very carefully calculated road to national leadership status among African-Americans at large: Jesse Jackson's presidential campaigns of 1984 and 1988; the conclusion of a "Sacred Covenant" between the Congressional Black Caucus and the NoI in 1993; the public reconciliation between Farrakhan and Betty Shabazz, the widow of Malcolm X, in January 1995; and the triumphal Million Man March in Washington, D.C., on October 16, 1995.

Together, these four developments have powerfully conditioned and propelled Farrakhan's quixotic political journey from the margins of African-American political respectability to a location, if not centrally within, at least proximate to, the national black political mainstream.

THE JACKSON FACTOR:
THE NATIONALIZATION OF LOUIS FARRAKHAN

If elections in liberal democracies have always been more emotional orgies than feasts of reason,[5] then it was perhaps especially appropriate that the quadrennial bout of sensory overload that an American presidential election typically occasions should form the catalytic engine of the entire Farrakhan phenomenon. For prior to 1984, Louis Farrakhan was a relatively marginal political figure for many black Americans and a wholly unknown one for the vast majority of non-blacks in both the United States and the rest of the world. Farrakhan's position as the leader of the recently revived NoI, an unorthodox and racially exclusive religious group that commanded few members—in either relative or absolute terms—among African-Americans and that preached a peculiar and uncompromising public gospel of racial separatism, made this fact (at best) unsurprising.

Within the space of a mere two years, however, between 1984 and 1986, Farrakhan found himself invited onto prime-time national television news and current affairs programs in the United States to give interviews about his religious beliefs and political aspirations; engaging in a remarkably well-attended and successful speaking tour of the fourteen most populous American cities in 1985; embarking in 1986 upon a series of international visits that took him around the world from Ghana and Pakistan to China and Japan (and that led to rumors of his facing possible prosecution by the U.S. Attorney General for violating federal prohibitions on travel to Colonel Gadhafi's Libya); and being subjected to vociferous, persistent, and near universal condemnation, by black and nonblack American political commentators alike, as a hysterical preacher of racial bigotry, sexism, and homophobic hatred—a veritable "black Hitler."

The rapid (and, for the minister, not unwelcome) transformation in Farrakhan's national public visibility was effected in two distinct, though related, stages during the period 1983–84. First, Farrakhan's initial entry into national black American politics occurred with his participation in the 1983 March on Washington. The march was a broadly based political gathering, organized both to commemorate the landmark civil rights mobilization of twenty years earlier and to bring substantial public pressure to bear upon the Reagan Administration and the U.S. Congress to halt, and subsequently reverse, the enactment of conservative economic and social policies that most black politicians deemed deeply inimical to mass African-American advancement.

The 1983 event represented an especially important attempt by the mainstream American civil rights establishment to reach out to a broader alliance of African-American and nonblack political forces that were all intent upon defending the hard-won liberal policy gains of the 1960s, an extremely heterogeneous political coalition that included democratic socialists, non-Marxist progressives, and black nationalists. Among the latter category, the NoI, as a result both of its historic longevity in the black community and its more recently revived urban activism, was undoubtedly the most significant nationalist group. Farrakhan, as its leader, was included as a principal speaker at the event, where he delivered an eloquent and well-received multiracial unity message to an ethnically diverse and racially mixed audience. For the Black Muslim minister, the content of his message was as uncharacteristic as the composition of his audience was unusual.

Both the message and the audience reflected the novelty of the event, which was particularly politically significant for Farrakhan's emergent national black leadership pretensions. Although he had previously attended black American political gatherings in the capacity of Elijah Muhammad's "national representative"—most notably, addressing the 1971 Black Solidarity Rally in Harlem and attending the 1972 National Black Convention in Gary, Indiana—the 1983 march represented Farrakhan's de facto national debut as the leader of the new NoI. For the first, but by no means the last, occasion in his intriguing career, Farrakhan achieved inclusion in a mainstream national political demonstration that drew extensive mass black American participation. Moreover, as Marable argued, the appearance of the NoI's leader on a national platform with figures such as Coretta Scott King was a powerful political symbol of elite, as well as popular, black legitimation, one that was not lost upon veterans of the civil rights movement.[6] That the putative heir to the black separatist tradition of Elijah Muhammad should now share a national platform with the widow of the most influential integrationist civil rights leader in American history was a cardinal political boost to Farrakhan's popular black standing and leadership credentials. In seeking both mass and elite black American legitimation, the march represented an initial, but vitally important, political victory for Farrakhan.

If the 1983 march signaled the tentative beginnings of Farrakhan's national political odyssey, however, the second and far more influential catalyst of his increasing national and international political prominence—indeed, the central, though inadvertent, launchpad for the entire Farrakhan phenomenon—occurred the following year, with the Reverend Jesse Jackson's insurgent campaign for the Democratic Party's presidential nomination.[7] The Jackson campaign of 1984 served, crucially, to nationalize Farrakhan's leadership status among African-Americans. Simultaneously, it cast the Black Muslim minister from a position of national obscurity (and almost total anonymity among white Americans) to one arousing widespread recognition, as well as a heady mixture of admiration and deep public animosity, across the entire United States.

The elevation reflected the landmark nature of the Jackson campaign. While it failed to secure him the party's nomination, the Jackson campaign nonetheless served as the principal political focus for a unity of purpose and an emotive and affective response among black Americans at the mass level that had rarely been in evidence since the high watermark of the civil rights movement, some twenty years previously.[8] Although its political significance remains widely and intensely disputed,[9] the evangelizing political crusade that Jackson tirelessly fought clearly succeeded in mobilizing large numbers of black Americans to register, vote, and take a new interest in political participation in general. Moreover, it established a wholly novel level of national media attention for Farrakhan in America and, in the intense furor over anti-Semitism that rapidly engulfed him, a deeply contentious issue that would subsequently become virtually inseparable from public discussions of the NoI's leader. In inadvertently ensuring him the vital American political oxygen of nationwide publicity and rapt media attention, the Jackson campaign thereby accorded Farrakhan the necessary ballast for his national African-American leadership aspirations.

Farrakhan's tentative entry into national U.S. politics was thus inextricably and very fortuitously bound to the four-yearly spectacle of the American presidential race and the intense concentration of media and public attention upon a set of tangible, concrete individual personalities that it invariably affords. Although it was not the first electoral campaign for the U.S. presidency mounted by an African-American, either within or outside the Democratic party, the Jackson bid did represent the first one to be accorded extensive news media coverage and to be treated by many political elites as serious in character, a requisite but insufficient condition of the aspirant's either winning the party nomination or exerting meaningful political influence subsequently upon the eventual nominee.[10]

Jackson's candidacy was the first by an African-American for the Democratic party's presidential nomination since Congresswoman Shirley Chisholm (D-NY) had made her disastrously unsuccessful and ineffectual bid in 1972. The twelve-year hiatus was itself of notable political significance. That a campaign by any African-American should have occurred in 1984 reflected three developments of increasing political import: the growing presence of black American activists and public officials within the ranks of local, state, and national Democratic party organizations; the contemporary imperative to challenge President Ronald Reagan's reelection effort; and the increasing desire of many African-American elected officials and voters loyal to the Democratic party to achieve a greater degree of responsiveness to their public policy concerns from its highest echelons than had hitherto been conceded by the party's elites, since 1980 at least.

In Jackson, however, that responsiveness was ironically sought through an insurgent African-American candidate who was expressly not an elected party official and who had never previously run for any elective public office in America: the quintessential "outsider" candidate. Despite the presence in the presidential race of white candidates whose commitment to civil rights and black American social and economic advancement was undeniably strong—most notably, former Vice President Walter Mondale and Senator Gary Hart (D-CO)—the entry into the Democratic party primaries of a fledgling black candidate who had never held a position of public authority represented an unusual and important political development, for both black (at both elite and mass levels) and white Americans.

Not the least of the politically significant aspects of the Jackson campaign was the manner in which it fully and dramatically encapsulated the acute dilemmas, for both aspirant and established national black American political leaders, that the polarizing figure of Louis Farrakhan would subsequently pose. It was also, moreover, replete with the many ironies that have surrounded Farrakhan's recent political rise and current national role. If, in effectively playing Hardy to Farrakhan's Laurel, Jackson found that the national political mess in which he was apt to be mired was worryingly deep and not prone to easy extraction, this was nonetheless a disconcerting discovery that other black American politicians would subsequently imitate, whether consciously or, more commonly, through strategic blunders and tactical miscalculations.

The genesis of the contemporary association was relatively recent. Jackson had asked Farrakhan in the winter of 1983 to participate actively in his prospective campaign for the Democratic party's presidential nomination. The links between the two black clergymen had been forged several years previously, however, in their common political and religious base of Chicago, Illinois. Both programmatic and strategic political factors had encouraged their informal political coalescence. The two ministers adhered to racially bounded capitalist economic tenets of self-help, individual entrepreneurship, and black private sector enterprise: Jackson through his modestly entitled organization, People United to Save Humanity (PUSH), founded in 1971; and Farrakhan, through the NoI's many and varied business enterprises and retail outlets. Jackson and Farrakhan also possessed very strong self-conceptions as the principal contemporary African-American heirs to the dominant black political figures of the 1960s and the political and racial traditions that they respectively embodied: the integrationism of Martin Luther King Jr., and the black nationalism of Malcolm X. Moreover, both ministers, albeit in dramatically different manners, were personally connected not only to their respective spiritual and political mentors, but also to their brutal assassinations.

Jackson's initial political socialization as a young assistant to King and an organizer in the civil rights movement was well-known to many black Americans. His presence at the Memphis, Tennessee, motel where King was shot on April 4, 1968, had accorded the young Baptist preacher a tragic but priceless personal legacy—and a controversial and contested one—that he readily and persistently attempted to exploit over subsequent years for political advantage. Implicitly and explicitly, Jackson sought as both a civil rights activist and an electoral candidate to enlist his links to the slain leader as one of the central foundations of his claims to be the rightful and appropriate successor to the reverend doctor's national political mantle among African-Americans for the 1970s and 1980s. In the latter decade, especially,

Jackson increasingly projected himself as the preeminent post–civil rights era legatee of King's fundamental goals of an integrated America, the achievement of a beloved interracial community, and the guarantee of economic security for minorities, the poor, and the disadvantaged of all races.

By contrast, Farrakhan's political inheritance was at once far more ambiguous, controversial, and unenthusiastically received by many black Americans at large. Befriended and tutored in the NoI by Malcolm X during the 1950s, Farrakhan's initially pronounced fraternal admiration for the charismatic black American political agitator had been rapidly transformed into an intense enmity and deep hostility by Malcolm's decisive break with the separatist organization in 1964–65.[11] Although regarded by some African-Americans (and nonblacks, too) as the effective successor to Malcolm's militant and uncompromising national black political mantle, the implication of Farrakhan in plots to assassinate the Black Muslim activist served as a political albatross for the NoI's leader among many American blacks. Until 1995, fully thirty years after Malcolm's assassination, rumors of the profound animosity harbored by the Shabazz family toward Farrakhan were accorded widespread credence in the black community in the United States.[12] By comparison even with Jackson, Farrakhan's reputation among African-Americans was, in consequence, far less than unimpeachable, and his legitimacy remained seriously tarnished and impaired.

Despite their divergent historical paths and distinct religious associations, however, Jackson and Farrakhan shared important political features that facilitated their coalescence. Most notably, both were ministers of faith, occupying positions with traditionally powerful historic roles in not only the spiritual, but also the secular and the political, lives of African-Americans generally.[13] Both were also accomplished, confident, and frequently compelling public orators whose mass black popularity and claims to political legitimacy rested to a substantial extent upon their self-evident possession of charismatic authority.[14] Unable to rely upon (or unwilling to attempt to achieve) the conventional forms of rational and legal authority that are typically conferred upon politicians by elective public office in liberal democratic polities, both Jackson and Farrakhan depended instead upon their personal qualities to win popularity and political support alike among black Americans.

Moreover, as "protest" leaders who possessed no formal public authority, both Jackson and Farrakhan stood demonstrably outside the increasingly dominant mode of political representation of black American interests in the post–civil rights era, that of black elected officialdom. Passage of the Voting Rights Act of 1965, enfranchising southern blacks, had powerfully assisted the growth of black American elected officials nationwide, from mayors and state legislators to members of Congress. Electoral channels represented the logical outgrowth of the pre-1965 protest and extrasystemic forms of black American political participation (such as sit-ins, boycotts, and marches) that had been advanced so effectively by the traditional civil rights movement. This new elective cadre of black politicians thus rapidly came to be viewed by many black Americans as not only the legitimate, but also as the principal, bearers of African-Americans' political, economic, and social interests.

Although few African-American civic leaders and elected officials believed that increased black political representation was itself sufficient to ameliorate black economic and social problems, putting black Americans into elective public offices nationwide nonetheless represented a necessary condition of collective black advancement. Moreover, the steady emergence of black elected officials as the de facto repositories of black Americans' public policy priorities and preferences was a development that was reasonably clearly delineated. Primary responsibility for the conversion of black Americans' social and economic interests into public policy agenda items and outputs increasingly resided with this new black political elite of elected officials, whose claims to democratic legitimacy could be tested transparently and whose institutional behavior in general (and voting records, in particular) could be made accountable to African-Americans by means of prescribed elections. Black political behavior in the post–civil rights era United States thus increasingly exhibited characteristics common to traditional modes of nonblack American politics.[15]

Two features of this "modernization" process among black American political elites were especially salient to the emergence of the Farrakhan phenomenon and to the evolving political fortunes of the NoI's leader subsequently. First, significant and persistent political tensions inevitably arose after 1965 between the growing set of African-American elected officials and the established constellation of protest-era black organizations, such as the National Association for the Advancement of Colored People, the Southern Christian Leadership

Conference, the Student Non-Violent Coordinating Committee, and the National Urban League. The claims of the latter organized black interest lobbies to fully representative status among African-Americans were now increasingly undermined—though not entirely endangered—by the democratically derived challenges posed by the new and expanding elected cadre of black American public officials.

Second, for black American elected (and appointed) officials themselves, loyalty to the Democratic party emerged as a fundamental article of political faith and typically a cardinal condition of personal career advancement (whether at the federal, state, or local level).[16] Efforts at independent African-American political campaigns or insurgent forms of activism were hence very powerfully constrained by the entrenched dominance of established party interests and the formidable boundaries to effective black political independence that these necessarily established.[17] A dual accountability structure within national black politics therefore emerged. On the one hand stood the increasing set of African-American elected officials, whose democratic political legitimacy was self-evident and transparent but whose jurisdictional bases were relatively narrow and whose political behavior was fundamentally conditioned by a near-universal one-party allegiance. On the other hand was the group of nonelected black American actors, whose racially organicist credentials (as representing all blacks) were still intact and were not subject to the demands of particular constituents, but whose effective and appropriate political roles in the post–civil rights era—which they had struggled so successfully to bring about—were far less certain and clear.

Most political and scholarly attention to this newly bifurcated structure of national black American politics was devoted to the new and increasing elite cadre of elected officials. Their growing numbers, novel political organizations, institutional behavior, and variegated policy influence encouraged extensive academic examination of the phenomenon of the so-called "new black politics."[18] (That the "old" black American politics persisted and remained influential was often complacently neglected or ignored.) Within this new structure of dual political authority, prior to 1984, both Jackson and Farrakhan occupied the more marginal and less academically noteworthy political positions in the protest category of nonelected, traditional black leadership. The entry of both into the conventional American electoral political arena—Jackson directly as electoral candidate, Farrakhan indirectly as his political confidant and zealous supporter—therefore represented a dramatic political development for African-Americans in general and national black political elites in particular. Jackson's candidacy attracted extensive media attention and comment in America and abroad. Not only did Jackson's entry into the Democratic party primaries in 1984 increase his personal name recognition and elevate the candidate's national political status among both black and white Americans, but national and international public awareness of Farrakhan was also wholly transformed as a result of the landmark Jackson presidential nomination campaign.

The two ministers certainly made for a peculiar political alliance: the Baptist progressive and King associate in search of an integrated, inclusive coalition of blacks, whites, labor, environmentalists, women, Latinos, Native Americans, Asians, and gays; and the fundamentalist Black Muslim separatist for whom the only color worth any apparent concern—to many of his critics at least—was black. The symbolic significance of their association was, by virtue of such manifest differences, both striking and substantial. The historic public and private divisions between the nonviolent, principally southern-based struggle for multiracial unity and integration personified by King, and Malcolm X's aggressive, and predominantly northern, urban militant black separatism were deep and, almost by definition, irreconcilable. For many black Americans, the *rapprochement* of Jackson and Farrakhan therefore represented an altogether new, regenerative, and welcome dimension of intraracial political unity, as an unprecedented coalition of traditionally distinct and antagonistic ideologies and religious tendencies around the common cause of black American political empowerment.

The political incentives structuring the association were distinct, but in essence complementary, for the two African-American preachers. For Jackson, Farrakhan's clear endorsement provided him with a particularly valuable political resource with which to appeal to the growing minority of American Muslims in the United States (although the NoI was unorthodox within this broader family, Farrakhan spoke Arabic sufficiently fluently to address Arab Americans on Jackson's behalf, for example). Also, and equally important, Farrakhan's imprimatur significantly enhanced Jackson's credentials among the more militant sections of the black nationalist movement in

America. Both groups represented constituencies traditionally uninvolved in, and generally very much opposed to, conventional forms of electoral and party politics in the United States.

Historically, the Nation of Islam had always rejected any participation in American politics in general, and electoral politics in particular. In a manner analogous to white Christian fundamentalist groups prior to their remarkable mobilization during the 1970s,[19] involvement in conventional, secular American political processes was seen as essentially sacrilegious by the Black Muslim movement. Moreover, the NoI viewed electoral participation as a strategy that was completely futile and ineffective for improving black Americans' social and economic conditions, the fundamental precondition of which remained (as chapter three explains in more detail) the complete and enduring separation of the races in the United States.

Nonetheless, despite facing significant internal NoI opposition, Farrakhan personally registered to vote at the Chicago Board of Elections on February 9, 1984.[20] The minister's expressed rationale for the novel departure from the NoI's traditional tenets of noninvolvement in American public life drew extensively upon claims that his spiritual father, Elijah Muhammad, had deemed electoral support for a black American candidate permissible in the event of that politician both emerging from within the black community in the United States and his additionally being fearless and unrelenting in pressing the cause of genuine African-American empowerment and liberation, conditions which Farrakhan made it abundantly clear during early 1984 that he held Jackson to have adequately and courageously fulfilled.[21]

For the leader of the NoI, the link with Jackson served two vital strategic functions in his personal political project. First, it accorded Farrakhan, an African-American figure even more obscure to most Americans than Jackson, national and international publicity; such attention represented an invaluable political asset for Farrakhan's burgeoning national black leadership ambitions. Second, the link encouraged Farrakhan's popular (albeit inaccurate and misleading) portrayal as a political radical, in the long historic tradition of black American progressives and liberals challenging established social, economic, and political structures. Although the sources and expressions of his purported radicalism were rarely accurately or fully disaggregated by most observers, either in the United States or abroad, Farrakhan's evident racial militancy accorded him significant political interest from leftist groups and African-American organizations alike. Jackson's political beliefs were, for most Americans, extremely liberal (and even unconventional) and a reasonable inference to make was that individuals especially close to his campaign broadly shared his political views. Given the persistently pronounced electoral support and political endorsements accorded ideologically liberal candidates by black Americans since 1965, Farrakhan's apparently radical, antiestablishment credentials thus served as a useful adjunct to his national black leadership claims and aspirations among African-Americans at large.

Although its early role was undeniably significant, the initial involvement of Farrakhan's NoI in the 1984 Jackson campaign nonetheless attracted relatively modest and circumspect media attention. The organization provided campaign workers for Jackson and, through its male and female Fruit of Islam guards, also provided personal security for the candidate, a function especially important in the initial stages of the campaign when the Reagan Administration denied Jackson the professional protection of trained Secret Service personnel. As the NoI's leader, Farrakhan personally and eagerly provided extensive political support to Jackson, through his weekly program on Chicago's WBEE radio station, in his public rallies and lectures (during which he regularly set aside time to encourage his black American audiences enthusiastically to register, turn out, and vote for Jackson), and by frequently serving as the warm-up speaker at campaign rallies immediately prior to Jackson's keynote addresses—sometimes even eclipsing the principal speaker in his oratorical zest and skill.

Anonymity and Farrakhan have been relatively rare bedfellows over recent years, however, and the initially limited media and popular attention was rapidly and definitively ended by the intense national political controversy that erupted in March 1984. The reaction of the NoI's leader to revelations in *The Washington Post* that Jackson had privately referred, in a conversation with one of the newspaper's black reporters, Milton Coleman, to American Jews as "Hymies" and to New York City as "Hymietown," strongly compounded Farrakhan's immoderate credentials. Jackson, in a remarkably inastute fashion, first denied making the statements, before stating that he had no memory of having made them, and then finally issuing a public apology for having made them. On February 25, 1984, in Chicago, Farrakhan came to the candidate's defense, standing beside Jackson and issuing an explicit warning to American Jews generally that, "If you harm this

brother, it will be the last one you harm." Farrakhan also threatened all
of Jackson's opponents with "retaliation if they harmed Jackson in any
way." Though the exact form that such retaliation would assume
remained unclear, the implicit threat of violence in Farrakhan's speech
was not lost upon even the least attentive of listeners. It was, moreover,
clarified further in Farrakhan's weekly radio broadcast on March 11,
1984, when he stated:

> But we're going to make an example of Mr. Coleman. I'm going
> to stay on his case until we make him a fit example for the rest
> of them. "What do you intend to do to Milton Coleman?" At
> this point, no physical harm. But at this point we're going to
> keep going until we make it so that he cannot enter in on any
> black people. One day soon we will punish you with death. [22]

American public outrage was nonetheless concentrated less upon
the Coleman threat[23] and upon Farrakhan's declaration that, if Jackson's candidacy was not taken seriously by white political elites, he
would "lead an army" to Washington, D.C., to "negotiate for a separate state or territory of our own,"[24] than upon the NoI leader's contemporaneous anti-Semitic comments. Most important, the national
mass media focused persistently upon Farrakhan's by now notorious
descriptions of Adolf Hitler as a "wickedly great man," and of Judaism
as a "dirty" and "gutter" religion—deliberately incendiary rhetoric
that one source persuasively held to have represented "the most serious injection of anti-Semitism into a national American political campaign in recent memory."[25] Despite his impeccably dapper personal
appearance, such calculated and provocative declarations ensured that
the NoI's leader provided a remarkably stark, controversial, and compelling contrast to the besuited and blow-dried politicians familiar to
most Americans from the 1984 presidential campaign trail.

In its intensity and scope, the ensuing national controversy represented the first instance of a pattern of reactions to Farrakhan that
was subsequently to become a familiar, repetitive, and (for him) generally beneficial feature of his gradual political ascendancy. The pattern comprised three interlinked stages: first, Farrakhan issues a
deliberately provocative public statement, one that inevitably and
deeply offends a sizeable section of the American populace; second,
outraged elite commentators (primarily, but not exclusively, white)

demand his immediate and unequivocal repudiation by prominent national black American figures for the offensive or defamatory remark; and third, those African-American figures variously comply, refuse, or equivocate in response, according to their personal circumstances, philosophies, and electoral imperatives. In this particular instance, Jackson disavowed Farrakhan's statements, but refused to repudiate the NoI leader's political endorsement, stating defiantly that "I am not going to negotiate away my integrity trying to impress somebody."[26]

That intrablack electoral imperatives powerfully informed and reinforced Jackson's personal integrity was readily apparent, but the candidate's refusal to denounce Farrakhan nonetheless prompted dozens of outraged editorial denunciations across America. The tactical exigencies and strategic imperatives of American party politics in 1984 sustained media and critical attention on Farrakhan and his immoderate political credentials still further. For the Democratic party, African-Americans constituted a core bloc of their general electoral coalition and their presidential base in particular, one that could be neither safely antagonized nor easily ignored. The New Deal policies of Franklin D. Roosevelt during the 1930s had initially begun an inexorable process of mass black electoral and political realignment away from the Republicans—the party of Lincoln, Emancipation, and Reconstruction.[27] Although that realignment was gradual, from the mid-1960s onward black electoral loyalty to the Democrats was comprehensive and near-complete.[28] Since 1948, and especially from 1968, a high black turnout in American elections emerged as crucial not only to the fortunes of the Democratic presidential nominee, but also to many of the party's incumbent and aspirant senators and representatives, especially in the South.[29] For many Democrats, therefore, inveighing too enthusiastically or strongly against Jackson was effectively to invite mass black disaffection and to court electoral suicide.

However, while Democratic party leaders risked seriously alienating black Americans if they denounced Jackson's informal associations with Farrakhan and his refusal fully to repudiate the NoI's leader, they also faced the deeply unattractive prospect of sacrificing significant Jewish American support—electoral, editorial, and financial—if they failed to do so. Although their relative proportions in the American population differed significantly, Jewish votes, money, and intellectual support for the Democrats were together vitally important

to the party's leadership and to many of its elected officials nationwide. Democratic leaders were therefore mired in a catch-22 political
predicament of epic proportions.

The tantalizing opportunity to accrue political profit from the
Democrats' dilemma was, for the Republican party, too obvious to
require either detailed elaboration or concerted pressure to exploit.
Then Vice President George Bush predictably attacked Mondale, Hart,
and Jackson collectively for their failure to denounce "the intrusion of
anti-Semitism into the American political process," arguing that American society possessed "no room for hate and no place for haters."[30]
President Reagan was also declared by White House spokesperson,
Larry Speaks, to be "forthrightly" against Farrakhan.[31] For the GOP's
campaign strategists, the incentive to denounce the NoI's leader was
as powerfully compelling as the imperative to appeal to black American voters at large was demonstrably slight. Writing off black voters
by vigorously attacking Farrakhan and Jackson was hardly a prohibi-
tive political cost, since African-Americans barely figured in the
Republican's electoral script in the first place. Highlighting the war-
ring forces within the Democratic base, by contrast, offered a likely
political reward from white voters well worth the minimal risk. If Farrakhan had not existed, the GOP's political operatives in 1984 would
have been especially eager to have invented him.

Republican party officials' denunciations of Farrakhan, deliberately aimed simultaneously at increasing the Democrats' acute political discomfort, attracting Jewish American votes, and exploiting
latent societal conflicts over race by exaggerating Jackson's political
role and influence within the party, also strongly implied that Farrakhan was no ally of American conservatives. Ironically, the message
was as formidably misleading as it was effective. Set against the deliberately bland—though electorally powerful—"Morning in America"
theme of Reagan's 1984 reelection campaign, Farrakhan symbolically
represented a hangover of a wake-up call to many white voters, as far
as Republican strategists were concerned, much as the figure of Willie
Horton would subsequently (though to far greater political effect) for
the Bush presidential campaign in 1988.[32] In the context of the 1984
campaign, Farrakhan served as a near-functional totemic equivalent
for animating white racial fears and arousing interracial animosities.
Although the wedge of the NoI's leader prised few voters from the
Democratic party, this was not for a want of effort on the Republicans'
part.[33]

By the summer of 1984, Jackson's prospects of retaining any of the marginal credibility that he still possessed with Jewish voters was rendered determinate upon his expressly repudiating Farrakhan. Though Jackson had asked the Black Muslim privately to refrain from public works for his campaign in March, only in June was a clearly negative evaluation of Farrakhan forthcoming. Benjamin Hooks, Executive Director of the NAACP, acted as a catalyst, when he issued a statement on June 27, 1984, in which Farrakhan's "inflammatory" statements were deplored and "such forms of racism and anti-Semitism," as he termed them, were wholly rejected. Farrakhan's inclusion within the remit of prejudice and bigotry was implicit, but unmistakable and significant nonetheless.[34] The denouement came two days later when a similar declaration was finally made by Jackson, in which he labeled Farrakhan's comments "reprehensible and morally indefensible" and publicly disavowed them. Too late to salvage Jackson's campaign, which had faltered long prior to June, neither did the declaration defuse Farrakhan's newly acquired national mantle of black American militant number one.

Consonant with that status, controversy surrounding Farrakhan did not abate either during or after the 1984 campaign. Farrakhan's position as a political pariah and a substantial albatross upon Jackson's electoral aspirations continued into the black Baptist's second unsuccessful campaign for the Democratic party nomination in 1988. Moreover, whereas the 1984 campaign had served the crucial function of nationalizing Farrakhan's name recognition and controversial public profile, the 1988 campaign accorded him a further political totem of substantial utility in his national African-American leadership bid: the full and exclusive mantle of the national black prophet of racial authenticity. In attempting, however ineffectively, to build a broader multiethnic and cross-class "rainbow" coalition in 1988—a bold strategy that necessarily entailed deemphasizing the centrally racial dimensions of his candidacy that he had stressed four years earlier—Jackson left open a vacuum into which Farrakhan eagerly stepped to claim his position as the true repository of authentic, collective black American interests. The critical value of the 1988 presidential campaign for Farrakhan thus resided, ironically, in eclipsing rather than confirming the racial foundations of Jackson's preeminent leadership status among African-Americans at large. For Farrakhan, the second Jackson campaign offered renewed opportunities to assume a national mantle as the dominant spokesperson for black nationalism. The legacy of prior attacks by whites, Jews, and established African-American politicians had also left Farrakhan sufficiently shrouded in an aura of racial martyrdom to render that new position especially congenial to such efforts.

According to the candidate's press secretary during that campaign, Jackson's proximity to Farrakhan over the years had occurred for "politically symbiotic reasons."[35] By 1984, Jackson had perceived himself unable to sever his ties with Farrakhan, in large part because it would have been viewed by black Americans as giving in to the demands of whites. Although Jackson dissociated himself from Farrakhan in 1984 and once again in 1988, the issue of explicit and unequivocal denunciation represented a de facto litmus test of the veracity of Jackson's denials of anti-Semitism, not only for whites in general (and Jews in particular), but also for many African-Americans. One Jewish editor of the *New York Times* stressed in 1988 that, "Until Jackson publicly breaks with Farrakhan and finally resolves that issue, he'll never be accepted by the Jews."[36] Whether he would be fully accepted even if he did publicly denounce Farrakhan remained unclear, at best; but denunciation of the NoI's leader represented a minimal, though not necessarily sufficient, condition of his attracting even marginal levels of Jewish support.

The continued significance of the Farrakhan factor to Jackson was evidently, but uncomfortably, manifest to the candidate. An anonymously authored background paper on "Jackson and his relationship to the Jewish community," issued to the press by his campaign organization during the 1988 primary season, contained an entire section devoted specifically to the subject of the candidate's fluctuating relations with Farrakhan. This elaborated Jackson's "final" position on the matter: the NoI leader was not a part of the 1988 campaign and Jackson had four years previously dissociated himself from Farrakhan's "objectionable" public remarks. It nonetheless also stated, explicitly and emphatically, that Jackson would never "repudiate the personhood of Farrakhan":

> This he refused to do! Rev. Jackson is a minister who believes in separating the sin from the sinner. One should condemn the sin, not the sinner. Black civil rights activists like Rev. Jackson repudiated the rhetoric and behavior of Bull Connor, Orval Faubus and George Wallace in the 1960s but did not repudiate their personhood. When Rev. Jackson debated with KKK head David Duke on television, he repudiated Duke's statements, his philosophy and his behavior—but not his personhood. In the nonvio-

lent tradition, this is perceived as strength (not as a weakness) in the civil rights movement.[37]

The gross political ineptitude of the Jackson campaign in this regard was especially striking, though not exceptional in the broader context of his still neophytic style of national electioneering. By making explicit the analogy between Farrakhan and the racist demagogues of the white far-right, the paper served inadvertently to fuel rather than to quell continued political suspicion of Jackson among Jews and other white (and black) Americans, to compound their marked antipathy toward Farrakhan, and to confirm their increasing ambivalence about Jackson. To place the NoI's leader on an equivalent political level with the white southern segregationists of the past and the vicious racists of the present—though in accord with the prevalent views of Farrakhan among many black and white American observers—was an effective (and astonishingly politically naive) admission of the unusual severity of Jackson's political problem. It conceded, in effect, that Farrakhan self-evidently stood outside the broad range of acceptable views in mainstream American politics in the 1980s. Moreover, it inadvertently lent some credence to Mayor Ed Koch's deliberately provocative claim during the New York Democratic party primary, that Jewish New Yorkers would have to be "crazy" to cast a vote for Jackson.

According to Elizabeth Colton, Farrakhan was completely "anathema to Jews and to many other sensitive whites and even some blacks who recognized the dangers he posed." One white Jackson aide questioned why the candidate himself seemed curiously unable to comprehend that "Farrakhan could reappear any day and wreck his campaign? He should renounce him once and for all." The more important factor in Jackson's continued refusal to denounce Farrakhan than his long-held philosophy of nonviolence, however, was the Baptist's acute political fear that an unequivocal renunciation of Farrakhan would alienate a substantial number of otherwise supportive black American voters. The electorally beneficial consequences of maintaining the appearance of collective intraracial unity still assumed a far greater political importance for Jackson than did the socially divisive interracial results of failing to condemn individual black American bigots and racists.

In retrospect, the political damage that association with Farrakhan caused Jackson's hopes of securing either the presidential or vice-presidential nomination of the Democratic party, in both 1984 and 1988, was probably not especially great in purely electoral terms. That the Farrakhan nexus contributed to the marked antipathy of established Democratic party elites toward the Jackson campaign and compounded the serious doubts of many black and nonblack American politicians regarding the candidate's credentials for elective office in general, much less the presidency in particular, is clear enough. But Farrakhan hardly cost Jackson the party's presidential nomination. Influential white and black Democratic public officials had been highly skeptical of the Jackson insurgency from the outset[38]; established party constituencies—labor, feminists, environmentalists, educationalists, and gay and lesbian activists—possessed their own formal and informal links to several other well-established candidates; and important aspects of Jackson's distinctive and unconventional political resume, such as embracing Fidel Castro and Yasir Arafat (both literally and figuratively), made him deeply unattractive to many Democratic sympathizers seeking a credible aspirant for the White House who could appeal to as broad a range of American voters as possible. The Farrakhan imbroglio served to confirm the preexisting negative dimensions of many Democrats' assessments.

Though no empirical evidence exists by which to evaluate the overall effect that the Farrakhan factor had upon Jackson's primary campaigns, some observers have argued that Jackson's urban victories could probably not have been achieved without Farrakhan's active and aggressive support.[39] But such assessments tend to exaggerate the Black Muslim leader's importance at the time and his substantive political influence among African-Americans at large. To the extent that Jackson's 1984 and 1988 victories relied overwhelmingly upon the support of black Americans who were not members of the NoI, the galvanizing effect of his campaign was in itself a sufficient political incentive for many blacks to have turned out to vote, Farrakhan notwithstanding. The balance of evidence suggests that the compensating gains among black American voters that Jackson achieved through refusing to denounce Farrakhan were probably not much greater than the nonblack votes he thereby forfeited from otherwise sympathetic and potentially supportive constituencies within the Democratic party.

For the NoI's leader, however, the Jackson association had no adverse political consequences of note at all. Rather, the two Jackson campaigns served the vital political goal of raising Farrakhan's public profile among black and white Americans in general, a necessary but insufficient condition of his ultimate admission to the national black political leadership cadre in the United States. Moreover, the 1988 campaign also allowed Farrakhan to present himself publicly to white and African-American audiences alike as the preeminent national black political spokesperson for collective black American interests: the definitive and exclusive repository of a putatively essential, universal black identity. Unburdened by the demands of compromise and conciliation that the coalitional requirements of conventional American electoral and institutional politics typically impose upon elected officials of all races, Farrakhan moved to occupy the ground of racial essentialism that Jackson had initially assumed in 1984, but forfeited in 1988. The mantle of defining racial authenticity among black Americans nationally—of what it meant to be truly "black" in character, values, and beliefs as well as physical appearance—had passed to a new and more enthusiastic torchbearer with whom it thereafter remained as a core feature of Farrakhan's leadership pretensions and claims to national black political authority.

Precisely how future black American presidential aspirants might treat the leader of the NoI remained unclear in the aftermath of the Jackson campaigns. That they would have to develop a strategy to do so, however, represented an unequivocal testament to the assumption of a powerful national leadership role and distinctive political appeal among many black Americans that Farrakhan had long craved, and subtly but surely achieved after the 1984 controversy first arose.[40] Subsequently, over a relatively short period of time, the NoI's leader consolidated his political position and advanced his national black leadership claims, at once purposefully, aggressively, and effectively. Farrakhan's initial dramatic burst upon the national political consciousness of America was dominated by elite discussions of the complete unacceptability of his iconoclastic public discourse and by a near-universal emphasis in popular commentaries upon the pressing imperative of his total exclusion from the ranks of mainstream African-American political leadership. Nine years later, however, it was the topic of Farrakhan's effective inclusion within those ranks that occupied most critical commentary.

SACRED COVENANTS: THE INCLUSION OF THE UNEXCLUDABLE

Farrakhan and the Congressional Black Caucus

By the early 1990s, it was increasingly apparent from both his tactical political behavior and his evolving public discourse that Louis Farrakhan coveted a more enhanced leadership role among black Americans at the national level. Since 1988, a gradual but unmistakable thawing of his conventionally cool and distant relations with other black social and political elites and with institutions traditionally anathema to the separatist NoI had occurred. Most notably, Farrakhan traveled the country in support of African-American congressional and municipal candidates in 1990 and conducted several extended interviews with nonblack national media outlets. In the latter, the markedly temperate tone of his language and the largely unobjectionable content of much of the agenda that he advanced—emphasizing the beneficial role of the NoI among inner-city black American communities and stressing the values of individual responsibility that he sought to inculcate among African-Americans—together suggested a mature moderation, a newfound responsibility, and a sincere desire to achieve a genuine and lasting national political legitimacy on his part.[41]

Not only did the conservative tenor of his public pronouncements on matters of personal morality and family structure accord strongly with other contemporary traditionalistic strains in American public life in the early 1990s but, more important, the fact of the NoI's new activism in deeply inhospitable urban environments was indisputable (although its motives and material effects were less universally agreed upon).[42] In 1990, for example, Farrakhan launched a nationwide "Stop the Killing" speaking tour of African-American urban centers aimed at highlighting and countering the terrible problem of black-on-black homicide. Not since the peak of its popularity in the early 1960s had the NoI achieved comparably effusive and positive critical commentary even from white Americans and won such widespread respect among black Americans at both elite and mass levels for its courageous and dedicated efforts to reduce drug consumption and to combat gang violence among urban blacks. Thus, it was upon this combination of his organization's practical achievements and the newly temperate and apparently conciliatory character of his public behavior—which even included a public rendition of a Felix Mendelssohn violin concerto as a symbolic gesture of reconciliation with American Jews[43]—that Farrakhan sought to advance his growing case for full and unequivocal inclusion among national black American political elites.

The most important indication that Farrakhan's shrewd and determined political strategy was reaping substantial rewards occurred

in 1993 at the "Race in America" panel of the annual legislative weekend of the Congressional Black Caucus (CBC), the organization of
African-American members of the U.S. Congress.[44] The September
gathering represented the Caucus's institutionalized national political
forum. A long-established opportunity for black American social, political, and business elites to converge on Washington, D.C., it had
evolved since the first dinner in 1971 as one of the most prestigious
and high-profile events in the national black American calendar. Democratic presidential aspirants were regular attendees, incumbent Democratic occupants of the White House often made speeches there, and
the national news media devoted substantial coverage to the glitter-
ing occasion.[45]

The 1993 CBC weekend assumed particular political significance
for the supporters and admirers of the NoI's leader. Having been controversially excluded from the previous month's thirtieth anniversary
of the 1963 March on Washington, Farrakhan was invited to attend
the CBC forum. Farrakhan had not previously been extended such an
invitation by the Caucus to share a national platform and the CBC,
like the vast majority of national black American politicians and organizations, had generally maintained a respectful but clear political distance from him and the NoI. The focus of the CBC session was the
grievous problem of intraracial crime, however, a subject that made
Farrakhan—given the NoI's increasing interventions in inner-city
black American neighborhoods—an especially appropriate and attractive candidate for inclusion on the Caucus panel.

The session received widespread media attention and was covered live by C-SPAN, and Farrakhan was well-received by the predominantly black American audience at the Convention Center in
Washington, D.C. There, Ben Chavis, the then recently appointed Executive Director of the NAACP, issued an unequivocal public apology to
the Black Muslim leader, describing his exclusion from the previous
month's march as "a mistake," a stark contrast to the principled
denunciation of Farrakhan nine years previously delivered by Chavis's
predecessor, Benjamin Hooks. Although Farrakhan was criticized at
times for attacking and belittling African-American politicians, the
general tone of the panel was incontrovertibly conciliatory, inclusive,
and forward looking. At the end of the session, to great applause, the
Caucus's aggressively independent-minded chairman in the 103rd
Congress, Kweisi Mfume (D-MD), solemnly pledged the CBC to enter
a "Sacred Covenant" with a range of black organizations, including

Farrakhan's Nation of Islam. Declaring that "no longer will we allow people to divide us," Mfume stated that:

> We will support the efforts of anyone committed to the restoration of hope through self-help and self-empowerment, whilst at the same time reserving the right to disagree on other matters of principle.[46]

Given its prestigious source, the announcement represented an especially controversial legitimation of Farrakhan and his organization. The CBC represented the most important national black political organization in America. It entered the 103rd Congress with substantially increased numbers from the 1992 elections. With forty members (the largest congressional delegation of blacks in American history), it also faced a Democratic president in the White House, Bill Clinton, for the first time since 1981. Through the covenant, black federal legislators publicly accorded the NoI a consultative role in formulating legislative proposals to bring before the U.S. Congress. They thereby implied that the NoI occupied an equivalent political position to the NAACP, with whom the Caucus had recently concluded a similar agreement: a group widely regarded as comprising extremist, sectarian bigots wedded to a bizarre cosmology now occupied the same moral standing as the oldest and most influential civil rights organization for blacks in American history.

The covenant effectively conceded Farrakhan's occupation of a uniquely influential position within national black American politics; its implicit message was that the issues of anti-Semitism and black racism that continued to shroud Farrakhan and his organization in a negative veil of the vilest bigotry were essentially secondary to the formulation of a common national black American political agenda.[47] There could be few more telling testimonies to Farrakhan's emergence as an African-American leader of singular and distinctive political importance and to the social concerns upon which he evidently touched among many African-Americans. Though the original catalyst for Farrakhan's rise to national prominence and the central explanation for the unprecedented involvement of the NoI in national American politics had occurred some nine years earlier in the Jackson campaign, the genie of separatist black nationalism, once released from the bottle of national public obscurity, had exploited his opportunity to gain political capital to the fullest and most substantial effect. With gradual but increasing assurance, the leader of the NoI had steadily inveigled his way from the obscure outer fringes toward the central arenas of mainstream national black American political leadership.

That political transition nonetheless remained incomplete. Moreover, at precisely the moment that Farrakhan's new leadership centrality was being consolidated, it was also deeply compromised. The catalyst was a series of remarkable revelations concerning a speech made at Kean College, New Jersey, on November 29, 1993, by Khalid Abdul Muhammad, Farrakhan's national spokesperson (and de facto second-in-command). Though unpublicized until January 1994, when the Anti-Defamation League (ADL) of B'Nai B'rith reprinted the full text of the address in an advertisement in *The New York Times*, the speech represented a profoundly embarrassing rebuke to those forces seeking a *rapprochement* with the NoI. Viciously anti-Semitic, anti-Catholic, racist, and homophobic in content, both the text and the African-American college audience's favorable reaction to the speech were widely publicized and roundly repudiated by the ADL. Nationwide editorial condemnation of the speech, Farrakhan, and the CBC covenant with the NoI followed its publication.[48] For many critics, the Muhammad speech represented the most dramatic, damning, and convincing refutation of Farrakhan's apparently newfound moderate credentials and constituted the clearest confirmation that the NoI's traditional racism, pervasive prejudice, and uncompromisingly exclusionary politics all remained intact.

Such adverse impressions were publicly compounded by the prompt actions of the U.S. Congress. The Senate forthrightly condemned Muhammad's remarks in a resolution offered by John Danforth (R-MO) and Edward Kennedy (D-MA) as an amendment to an education bill (H.R. 1804), on February 2, 1994, by a 97:0 vote. The House of Representatives followed by denouncing the speech in a resolution (H.R. 343) on February 23, 1994, which passed by a margin of 361 to 34 (with 29 members voting "present"). The principal sponsor of the motion, Rep. Tom Lantos (D-CA), argued compellingly that "When free speech is abused in a vile and vicious way to promote hatred and to incite murder on a gigantic scale, it is the duty of responsible legislative bodies to condemn such speech in clear and certain terms."[49]

The clarity, speed, and assurance of Congress's repudiation of Muhammad contrasted sharply with the responses of Farrakhan himself. For although Farrakhan subsequently removed Muhammad from his national post—after some predictable prevarication—his public assessment of the controversy was designed to fuel rather than diminish its political salience. Condemning in "the strongest terms" the malicious and mean-spirited manner in which Muhammad had made his comments, Farrakhan stated that he nonetheless stood by the "truths" that his assistant had inelegantly articulated. These "truths" included references to Jewish Americans as "blood-suckers" of the black community who controlled the White House, owned the Federal Reserve, and managed national policy from "behind the scenes"; descriptions of the Pope as a "no-good cracker" ("Somebody need to raise that dress up and see what's really under there."); and calls to black South Africans to kill their white compatriots (a later Muhammad speech also included professions of love toward Colin Ferguson, the young black American male who had indiscriminately murdered white passengers aboard a Long Island commuter train in December 1993). For good measure, Farrakhan added further that no rebuke would have been issued at all by him had Muhammad made the remarks in private rather than in a public forum, a statement hardly designed to bolster the minister's alleged newfound political maturity, increasing moderation, and putative mainstream leadership impulses.[50]

The controversy over the sickeningly offensive Muhammad speech served rapidly to reestablish the political distance between the CBC and the NoI. According to one source, the universal disgust and contempt occasioned by the pernicious and foul remarks ensured that the Caucus had no further formal contact with Farrakhan after the Khalid controversy.[51] But informal contacts continued to occur with representatives of the NoI, nonetheless. Moreover, the initial NoI coalescence with the CBC—however uncertain and tentative some of the latter's members undoubtedly were about the dangerous liaison—had itself represented a sufficiently clear and unequivocal confirmation of the dramatically altered dynamics of the relationship between Farrakhan and national black American political elites that had developed since 1984. That many Caucus members and other black politicians harbored profound reservations about, and deep disdain for, Farrakhan's values, beliefs, and methods is clear enough. Both privately and, less commonly, in public, several CBC members made their intense disquiet—and even anger—manifest.[52] Mfume also publicly revoked the previous fall's covenant, reluctantly conceding that the Caucus's ability to work for change with the NoI was severely jeopardized "as long as there remains a question by some of our membership about the Nation of Islam's sensitivity to the right of all people and all religions to be free from attacks, vilification and defamation."[53]

The very fact of the NoI's leader having been accorded a public platform at the Caucus's leading annual national gathering, however, had represented a development of cardinal political significance. Mfume's subsequent denunciation of Muhammad's speech had asserted that "nowhere" in American life could sanctuary be given to such appalling "garbage."[54] Yet the former Baltimore congressman's own organization had extended such sanctuary—albeit temporarily— to its most persistent, vociferous, and unrepentant African-American purveyor in national public life in America in modern times. As one of the Caucus's own members candidly observed (though without apparent irony or discernible regret), "Farrakhan in 15 minutes can draw more people than 40 members of the black caucus."[55] Clearly, for many black politicians, Farrakhan had emerged by 1993 as a national African-American leader at once too influential to be ignored and too controversial to be embraced.

Rapprochement and Reconciliation: the NAACP and Betty Shabazz

Even prior to the Million Man March, then, the CBC–NoI *rapprochement* had signaled Farrakhan's increasingly successful bid for an inclusive role within the national African-American leadership cadre. Two further developments over 1994–95 compounded the new environment of leadership inclusion that Farrakhan had long cherished and now enjoyed. First, Farrakhan's political ascent was assisted by the protracted, deep, and tragicomic convulsions that accompanied Ben Chavis's tenure as head of the NAACP during 1993–94. Facing profound political and financial difficulties upon his securing its Executive Directorship in 1993 (over Jesse Jackson, to the somewhat misplaced joy of the Clinton White House), Chavis pioneered a twin-track strategy to reinvigorate the prestigious civil rights organization: first, to champion aggressively the ecumenical cause of intraracial leadership inclusion, and, second, to target younger, militant, and nationalist black Americans for membership recruitment to the NAACP.[56]

Consonant with such an ambitious project, Chavis sought to incorporate Farrakhan, the itinerant *enfant terrible* and errant cousin,

fully within the national black leadership "family." The invitation that
he issued to Farrakhan to attend a two-day national African-American leadership "summit" in June 1994 served not only as a practical
attempt to realize the strained and intellectually challenged concept
of "operational unity" that had been widely and enthusiastically articulated at the previous year's CBC weekend, but also to demonstrate
publicly Chavis's apparently independent political credentials. In
forging closer links with Farrakhan, the NAACP Director issued
unmistakably clear signals of his unwillingness to be unduly influenced by either white American interest lobbies or adverse media
commentary, as well as his marked attentiveness to the urban African-
American constituency from which Farrakhan drew the bulk of his
popular black support.

The strategy's effectiveness was nonetheless strangled almost at
birth. Though it drew a chorus of criticism from white elites who had
traditionally been sympathetic to the NAACP,[57] the more telling influence upon Chavis's failure was internal. Chavis was forced to resign
his position after revelations that he had used over $300,000 of
NAACP funds to pay the legal costs of an action brought against him
by a former NAACP staffer, a black American woman, who had
charged Chavis with sexual harassment. The ultimate derailing of the
pronationalist strategy and the utter disgrace that enveloped Chavis
provided a peculiarly resonant image, curiously appropriate to his
fledgling political liaison with Farrakhan. Like Marion Barry previously, personal failure and political discredit served as particularly
strong incentives for Chavis to seek redemption through enlisting Farrakhan's approbation and assistance. Chavis represented another
example of the expanding ranks of what Reed termed the "rogues'
gallery" of disgraced malcontents and extremist black American figures whose dubious and doubtful causes Farrakhan rapidly embraced
and eagerly championed, and who thereby served as further proof for
the African-American public of Farrakhan's obligingly unqualified
and abundantly selfless "love" for his own race.

The second factor that embellished such a sensitive and nondis-
criminating affective emotional apparatus for his race and that eased
Farrakhan's hesitant entry into the portals of national black American
political leadership still further derived from a particularly unexpected quarter: Malcolm X's widow, Betty Shabazz. The persistent
controversy that had dogged Farrakhan since the assassination of Malcolm thirty years previously threatened to engulf him entirely in 1995

with the arrest of one of Malcolm's own daughters, Qubillah Shabazz, on charges of conspiracy to assassinate the NoI's leader. Rumors of the Shabazz family's deep antipathy toward Farrakhan had been widespread among African-Americans for many years after Malcolm's assassination. Betty Shabazz had persuasively labeled the NoI leader "an opportunist who creates public disarray" in 1985 and as late as 1994 described Farrakhan's incrimination in her husband's vicious murder as having represented "a badge of honor" for him in the NoI.[58] The possibility that one of Malcolm's daughters might enlist the assistance of a professional assassin to murder Farrakhan was therefore viewed as neither a preposterous nor an incomprehensible proposition.[59]

Ironically, however, the charges served as a particularly propitious political opportunity for Farrakhan to reestablish his national leadership credentials among skeptical African-Americans. Claims that the arrest was the result of a malicious plot by federal government authorities and white outsiders to divide the black American community were predictably but effectively invoked by Farrakhan to issue a national appeal for racial unity and political solidarity among African-Americans. At a New York City rally to raise funds for Qubillah Shabazz's legal defense costs in January 1995, the Farrakhan–Shabazz accommodation was tensely consummated.[60] Even Rep. Charles Rangel (D-NY), one of the most widely respected, influential, and electorally secure black members of Congress, felt it necessary to appear at the unity rally in Harlem in which Farrakhan was the principal speaker and main political attraction.[61] As ever, the NoI's leader once more sought successfully to make substantial political profit from apparently bankrupt leadership credentials.

The Farrakhan–Shabazz reconciliation not only constituted an apparent healing of a deep political wound between former black American allies, it also represented an invaluable symbolic seal of public legitimation that Farrakhan's inclusion within the ranks of national black American political leadership desperately required and that the Nation's leader deeply desired.[62] The emergence of Malcolm X as a popular contemporary black icon among African-Americans constituted a potentially more formidable barrier to Farrakhan's securing political support among many poorer, working class, and young black Americans than did the controversies over anti-Semitism by which so many white critics of the NoI's leader were persistently preoccupied. Farrakhan's historic role in Malcolm's murder, though decidedly unclear, had still cast an exceptional and substantial pall upon his leadership credentials among black Americans. In forging a new *entente* with Malcolm's widow and family—however much, even after the charges against Qubillah were dropped in May 1995, its genuinely cordial and sincere nature remained open to substantial doubt—Farrakhan thereby effectively neutralized an important political obstacle to his national leadership aspirations among many black Americans, aspirations that were ultimately realized in especially dramatic and decisive fashion on October 16, 1995.

THE MILLION MAN MARCH: FROM THE DREAM TO THE NIGHTMARE

The Million Man March represented the culmination of Farrakhan's bold attempts to achieve political legitimacy and full inclusion within the ranks of the national black American political leadership cadre.[63] To the deep chagrin of his many implacable opponents and ardent adversaries, it succeeded spectacularly. Farrakhan achieved a greater political legitimacy among African-Americans than ever before through the manifest success of the march's mass mobilization. Inspiring and organizing over 400,000 black American men to come to Washington, D.C., the march constituted one of the largest mass gatherings in the nation's capital in American history and represented an unprecedented affirmation of collective racial pride and self-love by African-American males.[64] By comparison even with the landmark 1963 March on Washington—whose striking numbers it more than doubled—the 1995 event was an undeniable and impressive political triumph for Farrakhan and the NoI in three important respects.

First, the 1963 march had occurred at the very height of the civil rights movement's protracted campaign to achieve effective southern desegregation. In converging upon Washington, the march had been founded upon a clear, noble, and broadly shared political objective: to bring irresistible public pressure to bear upon President John F. Kennedy and the Democratic Congress finally to enact a meaningful civil rights law that would give effective teeth to the Supreme Court's landmark desegregation ruling of 1954.[65] The practical goal of the march was integral to its purpose and assumed an importance that, in addition to being brilliantly encapsulated in King's soaring oratory, at least matched the great symbolic political significance of the mass gathering in the nation's capital.

By contrast, the 1995 event was far more symbolic than substantive in purpose. The declared public goals of the march were multiple and varied in emphasis both between its sponsors and over time: to counter the racist stereotype of all black American men as irresponsible, violent, and lazy; to serve as a reaffirmation of the commitment of African-American males to their families and local communities; and to register a clear and strong protest against the new Republican 104th Congress (1995–96). But beyond the notions of challenging prevailing stereotypes of African-American males and offering the latter an opportunity to atone for their errors (the October 16 date was symbolically selected by Farrakhan as the day of atonement from the Book of Leviticus), the march was entirely bereft of programmatic political, economic, and social content.[66] Lacking substantive programmatic purpose, with no intent to pressure either governing institutions, political parties, or corporate organizations, and pressing no concrete legislative agenda, policy program, or political strategy, the march represented a symbolic demonstration of collective racial pride and unity that advanced an unobjectionable and uncontentious vision, but one that simultaneously neglected to point the way forward to material socioeconomic or political achievements.[67]

The second factor that distinguished the march from its 1960s predecessor concerned its social composition. The 1963 march (and its successors in 1983, 1988, and 1993) had been an explicitly inclusive and ecumenical political initiative, an invitation to all Americans to consider the nature of U.S. citizenship, of what it meant fundamentally to be an American. Consonant with the integrationist objectives of its sponsors, the gathering was open to men and women of all races, religions, and creeds, a central explanatory factor in its effectiveness and eloquent affirmation of the irrelevance of arbitrary social and demographic distinctions to the possession of American citizenship. By contrast, the 1995 event was deliberately and consistently promoted as an event designed exclusively for black American males. Although some African-American women and nonblacks (including the author) attended the gathering, they had not been invited to do so. Powerfully reflecting the rotten core of Farrakhan's paranoid politics of hatred, polarization, and division, the march was infused by a dominant spirit of racial exclusion rather than inclusion—an emphasis on the myriad features that separated its attendees from other Americans rather than on what they shared in common.

The third factor differentiating the two marches was their wider public reception. The national civil rights leadership in 1963 had overwhelmingly—though by no means universally—agreed upon both the merits and objectives of the March on Washington. By contrast, national black American elected officials and civil rights leaders were deeply divided over both the virtues and the goals of the 1995 march.[68] Most significant, whereas the 1963 march had represented a collective interracial enterprise associated with a multiplicity of civic and political groups that were all dedicated to advancing the overarching goal of racial integration, the 1995 event was inextricably and principally linked to Farrakhan and the avowedly separatist NoI. The association of the gathering with such a divisive and polarizing public figure, and the potential prospect of Farrakhan's delivering an intemperate and bigoted tirade as the abusively offensive climax of the occasion, served greatly to quiet the enthusiasm of many black American elites for the march.

Thus, neither the NAACP nor the National Baptist Convention supported the march, while many prominent African-American politicians, such as Julian Bond and Douglas Wilder, refused to lend credence to its originator by attending. The several differences between the two occasions were most vividly personified by Rep. John Lewis (D-GA), the veteran civil rights activist whom *Time* magazine had once heralded as a "saint" for his incomparable courage and fortitude during the landmark Freedom Rides of 1963. Whereas, in that year, the then chairman of the SNCC had been pressured into rewriting and moderating the tone of his keynote speech and had, nonetheless, been the most progressive speaker on the platform, the increasingly influential black American congressman felt entirely unable to support its 1995 successor. The march's exclusionary nature, the central role of Farrakhan, and the occasion's strongly offending against the fundamental democratic values of "tolerance, inclusion and integration" were the proximate causes of Lewis's typically principled refusal.[69] For such a shining beacon of political and ethical integrity to dissociate himself from the 1995 march shed an abundant and humanitarian light upon its principal sponsor and ultimate political beneficiary.

For Farrakhan, however, the march represented a daring and eminently shrewd political gambit, the risk of which paid off very handsomely in the form of personal political and social profit. On the basis of a much smaller pool of potential participants, the 1995 event doubled the size of its predecessor of thirty-two years. It thus served simultaneously as the most foolproof manner for Farrakhan to once more gain unprecedented national and international attention and to mobilize collective action by African-Americans on a staggering scale, thereby confirming his national leadership credentials among both blacks and white Americans. The strategy that had informed the CBC–NoI coalescence in 1993 was revived and massively expanded in scope. By mounting an initiative whose ostensible political goals were fundamentally positive and universally unobjectionable to both black and nonblack Americans alike, Farrakhan posed established African-American political and civic leaders with an especially acute political dilemma: to oppose a novel and exciting initiative that sought to unite the black American community nationwide behind highly laudable civic and political objectives, or to support the march and thereby lend its leader and the bigoted creed that he consistently espoused an entirely new and potentially dangerous level of national political legitimacy. Eminently rational and reasonable impulses were thus cross-cut for many African-Americans, even as the principal object and political beneficiary of the march, Louis Farrakhan, became increasingly obvious to many of them.

Characteristically, then, the initiative was deliberately conceived by the NoI's leader to precipitate an extensive and intense nationwide political controversy, to advance a spurious unity through vigorously spreading the seeds of division. Within the African-American community, the principal focus of discontent centered upon the exclusion of black American women from attending the march, even as bystanders. The prohibition not only diminished the potential size of the crowd but also, more important, revived the accusations of rampant sexism that had previously been leveled at the NoI under both Farrakhan and, before him, Elijah Muhammad. The public rationale of Farrakhan and his spokespersons for the gender-based exclusion assumed two unconvincing forms: that the focus of the march—to challenge and alter perceptions of black American men—would be undermined if both sexes (and, of course, whites) participated, and that the march was, in itself, a manifest "tribute" to the dignity and burden of black American womanhood. Although neither explanation appeared persuasive to many female African-Americans, the exclusion nonetheless served its general political purpose of raising the public profile of the initiative among African-Americans at large.

The impact of the march was also greatly heightened by two entirely contingent political developments that dramatically accentuated its national and international public salience, again substantially to Farrakhan's benefit. Taking place less than two weeks after the former black football star O. J. Simpson was controversially acquitted of murdering his white wife and a male friend of hers, and in the midst of intense speculation about whether General Colin Powell would enter the 1996 presidential election, the march helped to concentrate national American public attention directly and explicitly upon matters of race (albeit for a short span) for the first time since the Los Angeles riot of 1992.

Simpson's trial and acquittal had occupied the national psyche and worldwide attention alike in a wholly unprecedented fashion. Replete with themes familiar to modern American life—the cult of celebrity, the taboo of interracial relationships, the frequently litigious destination of domestic strife, the sometimes dubious methods of police investigation, and the soap opera quality of national public affairs in the United States—the trial rapidly emerged as a peculiarly burlesque national spectacle unparalleled in its regular TV audience and curiously compulsive character. Yet, more than the verdict itself, America's deep racial fissures were starkly revealed in the contrasting reactions of the races to the jury's "not guilty" decision: on black Americans' part, jubilation and relief; on that of whites, disbelief, despondency, and anger. In a curious reversal of the more general historic pattern, the jury verdict suggested to many African-Americans that the criminal justice system for once worked and, to many more whites, that in this instance, it manifestly did not do so.

Most telling, the reactions themselves seemed to confirm to both groups the immeasurable distance that separated them from each other. For, unlike the King case, this was an instance in which both white and black Americans were overwhelmingly united as discrete national communities in desiring entirely different verdicts, and holding those, further, to be legally required; a satisfactory compromise was an impossibility. And the combination of the jury's composition and the actual verdict offered a disconcertingly clear lesson in modern racial politics: to blacks, that justice could be secured with a "fair" hearing only by a predominantly African-American jury; to whites, that black criminals would be acquitted by such a jury simply by virtue of their race. However mistaken those perceptions assuredly were, the evident separation, reciprocal incomprehension, and mutual hostility of black and white America were all glaringly on display in the trial's aftermath.

If the Simpson verdict confirmed both diffuse white suspicions of widespread African-American criminality and black American views of white indifference and hostility, Colin Powell—a figure who symbolically provided to whites proof positive of America's firm color-blind foundations and effective individualistic public philosophy—stood as a dramatic political counterpoint. Where Simpson had thrown aside a popular public mantle, Powell contemplated the most prestigious office that America could offer a citizen virtually being thrust upon him through the sheer brute force of a public clamorous for clear, decisive, and assured leadership. Where Simpson ostentatiously exhibited the many trappings of national celebrity, Powell consistently eschewed vulgar public displays. Where Simpson chose a white bride for his second wife, Powell's "blackness" remained a central—if complex—part of both his personal identity and his multiracial mass political appeal.[70] Where Simpson remained a fundamentally flawed and suspect figure to most white Americans even after the jury verdict was delivered, Powell's ethical credentials remained beyond reproach. Ironically, the only "blemish" upon them stemmed from Powell's responding to a Farrakhan phone call and contemplating attendance at the Million Man March, a lapse of political judgment uncharacteristic for the former general but a testament to the potent resonance of Farrakhan associations among white political elites.

Framed by these starkly polar symbolic visions of America's present and possible future racial relations, the march was critically important in confirming the disarray of national African-American leadership and black American elites' acute discomfiture in dealing with the growing political threat posed by Farrakhan. Once more, of all national black political, civic, and religious figures, it was Farrakhan—the most widely repudiated, divisive, and polarizing—who was determining the national African-American political agenda and conditioning the behavior of established national black American political elites, a plea for racial harmony articulated by the most deeply disharmonic of African-American voices. Although many of the speeches at the march, and much of the popular commentary upon it, focused upon the issue of black discontent with both the federal government and white American political leaders, the central political significance of the event was intraracial in character.

Thus, with black political representation at its highest-ever level in American history, the provocative revival of protest-era tactics by Farrakhan dramatically focused national American attention not only upon the failings of established African-American politicians, but also on the dynamism of the NoI's leader. The most common observation made by critics and supporters of the march alike (to which there were remarkably few dissenters) was that no one but Louis Farrakhan could have succeeded in mobilizing such an impressive demonstration of mass black American male unity; yet no black public figure was as divisive, despised, and polarizing a political actor in American racial politics. In a perverse inversion of Samuel Huntington's conceptual nexus of a disharmonic American polity in which conflict derived from universal consensus upon basic creedal values, here, instead, an event of broad intraracial consensus was the child that Farrakhan egregiously fathered from genes of pronounced interracial conflict.[71] Farrakhan's ascendancy to national black leadership was forged not so much despite, but precisely because of, what President Clinton persuasively termed his message of "malice and division."

Separating from the march that ignominious message and its ignoble messenger was a conceptual feat of which most of its participants and observers were eminently capable of achieving. Whether they actually should be so separated, however, represented a normative issue of more pressing political significance and extended elite–mass disagreement.[72] For no matter how subtle and carefully calibrated the distinctions they sought painstakingly to draw, the fundamental fact of the 1995 event was that a long succession of established and widely respected black American elected officials and civil rights activists eagerly assumed secondary positions behind the leader of the NoI. Jackson, Mfume, Rep. Donald Payne (D-NJ), Rangel, Rep. John Conyers (D-MI), Joseph Lowery of the SCLC, Betty Shabazz, Rosa Parks, and even Harvard's Cornel West—an erstwhile enlightened agitator for black-Jewish reconciliation—all gave their ringing personal endorsements to an occasion the principal organizing force and keynote speaker of which was one of the most controversial, heavily criticized, and polarizing figures in American public life; the platform of which was shared by the ranks of the politically disgraced and the disgraceful, a veritable who's who of zealots and demagogues, from Marion Barry through Gus Savage to Al Sharpton; and the spirit of which was infused by an uncompromising separatism and pleas for collective racial solitude as much as for black solidarity. For progressive critics who argue that the most important political dimension of Farrakhan's role is the threat that he poses to black Americans at large, rather than the racial animus that he promotes toward whites and Jews, the event was both a cause for sanguine reflection and a substantial confirmation of the deep dilemmas of contemporary national African-American leadership in general.[73]

For if, as Alonzo Hamby argues, the first essential of successful political leadership in America is "an ability to perceive the dominant needs of an era and to align oneself with them,"[74] Farrakhan achieved his epochal African-American leadership status by touching on some desperate and distressing racial imperatives. For many who watched the march, the peculiar spectacle of respected African-American politicians attending the court of an individual widely viewed as a combination of jester, bigot, and lunatic was as poignantly sad as it was politically significant and deeply discomforting.[75] The central irony of the peculiar plot of "Minister Farrakhan Goes to Washington" in 1995 was that many black American politicians were there many years before, and would remain long after, the NoI's leader opportunistically came and went; but that, thirty years after black Americans had achieved civil and political equality, many of their elected representatives who relied upon neither white votes nor white funds should line up behind an unelected, extremist, and bitterly divisive purveyor of political polarization and racial separatism represented a powerful indictment of the parlous and fissiparous state of contemporary racial relations in the United States. Where Malcolm X had once claimed that he would consider retiring if there were ten Adam Clayton Powells sitting in Congress,[76] now, with forty African-Americans there, it was the apparent redundancy of established black leaders that Farrakhan's day in the autumnal D.C. sun appeared to signal. Indeed, where Malcolm had once characterized the 1963 march as the "farce on Washington," now his verdict appeared to be premature by thirty-two years.

For Farrakhan's extraordinary political triumph was forged upon the fundamental failure—strategic, tactical, and otherwise—not only of U.S. public policy-makers in general, but also of black elected officials in particular, to address effectively the grievous socioeconomic problems of many African-American communities across the nation. Farrakhan enthusiastically exploited, and in exploiting knowingly aggravated, an edifice of racial antagonism that had been constructed upon the foundations of prejudice, discrimination, and despair. On a day publicly billed as one of mass black male atonement, the modern African-American leadership figure whose political career had been most strongly forged upon a path of unrelenting bigotry and prejudice offered no such personal precedents, only proverbial lessons in mass repentance to his assembled flock that once more demonstrated how glass houses remain vulnerable to their zealously stone-throwing occupants.[77] Although his political ascent had been gradual and occasionally halting, the Million Man March undeniably marked Farrakhan's firm incorporation within the national black American leadership cadre. From the grim ruins of King's noble dream had arisen the black phoenix of his ashen nightmare.

SUMMARY

Farrakhan's gradual but inexorable rise to a national political leadership position among American blacks in the 1990s was punctuated by several critical events, each of which contributed incrementally but positively to the increasing political legitimation of the NoI's leader among African-Americans at large. The Jackson association established Farrakhan's national political recognition by black and white Americans, at elite and mass levels, and eventually accorded the NoI's leader a unique and uncontested mantle of racial authenticity. The CBC's "Sacred Covenant" conceded Farrakhan's popular appeal among African-Americans and the NoI's effective activism in several urban black communities across America. The Shabazz controversy effectively neutralized the negative reactions among blacks to Farrakhan that derived from his implication in Malcolm X's assassination. The Million Man March provided a dramatic indication of Farrakhan's wholly exceptional capacity for national agenda-setting, mass mobilization, and widespread popular appeal among African-Americans. Though partial and unstable, rocked by tactical errors, and punctuated by impolitic pronouncements, the political legitimation that these developments afforded Farrakhan was nonetheless sufficiently deep and enduring to furnish him a clear mooring at the dock of national black American political leadership.

In seeking to explain Farrakhan's political rise and current influence, some critics draw parallels between Farrakhan and white right-wing extremists.[78] In issue concerns, organization, and rhetoric, comparisons with the white radical right are, to some extent, instructive in analyzing Farrakhan's role in contemporary American politics; but they are often invidious and tend to obscure as much as they reveal about the nature of the Farrakhan phenomenon. Admittedly, in several respects, Farrakhan and David Duke (the most common focus for comparative analysis) represent contemporaneous mirror images, adhering to parallel political analyses and policy prescriptions on the topic of America's racial ills, and having sought nationwide outlets for their unconventional views. In analyzing Duke's campaigns for the Senate and gubernatorial office in 1990 and 1991, respectively, Gary Esolen argues that the Louisianan's strategy resembled that of other latter-day "extremists-turned-moderates," among whom he included Farrakhan:

> The formula—develop a message acceptable in the mainstream, remake your image accordingly, keep at least one foot planted in your original constituency, and capitalize on personal notoriety and controversy—resembles the path taken by Louis Farrakhan, Yasir Arafat, and many others, with varying degrees of sincerity in their conversions. Some have succeeded in gaining a broader audience; many have failed.[79]

Both Duke and Farrakhan have certainly succeeded in winning a broader American—and even international—audience. But although Duke's efforts to improve his public image and enhance his electoral opportunities by moderating his rhetoric and approach were readily apparent (though assessments of his actual success vary), Farrakhan's conversion from extremist to moderate is difficult, by comparison, to discern as even remotely sincere. That Farrakhan has achieved a social impact which few would have anticipated upon his assumption of the NoI's leadership in 1978 is certainly manifest. That he has managed to do so by genuinely moderating his views is far less persuasive. Rather, it is the maintenance of an uncompromising conservative extremism and a comprehensive and distinctive political paranoia—one exclusive in its scope and intensity to Farrakhan among current national black leaders—that functions as the principal basis of the NoI leader's claims to political independence and, hence, political authority. Therein, moreover, resides the fundamental source of the threat that he poses to the established national black American political leadership cadre.

It may therefore reasonably seem to many that, like a bad bottle of wine, Farrakhan seems to immature with age, leaving the bitterest of tastes upon sensitive American palates. Upon being tentatively received anew, the grapes of black wrath and the old corrosive potion of racial animus and hostility invariably seep sourly through. At each point that Farrakhan has offered a fleeting and tantalizing glimpse of shedding a past of hatred, controversy, and demagogic confrontation, the minister has—unwittingly or intentionally—compromised a broader public acceptance through a return to his more intransigent and adversarial demeanor. The "World Friendship Tour" of 1995–96, which saw Farrakhan take his "message" to eighteen countries, including Iran, Iraq, and Libya, was only the latest and most spectacular instance of a well-established pattern of squandering newly acquired—if limited—legitimacy upon an altar of intense controversy.

However, the many controversies that have punctuated Farrakhan's political rise have served more to propel his elevation to the ranks of national African-American leadership than to limit the salience of his distinctive message among blacks at large, hence his apparent addiction to regularly stimulating such furors as a necessity for his leadership aims. Moderation, compromise, conciliation, pragmatism, and consensus are the dominant terms of conventional American politicians; they form the common currency of political exchange familiar to even the most cursory students of the dynamics of American politics. Farrakhan, however, bargains with a political capital culled unrepentantly from immoderation, nonnegotiable demands, dogmatism, intransigence, and incessant confrontation, in short, one that assumes an altogether different character to that of most American political actors and that ensures the NoI's leader of an exceptional niche within the ranks of black leadership.

Moreover, these controversies have also simultaneously rendered the substantive religious and ideological content of Farrakhan's distinctive message less clear than might otherwise have been the case, ironically, an important factor in explaining the mass black appeal that Farrakhan has achieved among both members and nonmembers of the NoI in the national African-American community. Precisely by virtue of the unconventional modes of political discourse and operation that have accorded him an ascendant position in national black politics, the content of his political and religious beliefs demands careful analysis. It is the peculiar nature of the belief system that Farrakhan propounds which we address next.

NOTES TO CHAPTER 2

1. William A. Henry, "Pride and Prejudice," *Time* 26 February 1994, pp. 21–27, at p. 21.
2. The song, from Reed's "New York" album (Sire Records, 1989), was an inventive attack upon anti-Semitic sentiments and prejudice that linked together Jesse Jackson; former Nazi, UN Secretary General, and

Austrian president Kurt Waldheim; and Pope John Paul II. Farrakhan is also mentioned by name in the late Frank Zappa's sharply satirical tribute to Jackson, "Rhymin' Man," from "Broadway the Hardway" (Zappa Records, 1989).

Farrakhan has also featured heavily in rap and hip-hop music, winning extensive support from black artists such as Ice Cube, Public Enemy, and Afrika Bambaataa. As Matthias Gardell observes, while some rap artists belong to the radical left, the majority of the more popular American rappers adhere to the broad black nationalist Islamic tradition. (See the discussion in Gardell, *Countdown to Armageddon*, pp. 293–301.) Ice Cube, in particular, has been one of the most consistent supporters of Farrakhan. Sleeve notes and photographs in his albums have variously encouraged membership in the NoI, praised Farrakhan, and depicted Cube reading the Nation's newspaper, *The Final Call*, backed by suitably stern-looking bow-tied Black Muslims.

3. This is not to suggest that the civil rights movement turned upon the Montgomery protest, but that King's particular role in the movement owed a substantial debt to his activism in the critical Alabama dispute. On the civil rights movement in general, and Montgomery in particular, see: Taylor Branch, *Parting the Waters: America in the King Years, 1954–1963* (New York: Simon and Schuster, 1988); the excellent rational choice treatment of the movement by Dennis Chong, *Collective Action and the Civil Rights Movement* (Chicago: University of Chicago Press, 1991); David J. Garrow, *Bearing the Cross: Martin Luther King, Jr. and the Southern Christian Leadership Conference* (London: Jonathan Cape, 1988); Doug McAdam, *Political Process and the Development of Black Insurgency, 1930–1970* (Chicago: University of Chicago Press, 1982); Aldon D. Morris, *The Origins of the Civil Rights Movement: Black Communities Organizing for Change* (New York: The Free Press, 1984); and Juan Williams, *Eyes on the Prize: America's Civil Rights Years, 1954–1965* (New York: Viking-Penguin, 1987).

4. On the tensions within American Islam, see: Amir M. Ali, *Islam or Farrakhanism?* (Chicago: Institute of Islamic Information and Education, 1991); and Marsh, *From Black Muslims to Muslims*, 1st edition.

5. The author first encountered the application of these terms to election campaigns in the conclusion to the volume by David Butler and Austin Ranney, eds., *Electioneering: A Comparative Study of Continuity and Change* (Oxford: Clarendon Press, 1992).

6. Marable, *Black American Politics*, p. 120.

7. The value of counterfactual speculation is inherently limited, of course. Nonetheless, it is difficult to conceive of Farrakhan achieving the leadership position that he has over the last two decades without the extensive publicity and acute controversy that attended his often stormy association with Jackson.

8. 1964 saw the passage of the most significant civil rights legislation in American history. For a detailed account, see Charles Whalen and Barbara Whalen, *The Longest Debate: A Legislative History of the 1964 Civil Rights Act* (New York: New American Library, 1985).

9. The most skeptical interpretation of Jackson's political role and substantive significance was first advanced by Adolph Reed in *The Jesse Jackson*

Phenomenon: The Crisis of Purpose in Afro-American Politics (New Haven: Yale University Press, 1986). For alternative, more sympathetic, but less persuasive, analyses, see: Lucius J. Barker and Ronald W. Walters, eds., *Jesse Jackson's 1984 Presidential Campaign: Challenge and Change in American Politics* (Chicago: University of Illinois Press, 1989); and Charles P. Henry, *Culture and African American Politics* (Bloomington: Indiana University Press, 1990).

10. On the role of the black vote and African American candidates in presidential elections, see: Ronald W. Walters, *Black Presidential Politics in America: A Strategic Approach* (New York: State University of New York Press, 1988); and Katherine Tate, *From Protest to Politics: The New Black Voters in American Elections* (Cambridge, Mass.: Harvard University Press, 1993).

11. Contrasting accounts of Malcolm X's evolving belief system and relations with the NoI can be found in: Steven Barboza, *American Jihad: Islam after Malcolm X* (New York: Doubleday, 1994); George Breitman, ed., *Malcolm X Speaks: Selected Speeches and Statements* (New York: Grove Press, 1965); George Breitman, ed., *By Any Means Necessary: Speeches, Interviews and a Letter by Malcolm X* (New York: Pathfinder Press, 1970); Louis DeCaro, *On the Side of My People: A Religious Life of Malcolm X* (New York: New York University Press, 1996); David Gallen, ed., *The Malcolm X Reader* (New York: Carroll and Graf, 1994); Benjamin Karim, *Remembering Malcolm* (New York: Carroll and Graf, 1992); Bruce Perry, *Malcolm: The Life of a Man Who Changed Black America* (Barrytown, NY: Station Hill, 1991); and Oba T'Shaka, *The Political Legacy of Malcolm X* (Chicago: Third World Press, 1983).

12. On the assassination of Malcolm X, see: George Breitman, Herman Porter, and Baxter Smith, *The Assassination of Malcolm X* (New York: Pathfinder Press, 1976); Michael Friendly, *Malcolm X: The Assassination* (New York: Carroll and Graf, 1992); Peter Goldman, *The Death and Life of Malcolm X*, 2nd ed. (Urbana: University of Illinois Press, 1979); and the brief discussion in David E. Scheim, *The Mafia Killed President Kennedy* (London: W. H. Allen, 1988), pp. 278–82.

13. The most accessible and influential works on the black religious experience and its influence in American politics are: Charles V. Hamilton, *The Black Preacher in America* (New York: William Morrow and Co., 1972); and C. Eric Lincoln, *The Black Church in the African American Experience* (Durham, N.C.: Duke University Press, 1990).

14. See Hans Gerth and C. Wright Mills, eds., *From Max Weber*.

15. For a concise summation of the changing environment of national black American politics after the civil rights movement, see Robert Smith, "Black Power and the Transformation From Protest to Politics," *Political Science Quarterly* 96, no. 3 (1981): 431–43.

16. On the consistent lock of the Democrats upon black Americans' voting loyalties, see Louis Bolce, Gerald De Maio, and Douglas Muzzio, "The 1992 Republican 'Tent': No Blacks Walked In," *Political Science Quarterly* 108, no. 2 (1993): 255–70.

17. The dominance of party interest derived from both electoral and institutional sources. Electorally, the vast majority of black Americans since 1964 have remained consistently, and disproportionately, loyal to Democratic

party candidates. At an institutional level, in addition, the Democratic party enjoyed a comprehensive lock upon the House of Representatives and (with the exception of 1981–87) the U.S. Senate in the years 1955–95. As the majority party in Congress (and in many state legislatures), black elected officials therefore had powerful institutional incentives to remain within the Democratic party fold.

18. See: Michael B. Preston, Lenneal S. Henderson, and Paul Puryear, eds., *The New Black Politics*, 2nd ed. (New York: Longman, 1987); and Clarence Lusane, "Black Political Power in the 1990s," *The Black Scholar*, January/February 1989, pp. 38–42.

19. Steve Bruce, *The Rise and Fall of the New Christian Right, 1978–1988* (Oxford: Clarendon Press, 1988).

20. See E. R. Shipp, "Candidacy of Jackson Highlights Split Among Black Muslims," *New York Times*, 27 February 1984, p. 10.

21. The reasons underlying Farrakhan's endorsement of Jackson are explained at length by the Nation of Islam leader in his article, "Farrakhan on Jesse Jackson: A Warning to Black Leaders, A Warning to Black People," in the black American female-oriented publication, *Essence*, February 1984, pp. 30–34. Therein, Farrakhan characterizes Jackson's candidacy as "one of the most far-reaching and significant events of this century" and argues that Jackson represented "an instrument that Allah is using for a much larger purpose than perhaps he [Jackson] himself realizes."

22. Farrakhan, "Register and Vote" radio address, 11 March 1984. Also quoted in McFadden-Preston, "The Rhetoric of Minister Louis Farrakhan," pp. 176–77.

23. The Reagan Administration's Justice Department did investigate the possibility of prosecuting Farrakhan for the threat, but rejected the notion on the grounds of insufficient evidential proof being available.

24. See *The New York Times*, 23 April 1984, p. 1.

25. Jerome H. Bakst, ed., "Louis Farrakhan: An Update," *Anti-Defamation League Facts* 30, Spring 1985 (New York: Anti-Defamation League, 1985), p. 1.

26. Faye S. Joyce, "Farrakhan Warns Press on Jackson," *New York Times*, 10 April 1984, p. 1.

27. See: Nancy Weiss, *Farewell to the Party of Lincoln: Black Politics in the Age of FDR* (Princeton: Princeton University Press, 1983); and Anthony Badger, *The New Deal: the Depression Years, 1933–1940* (New York: Hill and Wang, 1989).

28. On the pattern of black partisan allegiances, see: Louis Bolce, Gerald D. De Maio, and Douglas Muzzio, "Blacks and the Republican Party: The 20 Percent Solution," *Political Science Quarterly* 107, no. 1 (1992): 63–79.

29. See: Earl Black and Merle Black, *Politics and Society in the South* (Cambridge, Mass.: Harvard University Press, 1987) and *The Vital South: How Presidents are Elected* (Cambridge, Mass.: Harvard University Press, 1992); Alexander P. Lamis, *The Two-Party South* 2nd ed. (New York: Oxford University Press, 1990); and Nicol C. Rae, *Southern Democrats* (New York: Oxford University Press, 1994).

30. Joyce, "Farrakhan Warns Press on Jackson," p. 1.

31. "President Opposes Farrakhan," *The New York Times*, 28 June 1984, p. 22.

32. See Thomas Byrne Edsall and Mary D. Edsall, *Chain Reaction: The Impact of Race, Rights, and Taxes on American Politics* (New York: W. W. Norton, 1991).

33. Three out of every four Jewish Americans voted for the Democratic candidate, Walter Mondale, in 1984, a marginal increase from 1980 when a substantial minority of Jews voted for the independent candidate, John Anderson. See Paul R. Abramson, John H. Aldrich, and David W. Rohde, *Change and Continuity in the 1988 Elections* (Washington, D.C.: Congressional Quarterly Press, 1990), pp. 130–31.

34. *The New York Times*, 29 June 1984, p. 10.

35. Elizabeth O. Colton, *The Jackson Phenomenon: The Man, the Power, the Message* (New York: Doubleday, 1989).

36. Colton, *The Jackson Phenomenon*, p. 205–6.

37. Cited in Colton, *The Jackson Phenomenon*, p. 207–8.

38. On their skepticism in 1984, see: Lorenzo Morris, ed., *The Social and Political Implications of the 1984 Jesse Jackson Presidential Campaign* (New York: Praeger, 1990); Reed, *The Jesse Jackson Phenomenon*; and Maulana Karenga, "Jesse Jackson and the Presidential Campaign: The Invitation and the Oppositions of History," *Black Scholar* 15, no. 5 (September-October 1984). On the 1988 context, see: Paulette Pierce, "The Roots of the Rainbow Coalition," *Black Scholar* 20, no. 2 (March/April 1988), pp. 2–16; and Ronald W. Walters, "The American Crisis of Credibility and the 1988 Jesse Jackson Campaign," *Black Scholar* 20, no. 2 (March/April 1988), pp. 31–44.

39. See, for example, James Melvin Washington, "Jesse Jackson and the Symbolic Politics of Black Christendom," in *Annals of the American Academy of Political and Social Science* 480 (July 1985): 89–105, at 102.

40. Even an unannounced candidate, Colin Powell, encountered (in the context of otherwise near-universal praise) remarkably adverse critical comments for his speaking to Farrakhan on the phone about, and contemplating participation in, the Million Man March over the weekend of October 14–15, 1995. Though publicly rejecting the invitation as a result of book promotion duties in New York, the very fact that Farrakhan's contact cast a doubt upon his fitness for highest office says much about the litmus test that the NoI's leader has come to represent for many Americans.

41. See Bill Turque, Vern E. Smith, and John McCormick, "Playing a Different Tune: Louis Farrakhan Is Trying to Reach Out to the White Mainstream," *Newsweek* 121, 28 June 1993, p. 30.

42. See: Kenneth T. Walsh, "The New Drug Vigilantes," *U.S. & World News Report*, 9 May 1988, p. 20; and Lorraine Adams, "Nation of Islam: A Dream Past Due," *The Washington Post*, 2 September 1996, pp. A1, A8. Adams documents at length how the NoI and its related security offshoots became embroiled in severe debts by the mid-1990s and attracted strong criticism from housing tenants for their ineffectiveness and proselytizing on behalf of

Farrakhan, being "more concerned about converting people than security" (p. A8).

43. Farrakhan's rendition occurred as part of a three-day symposium, "Gateways: Classical Music and the Black Musician," at the Reynolds Auditorium in Winston-Salem, North Carolina, on 18 April 1993. He prefaced the recital by declaring that he would "try to do with music what cannot be done with words and try to undo with music what words have done." See Bernard Holland, "Sending a Message, Louis Farrakhan Plays Mendelssohn," *The New York Times*, 19 April 1993, p. C11. It is perhaps not inappropriate to treat the material political significance of the recital with a healthy degree of skepticism. One wonders, for example, whether black Americans would be persuaded of David Duke's sincerity in recanting his previous pronouncements upon race in the event of the Louisianan's publicly performing a Marvin Gaye tribute or Muddy Waters medley as a conciliatory message to African-Americans.

44. See Robert S. Singh, "The Congressional Black Caucus in the United States Congress, 1971–1990," *Parliaments, Estates and Representation* 14, no. 1 (1994): 65–91.

45. See William L. Clay, *Just Permanent Interests: Black Americans in Congress, 1870–1991* (New York: Amistad, 1992).

46. Quoted in Richard E. Cohen, "Hatred Covenant," *The Washington Post*, 15 October 1993, p. 25.

47. See: Cohen, "Hatred Covenant"; Lynne Duke, "Congressional Black Caucus and Nation of Islam Agree on Alliance," *The Washington Post*, 17 September 1993, p. A3; and Cameron Humphries, "The Sacred Covenant," *Diversity and Division* 3, no. 3 (Spring-Summer 1994).

48. See, for example: William A. Henry, "Pride and Prejudice," *Time* 143, 28 February 1994, pp. 21–27; Joe Klein, "The Threat of Tribalism," *Newsweek* 123, 14 March 1994, p. 28; Sylvester Monroe, "Khalid Abdul Muhammad: Is the Fiery Speaker Undermining the Nation of Islam?," *Emerge* 5, September 1994, p. 42; and Nat Hentoff, "Black Bigotry and Free Speech," *The Progressive*, May 1994, p. 20.

49. Cited in Janet Hook, "House Denounces Remarks as 'Racist' Speech," *Congressional Quarterly Weekly Report*, 26 February 1994, p. 458.

50. See Ian Brodie, "Muslim Racism Sparks Uproar," *The London Times*, 4 February 1994, p. 12.

51. David Bositis, *The Congressional Black Caucus in the 103rd Congress* (Washington, D.C.: Joint Center for Political and Economic Studies, 1994), p. 19.

52. See, for example, Juan Williams, "Hiding from this Rage Is Harmful," *International Herald Tribune*, 18 February 1994, p. 7.

53. Quoted in Janet Hook, "Mfume Cuts Renewed Ties to Nation of Islam," *Congressional Quarterly Weekly Report*, 5 February 1994, p. 219. See also Kevin Merida, "Black Caucus Says It Has No Official Ties with Nation of Islam," *The Washington Post*, 3 February 1994, p. A16.

54. Quoted in Brodie, "Muslim Racism."

55. Rep. Cynthia McKinney (D-GA), cited in Kevin Merida, "Lawmakers Uneasy Over Farrakhan: Black Officials Split on Summit Invitations," *The Washington Post*, 17 June 1994, p. A3.

56. See: Alex Kotlowitz, "A Bridge Too Far?," *The New York Times Magazine*, 12 June 1994, pp. 41–43; and George Curry, "Unity in the Community: Can Ben Chavis Pull It Off?," *Emerge* 5 (September 1994), p. 28.

57. See: Sylvester Monroe, "The Risky Association," *Time*, 27 June 1994, p. 39; Dorothy J. Gaiter, "Civil Unrest," *The Wall Street Journal*, 10 June 1994, p. A1; Denton L. Watson, "Chavis's NAACP: Embracing Farrakhan," *The Washington Post*, 29 June 1994, p. A23; and Nat Hentoff, "A Black Response to Black Bigotry," *The Washington Post*, 23 July 1994, p. A21.

58. See: *The Atlanta Journal*, 4 November 1985, p. A5.

59. See Tom Morganthau, "Back in the Line of Fire," *Newsweek*, 23 January 1995, p. 20.

60. Shabazz, eschewing any explicit talk of reconciliation, merely encouraged Farrakhan to continue broadening his "conceptual framework." See Malcolm Gladwell, "Farrakhan Seeks End of Rift with Shabazz; Apologizes for Hurt but Denies Involvement in Malcolm X Death," *The Washington Post*, 8 May 1995, p. A1.

61. Part of Rangel's calculations also involved the need to retain black support for his primary election constituency. Though he had triumphed easily over Adam Clayton Powell, the son of the (in)famous black congressman, in his October 1994 primary, the imperative to attend to the type of constituency to which Farrakhan targeted his general message clearly influenced the New York incumbent. Indeed, the following year, despite reports before the event that he would not attend at all, Rangel was also a featured platform speaker at the Million Man March in 1995.

62. See: Don Terry, "Shabazz Case: A Gain for Farrakhan," *The New York Times*, 3 May 1995, p. A15, B8; Charisse Jones, "Farrakhan-Shabazz Meeting Kindles Hope," *The New York Times*, 6 May 1995, p. 16, 23; and Joyce Purnick, "An Unlikely Matchmaker," *The New York Times*, 8 May 1995, p. B1, B12.

63. Given its notably more modest numbers and entirely stationary quality, the term is something of a misnomer, of course.

64. Farrakhan claimed 1.5 million African-American men had attended the march, and threatened to sue the National Park Service for its "racist" estimate of 400,000. It seemed to this author, both on the day and subsequently, that a figure somewhere between 400,000 and 600,000 was plausible—but no more than that.

65. *Brown v. Board of Education*, 347 U.S. 483 (1954).

66. The efforts to conduct a voter registration drive among black Americans that occurred on the day of the march and subsequently were not part of the original public literature promoting the event. Most of the emphasis upon African-American leadership inclusion and electoral influence that Farrakhan made occurred after, rather than prior to, the march itself. See, for example, Michael A. Fletcher and Hamil R. Harris, "Farrakhan Announces Voter Drive," *The Washington Post*, 19 October 1995, p. A3.

67. An implicit political goal of the march may, nonetheless, have been to demonstrate to black Americans both the possibility and the desirability of racial separatism. Many of the marchers commented upon the novelty of seeing so many black men gathered together, some recording that it felt as if they were in Africa. Given Farrakhan's separatist objectives, it seems plausible that the march was partly designed by him to encourage such sentiments and to reinforce the theoretical appeal of separatism by a practical demonstration of its putative viability.

68. For comparison with previous marches, see Marable, *Black American Politics*, chapter 2. One of the most lucid synopses of the arguments for and against participation in the 1995 march is made by A. Leon Higginbotham Jr., "Why I Didn't March," *The Washington Post*, 17 October 1995, p. A17.

69. Quoted in Martin Fletcher and Tom Rhodes, "Washington Mass Rally Rekindles Black Pride," *The London Times*, 17 October 1995, p. 11. It should be noted, though, that Lewis also relied upon, and enjoyed excellent relations with, white and Jewish supporters in his Atlanta district for his reelection to the House.

70. See Juan Williams, "President Colin Powell?," *Reconstruction* 2, no. 3 (1994): 67–78.

71. See Huntington, *American Politics*.

72. See: Richard E. Cohen, "Marching behind Farrakhan," *The Washington Post*, 19 September 1995, p. A18; E. J. Dionne, "So Many Could Have Been There," *The Washington Post*, 17 October 1995, p. A17; Matt Labash, "Inside the March: Farrakhan Is King," *The Weekly Standard*, 23 October 1995, pp. 26–29; and Glenn C. Loury, "One Man's March," *The New Republic*, 6 November 1995, pp. 18–22.

73. See the discussions in: Darryl Pinckney, "Slouching Towards Washington," *The New York Review of Books*, 21 December 1995, pp. 73–82; and Sean Wilentz, "Backward March," *The New Republic*, 6 November 1995, pp. 16–18. Many of Pinckney's points, especially on the respective racial dangers that Farrakhan poses, were also previously anticipated in Reed, "Behind the Farrakhan Show."

74. Alonzo L. Hamby, *Liberalism and Its Challengers: F.D.R. to Reagan* (New York: Oxford University Press, 1985), p. 9.

75. The international reception accorded the march provides interesting indications of the extent to which Farrakhan's rise has occasioned incredulity as well as curiosity outside America. Farrakhan was not only widely portrayed in the mass media in the United Kingdom, for example, as a racial extremist but was also ridiculed as a lunatic. See, for example, the references to the NoI as the "Nutters of Islam" in the satirical British fortnightly magazine, *Private Eye*, 3 November 1995, p. 15, and the question raised by the journalist Francis Wheen, as to whether Farrakhan was "loony as a coot?" in "Voice of Islam," *The Guardian*, 8 November 1995, sec. 2, p. 7. For black Americans who argued that distinctions needed to be made between the message and messenger, the international treatment of the march should serve as a

salutary reminder of the powerful symbolism that characterizes such events. Moreover, to the extent that advocates of the march sought to challenge the inaccurate and sometimes racist international perceptions of black American men that are represented in rap music and popular films, the external dimension of the coverage of the march assumed a particular importance. With Farrakhan as its principal sponsor, however, such stereotypes were apt to be less successfully countered than might otherwise have been the case. See also Martin Fletcher, "Prophet of Hatred Becomes Voice of Black America," *The London Times*, 18 October 1995, p. 11.

76. Malcolm X (with Alex Haley), *The Autobiography of Malcolm X* (New York: Penguin Books, 1968), p. 28.

77. Despite widespread anticipation that Farrakhan would use his keynote speech as an opportunity to offer public apologies for his own anti-Semitic and bigoted comments over the years (an anticipation admittedly tempered by Farrakhan's familiar reference to Jews as "bloodsuckers" in an interview the week before the march), the NoI leader scrupulously refused to apologize for his dubious record during his rambling monologue of over two hours duration. Though Farrakhan invited "dialogue" with Jewish leaders and others in the speech, his personal history provided few causes for optimism that such dialogues would either occur or produce tangible results in improved race relations.

78. See the lucid discussion in Dennis King, "The Farrakhan Phenomenon: Ideology, Support, Potential," *Patterns of Prejudice* 20, no. 1 (1986): 11–22.

79. Gary Esolen, "More Than a Pretty Face: David Duke's Use of Television as a Political Tool," *The Emergence of David Duke and the Politics of Race*, ed. Douglas Rose (Chapel Hill: University of North Carolina Press, 1992), pp. 136–55, at 140.

3

The Prophet Motive: The Theology and Ideology of Black Radical Reaction

Even Malcolm X . . . retreated from the impossible position of separatism.

Harold Cruse[1]

I really don't care if you think I'm a nut.

Louis Farrakhan[2]

Farrakhan's political ascendancy has been widely viewed as surprising by virtue of the anti-Semitism and racial militancy that pervade his national public profile in the United States. Perhaps the most common reaction among Americans to Farrakhan's public discourse, however, is not so much one of revulsion, outrage, or fear as sheer incredulity. Many can scarcely believe that a public figure articulating the beliefs that Farrakhan propounds can even take himself seriously, much less be taken so by others. The potent and eclectic amalgam of numerology, pseudo-history, theology, and prophecy that punctuates the Nation of Islam (NoI) leader's public pronouncements requires on the part of most listeners a willing suspension of disbelief to entertain even minimally. The veritable Stephen King of black nationalists, Farrakhan's fantastic world is inhabited by sinister Jews and malevolent Masons, spaceships waiting to drop bombs upon the Earth on an imminent judgment day, and African-American spirits miraculously returned from the dead. It is almost as if America patiently waits for Farrakhan eventually to smile, wink knowingly, and candidly concede that his political opportunism and vivid imagination are far more deeply entrenched and enduring than is the elaborate fictional landscape that he publicly relates.

Such reactions are certainly understandable. For though Farrakhan's rise to a position of national black American political leadership has afforded a reasonably large stock of public information and
commentary about the Black Muslim leader, much of this remains
essentially impressionistic, lacking comprehensive detail and accuracy. For most Americans, Farrakhan therefore continues to represent
a largely foreboding and mysterious black American figure of malice,
spite, and hatred. Relatively little is known at large of either his personal or political background beyond a national reputation rich in
racial militancy, vitriolically aggressive speeches, and barely coded
anti-Semitic public utterances. In short, many elite evaluations of, and
popular political responses to, Farrakhan occur against a background
of very partial and limited knowledge of the minister's substantive
political values, beliefs, and attitudes.

Farrakhan has, nonetheless, been active in the NoI for over forty
years. Having delivered literally thousands of speeches and sermons
across America, the Black Muslim has created a voluminous record of
his values and beliefs.[3] What that record clearly reveals is a minister
whose political project of racial regeneration is thoroughly infused by
a set of keenly held theological doctrines of a deeply unorthodox and
extremely tendentious hue, whose connection with orthodox Islam—
much less reality—is far more tenuous than certain. Although Farrakhan is a quintessential American political entrepreneur, highly attentive to opportunities to increase his personal role and influence
among African-Americans, his pragmatism is powerfully constrained
by the very distinctive religious and ideological beliefs that are
entirely inseparable from the minister's locus within the NoI. In this
regard, Farrakhan's extensive and varied experiences in the black separatist organization have altered few (if any) of the fundamental religious and ideological beliefs that first drew him to joining the NoI in
1955. What has changed significantly over subsequent decades, however, has been the lessons that Farrakhan has absorbed, adapted, and
reapplied about internal organization, self-publicity, and political
leadership.

As a political operator in recent American politics, Farrakhan's
sophistication is more pronounced than many of his critics are either
able to recognize or willing to concede. Moreover, the theological convictions that inform his political beliefs also render his public discourse somewhat more nuanced than is frequently admitted. Neither

the sensitivity of Farrakhan's political judgment nor the coherence of his belief system should be obscured by the apparent crudity of his public persona and by his regular public denials that he either is, or harbors aspirations to become, a national politician in America. For if Mahatma Gandhi can be said to have first invented the politician as saint, Farrakhan has equally vigorously promoted the self-proclaimed prophetic savior as politician.[4]

That this should be so reflects Farrakhan's distinctive organizational base. The NoI represents an esoteric and eccentric mix of cosmological, religious, and ideological tendencies that powerfully distinguish it from all other national political, religious, and civic organizations seeking black Americans' socioeconomic and political empowerment in the United States. Farrakhan's zealous adherence to the religious teachings of its founders, W. D. Fard and Elijah Muhammad, leads to his self-conception and national projection as a prophetic figure and race savior. That figure, however, is one who advances a public philosophy far closer to that of Jesse Helms than Jesse Jackson, a soothsayer whose offers of cathartic comfort to African-Americans conceal a deeply conservative and reactionary set of convictions and, moreover, a material practice that clearly contradicts those avowed political principles. The adverse and incredulous reactions that Farrakhan frequently elicits from his American compatriots are in this respect not merely eminently understandable, but are also in large part fully merited.

THE CHARMING DEMAGOGUE

Farrakhan's early personal background provided several useful preparatory experiences and skills for his eventual role as leader of the NoI. The minister's political socialization was founded upon formative experiences that subsequently enabled him to forge a public persona as readily able variously to identify with many African-Americans' concerns and aspirations from personal experience; to work with and across social classes among African-Americans; to be tutored in different styles of political and organizational leadership; to be afforded an early exposure to public performance, spectacle, and the critical importance of the mass media in personal political promotion; and to invoke Christian theological tenets and parables as a means of tempering and reinforcing his unorthodox Islamic message to black

Americans at large. The demagogic aspects of Farrakhan's political career and public persona have thus drawn deeply upon many important facets of his early life.

Minister Louis Haleem Abdul Farrakhan was born on May 11, 1933, in the Bronx, New York City. His mother, Mae Manning, had migrated to New York from the British colony of Saint Kitts, in the West Indies. She married a Jamaican, Percival Clark, who soon disappeared, before falling in love with another West Indian, Louis Walcott. Walcott fathered Farrakhan's older brother, Alvan, before Clark returned briefly and made Manning pregnant with a second child, prior to disappearing once more. Manning attempted to abort the baby three times with a coat hanger before eventually changing her mind and giving birth once again, at the age of 15. The child was given the name of Louis Eugene Walcott, after a man who was not his natural father and whom he would never know.

Three years after Louis's birth, Manning left for Boston, Massachusetts, where she raised the young child alone. Despite his lacking a father at home, Walcott's upbringing in the thriving West Indian neighborhood of Roxbury was conventionally middle-class in character. Walcott took up the violin from the age of five, for example, and received private music tuition. He also grew up as a devout Episcopalian, winning a place at the Boston Latin School (one of America's then best, and overwhelmingly white, state schools). After high school, Walcott gained a modest athletics scholarship to the Winston-Salem Teachers' College in North Carolina, a black academy where he majored in English. Returning to Boston with few serious prospects after college, Walcott married his high-school sweetheart, Betsy (later known as Khadijah). Walcott eventually fathered nine children by her, and has at least twenty grandchildren, some of whom have become active and influential members of the NoI and its several institutional enterprises and offshoots.

One of the first black Americans ever to appear on national television in the United States, Walcott achieved his initial exposure to a national American audience when he appeared on *Ted Mack's Amateur Hour*, playing the violin, in 1946. Soon taking up the guitar and the ukulele, he quickly assumed a journeyman role as a Calypso singer and dancer, rapidly gaining the affectionate sobriquets, "The Charmer" and "Calypso Gene." There, but for the grace of Harry Belafonte, Walcott might have remained.

Instead, Walcott's initiation into the NoI occurred in 1955, when (on a tour of Chicago nightclubs) he attended a lecture by Elijah

Muhammad, at the end of which he promptly joined the organiza-tion. Upon joining, however, he was instructed (whether by Elijah or by other members of the group is unclear) that life as a performer was incompatible with NoI membership. Now termed Louis X (the name "Farrakhan" does not appear to have been embraced by him until 1975), he thereupon gave up his fledgling performing career to partici-pate fully in the NoI through its Boston mosque. Nonetheless, his artistic bent still found typically didactic expression in several plays that he wrote—and, presaging his later political ambitions, starred in—that documented the nature and scale of black oppression in the United States at the hands of white Americans.[5] As Louis X, Farra-khan also went on eventually to release a calypso record redolent of his developing political and religious beliefs, "The White Man's Heaven Is the Black Man's Hell" (which won anthemic status within the NoI but achieved neither popular nor critical acclaim, although it was, admittedly, better received than his disc commemorating Amer-ica's first sex-change operation).[6]

In the Boston temple, Louis X was rapidly appointed to the rank of "Captain," in charge of training and instructing the male members of the NoI in the mosque. Outside the temple, he worked successively as a storm door and window salesman at a wage of $35 per week, as a dishwasher, and then in Boston's Garment District at $45 per week. Success as a Captain resulted in further rapid promotion to the presti-gious position of Minister of the Boston mosque, Temple No. 11, which subsequently emerged under his ministership as one of the fastest growing of the NoI's temples in the entire United States.

When Louis's early friend and mentor, Malcolm X, was brutally assassinated on February 21, 1965, the NoI was plunged into internal turmoil and the mosque in New York over which the latter had pre-sided was left in deep disarray. Louis was transferred by Elijah from Boston to act as minister of the prestigious Mosque No. 7 in Harlem, and shortly thereafter was selected to be Elijah's national spokesper-son for the NoI, in addition to his responsibilities in New York City. In the NoI's history up to that point, only Malcolm and Louis had been selected to serve as national spokespersons for the organization; both were personally chosen by Elijah for the role. The choice clearly reflected Farrakhan's diverse and compelling personal qualities: a man, according to C. Eric Lincoln, "of extraordinary charisma and charm, but, armed, with a rapier-like wit, he is well practised in polemical skills."[7] Such skills would be tested before a nationwide audience by the 1980s when Farrakhan's early reputation as the Charmer became largely and justifiably eclipsed by that of the Demagogue.[8]

THE NATION OF ISLAM: ELIJAH, MALCOLM, AND LOUIS

Farrakhan's early immersion in a religious environment was hardly unusual for an African-American of his generation, but his particular choice of organization was decidedly atypical for members of his race. For although religion and the institution of the Church have historically performed many vitally important social, economic, and political functions in the lives of most black Americans, the over-whelming focus of African-American religious allegiance in the United States has been Christianity.[9] The Islamic faith has never been adhered to by more than an extremely small proportion of Americans, either black or white, the vast majority of whom have remained firmly wedded to various denominations of the Christian faith. Thus, although in 1995 African-Americans made up 42 percent of the approximately five million Muslims in the United States, approximately 92 percent of all black Americans were Christians.[10]

In the African-American case, although Syrian Muslim immigrants and black returnees to Islam established local religious organizations as early as 1912 and 1913, respectively, it was not until the 1950s that a significant organization by orthodox Muslims on a national level was formed in America: the Federation of Islamic Associations (FIA). Established in June 1952, the Federation sought to promote the growth of Islam and to facilitate its greater understanding by the non-Muslim American majority.[11] The theological orthodoxy of the FIA, however, stood in sharp contrast to the Nation of Islam and the Bilalian faith to which its members subscribed.

Regarded by most Muslims as deeply unorthodox, Bilalian Islam arose from a belief system propounded and popularized by Robert J. Poole, a former automobile factory worker, before whom Allah—or God—allegedly appeared in the person of Master W. D. Fard Muhammad, in Detroit, Michigan, on July 4, 1930 (Poole later changed his name to "Elijah Muhammad," adopted as a symbolic rejection of all associations with white American society, its slave history and tainted legacy). Although few existing studies of the Black Muslim movement have commented upon it, the date of Fard's appearance was evidently of substantial political significance for African-Americans: American Independence Day. The arrival of Fard in the United States was intended to represent the day of future black American independence from the land of their enslavement and subjugation.

Bilalianism comprises six key beliefs: first, there is one God called Allah, who is identified as being black; second, Elijah Muhammad was his last messenger on Earth; third, heaven and hell are states that are deemed actually to exist on Earth and, therefore, there is no life after death; fourth, it is necessary to pray seven times daily and to fast each December; fifth, Elijah assumes the place of the Prophet (the justification for this is that Elijah knew Allah personally in the form of Fard Muhammad, which represents a double heresy in the orthodox Islamic faith, by making God both visible and personified in human form); and, sixth, Bilalians adhere to the notion of black supremacy, an inverted type of racism that characterizes Caucasians as intrinsically evil. Together, these six fundamental beliefs powerfully distinguish the Bilalian faith from orthodox Islam.

The Nation of Islam represents the institutional expression of Bilalianism in America. Established by Fard in July 1930—after the NAACP (1909) and the National Urban League (1910), but before the Congress of Racial Equality (1942), the SCLC (1957), and Jesse Jackson's Operation PUSH (1971)—the NoI's political locus was firmly within the relatively new ideological tradition of black nationalism in America. Though derided by early scholastic observers as a "voodoo cult"[12] and a "Muslim goon squad,"[13] the NoI has achieved an impressive institutional longevity that has eluded many other African-American organizations in the twentieth century. Much of the explanation resides in its consistently combining a distinctive theological belief system with a set of political goals, public rhetoric, and practical urban activism that have together singled out the organization as enduringly different from all other groups concerned with advancing African-American welfare in the United States.

Black Nationalism and the Early Nation of Islam

Nationalism is conventionally defined by political scientists as the belief of a group that shares (or alternatively, as a normative aspirational goal, ought to share) a common heritage of language, culture, and religion. Moreover, that heritage, way of life, and ethnic identity are conceived as being manifestly distinct from—though not necessarily superior to—those of other groups. Nationalists believe that members of a particular group ought to rule themselves and should enjoy

full autonomy in determining their own destinies. They should therefore be demonstrably in control of their own social, economic, and
political institutions, to shape entirely as they so desire.[14] The existence of such beliefs among African-Americans is conventionally
termed "black nationalism" and, although its particular political
expressions have differed both over time and among black nationalist
groups, it is within this basic conceptual notion that the NoI is most
clearly and appropriately located.[15]

Although its antecedents date at least as far back as Frederick
Douglas during the second half of the nineteenth century, black
nationalism first emerged as an influential political form and assumed
an identifiable organizational expression in the United States in the
years following the end of World War I. The contemporary political
environment was especially conducive to the development of a racially bounded nationalism in postwar America. Having risked their
lives in defense of American democracy abroad during the "Great
War," black servicemen returned from Europe to the United States to
face extensive racial discrimination and expressions of the deepest
prejudice at home. Black veterans confronted intense competition for
employment and housing opportunities, and many were subject to
grotesque forms of coercion and physical violence, including numerous lynchings. Moreover, far from actually challenging segregation,
the federal government itself perpetuated and spread segregated practices—both in and outside the South—through its own departments
and programs.[16] Many African-Americans therefore became especially
receptive to the political appeals of two nationalist movements then
emerging among U.S. blacks: the United Negro Improvement Association (UNIA) of Marcus Garvey and the Moorish Science Temple of Noble Drew Ali. The NoI's early development drew substantially—
though not exclusively—upon both the urban black constituencies and
the separatist beliefs of these two movements.

The NoI shared many ideological tenets with Marcus Garvey
and the UNIA, in particular.[17] Garvey had arrived in New York from
the Caribbean in 1916 and the following year established a Harlem
branch of the UNIA, which he had originally founded in Jamaica. The
U.S. organization rapidly acquired a membership estimated to exceed
one million black Americans by 1922. Vehemently rejecting the racial
integrationism of the fledgling NAACP, Garvey was the most influential early African-American exponent of a distinctive version of black

separatism: Pan-African nationalism. Garvey held that, ultimately, the only workable solution to black Americans' multiple problems in the United States was physically to leave America and to "return," albeit selectively, to Africa. Although the precise form of the African state that he hoped to establish has been the subject of academic dissensus, its initial intended foundation is generally agreed to have been the (now independent) state of Liberia, to which Garvey had sent several exploratory missions before Britain and France terminated the association.[18]

That Garvey's unequivocal racial separatism was wholly anathema to the integrationist ideals of many members of the black American middle class and intelligentsia was immaterial to the Jamaican agitator. Like Farrakhan subsequently, Garvey's principal target constituency was working class and deprived African-Americans. Seeking to increase their racial consciousness, Garvey vigorously exhorted the mass of African-Americans to revel and glory in their blackness, and argued—again anticipating Farrakhan by over half a century— that the white version of Christianity with which they had been indoctrinated since slavery was designed to achieve their collective racial subservience, not their true and lasting liberation. In its pernicious place, Garvey offered instead an explicitly black form of the Christian faith, complete with black icons, black parables, and a black Christ. Stressing the common origins and shared interests of black peoples throughout the world, Garvey advocated the selective emigration of black Americans to Africa in order to achieve their true freedom and independence.

The parallels with Farrakhan's NoI are at once several, striking, and significant. Drawing recruits largely from impoverished and disadvantaged black Americans in central cities in the Northeast and Midwest, Garvey's message was one of unabashed racial militancy, but one that neither offered nor demanded fundamental political or economic change in established American structures. In offering black Americans a new version of their collective history and in raising their racial pride, Garvey's movement was undeniably of dual political significance to African-Americans. Garvey, however, was fundamentally conservative in terms of his economic philosophy. He strongly urged his black supporters to emulate the white man's dedication to hard work, thrift, and individual responsibility, and called upon black Americans to establish separate industrial, commercial, and financial structures from whites, in order to counter white economic power in America. Enthusiastically championing black free market capitalism, the Jamaican fiercely attacked trade unions, socialists, and Marxists, all of whom he deemed to be implacable foes of black Americans. In the 1924 presidential election, Garvey even urged his (enfranchised) black followers to cast their votes for the Republican nominee, Calvin Coolidge, one of the most racially conservative candidates for the American presidency in the entire twentieth century. The jarring combination of racial militancy and deep conservatism of the Garvey movement thus powerfully presaged that of Farrakhan in these important respects. (Garvey was convicted of mail fraud after a campaign by integrationist activists, committed to prison in 1925, and deported in 1927, eventually to die in London in 1940. Deprived of its leader's crucial guidance, the UNIA rapidly experienced major internal divisions and soon atrophied.[19])

In contrast to Garveyite tenets, members of the Drewish cult essentially sought psychic rather than physical escape from white American oppression. Although both movements shared an abiding and fundamental belief in racial separatism as the only viable solution to black Americans' grievous problems in the United States, that of Noble Drew Ali (Timothy Drew) was essentially religious rather than political in character.[20] Black Americans were instructed by Ali that the white man's destruction both in and outside America was imminent, and that it would be signified by the appearance in the sky of a star with a crescent moon, the traditional symbol of Islam. Although most estimates of its membership put it at a maximum of 30,000, the eschatological beliefs of the Drewish cult accorded its members a collective racial self-confidence and an abiding contempt for white Americans that emboldened them greatly. The movement rapidly splintered, however, when Drew Ali attempted to prevent some of the cult's less spiritually inclined members from exploiting their cofollowers through selling goods and artifacts for profit. Ali was rapidly removed and eventually murdered, and the cult subsequently fragmented and ceased to be even a minimally influential force among urban black Americans by the later 1920s.

By 1930, the vacuum of racial militancy among black Americans caused by the decline of the Garvey and Ali movements was increasingly filled principally, though not exclusively, by Fard's fledgling Nation of Islam. Located within the same black nationalist and separatist traditions, the NoI vigorously espoused the merits of black capitalism and attempted strongly to recruit and win support from deprived urban blacks in central cities across America. Ironically, while its racial nationalism was pronounced, the Black Muslims (like the Garveyites previously) also celebrated and cherished many of the basic values and aspirations of the white petit-bourgeois American society that they superficially appeared to loathe and despise. Indeed, for all their virulent and contemptuous denunciations of the evil white man and congenitally oppressive "blue-eyed devils," the Black Muslims assiduously modeled themselves after certain familiar and conventionally "white" middle-class American ideals: personal cleanliness, fastidious care of the home, thrift, sobriety, diligent and honest hard work (even for a white employer), and obedience to civil authorities—except on grounds of religious obligation—all became moral duties incumbent upon NoI members. Although, therefore, the Black Muslims vehemently rejected the evil white man, they zealously embraced his Protestant ethic, nonetheless.[21]

Having rapidly acquired sufficient African-American supporters and finance to procure a temple for the NoI, Fard was thus able during 1930–33 to attract many of the former followers of Drew Ali and members of the much larger UNIA to join his fledgling black nationalist organization. Like the previous movements, the NoI's history was to prove extremely turbulent. Unlike its immediate spiritual predecessors, however, the NoI was destined to enjoy an institutional longevity and a political future of substantial consequence.

From Fard to Farrakhan: The Nation of Islam in Transition

Farrakhan's political and religious socialization within the NoI has evolved with each of the three distinct stages of political development that the organization has undergone since its initial establishment by Fard in 1930: fundamentalist separatism, liberalization and reform, and revived fundamentalism. Each period was associated with a particular leader of the organization, one who powerfully shaped its doctrinal beliefs and activities according to his personal tenets and particular perceptions of both the demands and opportunities of contemporary circumstances. The two earliest stages also contributed very powerfully to Farrakhan's theological and political education, providing him with the peculiar intellectual legacy and spiritual ballast that have robustly supported his gradual but inexorable ascent to the ranks of national African-American political leadership in the 1990s.

The first phase of the NoI's development, *fundamentalist separatism*, occurred between 1930 and 1964. It was during this period that the Bilalian faith to which Farrakhan so assiduously subscribes assumed its first coherent, if curious, shape. Fard, a traveling salesman, proclaimed in his teachings to black Americans in Detroit that he was a direct descendant of the Prophet Muhammad, his spiritual mission on Earth being to retrieve "The Dead Nation in the West." This nation comprised all American blacks, who had collectively lost their original Islamic faith and, with it, their true self-knowledge as Allah's chosen people, as a result of the peculiar institution of slavery and egregiously harmful white Christian indoctrination. Arrested in May 1933 in connection with a human sacrifice (described in police reports of the time as a "voodoo murder"), Fard was never charged, but was nonetheless ordered by concerned local authorities to leave Detroit.

Assuming the name Elijah Muhammad, Robert Poole rapidly took over the NoI's leadership from Fard. Widely held responsible for Fard's apparently mysterious and untimely disappearance, Muhammad fled several death threats from disgruntled NoI members and rapidly reestablished the organization in Chicago, Illinois, where he first enunciated two of the most important Bilalian doctrines: that Fard had in fact been Allah in human form, and that he, Elijah, was in turn the holy Messenger of Allah. (If necessity is indeed the mother of invention, this new doctrinal departure was certainly very convenient and effective for Elijah in explaining Fard's disappearance to his discontented followers.) Eventually arrested and incarcerated in 1942 for avoiding the U.S. military draft and allegedly being sympathetic to the Japanese cause during World War II, Elijah nonetheless continued to direct his movement from prison, with the outside assistance of his wife. Upon his final release in 1946, Elijah returned to his proselytizing religious work in full.

Under Elijah, Black Islam rapidly became synonymous not only with the Bilalian theology but also with the doctrine of black separatism, by now a well-established and increasingly important strand of American black nationalism. Elijah's NoI advocated separate black development in all spheres, and promoted both collective and individual racial self-reliance and self-assertion as the only legitimate and effective black responses to racial segregation in the United States (both de jure in the American South and de facto in the North). These injunctions essentially entailed the creation of an entirely separate black economy within the United States and the fostering of an identifiable and clear black American national consciousness. The black separatist creed was also a shrewd political recruitment strategy explicitly targeted at disadvantaged, poorer black Americans in the country's major urban centers. Combined with a rigorously conservative code of personal morality, the NoI promoted thrift and sobriety, and strongly disapproved of all displays of hedonism or frivolity, among both members and nonmembers, in African-American communities. Drinking, drug-taking, smoking, fornication, adultery, sexual promiscuity, gambling, lying, stealing, and all forms of idleness among black Americans were entirely prohibited by Elijah and were made punishable by suspension and, ultimately, expulsion from the organization.

The NoI's second stage, *reform and liberalization* (1965–78) was associated with the dramatic internal crisis of 1964–65, and the subsequent rebuilding process. The organization's activism and national public profile among both black and white Americans had received a particular boost during the late 1950s and early 1960s from the activism of the charismatic African-American figure, Malcolm X.[22] Although Malcolm's effective political career was relatively short—lasting from 1952 to 1965—and while several assessments persuasively concur that his political and social influence was much greater in death than during his life,[23] most of it was spent as a loyally devoted follower of, and an extremely dynamic and compelling spokesman for, Elijah Muhammad. Like many of the organization's recruits both before and after, the former drug pusher and pimp had first been converted to the Islamic faith and the NoI while in prison, and he subsequently rose rapidly within the organization to become one of Elijah's most effective, trusted, and dedicated lieutenants in the Black Muslim movement.

A combination, however, of Malcolm's formidable personal power base within the Nation of Islam, his growing popular support among black Americans at large, his increasingly critical attitude to traditional Bilalian doctrines, and his vocal criticisms of Elijah's personal conduct (after revelations concerning the latter's fathering several children through illicit relationships with female NoI members) caused pronounced tensions within the black organization. Malcolm's inopportune description of President John F. Kennedy's assassination, in November 1963, as a case of "chickens coming home to roost" provided Elijah Muhammad with an appropriately convenient pretext upon which to discipline and suspend his preeminent but increasingly errant disciple from the role of national representative, in late 1963 and early 1964.

These increasingly disturbing tensions were rapidly transformed into a formal and irrevocable split between Malcolm and the NoI after his return from a holy pilgrimage to Mecca in 1964, during which Malcolm had experienced a profound feeling of genuine brothership with Muslims of all races. The Mecca *hajj* encouraged Malcolm to convert to the orthodox Sunni Muslim faith and to found two new rival religious and political organizations to Elijah's NoI in the United States: the Muslim Mosque, Inc. and the Organization for Afro-American Unity, respectively. Although both organizations remained closed to white Americans, Malcolm now rejected the core Bilalian belief that whites were intrinsically evil and accepted the legitimate possibility of engaging in selective cooperation with politically sympathetic white Americans in pursuit of racial equality, comity, and economic justice in the United States.[24]

Such clearly heretical views inevitably earned widespread denunciation and fierce criticism from within the increasingly discordant ranks of the Nation of Islam, though not, publicly at least, from Elijah Muhammad personally. Farrakhan, despite (or, perhaps, partially because of) his previous closeness to Malcolm, notoriously denounced him as a "dog" in the NoI's house newspaper, *Muhammad Speaks*, declaring prophetically that:

> Only those who wish to be led to hell or to their doom will follow Malcolm. The die is set, and Malcolm shall not escape . . . Such a man as Malcolm is worthy of death.[25]

After receiving several death threats and surviving a bomb attack upon his family home, Malcolm X was eventually gunned down in controversial circumstances in Harlem's Audubon Ballroom, on February 21, 1965.[26] Although Farrakhan subsequently was widely incriminated in the plot to murder Malcolm, the minister reiterated in a speech in March 1994 that he had had "nothing to do with Malcolm's death." Farrakhan nonetheless conceded that he was among those influential contemporary black American figures who had "created an atmosphere that allowed Malcolm to be assassinated." Betty Shabazz, Malcolm's widow, was long convinced that

Farrakhan was indeed complicit in the murder, arguing that "every-body talked about it" and that its role for Farrakhan functioned as an invaluable, unmistakable, and morbidly distinctive "badge of honor" within the NoI thereafter.[27]

The NoI nonetheless gradually recovered from the consuming crisis precipitated by Malcolm's untimely demise. By the 1970s, the organization began to make an increasingly concerted political appeal to the growing black American middle class and to temper the more virulently offensive expressions of its traditional antiwhite racism. The NoI acquired a multimillion dollar corporate empire, including a bank, publishing facilities, an airplane, an import business, orchards, dairies, small businesses, 4200 acres of farmland, apartment com-plexes, a nationwide chain of supermarkets, barber shops, restaurants and clothing stores, over one hundred temples across the country, and a "palace" in Arizona. Its total assets were estimated by Lincoln to be worth between 80 and 100 million dollars.[28] Although several politi-cal, civil, and religious groups possessed significantly larger member-ships and greater national political legitimacy among African-Americans, few could claim comparably extensive financial support.

Following Elijah's death in 1975, his son, Wallace Deen Muham-mad, acceded to the NoI's leadership, as Farrakhan feared and many NoI insiders had both hoped and confidently predicted. As Marsh observed, upon assuming his father's leadership mantle, the strategic political choice confronting Wallace during the mid-1970s was between three stark alternatives: to continue to seek to change the nature of American society by acquiring a separate state, either therein or in Africa, exclusively for black Americans; to advocate the complete cultural separation of the races in America; or to alter sub-stantially the organization's religious and political doctrines to become more fully compatible with the pluralist nature of the United States' social and political structures. Wallace chose the latter course and, for the subsequent three years, advanced an extensive, unprece-dented, and extremely controversial reform process in the NoI.

The reforms ranged in both scope and importance. Most conten-tiously, the core doctrine of the intrinsic evil of whites was revised and modified to describe instead a more diffuse "devil mentality," which motivated some individual whites to commit evil deeds. Con-sonant with such reformist notions, whites were even invited by Wal-lace to join the organization. Demands for a separate American state for blacks were also abandoned, and members of the NoI were encouraged both to honor the American flag and to vote in elections to public office. The theological doctrines of the NoI were altered to conform more closely to orthodox Sunni Islam beliefs. Significantly, the interior decor of the NoI's mosques saw Arabic motifs replace the anti-American and anti-Christian symbols and slogans that had previously adorned the walls. The strict dress and grooming code of Elijah's organization was abandoned in favor of individual preferences, subject to the basic requirement that clothes remained neat, clean, and nondegrading to Islam. Presiding over such a radical relaxation of the NoI's strict codes of discipline, dress, and rules of personal morality, and dismantling the Fruit of Islam, the militia-style force of young men trained in martial arts (and sometimes firearms) who dealt with all aspects of the group's internal discipline and security, Wallace's leadership constituted the most profound and serious challenge to traditionalist conceptions of the Nation as an unorthodox black separatist, racist, and repressive cult.

Inevitably, such far-reaching reforms encountered strong internal opposition, sufficient ultimately to usher in the third and current stage of the NoI's development, *revived fundamentalism* (1978 to the present). The emergence of the third phase followed an irretrievably deep split between Wallace and Farrakhan, with the former becoming head of the larger and less sectarian World Community of Islam (WCI, within the United States, the American Muslim Mission [AMM]), while the latter assumed the NoI's leadership in 1978, announcing its eventual "rebirth" in January 1981. The WCI (disbanded in 1985) represented a nonexclusive entity that comprised Muslims who believe in Islam; rather than conceiving of themselves as Black Muslims, they were simply Muslims.[29] Farrakhan's group, by contrast, remained inextricably wedded to the unorthodox fundamentalism of Elijah's NoI.

The split—tellingly referred to in NoI circles subsequently as "The Fall of the Nation of Islam"—was occasioned by the increasingly stark and ultimately irreconcilable differences in opinion between Wallace and Farrakhan over the organization's racial vocation and religious philosophy after Elijah's death. Farrakhan had occupied a position as the international spokesman of the NoI under the Wallace interregnum but soon announced his departure in December 1977. He believed adamantly that the move to Orthodox Islam that Wallace had pioneered had caused a substantial decrease in the organization's financial assets and had also contributed powerfully to an increasing lack of discipline among its members, both individually and collectively. Farrakhan, as subsequent developments under his leadership would clearly demonstrate, maintained an uncompromising belief in the fundamentalist doctrines that had been enunciated and propagated by Wallace's father and by Fard Muhammad before him. As a matter of both theological faith and political strategy, Farrakhan held that the NoI's original doctrinal tenets were still central to its continued organizational vitality, its future prospects for recruiting new black members, and the likelihood of increasing its political influence among black Americans in general.

The internal power play also reflected the increasing marginalization of Farrakhan that Wallace Muhammad's acceding to the NoI's leadership appeared, at least to the former, clearly to presage. For Farrakhan, Wallace's assumption of the NoI's premier role entailed deep personal distress, as much for the manifest threat that it posed his demagogic national career prospects as for the material theological and organizational reforms that Wallace sincerely favored. Wallace Muhammad, for his part, perceived Farrakhan's new organization as markedly more political than religious in character. Elijah's son argued that it represented Farrakhan's attempt to stay abreast of the black political freedom movement.[30] The implicit critique was that Farrakhan's opportunism and desire for personal publicity as a serious player in national African-American politics weighed far more heavily upon his personal ambitions than did the Islamic faith to which he regularly paid the most lavish public tribute. Even the most charitable interpretations of Farrakhan's subsequent leadership of the NoI could not easily reject the accuracy of the Wallace interpretation.

For prior to Farrakhan's coup, most scholarly assessments of the NoI held the organization to have been of extremely limited political importance and effect in the United States. Prevailing views saw the black nationalist group as one that primarily promoted agitation and violence[31] and whose prison inmates could not safely be treated like followers of other religions[32]; as an unashamedly racist sect and a personality cult centered principally upon a visceral, collective black hatred of whites[33]; and as the religious dimension of racial strife in America and a genuine danger to American society.[34] In all these interpretations, however, the religious bounds to the NoI's activism were universally viewed as central. Resolutely eschewing participation in the growing civil rights movement, in which thousands of

African-Americans risked their very lives to achieve desegregation in the South, the NoI historically stood expressly outside that conflictual southern theater and, hence, occupied a place on the margins of black American society.

Critics such as Norton have therefore held the NoI's role among African-Americans to have been very limited. That the organization contributed to elevating black Americans' perceptions of their self-worth is conceded by him as an achievement of note. Even in increasing the level of collective race consciousness among northern urban black Americans, however, the NoI encouraged African-Americans to look beyond the NoI for effective political activism, thus compounding the group's political impotence and rendering it fundamentally unable to advance in either membership terms or national black prestige from 1965 onward. Marx, too, attributed the Black Muslims' fundamental lack of political success to the religiously derived separatist dimensions of the organization and to the related fact that black Americans "want in, not out" of mainstream America.[35]

The resurgence of the NoI under Farrakhan, however, has profoundly challenged such complacent assessments. Although Farrakhan's project has been unerringly attentive to opportunities for personal self-aggrandizement, the organization's revival and revitalization—and, not least, its securing new popularity, respect, and prestige—has also been integral to the minister's political advance. The third stage of the NoI's development reflects the dual forces of continuity and change upon which Farrakhan's strategic leadership calculus was originally founded: the former, in the decision explicitly to return the NoI to its traditional theological precepts and organizational disciplines; the latter, in the innovative and unprecedented participation of the NoI in American politics. Above all, though, the NoI's resurgent popularity and the success of the Farrakhan phenomenon have represented functions of the broader changes of post–civil rights era America, which have caused many black Americans to doubt both the possibility and the desirability of ever breaking "in" to the American political, social, and economic mainstream. In response, many have found in the NoI and its charismatic leader new and attractive sources of collective support, solidarity, and even potential salvation.

FARRAKHAN AS LEADER: THE POLITICS OF RADICAL REACTION

Although the political dimension of the NoI's activities under Farrakhan represented a substantial and dramatic departure from its traditional organizational role and doctrinal precepts, the group none-theless displayed substantial continuity with its first incarnation, under Fard and Elijah Muhammad. Upon assuming the leadership of the NoI in 1978, Farrakhan charted an explicit course of rebuilding and revitalizing the organization by reviving its original fundamental-ist theological values and beliefs, and by reintroducing the doctrinaire internal organizational codes and rigid practices that had existed under Elijah's lengthy period as leader. Farrakhan's leadership thus represented the most unequivocal rejection and comprehensive repu-diation of the liberalizing course upon which Wallace Muhammad had embarked in 1975.

Evaluations of the overall organizational success of Farrakhan's leadership strategy are heavily complicated by the unavailability of accurate statistics on the NoI's membership base. Speculative assess-ments by social scientists and media commentators have varied dramatically, even wildly. Dennis King, for example, estimated a membership of around 5,000–10,000 in 1985,[36] whereas Farzana Shaikh argued in favor of a figure of "less than 50,000" in 1990 (this compared with figures for the less sectarian AMM of between 150,000 and almost 1,000,000).[37] C. Eric Lincoln, however, contends that a black membership of between 70,000 and 100,000 in 1993 is "consis-tent with what is known about other aspects of the community."[38] Most critical estimates nonetheless tend to converge around an approximation of only 10,000–20,000 formal NoI members.

Evaluating Farrakhan's political achievement in recruitment terms alone, however, is a very misleading indicator of the effective-ness of his leadership of the NoI since 1978. The NoI's members and publications alike consistently and strongly emphasize that the orga-nization's influence within the national black American community and beyond should not be judged, either exclusively or principally, by the number of its formal, registered members, an argument that is largely persuasive in the light of its evolution during the last two decades. Members of the NoI adhere tenaciously to the (conveniently enigmatic) public maxim that "those who say they know don't know and those who know won't say." More important, however, Farra-khan's political ambitions upon assuming the organization's leader-ship were neither exclusively nor primarily concerned with recruiting new, bona fide members of the NoI. Rather, as Reed argued, the objec-tive that Farrakhan sought in terms of his popular appeal among African-Americans occupied an "intermediate zone" of mass black endorsement, lying somewhere between actual membership of the NoI and a more pro forma popular black American legitimation.[39]

That Farrakhan has largely achieved this core objective is especially notable when the actual content of the NoI's belief system is examined. For the NoI under Farrakhan comprises, at best, a very distinctive—even uniquely eccentric and bizarre—amalgam of cosmological, religious, and ideological currents. Together, these tendencies render the NoI entirely exceptional within the universe of national organizations in the United States dedicated to the improvement of black Americans' political, economic, and social fortunes in the post–civil rights era. Indeed, it is, ironically, in this very distinctiveness, in standing so vividly apart from other black organizations, that much of both the NoI's popular appeal and the most formidable limits to its potential social impact reside among the national African-American community.

Cosmology

The NoI's status as a cosmocentric community accords an exceptionally strong priority to two overarching organizational precepts: first, the need for complete conformity and obedience by its members to authority figures and established doctrines, and second, the preeminent and infallible role of the organization's leader. Membership in the NoI powerfully resembles that of a sectarian political movement, requiring energetic and complete devotion to the cause, enthusiastic imbibing of its canonical sources of collective wisdom, and regular recitation of the required mantras of faith.[40] To be a member in the NoI demands belonging fully to the group, in "body, mind, and spirit," in return for which the NoI belongs to its constituency, corporately and individually. The organization's achievements and mystique are thus replicated in each true believer. The group's primary unifying bond derives from direct, personal allegiance to its leader's exceptional vision, wisdom, will, program, and putative indestructibility. Salvation for individual members consists essentially in the recognition by, and approbation of, the leader, and hence is attainable in this life. In such an avowedly cosmocentric society, as Lincoln argues, "there can be but one loyalty, and it must be to one leader."[41]

The emphasis traditionally accorded the leadership role in the NoI has been of particular political importance for Farrakhan. It is the preeminence accorded the central role of unquestioned fidelity to the leader that Farrakhan has invoked not only to bolster his own position of political authority internally within the NoI, but also as an explanation—to both NoI members and outsiders—for his actions and pronouncements against Malcolm X in 1964–65. Thus, in explicit reference to the NoI's internal mores and codes of practice, in a speech in 1993, Farrakhan said of Malcolm's murder that, "if we dealt with him like a nation deals with a traitor, what the hell business is it of yours?"[42] According to Farrakhan, only the personal instructions of Elijah Muhammad not to harm Malcolm prevented him (and others in the Black Muslim movement) from engaging in more concerted and vigorous attempts to undermine Malcolm in order to assuage the compromised honor of the then leader of the NoI. The doctrine of leadership infallibility has thus served as an extremely useful and powerful legitimating device for Farrakhan, not only in defending his past actions as a loyal and dedicated follower, but also in compelling continual support among the NoI's members currently for his innovative strategic and tactical political decisions, and doctrinal interpretations, as the group's leader since 1978.

Theology and Ideology

Conjoined to its unusual cosmological currents is a distinctive ideological set of beliefs, one that is informed and driven by a theological foundation that is as logically coherent (accept its initial premise, and the rest follows logically) as it is intellectually vapid and morally bankrupt. At its most fundamental, the Nation's ideology combines a stridently aggressive black nationalism with a series of profoundly conservative economic tenets and social convictions. The peculiar combination of biblical allusion, racial militancy, and reactionary public philosophy is one that renders the NoI distinctive and unusual in comparative terms. It also serves to lend the organization and its leader a degree of public ambiguity, in terms of their appropriate ideological locus, that has strongly assisted the broad and amorphous appeal of Farrakhan and the NoI to African-Americans at large.

The NoI's separatist version of black nationalism is most obviously manifest in the organization's core political aims, which comprise: separate black economic and social development; employment and educational equality; freedom for black prisoners; rejection of all attempts at integration with whites; and the achievement of a separate, mineral-rich state (or states) for black Americans as minimum compensation for slavery.[43] Such goals represent relatively familiar core features of the ideological content of the programs of many black nationalist groups since (and, in some instances, prior to) the civil rights movement's landmark political successes during the 1960s.[44] Indeed, the symbolic continuity with the era of "black power" is made explicitly manifest through Farrakhan's personal links with prominent African-American agitators of the time, such as Kwame Toure (formerly Stokely Carmichael), probably the most influential popularizer of that famous slogan. Toure is one of a select group of favored black American political activists—past and present—regularly invited to address larger NoI gatherings, immediately prior to Farrakhan's keynote speeches. The racially separatist political goals of the NoI are not, then, particularly novel in comparison with other black American nationalist groups.

The separatist black nationalism of the NoI under Farrakhan, however, is infused by an explicitly religious dimension that is at once central, esoteric, and frequently overlooked or ignored in both elite and popular evaluations of the organization and its leader. The key feature of Farrakhan's public discourse is not so much its black nationalist or separatist character, which is shared in more or less muted forms by many historic and contemporary black political actors and organizations alike, but rather its particular and peculiar theocratic content, which is shared by none at all. For Farrakhan, neither he, the NoI, nor its members are primarily political actors, in the conventional sense of that term. Rather, they are religious disciples, spiritual warriors engaged upon a divine mission of racial revival and national salvation that is ultimately of nothing less than global importance. The political dimensions of the NoI's activities are principally a function (or, more accurately, an indirect consequence) of its central and dominant religious vocation. Although the theological and spiritual dimensions of Farrakhan's NoI are often neglected or minimized in popular accounts that tend to stress instead its racial militancy and uncompromisingly separatist creedo, the "Islam" component of the organization's title is in fact at least as significant as that of the "Nation." Moreover, the theological origins of Farrakhan's belief system have important political consequences in both ideological and strategic terms for Farrakhan's ongoing public praxis in and outside America.

Theology

Central to both Farrakhan's determined rise within the pre-1975 organization and his subsequent public activities and pronouncements as its leader since 1978 are the two key figures of W. D. Fard and Elijah Muhammad. Together, their theological teachings form the foundation stone upon which the entire edifice of Farrakhan's religious and political faith, and in turn public behavior, is shakily and unattractively constructed. As Elijah's former national representative to America and the world, and subsequently as leader of the NoI, Farrakhan's conception of his national role has been inextricably tied to these two men and their combined social and spiritual legacy: to representing his God (Fard) and spiritual father (Elijah) while the latter was alive and, subsequently, to resurrecting their divinely enlightened teachings after Elijah's death.

According to Bilalian tenets, Elijah was God's solitary student for three years and four to five months (that is, until Fard's untimely disappearance). Farrakhan was thus guided and taught by God, through his final messenger on Earth, Elijah. Thus, Farrakhan and members of the NoI are completely convinced in the fundamental rightness—indeed, the complete infallibility—of the values, analyses, and prescriptions to which they zealously adhere, since these are all divinely derived and therefore possess a uniquely righteous, and hence unchallengeable, authority. As Farrakhan's opening remarks to the National Press Club on July 30, 1984, proclaimed:

> I represent the Honorable Elijah Muhammad, a Messenger and Warner from Allah to Black people, and the world. I do not speak to you from mere personal desire, I speak in the Name of the God who raised up the Honorable Elijah Muhammad and I am backed by them both. [45]

Like Malcolm before him, Farrakhan frequently prefaces his public remarks by stating, "The Honorable Elijah Muhammad teaches that ..." Farrakhan's "voice" is therefore most assuredly not one of complete autonomy and independence, but rather that of the most loyal and assiduous student, articulating a litany of divinely revealed truths and prophecies, conveyed directly and personally by the holiest and most infallible of enlightened spiritual teachers.

Farrakhan's frequent self-reference as simply a dedicated student of Elijah serves three important political functions for the NoI's leader. First, it enables him to draw upon an historic lineage that is unavailable to many other contemporary national black American political leaders. Farrakhan's political entrepreneurship is not a matter of personal career aggrandizement or advancement, in this interpretation, but is instead located within deep historic roots and in direct encounters with (and instructions from) God's final messenger on Earth. Second, and connected to such a powerful historic lineage, the self-reference provides a useful pretext of personal modesty and deep humility to a political role that is, in every other respect, based upon the most persistent self-promotion and the steady but unrelenting accumulation of nationwide political attention centered unremittingly upon the individual leader. Third, the avowed student status underlies Farrakhan's recurrent public claims that both he and the organization that he leads are frequently misrepresented in and by the American mass media. Farrakhan's erroneous ascriptive designation as "leader" of the NoI by print and television commentators—when he is a mere representative and a follower of its genuine spiritual leader—is portrayed by him as an example of the deliberate failure (or the clear inability) of outsiders accurately and fully to understand the Black Muslim movement, its structure, and its most cherished beliefs.

As his Million Man March speech demonstrated to a national American audience, Farrakhan draws liberally upon both the Koran and the Bible to support his many claims. An accomplished and keen student of scripture, Farrakhan invokes apposite parables and verses at ease. The shrewd strategy reflects both his own early Christian upbringing and the tactical necessity of appealing to the mass of African-Americans by invoking their own religious beliefs. In doctrinal terms, however, the two most important sources of instruction for Farrakhan's theological claims and political arguments—as for Malcolm X before him—are Elijah Muhammad's treatises, *Message to the Black Man in America* and *The Fall of America*.[46] Together, these turgid tomes serve as the twin functional theological equivalents for Farrakhan that Karl Marx's secular *Communist Manifesto* and *Capital* once represented for Lenin and Trotsky. Farrakhan's contemporary public discourse and rhetoric flow directly from what Elijah taught him between 1934 and 1975 and from the divine pearls of collected wisdom contained in the two texts. If Farrakhan departs from Elijah's voice at all as the NoI's contemporary leader, it is merely to accord his mentor's beliefs greater conceptual clarity, and to lend them a more modern application, where such is either necessary or desirable (such as in endorsing Jesse Jackson's 1984 presidential bid as divinely sanctioned and blessed, for example).

Four distinct, though related, features of the religious dimension that is contained in Elijah's writings are especially prominent, important, and, to many Americans, utterly preposterous features of Farrakhan's public discourse: first, the biblical ancestry of African-Americans; second, the inevitable and violent fall of America in a global apocalypse; third, the overarching need for separation of the races in the United States prior to God's final judgment and the resulting Armageddon; and, fourth, Farrakhan's personal status as a messianic figure and prophetic race savior. Collectively, these beliefs serve powerfully to distinguish the NoI not only from other Islamic groups, but also from every other organization seeking currently to improve black Americans' political, economic, and social welfare in the United States. Together, the beliefs mark Farrakhan vividly apart from all other African-American leaders. Although muted or accorded varying degrees of emphasis according to the particular venue, occasion, and (actual or intended) audience, these four convictions are, nonetheless, absolutely fundamental to Farrakhan's worldview.

Central to the black nationalism of the NoI under Farrakhan is a core theological belief in the privileged biblical ancestry of black Americans collectively. In an ironic mirror of Judaistic belief in the Jews' role as the Almighty's "chosen" people, the 30 million-plus black Americans in the United States currently represent, for Farrakhan, "God's elect." According to Farrakhan, the "peculiar institution" of black slavery in America was an historic inevitability, since it was actually preordained and divinely sanctioned by Allah (God). The presence of blacks in America therefore assumes a major religious significance, their current condition being fundamentally prophetic in nature. The shameful and tragic character of blacks' history in America marks them out for their divine status. The Bible prophesied a people living at the temporal end of the world to whom a "warner" would be sent and, among the four "races" of the world (according to Farrakhan, Jews, whites, Muslims, and blacks), only blacks had not yet received such an enlightened visitor by 1930.

The basis for Farrakhan's idiosyncratic view, and the foundation upon which the NoI's predictive assertions of imminent black American deliverance rest, is typically identified as being the Book of Genesis, chapter 15, verses 13–14:

> And he God said unto Abraham, know of a surety that thy seed shall be a stranger in a land that is not theirs, and shall serve them, and they shall afflict them four hundred years; And also that nation whom they shall serve, will I judge; and afterward shall they come out with great substance.

Black Americans are argued by Farrakhan to be the direct descendants of the family of the biblical Abraham, the "lost-found nation of the tribe of Shabazz" and the seed of God. Forcibly removed from the continent of Africa in the 1500s, the descendants of the tribe were brutally imported, as private property, to the land that subsequently became known as America. The present black American population is thus the direct progeny of the original Shabazz tribe.

The peculiar institution of slavery in the United States was therefore unavoidable, since it formed part of a broader plan designed by God some 6000 years previously. However, after a period of 430 years of painful oppression, the Book of Exodus notes that the children of Israel eventually left their land of bondage to achieve their true liberation. The date of black Americans' freedom was thus set, according to Farrakhan, for midnight, December 31, 1985, some 430 years after their initial bondage in America. Fard's arrival in 1930 was designed to alert African-Americans to the circumstances of their plight and the methods by which freedom could be secured by that date, fifty-five years hence. Had Elijah not recognized his divine credentials, however, Fard would have left America earlier than 1934, and the fate of African-Americans would have thereby been irretrievably sealed in doom-laden perpetuity.[47]

This belief distinguishes Farrakhan sharply from the vast majority of contemporary national black American political and civic leaders in two key respects. First, while most black religious, civic, and political leaders would undoubtedly concur that black American history—and the turbulent shape of America's social and political development in general—has been profoundly influenced by African-Americans' forced importation to America as private property, few (if any) would accord the peculiar institution the pervasively malign influence that Farrakhan discerns. For Farrakhan, however, the present condition of blacks in America is by definition inseparable from, and is adequately explained by, the slave period. The origins of black Americans have ensured that they remain a totally "invented" people, without a homeland either in America or Africa, materially impoverished, emotionally crippled, and psychologically destitute. The Thirteenth Amendment admitted into American society as full participants a social group whose members were wholly unprepared and unsuited for their new status. Slavery was deliberately intended, originally, to bring about the creation of a new type of earthly being, neither necessarily nor fully human in character. According to Farrakhan, even the term "Negro" originated not from the Spanish word for "black," but rather from the Greek term "necropolis," meaning "cemetery" or "place of the dead." Black Americans are thus conceived by Farrakhan to be psychologically, spiritually, and emotionally dead and, hence, in need of the most complete and enlightened reeducation, a function that he and the NoI under him exist exclusively and selflessly to provide in the most generous of fashions.

The second consequential facet of black Americans' privileged ancestry concerns the date of their divinely prescribed release from collective racial bondage in the United States. The notion of black freedom being set for the beginning of 1986 onward has afforded a clear religious rationale—even a spiritual imperative—for Farrakhan's concerted efforts exponentially to increase the secular activism of the NoI in conventional American politics. Although occurring prior to the date of African-American freedom, the courageous activism of black American civil and political leaders such as Garvey, Du Bois, King, and Malcolm X was not entirely futile, in Farrakhan's view; it served as a necessary foundation for the current black political struggle. Nonetheless, black Americans at large only possessed sufficient potential to achieve their full mental and spiritual independence from 1986 onward. The imperative to reeducate them in order to ensure that they fully realized that potential has therefore served as the central basis for Farrakhan's leading the NoI into hitherto uncharted territories of mass mobilization and "mainstream" political activity, such as voter registration drives and election campaigning. Collective deliverance of African-Americans requires divinely influenced guidance; Farrakhan generously offers such enlightened and spiritually informed leadership at the appropriate historic moment for American blacks.

Linked to black Americans' uniquely privileged biblical ancestry and the momentous historic opportunities of the present is the second crucial constant in Farrakhan's theological black nationalism: belief in the inevitability of the decline, and ultimate fall, of the United States, in what the NoI's leader refers to variously as "the War" and the "Battle of Armageddon." Four centuries of brutal enslavement in America have left black Americans as the "lost sheep," "the dry bones in the valley," and the "despised and rejected." America represents the biblical Babylon; its president is the effective evil King of the corrupt, degenerate, and doomed land; and the cities of Los Angeles and San Francisco serve as its modern Sodom and Gomorrah.[48] Armageddon—the ultimate and decisive conflict between good and evil—will bring about the end of the present, evil, white-dominated world and the illustrious beginning of a newly righteous kingdom of God on Earth, one in which black Americans are finally spiritually, emotionally, and mentally reborn. Although the ensuing apocalypse will be global in scale, the war will commence in America, precisely because of its history of African enslavement and its subsequent mistreatment of American blacks. African-Americans will, nonetheless, emerge as the brave vanguard of human liberation in the war and as its clear eventual victors. Finally achieving true and complete emancipation, their role thereafter in the new righteous world will be to serve as its humanitarian leaders and hortatory teachers, offering appropriately enlightened spiritual instruction both to America and the rest of the world.

The inevitable global conflagration that awaits humanity gives logical rise to the third critical feature of Farrakhan's iconoclastic theological system, namely, the need for the full separation of the races in America prior to the imminent Armageddon. Racial separation is a necessary prerequisite and prelude to the collective judgment that is prophesied in Genesis as being inevitable for both Abraham's offspring and the corrupt Babylonian land that they currently inhabit. God did not desire his chosen people to be linked to their tyrannical master at the time of the latter's punishment, and he therefore encouraged the Israelites to leave the land of Pharaoh to establish their own independent nation. As Farrakhan observes:

> God raises up Moses not to tell Pharaoh "let's get chummy," not to tell Pharaoh "let's integrate," but God came to Pharaoh through Moses to warn Moses that . . . the time of Israel's deliverance had come.[49]

In this interpretation, the bondage of Jews by the Egyptians was not historical fact but rather prophetic allegory—the Jews of the Bible are the black Americans of today, not the Jews of ancient times.

The need for racial separation in America further reflects the inherent evil of the white race. Whites, along with all nonblack races, were originally conceived in a failed medical experiment on the island of Patmos by a mad black scientist named Dr. Yakub, a troublesome malcontent who was exiled from an original black Eden centered in Mecca, many thousands of years ago.[50] The most degenerate of all the half-breed races, whites were accorded the role of persecuting blacks, until the appearance of an enlightened Messenger (Fard). The Messenger would alert blacks to their true state, the real nature of their white oppressors, and the means by which genuine and lasting freedom could best be attained. Farrakhan's version of history also bears out the original doctrinal teachings of Fard, according to which whites have indeed been responsible for most of the evil that has occurred in the world. People of color, in particular, have consistently been the subject of white abuse and assault through colonialism, imperialism, and segregation, and so, for Farrakhan, the imperative for black Americans to distance themselves absolutely from such manifestly evil forces is self-evidently great.

The precise form that the necessary and complete separation of the races must assume has varied in character and over time, from an ambitious Garveyesque goal of physical and territorial separation to a somewhat more modest objective of mental and cultural retrenchment. Initially, the NoI sought the achievement of independent black territory or a block of mineral-rich American states to be set aside as a black homeland, owned, maintained, and developed exclusively for and by African-Americans. This remains the goal of the demands printed each week in *The Final Call*. Over recent years, however, the emphasis in Farrakhan's lectures and sermons has increasingly altered toward stressing a mental and cultural separation from white America.[51] Black Americans must, by this interpretation, studiously refrain from adopting "white" American norms, values, ideologies, mores, folkways, and lifestyles. Only through a true and complete knowledge of both Allah and self can black Americans achieve their full and authentic independence of thought and action as human beings. Whether physical or mental, though, the attempts that have been made in the postwar era in general, and the post–civil rights era in particular, to integrate the races in America have vividly demonstrated to Farrakhan the total futility of hope for peaceful coexistence between the races and the centrality of misguided integrative efforts to the United States' current (and, should such foolish efforts persist, future) racial problems.

The NoI's emphasis under Farrakhan on racial separation echoes the arguments of the Kerner Report on Civil Disorder in 1968, albeit with an implicit enthusiasm rather than explicit regret. Indeed, Farrakhan even cited Otto Kerner's famous conclusions in his speech at the Million Man March. Established by President Lyndon B. Johnson to investigate the sources of and potential solutions to America's urban crises of the mid to late 1960s, the Commission report represented a damning indictment of the contemporary condition of relations between black and white citizens in America. Prescriptively, Kerner argued that, in the absence of meaningful and effective public and private action to reduce the socioeconomic differences between the races, within twenty years the distance between black and white Americans would have become so wide as to be unbridgeable. Unity and comity would become impossible. Black and white Americans would physically inhabit the same nation but they would do so as two effectively separate, unequal, and hostile communities.

For Farrakhan, by the mid-1980s, American politics and society were indeed replete with multifarious indications of black and white relations in the United States having finally, completely, and irrevocably exhausted themselves. Among white Americans, the resurgence of the Ku Klux Klan, Aryan Nation, and other white supremacist groups; the several antiaffirmative action decisions of the U.S. Supreme Court under Chief Justices Warren Burger and William Rehnquist; the conservative policies of successive Republican administrations; and the incidence of sporadic, violent attacks upon black Americans and black institutions by whites all represented powerful symptoms of a white America that was attempting, increasingly and aggressively, to free itself from the troublesome aftermath of slavery and its unwanted black legacy. Among African-Americans too, growing disorder, rebelliousness, and disrespect for what were widely perceived as white-controlled institutions, laws, and practices suggested to Farrakhan that the great U.S. racial divide was widening even further in an inexorable fashion. Subconsciously, at least, black Americans were gradually responding to a majority-white nation that neither needed its black members any longer, nor cared for them, nor even knew precisely what to do with them. Otto Kerner's fears were thus being fully realized in the most dramatic and unequivocal of fashions.

Such clear signs of increasingly imminent racial crisis of course offered rewarding opportunities to advance the fourth feature of Farrakhan's theological worldview: his own, personal role as the prophetic race savior. The German philosopher Hegel once defined the "great man" as being the one "who actualizes his age." And in his words and deeds since assuming the NoI's leadership, Farrakhan manifestly conceives himself to be a great man—a messianic and prophetic figure of destiny whose historic hour had finally arrived. The biblical analogy is clear, after all. Black Americans resemble the people to whom Jesus arose, a people possessing eyes but not sight, ears but not hearing, tongues but not speech. Farrakhan views his national task as being to activate the dormant senses and the stunted critical faculties of black Americans at large. For Farrakhan, "Jesus" is a job description rather than the name of a particular historic figure—a revolutionary opponent of inequality, injustice, and prejudice whose passivity, patience, and tolerance in the face of oppression is a gross misrepresentation of the truth, originally perpetrated upon gullible black Americans by a manipulative and mendacious white slave-owner class, intent upon exercising complete social control and diffusing all forms of African-American protest. If the truth be told, there are in fact five entities known as Jesus, of which he, Farrakhan, (alongside the original Jesus, Fard, Elijah, and NoI members collectively) is one. The language in which Farrakhan's prophetic mission of racial salvation is described hence draws heavily upon resonant biblical images that project him as a beneficent savior of his long-oppressed people:

> I want to provide some comfort for the sheep of Almighty God who have not been led to green pastures, whose soul has not been restored, who have not been led in the path of righteousness for God's namesake. I want to be a good shepherd in the midst of a people who have had thieves and robbers in front of them as leaders.[52]

If the four claims that form the nucleus of Farrakhan's theology evince an undeniably coherent logic (bizarre and incredible, admittedly, but by no means incoherent), they nonetheless raise many more questions than they purport to answer. As a purely theological matter, for example, it is notably unclear how Farrakhan's claim that black slavery in America was preordained by God can be either fully or adequately reconciled with his argument that the United States is ultimately to be judged, and held to final account, by God because of its enslavement of blacks. It would appear, at best, perverse that God should hold to account a nation or people for a course that he had predetermined and for which they could hence exercise no free or conscious choice. The important argument for Farrakhan, though, is that Armageddon, the impending end of the existing (that is, white-dominated) pattern of race relations, and the full emancipation of black Americans is an historical inevitability, according to divine pre-scription. The apocalyptic conflagration of the races around the world is as inevitable as the sun's rising in the morning.

Of course, Farrakhan's manifest confidence in the inevitability of Armageddon also confronts certain evidential problems in terms of the accuracy of his prophetic analysis. For example, during the early 1980s, Farrakhan predicted—much as he has continued to do so sub-sequently—that the inevitable racial apocalypse was imminent. Presi-dent Ronald Reagan then represented a "blessing in disguise" to black Americans, a deliverance from God. Reagan professed a strong personal belief in good and evil; included among his Cabinet and White House staff evangelical Christians who themselves adhered to explicitly fundamentalist conceptions of the ultimate conflict between good and evil; presided over America at the date of blacks' release from the slave mentality (thus making the president the most impor-tant white man ever to have lived); and possessed a name (Ronald Wilson Reagan) whose letters, when added sequentially, totaled 666, the notorious biblical number of the Beast.[53] Although God knew that black Americans wanted former Vice-President Walter Mondale to win the 1984 presidential election, he apparently returned Reagan to the White House, in a landslide popular and electoral college victory, to give blacks not what they wanted, but what they instead needed to free themselves, according to Farrakhan. (No doubt the families and accountants of many professional political consultants and media advisors were especially appreciative of GOP operatives' ignorance about the presence of such decisively divine electioneering interven-tions in 1984.)

Reagan's momentous temporal presence, and the imminent glo-bal war that it presaged, thus strongly encouraged Farrakhan's ener-getic bouts of national activism. In typically individualistic and distinctive fashion, Farrakhan was one of the handful of outspoken national black American leaders during the 1980s to defend the con-servative Republican president's personal integrity:

> It is not that Mr. Reagan is insensitive. The man is looking at the economy of the country. You do not understand that the econ-

omy of the country is so weak today that Mr. Reagan must make cuts in order to save what he can. You know, if you're in an airplane and you lose an engine, they must look around for expendable baggage. "What can we jettison, what can we throw off to make it lighter?" I know you feel bad being in that position, as expendable baggage. Well, that's not Mr. Reagan's fault. That's our fault.[54]

Faced with such a grievously bleak picture, Farrakhan predicted that Reagan would soon proceed to undertake direct negotiations with the NoI's leader, personally, in order to save white America and that, unless this occurred, black Americans would either be "free or dead" by 1990. Americans probably needn't rush en masse to consult the history books at length to discover that these particular predictions were not, in fact, realized. Rather, they attested to a visionary quality on Farrakhan's part that remains more pathetically deficient than divinely prophetic in nature.

Perhaps, in this light, Farrakhan's many luridly colorful convictions should be dismissed as entirely irrelevant to his political importance. Whether on the grounds of the very tenuous and uncertain connection with reality that they manifest, or on the basis that they matter little to the true foundations of his popular appeal among African-Americans, such a view could certainly be plausibly advanced. While the religious beliefs that Farrakhan evinces are, however, at best distinctive and unusual in character, they nonetheless remain central to his view of the destiny of black Americans, as well as the ultimate fate of the United States and the entire world. Although his public discourse since the late 1980s has increasingly avoided a full enunciation of his theological beliefs (especially when white audiences are observing his pronouncements closely, as at the Million Man March), Farrakhan's values, attitudes, and prescriptions for black Americans' collective advancement are all inextricably bound to the revived fundamentalist theological foundation of the NoI. That the vast majority of African-Americans neither know of nor share his exotic theological views has not substantially inhibited his national political ascendancy thus far. Ironically, popular ignorance of Farrakhan's belief system represents a positive element in (and perhaps even a necessary condition of) his achieving mass African-American support. Nevertheless, the tangential relevance of Farrakhan's iconoclastic theology to his

popular black appeal hardly diminishes the profound significance—
and the peculiarity—of such an idiosyncratic public figure winning
broad African-American approval.

Ideology

The impressively eclectic theological dimensions of the Black
Muslim leader's worldview are important not only in themselves, but
also because they powerfully inform and shape the NoI's values, beliefs, and organizational practices more broadly. In particular, by
virtue of its connection to Farrakhan's avowedly theocratic, quasi-
Islamic, and separatist variant of black nationalism, the social, cultural,
and economic conservatism of the NoI is especially pronounced. On
matters of diet, gender, sexual and interracial relations, as well as
economic philosophy, Farrakhan's NoI endorses a markedly conservative—indeed, a quintessentially reactionary—agenda for African-
Americans and nonblacks alike. Like many conservatives, Farrakhan
zealously champions and celebrates what one critic has labeled the
"vigorous virtues" (most notably, independence, personal responsibility, and individual initiative).[55] Farrakhan's ideal American world,
however, is one in which professional women, unmarried mothers,
homosexuals, mixed-race couples, and free-thinkers are all decidedly
unwelcome. At once profoundly inegalitarian, strongly conformist,
deeply illiberal, and blessed by an expressly divine and infallible
imprimatur, Farrakhan's desperately bleak and dispiriting vision is a
reactionary's delight and an Epicurean's nightmare.

The critical religious and racial imperatives to reject dominant
American values, mores, and lifestyles that form such a prominent element of Farrakhan's worldview inevitably compel a profound alteration in the general behavioral patterns of the NoI's members.
Following Elijah's instructions and adhering to a strictly orthodox
interpretation of the Koran, strong emphasis therefore is attached
within the NoI to a very strict dietary code and to the tenets of personal discipline, respectable appearance and dress, individual responsibility, and an unremitting loyalty to the organization's leadership.

In achieving an effective mental and cultural separation from
whites, diet represents an especially important component of black
independence in modern America. Both Elijah and Farrakhan consistently stress the overarching imperative to end completely African-
American consumption of the "slave master's diet," and Elijah's

strictures and injunctions on the subject are regularly reprinted in weekly copies of *The Final Call*. For example, Elijah attributed the high incidence among black Americans of serious health problems, such as diabetes, heart disease, hypertension, and cancer, to an excessive intake by African-Americans of carbohydrates, sugars, and pork products, against which "divine" prohibitions were issued.[56] Fasting was also emphasized by Elijah as an especially desirable goal to which NoI members should dedicate themselves to achieving.

Farrakhan, too, has attributed the primary cause of many contemporary black health problems to African-Americans having never been properly taught how or what to eat, and hence having developed an unhealthy reliance principally upon food items produced by others, and in particular, by whites. To combat such deficiencies, dietary regulations of the NoI include eating only one meal in every twenty-four-hour period, and participating in a three-day fast at the end of each month. The general underlying goal is for blacks to strive to consume food in longer and longer intervals. The establishment of the NoI's Salaam restaurant on Chicago's south side, in 1995, represented a material realization of these convictions about the need for black autonomy in matters of diet (although, in common with the many inconsistencies that are a notable hallmark of the NoI under Farrakhan, its appetizing menus hardly represent great culinary frugality[57]).

Farrakhan's dietary prescriptions do not differentiate sharply between male and female NoI members, but the NoI leader's views on gender relations exhibit markedly traditionalist tendencies and deeply inegalitarian currents that draw very clear and rigid distinctions between the sexes. As can be inferred from the title of his mentor's main instructive treatise, the NoI's principal focus for attention has consistently been the black man in the United States. Nonetheless, Elijah Muhammad's message to the black American male also comprised an implicit, but equally fundamental, one to the black American woman: subordination. Thus, consonant with Bilalian biblical teachings, the role of women within the Black Muslim movement is carefully and deliberately prescribed, their being assigned to a fundamentally subordinate role within a patriarchal family, in which the functions of childbearing and childrearing assume their principal preoccupation and primary social importance. Farrakhan's (no doubt benevolent) paternalism is pronounced:

What black man can be a real man when he is unable to offer security to his wife and security to his children? Paul in the New Testament said, "As Christ is the head of the man, man is the head of the woman." But how can a man be a head of his woman, even be the head of his household, without knowledge, without wisdom, without economic wherewithal?[58]

For Farrakhan, the role of gender is fundamental not only in religious but also in historical terms for black Americans. As a result of white America's consistent and consciously destructive efforts, the black male in the United States has essentially been emasculated, and the black woman, in consequence, has been forced to bear a tremendous and excessive social burden. If the distant genesis of an emergent feminist discourse perhaps exists herein, however, it is nonetheless overwhelmed by Farrakhan's avowed view of the African-American woman's role. Following Malcolm X's epigrammatic advice that "to educate a woman is to liberate a nation," the unresolved issue in the modern NoI remains, educate to do what, precisely? Thus, Farrakhan's analysis typically conflates an apparently generous and lavish praise of black American women's ascribed personal qualities with interconnected explanations for the perceived failings and deficiencies of African-American males:

> . . . as Black men we've been castrated. We feel so threatened by the high degree of intelligence, aggressiveness, and forthrightness of our women. It only shows that we have not been afforded the opportunity under this social, economic, and political system to grow to our full potential as men. Our women have had a little more freedom to grow.[59]

That disproportionate African-American female liberty does not extend, however, to issues of reproductive rights, as far as Farrakhan is concerned. Abortion, for example, is opposed by the NoI's leader on the grounds that "when the black woman kills her unborn child, she is murdering the advancement of her nation."[60] Black Americans in general need to be taught techniques of "self-control" rather than birth control, according to the NoI's traditionalist social tenets.

While African-American women are admitted to the Black Muslim movement and have served selectively as both ministers[61] and security guards,[62] the NoI's prescribed views on gender roles are nonetheless stringently traditionalist and essentialist. Although Farrakhan appointed a female member of the NoI to the Mosque Maryam ministry in Chicago and has also made many public statements that apparently affirm the great importance of black women in the group, the internal organization of the NoI seems clearly to contradict such views. According to one female former NoI member, for example, upon joining the organization, black American women receive instruction in seven "basic" units: cooking; sewing; raising children; taking care of her husband; proper behavior inside the home; care of the home; and proper behavior outside the home.[63] Lest they be deluded into notions that such patronizing instruction might possibly hamper their full development as fundamentally equal human beings, NoI women are assured that they may pursue any area of interest and realize their many talents to the full—subject to the crucial condition that such ambitious endeavors do not compromise their "true nature." African-American women in Farrakhan's NoI are evidently intended to occupy a bleak state of "modified domestic purdah,"[64] such that even Murphy Brown might yearn for Dan Quayle's progressive and compassionate feminism by comparison.

The prohibition upon black American women participating in the October 1995 March on Washington was perhaps the most explicit and well-known example of the essentially patriarchal nature of the NoI's structure and public prescriptions. While black women were asked to assist in the national organization of the march, they were also requested not to participate or attend the event. The obvious tension was consonant with the subtly drawn distinction that Farrakhan offered in explanation, observing that "we are not saying that a woman's place is in the home; we are saying that a woman's base is in the home."[65] Although many black women attended despite the prohibition, the event was clearly intended by its organizers to be wholly exclusive in its gender, as well as in its racial, composition. While some critics attribute the patriarchal character of the organization to second-tier male administrators rather than to Farrakhan personally (despite his adamant rejection of female attendance at the march),[66] the hierarchical, leader-centric nature of the NoI strongly suggests that sexist stereotyping and paternalistic practices could effectively be eliminated if the NoI's leader so desired. That this has not occurred is a far more powerful indicator of the character of the NoI's gender politics

and its leader's convictions about the sexes than are Farrakhan's intermittent public commendations of the African-American woman's crucial social role and many admirable achievements.[67]

Almost inevitably, given his preoccupation with race as the sole
analytic category of social and political importance, issues of gender
relations are also crosscut by Farrakhan's unequivocal advocacy of
racial separatism in all social and cultural matters. Thus, paralleling
the prejudiced prescriptions of bigots, racialists, and white American
supremacist groups through the ages—and echoing the teachings of
Elijah and Malcolm X before him—Farrakhan opposes interracial relationships in the United States (in typically lurid and vitriolic terminology). The white American man having "pumped his blood" into
black females during slavery, African-Americans were as a result rendered persistently "weak and susceptible" to whites' "evil, filthy, and
indecent way of life." The prevalence among blacks of drug-taking,
alcohol consumption, prostitution, gambling, and other "sinful" activities can thus be directly traced to the forcible injection of impure and
degenerate "white" ideas into previously untainted and uncontami-
nated black American communities, through such brutally coercive
and vicious interracial liaisons. Black Americans must therefore steadfastly avoid further contamination by whites as a fundamental prerequisite of their collective purification and full redemption. Farrakhan's
antimiscegenistic message is, typically, directed at the African-American male:

> Take this beautiful Black woman—she's your Queen! She's your
> jewel! Don't let a white man get near this Black woman . . . And
> last but not least, Black Man, don't let that white man at anytime
> in your life give you his white woman! We don't want her! We
> don't want her![68]

Such puerile and base sentiments are, as far as groups such as the
Aryan Nation are concerned, evidently mutual. Moreover, given such
shared convictions, it is at best unclear as to whether Farrakhan
would agree—on either legal or normative grounds—with the
Supreme Court's landmark decision in 1967 that state prohibitions
upon interracial marriage violated the U.S. Constitution.[69] Farrakhan's organic conceptions of race are instead powerfully suggestive
of a wholesale rejection of the right of individuals to choose their

particular partners regardless of racial background; an anti-individualistic and morally contemptible position powerfully at odds with American creedal values, though not the nation's historic practice.

Farrakhan's views on sexual politics also encompass a miscellany of markedly illiberal and traditionalist views. The NoI's de facto constitution, "What the Muslims Want, What the Muslims Believe" (published in *The Final Call*), for example, calls for members found guilty of fornication or adultery to be suspended from the organization for certain prescribed periods of time (a suspension to which Elijah was, of course, notoriously and consistently exempt). Besides such immoral activity, though, Farrakhan also harbors a profound antipathy toward homosexuality, which he views as "submission to circumstances rather than anything genetic or innate." Derogatory references by Farrakhan to former New York City Mayor Ed Koch's alleged homosexuality and the vicious Kean College speech of his national spokesperson, Khalid Muhammad, attracted widespread accusations of virulent homophobia from gay rights groups. Viewing AIDS as an explicit and incontrovertible manifestation that "there is a problem somewhere in this kind of social behavior," Farrakhan advocates repressive measures to deal with both the disease and its carriers:

> . . . if AIDS is a communicable disease it has to be quarantined until we can correct it. If I were walking the streets with tuberculosis in the days when they didn't have the kind of cures for tuberculosis that they have today, it was almost mandatory that they take me off the streets. That's not a crime against my humanity; it is protection for my humanity and the humanity of others by taking me and putting me in a sanitarium until I can be relieved of that which I am suffering. Then I can enter back into society.[70]

Whether this entails the incarceration of all homosexuals as well as those diagnosed as HIV carriers is—no doubt deliberately—difficult to discern from Farrakhan's public comments. What is more certain, however, is that, as he argued in *A Torchlight for America*, homosexual behavior offends the proper standards of moral behavior established by God, and the "circumstances" that bring it about must be eliminated. Indeed, in encouraging less promiscuous sexual behavior, among both homosexuals and heterosexuals, Farrakhan even holds that ultimately AIDS "will turn out to be something good."[71] For

Farrakhan, fatal viruses evidently serve as timely and effective "cures" for sexually heretical behavior and inappropriate lifestyles.

Thus, in the conflict over issues of cultural values and "lifestyle" choice that has become such a prominent and divisive feature of recent national American politics, Farrakhan clearly occupies a strongly traditionalist rather than a progressive social stance.[72] The degenerative societal problem lies in the deficient behavior of particular individuals and social groups, not in the prejudiced attitudes of others toward certain modes of behavior. Were it not for the antiwhite bigotry in which they are frequently clouded, most of Farrakhan's traditionalist cultural values and moral convictions would be shared and heavily endorsed by Christian evangelicals such as Pat Robertson and Jerry Falwell, white conservative figures whose enthusiasm and activism on behalf of black American advancement have never assumed particularly prominent places on their political and religious resumes. Like them, too, Farrakhan's convictions on matters of morality and ethics tend to be strongly infused by the scapegoating discourse of censure and condemnation, to be dominated more by a lengthy litany of the many evils and vices that he is adamantly "against" than of the virtues that he is "for"—an exemplar of an antipolitics of familiar, though undistinguished, historical pedigree in the United States.

Farrakhan's cultural conservatism also encompasses his analysis of black Americans' current social and economic problems more generally, though. Paralleling his traditionalist views on matters of morality, Farrakhan's analysis of the so-called "Negro problem" is focused more on individual failings than on the historic, structural inequalities of American society, an analysis that—much as it targets homosexuals rather than homophobia for disapprobation and censure—frequently comes perilously close to blaming black people for not being economically successful. Farrakhan views the central societal problems confronting disadvantaged African-Americans in the contemporary United States through an ideological prism analogous to that of David Duke and the radical white American right, albeit one shaped by a peculiar theological derivation.[73] Given their shared belief in the notion of racial essences and purity, this interpretative commonality between Farrakhan and white racialists is hardly surprising. Nonetheless, it serves as yet another example of the very substantial distance that exists between Farrakhan and the vast majority of national African-American political actors.

Thus, in Farrakhan's view, the grievous maladies confronting many black American communities are neither exclusively nor primarily economic in character (poverty, unemployment, and dispossession) but are rather behavioral, attitudinal, and pathological in nature (drugs, crime, and general social dislocation). Separation of the races is hence, according to the Farrakhan analysis, fundamentally beneficial for African-Americans. Free from a malign white influence, black behavioral dysfunction can be diagnosed, challenged, and ultimately corrected under the beneficent auspices of the NoI. Consistent with such a notion, Farrakhan also holds that, historically, black-owned businesses were more numerous and successful under the legally sanctioned segregation of the Jim Crow era and, further, that the civil rights legislation that brought that era to an end has in fact caused black Americans general harm. Moreover, Farrakhan adamantly rejects the notion of governmental responsibility for citizen welfare in the United States and is, at best, ambivalent with regard to the secular character of the American state.

It is thus acutely ironic—and misleading—that many popular accounts often portray Farrakhan as the modern African-American national leadership successor to Malcolm X, as a comparable black nationalist icon for the 1990s. Certainly, Farrakhan and Malcolm share many beliefs regarding the cultural values that black Americans ought to adopt and profess. Malcolm X's ideological beliefs, however, evinced an enduring and marked hostility toward capitalism that contrasts sharply with Farrakhan's enthusiastic embrace of the free market. While some scholarly interpretations minimize the significance of Malcolm's prosocialist comments, arguing that these were made to marginal political groups and lacked either intellectual coherence, complexity, or sophistication,[74] such views are not especially compelling. Admittedly, Malcolm's beliefs were not definitively settled even at the time of his death. Nonetheless, the lack of faith in American capitalism that Malcolm displayed in the final eighteen months of his life was clearly substantial and evidently sincere. Certainly, Malcolm's anticapitalist convictions led progressive and socialist groups within and outside the United States, both at the time and subsequently, to claim his political legacy as their own, while characterizing its putative appropriation by Farrakhan as "distorted, caricatured, and sanitised."[75] Unsurprisingly, Farrakhan has consistently refused to compromise the notable popularity, among both African-Americans at large and leftists generally, that invariably attends such comparisons by conceding the profound ideological distance that has actually separated the two black American leaders—in death as well as in life.

Allied to its eschatological beliefs, leadership mystique, and black separatism, then, the NoI's pronounced cultural conservatism powerfully distinguishes Farrakhan's group from other African-American organizations—both integrative and separatist—concerned with improving black Americans' political, economic, and social welfare. Groups such as the NAACP or Urban League represent secular organizations that rarely issue recommendations of a cultural character (in relation either to their own members or nonmembers), concentrating their energies instead principally upon issues of economic and political empowerment. By comparison, Farrakhan's NoI adopts a very distinctive and unusual approach, even in its symbols. Following its conviction that blacks in America represent an oppressed nation within a nation, for instance, the organization developed its own flag to proclaim African-Americans' putative independence. Its symbols of the sun (representing freedom), moon (equality), and star (justice) are held by NoI members to render its flag superior to all others (including the Stars and Stripes) since none of these entities can be taken down by either government edict or military force. Again, the distinctive character of the NoI constitutes an important resource for Farrakhan's aspirations to national black political leadership, in affording him a status that is sharply differentiated from established African-American civic and political leaders.

Admittedly, on occasion, Farrakhan has issued public pronouncements that undermine the consistently conservative tenor of his worldview. The ideological identity of the NoI's leader has been complicated by Farrakhan's appeals to the progressive and liberal groups with whom a tactical alliance has frequently appeared both necessary and politically profitable. Neither the tactical appeals of the black nationalist nor the tentative embrace by political progressives is novel in historical terms, with white socialists and communists expressing interest in, and seeking to forge alliances with, black nationalist groups since the early part of the twentieth century.[76] As with black nationalists' efforts during earlier eras, the central features of Farrakhan's more recent attempts to create broader political links revolve around his rhetorical appeals for racial equality, the internationalist dimensions of his public discourse, and his calls for economic justice.

That Farrakhan strongly opposes black oppression by whites and sincerely seeks the improvement of African-Americans' economic and social welfare is clear from his many speeches and writings. The NoI's leader, however, has also made explicit attempts to appeal to nonblack racial and ethnic groups in America, in particular Native Americans and Latinos, to join black Americans in a broad-based anti-racist and antiestablishment coalition. Farrakhan issued such a call at the 1983 March on Washington, for example, and has often included Native and Latino Americans within the privileged ambit of his "black brothers." The actual strength of Farrakhan's commitment to multiracial and multiethnic unity both within and outside the United States, however, is implausibly great. It is at best difficult to reconcile such claims of inclusive humanitarian commitment with descriptions not only of Jews, but also of Arabs, Koreans, and other ethnic American groups as "bloodsuckers," for example. If it exists at all, Farrakhan's sincere desire to transcend racial and ethnic differences assumes such a minor role in his dominant political and religious agenda as to be effectively discounted.

In his apparent quest for an ecumenical racial unity, though, the NoI's leader has also sought to promote himself as an anti-imperialist, recalling the mantle of prior black leaders within the United States who had fought against American (and non-American) military involvement in foreign lands, such as Garvey, Du Bois, King, and Malcolm. Farrakhan's scathing criticisms of American foreign policy for being too favorable to the interests of Israel; his unrelenting defense of Palestinian rights; his personal ties to Arab regimes in general, and that of Gadhafi in Libya in particular; his close associations with African governments, such as that of Jerry Rawlings in Ghana; and his opposition to American sanctions against Cuba, Iran, Iraq, and other despotic regimes have provided overlapping areas of agreement for the NoI's leader with elements of the progressive Left in America.[77] In consistently opposing U.S. involvement in Central America and the Arabian Gulf, and in arguing that black Americans should never participate in any military action by the United States against black Africans, Farrakhan has evidently sought to echo the anticolonialist and anti-imperialist tenets of Malcolm X after his departure from the NoI. The relevance of such foreign policy positions to the advancement of African-American welfare in the United States is, nonetheless, at best marginal and indirect.[78]

An even more prominent theme in Farrakhan's speeches than foreign policy, however, is a recurrent call for economic equity between the races in America. Farrakhan has sought explicitly to deny the extent of his capitalist convictions by emphasizing his unyielding opposition to "exploitative" economic relations:

> I am not a capitalist, I don't believe in the exploitation of the wealth of the masses for the benefit of a few greedy people. I believe that since we are living in a capitalist society we should use the instruments of capitalism, but the ownership of everything must be the common ownership by the masses of the people. I don't believe the wealth of any nation should be in the hands of the few.[79]

The democratic-socialist and collectivist cast of Farrakhan's commitment to common ownership can nonetheless be heavily doubted. In 1985, for example, Farrakhan announced the establishment of a new and important NoI program, "People Organized and Working for Economic Rebirth" (POWER), which comprehensively embodied his black nationalist-capitalist tenets. The objective of POWER was to become a multiple-level business enterprise, marketing products produced and distributed exclusively by black Americans, for sale within and outside America. Farrakhan's goals were to tap into the estimated $200 billion purchasing power of African-Americans and to encourage a wholesale change in the prevailing patterns of their spending and saving habits. Black-owned firms would sell to black American consumers, with the resulting capital from sales being used to start small, all-black manufacturing companies. Based initially upon a black toiletries firm, Farrakhan's program for racial self-reliance invoked the inspirational argument that, if African-Americans continued to depend upon the white man for such intimate personal hygiene products, there would eventually be "a brown day in Detroit." Black Americans had, he eloquently averred, to attend assiduously to their own "wiping needs," free from the insidious and degenerative influence of the white man's toilet paper;[80] a noble, enlightened and compelling vision, indeed.

The program, which initially attracted significant support from black American businesspersons, reflected two of Farrakhan's core convictions: that African-Americans, with a "new" status as a freed people from 1986 onward, and a novel opportunity to be responsive to appropriately enlightened instruction, needed to be taught by example how to behave, and that economics represented the key mechanism by which collective black American advancement would most effectively be achieved. Prophesy and profit thus represented mutually reinforcing routes to collective black American emancipation, in Farrakhan's view. Subsequently, Farrakhan's entrepreneurial activities have increased in scope and diversity, though not at all clearly in terms of their commercial success.[81]

Farrakhan's core economic position is essentially a powerful echo of that of populists throughout American history, in its opposition to concentrations of economic power in the hands of wealthy conglomerates and in its antipathy toward multinational corporations. In favoring the "little man" against "big business," however, the racial twist to Farrakhan's American populism is manifest in economic tenets that are more deeply concerned with the racial control and size of the business than with challenging its capitalist mode of production. Although the little man may be an African-American, and the agents of big business white, the goals of Farrakhan's economic movement remain firmly located within the capitalist and free market tradition of American political economy. As Marable has argued, Farrakhan's economic philosophy essentially amounts to an ambitious black attempt to defeat the white American corporate elite by playing the free market game within its own rules of private enterprise.[82] Exploitation is directed by the NoI at the nonblack, rather than the African-American, poor in this guise. Farrakhan's strategy is therefore informed less by fighting social inequities and economic injustice per se than by simply inverting the identities of its victors and victims, according to race.

That Farrakhan's pronounced economic conservatism enjoys a deep historical lineage among African-Americans is clear enough, but this assumes a less significant role in terms of the minister's political ascendancy than does its current exceptionalism among national black American political elites. Certainly, the NoI's emphasis on self-help and economic individualism among African-Americans has a long historical pedigree. At the turn of the twentieth century, Booker T. Washington tirelessly advocated black capitalism and established the National Negro Business League to assist black entrepreneurship. A coalition of black businesspersons, the League promoted the development of all-black insurance firms, funeral homes, groceries, and retail establishments. In the 1920s, Garvey, too, endorsed similar race-bound economic tenets through his Black Star steamship line, which aspired to market black-produced goods to Africa and the Caribbean, and the Negro Factories Corporation, a group of black entrepreneurs that attempted unsuccessfully to dominate the black American consumer market.

However, the overwhelming majority of national black American politicians in the post–civil rights era have endorsed markedly liberal economic programs, social welfare assistance, and governmental regulation of economic affairs in a fashion wholly anathema to Farrakhan's laissez-faire precepts. As Charles Hamilton observed:

> Black Americans have always had to look to the national government for a more responsive hearing of their grievances . . . States' rights became synonymous with black oppression . . . (which) caused black political thought to be influenced very heavily by reliance on the federal government and to be very pessimistic about the ultimate willingness or ability of local governments to deal with black problems.[83]

By stark contrast, Farrakhan's combination of economic and cultural currents unmistakably mark him out as a conservative American populist. His avowed preference is consistently and overwhelmingly for order over freedom in social and cultural matters, yet simultaneously for liberty over regulation in economic ones. Equality does not figure prominently in his public philosophy beyond seeking an improvement of black welfare comparable to that of whites; redistributing resources within America on a more equitable basis is not the issue. On this point Farrakhan has substantially more in common with conservative white Republicans, such as Phil Gramm and Jesse Helms, than he does with liberal black Democrats, such as Jesse Jackson and John Lewis. Small wonder, then, that some critical observers were apt to doubt whether an imagined debate between Farrakhan and David Duke—an intriguing if deeply unedifying prospect—would witness any material disagreements arising between the two populist extremists, upon either the causes of America's racial problems or their most appropriate solutions.

That Farrakhan's conservatism has been largely ignored during his rise to national political attention is largely a consequence of the proximate causes of his increasing public notoriety. Although the ambiguous signals that his public pronouncements issued partly accounted for his ideological misplacement, the more influential sources of confusion surrounded his involvement in the Jackson campaign of 1984. A combination of the association with Jackson, the political capital that the Republican party sought to gain from the episode, and the intense and protracted political furor over his anti-Semitic remarks from 1984 onward, together conveyed a dominant media and public impression of Farrakhan as constituting simply a more extreme and crudely vitriolic version of the black American presidential aspirant himself. Since vigorously fighting against racial discrimination and prejudice necessarily entailed strong resistance to the status quo, and since Farrakhan appeared so obviously committed to challenging established structures in the most militant, aggressive, and uncompromising of fashions, the leader of the NoI was not easily cast as a conventional conservative.

More important, very few American political actors—black or white, progressive or conservative, supporters or opponents—have faced a sufficiently pressing political imperative or a compelling incentive actually to cast Farrakhan in such a light. Embracing Farrakhan's variant of right-wing conservatism was attractive to neither Republicans nor liberal Democrats. Although, for example, Charles Henry argues that Jackson's ultimate severance of his electoral ties with Farrakhan owed "more to the strategic needs and experience of each leader than . . . to ideological incompatibility,"[84] the latter was untested. Had it been, the substantial distance separating them would undoubtedly have become clear since, as Reed has compellingly and consistently argued, Farrakhan:

> weds a radical, oppositional style to a program that proposes private and individual responses to social problems; he endorses moral repressiveness; he asserts racial essentialism; he affirms male authority; and he lauds bootstrap capitalism.[85]

The Jackson-Farrakhan links were demonstrably less religious, philosophical, or ideological than politically pragmatic in their origins—a source of both their strength and frailty.

Abetted—inadvertently or intentionally—by his many erstwhile opponents, Farrakhan was therefore able to disguise a profoundly conservative political, economic, and social agenda behind his aggressively populist black nationalist public discourse, anti-Semitism, and his organization's direct action interventions in inner-city African-American communities to reduce black drug consumption and to combat black-on-black crime. The correct ideological locus of Farrakhan as an impassioned black conservative—indeed, as an African-

American exemplar of what might be most appropriately termed "radical reaction"—was thus left obscure for many Americans of all races.

A POLITICS OF CONTRADICTIONS: PROPHESY AND PROFITS

The most cursory examination of Farrakhan's prolific writings and speeches reveals that the minister eminently merits designation as a radical activist. In etymological terms, Farrakhan fully qualifies as an individual who vehemently believes in the overarching and immediate need to transform American society from its very roots, rather than through incremental changes, minor adaptations, and gradual reforms. Critical conceptions of both Farrakhan's personal politics and that of his organization are, nonetheless, frequently apt to diverge markedly between reformist and revolutionary interpretations.[86] Moreover, the notion of an uncompromising racial militant espousing deeply conservative, and even reactionary, positions and prescriptions renders the appropriate designation of Farrakhan particularly problematic.

Reformist social movements or political parties tend to be concerned with the achievement of incremental changes in existing patterns of political, economic, and social relations in a given polity. Their focus is upon the need to alter or repair laws, institutions, customs, or practices rather than to overhaul the prevailing system in its entirety. Revolutionary movements, by contrast, invariably emphasize the need for a complete regeneration of societal values and established institutional structures. They stress the desirability of either totally rebuking the old polity or bringing about an entirely new pattern of relationships between the individual and the state, between classes or ethnic and racial groups, and between individual citizens.

In this respect, Farrakhan occupies a political terrain decisively more reformist than revolutionary in nature. Admittedly, revolutionary themes and impulses infuse his public discourse. Farrakhan's NoI also advances a call for complete change in the values and priorities not just of American blacks, but also of the United States (and the West) as a whole. Farrakhan envisions an entirely new type of society, and a pattern of economic and political relations between the races, wholly novel and unprecedented in American experience. The NoI's theological precepts necessarily compel not a gradual and marginal set of alterations in existing structures and patterns of social and economic life in America, but their rapid, wholesale, and lasting transformation. Reformists, on the whole, tend not to endorse global Armageddon and all-consuming apocalyptic conflagrations as the most propitious incremental means by which existing political, economic, and social arrangements can best be improved to universal benefit.

Nonetheless, in demanding the full redress of black American grievances, Farrakhan advances no concrete plan or program of action, much less full-blown revolution. Although he explicitly and frequently directs American attentions to the socioeconomic gaps between blacks and whites in the United States, and demands their rapid and complete removal, there is surprisingly little in Farrakhan's public discourse that can be construed as even remotely encouraging the overthrow of the American state. The NoI's effective constitution, "What the Muslims Want, What the Muslims Believe," even includes a demand directed to the U.S. government to bring about "freedom, justice, and equality" for African-Americans, an explicit appeal to working within the existing state framework rather than threatening the polity's imminent demise. The organization has never engaged in extensive political activity to achieve a wholesale transformation of the state and of the established politicoeconomic system. Nor has the NoI resorted to coercive, violent, or terrorist acts to achieve its separatist goals. Farrakhan, it seems, desires power for himself and the organization that he leads. He wants to colonize governmental and civic institutions with his own loyal black forces, to bring about the multitude of comprehensive changes that he professes to desire. Were Farrakhan offered the U.S. presidency, he would most likely accept it as the most propitious national bully pulpit from which to press his radical transformation of American society.

The radical features of the NoI are a function of the centrality of race to Farrakhan's religious and ideological beliefs. Farrakhan's analysis of African-Americans' current woes consistently focuses on the racial rather than the class or economic causes of blacks' contemporary plight. Although the need for African-Americans generally to become economically self-sufficient is a prominent and critical theme in his speeches, that imperative is a product of the fact that black Americans have been mistreated and miseducated in the United States by virtue of their race, not their class positions. It is, therefore, in achieving a transformative racial unity that such deprivation must find its necessary, sufficient, and ultimate solution.

Thus, although Farrakhan's specific policy prescriptions on cultural and economic matters share substantially more in common with black American conservatives, such as Thomas Sowell or Clarence Thomas,[87] than progressives, the analyses of the NoI overlap with those of many avowedly liberal African-American politicians in their common emphasis on race. Unlike orthodox conservatives, both Farrakhan and progressive groups such as the CBC share a public dialogue whose preeminent analytic category—the cornerstone by which they assess policies, politicians, and institutions—is that of race. It is above all the racial variable that conditions the divergent collective fates of African-Americans and other social groups in the United States. Although their prescriptions for resolving the problems plaguing many African-American communities differ substantially, the source of those communities' difficulties is identified in remarkably similar fashion. For all their significant differences, the shared stress that is placed upon the achievement of racial unity by both Farrakhan and politicians such as Jesse Jackson reveals a basic commonality of vision and an adherence to a common notion of racial authenticity.

Consider, for example, Lani Guinier's definition of "authentic" black American leadership, regarding elected black officials: "Black Representatives are authentic because they are elected by blacks *and* because they are descriptively similar to their constituents. In other words, they are politically, psychologically, and culturally black."[88] Although Guinier and Farrakhan would disagree profoundly on what public policies black politicians should strive to enact in order to best benefit their African-American constituents, they share this fundamental notion that an authentic black persona can be identified, achieved, and (by definition) forfeited.

Moreover, in invoking race as the key prism through which prevailing public policies are evaluated, Farrakhan's prescriptions are precisely at odds with the calls from several influential African-American academics, such as the sociologist William Julius Wilson, for the development of a comprehensive and deracialized public policy program, capable of legislative passage and enactment, that can effectively address black Americans' social problems and economic grievances.[89] For Wilson and other neo-liberals, the grievous problems afflicting African-American communities require programs that do not make race their explicit basis or express goal in order to be effective. The deracialization of political discourse and the evolution of race-neutral public policy programs is a pressing necessity for the forging of multiracial, majority coalitions and a central precondition of the regeneration of many deprived and disadvantaged black communities across America. For Farrakhan, by manifest contrast, the extreme polarization of political forces and the explicit racialization of public policy is a requisite, though not sufficient, condition of meaningful black American empowerment.

Although, therefore, an explicit, pervasive, and important conflict exists between Farrakhan's militant racial posture, on the one hand, and his deeply conservative economic and social program, on the other, this does not represent a complete contradiction. Farrakhan's militancy is not only rhetorical but is also wholly compatible with the particular ideological nature of his demands. Much as Patrick J. Buchanan's increasingly aggressive promotion of a protectionist, nativist, and recidivist "America First" program since 1991 has hardly proven violative of an extremist and radical posture, so Farrakhan's "Black America First" discourse enthusiastically embraces rather than rejects deeply conservative and traditionalist tenets. Farrakhan represents a prophet of radical black reaction, propounding a populist right-wing message that, in order to achieve full emancipation, black Americans must adopt the avowedly conservative value system and the traditionalist behavioral modes that he vigorously espouses. Were his public philosophy to be articulated in similarly direct, vivid, and lurid terms by a white American politician, the latter would inevitably invite mass opprobrium and the ideas would probably compel censure rather than celebration or encouragement.[90]

Reed is thus absolutely correct to draw critical attention to the avowedly conservative nature of Farrakhan's agenda for black Americans.[91] One hundred years on, the NoI's leader essentially repeats Booker T. Washington's comprehensive indictment of black America during the 1890s for its collective failure to undertake proactive, private initiatives, to reject dependency upon government largesse, and to inculcate among black Americans responsible, bourgeois, and traditionalist cultural values in order to rejuvenate black communities. Like Washington previously, Farrakhan has come to national prominence in America at a moment of profound racial crisis, apparent impotence on the part of national black political and civic leadership, and increasing federal government retreat on matters of civil rights, welfare provision, and economic redistribution for African-Americans. Much as Washington's activism was centrally shaped by the collapse of the first Reconstruction, so Farrakhan's efforts have been directed at forging an influential popular base in the midst of the fragmentary remnants of the second.[92]

Admittedly, Washington was, unlike Farrakhan, ultimately an integrationist, and one whose genuine faith in the notion that separate could be equal remains in academic dispute. Nonetheless, his programs of self-help and moral regeneration bear substantial resemblance to the public prescriptions of Farrakhan's NoI currently. Espousing public policy positions that the Republican party in the House of Representatives under Newt Gingrich would mostly endorse with alacrity, it represents a signal achievement by Farrakhan that the full, repressive extent of his conservative agenda has not been effectively "smoked out" to the mass of black Americans. The threat that Farrakhan poses to his compatriots is far more potent in regard to black Americans than whites in its multifarious reactionary, authoritarian, and retrograde dimensions, a fact that many analyses of the Farrakhan phenomenon are apt to disregard or ignore.

The irony of Farrakhan's contemporary role, however, is not only a matter of his often mistaken and ambiguous ideological identity. It is also a function of the blatant contradictions between the conservative practices and autonomous modes of economic and social activity that the NoI publicly supports and the dependent state of its own private activities. Most notably, the free-market philosophy and self-sufficiency tenets that Farrakhan relentlessly advances in public forums across America is wholly belied by the extent to which his own organization's activities have depended on sources of substantial financial support that are external not only to the NoI, but also to the black American community in general. Thus, the POWER program, for example, was largely financed by an interest-free loan of $5 million from Libyan dictator Muammar Gadhafi (the second of three occasions, over twenty-three years, in which the dictatorial Libyan autocracy has financially assisted the NoI). Similarly, in 1993, a chain of health clinics run by a top NoI official willingly accepted federal monies to market a dubious "cure" for the AIDS virus, while at the same time the organization attributed the spread of that very virus among black Americans to a combination of deliberate federal governmental action and promiscuous homosexual activity among African-Americans.[93]

The NoI's efforts at reducing gang conflict and the drug trade in inner-cities through the Fruit of Islam and its several corporate relations have also relied critically, and controversially, upon the patronage of federal government funds. The NoI initially commenced voluntarily patrolling two housing projects in Washington, D.C., in April 1988. Subsequently, private security agencies affiliated with the NoI and the boards of which comprised NoI members—but which constituted legally separate and self-constituted corporations—secured in excess of $20 million of funds from local housing authorities for their activities in a total of nine American cities, in 1990–1995: D.C., Baltimore, Chicago, Dayton, Brooklyn, Buffalo, Philadelphia, Pittsburgh, and Los Angeles. The contracts were financed in part by funds that local authorities receive from the federal government, rendering the security firms subcontractors of the U.S. government.

Most accounts concur that the NoI security firms have been reasonably effective in tackling drugs and crime in the overwhelmingly black projects. The firms, however, hired almost exclusively black workers (in contravention of federal affirmative action guidelines on achieving racial and ethnic diversity in the workforce); invariably preferred NoI members over other African-Americans; numbered among their NoI employees many recently convicted black felons; and owed several thousands of dollars in back taxes. Moreover, the "firewalls" that existed between the NoI and the legally independent security agencies (the NOI Security Agency in Baltimore, the New Life Self Development Agency in Chicago, the X-Men Security Agency in New York, for example) were hardly thick,[94] while the evidence of proselytization by the latter on Farrakhan's behalf (from advertising his lectures to selling the NoI's newspaper and trademark bean pies in the blocks they patrolled) was considerable—all, indirectly, at American taxpayers' unwitting expense.

Nor was the suspicion that the federal government actively, though inadvertently and indirectly, subsidized the NoI laid to rest by congressional hearings on the matter in 1995. Replete with mutual recriminations and predictably hyperbolic accusations of "witch-hunts" being leveled at NoI investigators, the hearings revealed only that the security agencies' work won widespread plaudits from African-Americans in the projects and that their activities received federal support of a highly questionable (and likely illegal) nature.[95] The response of Henry Cisneros, then Secretary of Housing and Urban Development in the Clinton Administration, was to transfer the matter to the Equal Employment Opportunity Commission. Given the latter's two-year, 100,000 case backlog, the unrefuted charges against the NoI firms were thereby effectively buried (although eight security contracts at public or federally assisted housing projects in six cities either expired without being renewed or were terminated during 1995–96).[96]

For the frequency and ferocity with which Farrakhan preaches the merits of economic self-sufficiency and individualistic self-help, his organization practices a set of activities that is powerfully reliant upon sources of financial subsidy that are external to black Americans. No matter how effective they may have been in local black city communities, Farrakhan's organization and its affiliated security groups are markedly less self-sufficient than substantially subsidized (and, in spite of those subsidies, plagued by dire financial difficulties[97]). Much as Farrakhan's personally residing in a large mansion in a racially integrated neighborhood on Chicago's south side wholly contradicts his preaching in favor of separation of the races, so his practical business ventures are also directly violative of the self-help economic principles that he publicly promotes. But then, the NoI's leader would no doubt argue that the motives and methods of prophets throughout human history have frequently been misunderstood by the massed ranks of the infidels and the unenlightened.

SUMMARY

History may judge Farrakhan as neither an exotic political opportunist nor a certifiable madman. The esoteric religious dimensions of Farrakhan's message are nonetheless as central to his belief system and political behavior as his practice is violative of them. The Black Muslim leader's bizarre and byzantine theological analysis powerfully informs his explanations of black Americans' history, current position, and future social and economic prospects in the United States. Although distinctive to the point of being extraordinarily eccentric, risible, and repugnant, Farrakhan's political role and influence simply cannot be understood either fully or accurately apart from an appreciation of his prophetic self-conception and his profound, unshakeable conviction that he, personally, is imbued with divine influence and is set upon an irrevocable course of collective racial salvation. Farrakhan's theological beliefs remain fundamental to his leadership of the NoI—they form the fountain from which all his many other prescriptions and public behavior flow.

Farrakhan assuredly possesses the courage of his many colorful convictions. Those convictions, however, are deeply and overwhelmingly conservative in character. Indeed, if the project of many white

American conservatives over recent years has been to "take back" the United States by somehow transporting the country to an earlier period of its history (most typically, by reviving and recreating an idealized version of the 1950s), so Farrakhan's ultimate goal is to return black Americans to an earlier set of economic and social structures that shaped their development—albeit without the manifold black inequalities, indignities, and injuries so integral to the segregated system of Jim Crow. In advocating many of the reactionary positions he does, Farrakhan essentially calls for a return to the past in America: separate racial facilities and collective development; unequivocal and strong division of gender roles along traditionalist lines; an end to government programs to black American citizens; and a revival of traditional moral codes of behavior, subject to the strictest of sanctions for their violation. Louis Farrakhan's America is a nation in which all those many heretics who heinously breach his ascribed notions of racial authenticity and sexual and moral purity—fornicators, homosexuals, miscegenators, adulterers, drinkers, gamblers, and professional women—are effectively excluded; an imagined American community far less benignly beloved than brutally regimented, repressive, and deeply repugnant to civilized sensibilities.

Farrakhan therefore represents a substantially more reactionary than a progressive American political figure. Far less than three strikes would invite an "out" verdict under a Farrakhan regime, while the minister's great admiration of Saudi Arabian law and order methods suggests strongly that the conceptual (and constitutional) limits to "cruel and unusual punishment" in America would be tested to the full. Moreover, to the extent that his organizational practices are themselves clearly and deeply violative of his avowed public philosophy, Farrakhan also represents a fundamentally false prophet whose putative hopes for African-Americans are honed upon a hypocritical public praxis. Preaching a future panacea of racial separatism to deprived and impoverished blacks, Farrakhan resides in an integrated, affluent Chicago neighborhood; humbly affirming his essentially frugal and modest desires, he lives in resplendent luxury; persistently advocating black private enterprise and self-sufficiency, his organization depends crucially upon public subsidies and loans from foreign despots and international terrorist sponsors for its continued viability; and proclaiming deadly sexual viruses as of ultimately beneficial and cathartic social effect, the NoI markets dubious and doubtful cures for them. Professing a prophetic status, Farrakhan's plethora of promises and predictions emerges not only as bizarrely eccentric but also as a hollow and farcical fanaticist's facade. The conservatism and opportunism of Farrakhan's material practice dramatically contradict the supposed militancy and the elaborately principled character of his public preaching. The latter also marks him out, however, if not as insanely brilliant (or vice versa), at least as a modern exemplar of a distinctively black brand of American political paranoia.

NOTES TO CHAPTER 3

1. Cruse, *Plural But Equal*, p. 252.

2. Quoted in Martin Fletcher, "Anti-Semitic Gibes Mar Million Man March," *The London Times*, 16 October 1995, p. 10.

3. Most of Farrakhan's speeches are recorded, and many are sold by the NoI as cassette tapes. Some are also available as videos. In addition, collections of his speeches are contained in the following books: *Seven Speeches by Minister Louis Farrakhan* (New York: Ministry Class, Muhammad's Temple No. 7, 1974); and *A Torchlight for America* (Chicago: FCN Publishing, 1993). In addition to standard newspaper reports and interviews, a lengthy interview was also been published: *The Honorable Louis Farrakhan: a minister for progress; the complete historic interview with Michael Hardy and William Pleasant from The National Alliance* (New York: Practice Press, 1985). This pamphlet was reproduced in *Independent Black Leadership in America: Minister Louis Farrakhan, Dr. Leonari Fulani, Reverend Al Sharpton* (New York: Castillo International, 1990). See also "Excerpts of Interview," *The Washington Post*, 1 March 1990, pp. A16–17. I have drawn upon all of the available published sources, as well as audiocassette recordings of Farrakhan's speeches, to attempt to distill his biographical details and the nature of his belief system with a reasonable degree of conciseness.

4. The notion is that of the eminent Marxist historian, Eric Hobsbawm. See *The Age of Extremes: The Short Twentieth Century* (London; Abacus Books, 1995), p. 208.

5. Excerpts from one of Farrakhan's plays were featured in the 1959 documentary by Lomax on the Black Muslims, "The Hate That Hate Produced." Another, entitled *Orgena* ("A negro" spelled backward) satirized so-called "Americanized" blacks, from well-dressed businessmen to alcoholics. As well as writing, Farrakhan starred in the productions.

6. Although he does not refer to Farrakhan by name, the record is noted by James Baldwin as accurately expressing the sentiments of many black Americans outside as well as within the Nation of Islam (see Baldwin, *The Fire Next Time* [New York: Dell, 1963], p. 64). A less well-known Farrakhan disc from the 1950s was released, according to one account, to celebrate America's first sex-change operation. Both the general subject and the specific lyrics of the song (which include the memorable lines: "People came out of curiosity/To see this amazing freak of the century/With this modern surgery/

They change him from he to she/But behind that lipstick, rouge, and paint/I gotta know—is she is, or is she ain't?") rest somewhat incongruously with Farrakhan's subsequent public views on gender and sexual relations. See Francis Wheen, "Voice of Islam."

7. Lincoln, *The Black Muslims*, p. 268.

8. A detailed discussion of Farrakhan's demagogic status can be found in Julia E. Gaber, "Lamb of God or Demagogue? A Burkean Cluster Analysis of the Selected Speeches of Minister Louis Farrakhan" (unpublished Ph.D. thesis, Bowling Green State University, 1986). Gaber affirms the appropriateness of the designation to Farrakhan.

9. See: Hamilton, *The Black Preacher in America*; and Lincoln, *The Black Church in the African American Experience*.

10. The remainder were made up mainly by immigrants (and their descendants) from Saudi Arabia, Iran, Egypt, Pakistan, and Morocco. Personal communication, American Muslim Council, Washington, D.C., 19 October 1995.

11. Farzana Shaikh, ed., *Islam and Islamic Groups: A World Wide Reference Guide* (Harlow, UK: Longman, 1992).

12. Erdmann D. Beynon, "The Voodoo Cult Among Negro Migrants in Detroit," *American Journal of Sociology* 43 (July 1937—May 1938): 894–907.

13. Arna Bontemps and Jack Conroy, *Anyplace But Here* (New York: Hill and Wang, 1966), p. 230.

14. See: J. Herman Blake, "Black Nationalism," in *Annals of the American Academy of Political and Social Science*, 382 (1969): 15–25; and Essien-Udom, *Black Nationalism*, pp. 6–7.

15. See August Meier, Elliott Rudwick, and Francis L. Broderick, eds., *Black Protest Thought in the Twentieth Century* 2nd ed. (New York: Macmillan, 1971).

16. See King, *Separate and Unequal*.

17. My use of the term "ideology" reflects the basic definition offered by David Kettler: "a pattern of symbolically-charged beliefs and expressions that present, interpret and evaluate the world in a way designed to shape, mobilize, direct, organize and justify certain modes or courses of action and to anathematize others." See his discussion in *The Blackwell Encyclopaedia of Political Thought*, ed. David Miller (Oxford: Basil Blackwell, 1991), pp. 235–38.

18. On Garvey's pre-1925 beliefs, speeches, and writings, see Amy-Jacques Garvey, ed., *Philosophy and Opinions of Marcus Garvey* (New York: Universal Publishing House, 1923).

19. The two most impressive biographies of Garvey are: Edmund David Cronon, *Black Moses: The Story of Marcus Garvey and the Universal Negro Improvement Association* (Madison: University of Wisconsin Press, 1962); and Theodore G. Vincent, *Black Power and the Garvey Movement* (San Francisco: University of California Press, 1972).

20. See Arna Bontemps and Jack Conroy, *They Seek a City* (Garden City, N.Y.: Doubleday, 1945).

21. See Lawrence L. Tyler, "The Protestant Ethic Among the Black Muslims," *Phylon* 27, no. 1 (1966): 5–14.

22. Among the voluminous literature on Malcolm X, see, in particular: Cone, *Martin and Malcolm and America*; Perry, *Malcolm X*; and Eugene Victor Wolfenstein, *The Victims of Democracy: Malcolm X and the Black Revolution* (London: Free Association Books, 1989).

23. See, for example: David Mervin, "Malcolm X and the Moderation of Black Militancy," *PAIS Papers*, Department of Politics and International Studies, University of Warwick, Coventry, UK, Working Paper no. 107 (April 1992); and Frederick Harper, "The Influence of Malcolm X on Black Militancy," *Journal of Black Studies* 1, no. 4 (1971): 387–402.

24. See George Breitman, ed., *The Last Year of Malcolm X* (New York: Pathfinder Press, 1967).

25. Louis Farrakhan, "Boston Minister Tells of Malcolm—Muhammad's Biggest Hypocrite," *Muhammad Speaks*, 4 December 1964, pp. 11–15.

26. See Breitman et al., *The Assassination of Malcolm X*.

27. Quoted in M. A. Farber, "In the Name of the Father," *Vanity Fair* 58 (1995), pp. 52–60.

28. Lincoln, *The Black Muslims*, p. 264.

29. On the split, see Lawrence H. Mamiya and C. Eric Lincoln, "Minister Louis Farrakhan and the Final Call: Schism in the Muslim Movement," in *The Muslim Community in North America*, eds. Earle Waugh, Baha Abu-Laban, and Regular Querishi (Edmonton: University of Alberta Press, 1983), pp. 234–51. The AMM was eventually dissolved in 1985. Subsequently, other Black Muslim groups have sought to establish mass memberships among African Americans by adhering to orthodox Islamic doctrines and stressing their opposition to the sectarianism and racial separatism of Farrakhan's Nation of Islam—though without conspicuous success.

30. Cited in Marsh, *From Black Muslims to Muslims*, p. 97.

31. Wallace E. Caldwell, "Black Muslims Behind Bars," *Religious Studies* 34, no. 4 (1966): 185–204.

32. Wallace E. Caldwell, "A Survey of Attitudes Towards Black Muslims in Prison," *Journal of Human Relations* 16, no. 2 (1968): 220–38.

33. Scott Grant McNall, "The Sect Movement," *Pacific Sociology Review* 6, no. 2 (1963): 60–64.

34. Ernst Benz, "Der Schwarze Islam," *Zeitschrift fur Religion und Geistesgeschichte* 19, no. 2 (1967): 97–113.

35. Philip Norton, "Black Nationalism in America: the Significance of the Black Muslim Movement," *Hull Papers in Politics*, University of Hull, no. 31, 1983.

36. King, "The Farrakhan Phenomenon." See also Marable, *Black American Politics*, p. 287; and Christopher Thomas, "The Man Who Haunts Jesse Jackson," *The London Times*, 8 August 1984, p. 6.

37. Shaikh, *Islam and Islamic Movements*, pp. 268–72.

38. Lincoln, *The Black Muslims*, p. 266.

39. Reed, "All for One," p. 86.

40. It is striking how closely life in the NoI compares to that of splinter political parties and extremist organizations in terms of fulfilling the necessary requirements for membership, expending substantial personal resources (both in terms of time and finance) on the group, and in general ensuring that the organization assumes the preeminent focus of social life. For a non-U.S. secular comparison, see the study of Trotskyist "entryist" politics within the British Labour Party by Michael Crick, *Militant* (London: Faber and Faber, 1984).

41. Lincoln, *The Black Muslims*, p. 268.

42. The speech was made in Chicago and included in a 1995 documentary on Farrakhan's role in Malcolm's demise, *Brother Minister: The Assassination of Malcolm X*. The comments are also cited in *The London Times*, 13 January 1995, p. 13.

43. Shaikh, *Islam and Islamic Movements*, pp. 268–72.

44. See the examples in Meier et al., *Black Protest Thought in the Twentieth Century*.

45. Transcript of Farrakhan speech, 30 July 1984, National Press Club, Washington, D.C.

46. Elijah Muhammad, *Message to the Black Man in America* (Chicago: Muhammad's Temple No. 2, 1965); and *The Fall of America* (Chicago: Muhammad's Temple of Islam No. 2, 1973). See also Elijah's summation of the NoI's most important tenets in, "The Demands and Beliefs of the Black Muslims in America," *Islamic Review* 52, no. 10 (1964), pp. 25–27. Summations are also contained in Bernard Cushmeer, *This Is the One: Messenger Elijah Muhammad—You Need Not Look for Another* (Phoenix, Ariz.: Truth Publications, 1970).

47. Farrakhan's speeches attest to a view of history that is apparently determined in advance of itself by a council of Gods, in 25,000-year cycles. Fard, one of these Gods, dissented from their collective conviction that black Americans were beyond saving and came to America to warn them of their impending fate.

48. Among several other occurrences, Farrakhan predicted that the ensuing apocalypse would witness the destruction of the American 7th Fleet and the entire state of California collapsing into the Pacific Ocean, not as a result of the state lying on a fault line, but because of the corruptive and degenerate influence of the cities of Los Angeles and San Francisco.

49. Farrakhan speech, Cobal Hall, Detroit, 8 February 1985. Quoted in Gaber, "Lamb of God or Demagogue?," chapter 4, pp. 103–104.

50. Farrakhan confirmed in 1996 that he viewed the story of Yakub as fact rather than a metaphorical device, seeing the doctor as a "very real scientist." See his interview with Gates, "The Charmer," p. 124.

51. Although in an interview in 1990, Farrakhan restates his vision of a racial nightmare for America and the desirability of black Americans moving en masse to Africa. See Barbara Kleban Mills, "Predicting Disaster for a Racist America, Louis Farrakhan Envisions an African Homeland for U.S. Blacks," *People* 34, no. 11 (17 September 1990).

52. Quoted in Gaber, "Lamb of God or Demagogue?," p. 111.

53. Although an ingenious numerological device for identifying potentially satanic entities, it should perhaps be noted that, on this basis of inference, the number of Devils in the world is probably extremely large.

54. Quoted in Gaber, "Lamb of God or Demagogue?," p. 123.

55. Shirley R. Letwin, *The Anatomy of Thatcherism* (London: Fontana, 1992), p. 33–36.

56. Elijah Muhammad, *How to Eat to Live* (Chicago: Muhammad's Temple No. 2, 1968). *The Final Call* reprints Elijah's injunctions on health and diet in each issue, along with selective contemporary health briefs. One such example provided the striking warning (especially useful to academics) that "Students cannot pay attention and perform simple tasks after at least 22 days a month of marijuana smoking." See "Marijuana Use Impairs Performance," *The Final Call*, 3 April 1996, p. 28.

57. The restaurant was eventually completed and opened by Farrakhan in 1995. Its three separate areas included an array of dishes from curries to Creole cuisine and even permitted the sale of alcoholic beverages; food seems to be one of the few areas in which diversity evidently merits celebration and encouragement by Farrakhan and his organization.

58. Quoted in Gaber, "Lamb of God or Demagogue?," pp. 106–107.

59. Louis Farrakhan, *Independent Black Leadership in America: Minister Louis Farrakhan, Dr. Leonari Fulani, Reverend Al Sharpton* (New York: Castillo International, 1990), p. 47.

60. Cited in Robert Weisbord, *Genocide? Birth Control and the Black American* (Westport: Greenwood Press, 1975), pp. 96–104.

61. Farrakhan appointed a female African-American, Ava Muhammad, to the Ministry at the Nation's Chicago mosque (see R. X. White, "Minister Ava Muhammad: An Inspiration for Black Women," *The Final Call*, 27 January 1992, p. 17). The number of female ministers, however, still appears to be extremely limited and certainly not even in double figures as of September 1996.

62. Farrakhan's speech at Madison Square Garden on 7 October 1985 was the first and most notable occasion in which his normal guard of Fruit of Islam men was largely abandoned in favor of a phalanx of Black Muslim women. The decision evidently reflection a tactical ploy to counter accusations of sexism leveled at the NoI and to broaden Farrakhan's appeal among African-Americans of both sexes. A representative example of his views can also be garnered from his article, "Nation of Islam Offers True Liberation for Muslim Women," *The Final Call*, 24 August 1992, p. 28.

63. McFadden-Preston, "The Rhetoric of Minister Louis Farrakhan," p. 213, note 60.

64. Reed, "All for One," p. 87.

65. Quoted in Hamil R. Harris, "March of Black Men Is Planned in District; Farrakhan Seeks a Turnout of 1 Million," *The Washington Post*, 19 July 1995, p. B1.

66. See McFadden-Preston, "The Rhetoric of Minister Louis Farrakhan," chapter 6.

67. The suspicion that Farrakhan's personal values also encompass sexist notions is partially fuelled by some of his less sensitive public comments. One example was the interpretation that Farrakhan placed upon the conviction of the black boxer, Mike Tyson, for raping the African-American former beauty queen contestant, Desiree Washington: "You bring a hawk in at the chicken yard and wonder why the chicken got eaten up." Quoted in Richard E. Cohen, "Marching behind Farrakhan."

68. Farrakhan speech, "Black Solidarity Day Address," 2 November 1970. Reprinted in Farrakhan, *Seven Speeches by Minister Louis Farrakhan.*

69. See the aptly titled case, *Loving v. Virginia,* 388 U.S. 1 (1967). Virginia was one of sixteen American states in 1967 that still retained antimiscegenation laws that both prohibited and punished racial intermarriage. (Fifteen others had repealed such laws over the previous fifteen years.) In the Court's 9–0 decision to invalidate the Virginia statute as an invidious racial classification prohibited by the Equal Protection Clause of the Fourteenth Amendment, Chief Justice Warren held that, "Under our Constitution, the freedom to marry, or not to marry, a person of another race resides with the individual and cannot be infringed by the State" (p. 12).

70. Farrakhan, *Independent Black Leadership,* p. 46. The analysis is analogous to Farrakhan's argument that black Americans need to be taken "out" of American society and "cured" (clearly by the Nation of Islam, under his tutelage) before being allowed to return to play a full role therein. It also jibes with the views of "moral" crusaders such as Jerry Falwell, who have also advocated the quarantining of homosexuals as a proper and proportionate response to AIDS. See Dennis Altman, *AIDS and the New Puritanism* (London: Pluto Press, 1986).

71. Such pronouncements rest curiously with the Nation of Islam's attempts to market among African-Americans what most respected medical practitioners view as an entirely fraudulent cure for AIDS. See Gaines and Jackson, "Profit and Promises."

72. Isaac Julien has also drawn attention to the very narrow view of the African-American male that informs Farrakhan's racial essentialism. As Julien argues: "Black romanticism is high on the political agenda of people like Louis Farrakhan and the Nation of Islam and various rap groups prioritizing their very narrow versions of black masculinity. It mythologizes the past as it erases memory." See Julien, "Black Is, Black Ain't: Notes on De-Essentializing Black Identities," in *Black Popular Culture,* ed. Gina Dent (Seattle: Bay Press, 1992), pp. 255–63, at 257.

73. See Douglas Rose, ed., *The Emergence of David Duke and the Politics of Race* (Chapel Hill: University of North Carolina Press, 1992); and Sargent, *Extremism in America.*

74. See Mervin, "Malcolm X."

75. Keith Ovenden, *Malcolm X: Socialism and Black Nationalism* (London: Bookmarks, 1992), p. 9.

76. For example, see: George Breitman, ed., *Leon Trotsky on Black Nationalism and Self-Determination* (New York: Pathfinder Press, 1978); and Cedric J. Robinson, *Black Marxism: The Making of the Black Radical Tradition* (London: Zed Press, 1983).

77. See Marable, "In the Business of Prophet Making."

78. It may reasonably be argued that some of Farrakhan's international ties could yield benefits for American blacks. The refusal of the Treasury Department's Office of Foreign Assets Control to allow Farrakhan an exemption from U.S. sanctions on Libya, in September 1996, is one possible instance of this. Farrakhan had sought the exemption so that Colonel Gadhafi's pledge of $1 billion to assist American blacks economically and politically could be delivered. Even if the monies were indeed forthcoming, however (which may legitimately be doubted), the precise form of their proposed expenditure by Farrakhan and the NoI remained—much like the resources raised at the Million Man March—unclear.

79. Farrakhan, *Independent Black Leadership in America*, p. 42.

80. Quoted in Gaber, "Lamb of God or Demagogue?," p. 131.

81. See: Michael Sanson, "Farrakhan Means Business," *Restaurant Hospitality*, April 1995, p. 22; and Ron Stodghill, "Farrakhan's Three-Year Plan," *Business Week,*13 March 1995, p. 40.

82. Marable, "In the Business of Prophet Making," p. 24.

83. Charles V. Hamilton, *The Black Experience in American Politics* (New York: Putnam, 1973), pp. 245–6.

84. Henry, *Culture and African American Politics*, p. 86.

85. Reed, "All for One," p. 87.

86. See Shaikh, *Islam and Islamic Groups*; and O'Maolain, *The Radical Right*.

87. See, for example: Thomas Sowell, *The Economics and Politics of Race* (New York: Morrow, 1983) and *Civil Rights: Rhetoric or Reality?* (New York: Quill, 1984); and Walter Williams, *The State Against Blacks* (New York: McGraw-Hill, 1982).

88. Lani Guinier, *The Tyranny of the Majority: Fundamental Fairness in Representative Democracy* (New York: The Free Press, 1994), p. 56.

89. William Julius Wilson, *The Truly Disadvantaged: The Inner City, the Underclass, and Public Policy* (Chicago: University of Chicago Press, 1987); and "The Underclass: Issues, Perspectives, and Public Policy," in "The Ghetto Underclass: Social Science Perspectives," *Annals of the American Academy of Political and Social Science* 501 (January 1989).

90. Consider, for example, the censorious reaction among African-American and progressive political elites to the book by Charles Murray, *Losing Ground: American Social Policy, 1950–1980* (New York: Basic Books, 1984). Murray's prescriptions for ending welfare were in many respects merely a more rigorously detailed and coherent elaboration of Farrakhan's basic beliefs on the sources and consequences of African-American welfare dependency.

91. Reed, "All for One."

92. The most comprehensive scholarly account of Washington is the two-volume biography by Louis R. Harlan, *Booker T. Washington: The Making of a Black Leader, 1865–1901* (New York: Oxford University Press, 1972); and *Booker T. Washington: The Wizard of Tuskegee, 1901–1915* (New York: Oxford University Press, 1983).

93. NoI minister and head of the Washington, D.C. Abundant Life Clinic, Dr. Abdul Alim Muhammad, told a 1992 NoI convention in Atlanta that President Bush had played a "leading role" in the development of "a policy of genocide against non-white people," a direct consequence of which was the spread of the AIDS virus. In April 1993, the Abundant Life Foundation

won a federal grant of $213,000 to fund a one-year contract to treat AIDS patients in D.C., and a total of $571,521 of federal monies were received by the clinic 1993–95. See Gaines and Jackson, "Profit and Promises."

94. The Chicago company's chief executive, for example, was Leonard Farrakhan Muhammad, the NoI's "chief of staff" and Farrakhan's son-in-law.

95. The cry of "witch-hunt" was raised by Rep. Maxine Waters (D-CA), whose political career has been forged upon a well-earned reputation for racial militancy in her south-central Los Angeles district. See U.S. House of Representatives, *Security Contracts Between HUD or HUD Affiliated Entities and Companies Affiliated With the Nation of Islam.* As well as the hearings and documentary evidence in the report, see the account by Marshall J. Breger, "Discriminating in Favor of Farrakhan," *The Wall Street Journal*, 24 July 1994, p. A12.

96. According to Lorraine Adams, a contract with a federally subsidized housing project in Brooklyn and three publicly assisted but privately owned projects in Washington, D.C., remained in effect as of September 1996. See Adams, "Nation of Islam."

97. Adams's detailed investigation claimed that, in a "pattern of non-payment," the cumulative outstanding debts owed by the NoI in 1996 totaled $1.9 million (for which seventy-four lawsuits had been filed against NoI corporations and some of its key officials over 1986–96), in addition to which the organization owed $1.5 million in outstanding court judgments, unpaid liens, and secured claims. See Lorraine Adams, "Nation of Islam." Her findings corroborated entirely the previous research of David Gaines and William Jackson (dismissed by Farrakhan as a conspiracy) for *The Chicago Tribune*, in 1995.

4

The Paranoid Style in Black American Politics

We have a Congress, a Senate and a president working for the destruction of black people.

Louis Farrakhan, 1995[1]

The black community, as a product of their own experience, don't think that a conspiracy is such a bizarre phenomenon.

John Mack, Head of the Los Angeles Urban League, 1995[2]

To the extent that Americans have historically exhibited a marked proclivity toward embracing bizarre and ephemeral social and political phenomena, the political ascendancy of Louis Farrakhan is perhaps neither surprising nor entirely exceptional. What is truly unusual about the Farrakhan phenomenon, however, is not simply the confusion and ideological ambiguity that have enveloped the minister's controversial public persona in the United States, but more the unique brand of black separatist conservative populism that he so vigorously and consistently espouses. For Farrakhan represents far more than merely a conventional conservative authoritarian political actor or a right-wing black American populist. Rather, the NoI's leader constitutes the most powerful and comprehensive expression of political paranoia to be found in contemporary—as well as premodern—black American politics in the United States.

Although their religious and racial sources differ dramatically, Farrakhan's version of paranoid politics powerfully resembles that of many white American far-right extremist groups in its pronounced intensity, broad scope, and multiplicity of targets. Central to the worldviews of both the NoI's leader and the cadres of the white far-right is the concept of overarching conspiracy. Farrakhan consistently promotes the notion that a widespread and deeply rooted conspiratorial plot exists against African-Americans in the United States, and furthermore, the NoI leader publicly identifies the several agents of that sinister and far-reaching antiblack conspiracy. This dual project serves explicitly to draw popular African-American attentions to Farrakhan's own purported political autonomy and also to the relative moderation of the established national black American civil and political leadership elites in the United States. The political reactions that the minister thereby provokes from black and nonblack actors alike are invoked by Farrakhan to reaffirm and reinforce both the alleged veracity of his conspiratorial claims and his personal political authority as an independent, free-thinking, and courageous national black leadership aspirant. It is in his distinctive and fulsome embodiment of the paranoid style in contemporary black American politics that Farrakhan bases a substantial part of his national political leadership appeals as, simultaneously, a dedicated architect of African-American hopes and a forceful repository for white fears.

Farrakhan's novel locus in the paranoid hall of American political infamy is, moreover, doubly distinctive. First, expressions of paranoia in black American politics are relatively unusual (although certainly not unprecedented). At the very least, the legitimate concerns that many African-American politicians have often articulated over FBI surveillance and coercion, for example, are relatively few in comparison with the expansive scope and virulent nature of the many paranoid claims advanced by Farrakhan. Second, paranoid politics in the United States typically comprises, as a crucial feature, the notion of "un-American" activities and the identification of "un-American" conspirators. For Farrakhan, however, the claims of conspiracy that he persistently promotes are difficult to reconcile within the conceptual ambit of such notions. African-Americans have, after all, only been included in the United States as full citizens relatively recently. The ambivalence that many harbor toward their national identity—and both the historic and the contemporary inclusion of blacks within the broad "un-American" compass of many white paranoid groups—thus renders the relative absence of such claims from Farrakhan's brand of political paranoia rational and, at the same time, distinctive in comparative terms. While Farrakhan's paranoid convictions may therefore be incidental rather than central to his mass black support, they remain integral to his successfully stoking political controversy, and hence achieving national notoriety, which together have power-fully assisted his black leadership ambitions.

AUTHORITARIANISM, POPULISM, AND THE PARANOID STYLE IN AMERICAN POLITICS

In the years following World War II, in-depth examination of the social foundations of political authoritarianism (and, in particular, of anti-Semitic and fascist beliefs) became an important and understandable scholarly preoccupation for academics in general, and for European social scientists, in particular. The prewar rise of Nazism in Germany had powerfully spurred academic interest in authoritarianism as a culturally fostered personality trait during the 1930s. The banning and exile of leading members of the Frankfurt Institute during that decade led subsequently to their reconstituting at Berkeley, California, where they conducted the seminal sociological study of authoritarianism, *The Authoritarian Personality*. Drawing together the themes of anti-Semitism, discrimination, and political ideology, the text became a classic work of social science, "the most thoroughgoing attempt yet seen to . . . search for the roots of social action in personal motives displaced on public objects."[3]

Despite the book's controversial contemporary reception in the Academy and the widespread criticisms that were subsequently leveled at the very concept of an authoritarian personality, the notion has continued to retain a marked analytic resonance for social scientists. In 1984, for example, a special conference was convened on the topic of authoritarianism in Potsdam, New York. Several panels of the International Society of Political Psychology in 1990 were also devoted to reviewing four decades of research into the subject and, in April 1995, a workshop of the European Consortium on Political Research at Bordeaux, France, was convened upon the subject of racist political parties as a new authoritarian party "family."[4] The persistence of intolerance, prejudice, and discrimination against racial and ethnic minorities and the notable electoral successes of extremist right-wing political parties in several West European states during the late 1980s and early 1990s strongly encouraged renewed scholarly study of the social bases of their support.[5]

By comparison with Europe, however, the attention accorded American authoritarianism by political scientists has consistently been much more limited. The analytic imperative has traditionally been considerably weaker, given the very low incidence of mass-based, influential authoritarian American political movements. Such movements have confronted powerful and enduring societal and institutional obstacles to political success in the United States: a liberal political culture based upon a codified constitution and the protection of the fundamental civil liberties and rights of the individual citizen; the relative weakness and permeability of the American state; the complex division and pronounced fragmentation of governmental authority in America along both vertical and horizontal dimensions; extensive racial, ethnic, religious, and regional heterogeneity; and a dominant two-party system at once organizationally weak and ideologically inclusive. In consequence, authoritarian movements in America have been both more episodic and much less influential than their European counterparts.

Lack of political success has not deterred extremist American groups from persistent activism, though. Indeed, the significant popular attention devoted to white right-wing citizen militias and other extremist political activists during the mid-1990s has lent substantial credence to the conclusion of the most notable scholarly study of the authoritarian political fringe in the United States, published two decades earlier, that "the American population is still highly vulnerable to political extremism."[6] While the extent of that vulnerability may have been exaggerated in some of the more sensationalist of recent popular accounts, the novelty of extremist groups gaining growing public attention has itself been a noteworthy development in national American politics in the 1990s. It has also been one, moreover, that has offered a fittingly malevolent and macabre backdrop to the peculiar political ascendancy of Minister Farrakhan.[7]

An unusual constellation of factors encouraged the revival of both popular and populist coverage of extremist tendencies in American political life, and accounts for the renewed academic attention that the incidence and expressions of paranoid politics in the United States in general—and white right-wing authoritarianism, in particular—has increasingly received over the 1990s. The changing issue agenda of American politics, the perceived threats to domestic order from without and within the United States, and the dramatic and decisive victory of an increasingly conservative Republican party in the 1994 mid-term congressional elections together prompted editors and academics alike to analyze what some perceived as a sudden and alarming lurch to the right in American politics. Furthermore, over a relatively short period of time, the siege of David Koresh's sect of Branch Davidians at his ranch in Waco, Texas, in 1993; the fatal shooting of white extremist Randy Weaver's wife by agents of the Federal Bureau of Alcohol, Tobacco and Firearms in Rubyridge, Idaho in 1994; the bombing of a federal building in Oklahoma City (and arrest of suspect white supremacist Timothy McVeigh), in April 1995; the arrest of the Unabomber in March 1996; and the crude pipebomb attack on the Atlanta Olympics in July 1996 together concentrated national American attentions upon the activities of extremist right-wing individuals and organized groups (as well as the many allegations of conspiracy that they leveled at the federal government).[8]

The coincidence of these developments also focused attention upon deeper currents and fissures within the contemporary American polity. Perhaps most important, in the aftermath of the revolutions in Eastern Europe and the collapse of the Soviet Union in 1989 and 1990–91, respectively, the absence of an equivalent external threat to the national security of the United States cast open the opportunity for new and more concentrated attempts to identify possible internal sources of the various maladies and malaises afflicting American communities in the post–Cold War era: spiraling budget deficits, limited economic growth, diffuse perceptions of job insecurity in an era of rapid technological change, fear of violent crime, and widespread marital breakdown. In such a context, the politics of scapegoating—to which such a heterogeneous and diverse society has long been susceptible and has, on occasion, temporarily succumbed—enjoyed a new and unfortunate resurgence.

The political salience of attempts to identify internal sources of disorder also achieved an especially extensive reach in the context of the more conventional strains of American politics in the 1990s. Thus, some of the most dominant, recurrent themes of contemporary national political debate—crime, immigration, trade, and issues involving conflicts of cultural values (most notably, abortion, sexual orientation, and gun control)—were especially conducive to the eliciting of paranoid appeals. In particular, so-called lifestyle issues, which encompassed antagonism over moral and ethical values, were apt to animate the most fundamental and visceral bases of many Americans' outlooks upon both their individual lives and their nation as a whole. As Michael Barone and others have persuasively argued, the most acute, prolonged, and painful conflicts in American politics have derived as much, if not more than, from dissension over issues of culture, morality, and ethics than over ones involving economics.[9] Social issues, such as abortion rights and gun control, invariably force American citizens to address some of their most deeply held cultural beliefs and personal values.[10] For many Americans such issues have been prone to animate greater political interest and to encourage more extensive political mobilization than complex and abstruse public policy questions such as the federal budget deficit or social security reform. Although the Federal Reserve may be a target of their righteous animus, for example, few militias have actually formed around the cause of reforming national monetary policy.

Moreover, by virtue of their widespread salience to ordinary American voters and citizens, established politicians and aspirants to governmental office alike frequently felt compelled to make public pronouncements upon such issues themselves. Consequently, both the issue agenda of American politics and the substantive positions held by many national politicians were framed by, and often occupied ground that either overlapped with (or was not notably dissimilar to), the dominant concerns of the cults and extremist groups associated with the Texas, Idaho, and Oklahoma disasters. The political context of national U.S. politics was, after all, one in which a prime-time speech at the 1992 Republican convention included explicit references to the "cultural and religious war" allegedly being waged in America and in which the candidate making that acerbic speech, Pat Buchanan (who had not previously been elected to any public post), was subsequently treated by many media commentators and GOP operatives alike as an important force in the 1996 Republican presidential nomination battle, representing a sizeable—albeit somewhat disparate and inchoate—popular constituency.

The GOP's victory in the 1994 mid-term congressional elections also compounded popular perceptions of a dramatic and historic shift having occurred in the traditional social bases and issue concerns of American politics. In securing control of both houses of the U.S. Congress, the Republicans dramatically ended the brief return to unified party control of national government that Bill Clinton's election had heralded in 1992. Forty years of entrenched Democratic dominance of the House of Representatives was dramatically and surprisingly brought to an end. The Republicans triumphed, moreover, on the unusual basis of a program of government, the "Contract with America," which represented a decidedly conservative set of policy proposals. The new Speaker of the House even spoke publicly in terms of "renewing American civilization," bombastic language calculated intentionally to cast opponents of the Gingrich project on the side of the forces of barbarism. The marked enthusiasm of populist right-wing radio talk-show hosts, such as Rush Limbaugh, Oliver North, and G. Gordon Liddy, for the new GOP majority, and its electoral support by a majority of white southerners for the first time in the region's history, suggested that a politics of extremism that had traditionally been confined to the outer fringes of national American political life was increasingly entering the corridors of the Congress itself, a view that the politics of the 104th Congress did relatively little to disturb.[11]

The combination of these influences contributed powerfully to a revival of critical interest in extremist politics in America, but the overwhelming focus of such concern remained the extreme white right-wing. In this respect, the marginal attention that had always been accorded the incidence of authoritarian and conservative impulses among African-Americans was once more compounded. Traditionally, two factors have occasioned limited intellectual attention to be devoted to the phenomenon of black political extremism in the United States. First, and most notable, the combination of the absence of a substantial historic conflict over the institution of private property and the demagoguery of McCarthyism during the 1940s and early 1950s have together encouraged most postwar studies of American authoritarianism to examine white extremist groups, generally of the far-right.[12] Second, since black Americans have historically been among the most common targets of such white authoritarians, and since African-American extremism has traditionally been associated with leftist ideological tendencies, few political scientists have analyzed the black right-wing in general, or the Nation of Islam (NoI) in particular.[13] In addition, of course, as a secretive, racially exclusive organization, the NoI has not been readily amenable to conventional methods of scholarly investigation. Nonetheless, Farrakhan's NoI represents as powerful an exemplar of American conservative authoritarianism in its paranoid form as white far-right groups in the United States; albeit with its own particular, distinctive sets of racial, religious, and political identities and sources of popular black American support.

FARRAKHAN, POPULISM, AND PARANOIA

Despite the factors that have reliably informed the reluctance of scholars of American politics to apply extremist analyses to black leaders and African-American organizations in the United States, such a lack of attention is at once intellectually surprising and mildly disappointing: surprising, because extremist and unconventional politicians have certainly been present and active in black American politics during the twentieth century; and disappointing, because the absence of academic attention leaves something of an intellectual vacuum in the literature on modern black politics in the United States. Precisely because black American history has been so dominated by the long and inordinately costly struggle against their political, economic, and social deprivation, both the general absence and the occasional incidence of successful extremist political movements and currents among African-Americans in the United States merit the considered attention of researchers.[14]

The roots of political extremism in America are conventionally traced by political historians to early anti-immigrant or "nativist" social movements, which were invariably dominated by white Americans. "Aliens," whether foreign or indigenous, typically occupied the animus of such groups. Although some of the social and political movements, as well as the ideologies of both the left and right in America, admittedly manifest external origins and foreign influences of varying consequence (most typically, forms of Marxism for the left, and National Socialism and fascism on the right), many extremist groups in the United States have drawn heavily upon a distinctively homegrown American brand of populism.

Originating during the later nineteenth century, populism was a quintessentially American political movement, centered upon the rural and small-town Midwest and South. Two features were traditionally central to populist appeals: first, a demand for government intervention (whether state or federal) to aid particular groups that had fallen into social or economic distress, such as farmers; and, second, an appeal for effective political reforms to give the average American citizen more power in relation to public officials and large corporations. Neither component in themselves suggested, of necessity, especially adverse political results for African-Americans. If anything, in fact, the populists' demands for enlightened state intervention and assistance to the ordinary American citizen invariably promised beneficial consequences for often-deprived minority communities.

In addition, however, the role of race has been fundamental to American populism through the ages; so fundamental, in fact, as to encourage a near-exclusive concentration on white populist agitators in the United States by social scientists. Nineteenth century populists were frequently—and their twentieth century successors remain similarly—divided over the social cleavage of race. In the American South and southern parts of the Midwest, in particular, populists were generally extremely conservative on issues encompassing race and, in many cases (such as that of Alabama Governor and 1968 American Independence Party presidential candidate, George Wallace) made brutally racist political appeals. Even today, while the extreme left in the United States tends strongly to favor attempts to integrate the races and heartily supports racial and ethnic assimilation as a positive social ideal, the extreme right generally favors racial separation, either explicitly or implicitly. A substantial part of the extreme right (though not all) identifies America as a quintessentially "white" nation whose social, political, and cultural roots reside in northern Europe. Many such groups also incorporate into this essentialist vision of the United States additional notions of America as a fundamentally Anglo-Saxon and Christian democratic republic.[15] The formal, definitional neutrality of populist origins in theory has thus been frequently belied, and often very brutally and inhumanely so, by its historic practice in the United States.

The marked prevalence in the social science literature of studies of right-wing white American authoritarians is therefore eminently understandable in historical terms. Nonetheless, in generally eschewing consideration of nonwhite extremists, such studies provide a decidedly partial focus upon American extremist tendencies in general. This is particularly the case with regard to the NoI, in both its traditional and, especially, its modern guise under Farrakhan. For Farrakhan is most appropriately viewed not only as a conservative African-American populist, but also as an excellent contemporary example of the "paranoid style" in American politics.

Richard Hofstadter and the Paranoid Style in American Politics

Paranoia is conventionally defined as comprising, first, some form of mental disorder (typically characterized by persistent delusions of persecution and self-importance) and, second, an abnormal tendency to suspect and mistrust others.[16] Its most familiar and influential public exponent and arch-exemplar in modern American history, Senator Joseph Raymond McCarthy (R-WI), stimulated extensive academic inquiry into the origins, role, and consequences of paranoia within

U.S. social and political life.[17] Most notable, in order to locate McCarthy within his appropriate national historical setting, the late political historian Richard Hofstadter drew upon the standard definition of paranoia in order to develop the more specific notion of the American political paranoid. In so doing, Hofstadter's sweeping survey of American history since the republic's founding isolated the paranoid as an identifiable, distinctive, and peculiarly recurrent style in American politics through the ages.[18]

The paranoid politician represents an especially curious and compelling, though deeply unattractive, American public figure. In marked contrast to most politicians active in American national life, the political paranoid constitutes a distinctive activist. Most obvious, the stuff of "normal" politics—moderation and courtesy, comity and mutual cordiality, civility of manners and discourse, a consistent striving for conciliation and compromise—is not for the paranoid actor, for whom blandness and uniformity are traits to be zealously avoided at almost all costs. Indeed, it is partly by virtue of his vivid differentiation from conventional American politicians that the paranoid bases and sustains his public appeals and aspirations to mass popularity. Although it is unclear whether his typology is fully exhaustive, the paranoid exhibits six distinctive characteristics, according to Hofstadter. Possession of any one would classify the individual as an unusual political actor, but collectively they render the paranoid a distinctive and especially troubling political figure.

First, the perceived existence of an all-encompassing conspiracy is fundamental to the paranoid *Weltanschauung*, or worldview. The core feature that distinguishes paranoids from authoritarians—and that can be said, in an historic European context, to have separated Hitler from Mussolini during the 1930s, for example—is the former's vision of a vast and unrelenting conspiracy as the dominant force in human history. The central case advanced by the paranoid is that of "a gigantic yet subtle machinery of influence set in motion to undermine and destroy a way of life."[19] The paranoid is confronted by opponents whose goal is not merely the enactment and implementation of particular public policies but also, thereby, the effective eradication of an entire cultural or political tradition and, in the most extreme instances, the elimination of a whole people. Moreover, the latter is absolutely integral, not incidental, to the conspiratorial project. The paranoid thus constantly lives at an historic turning point, with time rapidly ebbing away and demanding a suitably forceful and prompt response from those under threat, should they wish to survive. The unavoidable choice that confronts the threatened group is between immediate, organized action to resist the conspiracy or its collective subjection to potentially apocalyptic consequences.

Second, the paranoid differs from most conventional American politicians in the fundamental nature of his political demands. The paranoid is a demonstrably militant leader, for whom the necessities and niceties of conventional politics are essentially tantamount to acquiescence in defeat. Compromise, concessions, consensus, and conciliation are the bankrupt political currency of appeasement. The paranoid's demands are, by contrast, wholly unavailable for bargaining and exist to be met in full rather than being mediated or compromised. Such militancy is a vital feature of the paranoid's public praxis. The strength, sophistication, and persistence of the conspiratorial forces ranged against the paranoid requires his opposition—and that of the vulnerable group whose cause he selflessly champions—to be full, unequivocal, and uncompromising.

Third, the paranoid explicitly identifies and demonizes political opponents—both domestic and foreign—as enemies. As Sargent argues, the identification of a conspiracy permits one to know who the enemy is, and the existence of enemies represents a constant and central feature of the American paranoid's peculiarly distorted political vision.[20] Those who participate in the conspiracy against a particular group or established way of life (whether directly or indirectly) represent far more than mere political opponents. So great are the stakes involved, and so fundamental and intense are the differences in respective worldviews, that the relationship between the paranoid and his political protagonists merits characterization in terms analogous to war. Moreover, the enemy is both readily identifiable in the paranoid mind-set and bears direct responsibility for many current maladies and for the threat of future disasters to come. (Ironically, however, precisely by virtue of his impressive political skills and potentially overwhelming power, the enemy also elicits from the paranoid a grudging admiration and even imitation.[21])

Fourth, in the intense and unrelenting struggle between virtue and vice, good and evil, the possibility of redemption as well as treason is an important paranoiac belief. Although the symbolic attractions and material blandishments of the conspirators' cause may frequently be great, the possibility exists that even members of the

enemy's malign coalition may later be persuaded to reform their misplaced and dangerous views. Thus, the convert occupies an especially
prestigious status in the paranoid world, serving as "living proof that
all the conversions are not made by the wrong side."[22] The confessions
of subversives in the federal government during the McCarthy era, for
example, provided to many American observers clear and irrefutable
confirmation of the truth of the Senator's claims of internal conspiracy
and, thereby, further fuel for his anticommunist political project and
zealous self-promotion.

Fifth, the paranoid possesses an abiding ambivalence—tending
to outright hostility—toward abstract thought in general, and toward
its practitioners in the academy and the mass media in particular.
Frequently aiding and abetting his enemies directly, the intellectual
represents a particularly grave political threat, given the authoritative
professional status of the critic and the associated ability of such a
thinker to undermine the veracity of the paranoid's case solely
through rational argument. Nonetheless, the intellectual can also, by
virtue of the very same mental resources and prestigious social status,
confer a desirable degree of outside credibility upon the paranoid's
claims, as both a source of independent and "objective" advice and as
a counter to the enemies' arsenal of intellectuals.[23]

Sixth, the diverse movements manifesting the paranoid style
tend to be episodic rather than enduring in character. The essentially
temporary and transient nature of paranoid political forces suggested
strongly to Hofstadter that the:

> . . . paranoid disposition is mobilized into action chiefly by
> social conflicts that involve ultimate schemes of values and that
> bring fundamental fears and hatreds, rather than negotiable
> interests, into political action.[24]

Thus, conflicts over complex but essentially incremental questions of
fiscal or monetary policy, for example, are not the paranoid's preoccupation. Rather, catastrophe, tragedy, and disaster (or the fear and
threat thereof) are most conducive to eliciting paranoid appeals. The
paranoid tendency is aroused by a conflict of interests that the protagonists in the struggle perceive (rightly or wrongly) to be wholly and
enduringly irreconcilable and that, therefore, are also entirely unamenable to resolution by conventional political processes and established procedures; an environment exacerbated further when the

representatives of a particular social group or collective interest perceive themselves to be unable materially to influence either the political system or the governmental process to discernible effect. Ethnic, religious, and class conflicts have hence tended to constitute the major foci for paranoid politics in America, forming the main stages of the democratic theater upon which the various demagogues have strutted and starred.

Farrakhan and the Paranoid Style: A Suitable Case for Treatment?

Although Hofstadter referred in passing to the Black Muslims—observing that paranoid tendencies existed on both sides of the racial divide in the segregated America of the 1950s—the principal focus of his seminal treatise on paranoid politics was the American white far-right, and its specific expressions in McCarthyism and the John Birch Society, in particular. Farrakhan's distinctive brand of conservative black nationalism nonetheless merits analysis according to the basic framework of paranoid politics that Hofstadter outlined. For, although some popular commentaries have drawn attention to the paranoiac character of Farrakhan's public discourse,[25] the extent to which the categories identified by Hofstadter clearly and fully encompass Farrakhan is both striking and politically significant. Of course, many of Farrakhan's more remarkable paranoid claims derive—either directly or indirectly—from his eccentric theological beliefs, discussed in the previous chapter. Others, however, remain entirely separate and distinct from Farrakhan's unusual religious convictions. Whatever their source, though, they suggest that the Black Muslim minister meets Hofstadter's six paranoid criteria in full: belief in conspiracy; militancy; identification of enemies; faith in redemption; ambivalence toward intellectuals; and an essentially episodic character. Let us deal with each in turn.

An explicit and central feature of Farrakhan's worldview is his resolute conviction that a deep, far-reaching, and formidably powerful conspiracy—comprising both general and particular dimensions—currently exists against black Americans in the United States. Just as previously, for McCarthy, communist subversion within the U.S. federal government constituted the only persuasive explanation for postwar Soviet expansionism and the "loss" of China, so, for Farrakhan, the existence of a diffuse antiblack conspiracy represents the sole compelling rationale for the grievous socioeconomic plight of many African-

Americans in the post–civil rights era and the devastated character of many black communities across America currently. Only the fact of secret plots, premeditated machinations, and malign plans that are all deliberately designed to ruin African-Americans can adequately account for the atrophy, despair, and seemingly unremitting downward spiral of so many black lives.

Admittedly, a substantial component of Farrakhan's outspoken public lexicon emphasizes both the individual and the collective responsibilities of African-Americans themselves for their fate. Following his religious precepts, Farrakhan consistently and vigorously encourages black Americans to assume the responsibility for their own welfare, reject government programs as appropriate palliatives or effective solutions to current black problems, and adopt private, proactive initiatives to regenerate and revitalize African-American communities across the United States. Engendering such tenets of individual and collective responsibility among blacks, however, essentially represents a necessary response to conditions that have been externally created, imposed, and perpetuated by whites. In this context, African-Americans in the United States are:

> . . . of no further use to the children of our former slavemasters and when a thing loses its use or utility, it loses its value. If your shoes wear out, you don't keep them around. Once it loses its utility, you move to get rid of it . . . We cannot accept the fact that they think black people have become a permanent underclass . . . If we have become useless in a racist society, then you must know that, not public policy, but a covert policy is being formulated to get rid of that which is useless since the economy is going down, and the world is going down.[26]

Black citizens in America must recognize, according to Farrakhan, that they continue to suffer terribly from a dependent, welfare mentality and that, even in the 1990s (as a result principally of the peculiar institution of slavery), "we as a people are sick." Nonetheless, black Americans collectively are essentially absolved by Farrakhan from the full responsibility for their ignoble and parlous contemporary state; the overwhelming—though not the exclusive—locus for their tragic and disheartening modern condition remains essentially external. Thus, for example, the type of devastating fratricidal conflict in which almost 96 percent of the crime and violence in the African-American community is perpetrated by blacks upon other blacks, represents ". . . a field in which the wicked manipulate our ignorance to create genocide, but using our own hands as the destructive force."[27] African-Americans are essentially unwitting pawns, black dupes in a concerted and comprehensive (although heavily disguised) national project of racial genocide, one that is fundamentally determined, devised, and dominated by whites.[28]

The particularistic dimension of the antiblack conspiracy concerns the incessant harassment of national black U.S. politicians and the existence of recurrent, premeditated attempts at the complete destruction of "authentic" black American political and civic leaders. Militant black public figures who either achieve mass followings among African-Americans or who attain influential political roles are invariably made the subject of persistent and vicious attacks by a fearful, cowardly, and intimidated white establishment. For Farrakhan, such black leaders encompass a range of historic and contemporary African-American figures, from the controversial and flamboyant black congressman Adam Clayton Powell ("lynched because he got too close to the juice box"[29]) and Jesse Jackson, to former Chicago congressman Gus Savage, and Washington, D.C., mayor Marion Barry. Although the specific authors of such dastardly attacks and their exact methods are rarely identified by Farrakhan, their political goals nonetheless remain self-evident: the destabilization and eventual destruction of African-American political leaders who fearlessly represent and accurately articulate the true interests of black Americans. The long and distinguished list of black politicians in the United States who have been subject to external surveillance and various forms of political, economic, and social intimidation is ample proof of the many malign forces ranged against courageous African-American leaders.[30]

In this specific generic context, Farrakhan also perceives the existence of sinister and malevolent forces that are dedicated to achieving his own elimination. That this should be the case is not particularly surprising. Since the NoI's leader clearly views himself as the most honest, dedicated, and complete personification of authentic collective black interests in America, it is only to be expected that the many dangerous forces ranged against those interests in general should isolate Farrakhan in particular for especially concerted, aggressive, and persistent attack. Indeed, in this respect, the sheer number and diversity of these hostile anti-Farrakhan forces is impressive. Thus, for example, Farrakhan held (in 1990) that President George Bush wanted to have him murdered,[31] while the implication of Farrakhan in Malcolm X's assassination was, furthermore, inextricably linked to the deliberate, discrete attempt to discredit his increasingly influential political role as an African-American leader that has occurred since 1984. The revival of popular and elite black interest in Malcolm during the 1990s resulted from a long-term conspiracy to undermine the minister's increasing popularity among black Americans at large:

> . . . it is because I am popular today, and there's only one Black man in the Black community who has popularity dead to match my popularity living and that's Malcolm X and/or Martin Luther King [sic]! So if you can tie me to the murder of Malcolm X you can put a cloud over Louis Farrakhan and diminish him in importance to this community—and perhaps you can incite someone to murder him. That's the plot. That's the plan.[32]

The arrest of Malcolm's daughter, Qubillah Shabazz, in 1995, on a nine-count federal indictment that charged her with complicity in an assassination attempt on Farrakhan—and that ultimately resulted in the trial's abandonment—was yet another powerful example of the lengths to which antiblack conspirators would go in order to undermine the Black Muslim's increasing leadership credentials among the minority American community. It showed clearly that the "ultimate aim of this government is to destroy Louis Farrakhan by planting the seeds of public contempt and hatred" through a compliant news media, thus "setting the stage for my incarceration or assassination."[33] That homicidal stage was also powerfully aided by Farrakhan's 1996 World Friendship Tour "interfering with America's foreign policy objective in Africa and in the Middle East," interference that the minister held had prompted intense discussions in both the White House and the Congress as to how best to silence him.[34]

The unremitting and increasingly desperate attempts to isolate and discredit Farrakhan also include deliberate, concerted efforts to attack and undermine his popular political base, as well as his prestigious personal reputation. Thus, even the spread of crack cocaine and other "hard," addictive drugs in America's inner cities—the NoI's principal recruiting sites and mass constituency—since the early 1980s is explicable in terms of anti-Farrakhan conspiracies:

> I have noticed that since my coming to tremendous popularity, crack has come to prominence in the various metropolitan centers of this nation. I don't think this is accidental. I do believe with all my heart that there is a purposeful destruction of the black community.[35]

Indeed, according to Farrakhan, a revelatory series of investigative articles in the *Chicago Tribune* in March 1995, which persuasively argued that the NoI was an organization pervaded by debt, dominated by nepotism, and rife with corruption, was itself part of an ongoing conspiracy between American journalists and "international bankers" to destroy the NoI's leader.[36] Only the fortuitous combination of Farrakhan's immense vigilance, infallible judgment, and acutely sensitive political antennae have thus far foiled these accumulated foul and fiendish plots. A representative example of his unintimidated third-person response to his many unidentified and absent enemies occurred in 1991:

> Everything you try to do to destroy Farrakhan, it backfires on you and now you're just about at your wit's end! You really want Farrakhan? Well, here I am! I ain't going nowhere![37]

Unbowed, unbossed, and undefeated, Farrakhan clearly views himself as the most vilified black American man in the history of the United States; vilification that serves as yet further proof, were any either warranted or required, of the fact of his articulating eternal truths in the most brave and fearless of fashions. Farrakhan's opening remarks to a speech to the National Press Club in August 1984, for example, included a reference to his having "the distinction of being the most openly censured and repudiated black man in the history of this country,"[38] a spectacularly impressive political performance for a figure unknown to the vast majority of Americans a mere six months previously. Nevertheless, according to the NoI's leader, of all contemporary and prior black American political figures, only Malcolm X even approximates the disgraceful level of national (and international) vilification and censure directed at Farrakhan over recent years.

That unrelenting vilification also serves to embellish Farrakhan's claims of prophetic stature since, like the Messiah, he must of necessity suffer widespread insult, injury, and indignity before rising to appropriate public recognition and full and unchallenged leadership status among his people. Moreover, Farrakhan is evidently convinced that, like Jesus previously, his personal destruction is not merely political or social in character but necessarily encompasses his actual physical assassination. Public espousals of a belief in an all-encompassing conspiracy—the leitmotif of paranoids and demagogues around the world and through the ages—is thus a conspicuously prominent feature of Farrakhan's distinctive worldview.

That Farrakhan also merits appropriate designation as a militant is no doubt clear and compelling by now. Farrakhan's political, economic, and social demands are nonnegotiable in character. For Farrakhan, the constant and fundamental imperative to challenge the blindness, deafness, and muted character of his African-American audiences necessarily entails that his public rhetoric be consistently as clear, strident, and provocative as possible. To awaken a sleeping race (Farrakhan once even entitled a suitably modest and circumspect monograph, "I Am an Alarm Clock"), his message must be propounded in an uncompromisingly aggressive, articulate, and vocal fashion. Thus, the minister's sermons and speeches are incontestably infused by political extremism, and Farrakhan consistently and publicly condemns "crossover" black politicians who sell out by egregiously compromising with "the system." The establishment of a separate black American homeland; the quarantining of AIDS carriers (and, implicitly, homosexuals in general); the essentially domestic, secondary, and family-centered role of African-American women; the implacable opposition to abortion rights all clearly testify to a political figure whose values and policy prescriptions do not admit of compromise and are unavailable for negotiation. "Coalition-builder" is more a term of abuse than one deserving approbation in Farrakhan's militant political lexicon.

Indeed, even Farrakhan's lectures and rallies are frequently not public in the proper sense of the term; both African-American women and whites have frequently been excluded from attending. Admittedly, many private organizations scrutinize the credentials of those attending their meetings before allowing them admission. They tend, however, neither to exclude individuals merely on the basis of their race or gender, nor to deny entry to those citizens wishing to attend from genuine interest rather than a desire to cause disruption. Of course, in more general terms, given the context of America's inevitable fall and the imminent global apocalypse, compromise and conciliation would be manifestly self-defeating for Farrakhan and the NoI, black Americans collectively, and (indirectly, at least) the human race in general. Hardly surprising, then, that Farrakhan has frequently subscribed—both explicitly and implicitly—to the clear, simple, and uncompromisingly militant dictum that, "if you are not for us, you are against us."[39] Farrakhan's black and white view of the world is as wide-ranging in its inclusive compass as it is certain of its infallible veracity.

An additional, and very important, dimension to Farrakhan's militancy clearly fulfills the third of Hofstadter's paranoid criteria: the NoI leader frequently and relentlessly demonizes his many political opponents as either malign, misguided, or foolish enemies. Such demonization is in part a function of the pressing need to awaken black Americans from their slave-induced mental and spiritual slumber in order to reeducate them to their true worth, path to salvation, and proper national (and ultimately global) vocation. It also represents, however, a genuine reflection of Farrakhan's theological beliefs concerning the imminent worldwide conflict between the races and the Armageddon that this conflict will occasion. Given the immense magnitude of the stakes involved—apocalypse, global war, and the final emergence of God's righteous kingdom on Earth—demonization of opponents is less a risky gamble than a necessary condition of Farrakhan's preparatory teachings of black Americans prior to their full and enduring emancipation. It is in this aspect of the paranoid demeanor, in particular, that Farrakhan's prominent role as an assiduous architect of fear in contemporary America is most centrally to be found and that has occupied the dominant focus of national and international media coverage of the NoI's leader.

Although—like McCarthy previously—he rarely mentions specific individuals by name, preferring instead the characteristically comfortable demagogic luxury of anonymity and sweeping generalization, Farrakhan frequently invokes indirect assistance (generally of a divine nature) in explaining the existence of antiblack conspiracies and in ascertaining the identities of the various antiblack conspirators. He has referred most notoriously (in a richly exotic plot worthy of George Lucas or Isaac Asimov), for example, to a vision of being transported in 1985 to a spaceship hovering forty miles above the Earth, where Elijah Muhammad issued him instructions and prophesied the 1986 U.S. bombing raid on Tripoli, Libya.[40] Access to such privileged cosmic assistance has enabled Farrakhan to divine, and explicitly to identify for a mass black public, the several conspiratorial forces that are responsible for African-American disadvantage and degradation, both historically and in the modern era in the United States. Four of these malevolent agents of destruction are especially noteworthy and feature prominently in Farrakhan's regular public indictments of the enemies of black America: Jews, the U.S. federal government, white Americans, and black accommodationists.

Unlike both Elijah Muhammad and the pre-1964 Malcolm X—for whom white Americans in general were intrinsically evil devils and among whom neither made substantial distinctions—Farrakhan has increasingly isolated Jews (both within and outside America) as a particularly influential source of mass black oppression in the United States. Most notable, Farrakhan vigorously defended Jesse Jackson's "Hymietown" reference in 1984 and held Jewish groups responsible for anonymous death threats that were issued against Jackson during that year's presidential campaign. Almost a decade later, in January 1994, Farrakhan informed an African-American audience at the New York City Regiment Armory that "Jews are the most organized, rich and powerful people, not only in America, but in the world. They're plotting against us even as we speak." Farrakhan has also argued that Jews dominated the slave trade and has speculated that Jewish doctors deliberately inject the HIV virus into black American patients in order to advance black genocide, endorsing a Black Muslim aide's statement to this effect as "the truth."[41]

The themes of hatred, physical violence, and death represent regular components of Farrakhan's public references to or about Jews. Such ominous references are, of course, neither coincidental nor unintentional. As a rhetorical device, however unsophisticated, the premeditated and deliberate emphasis upon violence is one that is not only calculated to create the maximum possible amount of rapt audience reaction and media attention but also—given the systematic murder of millions of Jews in death camps under Nazi Germany (and the brutal incarceration and grotesque mistreatment of many others)—one that is especially powerful, deeply distasteful, and grievously offensive to many individuals, Jewish and non-Jewish alike. Farrakhan's most notorious comments, made during a radio address in Chicago in March 1984 are a good example of his more general rhetorical approach to black-Jewish relations in America:

> The Jews don't like Farrakhan, so they call me Hitler. Well, that's a good name. Hitler was a very great man. He wasn't great for me as a black person, but he was a great German . . . He rose Germany up from nothing. Well, in a sense you could say there's similarity in that we are rising our people up from nothing. What is it about Hitler that you love to call every black man who rises up with strength a Hitler? What have I done? Who have I killed? I warn you, be careful, be careful. You're putting yourself in dangerous, dangerous shoes. You have been the killer of all the prophets. Now, if you seek my life, you only show that you are no better than your fathers.[42]

Despite his apparently sincere expressions of personal admiration for many individual American Jews, and for the Jewish people as a whole, few of Farrakhan's public discussions of Jews omit a fulsomely lurid lexicon of murder, destruction, and retaliation. For example, the minister claimed, in a speech at the University of the District of Columbia in March 1988 that, "You (Jews) want my people to kill me."[43] The NoI even attributed the revival in 1994 of allegations concerning Farrakhan's complicity in Malcolm X's assassination to a Jewish plot, led by the New York-based Anti-Defamation League, to "incite the murder" of its leader. Farrakhan's many enemies having "already determined that I must die," Jewish-controlled media had shrewdly sought to enhance Malcolm's image in order "to use a dead man against the only living black American . . . who can't be bought."[44] In the same year, the universally negative and hostile nationwide media response to Farrakhan's "rebuke" of Khalid Muhammad's New Jersey speech also affirmed, for the NoI's leader, the stark reality of the continued Jewish conspiratorial project: "I see a conspiracy. I don't know what others see, but the conspiracy is to destroy Louis Farrakhan and the Nation of Islam."[45] As for those who hold Farrakhan's vision to be less than 20–20 and more than a little impaired, his morbid preoccupation with death and destruction reflects the obvious fact that, according to the NoI's leader:

The germ of murder is already sewed into the hearts of Jews in this country . . . The Jews talk about "Never again." Well, I am your last chance, too, Jews. Listen, Jews, this little Black boy is your last chance because the Scriptures charge (you) with killing the prophets of God. But if you rise up to try to kill me, then Allah promises you that he will bring on this generation the blood of the righteous. All of you will be killed outright . . . You cannot say "Never again" to God, because when He puts you in the oven, "Never again" don't mean a thing.[46]

Imitating the viciously unrelenting and unapologetic anti-Semitism of the Irish-American priest, Father Charles Coughlin, during the New Deal, Jews occupy a central role for Farrakhan. Instead of the three interlocking conspiracies of the 1930s that Coughlin identified (the New Deal, communism, and international banking), however, it is the Jews' alleged historic role in slave-ownership and their putative dominance of the American mass media and entertainment industries that occupy the focus of Farrakhan's virulent anti-Semitism. Thus, according to the Black Muslim, the United States is "being made ripe for a take-over from without" through a Jewish plot to use Hollywood and the music industry to corrupt Americans through the "sexual drive." That many Jewish writers, directors, and producers of films have sympathetically addressed the subject of black disadvantage in America (such as Steven Spielberg's adaptation of *The Color Purple*, a novel by the black American feminist Alice Walker), and that much of the most lurid, savage, and rabidly misogynistic sexual imagery in contemporary popular music is to be found among the recorded work of black American artists (including some of Farrakhan's most enthusiastic and outspoken public supporters, such as the rapper Ice Cube[47]), are facts that rarely seem to disturb the NoI leader's simple analysis of the key sources of "corrupting" influences in contemporary American society.[48]

For many Americans, Farrakhan's unrelenting public hostility toward Jews is more than a matter of its intensity and depth. Farrakhan's thuggish animus is also seen by several commentators as being sinister and politically dangerous, in comparison with both Coughlin previously and other anti-Semites currently.[49] This view is to a large extent attributable to the post–civil rights era political context of black-Jewish relations having been altered in ways that have increased the potential for economic competition, and for social and political polarization, between the two minority American communities.

First, the shared moral commitment that strongly informed black–Jewish cooperation in the civil rights movement during the 1950s and 1960s subsequently foundered on class and ethnic conflicts over affirmative action, education, urban violence, the Middle-East, and Africa.[50] Second, whereas shared working class origins and the political institutions of organized labor and the Democratic party mediated conflict between Jews and both Irish and African-Americans (and thereby limited Coughlin's appeal) in the 1930s, the contemporary political environment is characterized by largely dissimilar class interests and electoral affiliations between blacks and Jewish Americans. Although a decisive majority of Jewish Americans remain supportive of the Democratic party, their identification with, and loyalty to, the party's candidates is neither as overwhelming nor as reliable as that of African-Americans.

Third, Farrakhan's anti-Semitism encompasses an important foreign policy dimension that was wholly unavailable to Father Coughlin during the 1930s: opposition to the state of Israel and its international allies. Antipathy toward Israel among Americans is hardly confined to the NoI, of course; many others share Farrakhan's view of U.S. foreign policy toward Israel as being unduly favorable and as deriving principally from the "abnormal . . . power of the Jewish leadership."[51] Typically, though, few express it in the virulently aggressive and disparaging terminology of Farrakhan, for whom those nations that assisted in the original establishment of the state of Israel (an "outlaw act") and who currently lend it financial assistance, military aid, and diplomatic support constitute nothing less than "criminals in the sight of Almighty God."[52]

Farrakhan has nonetheless insisted that such adamant opposition to Israel is entirely unrelated to issues of anti-Semitic belief on his part, explaining that:

> When I made the statement that Israel had not had any peace in forty years and will never have any peace because there can be no peace structured on injustice, lying, thieving, and deceit, using God's name to shield your dirty religion or practices

under His holy and righteous name, this was termed to be an attempt on my part to discredit Judaism as a religion.[53]

Farrakhan's appeals frequently seek to invoke such allegedly neutral, nonreligious, anti-Israeli sentiments in order to reach across racial and ethnic lines to "patriotic" Americans generally:

> I am very concerned, not just for Black people, but for America. I see America like ancient Egypt, Babylon, and Rome, going down the tubes—not from external aggression, but from internal corruption. When a strong Jewish lobby can control the United States Senate, where anything Israel wants, she can get. This kind of lobby robs the American people of their vote when they have voted for representation in the Congress and that Congress is manipulated by a Jewish lobby and other lobbies, then this strangles the democratic process and, in my judgement, is the great danger to America's future.[54]

That Farrakhan's concern for the American nation as a whole rests curiously and uneasily with his stinging rebukes of black American parents for bringing up their children to "salute the conqueror's flag"[55] (i.e., the Stars and Stripes) is suggestive of either a somewhat confused intellectual apparatus or more than a mild deficiency in the minister's political sincerity. The NoI's own flag, after all, represents the Black Muslims' core belief in the status of black Americans as a nation within a nation, and Farrakhan has stated explicitly that, "As a Muslim, I cannot pledge allegiance to the flag; my allegiance is to God."[56] Much as Farrakhan condemned the U.S. Constitution as "racist" in the 1980s only to praise its First Amendment guarantee of freedom of speech in his Million Man March speech of 1995, so Farrakhan's economy with the truth about America's plight (not to mention his personal love of an America whose incipient destruction at Muslim hands he eagerly related to an Iranian audience as an impending and welcome "privilege") is such as to assure him of every award in the patriotic parsimony stakes.[57]

Nonetheless, such allegedly sincere patriotic appeals win Farrakhan political admirers and potential allies in what might otherwise be viewed as an unexpected quarter: far-right white American supremacist groups, such as the Ku Klux Klan and Aryan Nation. It is in their shared—and deeply rooted—perception of both Jews and the U.S. federal government as the true enemies of the American people that Farrakhan secures enthusiastic political support from white supremacists who zealously adhere to notions of the intrinsic inferiority of his own race. Roy Frankhouser, a former KKK Grand Dragon, for example, expressed the consensus of a meeting in October 1985, in Michigan, of over 200 neo-Nazis and Klansman nationwide that, "Louis Farrakhan is a man who understands the problems of this country the same as we do, and patriots shouldn't shy away from someone who speaks the truth, no matter what color he is."[58] Tom Metzger, whose KKK career was superseded by his heading the equally racist Aryan Nation, also attended Farrakhan's 1985 rally in Los Angeles, donating $100 to the NoI. Informal contacts between the NoI and far-right groups were established around this time, though the substantive results of their bigoted liaison remain unknown.

Although it remains one of the exceptional examples of Farrakhan actually serving as an agent for encouraging a curious form of black–white "understanding," the racist rapprochement was in some respects unsurprising. For while white hate groups retain their fundamental belief in the inherent racial inferiority of African-Americans, it is the Jewish community and the federal governmental institutions of Washington, D.C., that are increasingly viewed as the genuine political threats and the real controlling forces that are responsible for America's recent relative economic decline and current societal woes. As one Klansman argued:

> The Klan in the 20s made a mistake thinking that evil resided in men who came home drunk or in Negroes who walked on the wrong side of the street. Today we see the evil is coming out of the government. To go out and shoot a Negro is foolish. It's not the Negro in the alley who's responsible for what's wrong with this country. It's the traitors in Washington.[59]

It is difficult to identify anything in the above statement with which Farrakhan—for whom Washington, D.C., also represents the avowed "capital of oppression"—would disagree. In judging one's political allies according to the inverted logic of the traditional, strategic tenet of possessing shared enemies, the Jewish community within and outside the United States represents a central fulcrum of political friendship for black and white extremists in America.[60] By the very same logic, of course, the fact that Farrakhan's more enthusiastic admirers include such racist and terrorist groups is itself eloquent testimony to many black Americans as to the dubious—even disreputable—ethical and political credentials of the NoI's leader.

Though of course striking, neither the acute irony nor the historic precedents of these unholy extremist overtures are lost on many observers.[61] After all, such unlikely associations represent nothing new or original in the politics of race in the United States in the postwar era. American Nazi party leader George Rockwell, for example, attended a Black Muslims Washington, D.C., rally in 1961, observing that he and Malcolm X were in complete agreement about the causes of and solutions to the problems of race relations in America, and donating twenty dollars to the NoI.[62] (Subsequently, he was a featured speaker at the NoI's Savior's Day convention in Chicago in 1962, declaring to warm African-American applause his strong belief that Elijah Muhammad was "the Adolf Hitler of the black man.") Moreover, in 1964, Malcolm X argued in favor of conservative Republican presidential candidate Barry Goldwater's dictum that "extremism in the defence of liberty is no vice, moderation in the pursuit of justice is no virtue."[63] Without engaging in speculations upon the geometric configuration of the shape of ideological fissures in American public opinion in the 1990s, the consonance in the positions of extremists of the left and right across several issue dimensions is commonplace in current U.S. politics, but in particular with regard to issues involving race. Admittedly, Farrakhan and David Duke represent imperfect political parallels; nonetheless, the distortion of their ugly mirror image is more one of degree than of nature.

The biracial animus directed at Jews by the white far right and the NoI is also invoked by Farrakhan as a central explanation of his isolation by Jewish groups for particularly vehement and unrelenting public attack. Farrakhan holds that the vigor with which he has been condemned by Jewish groups is in fact entirely unrelated to his alleged anti-Semitism. Rather, he attributes such attacks to growing Jewish fears that non-Jewish white Americans will be alerted by Farrakhan's vocal, persistent, and increasingly effective activism to the disproportionate political, financial, and cultural influence that Jews, a mere 6 percent of the American population, wield in the United States. In this respect, much as Farrakhan seeks to teach his race the "truth" about America, so white supremacist groups are intellectually in advance of their racial compatriots in persistently and vigorously emphasizing both the scope and depth of Jewish domination of America. Hence, Farrakhan has even lavished fulsome praise upon *None Dare Call It Conspiracy*, an unrelentingly anti-Semitic tract penned by the self-confessed white supremacist, Gary Allen. The vociferousness with which Farrakhan refers to Jews is not aimed exclusively at black Americans, but also targets white Americans in need of patriotic "education" to the insidious clout of Jewish America.

Nonetheless, Farrakhan vigorously denies the charge of anti-Semitism, a denial that assumes two main forms. The first rebuttal charges that accusations of anti-Semitism are the invidious product of the misrepresentation of his views by the American mass media. In this respect, it is certainly true that Farrakhan's articulation of sentiments that express deep animus toward Jews and Judaism have been a relatively recent part of his public discourse in America. Prior to 1984, such references were relatively rare in his speeches. Moreover, it clearly has also been the case that media representations of some of his public speeches have—whether deliberately or unintentionally—omitted particular nuances that enter his public discourse, such as leaving out the qualification of "wickedly" from press and TV reports of Farrakhan's descriptions of Hitler as "great." Notwithstanding this, however, the argument that selective quotations taken out of their full context are responsible for erroneous notions that Farrakhan is an anti-Semite is extremely difficult—indeed impossible—to sustain. Even as late as 1995, for example, Farrakhan continued to inform worshippers in Chicago that Hitler's genocidal project had actually been bankrolled by Jewish financiers:

> Little Jews died while big Jews made money. Little Jews being turned into soap while big Jews washed themselves with it. Jews playing violin, Jews playing music, while other Jews (were) marching into the gas chambers.[64]

Most observers might be forgiven for wondering, if Farrakhan's many well-documented public comments do not qualify as anti-Semitic, how lurid, derogatory, and vicious must a defamatory public statement about an entire social group be to permit the designation as an accurate rather than an invidious one.

Second, Farrakhan invokes the claim that it is simply impossible for African-Americans to be racist. In an argument that has gained significant support among African-Americans at both elite and mass levels, Farrakhan contends that "For a black man to become a racist he must first have power."[65] Racism as a generic term, however, comprises three distinct meanings: a belief in the superiority of a particular race and prejudice based upon this belief; antagonism toward other races based upon this belief; and the theory that human abilities are essentially determined by race. Wielding power is not, and never has been, a necessary condition of professing racist views.

Of course, the adverse consequences for others of a belief among African-Americans of their own superiority or of racially predetermined differences in human abilities are limited, given the disproportionate exclusion from economic and political resources of African-Americans. Their situation hardly parallels the old white minority in apartheid South Africa or Hitler's Nazis after 1933. While they could only implement their genocidal policies once acceding to state power, however, the Nazis—themselves well-versed in the populist rhetoric of exclusion, disadvantage, vicitimization, and conspiracy—were no less racist in their beliefs prior to Hitler's becoming German Chancellor than subsequently. Power facilitated their carrying out their racist convictions as public policy, but the convictions preexisted.

Moreover, the possibility that prejudiced beliefs exist among African-Americans is a very real one, and indeed the notion of an inherent black racial superiority has traditionally been one of the doctrinal mainstays of the NoI. Even Farrakhan himself, both in his rebuke of Khalid Muhammad and in his unconvincing claims that the NoI has abandoned the notion of whites being congenitally evil devils, at least implicitly concedes that prejudice and bigotry can be harbored by members of any—and potentially all—social, racial, and ethnic groups. The notion that Farrakhan's contention that blacks cannot be racist actually exculpates him from the legitimate charge of anti-Semitism is a spurious and unconvincing one.

Still, Jewish conspirators constitute only one—albeit an especially influential—component of the multiplicity of nemeses and nefarious forces arrayed against African-Americans. Although Farrakhan holds Jews responsible for many of the most serious problems facing black (and white) Americans, the scale of organization necessary to import the quantity of hard drugs and to spread HIV sufficiently to wreak social and economic devastation among urban black American communities requires assistance by the one U.S. institution capable of concerted national and international action: the federal government. The federal role in the oppression of black Americans is substantial, and assumes a twofold dimension in Farrakhan's paranoid analysis.

First, through the combination of its inaction against black-on-black crime, its refusal to undermine indigenous and foreign drug barons and cartels, insufficient funding of AIDS research, and progressive regulations regarding homosexual relations, the federal government has effectively abetted black American genocide. Indeed, the secretive and sinister plots of the U.S. national authorities against African-Americans seem to know few apparent bounds. According to Farrakhan, the primary reason that the government has done nothing meaningful to stem intrablack crime, for example, is the increasingly desperate need among white Americans for organ donors.[66] As if this were not sufficiently obvious and compelling evidence of the government's anti-black malevolence, Farrakhan also argues that:

> ... the government has done nothing to stem the tide of alcohol, which is the number one destroyer of the people, and tobacco, which is of course killing our people; the chemicals that they are putting in the foods are killing the people.[67]

That tobacco and alcohol companies represented some of the largest corporate donors to the CBC annual legislative weekend—presumably unprompted by the federal government—which Farrakhan enthusiastically attended in 1993, evidently escaped his otherwise wide-ranging attention, not to mention his righteous censure.[68]

The all-encompassing dimensions of the governmental conspiracy (like the multiplicity of anti-Farrakhan forces in existence) are indeed almost staggering to the uninformed and unenlightened mind. Thus, Farrakhan argues:

> Don't you know the wicked ones today don't need ovens like they did in Germany for the Jews? Chemical death can do the job just as easily. A little dab of this in the water, you don't know what it is, you don't know what effect it has on your reproductive organs. You're drinking water that is death. You're breathing air that is death. You're eating food that is death because you're too lazy to get up and do for yourself.[69]

The racially discriminatory properties of water and air may no doubt represent as yet undiscovered facts for most Americans, not to mention natural science in general. (Although, in this context, Farrakhan's otherwise surprising defense of the "crossover" black popular music icon, recluse, and androgynous oxygen tent–enthusiast, Michael Jackson, perhaps becomes a little more understandable.[70])

Farrakhan has also occasionally argued that the federal government positively assists in the importation of drugs and dissemination of HIV among African-Americans. In 1990, for example, the minister argued that "there is a war being planned against black youth by the government of the United States under the guise of a war against drugs and gangs and violence."[71] Myriad as the problems that face the U.S. government and successive administrations typically are, both a compelling imperative and sufficient resources evidently exist for federal authorities to devote to devising and implementing the destruction of over a tenth of the nation's population.

The second manner in which the national government acts against black Americans at elite and mass levels is through the Federal Bureau of Investigation. The FBI's historic record of black harassment extends from Martin Luther King through the Black Panthers to members of Farrakhan's NoI. Marion Barry's arrest in 1990 on felony charges and the 1995 trial of Qubillah Shabazz, over an alleged FBI-orchestrated plot to hire a professional assassin to kill Farrakhan, represent two of the more recent examples of the Bureau's deep complicity in the premeditated and deliberate destruction of national black American political leadership. The latter, in particular, was attributed by Farrakhan to an attempt by the FBI (in alliance with the Justice Department of the Clinton Administration) to create "conflict and hostility" between the NoI and the family of Malcolm X.[72] At base, the FBI functions essentially as a coercive force against those blacks who reject the compromises and coalitional requirements of conventional American politics.[73]

If the FBI's role in seeking to undermine black leaders historically has been well-documented, the contemporary scope of such efforts has been less clearly proven to be either as broad or anywhere near as sinister in nature as Farrakhan holds. Barry, for instance, was certainly the subject of a well-planned and orchestrated sting operation; but not so much on the basis of his race or the novelty of drug use as for egregiously abusing his public office as mayor of the nation's capital. Antipathy toward the Bureau ironically is another area in which the parallels between Farrakhan and white extremist groups is especially marked. For the latter, the coercive tactics and surveillance techniques of the FBI are deployed not against genuine subversives but rather against patriotic and loyal Americans, such as Randy Weaver, who are simply gun owners and enthusiasts seeking to protect "their" nation. Although the motives and sources of the FBI's actions in such cases demonstrably differ, the persecution to which black leaders and white patriots alike are subjected is evidently common in the paranoid lens.

The racial identities of other American conspiratorial forces are less clearly or fully shared between Farrakhan and his many white supremacist admirers and putative allies, however. Just as white supremacist groups remain wedded to notions of the inherent racial inferiority of blacks, so Farrakhan's organization is still committed to a belief in the fundamental racial superiority of African-Americans. Although he claims to have "long ago left the language of White devils behind,"[74] Farrakhan views white Americans as being fundamentally antiblack in their values, attitudes, and behavior. Whether through direct participation or acquiescence in black American oppression, whites are universally guilty. Farrakhan has referred to whites, for example, as "the enemy" that trains black American babies subversively in order to undermine collective black solidarity. Whites have been "chemical engineers of death" and have "practised a form of genocide" toward dark-skinned peoples in America and toward people of color all over the world.[75] As the minister told a black City College audience in New York:

> The white man is our mortal enemy, and we cannot accept him. I will fight to see that vicious beast go down into the lake of fire prepared for him from the beginning, that he never rise again to give any innocent black man, woman or child the hell that he has delighted in pouring on us for 400 years.[76]

White Americans' fundamental antagonism toward blacks is also manifest in racial disjunctures in partisan preferences in recent elections in the United States. Democratic presidential candidates have never secured a majority of the white vote since African-Americans achieved civil and political equality in 1964 and 1965, respectively, whereas blacks have overwhelmingly supported the Democratic party at all levels.[77] Even within the Democratic party, the Jackson campaigns demonstrated the pronounced reluctance of white Americans actively to support a black American candidate for public office; a reluctance manifest also in the narrowly successful campaigns of Harold Washington, David Dinkins, and Doug Wilder in the traditionally Democratic bastions of Chicago, New York City, and Virginia, respectively.[78]

For Farrakhan, the disastrous defects of white America are many, deep, and distressing to behold. Addressing a rally at the Washington Convention Center in July 1985, Farrakhan explained that, "It's because you (whites) are wicked and you fear in the sickness of your mind that you must control everybody . . . I say you're sick and you need a doctor or you need to be buried." The minister holds that it represents "an act of mercy to white people that we end your world" and a pressing imperative for black Americans to do so, since "Your world is killing you and all of humanity. We must end your world and bring in a new world."[79] At the NoI's annual Savior's Day Convention, in February 1994, Farrakhan also stated that whites' "history is written in the blood of the human family . . . Murder and lying comes easy for white people. . . . Your history is shedding the blood of all human beings." Such remarks powerfully negate the less-than-subtle analytic distinction that the NoI leader sought suddenly to draw in his Million Man March speech, between individual evil whites and the "mind-set" of white supremacy. That Farrakhan's rebuilding of the NoI since 1978 has entailed the explicit and complete reiteration of its founders' original teachings about the nature of Allah, the prospective racial Armageddon, and the character of whites "without change"[80] powerfully suggests that its traditional racism endures, robust and irrevocably central to Farrakhan's worldview.

The racial antagonists and enemies of African-Americans, however, are not exclusively white in identity. Abetting white American conspirators—whether intentionally or unconsciously—are black American allies of white political and economic power structures. For Farrakhan, such black Americans represent the functional political equivalents of citizens in an occupied nation who traitorously collaborate with their invaders and oppressors. In the contemporary United States, the main group of such treacherous accommodationists comprises so-called crossover black politicians who seek to build biracial coalitions and to practice the logrolling and exchange of favors that are central to conventional American politics. Farrakhan has thus strongly criticized black elected officials such as William Gray, Dinkins, and Wilder for their consensual and pragmatic approach to public office:

> America is willing to use safe black men, non-threatening black men who will not rock the white boat by crying out for justice for black people.[81]

In Farrakhan's turbulent world, disturbing the white boat represents a de facto litmus test of racial purity for African-American elected officials and blacks in general; antagonism toward whites constitutes the anchor of black authenticity. Thus, Farrakhan's threat to the black *Washington Post* reporter who initially broke Jackson's "Hymietown" remark that, "One day we will punish you with death. . . . we're going to make an example of Milton Coleman," was also intended to be a dire warning to other black American members of the press corps who failed the demanding tests of racial essentialism and black authenticity established by the NoI's leader. Such threats of fatal retaliation remarkably extend as far as to encompass potential future race traitors who depart from Farrakhan's many prescriptions for collective black regeneration. Discussing the rebirth of black America after Armageddon under his divinely beneficent tutelage, for example, Farrakhan projects an American future abundant with employment opportunities for blacks. For African-American hustlers and drug dealers, however, "if you don't take that job and continue to deal death to our people, then we will deal death to you, make no mistake about it,"[82] an assuredly novel form of work incentives in a full employment economy.

Farrakhan has even held "moderate" black American politicians partly responsible for the fall of "authentic" black leaders:

> May I remind you that whenever a strong black leader made a revolutionary stand, the moderate black leaders condemned that revolutionary leader, giving the signal that it was alright to move against him. That is how we have lost most of our brilliant leaders.[83]

To be more specific:

> The moderate black leaders opposed Malcolm X and the Honorable Elijah Muhammad, and that gave the government the

signals that it could destroy those leaders and their organizations. When Martin Luther King, Jr. spoke out against the war in
Vietnam, moderate black leadership stood against Dr. King, and
the signal was clear to the forces that wanted to destroy him that
this was the right moment to do so.[84]

The parallels with Farrakhan's own controversial position in modern
black politics are often drawn explicitly by the NoI leader and are
sometimes left implicit for his audience to infer autonomously.

Notwithstanding the flawed history and conspiratorial cast, the
organicist and racially essentialist worldview that such statements
reveal serves not only as a useful strategic mechanism by which Farrakhan seeks to rally the black American masses to his eclectic, idiosyncratic, and bigoted banner—and to intimidate his more conventional
elite black opponents and detractors. Such allegations also serve to
reinforce prevailing perceptions among many white Americans of the
fundamental homogeneity of black American culture and values, and
the continued need for an identifiable, preeminent black political
leader (titular or otherwise), exempted from the accepted tenets of
democratic accountability and legitimacy that characterizes white,
mainstream American politics.[85] (It is in this respect that, by adopting
secondary roles in the Million Man March, other black leaders reinforced many white Americans' inferences of the failure of black leadership as being primarily a function of the absence of a single,
dominant black leader.) Although many distinguished, responsible,
and courageous African-American politicians refused to participate in
the Million Man March, these "inauthentic" blacks are—along with
Jews, whites, and the federal government—among black America's
central and most consistently disturbing enemies.

While the notion of having enemies rather than mere opponents
is one wholly alien to most American politicians and decidedly
unusual in the general tenor of public discourse in the United States,
it nonetheless serves as still further evidence to Farrakhan (in the very
unlikely event that any were needed) of the fundamentally correct
character of his analysis. Having been strongly criticized by the black
activist, Paul Robeson, for having made enemies among the wrong
people, for example, the Black Muslim leader's response was to seek
to diminish the force of the criticism by invoking claims of his significant popular black American support. In an argument somewhat
strained in coherence and clarity, Farrakhan responded that:

> Well, I'm not the first to make enemies among the wrong people.
> The question is, are the wrong people the oppressors of the right
> people? No, I have impressed the *right* people—the masses.[86]

In sum, then, the existence of enemies of black America is a central
and vital component of Farrakhan's public discourse.

Nonetheless, for Farrakhan, the possibility of black American
redemption also represents a necessary and important feature of his
religious and political worldview. Providing that they listen carefully
to his enlightened warnings and vigorously adhere to his divine prescriptions, black Americans can successfully cast off their slave mentality and experience a complete spiritual, psychological, and mental
regeneration, attaining a resplendent revival through embracing reaction, in effect.

Moreover, the possibility of mass black redemption is regularly
reaffirmed by the addition to the NoI of new African-American members and by its popularity among disadvantaged urban blacks, black
college students, and black celebrities. That Farrakhan commands
speaking fees for college lectures far in excess of other national black
politicians provides one indication of his exceptional leadership position among African-Americans. Furthermore, the embrace of Islam by
disgraced black Americans in politics and entertainment/sport, such
as former convicts Barry and boxer Mike Tyson, respectively (as well
as black entertainers such as the rap and film star, Ice Cube), all provide additional—and very visible—examples of successful conversion. In Barry's case, the mayor's apparent spiritual and political
rejuvenation was an especially piquant redemptive victory for Farrakhan, who had denounced him in 1990 as an immoral drug fiend,
prior to Barry's subsequently embracing the NoI.[87] The public notoriety of figures such as Johnnie Cochran, the leading O. J. Simpson
defense attorney, being escorted to court by Fruit of Islam guards also
undoubtedly lends the NoI a particular social cache among many
black Americans. The example of individual black Americans, apparently at the very depths of social life in America, being "raised" and
rejuvenated by the NoI is a powerful religious metaphor and also a
political symbol of manifest significance.

A distinct, though complementary, feature of Farrakhan's paranoid politics is his anti-intellectualism, which is in turn linked to a
broader antielitism that frequently animates the NoI's leader and
informs his public discourse. Given the divine source of his belief

system, the hostility evinced by Farrakhan toward intellectuals is hardly surprising. Since the values, beliefs, attitudes, and prescriptions that the NoI's leader advances are by definition correct and wholly irrefutable, given their directly divine derivation, the position of most intellectuals is necessarily marginal and fundamentally redundant. In terms of recruitment to full membership in the NoI—as Malcolm X eventually found to fatal cost—independent thinkers need not apply. Critical faculties must essentially be sacrificed upon the altars of leadership loyalty and conformity to the prescribed NoI faith.

Nonetheless, a degree of ambivalence characterizes Farrakhan's antipathy toward the thinking and writing classes in America. Most notable, Farrakhan simultaneously denounces intellectuals who challenge the NoI's mass black credibility and eagerly cites those who either directly or indirectly affirm his own eclectic positions and esoteric arguments. Enlisting unspecified authorities or experts in the Farrakhan cause is a common rhetorical tactic:

> According to demographers, if the plummeting birth rate of white people in America continues, in a few years, it will reach zero population growth. As for blacks, Hispanics, and Native Americans, if their present birth rate continues, by the year 2080, demographers say, blacks, Hispanics and native Americans will conceivably be 50 percent or more of the United States population . . . If things continue just birthwise, we could control the Congress, we could control the Supreme Court, we could control state legislatures and then "Run, Jesse, run" or "Run, Jesse Junior, run," or "Run, Jesse the Third, run."[88]

The NoI's February 1985 Savior's Day convention also featured a major speech by Dr. Arthur Butz, a leading Holocaust "revisionist" historian and a prominent associate of white American neo-Nazi groups. The imprimatur of intellectual credibility is one eagerly sought by Farrakhan from either anonymous or unusual (and flawed), critical sources.

Farrakhan also frequently cites *The Secret Relationship Between Blacks and Jews*, a NoI text controversially adopted by Tony Martin, a black American professor in Wellesley College's African Studies Department, as authoritative confirmation of the Jewish role in black enslavement. Persuasively labeled the "bible of black anti-Semitism" by Henry Louis Gates, the book provides a fascinating window on the black paranoid disposition in general in the United States and toward intellectuals in particular. Vigorously promoted by Farrakhan and his followers, the book serves as the functional contemporary equivalent for the NoI that the *Protocols of the Elders of Zion* has done previously for many anti-Semitic groups. Most of its central arguments have been strongly countered and convincingly disproved. Contrary to its central argument, for instance, the existence of slavery in Africa was a Muslim invention long before the white man colonized the continent. Moreover, nothing in the orthodox Muslim writings of the Prophet forbids the institution of slavery, which is one of the central reasons for its development into an extremely profitable business dominated by Arabs. For Farrakhan and the NoI, *The Secret Relationship* (compiled by the NoI's "historical research department") represented a useful pseudo-intellectual attempt to neutralize such inconvenient facts.[89]

Although its distortive allegations were both condemned by the Council of the American Historical Association (in January 1995) and emphatically refuted in an extremely detailed, point-by-point analysis by the distinguished historian, Harold Brackman[90] (invoking in their full and accurate context many of the sources misused and misquoted in Farrakhan's version), the NoI book rapidly became a best-seller among black Americans. As the cultural critic Robert Hughes has persuasively argued, in spite of Brackman's extensive research, the author's clear exposure of the NoI text's pseudo-history:

> . . . could not penetrate the black community as *The Secret Relationship* has done, since it is in the nature of paranoid texts to inoculate naive readers against their rebuttal; any reply becomes part of the huge global conspiracy itself.[91]

Indeed, the particular instance of *The Secret Relationship* manifested a more broad and serious dilemma for Farrakhan's opponents generally. As the NoI's leader is evidently well aware—and as some of his strongest and most courageous critics, such as the *Washington Post* journalist Juan Williams, regularly point out—the challenge to or condemnation of Farrakhan's paranoid claims has a tendency to rebound and reinforce the claims' political salience and popular black appeal in inverse proportion to the ferocity of the attacks. For Farrakhan's political opponents, the strategic dilemma is one that is not only acute but also essentially intractable: on the one hand, to seek to refute Farrakhan's claims, and thereby to lend him an importance through dignifying his outrageous charges that he might otherwise forfeit; or, alternatively, to ignore the claims, and (as was previously the case for McCarthy's anticommunist allegations) thereby to provide an implicit and tacit acceptance of their veracity from the very groups whom Farrakhan accuses of continually conspiring against African-Americans.

Much as Hofstadter observed that, for American paranoids generally, the greatest evidence for the existence of an all-consuming conspiracy is the complete absence of such evidence, so, in Farrakhan's particular case, the greater the frequency and the more intense the vigor with which Jewish groups and others seek to refute his conspiratorial claims and "historical" arguments, the more those claims thereby acquire the status of potentially accurate and legitimate political views and perspicacious historical interpretations among many black Americans. Certainly, Farrakhan takes great nourishment in such attacks, which seem only to confirm the accuracy of his allegations about his enemies' diabolical motives and their unremitting personal animus. After all, a basic logic suggests that, if the claims that Farrakhan advances were so manifestly wrong or obviously preposterous, why bother to seek to repudiate them with such vigor and passion at all?

Although the bulk of Farrakhan's anti-intellectual critique is aimed at nonblack Americans, it also comprises a racial dimension that is addressed specifically and exclusively to black American professionals. Criticisms of African-American intellectuals and professionals are a regular feature of Farrakhan's speeches. For the NoI's leader, such African-Americans neglect their solidaristic duties to their race by working for white-dominated corporations, such as IBM and Microsoft, and by pursuing their individual careers at the expense of the collective social group. The mental resources and physical effort that they devote to furthering the corporate interests of such white businesses ought to be more effectively and responsibly employed in intrablack social and economic affairs. Along with white American critics in general, African-American intellectuals in particular therefore represent important objects of Farrakhan's fiery disapprobation.

That Farrakhan meets the first five of the six criteria of paranoia identified by Hofstadter appears incontrovertibly to be the case.

What, though, of the traditionally temporary and transient nature of the paranoid disposition and its multiple organizational expressions? Paranoid movements such as McCarthyism, and extremist forces in American politics in general, are largely ephemeral phenomena, the product of very specific, unusual, and transitory conditions, according to most analyses.[92] For Hofstadter, in particular, this observation was at once a cause for both optimism and caution: the former, in pointing to the fundamental resilience of the political moderation, liberal tolerance, and inclusive pluralism of American culture; and the latter, in the tenacious tendency of paranoid movements to reconstitute and reappear over time in a variety of distinct forms.

In this respect, Farrakhan and his organization could be argued to be manifestly ineligible for the paranoid designation. In particular, after sixty-seven years, the NoI represents a more enduring than ephemeral component of American authoritarianism in general, and black American social and civic life in particular. To this extent, both the specific organization, and the longevity of black American separatist political thought generally, might together be held to disqualify Farrakhan from the paranoid category of American authoritarians and extremists. Not only is his organization effectively institutionalized in the United States (despite its intermittent internal feuds and alleged factions), but Farrakhan fits into a political and ideological locus in American politics more permanent than transient during the twentieth century as a whole.

While the NoI does constitute an enduring component of the universe of American authoritarian movements this century, however, Farrakhan clearly represents an entirely novel leader of the organization in terms of his political strategy, tactics, and, most important, his broad social impact. The NoI's political activism, in particular, is unprecedented, and unquestionably represents Farrakhan's most important and innovative strategic contribution since he assumed its leadership in 1978: in 1984, Farrakhan registered to vote, a first for any member of the sect, and cast his vote for Jesse Jackson in the Illinois Democratic Party primary election of that year; the Fruit of Islam provided security for Jackson's 1984 campaign, and Farrakhan took a keen and supportive interest in the candidate's affairs; in 1986, Farrakhan's fund-raising world tour included visits to China, Ghana, Iran, Japan, Libya, Pakistan, and Saudi Arabia; Farrakhan has frequently addressed the national and international media and appeared on national television, in a fashion that both Elijah Muhammad and

Malcolm X largely eschewed; three NoI members unsuccessfully sought elective office in Washington, D.C., in 1990; during 1992–96, relatively successful overtures were made by Farrakhan toward mainstream black organizations and elected officials; October 16, 1995, saw Farrakhan organize and lead an unprecedentedly large national gathering of African-Americans in the Million Man March on Washington, D.C.; the beginning of 1996 saw Farrakhan once more travel across Africa and the Middle East, often to be treated by his hosts in the manner normally accorded a head of state; and Farrakhan mounted a campaign to register black, Arab, and Muslim voters in 1996, ostensibly in order to forge "a third force" that would be effective in the United States in defending their interests and ensuring their rights.[93] None of these initiatives had previously been advanced in theory or executed in practice by either Elijah Muhammad or Malcolm X.

The NoI's permanence should not, therefore, obscure the essentially episodic character of the Farrakhan phenomenon, insofar as it represents neither an extension of Elijah's leadership nor a guarantor of substantial political continuity under Farrakhan's potential successors.[94] Farrakhan's personal contribution as leader of the NoI has been critically influential in his achievement of national leadership status among African-Americans in the 1990s. In his strategic and tactical choices, his adaptation and contemporary reapplication of Elijah's original teachings, and his evolving relations with other African-American religious and political leaders, Farrakhan has displayed a wholly distinctive, entrepreneurial, and individualistic approach, neither imitative of, nor emulated successfully by, other black American actors. To this extent, Farrakhan evidently meets the sixth of Hofstadter's criteria of American political paranoia.

In sum, then, Farrakhan powerfully exemplifies an exceptional, black variant of the dominant tradition or "style" of political paranoia in American politics. The NoI's leader is, of course, only one (albeit particularly visible and controversial) exponent of paranoid politics in the contemporary United States. Both other black American activists, such as Sharpton and Leonara Fulani, and nonblack politicians, from Duke and Buchanan on the conservative far-right to former California governor Jerry Brown on the progressive left, manifest varying degrees of paranoia in their political critiques and policy prescriptions. Their fears, frustrations, and resentments are also unquestionably shared by substantial numbers of ordinary American citizens. Most notable, deep antipathy to government in general, and the federal government in particular, is a long-established but still extremely potent target for the expression of popular anger and mass disenchantment in the America of the 1990s.

The articulation of citizen grievances that such figures address has constituted a central feature of populist politics in general over the course of American history. In constructing a political battle centered upon a bitter struggle between "us" and "them," based on an apparently irreconcilable conflict of fundamental values that admits of no obvious compromise, populists seek to exploit genuine fears and resentments among sections of the citizenry by expressing such sentiments and allocating blame upon particular groups or institutions. Partly by virtue of the nation's long and rich history of representing a welcoming home to immigrants from all corners of the world, the populist strain in politics in the United States—one that stresses the precedence of values of social order and equality over freedom—is essentially as American as apple pie (if not always as palatable). Indeed, it is mildly ironic that aliens of some or another type have been—and remain—so evidently integral to America's social, political, and economic development and yet have so frequently formed the target for concerted and vitriolic attack. The politics of scapegoating that is rarely far from the surface of such populist appeals is a sadly familiar, recurrent, and unattractive feature of the American political landscape.

Political paranoia, by contrast, is not so clearly an integral feature of the American polity, however much it is a transparently recurrent one. The articulation of conspiracy theories is not a necessary feature of populist rhetoric. It is absolutely central, however, to the paranoiac's political praxis. Moreover, not only is it the case that few contemporary political figures fulfill the analytic criteria of American paranoid politics identified by Hofstadter as does Farrakhan; but, in addition, still fewer have achieved the notable social and political impact of the NoI's leader over recent years. As the head of a national organization of long historical standing, Farrakhan possesses an organizational base and an established mechanism of institutional support denied more marginal and sensationalist local political figures, such as Sharpton. Perhaps most significant, Farrakhan's political locus in the NoI accords him an historic and ideological legacy upon which to draw that few other contemporary African-American politicians can rely on in comparable fashion.

In addition, of course, the impact that Farrakhan has achieved has occurred as a member of a minority racial group that has been subject to grievous harms and deliberate mistreatment over the course of American history. The potency of Farrakhan's political paranoia consequently has assumed threatening dimensions to many non-black observers of his political rise. With the notable and mercifully brief exception of McCarthyism, the incidence of paranoid appeals among white Americans has conventionally been greeted by a curiosity and bewilderment that has been tempered by the confident expectation of its effective containment by the majority-white population. Its occurrence among a racial minority still suffering from disproportionate social and economic grievances during the 1990s is less deserving of a sanguine response, for many white and black Americans alike; not least when whites in general, and Jews in particular, are isolated as being particularly culpable for the distressing plight of the black disadvantaged in the modern United States.

It is in this respect that Farrakhan occupies an especially important and exceptional status among contemporary African-American political, civic, and religious leaders. The incidence of paranoid appeals among African-Americans is of vital importance in understanding Farrakhan's political rise and national role. As Andrew Hacker has compellingly argued, the fear that black Americans achieving political power will exact retributive justice upon whites for white Americans having previously treated blacks unfavorably is a powerful and widespread dread that continues to animate the white psyche and to condition relations between the races in contemporary America. Typically, though, few national political figures of either race have publicly interpreted the latent sensibilities of whites as succinctly and brutally as Farrakhan did when he stated that, "You fear we'll do to you what you did to us."[95] It is upon such deeply held (though rarely articulated) fears and resentments, among both blacks and nonblacks, that much of Farrakhan's public discourse is forged and that his viscerally reactionary and paranoid political appeal among many African-Americans is in part based. The scar of race is an ugly abrasion that Farrakhan invokes as a political scare tactic, simultaneously to provoke and embolden African Americans and to shock and intimidate white Americans—to significant political and social effect.

The fractious "threat" that Farrakhan personifies to many whites is therefore perceived by some critics to be especially great, by virtue not only of the glaring and incontrovertible historic fact of black mistreatment, subjugation, and murder in the United States at white American hands, but also as a result of the obvious deterioration in the quality of life and the socioeconomic infrastructure of many black communities since achievement of formal civil and political equality, in 1964 and 1965, respectively. For many people, Farrakhan represents the formidable symbolic and (rhetorically) violent African-American political repository of a powerful, constant, and barely suppressed black rage, a rage directed not only toward their historic mistreatment but also to their contemporary deprivation. More than "the hate that hate produced," the Farrakhan phenomenon constitutes the hate that equality before the law, growing black political representation, and the formal prohibition of public discrimination by race in America have together failed to quell in the post–civil rights era. The anger and disappointment that fuel Farrakhan's racial animus are of extensive and deep historical lineage.

Thus, in invoking the claims that Farrakhan does, the Black Muslim leader uses political paranoia for a dual political purpose. First, the extreme nature of his claims and the uncompromisingly aggressive rhetoric in which they are couched draw popular attention to the relative moderation of both the content and the style of established national black politicians' public discourse. In presentational and discursive forms, the NoI's leader vividly recalls earlier periods of American history in which apparently isolated African-American political, civic, and religious leaders waged entrenched battles against many powerful opponents and seemingly insurmountable odds. Eschewing appeals to the forging of broad-based coalitions, consensus, and interracial harmony, Farrakhan instead enthusiastically embraces a strident, radical rhetoric that most—though not all—black elected officials long ago discarded as outdated, inappropriate, and fundamentally self-defeating, both for them individually and for African-Americans collectively. Farrakhan, like his one-time friend and mentor, and subsequent enemy, Malcolm X, stands in sharp and vivid contrast to the bulk of contemporary black civic, religious, and political leaders. Like Malcolm before him, Farrakhan wins many thousands of adherents and plaudits among African-Americans—as well as many critics and opponents—for the caustic candor by which he "tells it like it is"; even, and especially, when he tells it like it is not.

Second, in making the exotic claims he does, Farrakhan invokes paranoia as supportive evidence of his extraordinary and exceptional political independence, and hence unique political authority, among national black political leaders. Uncompromised by the political demands of consensus-building and conciliation that typically confront elected or appointed black American public officials in the

United States, Farrakhan seeks to reinforce his "outsider" political credentials as an incorruptible and immutable voice on behalf of African-Americans' true, enduring, and shared collective racial interests. It is by a very deliberate and carefully constructed contrast with the established cohort of elected black officialdom—and the pluralist traits that it increasingly manifests—that Farrakhan seeks to embellish his putative essentialist credentials as the preeminent repository, indeed the personification, of his race's authentic values and aspirations. Thus, according to Farrakhan's own characteristically humble and unassuming assessment:

> . . . my experience today, standing up against the manipulation of Black politicians and Black organizations by elements of the white community, particularly Jewish persons, has created a crisis in Black leadership. You see, there was no crisis so long as nobody could present some alternative to what they are offering. It only became a crisis when another voice stood up that was not controlled by those same persons that they are responsible to. The pressure is put on them to repudiate this voice. So, then there is a big crisis.[96]

Unflinchingly independent, fearless, unbowed, and eloquent, Farrakhan stands fast as a uniquely outspoken and independent black leader who insouciantly treats sacred cows as mere ordinary heifers. Political disagreement with, or opposition to, Farrakhan among African-Americans is (according to the notions of collective group purity that informs his particular diagnosis of American racial dynamics) effectively suggestive of either control by nonblack forces or amounts to a form of racial "false consciousness" among black Americans. The political strategy represents, in effect, an external projection upon blacks nationwide of the internal loyalty and discipline that Farrakhan commands in the NoI. Fidelity to the race and its assumed homogeneous collective values and interests overwhelms the pluralism, diversity, and heterogeneity that black Americans in fact clearly, and increasingly, exhibit in political, economic, and social terms in the post–civil rights era. In vigorously projecting himself as the prophetic personification of black Americans' genuine individual and collective racial interests, and as the divinely ordained savior of their fate as a social group in the United States, Farrakhan makes extraordinary claims that few other national black leaders either could, or would, dare to advance. Therein resides some of the most curious but crucial features of his contemporary popular African-American appeal and political success.

SUMMARY

Farrakhan's religious and racially bounded conservative authoritarianism exists within the broader historical tradition of paranoid politics in America. Farrakhan is richly endowed with the several constituent attributes of political paranoia: his belief in the existence of antiblack conspiracies; strident racial militancy; ready identification and frequent demonization of opponents as political enemies; pronounced faith in the possibility of collective African-American redemption; ambivalent anti-intellectualism; and his distinctive leadership contribution to the NoI since 1978. Together these influences distinguish the minister as an unusually powerful contemporary black exemplar of the paranoid style in American politics. In combination with the distinctive cosmological, religious, and ideological positions to which the NoI's leader adheres, Farrakhan's unique black brand of American political paranoia accords him a wholly exceptional leadership status within contemporary U.S. politics in general, and national African-American politics in particular.

Farrakhan represents a reactionary and paranoid political figure whose public rhetoric is deeply imbued by the clearest and most unyielding expressions of hatred, ridicule, and loathing. Admittedly, no list of hate groups has ever been officially compiled by the federal government. Although it maintained a committee in its national legislature dedicated to the monitoring of "un-American activities," the term "hate group" itself has no legal definition, meaning, or judicial standing in the United States. While the FBI maintains a list of active domestic terrorist groups in America, the NoI has not merited inclusion thereon. (Unlike many white supremacist groups and citizen militias, the NoI has not, thus far, engaged in acts of direct physical violence against its many sworn enemies.) Nonetheless, Farrakhan's public discourse is pervaded by expressions of the deepest racial animus and clearest contempt. Although not alone in so doing, the NoI's leader deeply compromises and taints the tone of public life in America by the unceasing venom, vitriol, and viciousness with which he attacks those who he deems to be enemies; and, thereby, at minimum, Farrakhan contributes to an environment that is conducive to further assaults upon them, both verbal and otherwise.[97]

That Farrakhan represents a distinctive, vociferous, and disturb-ingly dangerous voice among African-American political and reli-gious leaders—and one that many Americans of all races would prefer to be strongly muted or to fall completely silent—is, by now, no doubt clear. Two distinct though related issues that are central to the political evolution of the Farrakhan phenomenon, however, thus far remain unresolved: first, the full extent of the popularity of Farra-khan's particular black brand of political paranoia among African-Americans, and second, its causes and consequences for national black political leadership and American politics more broadly. It is the former that we examine in chapter five.

NOTES TO CHAPTER 4

1. Farrakhan speech at Harlem's Apollo Theatre, New York City, 7 May 1995. Quoted in Malcolm Gladwell, "Farrakhan Seeks End of Rift."

2. Quoted in Martin Walker, "America's Great Divide Widens," *The Guardian*, 2 September 1995, p. 25.

3. M. B. Smith, "Foreword" to J. P. Kirscht and R. C. Dilleehay, *Dimensions of Authoritarianism: A Review of Research and Theory* (Lexington, Ky.: University of Kentucky Press, 1967), p. vi.

4. For a summation of the results, see Cas Mudde, "The War of Words Defining the Extreme Right Party Family," *West European Politics* 19, no. 2 (1996): 225–48.

5. Among the most notable studies are: Hans-Georg Betz, *Radical Right-Wing Populism in Western Europe* (Basingstoke: Macmillan, 1994); Luciano Cheles, Ronnie Ferguson, and Michael Vaughan, eds., *Neo-Fascism in Europe* (New York: Longman, 1991); and Hainsworth, *The Extreme Right in Europe and the USA*.

6. Lipset and Raab, *The Politics of Unreason*, p. 508. See also: Richard Orr Curry, *Conspiracy: The Fear of Subversion in American History* (New York: Holt, Rinehart, and Winston, 1972); David Brion Davis, ed., *The Fear of Conspiracy: Images of Un-American Subversion from the Revolution to the Present Day* (Ithaca, N.Y.: Cornell University Press, 1971); George Johnson, *Architects of Fear: Conspiracy Theories and Paranoia in American Politics* (Los Angeles: J. P. Tarcher, 1983); and Sargent, *Extremism in America*.

7. In this context, see the examples discussed in Zillah Eisenstein, *Hatreds: Racialized and Sexualized* (London: Routledge, 1996); and the excellent review essay by Garry Wills, "The Militias," *The New York Review of Books*, 10 August 1995, pp. 50–55.

8. On the Waco controversy, see Stuart A. Wright, *Armageddon at Waco: Critical Perspectives on the Branch Davidian Conflict* (Chicago: University of Chicago Press, 1995).

9. See: Michael Barone, *Our Country: The Shaping of America from Roosevelt to Reagan* (New York: Free Press, 1990); and Huntington, *American Politics*.

10. On these, see respectively: Barbara Hinkson Craig and David M. O'Brien, *Abortion and American Politics* (Chatham, N.J.: Chatham House, 1993); and Robert J. Spitzer, *The Politics of Gun Control* (Chatham, N.J.: Chatham House, 1995).

11. See Norman Ornstein and Amy Schenkenberg, "The 1995 Congress: The First Hundred Days and Beyond," *Political Science Quarterly* 110, no. 2 (1995).

12. See note 3 .

13. See note 3. None of the studies refer to the incidence of right-wing authoritarian appeals among black Americans in general, much less Farrakhan and the NoI in particular.

14. It is significant, for example, that even in a recent undergraduate textbook on the role and influence of racial minorities in American politics, no reference at all is made to Louis Farrakhan, whereas David Duke and other expressions of antiblack animus receive attention. See Paula D. McClain and Joseph Stewart Jr., *"Can We All Get Along?" Racial and Ethnic Minorities in American Politics* (Boulder, Colo.: Westview Press, 1995).

15. See the collection of primary sources compiled by Sargent, *Extremism in America.*

16. Allen, *The Concise Oxford Dictionary of Current English,* p. 863.

17. Among the most impressive works in an extensive scholarly literature on McCarthy and McCarthyism, see: John G. Adams, *Without Precedent: the Story of the Death of McCarthyism* (New York: Norton, 1983); Edwin R. Bayley, *Joe McCarthy and the Press* (Madison: University of Wisconsin Press, 1981); Richard M. Fried, *Men Against McCarthy* (New York: Columbia University Press, 1976) and *Nightmare in Red: the McCarthy Era in Perspective* (New York: Oxford University Press, 1991); Robert Griffith, *The Politics of Fear: Joseph McCarthy and the Senate* (Rochelle Park, N.J.: Hayden Book Company, 1970); Allen Joseph Matusow, ed., *Joseph R. McCarthy* (Hemel Hempstead: Prentice-Hall, 1970); Richard Rovere, *Senator Joe McCarthy* (New York: Harper and Row, 1973); and Thomas C. Reeves, *The Life and Times of Joe McCarthy: a Biography* (London: Blond and Briggs, 1982).

18. See Richard Hofstadter, *The Paranoid Style,* pp. 3–40.

19. Hofstadter, "The Paranoid Style," p. 29.

20. Sargent, *Extremism in America,* p. 2.

21. A relatively recent example from the white radical right is the white supremacist organization established by David Duke, the National Association for the Advancement of White People. The group's title was a deliberate variant of that of the preeminent civil rights organization for black Americans, the NAACP. See Rose, *The Emergence of David Duke.*

22. Hofstadter, "The Paranoid Style," p. 35.

23. On the general political context and role of the intellectual in American political history, see Richard Hofstadter, *Anti-intellectualism in American Life* (New York: Knopf, 1963).

24. Hofstadter, "The Paranoid Style," p. 39.

25. See, for example: Lynda Wright, "Farrakhan's Mission: Fighting the Drug War—His Way," *Newsweek,* 19 March 1990, p. 25; and Howard Fineman

and Vern E. Smith, "An Angry 'Charmer'," *Newsweek*, 30 October 1995, pp. 42–46.

26. Farrakhan speech in New Orleans at the African American Summit 1989, 23 April 1989, cited in Edsall and Edsall, *Chain Reaction*, p. 238.

27. Farrakhan, *Independent Black Leadership in America*, p. 51. Also, see Farrakhan's interview with John F. Davis, "Farrakhan Speaks," *Village Voice* 29 (22 May 1984) pp. 15–18, 20.

28. See also Farrakhan's address, "Countering the Plan of Genocide Against the Black Male in America," delivered at Bethel A.M.E. Church, San Francisco, 13 September 1995 (audiotape).

29. Louis Farrakhan, "I Am an Alarm Clock," *Black Scholar*, January/February 1979.

30. Of course, ample documentary evidence exists to support the argument that many black American organizations and individuals have indeed been targeted by the FBI—especially under J. Edgar Hoover—for surveillance, infiltration, and destabilization. In this particular instance, it is not the fact of historic FBI intrigue that is notable but the vast scope and unrelenting character of the Bureau's efforts that distinguishes—and substantially diminishes—Farrakhan's case.

31. See Lynda Wright, "Farrakhan's Mission."

32. Farrakhan, *Independent Black Leadership in America*, p. 32. See also the Farrakhan address, "Farrakhan: The Marked Man for Death!," delivered at Mount Zion Baptist Church, Miami, Florida, 2 October 1995. That Farrakhan has admitted to personally contributing to the atmosphere in which Malcolm was murdered makes one wonder whether the minister holds even himself to be part of the anti-Farrakhan conspiracy.

33. Farrakhan speech, Mosque Maryam, Chicago, 17 January 1995. Quoted in Edward Walsh, "Farrakhan Says U.S. Concocted Plot Charge," *The Washington Post*, 18 January 1995, p. A3.

34. Transcript, Farrakhan's interview with Mike Wallace, "60 Minutes" 14 April 1996 (New York: CBS News, 1996).

35. Farrakhan interview with Mills, "Predicting Disaster." When asked whether he possessed hard evidence to support his assertion about crack dissemination, Farrakhan argued simply that, "Statistics on drug usage will bear me out."

36. See Mark Fitzgerald, "Farrakhan Denounces Critical Stories," *Editor and Publisher*, 8 April 1995, p. 11. The findings of the original four-part series by Gaines and Jackson, "Profit and Promises," were reaffirmed in the two-part investigation by Lorraine Adams, "Nation of Islam."

37. Quoted in Lynne Duke, "At the Core of the Nation of Islam: Confrontation," *The Washington Post*, 21 March 1994, p. A1.

38. Quoted in Thomas, "The Man Who Haunts Jesse Jackson," p. 6.

39. See Farrakhan's article on Jesse Jackson in *Essence*, February 1984.

40. According to Farrakhan, a giant spacecraft called the Mother Wheel floats approximately forty miles above the Earth, in anticipation of the day of divine judgment, when it will release its load of bombs upon whites, while blacks who have embraced the Nation of Islam will be lifted to their

full and appropriate majesty (the fate of other blacks is presumably the same as that of whites, though this is not entirely clear from Farrakhan's speeches and writings). Farrakhan stated in 1985 that he had been seized by a vision in which he was taken on board a smaller spaceship, which transported him through a beam of light to the Mother Wheel and where, once docked, Elijah Muhammad spoke to him at length. See Gaines and Jackson, "Profit and Promises."

41. See Gareth G. Cook, "Race: Feeding the Fire," *U.S. News and World Report*, 7 February 1994, p. 12.

42. Cited in Jonathan Kaufman, *Broken Alliance: The Turbulent Times Between Blacks and Jews in America* (New York: Scribner, 1988), pp. 219–20.

43. Quoted in David Kurapka, "Hate Story: Farrakhan's Still at It," *The New Republic* 198, 30 May 1988, pp. 19–21, at 20.

44. The comments are from a Farrakhan speech in Fresno, California, 19 March 1994. Quoted in "Conspired against, Farrakhan says," *Christian Century*, 6 April 1994, p. 347.

45. Quoted in "Farrakhan Sees a Plot Against Him," *The New York Times*, 21 February 1994, p. A11.

46. Cited in Michael Kramer, "Loud and Clear: Farrakhan's anti-Semitism," *New York Magazine*, 18, no. 41 (21 October 1985). Other examples (and discussions) of Farrakhan's anti-Semitic diatribes and warnings of retribution are contained in David Evanier, *The Anti-Semitism of Black Demagogues and Extremists* (New York: Anti-Defamation League, 1992); Lori Linzer, *The Nation of Islam: the Relentless Record of Hate* (New York: Anti-Defamation League, 1995); and Kenneth Stern, *Farrakhan and Jews in the 1990s* (New York: Institute of Human Relations, 1994).

47. Cube has included explicit praise of both Farrakhan and the Nation of Islam in his lyrics and the liner notes of some of his albums, in between his descriptions of black American women as "bitches" and "hos." His fellow rapper, Ice-T, also thanks Khalid Muhammad, Farrakhan's even more vulgarly loquacious lieutenant, in the notes to his 1993 album, "Home Invasion."

48. Farrakhan has also issued rhetorical questions as to why no black American equivalent of the attention devoted to the Jewish holocaust by Spielberg's film, "Schindler's List," exists. The question is typically posed as yielding only one adequate answer: Jewish domination of the film industry that invariably ignores African-American problems. It is less common to hear Farrakhan advocating that the newly emergent group of prominent black filmmakers, such as Spike Lee, John Singleton, and Mario Van Peebles, address their attention to the historic sufferings of African-Americans rather than projecting unsympathetic and negative images of violent and abusive black American males to cinema audiences around the world.

49. See, for example, the discussions in: Kenneth S. Stern, *Farrakhan and Jews in the 1990s*; Paul Shore, "Farrakhan and the Filling of the Mythic Gap," *The Humanist*, July-August 1994, pp. 4–6; Frank Rich, "Bad for the Jews," *The New York Times*, 3 March 1994, p. A17; and Julius Lester, "Blacks, Jews, and Farrakhan," *Dissent* 41, no. 3 (Summer 1994).

50. See: Milton D. Morris and Gary E. Rubin, "The Turbulent Friendship: Black-Jewish Relations in the 1990s," in "Interminority Affairs in the U.S.: Pluralism at the Crossroads," ed., Peter Rose, *The Annals of the American Academy of Political and Social Science* 530 (November 1993); and Edwin Black, "Farrakhan and the Jews," *Midstream* 32 (August-September 1986), pp. 3–6.

51. Cited in Thomas, "The Man Who Haunts Jesse Jackson," p. 6.

52. See Penelope McMillan and Cathleen Decker, "Israel Is a 'Wicked Hypocrisy'," *Los Angeles Times*, 15 September 1983, p. 1, 3.

53. Cited in Christopher Thomas, "The Man Who Haunts Jesse Jackson," p. 6.

54. Cited in "The conscience of Louis Farrakhan," *Dallas Times Herald*, 8 December 1985; and King, "The Farrakhan Phenomenon," p. 20.

55. *The (London) Times*, 26 March 1985, p. 5.

56. Transcript of news conference at the National Press Club in Washington, D.C., 14 March 1996. Also cited in "Media Eye on Farrakhan," *The Final Call* 15, no. 11 (3 April 1996), p. 21.

57. See Adam Gelb, "Farrakhan Calls U.S. Constitution Racist," *Atlanta Journal and Atlanta Constitution*, 13 September 1987, p. E24. The Million Man March was also almost completely bereft of American flags—certainly the largest demonstration in Washington, D.C., in American history to witness so few Stars and Stripes among the crowd.

58. Cited in Erwin Suall, "Look who's in Farrakhan's Corner," *ADL Bulletin* 42, no. 10 (December 1985).

59. Quoted in *Newsweek*, 4 March 1985, p. 25.

60. It was also interesting to observe the presence of white American supporters of Lyndon LaRouche at the Million Man March in Washington, D.C., in October 1995. They had evidently identified a Farrakhan audience as one whose members would potentially be receptive to their own eccentric brand of paranoid and quasi-fascistic politics.

61. See: King, "The Farrakhan Phenomenon"; and Reed, "All for One."

62. Baldwin, for example, makes note of this in *The Fire Next Time*, p. 112.

63. The dictum was first enunciated by Goldwater at the 1964 Republican National Convention, in response to some supporters of Nelson Rockefeller who had sought to portray the Arizona Senator as an unacceptable extremist. A central part of the explanation for Goldwater's winning the electoral college votes of five Deep South states in the 1964 presidential election was his vote against the year's landmark civil rights legislation for southern blacks.

64. Quoted in Bone, "Prophet of Hate." Even some of Farrakhan's most prominent public supporters have disavowed the parts of the NoI leader's belief system that are clearly anti-Semitic. See, for example, "The Andrew Billen interview: Spike Lee," *The Observer*, 14 January 1996, pp. 11–12.

65. Quoted in Munnion, "Farrakhan Tells Whites to Atone for Apartheid."

66. See Nicoll, Ruaridh, "Black Pride on the March Again," *The Observer*, 1 October 1995, p. 23.

67. Farrakhan, *Independent Black Leadership in America*, p. 46.

68. On the links between black American political organizations and white corporate largesse, see Viveca Novak, "Conservatives and Corporations Plug Into Black Power," *Business and Society Review* 71 (Fall 1989): 32–39.

69. Quoted in Gaber, "Lamb of God or Demagogue?," p. 108.

70. It may be, alternatively, that Jackson's inclusion of derogatory references to Jews in his 1995 release, "HIStory" (subsequently withdrawn and reissued without the offending lyrics), outweighed his androgynous sexuality and crossover popular appeal in Farrakhan's evaluation of the singer's racial authenticity.

71. Quoted in Lynda Wright, "Farrakhan's Mission," p. 22.

72. See: Peter Pearl and Edward Walsh, "Muslims Accuse U.S. of Creating Farrakhan Plot," *The Washington Post*, 14 January 1995, p. A1; and Tom Morganthau, "Back in the Line of Fire."

73. On the FBI and black activists, see Nelson Blackstock, *Cointelpro: The FBI's Secret War on Political Freedom*, 3rd ed. (New York: Pathfinder Press, 1995).

74. Most of Farrakhan's public speeches and interviews since 1984 do not include any references to white Americans as "devils." The extent to which such an omission merely represents a strategic political ploy rather than a reflection of a genuinely changed view of whites, though, remains unclear. Given the nature of Farrakhan's theological beliefs, outlined in chapter 2, it seems unlikely that his conception of whites as devils has altered, not least since this alteration would entail a violation of the divine doctrines of Fard and Elijah Muhammad about the essential nature of whites in America. Moreover, in an interview with the BBC's *Panorama* current affairs program ("An American Apartheid?," broadcast in November 1995), Farrakhan stated defiantly that he didn't originally define whites as devils, but God did.

75. Wright, "Farrakhan's Mission," p. 22.

76. Quoted in Gaines and Jackson, "Profit and Promises," p. 10.

77. On the racially driven transformation of American politics, see Edward G. Carmines and James A. Stimson, *Issue Evolution: Race and the Transformation of American Politics* (Princeton, N.J.: Princeton University Press, 1989).

78. On the apparent reluctance of whites to support African-American candidacies, see: Barker and Walters, *Jesse Jackson's 1984 Presidential Campaign*; Colton, *The Jesse Jackson Phenomenon*; and Abdul Alkalimat and Doug Gills, *Harold Washington and the Crisis of Black Power in Chicago* (Chicago: Twenty-First Century Books, 1989).

79. Quoted in Christopher Thomas, "Idol Who Strikes Terror Into Whites," *The (London) Times*, 26 March 1985, p. 5.

80. The term is that of Lincoln, in *The Black Muslims*, p. 269.

81. Cited in J. L. Hochschild, "Blacks and the Ambiguities of Success," in *Prejudice, Politics and the American Dilemma*, eds., Sniderman, Tetlock, and Carmines, pp. 148–72, at 159.

82. Quoted in Gaber, "Lamb of God or Demagogue?," p. 124.

83. Farrakhan, "Farrakhan on Jesse Jackson."

84. Farrakhan, "Farrakhan on Jesse Jackson." Even if governmental involvement in the assassinations of Martin and Malcolm is accepted, no allegations of government complicity in Elijah's death—which occurred of natural causes—have been made by any persons other than NoI members.

85. For an account of this interpretation as applied to Jackson, see Reed, *The Jesse Jackson Phenomenon*. Reed's assessments of Farrakhan in his popular writings also support this argument further.

86. Farrakhan, *Independent Black Leadership*, p. 41.

87. For an account of their reconciliation, see Sullivan, "Call to Harm."

88. Farrakhan, New Orleans speech, quoted in Edsall and Edsall, *Chain Reaction*, p. 238.

89. The reluctance of the Nation of Islam under Farrakhan to condemn present-day slave practices is itself a significant indication of the ambivalence that surrounds the organization's pronouncements upon the issue. See: Paul Liben, "Farrakhan Turns Blind Eye to African Slave Trade," *Human Events* 51, no. 20 (26 May 1995); and Minoo Southgate, "Slavery Ignored," *National Review*, 23 October 1995, pp. 26–27.

90. Harold D. Brackman, *Ministry of Lies: The Truth Behind the Nation of Islam's "The Secret History between Blacks and Jews"* (New York: Four Walls Eight Windows, 1994).

91. Robert Hughes, *Culture of Complaint: The Fraying of America* (London: Harvill, 1994), p. 122.

92. See, in particular: Hofstadter, *The Paranoid Style*; and Lipset and Raab, *The Politics of Unreason*.

93. Quoted from Jim Drinkard, "Farrakhan Denied Permission to Take $1 Billion Libyan Donation," Associated Press Report, 4 September 1996.

94. This ought, in the context of Farrakhan's popularity during the 1990s, to be a source of some political comfort to his critics, at least to the extent that Farrakhan is unable—and perhaps unwilling—to perpetuate his influence through grooming a successor.

95. Quoted in Hacker, *Two Nations*, p. 206.

96. Farrakhan, *Independent Black Leadership in America*, p. 39.

97. In this context, Arthur Magida provides one example of a Jewish man who, having requested to an apparently gracious Farrakhan on an airplane flight in 1994 that the minister "tone down" his rhetoric about Jews, was followed on landing by one of Farrakhan's guards through the airport, who repeatedly muttered, "You fucking Jew bastard. We're gonna get you. Motherfucker. Motherfucker. Fucking Jew bastard." See Magida, *Prophet of Rage*, p. xxiii.

5

The Popularity of Paranoia

. . . there can be no substantial or disruptive political action by the Nation of Islam other than akin to the campus gadfly—a nuisance, mildly frightening, but actually not as deadly as the Tse-tse fly. Yet a frightened public or civic authorities, incensed by a sensationalist press, may well be led in such a way to precipitate the fulfilment of alarmist prophecies.

E. U. Essien-Udom, 1962[1]

Anyone who can pull an audience of 10,000 without the benefit of an electric guitar is worthy of some attention.

Richard E. Cohen, 1985[2]

Louis Farrakhan is considerably more than a one-chord paranoiac wonder, but the harmonic strains of his public discourse are far outweighed by its more deeply discordant tones. Nonetheless, it is precisely through his almost unerring ability to achieve and exploit political controversy that Farrakhan has managed to secure his intermittently disturbing fifteen-minute bouts of national American infamy over the past decade—an ability that has relied centrally upon the eagerly receptive and rapt attentions of the press and television media alike. For while no paranoid political figure in the United States, either previously or subsequently, has exercised a political influence even remotely comparable to that of Senator Joe McCarthy during the early 1950s, Farrakhan, like the Wisconsin Senator before him, has clearly benefited to a substantial degree from the extensive coverage that has been accorded him by the modern American mass media.

The media's role has been crucial to Farrakhan's evolving political career, representing a necessary (if insufficient) condition of his national ascendancy. The central foundation upon which the minister's emergence as a national political phenomenon of consequence has rested has been the increasingly common perception, among both black and white American political elites, that Farrakhan has forged a significant mass base of support among African-Americans at large. Particularly for white Americans, that disconcerting view—that Farrakhan's popular black foundations extend far beyond the narrow ranks of the Nation of Islam (NoI)—has been one whose popular acceptance has been powerfully abetted, if not actively promoted, by the national (and international) media. For many professional journalists and editors, the inviting "story" of racial controversy that Farrakhan regularly stokes has invariably been as difficult to resist replaying in its various dramatic guises as its paranoid protagonist has been a consistently compelling political figure to cover. John Lewis's forceful assessment of the civil rights movement—that, without the accompanying national and international media coverage, it would have constituted "a bird without wings"—is equally applicable to the Farrakhan phenomenon in the post–civil rights era.

The full extent of popular black American support of Farrakhan has hence been strongly challenged by many politicians, media commentators, and academics. Critics of Farrakhan have dismissed the Black Muslim minister as, variously, an ephemeral social force, a marginal political figure, and an essentially hollow and vapid "media creation" whose national public profile is entirely disproportionate to his actual mass black appeal. For still others, however, the jarring combination of Farrakhan's eccentric theological beliefs, extremist political views, and apparent popular black support has instead accorded the NoI leader an especially unusual and dangerous niche in contemporary American politics, one that print and television journalists alike face a responsibility not only to address, but also to challenge strongly and convincingly.

In fact, according to the limited indicators thus far available, Farrakhan does indeed enjoy a broad, supportive political constituency among black Americans. Admittedly, the depth and resilience of that popular appeal remains somewhat unclear and uncertain. Farrakhan elicits very strong disapproval from sections of the national black American community, and it remains the case that the overwhelming majority of African-Americans simply do not share the Black Muslim's beliefs in their entirety. Nonetheless, the minister does receive very positive evaluations from black Americans across a range of important indices. Moreover, Farrakhan's notable political longevity and broad black support in the face of intense, widespread, and persistent personal criticism clearly indicate that the NoI's leader enjoys a level of popular political backing from many African-Americans that is at once significant and surprisingly resilient. However uncomfortable, difficult, and worrying it may be for many Americans to accept the notion of Farrakhan's reactionary and paranoid form of politics securing substantial mass black support, the fact of its occurrence can be neither easily nor convincingly denied.

POPULARITY, CONTROVERSY, AND INFLUENCE: TELLING IT LIKE IT IS?

Students of American politics seeking definitive answers to the questions that are frequently posed about the influence of an individual political institution or actor in the United States invariably encounter powerful conceptual obstacles and methodological difficulties. In providing responses to enquiries about how effective an individual president is, for example, evaluations of the extent of a chief executive's political success must first establish the precise criteria by which to define, and the methods by which to measure accurately, the somewhat inchoate notion of "presidential success." Even if appropriate indices of influence can be clearly defined, their ranking in terms of priorities is itself an often disputatious and contentious intellectual matter. The grounds for meaningful comparison, and the quantification of appropriate indicators of influence, only rarely admit of broad-based and lasting critical agreement.

If the influence of an individual politician is frequently difficult to assess accurately, the project of evaluating such influence is exacerbated even further in the case of nonelected political figures, whose leadership status and claims of public support are not subjected to political accountability through the democratic test of free, fair, and regularly prescribed elections. Although an assuredly imperfect and decidedly partial method of assessing influence, elections are widely accepted in liberal democratic regimes as the most reliable and appropriate opportunities for citizens to express their political will and articulate their preferred policy options by choosing between different candidates or political parties for public office. At a minimum, elections provide some basic indicators of mass approval, and thereby confer upon elected officials a popular legitimacy, however limited and imprecise, that is denied many nonelected activists.

It might be argued, therefore, that attempting to reach accurate, informed, and comprehensive conclusions about the extent and nature of Farrakhan's contemporary political influence in American politics is plagued by intractable, and perhaps even insurmountable, intellectual and methodological hurdles. Not the least of these is the fact that, as a nonelected African-American activist whose organization's precise membership remains unknown, the indices by which to assess the minister's political influence are few in number and weak in character. Reliable, hard, and fast conclusions about Farrakhan and the Black Muslim movement seem to be especially elusive. To move beyond merely impressionistic and tendentious assessments, evaluations of Farrakhan's political impact must, of necessity, draw upon empirical findings from outside the province of American elections and voting behavior studies.

Naturally, the extent to which such an enterprise is useful may quite reasonably be doubted. Contemporary American political scientists, in particular, tend to view with a skepticism verging almost on scorn scholarly inquiries that lack sufficiently abundant, rigorous, and supportive quantitative evidence for their arguments. Nonetheless, few political scientists deny that Jesse Jackson, for example, has represented a key national black American political leader since at least 1984, though until 1990 he had not been elected to any public office and his claims to national African-American leadership rested on limited, unconventional, and contentious grounds. The logic of denying the existence of political significance or influence to an individual on the basis of his not standing for elected office—and therefore being beyond the bounds of standard methods of verifiable quantitative investigation—is both intellectually perverse and extremely stifling to scholarly inquiry, not least in the context of such influential nonelected black American figures such as Martin Luther King Jr., Thurgood Marshall, and Clarence Mitchell.

If elections cannot furnish us with information about Farrakhan's mass black American appeal, some of the available indications of the minister's political ascendancy can nonetheless be located in the sheer quantity of media attention that his various activities have increasingly received over the 1990s. The popular attention and media coverage devoted to Farrakhan during the previous decade had been intermittent, generally being occasioned by Jackson's two presidential nomination campaigns and the accompanying national political furors over alleged anti-Semitism. The 1990s, however, have witnessed a more consistent and stable level of mainstream media coverage of Farrakhan and the NoI, one that has also broadened in scope and acquired a more temperate tone.[3] Primary attention was still devoted to Farrakhan's extremist credentials, paranoid politics, and anti-Semitic pronouncements.[4] In addition, though, more extensive and balanced coverage was accorded the NoI's interventions in inner cities to reduce drug consumption and gang violence[5]; the organization's varied business concerns and plans[6]; the lingering controversy over the circumstances of Malcolm X's assassination and Farrakhan's role therein[7]; and a newfound willingness on Farrakhan's part to grant newspaper interviews and make personal appearances on national network and cable television programs. Speculation that Farrakhan had moderated was a new twist and an unexpected addition to the traditional catalog of post–1984 media spins on the NoI's leader, and contributed to a discernible tempering of the critical tone in which he was conventionally treated in many journalistic accounts.[8] Consonant with this changing political environment, Farrakhan was even accorded the 1995 "Newsmaker of the Year" award by the National Newspaper Publishers Association in Washington, D.C., before being subsequently anointed by *Time* magazine, in 1996, with the accolade of being one of America's "25 most influential individuals."[9]

The new media attention notwithstanding, however, four distinct developments provided important indicators of Farrakhan's increasing political influence and social impact among African-Americans at large during the 1990s. First, Vice-President Al Gore, the U.S. Congress, and the U.S. Commission on Civil Rights independently criticized (and Jewish groups ran full-page newspaper advertisements denouncing) Farrakhan and the NoI, during 1992–96. Most significant, as chapter two noted, the U.S. House of Representatives and Senate approved resolutions explicitly condemning the Kean College remarks of Farrakhan's chief aide and spokesperson, Khalid Abdul Muhammad, as "hate-mongering" and "vicious," by margins of 364:34 (29 voting "present") and 97:0, respectively, in February 1994. Furthermore, in 1995–96, the House convened hearings on the NoI's involvement in obtaining security contracts for inner-city housing projects and on Farrakhan's ongoing relationship with several foreign despots and "rogue regimes."[10]

The 1994 initiative by the federal legislature was especially remarkable. The denunciation of Khalid's speech constituted a rare—

and, according to Rep. Don Edwards (D-CA), then chairman of the House Judiciary Committee's Subcommittee on Civil Rights, wholly unprecedented—instance of the U.S. Congress officially condemning a political speech by an American citizen. An unusual occurrence in any circumstances, such governmental censure would seem especially peculiar if directed against a member of an organization of marginal social consequence or political importance. Moreover, the congressional action also contrasted powerfully with two expressions of antiblack sentiment in America that notably escaped the national legislature's unequivocal censure, one historic and the other more recent.

In terms of the former, the isolation and condemnation of the NoI's spokesperson contrasted sharply with the essentially benign treatment accorded the Ku Klux Klan (and other racist vigilante groups) by Congress in the 1920s and 1930s, when the white supremacist group was enjoying substantial membership and exercising considerable political influence, particularly within southern state Democratic parties.[11] Unlike the KKK, the NoI had committed no documented acts of violence, vigilantism, or terrorism, nor were members of its security arm, the Fruit of Islam, permitted by their own organization to carry offensive weapons of any type. That an organization such as the NoI should merit adverse congressional attention was thus wholly exceptional, even within the peculiar generic family of extremist American cults and militias.

Historic disjunctures, however, were not the only contrast in congressional attentiveness to the incidence of expressions of bigotry and racial animus. Contemporaneous to Khalid's viciously defamatory speech, the Democratic Senator for South Carolina, Ernest "Fritz" Hollings, made a series of deeply offensive remarks about a delegation of black Africans attending a conference in Geneva. Not a politician noted on Capitol Hill for being especially overburdened by either intellect or sensitivity, Hollings referred to the Africans as potentates and cannibals, "in search of a good meal." Although then-CBC chairman Mfume attempted to attach an amendment condemning Hollings's comments to the motion censuring Muhammad, the House of Representatives refused to accept it, while the Senate typically eschewed censuring one of its own.

Although neither the scope of Hollings's remarks nor the form of their expression approximated the comprehensive range and vituperatively virulent nature of Muhammad's speech, the apparent double standard for condemnation of transparently bigoted comments was obvious. That the national legislature of the United States should engage in censure of a member of the NoI was not so much an indication of a newfound sensitivity to prejudice and bigotry on the part of American federal legislators, but more a clear sign of two political developments: first, the increasingly widespread perception and broadly shared consensus in the Congress of the gravity of the threat that Farrakhan's organization represented to social comity and harmonious relations between the races in America; and second, the exclusively beneficial results and political profit to be accrued for almost all congresspersons from attacking Farrakhan and the NoI, a political capital decidedly less marked and far more uncertain for many representatives and senators in the case of repudiating Hollings's offensive remarks.

The decisive and hostile (though inconsistent) response of U.S. federal legislators to the NoI thus offered one indication of Farrakhan's growing political impact. Another, and in many respects more important, set of signals of the minister's rise was provided by the large audiences that Farrakhan's sermons and rallies attracted and by public opinion surveys of support for the Black Muslim minister among African-Americans at large. Both indices powerfully suggested that Farrakhan's popular appeal among black Americans was substantially increasing. Although the material significance of both the rallies and the poll data is open to challenge, it is unusual that a member of a relatively small, unorthodox, and isolated minority religious sect should attract such huge numbers of attenders to his rallies and win widespread approval in opinion surveys of African-Americans at large, and that, partly as a result, Farrakhan should be intermittently accorded the star turn before the world's press corps. Farrakhan's claims of popular legitimation had evidently secured strong sources of popular sustenance and support.

The Million Man March may have easily been his greatest political achievement in mass black mobilization, but Farrakhan's public lecture tours since 1984 have frequently drawn substantial African-American audiences, often of between fifteen and twenty thousand people and rarely fewer than five thousand. His 1985 tour of fourteen American cities, for example, pulled in impressive black American crowds of six thousand in Detroit, Michigan; seven thousand in Atlanta, Georgia; five thousand in Houston, Texas; and seven thousand in Philadelphia, Pennsylvania, all of whom paid $2–3 for the privilege of temporary admittance to Farrakhan's traveling court of

reaction and paranoia.[12] Although Reed, in 1991,[13] somewhat causti-
cally and casually dismissed mass African-American attendance at
such rallies as a temporarily fashionable act of black radical chic, but
one of minimal substantive consequence among African-Americans—
akin to attending concerts of the then trendy rap star M. C. Hammer—
the consistently large audiences that Farrakhan commands over a
remarkably prolonged period of time belies such a complacent interpretation. If Reed's analogy held firm, Farrakhan would have (like
Hammer) exited the political pop charts of African-America by the
mid-1990s. Instead, the minister's paranoid and reactionary mantra
has attracted many more black American buyers and perhaps adherents. (Lincoln, for example, argues that the NoI's newspaper, *The Final
Call*, claims the largest regular circulation of any specifically African-
American periodical in the United States, at around 600,000 per
week.[14])

Farrakhan's exceptional ability to inspire such incredible numbers of ordinary black American citizens to attend his lectures and sermons is indeed striking. The substantial size of the audiences that
Farrakhan draws is truly impressive, no matter what comparative
standards are invoked. Few, if any, other national black or nonblack
American political leaders could aspire to Farrakhan's heights. The
minister's rally at New York City's Madison Square Garden in October 1985, for example, drew in excess of twenty thousand African-
Americans to the stadium, with another five thousand watching on
closed-circuit televisions in a neighboring building, despite (or, more
accurately, partly because of) widespread efforts by local black and
nonblack public figures to discourage African-Americans from attending the event. In 1992, while 53,000 fans turned out for the opening
game of the baseball World Series in Atlanta's Fulton County Stadium, over 60,000 black Americans attended a Farrakhan rally in the
Georgia Dome just one mile away—at an entrance fee of $15 per
head.[15] And in 1994, approximately 25,000 African-Americans filled
the Jacob Javits Convention Center in New York City to listen to Farrakhan's lengthy address. Such startling figures are quite impossible to
dismiss as being merely ephemeral social products of passing, fad-
dish, or marginal political significance.

This is especially so given the character of the African-American
audiences that the NoI's leader attracts to his rallies. The social composition of those attending Farrakhan's public sermons and lectures is

generally far from being homogeneously deprived and disadvantaged in socioeconomic terms. While the majority of attenders are indeed working class and underprivileged black Americans, Farrakhan's meetings also consistently attract large numbers of middle income and relatively affluent African-Americans. One observer, who attended more than 200 such meetings over a twelve-year period, related that Farrakhan's audiences comprised an extremely heterogeneous range of African-Americans, from single black American females to professional football players, accountants, pop singers, physicians, and the unemployed.[16] Moreover, the overwhelming majority of these African-Americans are, of course, not NoI members, either prior or subsequent to attending the Farrakhan rallies.

The impressionistic evidence that such events regularly provide has been supplemented and largely supported by public survey data on Farrakhan. The limited but increasing public opinion poll evidence that exists about the Black Muslim minister has tended to indicate a broad level of support for Farrakhan among black Americans at large, although the exact strength and depth of its foundations remain open to question. An October 1985 poll of African-Americans (commissioned by the Simon Wiesenthal Center), for example, found that Farrakhan had rapidly emerged as the third best-known national black political spokesman, after Jesse Jackson and Andrew Young. It is significant that two-fifths of those African-Americans surveyed who had heard of Farrakhan at the time also wanted to see his political influence increase.[17]

Of course, such an impressive level of name recognition may plausibly have been simply a direct, isolated, and unrepresentative response to the furor over Farrakhan that erupted during the previous year's presidential election campaign. Moreover, name recognition does not necessarily imply public approval. Nonetheless, almost a decade later, according to the University of Chicago's 1993–94 Black Politics Study, in response to the question, "Do you think Farrakhan is a good leader or a dangerous force in the black community?," two-thirds of those African-Americans who answered (67 percent) deemed him a good leader, while a relatively modest 28 percent viewed the minister as dangerous (4 percent said both). On a separate scale of 0 to 100 (from cold to warm), Farrakhan scored 59, a "moderately warm" response. Almost one-third of those African-Americans surveyed, however, failed to answer either question. Michael Dawson, one of the study's coauthors, suspected that Farrakhan's approval rating would have been even higher had more black Americans actually responded.[18]

Such indicators of Farrakhan's mass appeal are also supported by several other surveys that suggest that the minister's role and analyses of black Americans' contemporary plight resonate strongly with many African-Americans nationwide. A Gallup poll in April 1991, for example, revealed that 34 percent of black American respondents believed that African-Americans would benefit if Farrakhan assumed a larger leadership role in their affairs. This figure compared to 72 percent for Jesse Jackson, 42 percent for Colin Powell, and 29 percent for Doug Wilder. By comparison, only 8 percent of white American respondents felt that a larger leadership role for Farrakhan would benefit black Americans, compared to 54 percent for Powell, 46 percent for Jackson, and 18 percent for Wilder.[19] A 1994 poll for *Time* also revealed that 70 percent of African-Americans felt that Farrakhan "says things the country should hear"; 67 percent saw him as an "effective leader"; 62 percent held him to be "good for the black community"; and, perhaps most important, 63 percent believed he "speaks the truth." Only 34 percent of blacks saw him as a bigot and a racist.[20] (These figures compare ironically with an August 1993 Gallup poll that found only 1 percent of African-American respondents citing Farrakhan when asked to name "black leaders."[21])

The reasons for the significant discrepancy in survey evidence are unclear and encompass several plausible possibilities: an understandable reluctance among black American respondents to reveal political support for Farrakhan in public; genuine popular indifference to, or disapproval of, Farrakhan and the NoI; ignorance about the NoI's leader; and attitudinal reactions among African-Americans who may have been conditioned in the post–civil rights era to respond to inquiries about leadership among blacks in terms of conventional, elected officials rather than protest or extrasystemic political actors.

Juan Williams argues that the figures suggest that Farrakhan is not actually viewed by the mass of African-Americans as a leader but that, through repeated exposure by the mass media, he is nonetheless granted authority as an opinion maker.[22] If the core of Williams's argument, however, is that African-Americans do not subscribe wholly, and will not follow unthinkingly, an activist such as Farrakhan, then precisely the same point could be made in regard to virtually any other black American politician, from Jesse Jackson to Baltimore Mayor Kurt Schmoke. Williams's view does not negate the notion that Farrakhan's political support is indeed significant; the generally favorable responses that the Black Muslim receives when his name is mentioned to African-Americans and the sizeable proportions of respondents who publicly endorse an enhanced leadership role for him indicate that both his name recognition and substantive approval among black Americans at large are extensive. Leaders require supporters, however selective and qualified their endorsements, more than sycophants and blind followers in order to propagate their views, acquire national legitimacy and, ultimately, effect meaningful social and political change. And the combination of survey evidence and mass attendance at Farrakhan events clearly suggests that the popular constituency among African-Americans to which the minister successfully appeals for mass black support is far more substantial than negligible in scope.

In addition to his substantial mass African-American approval, the third development indicative of the Black Muslim's increased impact was the growing attention that Farrakhan received from, and his generally improved and increasingly conciliatory relations with, other national black American political and civic elites. The most important political development in this respect was his rapprochement in the early–mid-1990s with the CBC under Mfume and the NAACP under Chavis (discussed in chapter two). Through his resulting partial inclusion in the elite cadre of national African-American political leadership, Farrakhan achieved a notable political triumph that had eluded many black nationalist political activists and organizations in the United States previously. That his inclusion was largely conferred upon him by other elite African-American political actors (some of whom, such as Chavis, occupied leadership positions through bureaucratic patronage politics rather than direct popular election) was of less political importance to Farrakhan's burgeoning leadership role than was his mere presence at national black political leadership forums. The enthusiastic responses of both other panel members and the audience at the 1993 CBC legislative weekend, for example, provided strong confirmation of the important role (as well as fundamental legitimation of the increasing political influence) that the NoI's leader had achieved by 1993. That Farrakhan should have merited such inclusion was testimony to his appeal to a broad social constituency among American blacks.

Fourth, and most incontrovertible, Farrakhan's 1995 Million Man March on Washington, D.C., demonstrated to the entire American nation an exceptional ability on the NoI leader's part to mobilize collective action by African-Americans on an unprecedented and dramatic scale. Although estimates of the true size of the march varied greatly, the remarkable political achievement of the occasion could hardly be disputed.[23] No other contemporary black American political leader could have even contemplated the organization and successful execution of such an impressively well-attended national political event. Indeed, the most emphatic statement of the changing internal balance of the national African-American leadership cadre could partially be inferred from two starkly contrasting demonstrations of 1995. In the spring of that year, Jesse Jackson had barely been able to muster 300 marchers to walk to Martin Luther King's grave in Atlanta, Georgia, to protest against possible federal reversal of affirmative action policies under the Republican-controlled 104th Congress and the Rehnquist Supreme Court. But by October 1995, the man whose public pronouncements Jackson had eventually repudiated a decade previously headed a gathering of over 400,000 African-American men in the nation's capital, striking numbers that were powerfully suggestive of an extensive political reach and a broad social impact wholly exceptional among current national black American political leaders.

Opinion surveys taken both prior and subsequent to the march also provided further confirmation of Farrakhan's popular, if by no means universal, political appeal among black Americans. A *Washington Post-ABC News* poll prior to the march, for example, revealed that over half of all black Americans knew of the march and an overwhelming majority (84 percent) approved of the initiative. Many respondents nonetheless drew a distinction between the public goals of the march, which were overwhelmingly supported, and the character of its principal organizers: both Farrakhan and Chavis had at least as many black detractors as supporters in the poll.[24]

Polls taken subsequently, however, at the time of the march and thereafter, revealed an alternative set of popular black views of Farrakhan. Although, as table 5.1 shows, a mere 5 percent of marchers participated in order specifically to express support for Farrakhan, fully 87 percent of the marchers expressed a favorable opinion of the NoI's leader, while a slightly larger proportion (88 percent) also endorsed his organization. These figures exceeded approval of Jesse Jackson by 15 percent and Bill Clinton by over 30 percent. Most African-Americans

---

TABLE 5.1   The Million Man March*

Single most important reason for participation?

Support for black family	29
Support for black men showing more responsibility	
for families and communities	25
Support black unity	25
Support black economic strength	7
Support for Farrakhan	5

Favorable or unfavorable impression of:

Nation of Islam	88	Clinton	54
Farrakhan	87	Jewish people	41
Chavis	77	White people	31
Jackson	73	Criminal justice system	15

As a result of the march, will Farrakhan have more influence among black leaders in the African-American community?

	MMM Participants	Blacks Nationally
Yes	80	34
No	14	27

Will Farrakhan have more influence among political leaders in Washington?

	MMM Participants	Blacks Nationally
Yes	55	34
No	14	41

Age		Education		Marital Status	
18–30	33	Less than HS	5	Married	42
30–44	42	HS graduate	22	Single	46
45–60	20	Some college/college grad.	59	Divorced	10
61+	4	Post–graduate	14	Widowed	1

Religion

Protestant	52	Muslim	6	None	14
Catholic	7	Nation of Islam	5		

---

*Figures are percentages of total number of respondents
Source: *The Washington Post*, 17 October 1995, p. A23.
N=1047, sampling error of +/- 3 percent.

also expected Farrakhan to achieve a more influential role among national black leaders as a result of the successful mass mobilization.

Moreover, one of the most important features of the poll in this respect concerns the demographic bases of Farrakhan's support and approval. For in terms of both age and education, in particular, the pool of African-American respondents professing their approval of Farrakhan and the NoI was notably mature, educated, and middle income in character. That Farrakhan should elicit such markedly high approval ratings from a middle-income group of black American males is especially significant. Dismissing the mass black American constituency to which Farrakhan appeals as essentially comprising only the most impoverished, underprivileged, and unrepresentative segment of African-Americans is hence impossible. Although this segment is undoubtedly the mainstay of the NoI's mass base, the minister's signal political achievement is that, as the table clearly shows, his reach actually encompasses very diverse and disparate sections of the national black American community.

Perhaps even more telling than the *Post*'s survey were the results of two opinion surveys for the magazines *Time* and *Newsweek*.[25] The former revealed that the ratio of positive to negative evaluations of Farrakhan by black Americans had hardly altered between February 1994 (at the height of the national furor over Khalid Muhammad's Kean College speech) and October 1995. Almost half of black respondents (48 percent) held that Farrakhan was not a bigot and a racist, while well over half believed him to speak the truth (59 percent). Half of all black respondents also viewed him as a good role model for black youth (59 percent) and as a positive force in the black community (50 percent).

Farrakhan's support admittedly remained far from universal: 36 percent of black respondents held Farrakhan to be a bigot and a racist, and 30 percent did not view him as a good role model for black youth. The *Newsweek* survey also recorded that, while 41 percent of black Americans harbored a favorable opinion of Farrakhan, exactly the same percentage had an unfavorable view of him. Even in the hour of his greatest political triumph, then, the Black Muslim minister found himself unable to command anywhere near universal African-American support.

Such persistently skeptical and hostile responses to Farrakhan from many black Americans serve as the clearest repudiations of naively critical assessments that portray the minister as having won overwhelming and uncritical endorsement and support from American blacks, or as somehow having become the titular "leader" of African-Americans. That the leader of the NoI elicits negative reactions and unfavorable evaluations from many African-Americans is clear and beyond refutation. Given both the esoteric content of his religious and ideological beliefs and the concerted public attacks to which he has so long been subject from black and nonblack American elites, however, this is neither especially surprising nor of momentous political (or analytic) significance. Indeed, it would be far more notable—and immeasurably more worrying for white Americans—if Farrakhan elicited either exclusively, universally, or overwhelmingly positive and favorable responses from black Americans in general.

Far more significant than the fact of negative reactions persisting among blacks toward the NoI's leader, however, is the remarkable proportion of African-Americans who do respond positively to Farrakhan. A sizeable proportion of black Americans consistently view Farrakhan favorably and warmly, seeing him as a positive force within black communities.[26] Moreover, it seems reasonable to assume that a significant percentage of those respondents who either do not answer such surveys or, if they do, answer "not sure" to questions about Farrakhan, also harbor positive dispositions toward the minister. In sum, although the evidence by which to evaluate the question of Farrakhan's popularity and political influence is incomplete, and by no means provides a definitive answer, the achievement by Farrakhan of a substantial political and social impact among African-Americans in the 1990s is extremely difficult—indeed, impossible—to reject. Farrakhan's wary treatment by nonblack politicians and political lobbies, the several indices of his mass black approval, the vacillating responses of black political and civic elites, and the manifest success of the Million Man March together testify to the minister's achievement of an exceptional leadership position among African-Americans at large.

THE FARRAKHAN PHENOMENON: A MEDIA CREATION?

Although the indicators of his increasing mass appeal among black Americans are multiple and undeniably persuasive, the precise extent and nature of Farrakhan's political influence have nonetheless been strongly contested by political commentators in both the American Academy and the mass media. For several critics, Farrakhan's recent national rise essentially provides yet another unfortunate example of the pervasive, if generally unintentional and often adverse, influence of the modern mass communications industry in recent American politics.[27] The necessary political fuel for the Farrakhan phenomenon, in this interpretation, is largely provided by an American press and televisual corps whose principal fascination about national politics in the contemporary United States is dominated by the compelling political dramas of sleaze and sensationalism (whether racial, sexual, or financial), and which appears almost congenitally predisposed to reducing complex and difficult political issues into simplistic and inaccurate narratives. In place of both abstract entities, such as political parties, and substantive issue-oriented national policy debates, a candidate-centered, personality-driven politics and an artificially constructed adversarialism instead increasingly inform the American public's limited consumption of political news.

Certainly, few political scientists dispute the extensive political influence that the fourth estate now exerts in liberal democratic regimes in general and the United States in particular.[28] Far from being a neutral observer of political events, the media, in particular television, has become a central player in political matters in contemporary America, particularly in national and statewide election campaigns.[29] Through its decisions either to run or ignore particular stories and, indeed, through the very decision that a particular event actually merits designation as a story worthy of dissemination to the public, the media participates powerfully in determining the national political agenda. Media journalists both select and screen the political information that American citizens receive. Moreover, not only does that selection process determine what counts as news, but the spin that a story receives from the media also shapes its general, diffuse reception by the mass American public. Television and print editors and reporters thus consistently act as professional gatekeepers to political information, determining what citizens know and the manner in which what they deem relevant information is imparted to the public—a process that powerfully shapes, even if it can neither fully nor consistently determine with precision, what the responses of news watchers are likely to be.

That Farrakhan's politics should have been profoundly affected by the mass media is hardly a shocking or unreasonable proposition, then. Indeed, the American media can be argued to have performed a doubly critical role in shaping Farrakhan's political ascendancy. First, the media have been of cardinal importance in terms of the sheer volume of print and televisual coverage devoted to the NoI's leader since 1984, both of which have increased almost exponentially in scope. Second, the evolving political salience to, and the varied reception of Farrakhan among, the American public has been greatly influenced by

212 The Popularity of Paranoia

the invariably negative character—whether excessively or insuffi-
ciently so, according to particular subjective tastes—of much of that
media coverage. Farrakhan's national public visibility among both
black and nonblack Americans has thus been crucially raised—and
his political career thereby vitally advanced—by generous, if intermittent, media attention. In both assisting in the initial creation of the Farrakhan phenomenon as a national force, and in subsequently reviving
and sustaining its political momentum, the U.S. media has incontrovertibly played its part in contributing to the minister's national political ascent.

To deny that this is the case would certainly be ludicrous. The
precise extent to which the media has either created or driven the Farrakhan phenomenon, however, remains unclear. Farrakhan's gradual
but inexorable political rise to a position of national influence and
leadership among African-Americans over the past twelve years has
been viewed almost universally as being vitally assisted by the disproportionately large amount—and occasionally histrionic and near-hys-
terical style—of coverage devoted to the Black Muslim leader by
television and, in particular, print reporters. Farrakhan has, by this
interpretation, invoked Marshall McLuhan's most famous dictum to
devastating demagogic effect. If the medium is the message, the message that the combination of the cathode ray and the nationally syndicated column has assisted Farrakhan to propagate across America has
been one of paranoia, fear, and mutual racial animosity combined.
Moreover, in focusing mainly upon the concrete and charismatic individual behind that unedifying message, the media has in effect not
only disseminated his pernicious views but has also elevated—even
transformed—the political legitimacy and social status of the messenger.

Dennis King, for example, views Farrakhan as "very much a
media creature":

> As with many such figures a theatre of illusion is created com-
> prising rhetorical violence, cheering crowds, TV cameras and
> hysterical newspaper editorials. In short, it becomes easy to
> ascribe to Farrakhan an importance much greater than he actu-
> ally possesses.[30]

In arguing further (and persuasively) that the direct threat to American Jews that Farrakhan poses has been vastly overdrawn, King notes

the total absence of physical violence committed by the NoI upon its many enemies. In contrast to many white supremacist American groups, for whom the violence of their racist rhetoric has frequently been matched by the brutality of their actions, no physical attacks on Jews or synagogues or incidents of cemetery desecration have ever been directly traced to the NoI, under either Farrakhan or his predecessors.[31]

King also argues less compellingly that the support that Farrakhan receives from educated and middle-income black Americans is fundamentally "a passive form of support, the product of media hype more than of any organizational skill on Farrakhan's part." In this, Juan Williams, too, concurs that it is the attention that Farrakhan actively and assiduously pursues, and regularly and readily receives, from the American mass media that serves as the necessary fuel for his public notoriety and his national African-American political leadership pretensions.[32]

The central theme of such arguments tends to converge upon a shared notion that Farrakhan has essentially been propelled into a position of national public prominence in America by a media-driven politics of racial sensationalism. In creating a political climate in which demands either for Farrakhan's vigorous denunciation or for solidaristic rallies to his support are easily generated, the media inevitably stokes (and even causes) the controversies and "scandals" surrounding Farrakhan and, thereby, animates the visceral bases of his popular black American appeal. Such are the depths to which contemporary black-white relations have plunged that, as Manning Marable argued, many black Americans "instinctively" recognize that any African-American public figure who so unerringly evokes harsh contempt and unrelenting condemnation from white religious and political leaders in the United States must "necessarily" have something meaningful for them in his program.[33] Black Americans are prompted to rally to Farrakhan mainly because he is quite correctly perceived to be the object of persistently disparaging, abusive, and derogatory public attacks, especially by members of other, nonblack social groups— attacks that, when they occur, are assiduously and expansively featured in national newspaper opinion pages and evening news bulletins.[34] Thus, in encouraging public responses and in relaying nationwide reactions to Farrakhan, the news media thereby contributes to his emergent status as an embattled and courageous black political martyr, boldly seeking to advance African-Americans' collective well-being (whether wisely or misguidedly is essentially beside the point here; the laudatory effort is all that is relevant), but being denounced and defamed by nonblacks in that admirable process.

Such arguments are frequently linked to vehement rejections of the various theses that advance Farrakhan's growing status as an influential national political actor among African-Americans. These rejections tend to adopt one of two interpretive strategies: either to deny or refute the notion that Farrakhan performs a role of some consequence in black American politics at present, and hence to infer that media attention accorded the NoI's leader is entirely unmerited, malapportioned, and inflammatory; or, alternatively, to acknowledge the significant social and political impact achieved by Farrakhan among many African-Americans at the mass level, but to identify this principally as the product of undue and excessive media attention. Thus, in constituting some type of militant, totemic racial figure of paranoid extremism, mass black American support for the NoI's leader is viewed by such critics as being either limited, weak, and fundamentally transient or, alternatively, an artificial consequence of media hyperbole. The inherent contradiction in the two arguments is no doubt sufficiently manifest, but each nonetheless possesses a particular, distinctive, and coherent internal logic. Let us therefore deal with them each in turn.

The first interpretive course tends to reduce Farrakhan's influence to a matter of essentially transient popular symbolism, what can perhaps be defined most appropriately as the "media event" school. According to this reductive line of argument, Farrakhan represents a particularly virulent and compelling example of the increasingly disturbing conflation between sensationalist politics and entertainment that the modern mass media and the phenomenon of "video politics" has wrought in the United States and elsewhere.[35] Farrakhan, in this view, essentially forms part of a continuum of popular cultural references that advance a dual message of collective black American uplift and increasing interracial animosity in the United States. Thus, the NoI's leader occupies an ignominious place in the media's broad spectrum of ugly but compelling social and political ogres, "somewhere between Ice-T and the Ayatollah Khomeini," as Joe Klein memorably put it.[36] Attendance at Farrakhan rallies and lectures represents little more for African-Americans than an essentially vicarious experience of a temporarily fashionable racial fad, of (at best) primarily cathartic value in contributing to those blacks attending a brief and necessarily ephemeral moment of racial pride and uplift—miniature-scale, localized versions of the Million Man March, in essence.[37] Farrakhan's public discourse is merely a marginally more elaborate and pseudosophisticated version of the sounds of gunshots aimed by black Americans at a white victim that introduce a new gangsta rap album.[38] The consuming hatred and the implicit threat of violence that pervade Farrakhan's speeches together contribute to a compulsively marketable national package, fastidiously tailor-made for the mass American public's contemporary consumptive tastes. Shocking and outrageous, to be sure, at times even scandalous, but of neither fundamental, serious, nor lasting material consequence for white America.

The alternative interpretation is at once less hasty and more uncertain that Farrakhan's influence among black Americans at large is either overestimated or can legitimately be viewed as analogous to the consumption of the various visceral racial messages and symbols of interracial dissensus that are invariably disseminated by the modern mass entertainment industry in America.[39] Unlike the media event school, adherents to the "media irresponsibility" interpretation broadly accept that Farrakhan has achieved an influential and serious national political role among African-Americans. Still, they attribute this largely to the very coverage of the NoI's leader in which they and their colleagues themselves frequently engage. The national attention and ready journalistic access that the media typically grant Farrakhan (however intermittently) ensures that his poisonous and pernicious racial message achieves a uniquely privileged political outlet. The minister hence receives a wide and—given the inflammatory nature of the news—unusually attentive American audience; one, moreover, that would otherwise not exist or, at a minimum, would be considerably narrower in scope.

A representative example of this interpretive school is the nationally syndicated black American journalist Carl Rowan, who best encapsulated its outlook when Farrakhan first won widespread media attention and criticism in 1984:

> I cannot silence Farrakhan. I cannot stop the media from exploiting him. I can, I hope, make some of my media colleagues understand the damage they do in chasing down black demagogues and making them national figures.[40]

Rowan subsequently speculated further:

> Media mirror on my wall, who's the dumbest of 'em all? Those
> of us . . . who are making Mr. Farrakhan one of the best-known,
> most-listened-to black persons on earth, even though he offers
> nothing more than religious bilge and racial hatred and is
> preying on the frustrations, the rage, of millions of black
> Americans.[41]

Twelve years on, and Rowan grew ever more frustrated and exasperated that, in the face of the national media's continued and seemingly unremitting, deer-in-the-headlight-like fixation upon Farrakhan, "those blacks to whom America's leaders and power-brokers ought to be listening can rarely get a fair hearing."[42]

Another, equally disenchanted, subscriber to the "media irresponsibility" thesis, political scientist Martin Kilson, also holds that the American print and televisual media have accorded grossly "disproportionate attention to leaders of the black disenchanted," such as Farrakhan and Sharpton. "Pseudo-event politics," that is, media-hyped politics, attempts to equate what Kilson sees as a minority and marginal strand of ethnocentric black American nationalism with the more mature, pragmatic, and important electoral "mainplot" of African-American politics.[43] In paying attention to Farrakhan at all, the U.S. media effectively serve the deeply deleterious political function of legitimizing his otherwise extremely limited and contentious national leadership claims as equivalent, though by definition different (and, for Kilson and many others, wholly deficient) to those of established black American elected and appointive officials.

Although these two interpretations are analytically distinct, the basic logic that informs their core arguments is nonetheless shared, simple, and clear. Since the media bear a disproportionate burden of the unenviably heavy responsibility for Farrakhan's rise, they also possess the power—and should rapidly grasp the political opportunity—to precipitate his decline: either by ignoring or reducing substantially their excessive coverage of his public speeches and the NoI's activities (Rowan and King's preferred solution), or by making absolutely clear the complete unacceptability of Farrakhan's rampantly paranoid bigotry in American public life (the course preferred by Cohen, Williams, and Klein). As with McCarthy in the 1940s, the coverage of Farrakhan's activities and paranoid allegations by the print and television media renders those newsworthy in a manner in which they would otherwise utterly fail to be. Thus, for Farrakhan, the unmerited and invariably hostile coverage directed toward his speeches and sermons serves strongly to amplify rather than to diminish the extent of his popular African-American support and, hence, to exaggerate rather than reduce the more general political threat that he is perceived to represent. National notoriety, ipso facto, equals news; and notoriety is conferred upon Farrakhan through and by the media, whose unceasingly formidable appetite for the sensational is fed, but rarely satiated, by the minister's more inflammatory public claims, statements, and threats.

Such arguments are, however, neither internally coherent nor especially intellectually convincing. Let us concede, for the moment, that the Farrakhan phenomenon is predominantly, or even exclusively, a media-driven entity. The proposed solution to the minister's national rise—withdrawing or decreasing the level of media attention—seems wholly insufficient to accomplish its instrumental goal of a diminution in Farrakhan's political and social influence. Notwithstanding its ascribed origins, the current popularity of Farrakhan among black Americans is such that simply ignoring his role in current African-American politics would do little, if anything, to modify or dilute his popular black appeal.

In much the same way that Jackson successfully achieved a preeminent leadership status by 1984 as a result of his spectacularly unsuccessful campaign for the Democratic party presidential nomination, which media inattention thereafter did not diminish, so, for Farrakhan, his social impact has reached levels—and his organization achieved a sufficiently widespread mass black admiration and respect—that transcend any coverage the mainstream press and television may now accord him. If the media are either wholly or primarily culpable for releasing the black American demagogic genie from the bottle of racial hatred, it is unclear how the lax and complacent professional culprits can either easily or completely return the bigoted escapee to his original isolated, unfamiliar, and appropriate political home. Containment of those contaminated by such unapologetic racial animus requires far more than a willing suspension of disbelief and pretenses that Farrakhan is an inconsequential national African-American figure.

It is at the very least unclear, though, that the notion that the media created the Farrakhan phenomenon should be accepted at all. Indeed, in searching for plausible explanations for Farrakhan's political rise, the notion that "the media did it" is one that is inherently and deeply flawed in two key respects. First, in sharp contrast to Jackson, the NoI's leader has generally explicitly avoided mainstream media outlets until relatively recently in his leadership career. Of the 110 television channels and 50 radio stations across America (listed in *The Final Call*) that Farrakhan could be heard or seen on in May 1996, for example, no more than a handful could even optimistically be described as "mainstream."[44] Indeed, Farrakhan maintained a complete vow of silence in relation to white media outlets until well into the 1980s, a practice which in part accounts for the striking paucity of both popular and scholarly articles on him prior to 1984, and the relative dearth of them even between 1985 and 1990.[45] Second, when Farrakhan has subsequently appeared on network television or granted lengthy interviews to particularly well-respected newspapers during the 1990s, the content of his core message has barely altered, even though the style of his delivery has softened noticeably from his typically intemperate stump tirades.[46]

Thus, in attributing *Larry King Live*, *The New York Times*, or *Washington Post* op-ed pieces with providing the complicitous fuel for erroneous claims of Farrakhan's political leadership status among black Americans, media critics seem guilty of an interpretive faculty that is unduly conditioned by the Beltway mentality. One might greet with a reasonably healthy degree of skepticism, after all, the notion that sixty thousand black Americans paid $15 each in Atlanta in 1992 to listen to the NoI's leader because they had been fooled by such editorials— or by appearances on *Donahue*—into thinking that Farrakhan had more to say than he actually did. African-Americans attend because they want to hear Farrakhan's message undiluted, unabridged, and unadorned by commentaries, even if they may neither agree with nor endorse that message in its entirety.

Moreover, to compare Farrakhan's rallies to concerts by popular musicians wholly neglects the explicitly political content—and hence the unusual political significance—of the former. When an accomplished and militant black American agitator, whose speeches consistently feature vicious attacks upon a variety of specified enemies (both in and outside the United States) and whose rhetoric is deliberately infused by incendiary references to violence and death, can pack to overflowing stadia that many popular entertainers can never hope to fill, far more fundamental political questions are involved than that of mere media attention, particularly given the clear longevity of

Farrakhan's mass African-American appeal and the fact that white media are more often absent than present at NoI rallies. The persistence of large black American audiences attending such lectures and rallies over a twelve-year period since Farrakhan's effective national media debut in 1984 is powerfully suggestive of a political appeal among African-Americans at large that stretches far beyond that of mere novelty and cathartic psychological value, or some transient, collective racial fashionability.

If the media event school of interpretation is unconvincing, the irresponsibility variant of the media creation argument, as applied to Farrakhan (and others before him), also seems very weak. For its proponents, such as Kilson and Rowan, the essence of their argument is that coverage devoted to the Black Muslim leader is grossly malapportioned to his original political influence among African-Americans, prior to such undue media attention. They must then, however, confront the vexing issue of defining what would constitute a proportionate level of coverage of Farrakhan. In fact, it is not so much the quantity of coverage that is the real cause of their disapprobation, but the substantive content of the subject's message and the fact of its positive reception among many African-Americans. Farrakhan's face on the cover of *Time* magazine in February 1994 would in itself have been unremarkable, and impossible, were it not for the combination of the reactionary and paranoid content of his discourse and its evident popular appeal among black Americans at large. If Farrakhan's influence is indeed exaggerated, then denunciations would seem wholly out of place; the logic in vigorously denouncing an entirely irrelevant, fatuous, or marginal political force (Lyndon La Rouche, say) is not readily apparent. If, however, Farrakhan's influence is instead conceded to be tangible, ignoring the Black Muslim leader (as Rowan recommended) would appear to be neglecting a pressing responsibility—even a civic imperative—to challenge his pernicious message and to combat his harmful political aspirations. Direct and full engagement is otherwise subsumed by wholesale avoidance, when a combative, candid dialogue and an analysis of the real sources of Farrakhan's mass appeal seems of cardinal importance.

The line between being "merely" a media creation and constituting "more than" a media creation is admittedly as thin in modern American public life as the gulf between the television news headlines and the range of important political events that actually occur in the world is wide. Indeed, in the context of an American politics wherein the two major parties' national conventions were literally made for TV in 1996, separating the media out from "real" politics at times seems an almost futile project. The actual causes of Farrakhan's increasing influence, however, are more appropriately identified elsewhere than in either the American mass media's structural and political biases or its sensationalist predispositions. The blight of many predominantly black-populated urban centers across the United States; the persistence of racial prejudice and discrimination; the increasing social and economic problems affecting many black American communities; the perceived inability of national black political elites—and apparent unwillingness of many whites—effectively to ameliorate and rectify such serious problems together form a critical set of underlying conditions that are especially ripe for Farrakhan to exploit. (The next chapter examines these bases of the Farrakhan phenomenon in detail.)

That mass media attention has substantially assisted the dissemination of Farrakhan's activities and views among both black and nonblack Americans is, of course, undeniable. Farrakhan himself regularly addresses parts of his sermons specifically to the assembled press corps and, in the aftermath of his 1996 World Friendship Tour, ironically thanked CNN for increasing his international stature by its extensive coverage of the Million Man March.[47] The extent to which this has been the central, rather than an admittedly important, contributory factor in the minister's growing role and influence is much less certain. Arguments that the media are responsible for, rather than simply culpable in, Farrakhan's rise are too tenuous, counterfactual, and tendentious to be convincing.

Indeed, the view that sensationalist media attention to, and portrayals of, Farrakhan have been responsible for his political rise also rests uneasily with two distinct (though related) issues of intellectual consistency and reporting double standards. Both concern the full repudiation of bigoted sentiments, no matter what the locus thereof may be. Williams, for example, has argued that black American leaders and elites cannot simply ignore Farrakhan's incandescent rage. Richard Cohen has also held that the media and public attention devoted to Farrakhan and his aides' anti-Semitism is insufficient, and contrasts this with an imaginary white bigot who made equally defamatory remarks about black Americans on a regular basis.[48] Both are surely correct, and it is certainly surprising that even some academic commentators treat Farrakhan's anti-Semitism as a matter merely of "unfortunate" rhetoric.[49] For other critics, though, such as Adolph Reed (as far from being a defender of the NoI leader as any), the opprobrium that is legitimately and deservedly heaped upon black American bigots such as Farrakhan, Leonard Jeffries, and Public Enemy is considerably less than that addressed to the many white Americans who engage in similarly offensive and defamatory expressions of racial prejudice and sexism, from David Duke through right-wing radio "shock jocks" to the rock group Guns'n'Roses.[50]

Condemnation of Farrakhan's more rabidly prejudiced comments is a necessary part of any strategy aimed at effectively confronting his political challenge. But it is also an insufficient one, and one that must be accompanied by a full and frank assessment of the broader and very real conditions to which Farrakhan forcefully speaks, however falsely. Consistency demands an equally forceful repudiation of the Dukes and Helmses and Hollingses, however coded or allegedly jocular a veil the various appeals to baser sentiments of antiblack bigotry in their messages frequently assume. Nonetheless, the prevalence of persistent and grievous historic injustice and discrimination by some white Americans against their black compatriots fails to render African-Americans wholly free from the legitimate accusation of racism. The fact of white prejudice does not exculpate Farrakhan from the fullest and clearest repudiation for the bigotry that he evinces and the manifest injury to racial comity that he causes. Journalists and academics alike face this responsibility, for the bifurcation in racial attitudes and responses to Farrakhan is one that pervades not only popular perceptions but also divides intellectual elites—a powerful testimony to the substantial disjuncture in perceptions about race that characterize current attitudes among black and white Americans in general.

None of the preceding discussion is intended to suggest that Farrakhan has achieved his current status unassisted by the media, nor that the Black Muslim has not zealously sought to exploit the media as often as possible for his own political purposes. It is clear that Farrakhan has seized with increasing eagerness every opportunity available to utilize media outlets in order to disseminate his message as widely as possible. Jackson's 1984 campaign, for example, was interpreted by the NoI's leader as a mechanism that Allah grasped in order to make Farrakhan known to greater numbers of black and white Americans alike.

Farrakhan has also deliberately created media opportunities designed to achieve maximum nationwide publicity for his paranoid views, particularly through his international links, in which Libya looms especially prominent. The minister's attendance at the Second Mathaba in Tripoli in 1986, despite threats of possible arrest and federal prosecution subsequent to his return to the United States, was deliberately intended to provoke the maximum amount of outrage by white American politicians and to ensure that his message was heard in the highest echelons of the federal government.[51] A decade later, Farrakhan's return to Libya to receive that year's "Gadhafi International Human Rights Prize" (surely the ultimate definition of a tragicomic oxymoron) once more yielded outraged coverage in the United States.[52]

Farrakhan's meeting Nelson Mandela in January 1996 was similarly designed to achieve maximum media attention and to compound the increasingly widespread American perceptions of his new political influence that he had elicited in the United States since the Million Man March. Farrakhan's audiences with an unedifying gallery of tyrants and terrorist sponsors in Libya, Sudan, Nigeria, Iran, and Iraq and his public comments on the ultimately doomed fate of the United States were private affairs, of course. But they were also aimed, simultaneously, at provoking the strongest and most hostile of white reactions across America which, he hoped, would once more consolidate his putative martyr status on behalf of African-Americans and the oppressed. The World Friendship Tour epitomized Farrakhan's strategy of winning incredulous headlines and outraged editorials, and thereby political martyrdom, at home by declaring verbal war on America from abroad. As he put it, addressing the U.S. government upon his return from the trip, "I know you want to kill me, but I just raised the price . . . Whatever you do to me over here, they're going to do to you over there."[53] Such provocative proclamations are invariably designed to maximize the amount of public attention and fury that Farrakhan receives from press and television alike; and they frequently succeed in so doing. Witness, for example, the grossly exaggerated assessments of Farrakhan's having graduated from being a "national nuisance" to "a national security threat."[54]

Moreover, media coverage of Farrakhan is used by the leader of the NoI to support his own claims about the deliberate misrepresentation of his views by fearful and furious white elites. The factors that encourage structural bias in American television coverage generally

(time constraints, revenue demands from advertisers, fairness doctrine requirements) preclude a full discussion of Farrakhan's public
statements in general, and theological beliefs in particular, on network news or elsewhere. Farrakhan is thus able to invoke claims that
his real message is deliberately being distorted by a hostile white/
Jewish media in order to undermine both his existing and his potential political support among black Americans.[55] Of course, the accusation of distortion ironically is itself a strategy designed to attract
additional African-American supporters. Although it is necessarily
speculative, it seems reasonable to assume that at least some of the
black Americans who attend Farrakhan's rallies and lectures do so
from a genuine desire to discover for themselves whether or not the
image of the NoI's leader that they have received from media coverage in fact comports with what he represents in person. The charge of
media bias is therefore one that functions not only to shield Farrakhan from criticism but also to assist mass black attendance of his
public events.

Just as few analysts today, however, would attribute Malcolm
X's political influence among American blacks during the 1960s (and
subsequently) mainly to the controversy sparked by the Mike Wallace
"hate that hate produced" documentary, so Farrakhan's more recent
rise rests heavily upon foundations that are far more extensive, deep,
and enduring than simple media coverage alone. The intermittent
and generally hostile attention of the mainstream print and televisual
media has represented an integral and necessary, but far from a sufficient, condition of the NoI leader's political ascendancy and current
influence among African-Americans at large. Although the mass
media have strongly assisted the faltering propulsion of the Farrakhan roadshow, and continue to cover its more well-attended, important, and exotic stopovers, they certainly did not invent the unseemly
spectacle.

THE NEW AND OLD POLITICS OF PARANOIA

The important, but nonetheless limited, extent of the mass media's
role in Farrakhan's rise can most appropriately be examined by contrasting the Black Muslim leader with a more familiar American
exemplar of traditional paranoid politics from the paranoid white far-
right: David Duke. The former KKK leader represents probably the

most well-known hate figure on the white radical right in the modern United States. Like Farrakhan, Duke's past associations and activities were extremely dubious and controversial and have rendered him, at times, the brief focus of intense national political attention in America. Unlike Farrakhan, however, Duke sought deliberately and explicitly to moderate his extremist public persona by rejecting elements of his previous behavior as merely the product of youthful indiscretions or harmless mischief. In addition, the process of achieving a mass influence depended for Duke upon the successful cultivation of a conventional and widely acceptable political image via the mass media, and through television in particular. For thousands of white Louisiana voters, by 1990, Duke had done precisely that. In appearance, delivery, and style, Duke's demeanor was virtually inseparable from that of the majority of nattily besuited, softly spoken, and carefully coiffured candidates for federal or state elective office in America.[56]

In contrast to Farrakhan, the Louisianan's rise to statewide, and subsequently national, political attention was accompanied by electoral campaigns for specific elective offices. Prior to his successful bid for a seat in the Louisiana state House of Representatives in 1989, Duke was known only to those active on the fringes of the American far-right. Not until his 1990 campaign for the U.S. Senate and, in particular, his 1991 campaign for gubernatorial office in Louisiana, did Duke reach a national—and international—audience. Moreover, after his abortive bid for the Republican presidential nomination in 1992, Duke's coverage in the mass media dropped precipitously, recovering only slightly with his second abortive Senate bid in 1996. The appropriation of many of his themes by Republicans with less controversial personal histories and associations was one factor in this. Duke's appeal, however, had always been based on a relatively narrow and ephemeral set of state-specific conditions. The centrality of media attention was therefore especially important to his prospects for popular attention, name recognition, and ultimately, elective success.

Farrakhan, by comparison, occupies an entirely different national political milieu. First, he personally has never run, and harbors no apparent ambitions to run, for elective political office in the United States, at any level. In contrast, the electoral process was fundamental to Duke's rise and fall. Duke was in part defeated because of the response of those white Louisianans (and the state's business community, in particular) who recognized the many dangers that the achievement of political office by Duke could potentially pose to their material socioeconomic interests. The symbolism of a former Grand Wizard of the KKK occupying the governor's mansion in Baton Rouge was conjoined to the substantial powers that the gubernatorial office possessed in concentrating both black and white voters' minds in the state. Whatever threat Farrakhan poses, by contrast, derives from factors that are entirely unassociated either with his seeking state power or with the prospect of his attempting to achieve elective public office.

Second, Farrakhan heads a national organization of long-standing (if changeable) repute among black Americans. The Nation of Islam may be a relatively minor player in America's racial politics, but it is not an ephemeral entity in African-American social and political life. With or without the attention of print journalists and television pundits, the organization's laudable and brave efforts to police central city areas, reduce drug consumption, and mediate in gang disputes among African-Americans would doubtless continue apace. The media critique of Farrakhan is thus somewhat misplaced. If he and the NoI have been "discovered" by the media, that discovery has been far more for white American audiences than for black ones. Duke, by comparison, was not only found but was also assiduously amplified to white and black Americans alike, both within and beyond the state of Louisiana, by the media's attention from 1989 to 1992.

Third, the substantive content of media coverage of Duke and Farrakhan emphasizes quite distinctive features in each case. In Duke's, press attention invariably stressed the Louisianan's Klan background and white supremacist associations. A prominent subtheme, however, was the common political agenda and policy preferences that Duke shared with the modern Republican party. Commentators drew attention to the difficulty that Duke posed for then president Bush, whose eventually reluctant approval of the 1991 Civil Rights bill (after he had vetoed the previous year's proposal) was attributed largely to the negative public effects of the Duke candidacy for the GOP nationally. As Duke went down to a decisive defeat against Edwin Edwards in 1991 (one in which he nonetheless captured a majority of the white vote in Louisiana, as he had done previously, in 1990), Kirk Fordice won the neighboring gubernatorial race in Mississippi (and repeated his electoral success in 1995) on a markedly similar platform: addressing welfare beneficiaries, crime, affirmative action, and the status of the United States as an avowedly "Christian nation." Although the racial code words were barely different in the two Deep South state races, Fordice received the Republican National

Committee's assistance while Duke received the mild opprobrium of its chairman and of the then president.

In Farrakhan's case, by contrast, the emphasis of much popular coverage is the express distance between the NoI's leader and other national black American politicians and civil rights figures. By stressing the respectable political credentials of the latter, in order to frame Farrakhan as a markedly unsavory and exceptional extremist figure, the terms of debate are, ironically, drawn so starkly and simplistically that the ultimate strategic advantage frequently accrues more to Farrakhan than to established African-American political leaders. The conceptual prism by which black American leadership is viewed by African-Americans at large is one in which white assessments frequently function as influential mediating agents. The content of the bulk of white media coverage of the NoI is clear, however. Farrakhan, in diametric contrast to Kilson's view, is not typically equated with established African-American leaders—the threat that he poses them is an important, though not always explicit, theme in the coverage of his activities, just as the fact of Farrakhan's winning support is treated as surprising, not understandable, in most popular accounts.[57] Duke, by comparison, was rarely interpreted in terms of posing anything approximating a threat to national white American politicians, whom he sought to imitate as much as to condemn.

Critics such as Esolen, who view both Duke and Farrakhan as more or less equivalent opportunistic fame seekers and extremists-turned-moderates whose appeals to the media conditioned their changing political creeds, therefore miss the paranoid mark somewhat. Dapperly besuited, bejewelled, and bow-tied though he may be, Farrakhan has done nothing to approach either a blow-dried image or a moderated, inclusive message. Although Farrakhan's oratorical abilities and rhetorical style attract some media attention, many established black leaders also exhibit an impressive and varied range of public-speaking credentials. The fact that a politician such as Bill Gray, John Lewis, or Mike Espy is able to adopt a presentational style that is well-suited to the televisual medium does not preclude their still possessing a formidable array of oratorical skills in alternative contexts. Espy, for example, was as comfortable displaying a markedly "southern" style of speech in his reelection activities "at home" as in moderating his stentorian Mississippian tones on the Hill.[58] That Farrakhan can alternately rant and rave as a prophet of rage at his NoI rallies only to soothe subsequently on national television as a lucid voice of reason and calm says much about his shrewd intelligence and presentational skills, but very little about an allegedly moderated belief system.

Farrakhan has provided as few reasons for the American public to accept that his traditional views on racial Armageddon, whites, and Jews have sincerely altered as Duke has done for that public to believe that he has genuinely recanted his long-held prejudices about, and barely latent antagonism toward, African-Americans. Both have acquired a natty sartorial sense while neither has shed the nasty opinions of old. Perhaps, since the subtleties and nuances of the peculiarly flawed architecture of their respective belief systems has never attracted either substantial or enduring attention from most Americans, that may not actually matter very much. Hacker's view, for example, that "Farrakhan and Duke are more ideological symbols than expositors of intellectual positions" has some evident merit.[59] The importance of symbolism in American political life, however, is frequently substantial.[60] The Republicans' platform for the 1994 congressional mid-term elections, the "Contract with America," for instance, was a largely symbolic document; but its electoral and policy consequences were marked. Farrakhan's public discourse may similarly contain relatively little that poses as either intellectually distinguished, impeccably rational, or even minimally respectable, but the importance of what he says is substantial nonetheless, if only because many African-Americans listen assiduously to, and frequently agree with, much of the reactionary and paranoid case that he advances.

To exaggerate unduly either Farrakhan's mass appeal to black Americans or the political threat that he represents to whites would be a grave and foolish error. Contrary to many fanciful popular beliefs, the minister has achieved neither universal nor uncritical endorsement from African-Americans. Nor is Farrakhan poised to mount some swift takeover even of Black America, much less the United States. Despite his gruesome links with Gadhafi and other tyrants, Farrakhan poses no clear and present danger to American society. Reed is absolutely right to remind Americans that, unlike David Duke, the NoI's leader has never once held public office in the United States; has never had the slightest input to public policy outcomes at state or local, much less national, levels; and has never enjoyed access to state power or to positions of institutional authority within policy-making bodies.[61] It is as laughable as it is incredible to imagine Farrakhan leading some Black Muslim (presumably non-alcoholic) beer-hall putsch or heading a successful fascistic coup d'état in America.

Still, lack of imagination is a deficiency that rarely justifies wholesale neglect of the substantive threats that even small-time demagogues and fanatics may ultimately represent.[62] The complacently indulgent refrains of the Weimar Republic of 1930 are hardly resonant in the minuscule political threat that Farrakhan personally or the NoI corporately poses to the American nation in the late 1990s. Notwithstanding the extensive media coverage that he frequently receives, however, Farrakhan possesses the resources, ambition, and leadership skills to assume an increasingly important political role among African-Americans. Although a preeminent leadership role among black Americans—a primus inter pares niche in the realms of African-American statesmanship—will doubtless elude him in his remaining years, Farrakhan still retains the disturbing potential to deepen America's yawning racial divide to a profound and perhaps even precipitous point. That prospect, moreover, should be sufficient cause to occasion at least informed and attentive public concern, if not pronounced alarm.

SUMMARY

Farrakhan has emerged in the 1990s as a political leader of substantial popular appeal among African-Americans at large. Although popularity is, of course, only one resource for a political leader seeking influence in the United States, it nonetheless represents an extremely important and valuable commodity, and one that many American public figures find exceedingly difficult to both achieve and sustain. Few politicians in America, from presidents to school board members, are eager to forfeit the considerable political capital that widespread and lasting popular support affords. Moreover, for other envious and fearful political actors, the fact of Farrakhan's popularity partly conditions their own strategic and tactical political behavior. To the extent that other political actors must take his popularity into account in calculating their own electoral interests, determining their voting behavior, and shaping their general political approaches, Farrakhan's political influence may be indirect within the ranks of national African-American leadership. Nonetheless, it remains of manifest political significance.

Like all demagogues through the ages, Farrakhan relies strongly upon the spoken word through which to exert political influence and to forge a popular base. Although the mass media in America have clearly assisted his political rise, however, Farrakhan represents much more than merely an ephemeral or a marginal media creation. The minister's mass appeal among African-Americans has been far more helped than hindered by the recurrent attention of mainstream television and print media, even in its more critical and adverse forms. Nonetheless, Farrakhan's longevity is also powerfully suggestive of a broad political appeal that far transcends the intermittent bouts of national attention accorded by the American news media to his more extreme public pronouncements and quixotic political initiatives.

While the fact of Farrakhan's significant—though limited—mass black American appeal is demonstrable, however, the reasons for the popularity of such an unorthodox, extreme, and polarizing minority religious and political figure have yet to be fully analyzed. By virtue of his theological convictions, reactionary political beliefs, and paranoid political claims, Farrakhan occupies a peculiar and distinctive contemporary niche in national black American politics. That the leader of the NoI should have achieved the social impact and mass appeal among African-Americans that he has over recent years obviously demands explanation. It is to the proximate causes of the minister's political ascendancy and the multiple foundations of the Farrakhan phenomenon that we hence turn next.

NOTES TO CHAPTER 5

1. Essien-Udom, *Black Nationalism*, p. 339.
2. Richard E. Cohen, "Farrakhan and Anti-Semitism," *Torrington (CT) Register-Criterion*, 28 July 1985, p. 15.
3. Mention of Farrakhan in the indexes of newspapers such as *The New York Times* and *The Washington Post* from 1990–1996, for example, was almost twice that of 1984–89.
4. See, for example: Richard E. Cohen, "Farrakhan Too," *The Washington Post*, 16 May 1995, p. A17; Chris Bull, "Farrakhan Under Fire," *The Advocate*, 8 March 1994, p. 25; Thomas W. Hazlett, "The Wrath of Farrakhan," *Reason*, 26 (May 1994), p. 66; and Sullivan, "Call to Harm."
5. See, for example: Lyons, "Muslim Guard Service Grows"; Nathan McCall, "D.C. Council Votes to Praise Farrakhan's Anti-Drug Work," *The Washington Post*, 25 October 1989, p. A1; Sylvester Monroe, "Doing the Right Thing: Muslims Have Become a Welcome Force in Black Neighborhoods," *Time*, 135, 16 April 1990, p. 22; William K. Stevens, "The Muslims Keep the

Lid on Drugs in Capital: The Dealers Simply Move to Another Area," *The New York Times*, 26 September 1988, p. 8; and Wright, "Farrakhan's Mission."

6. Sanson, "Farrakhan Means Business"; and Stodghill, "Farrakhan's Three-Year Plan."

7. See: Farber, "In the Name of the Father"; Purnick, "An Unlikely Matchmaker"; and Terry, "Shabazz Case."

8. See, for example, Turque, Smith, and McCormick, "Playing a Different Tune," p. 30.

9. The association represents approximately 200 black-owned newspapers across the United States and awarded Farrakhan the honor (on 14 March 1996) for his "vision" in putting together the previous year's Million Man March.

10. See the transcript, "Attempts by Rogue Regimes to Influence U.S. Policy," Hearing before the Subcommittee on International Operations and Human Rights, Committee on International Relations, U.S. House of Representatives, 19 March 1996.

11. Perhaps the most notorious instance of congressional insouciance regarding the Klan at this time concerned the 1937 confirmation of former KKK member and then Alabama Senator Hugo Black, as an Associate Justice of the United States Supreme Court. See William E. Leuchtenberg, "A Klansman Joins the Court: The Appointment of Hugo L. Black," in Leonard Dinnerstein and Kenneth T. Jackson, eds., *American Vistas: 1877 to the Present*, 5th ed. (New York: Oxford University Press, 1987), pp. 187–215.

12. Christopher Thomas, "Idol Who Strikes Terror into Whites," *The (London) Times*, 1985, p. 5.

13. See Reed, "All for One."

14. Lincoln, *The Black Muslims*, p. 272.

15. The figure is from Lincoln, *The Black Muslims*, p. 270. Other sources claim that the total number at the Atlanta rally was closer to 40,000. See, for example, Lynne Duke, "Farrakhan Defends Clinton, Asks Critics to 'Get to Know Me Better'," *The Washington Post*, 5 May 1993, p. A22. Whichever figure is the more accurate, the numbers are clearly substantial.

16. McFadden-Preston, "The Rhetoric of Minister Louis Farrakhan," p. 160.

17. *A National Survey of American Blacks* (New York: Simon Wiesenthal Center, December 1985).

18. Dawson made the remarks to (and the figures are also cited by) Juan Williams, "The Farrakhan Paralysis: How the Demagogues of the Disenfranchised Are Silencing Black Leaders," *The Washington Post*, 13 February 1994, p. C2.

19. See "The New Politics of Race," *Newsweek*, 6 May 1991, p. 23.

20. See Henry, "Pride and Prejudice," p. 22.

21. In addition, see Michael Kagay, "Poll Finds Most Blacks Reject Farrakhan's Ideas as Theirs," *The New York Times*, 5 March 1994, p. 8.

22. Williams, "The Farrakhan Paralysis."

23. The most ridiculously inflated estimate of the march's crowd that has been publicly advanced thus far has come from the filmmaker Spike Lee.

Though he didn't personally attend the gathering (instead watching it on television as a result of a medical operation), Lee confidently told a British audience to discount suggestions that only 500,000 African-Americans had attended, stating for the record that, "Two million black men assembled in the nation's capital . . ." See "Why Do the White Thing?," *The Guardian*, 18 November 1995, p. 32.

24. See the poll surveys in *The Washington Post*, 9–10 October 1995, Sec. A.

25. See, respectively: Monroe, "The Mirage of Farrakhan"; and Fineman and Smith, "An Angry 'Charmer'," pp. 42–46.

26. A comprehensive poll by CBS news, for example, revealed that 30 percent of blacks believed that Farrakhan and the NoI "represent the views of most black people in America," while 22 percent of blacks "generally agree" with Farrakhan's positions. Although this may be treated as a relatively small proportion, a further 40 percent of respondents were "not familiar enough" with Farrakhan's views to state an opinion. See "60 Minutes Poll: Louis Farrakhan and Public Opinion, March 27–28, 1996" (New York: CBS News, 1996).

27. See, in particular: Klein, "The threat of tribalism"; King, "The Farrakhan Phenomenon"; and Reed, "All for One."

28. See the excellent volume by Doris Graber, ed., *Mass Media and American Politics* (Washington, D.C.: Congressional Quarterly Press, 1993).

29. See: Butler and Ranney, *Electioneering*; Paul Herrnson, *Congressional Elections* (Washington, D.C.: Congressional Quarterly Press, 1995); Larry Sabato, *Feeding Frenzy: How Attack Journalism Has Transformed American Politics* (New York: The Free Press, 1993); and, on the media's effect on the changing role of national party conventions, Byron E. Shafer, *Bifurcated Politics* (Cambridge, Mass.: Harvard University Press, 1988).

30. King, "The Farrakhan Phenomenon," p. 17.

31. Though King's argument is compelling, it largely neglects the potential indirect consequences of the violent rhetoric of Farrakhan and many of his followers. According to one Anti-Defamation League report, for example, the incidence of anti-Semitic conflagrations on college campuses increased from 54 in 1988 to 114 in 1992–93. This latter figure, an increase of thirteen from 1991, coincided with an 8 percent drop in the number of anti-Semitic incidents reported nationwide during 1992–93. The ADL attributed the increased incidence of campus harassment of Jews in part to the messages of Farrakhan and other black speakers popular with many African-American students.

The issue of violence that surrounds Farrakhan's rhetoric is one that other scholars have also isolated for particular attention. Gaber, for example, in cautioning against devoting attention to the socioeconomic grievances among Farrakhan's supporters, argues that "when violence is finally committed by people full of hate, it hardly matters that they have other, genuine, grievances. What matters is that the innocent get hurt for no good reason." See Gaber, "Lamb of God or Demagogue?," p. 167. Insofar as Farrakhan himself has conceded, in the context of Malcolm X's assassination, that he contributed to the atmosphere in which Malcolm's murder occurred, so it seems

plausible to argue that a persistently violent rhetoric directed toward a particular social group by members of another is indeed likely to contribute toward
the incidence of at least some antagonistic and potentially violent confronta-
tions. There is no evidence, however, that innocents (the NoI may not accept
the term's usage, of course) have been directly harmed by Farrakhan's followers.

32. Williams, "The Farrakhan Paralysis."

33. Marable, "In the Business of Prophet Making."

34. See Reed, "All for One."

35. For expositions of this position, see: Giovanni Sartori, *Comparative
Constitutional Engineering: An Inquiry into Structures, Incentives and Outcomes*
(London: Macmillan, 1994); and his article, "Video-Power," *Government and
Opposition* 24, no. 1 (Winter 1989): 39–53.

36. Klein, "The Threat of Tribalism," p. 15.

37. Dennis King, Manning Marable, and Adolph Reed all subscribe to
this basic view of Farrakhan's rallies. The commentaries by, among others,
Richard Cohen, Julius Lester, and Andrew Sullivan are altogether less sanguine in this regard.

38. Ice Cube, *Lethal Injection* (Fourth and Broadway, 1994).

39. On the subject of the representation of African-Americans in popu-
lar culture and by the mass media, see: Richard M. Merelman, *Representing
Black Culture: Racial Conflict and Cultural Politics in the United States* (New
York: Routledge, 1995); Dent, ed., *Black Popular Culture*; and Van Deburg, *New
Day in Babylon*.

40. Carl Rowan, *The Washington Post*, 6 August 1984, op-ed.

41. Carl Rowan, "Antidote to Louis Farrakhan: Ignore Him," *The New
York Times*, 25 September 1985, p. 22.

42. Carl Rowan, "Farrakhan's Poisonous Journey," *The Buffalo News*, 28
February 1996, p. 3B.

43. Martin Kilson and Clement Cottingham, "Thinking About Race
Relations: How Far Are We Still From Integration?," *Dissent*, Fall 1991, pp.
520–30, at 525.

44. Figures calculated by the author from *The Final Call*, 15, no. 17 (21
May 1996), p. 11.

45. For a breakdown of the latter, see Gaber, "Lamb of God or Demagogue?"

46. For examples of the latter, see Farrakhan's appearances on: *The Phil
Donahue Show*, 13 and 15 March 1990; *The Arsenio Hall Show*, 25 February 1994;
and *Larry King Live*, 16 October 1995.

47. See Byron White, Jerry Thomas, and Shirley Salemy, "Farrakhan
Defends World Tour: Nation of Islam Leader Welcomes Showdown," *Chicago
Tribune*, 26 February 1996, p. 1.

48. Richard E. Cohen, "At Nuremberg-on-Potomac," p. 7.

49. Washington, "Jesse Jackson," p. 93.

50. Reed, "All for One."

51. See McFadden-Preston's account of Farrakhan's "triumphant
return" address, in "The Rhetoric of Minister Louis Farrakhan," chapter five.

52. Farrakhan was the guest of honor at celebrations in September 1996 to commemorate the twenty-seventh anniversary of the coup that overthrew Libya's monarchy and installed Gadhafi as leader. In accordance with the decade-long American sanctions on most financial transactions between the United States and Libya, Farrakhan was banned by the U.S. Treasury Department from accepting the $250,000 prize that accompanied the award.

53. Quoted in White, Thomas, and Salemy, "Farrakhan Defends World Tour."

54. Peter King, "'PC' Handling of Farrakhan Is Wrong," *Newsday* (Nassau Edition), 8 March 1996, p. A47.

55. An editorial in *The Final Call*, for example, claimed in relation to Farrakhan's World Friendship Tour that the "national mainstream media fuelled a frenzy when they misportrayed the purpose of the tour," while then giving scant coverage to Farrakhan's explanatory press conferences and speeches upon his return home. See "Media Consistent on Farrakhan Coverage," *The Final Call*, 21 May 1996, p. 16.

56. See the collection of essays in Rose, *The Emergence of David Duke*. A more polemical discussion is contained in Clarence Lusane, *African Americans at the Crossroads*, pp. 87–92.

57. See, for example, Fred Barnes, "Farrakhan Frenzy: What's a Black Politician to Do?," *New Republic*, (28 October 1985), pp. 13–15.

58. See, for example, the account of Espy's electioneering style in Rob Gurwitt, "A Quest for a Breakthrough," *Congressional Quarterly Weekly Report*, 25 October 1986, pp. 2645–46.

59. Hacker, *Two Nations*, p. 150.

60. Murray Edelman, *The Symbolic Uses of Politics* (Urbana: University of Illinois Press, 1964).

61. Reed, "Behind the Farrakhan Show," p. 16.

62. It was partly for this reason that the Clinton Administration's refusal to allow Farrakhan to accept the financial assistance offered by Gadhafi to the NoI elicited such widespread approval in both the United States and Europe in September 1996.

6

Explaining Farrakhan

Black people exist on the edge of outrage against white people.
Farrakhan provides an outlet. He gives whitey hell.

Reverend Wyatt Walker[1]

This is a man whose political identity is constituted by antago-
nism to the self-image of America.

Henry Louis Gates[2]

Popular interpretations of the Farrakhan phenomenon frequently
present a racial hatred borne of the most widespread disillusion and
deep black despair as the exclusive foundation of the minister's charismatic version of paranoid American politics; all else is embellishment and detail. E. J. Dionne, for example, encapsulates the views of
many critics of the Nation of Islam (NoI) leader when he attributes
the source of Farrakhan's popularity among African-Americans to "a
loss of faith" by the black community in white U.S. society.[3] William
Schneider, too, viewed Farrakhan's political ascent as essentially a
reflection of increasing black–white antipathies, as signaling "a new
direction in black politics and a new division between the races."[4] A
leading international newspaper even identified a distinctive "Farrakhan style of leadership," entailing that African-American politicians
behave "outrageously" and shout "that your critics are racists until
they shut up."[5] For such commentators, Farrakhan's rise is fundamentally a matter of unfavorable black responses to white Americans. It
reflects, in large part, what Adolph Reed identified as the central fascination that many whites invariably find in the Farrakhan phenomenon and in the vexed issue of race more generally: what do black
Americans think about whites?[6]

Such interpretations, focusing upon a diffuse African-American despondency and disillusion, are superficially compelling in their appeal, and they comport with many popular conceptions of current black–white disjunctures in beliefs, values, and attitudes. These views, however, obscure the pronounced complexity of the causes of Farra-khan's growing appeal and social impact among African-Americans. Moreover, in their monodimensional aspect, they also evince a some-what paternalistic and inaccurate interpretation of black Americans' views of the most propitious prospective forces for their own social and economic advancement in the post–civil rights era (i.e., whites) and the most effective method of African-American leadership (i.e., a single heroic figure capable of somehow transforming their collective fortunes).

Of course, Farrakhan is a manifestly charismatic black American political leader. An accomplished and often compelling orator, the minister seems able mellifluously to tap deeply and powerfully into mass black hopes and fears, almost at will. In full flow, Farrakhan frequently appears able to steal the sunrise past the proverbial rooster. Farrakhan's popular appeal among African-Americans, how-ever, relies upon a multiplicity of factors, most of which are far more complex in character than simple notions of a Weberian type of charis-matic authority are able either to capture or convey. In Farrakhan's case, the individual leader and the collective social group to which he addresses his activism are frequently—and falsely—conflated. As Harold Cruse argued three decades previously, this problem of con-fusing the individual black leader with the broader African-American political movement (and of his personality with the wider societal forces and fissures upon which his support is based) is a familiar one over the course of black American history:

> Individual leaders can project ideologies of many kinds and color them with the hues of their own personal aspirations which very often obscure the very fundamental issues which are of crucial interest to the people for whom the leaders speak. Then historians come along and completely forget or overlook what the basic issues were for the people in the mass, and center their attention on the personal characteristics of the leaders.[7]

The caution expressed by Cruse is especially apposite to analy-ses of Farrakhan, wherein disproportionate attention to his extreme rhetoric and paranoid tendencies can overshadow the extent to which a significant number of his public views clearly accord with many mass black American beliefs, attitudes, and values. (Moreover, of course, if the mere possession of charismatic authority was the principal basis of Farrakhan's political rise, many other African-American politicians who also display great personal qualities of charisma, such as Julian Bond and Ron Dellums, ought logically also to have established more influential national political roles over recent years.) Farrakhan's leadership role relies heavily upon several foundations that far transcend his prodigious charismatic appeals.

The sources of Farrakhan's political ascendancy are at once multiple, distinctive, and interconnected. Farrakhan has achieved an influential political role in the 1990s partly through a combination of innovative political leadership of the NoI and sensitive political judgment of the opportunities and constraints facing an African-American "protest" leader in the post–civil rights era. While Farrakhan has certainly exploited the manifest crises of many black Americans in the post–civil rights era to great personal advantage, however, it is not only a loss of confidence in the possibility of achieving an integrated America (and of black and white citizens' support for that ideal) that is central to his popular appeal among African-Americans. It is also, crucially, the confusion and negative attitudes that black Americans harbor toward members of their own communities; the increasingly distant prospect of the socioeconomic regeneration of many central cities at a time of pronounced fiscal constraint; the sometimes remarkable dissonance between the policy preferences of African-Americans at large and their putative national political leaders, along several issue dimensions; the material actions and achievements of the NoI among black city communities; and Farrakhan's running for black leadership by running against black leaders that are together fundamental to the minister's contemporary political role, popular appeal, and national influence. In sum, divisions among black Americans, as much as between blacks and whites, are critical in accounting for Farrakhan's contemporary black appeal.

THE TWO CRISES OF BLACK AMERICA

Like his white right-wing paranoid predecessor, Senator Joseph McCarthy, Farrakhan's recent ascendancy in national American politics has depended upon two analytically distinct but closely related factors: first, the existence of a manifest sense of crisis and the presence of seemingly intractable social, economic, and political problems affecting American citizens in general, or a particular, discrete group thereof; second, the plausibility of the aspirant leader's claims as to both the origins of the crisis and the most effective means of its possible resolution. The more acute the nature of the crisis, the more plausible and legitimate (even rational) a status otherwise unconventional analyses and simplistic political solutions are apt, respectively, to assume for many of those either affected by or concerned with the cataclysmic situation at hand. Although, like McCarthy previously, Farrakhan certainly does considerably more to aggravate than ameliorate the dual crises, his persistent activism serves, simultaneously, to elevate his personal public recognition to national and international dimensions—a critical feature of the demagogue's political project.

For Joe McCarthy, the crisis-level problems confronting Americans in the immediate postwar era were notoriously cast in terms of the apparently relentless advance of atheistic international communism and the cardinal threat that this was held to pose to America's vital political, economic, and security interests. The preferred solution that the senator consistently and confidently advanced—vigorous diplomatic and military defense of those interests abroad by the United States and unrelenting domestic vigilance against the many alleged subversive enemies and radical malcontents at home—was at once straightforward, clear, and (lest it be forgotten) widely appealing.[8]

That appeal achieved a pronounced political salience and won significant popular support among Americans not least as a result of its immediacy. The clear emergence of the United States as the world's foremost—indeed, hegemonic—superpower after 1945 was very rapidly accompanied by broad and acute fears of foreign military aggression, domestic political subversion, and the prospect of an incipient, third, catastrophic global war. McCarthy's activities were therefore undertaken in the context of a wholly new, complex, and disturbing national and international environment. Although, from the perspective of the post–Cold War era (and with the benefit of the impeccable clarity of analytic vision that hindsight invariably affords), the structure of superpower relations from 1947 to 1989 was in fact relatively clear and stable, its initial emergence in the late 1940s was then characterized by profound confusion and deep dissensus; an uncertainty paralleled currently by the continuing search for an appropriate paradigm by which U.S. foreign policy should be conducted in the 1990s.[9]

McCarthy's paranoid claims—and his mercifully brief political ascendancy, from 1950–1954—were therefore advanced during a period of profound American unease over the prospective shape of international relations.

By comparison, in the post–civil rights era, the political, economic, and social development of black Americans has provided an especially fertile environment in which Farrakhan's demagogic and paranoid appeals have been able to achieve a national political salience and mass popularity. For many blacks, material social and economic conditions lend their desperate circumstances a critical status. In turn, Farrakhan's analyses are widely accorded elements of persuasiveness, however repugnant or ludicrous these appear to most black and white Americans. To many African-Americans, Farrakhan's prescriptions for improving black socioeconomic welfare assume a political importance that extends far beyond their cathartic and uplifting psychological value. The NoI's leader does not promise salvation in an afterlife, but constantly stresses instead the achievability of human dignity and a decent material and spiritual life on Earth. The current appeal of that promise is an extremely sad, but very powerful, indictment of many black Americans' parlous social and economic position in the most prosperous nation-state on the planet at the close of the twentieth century.

Moreover, compared to McCarthy's paranoid assertions, Farrakhan's unremitting claims of a conspiracy against black Americans are forged upon a basis prima facie more plausible to many African-Americans, given two hundred years of slavery, de jure and de facto segregation, racial discrimination, and prejudice. Whereas the Cold War was, even at the height of McCarthyism, a relatively new international political phenomenon,[10] and fear of foreign threats fundamentally a psychological condition, the plight of disadvantaged African-Americans is one of the more enduringly undistinguished—and the brute fact of black political, economic, and social inequality one of the most depressingly constant—and objective features of American historical development since the republic's founding in the eighteenth century. What is perhaps most surprising, in this context, is not so much that an unprepossessing national figure such as Farrakhan has arisen in the dramatic fashion that he has over recent years, but more that it has taken so long for this actually to have occurred.

Indeed, the very longevity of broadly based black American inequality—the enduring and disproportionate disadvantage faced by

African-Americans—serves as an important focus for starkly dissonant interpretations of Farrakhan's reactionary and paranoid praxis.
Conspiracy theorists typically invoke their claims of malevolent and
secret plots in order to account for a set of events or developments for
which no otherwise obvious or immediate explanation seems plausible, that is, to explain a situation which is, in most respects, inexplicable. In the nineteenth and early twentieth centuries, for example,
mass immigration into the United States (particularly from southern
Europe) was viewed by nativist American groups as grievously
undermining the purported unity of the young nation through irrepa-
rably disturbing its relative ethnic homogeneity. The only reasonable
explanation for the influx of such "aliens" had, for many established
Americans, to reside in the sinister conspiratorial activities of elite
governmental authorities.

In the twentieth century, the steady spread of international communism, to which the United States appeared passive and irresolute
in effectively opposing, was similarly attributed by McCarthy and others largely to internal forces of subversion. In the 1950s and 1960s, the
decisive intervention of the federal government in advancing desegregation of public facilities in the South was viewed by many white
southerners as being inherently rooted in antisouthern conspiracies
and elitist northeastern seaboard designs deliberately hatched to
destroy traditional ways of life in Dixie. The presence of communists
and Jews in the civil rights movement appeared to lend some credence to many southerners' suspicions (along with the tacit, and
sometimes outspoken, agreement of FBI head J. Edgar Hoover). Subsequently, in the 1970s and 1980s, attempts by the federal and state
courts to achieve racially integrated schools through busing; to provide welfare benefits to indigents; to outlaw prayer in public schools
while permitting sex education, legalized abortion, and "obscene" art
and literature have all suggested to discrete groups of Americans the
existence of a destructive conspiracy of unrepresentative and effete
elites in Washington, D.C. The historical lineage and extensive scope
of conspiratorial claims is therefore pronounced in American public
life.

The invocation of such assertions of conspiracy is largely associated with (though not exclusively confined to) periods of rapid political, social, and economic change. As Lipset and Raab rightly observe,
extremist movements have historically been movements of disaffection that typically occur during periods of incipient, but potentially

broad-ranging, change in traditional modes of life and established customs. Such movements invariably address social groups that have either already been, or are about to be, deprived of something they perceive to be important or, alternatively, that experience rising aspirations that lead them to feel that they have always been deprived of something that they now strongly desire. Such a widespread sentiment of deprivation is typically accompanied by a profound sense of political dislocation, with the groups concerned casting increasingly unfavorable, suspicious, and wary eyes upon an established polity (and, especially, an existing party structure) that no longer seems able to serve their needs or wants.[11]

At such transitional moments, traditional patterns, structures, and established ways of life are threatened by being forced—by hostile outside entities—to undergo dramatic and rapid transformations. Where this "threat" seems especially potent, and the scope of change particularly great, the popular plausibility of conspiracy theories— and the accompanying mass appeal of their most articulate, vigorous, and skillful proponents—has been considerable. For many Americans at the time, for example, the international advance of communism in Europe (Eastern and Western), Asia, Africa, Latin America, and the Caribbean during the 1950s did indeed appear to be peculiar, dangerous, and virtually inexplicable. For many white southerners then, and over subsequent decades, the external federal government "interference" in regional practices that had been established for well over sixty years did seem not only shocking, but also without legitimate precedent or adequate explanation; the region seemed to many to be subject to special and intensely adverse treatment. Only the existence of malign forces conspiring to advance deleterious sectional goals appeared to be a sufficiently persuasive explanation to account for the rapid changes that were occurring to traditional forms of racially segregated existence in Dixie.

In its many distinct guises, the disconcerting process of change has therefore rendered many millions of Americans particularly susceptible to the proponents of conspiratorial analyses at different points in American history. In the case of African-Americans, however, the brute historic fact of persistent and disproportionate political, social, and economic inequality is so self-evident—and its causes so lengthily and well-enumerated—that no pressing imperative to invoke conspiracies seems to be incumbent upon analysts of the racial minority's plight. There are few, if any, mysteries about the state and the multiple sources of black deprivation. The manifest character of black American history provides a dramatic and powerful indication of the perversity of claims of the existence of an insidious, widespread, and sinister antiblack conspiracy on the part of Jews, whites, or the federal government. Conspiracies are normally invoked to explain the existence of a phenomenon that seems otherwise inexplicable, but compelling explanations for black American disadvantage do not require such invocations of conspiracy theories to be sufficiently persuasive.

For many African-Americans however,—and in particular for those blacks whose political socialization has been shaped in and by the politics of the post–civil rights era, with the experience of de jure segregation a relatively distant memory—the persistence of grievous and disproportionate maladies among black communities nationwide renders such claims of an antiblack conspiracy more palatable and plausible. This is so, in particular, because the prescriptive content of Farrakhan's analysis rests upon such stark and persistent indices of many African-Americans' continued material social and economic dislocation since 1964–65. Both the critical and popular recitation of figures detailing black socioeconomic deprivation in the post–civil rights era have admittedly become so frequent in recent years as to render the notion of disproportionate problems affecting African-Americans familiar to all. But the sheer scale and scope of the social and economic devastation that afflicts many predominantly black urban communities nonetheless require particular emphasis and are worth detailed elaboration so as to be absolutely clear about their dramatic and critical qualities.

Even the most cursory glance through studies of contemporary black American socioeconomic conditions makes for deeply distressing reading. Both absolute and relative indicators of social and economic well-being register demonstrably poor advances for millions of blacks in the post–civil rights era. In 1990, for example, African-Americans were collectively:

> . . . over twice as likely as whites to be jobless. The median black family income is 56% of a white family's. Nearly a third of all blacks, as against 10 percent of whites, live below what is officially reckoned to be the poverty level. A new-born black baby is twice as likely as a white baby to die before its first birthday. The 31 million or so blacks are 12 percent of America's population but supply nearly half its prison population. A black man is

six times as likely as a white man to be murdered; homicide is the leading cause of death of young black men.[12]

For some social scientists, such as William Julius Wilson, these statistics, while in the main accurate, nonetheless obscure a crucial point: that the problems conventionally associated with issues of race are in fact problems more accurately and comprehensively linked to issues of social class.[13] Such analysts are prone to adopt more optimistic diagnoses for the future of America's blacks (and for U.S. race relations in general) than are others for whom the scar of race is emphatically the central and dominant explanatory variable in the marked disjunctures in black/white life chances. According to this class-centered view, the relentlessly broad scope and seemingly intractable character of the socioeconomic problems facing many African-Americans is at least partially alleviated by the growing economic security and increasing prosperity of the substantial black middle class, even though, for those many blacks excluded from its burgeoning ranks, the statistics remain a lengthy litany of acute and broadly based pain.[14]

Thus, for example, the 1990 American census found that of approximately 30 million black American citizens, over 9 million lived in households with a total annual income of $35,000 or more, the conventional definition of a middle-income status in contemporary America. Clear and substantial black progress has also occurred along several other important socioeconomic dimensions. In educational terms, for example, in 1965, there were five times as many high school dropouts among black Americans as there were college graduates. By 1995, among blacks aged 25–44, the figures were even. In 1970, only 15.3 percent of black Americans had any college education or better; twenty-five years later, fully 48.3 percent did (compared to 59.8 percent of whites). Moreover, in many suburban residential areas across America, such as Carson, California, and Queens, New York, the median black household income is equal to, or in excess of, that of whites. A generation on from the civil rights era, material progress is indeed a reality, not an illusion, for millions of black Americans.

Nonetheless, while such figures (and the analyses of scholars such as Wilson) provide some significant grounds for optimism about many black Americans' life prospects, the differences between the races on many important indices of collective social and economic welfare remain nothing less than startling in the 1990s. Overall, for example, the average black household income is currently a mere 63 percent of that of white Americans. In 1993, almost one-third of all African-American families (31 percent, or 2.5 million) were officially designated as poor, compared to just under one-tenth (9 percent, or 5.4 million) of white families. No temporal progress was in evidence here. African-American families were more than three times as likely as white families to be poor in 1993, a ratio that was actually somewhat larger than that obtained in 1969 (28 percent compared to 8 percent). Fully 33 percent of black Americans were poor in 1993, an overall increase of 1 percent from 1969, while the poverty rate for blacks was more than twice that for whites (at 12 percent), in both 1993 and 1969.[15] Thus, almost a quarter-century of post–civil rights era development has witnessed no enduring progress for black Americans, collectively, in comparison with whites.

Furthermore, black Americans are also twice as likely as whites to be unemployed, three times more likely to be recipients of welfare, and four times more likely to be serving time in prison than are whites. In both 1993 and 1980, the civilian unemployment rate for African-Americans was more than twice that for their white compatriots (14 compared to 6 percent). The unemployment rate for black Americans grew from 14 percent in 1980 to a high of 20 percent in 1983, before dropping to 11 percent in 1989, and then rising again to 14 percent in 1993.[16] Black American teenage males are also six times more likely to be murdered than their white counterparts currently, and homicide is the leading cause of death among black males aged 15–24. Although representing only 6 percent of the national population, black American men constitute a massive 47 percent of the total U.S. prison population. A study by the National Center on Institutions and Alternatives discovered that, on an average day in 1991, fully 42 percent of the black male population of Washington, D.C., aged 18–35, was either incarcerated, on probation or parole, awaiting trial, or being sought by authorities on an arrest warrant.[17] In 1995, one in three black men in America was in some form of penal care. Clearly, this terrain is depressingly barren, but it also provides demonstrably fertile and propitious ground for Farrakhan's many appeals to resonate among African-Americans.

Moreover, even the notable expansion of the black American middle class over recent decades—a development that might be thought partially to retard the nascent appeal of the NoI's leader—offers significant opportunities for Farrakhan to secure substantial political support for, if not actual recruits to, his separatist organization. Deprivation in the black community, after all, assumes both absolute and relative forms. As Lipset and Raab argued during the 1970s, the very improvement of the material circumstances of some African-Americans can actually serve to aggravate the sense of deprivation harbored by many others, providing additional reasons for alienation, beyond the absolute deprivation experienced by many vis-a-vis the white American community.[18] Such a crisis of rising expectations has, historically, been among the most influential catalysts for revolutionary and protest movements, from the French Revolution of 1789 to the anti-Vietnam war demonstrations of the 1960s. The unique status of black Americans as the only social group in the United States to be depressed by American society, rather than by their countries of origin, plausibly adds a further sense of collective bitterness to their mood and accentuates demands for immediate and effective remedies: for reparations as well as progress.

The claims of an antiblack conspiracy that Farrakhan regularly advances are thus neither outlandish nor preposterous to the hard-pressed inhabitants of metropolitan areas of America, urban landscapes that resemble not so much the central cities of the most prosperous nation in the world but more battle zones of an undeveloped country teetering in the bloody throes of an ongoing civil war. Such inhospitable areas are more than merely "no-go" zones for whites who happen to value their lives. They also represent Hobbesian territories that are fundamentally off bounds and wholly unknown to the majority of black Americans. In appalling conditions barely fit for human habitation, in which life is assuredly nasty, brutish, and short, the conspiratorial claim that only inhuman forces can have allowed these areas to deteriorate to such a barbaric state of nature is not prima facie implausible. Thus although, for example, many black Americans would vigorously disagree with paranoid claims that the "war on drugs" of the Reagan and Bush administrations actually constituted a deliberately coercive and genocidal government effort directed at further dislocating black Americans in U.S. inner cities, few would deny that it was almost totally ineffective in stemming the spread of hard drugs and drug-related crime.[19]

For the NoI's principal target group of inner-city blacks, in particular, the ravaged urban environment therefore represents a much more visible confirmation of the plausibility of claims of a conspiracy's existence than did McCarthy's communists to many Americans previously. In comparative terms, the loss of China and the communist threat to Korea were far more abstract and much less substantial blows than the devastatingly tangible losses of work, family, or life, the deep symbolic significance of the former notwithstanding. Farrakhan and the NoI target such deprived city areas, rather than prosperous black American suburbs, for the most obvious and simple of strategic reasons: the prospects for a sympathetic hearing are especially great in the former. Farrakhan's central message certainly encompasses middle-income "Buppies," but it is directed primarily toward reaping a harvest of new adherents and supporters from the many seeds of acute despair that are scattered throughout inner-city black communities across America.

The disproportionate dimensions of black disadvantage also render conspiracy theories especially plausible for many African-Americans. While the threat of Soviet and Chinese expansionism in the postwar years did not discriminate between Americans by race or ethnicity, the socioeconomic plight of African-Americans has always been, and remains, especially acute compared to that of other social groups in the United States. Farrakhan consistently challenges Americans of all races to look directly at the persistently skewed racial distribution of social and economic deprivation in the United States ". . . and tell me if there's not a plot. Twenty-five percent of our black youth in prison, black males destroyed in the cities . . . the black man crushed."[20] As many black politicians often argue, were such dramatic proportions of white America to be afflicted by similar social and economic problems, a full-scale national emergency would likely be declared and prompt ameliorative action undertaken as a matter of course.

In addition to the basic socioeconomic conditions being ripe for notions of a conspiracy's existence to take hold, more black Americans (in relative, and perhaps also absolute, terms) have directly encountered adverse experiences with the putative agents of Farrakhan's claimed conspiracies—Jews, whites, the federal government, and accommodationist blacks—in the postwar years than had Americans in general personally encountered communists in the 1940s and 1950s. Admit the possibility of the conspiracy, and the existence and identification of those forces that target its victims become both necessary and desirable. In this respect, the dismissal of Farrakhan's supporters and sympathizers as somehow naive (or worse), by virtue of his conspiratorial claims, reveals a surprising and significant degree of ahistoricism. Many more Americans adhered to McCarthyite tenets about the extent and multiple forms of domestic communist subversion on the basis of more meager and tendentious information and limited personal experience. It is worth recalling, after all, that Farrakhan, unlike McCarthy, occupies no position of institutional influence that requires that U.S. presidents must consider his reactions when contemplating their future policy options and public pronouncements.

If the potential for African-Americans encountering the alleged agents of antiblack conspiracies is, in principle at least, greater than that of discovering communists was during the 1950s, it is also clear that Farrakhan's anti-Semitism taps into a sizeable reservoir of latent prejudice among some African-Americans toward Jews.[21] Anti-Semitism admittedly has never acquired a mass political following among black Americans, and the vast majority of black Americans have probably not directly encountered Jewish Americans at all.[22] Shared experience of discrimination and prejudice has, historically, constituted the basis for a consonance of political goals and a remarkably resilient relationship between the two groups. Moreover, the incidence of such prejudices has been viewed by some social scientists as being merely the particular expression of a more diffuse antiwhite sentiment among African-Americans, rather than reflecting a specific anti-Semitic bias and antagonism.[23]

Some blacks, however, clearly do harbor prejudices toward Jews regardless of the presence or absence of their personal contact with members of the latter social group. Moreover, these prejudices extend beyond the narrow perceptions of economic exploitation that resulted from historic patterns of black migration during the first half of the twentieth century, which saw disadvantaged African-Americans move into urban areas in which Jews ran businesses and owned dwellings (prejudices that rest uneasily with the social groups, such as Koreans, currently owning businesses in central cities). The breakdown of the black–Jewish alliance of the civil rights era has fissiparous roots that extend deeply, and black American stereotyping of Jews (as more loyal to Israel than America, and as aggressive and therefore irritating, for example) is not restricted to economic issues, no matter how central to anti-Jewish prejudices such issues remain.[24]

In some respects, the crude anti-Semitism that Farrakhan exploits and promotes resembles not so much interracial hatred as more ethnic rivalry. The principal locus of conflicts between blacks and Jews have been the cities of New York and Chicago, historic migrant magnets whose conurbations comprise significant proportions of both populations. The competition over economic resources and political power that is endemic between American ethnic and social groups in general also informs black–Jewish rivalries in particular. In this sense, the extent and importance of anti-Semitic attitudes among black Americans is perhaps exaggerated and overstated.

Nonetheless, the gratuitous opprobrium regularly heaped upon Jews by Farrakhan and his NoI acolytes is exceptional. No other American ethnic group in the modern era faces the type of recurrent public vilification and intense hostility from a national political figure that Jews regularly confront from Farrakhan and his followers. The NoI's leader may, very plausibly, forfeit more potential African-American support than he attracts through his anti-Semitic appeals. Many of the working class and poor black Americans to whom his message appeals would no doubt be equally supportive and appreciative of Farrakhan without the virulent tirades against Jews. More affluent and educated African-American elites would also, almost certainly, be far more willing to accord Farrakhan greater legitimacy and respect in the absence of such pernicious and repugnant comments. The critical attention and national visibility that attends the more controversial public pronouncements that Farrakhan makes, however, are central to both his public profile and political ascendancy. In affording him notoriety as an allegedly independent and outspoken leader, anti-Semitism is inextricably bound to Farrakhan's rise, even if it does not constitute either a necessary, dominant, or sufficient part of his mass black American appeal.

The litany of socioeconomic woes that plague black Americans is, therefore, evidently critical to the popularity of the NoI leader. To attribute Farrakhan's political ascendancy to the existence of persistent social and economic problems among many black American communities, however, is an interpretation that is too simplistic and ahistorical to be intellectually convincing. By comparison, for example, the 1920s and 1930s, periods of deep economic dislocation among African-Americans, witnessed relative moderation among black political and civic elites. Garvey's pan-Africanist movement was eclipsed and undermined by the integrationist NAACP by the early 1920s and failed to revive during the acutely harsh economic conditions of the post–1929 Depression. Noble Drew Ali's Moorish Science movement was never more than a tiny cult. Even the original NoI's period of substantial growth in membership occurred during the late 1950s and early 1960s, years of sustained (though, for African-Americans, unevenly distributed) economic growth. Economic deprivation is therefore very much a necessary and important, but by no means a sufficient, condition of the contemporary success of the Farrakhan phenomenon.

For it is not only the existence of deeply adverse socioeconomic conditions among many black American communities that informs Farrakhan's rise. The responses of elite American actors—both white and black—have also critically shaped Farrakhan's fluctuating political fortunes. In particular, the reactions of African-American political, economic, and social elites to the Black Muslim have powerfully conditioned his emergent role and influence. As C. Eric Lincoln argued, it is Farrakhan's:

> . . . inexplicable attractiveness to the responsible element of the black community that constitutes the major source of threat and irritation that the Muslim leader seems to pose.[25]

In fact, however, Farrakhan's resonance with middle-class black Americans is by no means inexplicable. Central to Farrakhan's popular appeal is an unusual ability, derived principally from the more ambiguous elements of the ideological message that he propounds, effectively to exploit both elite and mass intrablack cleavages. Farrakhan falls squarely within the category of "preservatist" right-wing American movements, which typically require some type of symbiosis or ongoing commonality of interests between members of the upper and the lower economic stratas in order to achieve significant and lasting political influence. Such movements:

> . . . are guarding different kinds of self-interest together. The common grounds they find are some symbolic and effective aspects of the changing times: a disappearing way of life, a vanishing power, a diminishing group prestige, a heart-sinking change of social scenery, a lost sense of comfort and belongingness. This is status deterioration which is seen in political terms as a general social deterioration.[26]

Farrakhan has sought deliberately, consistently, and carefully to safeguard together quite distinct types of particular, discrete black

American interests within the same collective, universal, and organic racial message. In doing so, his political appeal has essentially cut across intrablack cleavages of social class, gender, age, religion, and region to forge a broad base of pro forma African-American support. The NoI's free-market economic principles, for example, coincide substantially with the dominant economic agenda of the black American petit bourgeoisie. However objectionable many middle income African-Americans find his bizarre theological claims, militantly unrepentant anti-Semitism, and traditionalist cultural prescriptions, Farrakhan's avowed brand of economic individualism resonates among black American elites. Even Coretta Scott King—whose personal history is so intimately linked to the philosophy of racial integration and the achievement of a multiracial democracy—argued that Farrakhan's self-help philosophy is "something we can all agree on."[27] The frustrations and anger that middle-class black Americans feel as members of a racial minority still subject to prejudice and discrimination and their conventional American aspirations to a secure, prosperous, and affluent lifestyle intersect in Farrakhan's distinctive combination of cathartic racial militancy, black nationalism, and economic conservatism.[28]

Conversely, for many poorer and disadvantaged black Americans, the combined appeal of the NoI's noneconomic message and the organization's direct action interventions to reduce drug consumption and combat intrablack crime in disintegrating urban centers far outweighs the more negative features of Farrakhan's antigovernment, laissez-faire agenda. Noneconomic demands to rid inner-city communities of dope addicts, beggars, and gangsters win support from those many black Americans who have to confront that decaying and dangerous urban environment on a routine basis. Thus, when otherwise sharply astute critics (such as Richard Cohen) casually compare defenders of Farrakhan to those of Benito Mussolini, for reserving their full disapprobation and unequivocal censure on account of the good works that the authoritarians have achieved, they miss a vitally important distinction: the NoI's efforts to improve black city communities assume an entirely different qualitative—and an immeasurably more pressing—human importance than simply "making the trains run on time." For many black Americans, the NoI is bravely engaged in nothing less than a struggle of life and death.

Moreover, popular African-American demands are frequently matched, however imperfectly, by the NoI's organized actions. The Nation of Islam Security Agency, a licensed corporation and business unit of the organization, secured contracts to patrol apartment complexes in crime-ridden areas of Washington, D.C., Chicago, Baltimore, and Los Angeles, where its presence has been widely accredited with achieving a tangible difference in the quality of life of these areas' inhabitants. The Black Muslims commenced patrols of Mayfair Mansions and Paradise Manor (two housing projects in Washington) in 1988, and won notable praise from both tenants and police officers for their dedicated efforts. According to the former, the NoI's guards were not only more committed than were regular police officers to the pressing goals of crime reduction and community regeneration, but they also commanded more popular respect among African-Americans at large, not least from some of the initially skeptical black elderly residents in the projects.[29] The licenses that NoI-affiliated groups secured from local government authorities testified both to the deeply inhospitable nature of the central city environs and the almost total lack of competing sources of effective security for their beleaguered residents.

The response of the late black American novelist, James Baldwin, to Elijah Muhammad's NoI in the early 1960s is indicative of the type of emotions aroused by the actions of Farrakhan's organization (and its offshoots) during the 1990s. Baldwin, as both an avowed and courageous opponent of racial separatism and an outspoken, cosmopolitan homosexual, was by no means a sympathetic observer of Elijah's NoI. Nonetheless, though he wrote about Elijah, Baldwin expressed laudatory sentiments that are equally applicable to Farrakhan's organization currently, for many blacks:

> [He] has been able to do what generations of welfare workers and committees and resolutions and reports and housing projects and playgrounds have failed to do: to heal and redeem drunkards and junkies, to convert people who have come out of prison and to keep them out, to make men chaste and women virtuous, and to invest both the male and the female with a pride and serenity that hang about them like an unfailing light. He has done all these things, which our Christian church has spectacularly failed to do. How has Elijah managed it?[30]

Substitute Farrakhan's name for that of Elijah, and it should become apparent that, despite the many contradictions and controversies that surround the NoI's activities, it is extremely difficult—if not entirely impossible—for many blacks unequivocally to reject the minister. There are some elements of Farrakhan's public message and his organization's activism that are accepted, admired, and approved of by most African-Americans. Therein resides one of the most important features of Farrakhan's mass black appeal.

Unhindered by the demands of public office, in which his many avowed convictions and prescriptions would require support through roll-call votes, legislative results, and effective implementation, Farrakhan's protest-centered posture permits the vigorous articulation of policy positions, economic self-help programs, and proactive social initiatives that—shorn of their eccentric theological accompaniments—few African-Americans would dismiss in toto. The combination of public prescriptions that are shared by many blacks and tangible social and economic accomplishments in central cities that are admired by still more represents an especially powerful resource for Farrakhan consistently to extol and to capitalize upon for substantial personal political advantage.

INTER- AND INTRA-RACIAL DIVISIONS

Interracial Dissensus

Farrakhan has zealously exploited the fact of pronounced interracial tension in America, the existence of which undeniably remains one of the nation's most prominent and persistent societal features. The NoI's leader has been assisted in this undistinguished task by the continued existence in the post–civil rights era of pronounced socioeconomic disparities between white and black America. The massive growth of the African-American middle class since the mid-1960s has not caused two fundamentally separate and estranged black and white American societies to converge to any meaningful extent.

Dionne was thus quite correct to argue that mass black disillusionment with white America has had a fundamental and extensive role to play in enlarging Farrakhan's effective political and social constituency among African-Americans over recent years. This process, however, has occurred in three quite distinct ways that, when isolated into their component parts, go considerably beyond a simple loss of faith among African-Americans in whites' idealism, benevolence, and support for black aspirations in the United States, and instead imply a far more deep racial chasm, a chasm that Farrakhan at once exploits and exacerbates still further.

The first dimension—which forms the implicit but dominant theme of Dionne's argument—is that black and white Americans harbor strongly divergent and discrepant opinions upon both the extent of, and the explanations for, current African-American socioeconomic deprivation (both relative and absolute). Opinion surveys clearly and consistently demonstrate that black Americans powerfully disagree with white Americans on a range of important questions: on whether the post–civil rights era economic situation has improved for blacks; on whether more opportunities for racial minorities exist in the 1990s; on whether interracial competition for employment now occurs on a fair and equitable basis; and on whether the extent of white racism and prejudice toward blacks in America has diminished.[31]

In addition, and most important, clear and persistent racial disjunctures exist in relation to the appropriate role of government in general—and the U.S. federal government in particular—in promoting black American welfare. The majority of African-Americans continue to believe that the American state has a moral obligation to provide entitlement programs and other forms of public benefits to black (and also nonblack) U.S. citizens. Compared to white Americans, most blacks are particularly supportive of the notions that jobs should be guaranteed by the federal government and that the government should ensure a decent standard of living for all of its citizens. According to the most comprehensive database available—the 1988 Black Election Study—African-Americans decisively support greater spending by the government than do whites in all policy areas, bar defense, the environment, and space/scientific research (see table 6.1).

Black Americans' enduringly robust support for an active and interventionist federal government has represented one of the most consistently important and manifest differences between the races in the post–civil rights era. Moreover, it substantially (though not completely) explains the striking racial differences in electoral support for the two main American political parties since 1968.[32] The vast bulk of black Americans continue in the 1990s to favor the type of purposive government intervention, redistributive economic policies, and comprehensive social welfare programs that have historically been associated with the post–New Deal Democratic party. White Americans, who in the main do not endorse such interventionist policies, tend instead to support the GOP in national elections, particularly—though not, as the 1994 mid-terms revealed, exclusively—in the quadrennial presidential elections. The Democratic party has thus emerged in the post–

TABLE 6.1. Differences between White and Black Public Opinion

Issues	Whites	Blacks	+/-
Support increased spending on government services	33	63	30
Support decreased defense spending	31	47	16
Support government health insurance	39	49	10
Believe government should provide jobs and a good standard of living	21	57	36
Support increased federal spending on:			
Social security	53	82	29
Food stamps	16	49	30
Fighting AIDS	71	83	12
Protecting the environment	64	58	-6
Financial aid to college students	39	72	33
Assistance to the unemployed	24	65	41
Child care	53	78	25
Public schools	61	83	22
Care for the elderly	73	90	17
Homeless	61	90	29
War on drugs	74	82	8
Support decreased federal spending on:			
Aid to Nicaraguan Contras	50	51	1
Star Wars	40	53	13
Space and scientific research	31	25	-6
Political identifications:			
Consider self a liberal	27	41	14
Consider self a Democrat	40	83	43
Like something about the Democratic party	51	63	12
Dislike something about the Democratic party	48	20	-28
Like something about the Republican party	52	22	-30
Dislike something about the Republican party	47	50	3

Sources: Adapted by the author from: 1988 American National Black Election Panel Study; and Michael Dawson, *Behind the Mule: Race and Class in African American Politics* (Princeton, N.J.: Princeton University Press, 1994), p. 183.

civil rights era as the party of racial liberalism, whereas the Republican party has taken up the banner of racial conservatism with increasing alacrity and enthusiasm.

While the GOP's racial conservatism may be driven largely by a (theoretically, at least) "race-neutral" economics and by opposition to an activist federal government among whites, not by the crudely overt racism of the old Dixiecrat, the role of race still remains a crucial one for Republicans. Considerations of race have become so deeply embedded in the strategy and tactics of modern U.S. politics, in competing conceptions of the appropriate role and responsibility of the federal government, and even in American voters' very conceptions of moral and partisan identity, that few national elections now occur without some reference to latent racial tensions and ongoing conflicts. As Stanley Greenberg's influential research into the "Reagan Democrats" of the 1980s found, white Democratic defectors expressed a "profound distaste for blacks, a sentiment that pervades everything they think about government and politics." African-Americans constituted "the explanation for their (white defectors') vulnerability and for almost everything that has gone wrong in their lives; not being black is what constitutes being middle class; not living with blacks is what makes a neighborhood a decent place to live."[33] The combination of an antigovernment appeal and either explicit or implicit racial signals in Republican campaigns (busing, "law and order," the "welfare queen," minority quotas, Willie Horton) has hence proven to be a reliable midwife to the regular delivery of powerful electoral bases for GOP candidates—federal, state, and local—since 1968. A clear result has been that racial disjunctures in partisan identification, affiliation, and electoral support have emerged in the past thirty years as more profound and persistent than ever.[34]

Although Farrakhan's economic beliefs enthusiastically embrace laissez-faire principles more congenial to Republicans than liberal Democrats (rather than government-oriented programs), the disjuncture in racial attitudes to black American welfare nonetheless provides an attractive opportunity for him to exploit for political gain among black Americans. The core themes that Farrakhan relentlessly develops and advances in his public discourse—that white America is largely responsible for black problems and that whites collectively desire to be rid of African-Americans entirely—are themes that the differences in racial attitudes outlined above seem, to many African-Americans, to confirm. A government ostensibly of all Americans appears to some blacks to be implacably unwilling to address the needs and desires of a long-oppressed racial minority, whose historic deprivation is thereby effectively sanctioned, perpetuated, and worsened. Although the reasons for white Americans' opposition to new government programs to benefit blacks are far more complex than simple racial prejudice alone—and while white opposition to such programs is far from being either universal or immutable in character[35]—the very existence of white opposition is a sufficiently galvanizing force for Farrakhan's attempts to win mass political support through stoking up black American animosity and thereby exacerbating interracial tensions still further.

Dissensus over economics therefore strongly informs continued discrepancies in racial life chances and powerfully buttresses Farrakhan's frequent assertions of the incompatibility of the races in America: in this view, even peaceful coexistence between black and white Americans represents a chimera. While interracial differences in opinions, however, are principally focused upon distributive and redistributive policy concerns, the clear disjunctures in attitudes between the races also extend far beyond narrowly economic issues. Especially in regard to some of the most notable foci of societal conflicts involving race in recent years, such as the Rodney King beating in 1992 and the O. J. Simpson trial of 1994–95, black and white Americans differed dramatically in their assessments of the relative and absolute guilt and innocence of the involved parties.

Consider, for example, the reaction to the King beating and the subsequent Los Angeles riots of April 1992. Although an overwhelming majority of both black and white Americans believed that the four white police officers found not guilty of beating King should have been found guilty, the broader inferences that they drew from the affair diverged dramatically. For example, while 78 percent of black Americans agreed that the King verdict demonstrated that blacks simply cannot achieve justice in America, only 25 percent of whites (admittedly, a significant figure in itself) concurred with that view. Only 1 percent of African-Americans, compared with fully 47 percent of whites, held that the police in most U.S. cities treat blacks as fairly as whites, while a mere 8 percent of blacks (against a substantial 46 percent of whites) believed that black Americans and other minorities received equal treatment in the American criminal justice system as a whole.[36] The vast gulf between the races in their dissonant perceptions of the same evidence, events, and politicosocial institutions is such that Farrakhan's repetitive central message—that America's racial chasm is now beyond the reach of any bridge—is one that resonates with increasing popular force.

Farrakhan's popularity among many black American college students, as well as inner-city blacks, also reflects this pronounced gulf and the marked extent to which even middle-income black Americans in the post–civil rights era still hold race to be a formidable obstacle to their individual advancement and to the enjoyment of full citizenship in the United States. Simplistic characterizations of Farrakhan as the "gangsta of choice on college campuses, a trendy demagogue"[37] entirely fail to address the complex intraracial cleavages and the particularly salient issues upon which the Black Muslim's appeal among educated (as well as uneducated) black Americans is founded. The centrality of race that Farrakhan invokes constantly in his analyses of America's plight is a factor that middle-class black Americans, aspiring to upward social and geographic mobility, also perceive to be absolutely fundamental—and far more often constraining than beneficial—to their own individual and collective futures. Disjunctures between black and white conceptions along a range of important questions are thus a crucial feature of the interracial conflict that Farrakhan invariably highlights.

The second dimension in which Farrakhan's appeals win popular black American support, however, is based more clearly and comprehensively on a shared black antipathy toward white Americans and/or the governmental and political institutions that are perceived to be dominated or controlled by them. Several of the paranoiac themes that Farrakhan emphasizes in his public discourse are themes that evidently resonate with popular black American attitudes. In particular, the pronounced mistrust of government in general, and the federal government in particular, shared by both Farrakhan and white supremacists—albeit for different reasons and from discordant motives—is one that many blacks at the mass level also demonstrably harbor. A poll in the *New York Times* in 1990, for example, revealed that 77 percent of black Americans (compared with 34 percent of whites) think it either "true, or most likely true" that the government singles out African-American politicians for investigations in order to discredit them. Fully 60 percent of black Americans (compared with only 16 percent of whites) believed that the government intentionally makes drugs easily available in poor black neighborhoods to harm African-Americans. In addition, a remarkable 29 percent of African-Americans (but just 5 percent of whites) thought that it was true, or possibly true, that the AIDS virus was created deliberately to decimate the black population and to advance its genocide.[38]

What is most striking about these figures is not simply the substantial proportion of black Americans who adhere to these notions—although, obviously, this is itself impressive—but also the clear and marked differences that exist between the races on the above questions. The figures indicate very strongly that not only does a significant pool of potential black support for Farrakhan exist when he addresses issues such as FBI harassment of black American politicians and the dissemination of hard drugs and the HIV virus in black neighborhoods, but also that the minister's linking these themes to prevailing conceptions of a diffuse white American hostility or increasing indifference toward African-Americans compounds their popular appeal among many blacks. No matter how ludicrous, preposterous, and repugnant the propositions are to many white and black Americans alike, Farrakhan unapologetically articulates sentiments about drugs and AIDS that are shared by substantial numbers of blacks.

Farrakhan's demonization of whites and the federal government as enemies of black Americans is not, therefore, as much a high-risk strategy as it is one that is certain to accord favorably with many popular black attitudes. If white Americans and a white/Jewish-run federal government truly are capable of deliberately disseminating lethally addictive drugs and deadly sex-related viruses among blacks in order to hasten African-American genocide—as many blacks currently believe is the case—it is hardly surprising that Farrakhan's strident calls for racial separation (whether cultural or physical) in the United States win him significant popular black support. It would be immeasurably more surprising, in fact, if his vocal pleas actually fell upon deaf ears, in this context. Separate racial development represents not just a matter of empowering black Americans politically, economically, and socially, by this interpretation. It is also a fundamental prerequisite for the very survival of the African-American race in the United States. Farrakhan's militant demeanor and uncompromising demands are thus entirely appropriate to—and even required by—the broader context of deteriorating U.S. race relations for many African-Americans.

The third facet of popular black American disillusionment with whites concerns the widespread perception among African-Americans of a deep and growing white political backlash against the landmark black political and social gains secured, after protracted and costly struggle, during the 1960s. The roots of the Farrakhan phenomenon thus extend beyond simple white indifference about, or neutrality toward, African-Americans or black welfare in the 1990s. Rather, several recent developments in national American politics instead point clearly toward an increasing and dangerous level of white hostility to blacks, with white Americans actively and aggressively seeking to reverse established public policies that were originally designed to assist black Americans in particular.

The most significant historical development in this respect was the election and reelection of Ronald Reagan to the United States presidency in 1980 and 1984, respectively. The civil rights gains of the 1960s and 1970s appeared to come a screeching halt with the election of one of their most vocal and consistent conservative opponents. As a presidential candidate more broadly and deeply despised by black Americans than any since George Wallace, and as a president whose political aspirations were more distant from those of African-Americans than any occupant of the White House since Herbert Hoover, Reagan undoubtedly—though inadvertently—antagonized, galvanized, and politicized blacks nationwide. In many respects, in fact, Reagan was the perfect national white foil for expanding Farrakhan's popular black political base. For many African-Americans, the president vividly personified the racial insensitivity, indifference, and ignorance of white America and, moreover, fathered the socioeconomic conditions that gave rise to the antiblack backlash of the "angry white male" during the 1990s.[39] Although his unabashed conservatism was viewed by Farrakhan as being ultimately beneficial to the cause of racial separatism (Reaganite attacks upon public welfare programs were seen by the minister as evidence that the president had been dispatched by God to set blacks free), the very values that led African-Americans ardently to oppose Reagan and to support Farrakhan ironically saw the latter deliver the president's own brand of conservative individualism back to them once more, albeit this time in a racially militant and paranoid black separatist guise.

That hostile national political environment—the sense of a white America that no longer needs, but does not know precisely what to do with, African-Americans—has in several respects been exacerbated even further since Reagan's departure from Washington in 1989. After two decades as mainstream public policy items, for example, both the United States Supreme Court and Republican elected officials in federal, state, and local office have struck down affirmative action policies and minority set-aside programs that had been specifically designed to assist black Americans' opportunities for education, employment, and private enterprise. Having upheld the practice of concentrating racial minorities into particular congressional districts in order to increase black representation in representative assemblies in 1986 (a process dubbed "affirmative gerrymandering" by its critics), the Supreme Court moved in four critical decisions during the 1990s to reverse that policy, condemning it as a form of "political apartheid" repugnant to both a color-blind U.S. Constitution and civilized American sensibilities. Having won control of both houses of Congress in 1994, the GOP majority even managed to abolish the relatively meager support services and limited funding of minority congressional caucuses (such as the Black and Hispanic Caucuses) on the first day of the 104th Congress.[40] And, in 1995–96, a wave of arson attacks on over thirty black churches—what the SCLC's Joseph Lowery termed "the soul of the black community"[41]—across the American South vividly recalled the most brutal terrorist attacks of white supremacist groups during the 1960s.

In sum, a deepening racial tumult seemed to have engulfed American race relations. At a popular level, opinion polls also revealed the growing mutual animus that animated racial attitudes to national public policy debates. By 1995, only 12 percent of black Americans and a mere 23 percent of whites held race relations to be either "excellent or good." Of white Americans, 54 percent professed to a belief that "we have gone too far in pushing equal rights in this country," while a decisive 73 percent opposed giving "special consideration" to black Americans in opportunities for college places, jobs, and employment promotions. Of African-Americans, 70 percent (compared with only 25 percent of whites) held it to be "very important" that legislative districts remained drawn to increase black representation in assemblies.[42] Two-thirds of white Americans believed that "it is their own fault that blacks cannot get ahead," with only one-third attributing lack of black progress to the persistence of racial discrimination, figures that represented a complete reversal of the proportions that had obtained thirty years previously.

For some observers, locating the origins of this third dimension of interracial dissonance in collective white anger, fear, and resentment was a profoundly misplaced and misleading exercise. White Americans' attitudes toward black Americans was, in this context, not so much one of overt hostility or pronounced disinterest, but rather of fundamentally benign indifference. Some of the more strident of these critics, such as Jared Taylor, author of *Paved with Good Intentions: The Failure of Race Relations in America*, locate the core of contemporary tension between the races in America instead at a problem of black

Americans viscerally hating whites. Taylor identifies an all-consuming black American racial hatred, an antipathy expressed in the ferocious and violent rhetoric of rap music; manifest in the incidence of black American criminal acts against white citizens (such as the appalling rape of a white woman jogger in New York's Central Park in 1990, the beating of Reginald Denny in Los Angeles in 1992, and the indiscriminate mass murder of white passengers committed by Colin Ferguson on a suburban Long Island commuter train in December 1993[43]); discernible in widespread white perceptions of an underlying mood of sullen, smoldering rage among African-Americans in general; and articulated with varying degrees of eloquence and bile by figures such as Farrakhan, Fulani, Sharpton, Savage, and the notorious Sister Souljah.

The harsh tone of Taylor's conservative treatise and the condemnatory critical responses to it both testified to the stark interracial dissensus in which American public life has become so thoroughly mired during the 1990s.[44] Although, in looking to the future, whites remained more optimistic that the pattern of contemporary race relations could improve than did blacks (according to Taylor), the fact of enduring and extensive interracial animus remained brutally clear, whatever its principal motivating locus.[45] So, while Andrew Hacker is undoubtedly correct that effective political measures intended to redress relations between the races require from white Americans either "support, neutrality or indifference,"[46] it remains the case that, over recent years, issues of race have become far too salient to elicit indifference, too controversial to allow neutrality, and too divisive to produce decisive white support. With such a febrile social canvas as his striking backdrop, it should hardly be surprising that Farrakhan's inflammatory picture of an incipient American racial nightmare should both catch and retain the attention of so many African-Americans.

Intraracial Dissensus

The existence of pronounced interracial cleavages is a familiar enough theme in American politics, even if the three dimensions of interracial dissensus and disaffection outlined above are only infrequently delineated with particular clarity or precision. The disaggregation of the distinct components of the factors animating black–white tensions provides clear and substantial evidential support to

the arguments of Dionne and other critics that the basis of Farrakhan's mass black political appeal resides in his unremitting exploitation of (and impressive contribution to) a diffuse but palpable sense
of growing racial antagonism in contemporary America.

Conflict and antipathy between the races nonetheless forms only
one of the core foundations for Farrakhan's rise, albeit a very important one. The external focus upon white Americans that is commonplace in critical commentaries on Farrakhan substantially obscures the
internal African-American dynamics that also powerfully inform the
Black Muslim leader's politics. For not only is interracial antipathy a
critically important theme in the Farrakhan phenomenon, but intraracial differences and heterogeneous black attitudes are also influential
in expanding the NoI minister's popular appeal among African-Americans. Farrakhan's persistent (and largely successful) provocation of
extensive dissensus within, as well as between, the races is a central
and often-neglected component of his political ascendancy and of the
continuing political controversy that has conditioned his gradual but
steady path to national notoriety.

In this respect, the central intellectual problem posed by the general phenomenon of political authoritarianism and first identified by
Adorno et al.—its being a function principally of either personality or
ideology—is especially relevant to explanations of Farrakhan's ascendancy. In particular, the existence among many black Americans of
markedly negative self-images provides a rich and propitious basis
for Farrakhan's demagogic, reactionary, and paranoid appeals to
secure popular African-American support. Paul Sniderman and Thomas Piazza, for example, record how, on a series of explicitly negative
stereotypes of African-Americans, black respondents actually concurred with every one of the characterizations even more than
whites.[47] As table 6.2 shows, the median level of black American
agreement on the five selected negative racial stereotypes of blacks
exceeds that of white Americans by over 10 percent.

Such findings are striking and powerful, and they go a long way
toward accounting for Farrakhan's recent popular appeal among many
black Americans. Farrakhan's core political message of individual
responsibility, personal discipline, and collective black racial pride is
likely to find a responsive and receptive African-American audience
far beyond the comparatively few members of the NoI: among black
Americans both disillusioned at the increasing disintegration of black
communities and disgruntled at existing African-American politicians

TABLE 6.2. Acceptance of Negative Stereotypes of African-Americans by White and Black Americans

Stereotype	*Percent in Agreement*		
	Whites	*Blacks*	*Difference*
Blacks are more aggressive or violent	52	59	7
Blacks are boastful	45	57	12
Blacks are complaining	41	51	10
Blacks are lazy	34	39	5
Blacks are irresponsible	21	40	19
Median	38.6	49.2	10.6

Source: Adapted from Paul M. Sniderman and Thomas Piazza, *The Scar of Race* (Cambridge, Mass.: Harvard University Press, 1993), p. 45, and the 1991 National Race Survey. N=1744 whites, 182 blacks.

Note: Acceptance is defined by assigning a value of 6 or higher on a scale of 0 to 10.

and other established civic leaders. Reed speculated in 1991 that Farrakhan's political aspirations were staked upon a terrain somewhere between actual mass membership of the NoI and a more limited form of pro forma black support.[48] According to these figures that ground is exceedingly responsive to the discordant seeds of bitterness that Farrakhan sows.

It was, of course, precisely that fertile terrain that Farrakhan exploited through the Million Man March and its central theme of black male atonement, at once an opportunity for individual atonement and collective African-American redemption and an explicit admission of both individual sins and collective guilt. The inward-looking parochialism manifest in the march—the exclusive focus on intrablack affairs and the often errant practice but great potential of black American males—was without precedent for such a mass gathering in Washington, D.C. Never before had so many American citizens gathered together in the nation's capital to engage in an explicitly celebratory occasion that was so deeply suffused by self-recrimination, regret, and remorse. Whatever its subsequent material effects, the march represented an unequivocal, public mass black confession, a national expiation that spoke directly to the negative self-evaluations of—as well as the adverse external stereotypes widely held about—African-American men.

In addressing those self-evaluations, some of the march's success (and of Farrakhan's visceral appeal to black men generally) relied
on the gender differences within African-American communities that
have fueled widespread popular perceptions of the black male as
being increasingly emasculated. Farrakhan publicly seeks, and pur-
ports in his prescriptions to offer, the restoration of male authority—
an authority that the growing employment and educational achievements of African-American women are easily portrayed as undermining. In socioeconomic terms, for example, by March 1993, the civilian
U.S. labor force was populated more by black women than men; African-American women's educational attainment levels exceeded those
of African-American men; and a higher proportion of black women
than men were employed in managerial and professional jobs, as well
as service occupations, by 1994.[49] The latter disjuncture, especially,
represented not only a matter of black females constituting a decisive
majority of the total number of African-Americans occupying such
positions, but also of the diminishing opportunities for black men to
obtain traditional blue collar and public sector employment that had
occurred since 1980.[50]

Although the discrepancies between male and female black
income, educational achievements, and employment prospects are
not as pronounced as among other American racial and ethnic
groups, the substantial differences that clearly do exist are nonetheless important in conditioning Farrakhan's appeals to black men. For
all his protestations about the heavy burdens of black American
women, Farrakhan's message (like that of his mentor, Elijah) is concentrated primarily upon the regeneration of male responsibility, the
revival of male authority, and the reinstitution of an essentially patriarchal and paternalist sexual order. The compelling image of the African-American male as not only endangered but as also emasculated is
a constant refrain in Farrakhan's pronouncements. When conjoined to
the statistics of the likelihood of black men being homicide victims or
convicted criminals, and of U.S. Census Bureau conclusions that "less
than 3 out of 4 Black women will eventually marry,"[51] for example, it
is also an image that becomes especially resonant—and understandably so—with many popular black sentiments.[52]

The resonance of such an appeal and the figures contained in
table 6.2 clearly undermine the argument that it is either exclusively
or primarily a loss of black Americans' faith in white support or

benevolence that explains the rising popularity over recent years of black nationalist sentiment in general among African-Americans, or Farrakhan's variant thereof, in particular. Central though perceptions of white Americans' indifference and hostility to black interests and aspirations undoubtedly remain to popular African-American support for the NoI's leader, it is also the complex nature of contemporary intrablack attitudes and elite–mass relations within the black community that is critical to the increasingly advanced political effectiveness of Farrakhan's reactionary and paranoid appeals.

Farrakhan's political strategy is to confirm rather than deny the accuracy of these adverse self-perceptions among black Americans. As the minister succinctly observed in his Million Man March speech, "I point out the evils of black people like no other leader alive."[53] His explicit public message is that many African-Americans are indeed irresponsible, lazy, dependent, and so forth. Issued by any white American politician (and most black ones, too), such negative remarks would naturally invite wholesale censure. Farrakhan, however, qualifies his aggressive and repudiative rhetoric by invoking two (admittedly unsubtle) qualifications: first, that the institution of slavery is held responsible for leaving blacks in America in such a profound state of collective emotional and psychological disarray; second, that that abject state is one that is open to challenge and change, providing that black Americans heed Farrakhan's message and "fly to Islam." The reeducation of black Americans is thus premised upon their purported existing mental, social, and psychological inadequacies and the fundamental mutability of those deficient characteristics.

Of course, Farrakhan's exploitation of negative black American self-images also comprises an explicit attempt vigorously to challenge and change them for the better. Such challenges are common enough among more conventional political, religious, and civic figures in black American communities, dating back to the earliest days of the republic. What distinguishes Farrakhan's appeals from those of other African-American leaders, however, is his intensity, his theologically derived analysis, and the notable public alacrity and marked insouciance with which he persistently charts black Americans' purported defects and deficiencies. Established black American leaders do not stress the alleged consuming emotive and psychological poverty of the mass of African-Americans with either the frequency, emphasis, or eloquence that Farrakhan does as a matter of course. Other African-American leaders do not share the minister's religious beliefs in the divinely ordained crippling of American blacks' individual and collective wills. However much its derivation is ultimately premised upon love and respect, Farrakhan's public message is one of apparent revulsion for many of his black compatriots and one that is delivered, it should be added, almost with relish.

Indeed, it is ironic that, for a national black leader who invariably places such pronounced importance upon racial exclusivity, essentialism, organicism, and unity—to the extent of excluding nonblacks and African-American women from his lectures and rallies—Farrakhan harbors so few public inhibitions about discussing black deficiencies in the presence of nonblacks. Since his controversial national media debut in 1984, Farrakhan's willingness to engage in public declarations about the many maladies of African-Americans and to offer elaborate explanations of black American malfeasance in a variety of nationwide forums has increased exponentially. By 1990, even the Phil Donahue show—with a mostly white studio and non-studio audience alike—was graced by the Black Muslim leader's presence.[54] In front of a predominantly white audience, Farrakhan proceeded to articulate in detail, and without circumspection or reticence, his firm belief in black Americans' welfare mentality and the infantile mental state of African-Americans at Emancipation. For many other black American public and private elites, such public candor is far less appealing and wholly self-defeating in seeking to challenge and alter preexisting racial stereotypes of African-Americans as incompetent, amoral, violent, and bestial savages. It is inconceivable that a white American politician could engage in similar rhetorical gambits without provoking an intense national controversy and inviting justifiable public censure.[55] Furthermore, were any other established black American politician to do so, the grave charges of race betrayal and Uncle Tomism would no doubt be forthcoming.

For Farrakhan, however, such marked discrepancies in approach are themselves effectively demanded by the strategic and tactical political deficiencies of the existing national black political leadership cohort in America. As the minister noted (with a characteristically ambiguous mixture of pride and regret) during his keynote speech at the Million Man March, of all contemporary black American political figures, only he assiduously draws attention to the evils that many African-Americans commit. In order to encourage African-Americans to achieve moral rectitude, Farrakhan must apparently first highlight black failings. In conferring a nobility upon the black dispossessed,

Farrakhan must, of necessity, address the more base aspects of African-American actions and attitudes.

Moreover, not only do negative self-images evidently exist among African-Americans and demand to be squarely confronted and challenged, but the inadequate and inaccurate representation of black American interests by black elite organizations and elected politicians is also an important contributory factor abetting Farrakhan's national political ascent. Thus, in addition to the notable political capital that the NoI's leader gains from challenging negative self-conceptions at the mass level, Farrakhan's popular appeals are also in part based upon his persistent exploitation of the disjunctures between elite black attitudes and popular African-American beliefs. In particular, Farrakhan's authoritarian and traditionalist prescriptions mirror the existence of majorities among African-Americans favoring conservative policy preferences, particularly on so-called "social issues," that is, those issues that encompass conflicts over cultural and moral values. Farrakhan's strong endorsement of traditionalist and morally repressive stances and his adamant rejection of negative conceptions of liberty (in essence, the notion of "freedom as license" and the absence of constraints upon autonomous individual action) clearly strike a resounding chord with African-Americans at a mass level.

Although most pronounced among southern blacks, this traditionalism also encompasses nonsouthern blacks. In fact, by some indicators, social conservatism is actually significantly more pronounced among black than white Americans, and has been so for many years. In 1980, for example, 50 percent of black Americans replied "harmful" or "unsure" when asked about the benefits of social welfare programs, while 52 percent said "no" to legalized abortion for women, even if married.[56] Fewer African-Americans than whites approve of married women working (70 versus 76 percent) or like the idea of female politicians (65 versus 75 percent). More black Americans than whites, however, favor prayer in public school (82 percent of blacks versus 68 percent of whites). More black Americans than whites also disapprove of abortions on demand (41 versus 28), though blacks and whites are evenly divided against abortion restrictions on the victims of rape and incest (47 versus 46 percent). A survey of 750 African-Americans by the Joint Center for Political and Economic Studies, in June 1992, found one-third of respondents agreeing that abortion should be legal under any circumstances and an additional 47 percent favoring its legality under some circumstances. A poll of black activists for the magazine *Emerge* at the 1992 Democratic Convention also found that 50 percent agreed that abortion should always be legal, with only 4 percent believing it should never be legal. Nonetheless, even among these activists, 38 percent agreed with the statement that "abortion is genocide"[57]—precisely the view of the NoI's leader.

Stereotypical conceptions of black Americans as overwhelmingly liberal in values and beliefs, while generally accurate when confined exclusively to economic questions, tend to neglect the strong cultural conservatism of many African-Americans, a conservatism that comports well with the avowed preference of Farrakhan for well-ordered and traditionalistic social relations among black Americans.[58] As with empirical indicators of Farrakhan's popularity among black Americans, opinion poll evidence is by no means conclusive or foolproof and should not be taken as such. Increased support for Farrakhan, however, is certainly consistent with the well-documented trend away from blacks describing their ideology as "liberal" and with critical arguments that "Black support for conservatism is likely to accelerate, as gaping cracks and fault lines appear in black liberalism."[59] At a minimum, the figures in table 6.2 suggest strongly that the deeply conservative cultural convictions of the NoI's leader are also attractive to a significant proportion of African-Americans at large.

Moreover, these traditionalist political positions are only infrequently reflected in, for example, the roll-call voting of CBC members and the public statements of other organized black interest lobbies, who consistently adopt more liberal and socially progressive positions on issues such as federal government funding for abortion clinics or public school prayer than do black Americans at large. Indeed, the disjunctures between the opinions of the mass of African-Americans and black elites are pronounced, especially on issues of a noneconomic nature. A poll by the American Enterprise Institute—contrasting a black "leadership" sample with a "national" black sample—found that 83 percent of the national sample approved of prayer in public schools, compared with only 40 percent of the leadership sample; 53 percent of the national sample approved of the death penalty, compared with only 33 percent of the leadership; and 53 percent of the national sample opposed busing for school integration, compared with 68 percent of the leadership who favored the policy.[60] Many of these differences clearly reflect divergent concerns between elite and mass blacks. On the death penalty, for example, as the conservative black economist Glenn Loury has observed, for black political and civic leaders, the

issue of criminal justice is primarily one of police brutality and coercion; for many ordinary blacks, however, intraracial violence has
caused them to view the death penalty as a means of improving the
fragile security of their inner-city neighborhoods.

Thus, for many black Americans, the NoI's religious doctrines
and Farrakhan's eclectic theological claims are most appropriately
regarded as representing merely the embellishment of more fundamental traditionalist and populist political tenets: respect for the institution of the family; clear demarcation of strictly defined, traditional
gender roles; condemnation of nontraditional sexual practices; and
disapproval of stimulants of all kinds. Explanations of Farrakhan's
ascendant leadership status among African-Americans must, to be
accurate, take appropriate account of more than just interracial differences. The Black Muslim's mass black appeals are vitally founded not
only upon the profound differences in political values and attitudes
that exist between black and white Americans, but also upon the partial failure of black political elites faithfully and consistently to represent the policy preferences of African-Americans at a mass level.

Both intra- and inter-racial cleavages therefore inform Farrakhan's popular appeal among African-Americans. As Carol Swain
argues, for effective political representation on these types of social
issues, blacks currently need to look beyond both the Democratic
party and their established national political representatives, whether
African-American or nonblack.[61] For many blacks, they evidently
find an approximation of or a functional substitute for such representation in Farrakhan. By virtue of his nonelected status, that representation is necessarily imperfect in ensuring the achievement of an
effective contribution to national public policy processes and their
ultimate policy outputs. Nonetheless, Farrakhan's appeals partly rest
upon the clear conviction that conventional political methods have
failed, and will remain inadequate, to redress fully black American
grievances and demands. Changes in the social behavior and attitudes of both individuals and groups can assuredly be effected by
methods other than the passing of laws and resolutions by governmental institutions. Indeed, the NoI's political strategy is precisely to
prove the accuracy of that contention through its proactive private
initiatives and interventions in urban centers across the United States.
If Farrakhan and the NoI stand squarely and uncompromisingly
outside established institutions, and are hence denied an influence
upon their internal deliberations and decisions, this serves more as an

indication of their strength than their weakness, an unmistakably clear sign of their incorruptibility and dogged resistance to the established system of oppression.

Thus, it is partly upon the indices of traditionalist and illiberal attitudes outlined above that Farrakhan carefully cultivates a broader supportive mass African-American constituency, far beyond the NoI's narrow membership base, much as Malcolm X has become a popular black American icon more by virtue of the secular, nonreligious values he is widely perceived to symbolize than either his religious convictions or his material political, economic, and social achievements.[62] Malcolm's charismatic personal leadership qualities—stridency, courage, fearless desire to challenge, eloquence, and political commitment—constituted a substantial part of his popular mass black appeal, both during his lifetime and subsequently. His status as an "authentic" black man, unbowed, unbought, and unbeaten by the very formidable pressures of being an African-American in the United States in the middle years of the twentieth century, was central to his mass black American popularity, both then and over subsequent decades.

Like Malcolm X, Farrakhan's exceptionally charismatic and stylistic qualities—not least his ability to "tell it like it is"—powerfully assist the winning of many African-American adherents and sympathizers in the 1990s. Like Malcolm, too, Farrakhan's proselytizing politics is also premised upon a bifurcated black public appeal of racial love and hate. As Reverend Walker rightly observed, Farrakhan eagerly serves as an outlet for African-Americans' angst, anger, and antipathy, for black rage against the failure of America to include blacks as substantively equal members of its polity: Farrakhan gives whitey hell. That dubious but recurrent donation is a central, unedifying, and wholly inextricable part of his popular appeal among African-Americans. Nonetheless, like Malcolm previously, black Americans do not escape Farrakhan's fulsome censure and venomous fury either.

Unlike Malcolm, however, Farrakhan's consuming racial wrath and his righteous rebuke of his fellow black Americans occasionally approach a form of almost megalomaniacal loathing and contempt, in both its content and tone. Addressing the (white) editorial board of the markedly conservative Liberty Lobby's house journal, *The Spotlight*, for example, Farrakhan explained:

Not one of you would mind, maybe, my living next door to you, because I'm a man of a degree of intelligence, of moral character.

I'm not a wild, partying fellow. I'm not a noisemaker. I keep my home very clean and my lawn very nice . . . With some of us who have learned how to act at home and abroad, you might not have problems . . . Drive through the ghettos, and see our people. See how we live. Tell me that you want your son or daughter to marry one of these. No, you won't.[63]

As such comments amply demonstrate, Farrakhan makes deeply derogatory pronouncements about the African-American community that other black political leaders either do not believe or will not state publicly, for a multiplicity of understandable reasons. The gratuitous and deep opprobrium that Farrakhan frequently directs at both black and white races in the United States—their distinct motivations and effects notwithstanding—assumes a crucial constituent of his popular black American appeal. So, too, does the generally adverse and hostile attention that Farrakhan directs at elite black American actors in general, and the established national African-American leadership cadre, in particular.

SPATIAL LEADERSHIP: RUNNING FOR BLACK LEADERSHIP, RUNNING AGAINST BLACK LEADERS

Although Farrakhan has never publicly articulated a desire to win elective office in America, the NoI's leader has effectively exercised a distinctive version of what the British political scientist Michael Foley terms "spatial leadership."[64] Drawing upon the seminal research of the distinguished American scholars, Richard Fenno and Morris Fiorina, on incumbent behavior in the United States Congress, Foley refined further the notion of running *for* public office by running *against* the institution to which one actually aspires to join or become a part of.[65] The attack upon the particular institution is, ironically, an especially advantageous method of achieving membership therein. In particular, when the institution is one that is collectively perceived as unpopular or ineffective, the individual-level strategy of presenting oneself as an outsider, untainted by the institution's faults and (potentially, at least) able to clean it up and rectify its many defects, is politically very attractive.

Farrakhan, by analogy, seeks neither to join a representative assembly nor a branch of government in the United States, nor directly as a candidate to challenge incumbent African-American elected officials (or others); but the Black Muslim leader assiduously runs for national

African-American leadership by running against the cohort of established black American leaders. This is not to imply a deliberate or concerted political campaign by Farrakhan but simply to observe that, both implicitly and explicitly, the NoI's leader persistently focuses popular black (and nonblack) American attentions upon the particular crisis of national African-American political leadership, as well as that of many black American communities more broadly. In so doing, Farrakhan deliberately seeks to draw a clear, powerful, and unmistakable contrast between what is being done by the NoI under his inspirational leadership to resolve the problems of blighted African-American communities, in comparison with the more limited and largely ineffective efforts of elected black officials and black interest lobbies. Thereby Farrakhan also highlights, and seeks to enhance, his relative leadership credentials compared to the latter, established national black American political leadership cadre.

Farrakhan shrewdly aspires not to government but instead to orchestrating the diffuse forces of African-American protest against the status quo, to shaping those sonorous and disparate voices of black disaffection into a commanding crescendo of righteous and invincible anger whose militant chorus sings exclusively from his personal hymn sheet of malice and hatred. Farrakhan persistently presents himself as an outsider to established black American leadership (a status that the public demands for, and accompanying expressions of, his repudiation serve consistently to assist) who, by virtue of that external locus, can inject the necessary vitality, innovation, and integrity to bring about its more general revival. As an avowed spiritual redeemer, from outside the conventional political realm and hence untainted by its corrupting demands and cooptive tendencies, Farrakhan and the NoI can purify black American civic and political leadership and thereby regenerate black communities nationwide.

As Reed argued, Farrakhan shares with Ronald Reagan the same essential style of self-promotion, as the redemptive vanguard of an antipolitical politics, a politics largely bereft of substantive commitments and programmatic specifics and instead heavily reliant upon a rich catalog of comforting homilies to the fundamental goodness of the ordinary citizen, along with caustic criticisms of the sellouts and betrayals of that citizen by corrupt, venal, and even degenerate national political elites. Similar to the inchoate antiestablishment appeals that informed both H. Ross Perot's 1992 independent presidential candidacy and the substantial popular support for a potential Colin Powell bid for the Oval Office in 1996, Farrakhan's leadership aspirations are founded upon an explicit leadership status as being expressly outside the established political arena.[66] Farrakhan's legitimacy is partially founded upon this expressly external locus, as apparently representing a genuinely formidable challenge to the political establishment and the governmental status quo.

Thus, Farrakhan's distinctive, paranoid brand of spatial leadership invokes his pronounced ideological, religious, and stylistic distance from mainstream black American politicians precisely in order to gain entry into the ranks of national African-American leadership. Farrakhan argues, for example, that the "current crop of leaders, black and white, have been ineffective in purging black communities of drugs, crime, and other social ills." In archetypal American populist mode, the minister excoriates African-American politicians who "used the people to get what they want, then forget to serve the people." After Mayor Barry's infamous drug bust in Washington, D.C., in 1990, Farrakhan promised that Black Muslim politicians—a notion that would have been entirely oxymoronic in Elijah Muhammad's days as the NoI's leader—would provide "upright alternatives." Alternative black American leaders' analyses—should they depart from Farrakhan's—are, by definition, incorrect and misleading, lacking both the divine derivation accorded the NoI leader's interpretations and the minister's full and unbowed political independence. In acidly attacking existing black politicians, Farrakhan aspires to secure increasing national recognition as an authoritative and independent black leadership figure.

In his more vituperative mode, Farrakhan's populist critique of established black political leadership becomes dramatically more extreme, acerbic, and vehement in its explicit denunciations:

> Black leaders have become whores, and we sell ourselves to whomever pays the bills and so we don't have too many independent Black leaders who have their hands in their own people's hands exclusively. They have one hand or finger in the Black community's hands and nine fingers and their feet under the table of some white person.[67]

By implication, of course, Farrakhan's ten dextrous digits are firmly and irrevocably entwined in those of African-Americans nationwide. Or, as his NoI lieutenant Khalid Muhammad summarized the dilemma facing authentic black leaders such as Farrakhan and himself (typically, in even more luridly offensive and vulgar fashion than his own superior):

> When white folks can't defeat you, they'll always find some Negro, some boot-licking, butt-licking, bamboozled, half-baked, half-fried, sissified, punkified, pasteurized, homogenized nigger that they can trot out in front of you. [68]

Unconstrained by representing a particular, discrete constituency of black Americans to which he is politically accountable by formally prescribed mechanisms, such as free and fair elections, Farrakhan instead projects himself (and is zealously promoted by erstwhile supporters such as Khalid) as the representative of all, the ultimate and exemplary repository of collective black interests. As the prophetic and enlightened savior of the entire black race, Farrakhan modestly desires simply to be a "good shepherd" for a race of people who have had "thieves and robbers in front of them as leaders."[69] To this noble end, by 1988, even Jesse Jackson was described by Farrakhan as possessing a "slave mentality,"[70] whereas, eight years later, those African-Americans who publicly raised concerns that Farrakhan was opportunistically exploiting his post–Million Man March fame as a vehicle for pursuing his own religious and political agenda overseas were roundly ridiculed by the humble minister as being blinded by the fear of whites, as constituting black critics who slavishly "live in the ghetto, stay in the ghetto, and . . . only go where the master says it is safe."[71]

The overarching purpose of such virulent attacks upon the established cadre of black American political leaders is clear. Denigration and ridicule of his African-American political peers is designed by Farrakhan to secure mass black support as an outspokenly independent force for meaningful social change and, by virtue of that popular support, to obtain the respect, envy, and fear of other black leaders. The link between the bleak and deteriorating conditions of many black American communities in the post–civil rights era and the apparent failure of established black leaders to halt and reverse that devastating decline is one that is designed to bolster powerfully Farrakhan's personal claims to legitimate national leadership status among African-Americans. As Marable argued, "Black people don't listen to Farrakhan because of his anti-Semitism. They listen to him because

the traditional civil rights establishment and most black elected officials have failed miserably in providing any effective leadership or
vision."[72] It is in the de facto co-optation of black leadership by establishment forces, which Farrakhan explicitly identifies, that the minister simultaneously locates much of the responsibility for African-
American communities' continued socioeconomic problems and also
isolates one of his most vulnerable elite targets for unrelentingly populist attack.[73]

Farrakhan uses his various aggressive appeals, denunciations,
and claims of popular black American support to demand a "seat at
the table" of the national African-American leadership cadre, in a
manner analogous to Jesse Jackson's attempts to gain respect and recognition from Democratic party elites during the party's primaries
and conventions in 1984 and 1988. Although neither of the African-
American preachers had won election to public office (the most conventional, if limited, indication of public support in liberal democratic
regimes), both used their claims of widespread popular support to
achieve effective recognition from recalcitrant, unenamored, and skeptical political elites: Jackson, in the form of party delegate selection
rules changes, particular platform planks, and prime-time convention
speeches; Farrakhan, in the form of public tributes, media attention,
and inclusion in black American umbrella organizations and special
national black events.

Moreover, despite the fact that their presence and activism in
African-American communities could be assessed in terms of
decades, both Jackson and Farrakhan's distinctive exercise of spatial
leadership enabled them, at different times, successfully to develop
and project public images as new entrants into national black political
life. For Jackson, the presentational task was rendered possible by the
mass media's focus upon the novelty and significance of the first "serious" campaign for the Democratic party's presidential nomination to
be mounted by an African-American. For Farrakhan, the media's assistance principally assumed the form of disseminating his reactionary
and paranoid message (and the accomplished demagogic style in
which it was invariably delivered) to as wide a national American
audience as possible. The more years that have passed in the post–civil
rights era, the greater the contrast (if not the conflict) has become
between protest agitators and increasingly well-established and experienced elected black political leaders. In achieving formal political
equality and expanding the ranks of black American elected officials

operating "inside" the American political system, the old protest credentials of extrasystemic African-American actors were ironically accorded a peculiar novelty and an intrinsic value that facilitated the presentation of Jackson and Farrakhan as new outsiders.

That status, as essentially outside the increasingly dominant domain of black American politics has also, necessarily, encompassed a locus beyond the conventional realms of mainstream U.S. party politics. Farrakhan's political appeal is based to a substantial extent upon—and seeks consistently to exploit—the continued strategic dilemma facing black American elected officials in particular and African-American voters in general in the U.S. two-party system. Farrakhan vigorously promotes himself as an unceasingly independent voice for black America and for black political autonomy, whether in the form of an independent black American political party or presidential candidate in national American elections—a strategy that has often been advanced by African-Americans but, thus far, never realized.[74]

That this should be the case is unsurprising. The institutional logic imposed by the plurality American electoral system upon its party system is fundamentally coalitional in character. Independence is either impossible or self-defeating.[75] Continued participation in and loyalty to the Democratic party, however, has won insufficient concessions in the form of material public policy outputs and redistribution of resources to improve the quality of life of millions of African-Americans. For Ronald Walters, black Americans occupy a position of "dependent-leverage."[76] As a minority group operating in a political system replete with other minorities, blacks must necessarily compete within the same distributional framework as all other American social groups. Securing distributive benefits depends centrally, as for those other groups, on the political and economic capital that African-Americans can muster, either to exchange favors, demand concessions, or bargain effectively in policy-making institutions. Black Americans' status as a numerical rather than a racial minority of the U.S. population is shared by all other social groups. The manifest urgency of black American demands, however, is a factor that is of at best marginal consequence to most other groups in either American election campaigns or the institutional distributive bargaining nexus that ultimately determines public policy outcomes. The policy benefits eventually accorded black Americans are therefore limited in volume and scope and remain woefully inadequate to change the plight of depressed black communities materially and decisively for the better.

The resulting mass–elite disjuncture in attitudes toward the Democratic party among African-Americans is hence especially pronounced and deeply problematic. As Marable and other African-American critics have argued, most contemporary black American political leaders are mentally, emotionally, and ideologically committed to the Democratic party, even if many of their African-American constituents increasingly are not.[77] For Farrakhan, such a tenacious attachment represents yet another particular political expression of the more generally compliant, unchallenging, and self-defeating slave mentality the long-lasting presence of which among black Americans the minister constantly bemoans and seeks to challenge. In this sense, Farrakhan's consistent message to African-Americans to achieve collective autonomy and complete independence represents as much a desperate cry of black American political frustration as it does one of either political defiance or hope.

Indeed, with regard to Farrakhan's exploitation of black American disaffection from the established political system in general, the reactions of Jesse Jackson's delegates to Farrakhan at the Democratic party's national convention at San Francisco in 1984 were also revealing. As table 6.3 demonstrates, whereas only 5 percent of Walter Mondale and 3 percent of Gary Hart's delegates were at all favorable to Farrakhan (presumably comprising mostly their respective black American delegates), fully 65 percent of Jackson delegates had a positive impression of the NoI's leader, and more than a quarter had a "very favorable" view.

Robert Newby's conclusion, that the gap "marks the vast ideological differences that separated the Jackson candidacy from that of the more mainstream candidates" is, however, unpersuasive.[78] That affinity for Farrakhan among Jackson delegates was partly a function of the minister's deep disdain for "the system" is certainly plausible. The ideological content of this view, though, is at best marginal. Rather, it is the unusual mixture of ideological dimensions—a reactionary set of cultural values combined with an unremitting commitment to black separatism—that is central to Farrakhan's public message, and the resulting ambiguity (one that nonetheless comprises no obvious internal contradictions), couched in the most strident black nationalist rhetoric, that is fundamental to his cross-cutting appeal among African-Americans at large.

TABLE 6.3. Delegate Views of Minister Louis Farrakhan by Candidate, Preference (%)

Views on Farrakhan	Candidate Preference		
	Mondale	*Hart*	*Jackson*
Very favorable	0	0	27
Somewhat favorable	5	3	38
Somewhat unfavorable	16	22	14
Very unfavorable	56	58	8
Not aware of him	23	17	13
Total %	100	100	100
*of responses	(N=1699)	(N=1111)	(N=305)

Source: Los Angeles Times Delegate Survey. Cited in Lucius J. Barker and Ronald W. Walters, *Jesse Jackson's 1984 Presidential Campaign* (Chicago: University of Illinois, 1989), p. 171.

That appeal is itself built, fragilely, upon a telling paradox. For though Farrakhan persistently preaches a public gospel of intraracial unity and self-love among black Americans, the minister's national leadership aspirations and popular support have depended critically upon his identifying and magnifying the available forces of disharmony, disunity, and disaggregation among African-Americans. Professing to be seeking black harmony, Farrakhan attacks African-Americans who do not subscribe to his views, who dare to criticize his beliefs and methods, and who depart from his divine script of racial salvation. The minister may be no modern Machiavelli, but Farrakhan's politics of intraracial love and reconciliation is premised fundamentally upon one of the oldest but most effective political tactics of divide and conquer, reflecting a deliberate and consistent strategy of provoking racial polarization and division nationwide, not just between black Americans and whites, but also, crucially, among African-Americans themselves. By making scrupulous support for Farrakhan a de facto litmus test of unswerving fidelity to the race and of black authenticity, the NoI leader effectively guarantees that dissension, division, and fragmentation all prosper within black ranks.

For other black American politicians, however, the Farrakhan phenomenon is an especially difficult one to deal with and to counter successfully. In 1985, for example, Mayor Tom Bradley of Los Angeles—an exemplar of the type of effective biracial coalition-builder that

Farrakhan regularly lambastes as treacherously selling black Americans out—was asked by local Jewish leaders to denounce the minister prior to the NoI's leader delivering an address in the city. Bradley refused, on the basis of an informal agreement that he had concluded with Farrakhan, in which the latter vowed to keep his upcoming speech entirely free of anti-Semitic remarks. Predictably enough, the agreement meant nothing. Farrakhan insouciantly proceeded, as he had in other major cities that year, to articulate explicitly anti-Jewish sentiments in the speech, and Bradley duly denounced the NoI's leader.[79]

The Bradley experience was not, however, an isolated or exceptional instance.[80] For established black American politicians more broadly, reaching an effective accommodation with Farrakhan represents a delicate enterprise fraught with many potential political costs and few substantive rewards. For the leader of the NoI, by contrast, the exercise of spatial leadership is one that entails very few political penalties of consequence and offers many welcome benefits. Most important, the fact that established African-American leaders feel it necessary to forge tentative and amorphous agreements—whether formal or informal—with Farrakhan serves to bolster his burgeoning political credentials and claims of leadership respect, while Farrakhan's ability nonchalantly to flout such agreements serves only to embellish his claims of political independence and autonomy.

The immense political difficulty that black leaders confront in dealing effectively with the NoI's leader is therefore one that is also central to Farrakhan's rise. As table 6.4 shows, the divisions within the then 38-member Congressional Black Caucus on the vote to condemn Khalid's Kean College diatribe closely reflect such strategic and tactical calculations. CBC members' votes did not reflect differential black voting age populations in their districts; if the votes for the resolution are compared with those who voted either against, present, and did not vote or make a position known, the difference is less than five percentage points. Nor did the intra-CBC dissension reflect differences in seniority in the House, the median term length being five terms for those voting for, four for those voting against. For most CBC members, the vote was evidently more a matter of personal philosophy and tactical convictions regarding Farrakhan and the NoI. As such, the marked dissensus within the CBC spoke powerfully to the difficult political dilemmas that Farrakhan and his followers have continued to pose his erstwhile black leadership allies.

TABLE 6.4. CBC Votes on Khalid Resolution*

CBC Member	State/ District	Black VAP	Term	Vote	CBC Member	State/ District	Black VAP	Term	Vote
Dixon	CA 32	40	9th	Y	Dellums	CA 9	29	13th	N
Tucker	CA 37	34	2nd	Y	Waters	CA 35	44	3rd	N
Franks	CT 5	5	3rd	Y	McKinney	GA 11	60	2nd	N
Brown	FLA 3	50	2nd	Y	Rush	ILL 1	68	2nd	N
Meek	FLA 17	54	2nd	Y	Fields	LA 4	63	2nd	N
Bishop	GA 2	52	2nd	Y	Thompson	MS 2	58	2nd	N
Lewis	GA 5	57	5th	Y	Clay	MO 1	48	14th	N
Reynolds	ILL 2	66	2nd	Y	Payne	NJ 10	57	4th	N
Collins	ILL 7	60	12th	Y	Towns	NY 10	60	7th	N
Jefferson	LA 2	56	3rd	Y	Watt	NC 12	53	2nd	N
Wynn	MD 4	56	2nd	Y	Washington	TX 18	49	3rd	N
Conyers	MI 14	65	16th	Y					
Wheat	MO 5	21	7th	Y	Mfume	MD 7	68	5th	P
Owens	NY 11	72	7th	Y	Collins	MI 15	68	3rd	P
Rangel	NY 15	47	13th	Y	Clayton	NC 1	53	2nd	P
Stokes	OH 11	55	14th	Y	Ford	TN 9	54	11th	P
Blackwell	PA 2	58	2nd	Y					
Clyburn	SC 6	58	2nd	Y	Hilliard	ALA 7	64	2nd	?
Johnson	TX 30	47	2nd	Y	Hastings	FLA 23	46	2nd	?
Scott	VA 3	61	2nd	Y	Flake	NY 6	54	5th	?
					Median				
					Votes For	—	50.6	5th	—
					Votes Against	—	55.3	4th	—

*H. Res. 343. Adoption of the resolution to express the sense of the House condemning the "hate-mongering" and "vicious" speech given by Khalid Abdul Muhammad at Kean College in Union, N.J., on 29 November 1993, and condemn all anti-Semitic, anti-Catholic, and racist forms of expression. Adopted 361–34: R 169–2; D 192–31 (ND 126–22, SD 66–9); I 0–1, Feb. 23, 1994.

P= voted "present," ? = did not vote or otherwise make position known.

Source: Adapted by the author from *Congressional Quarterly Weekly Report* 52, no. 8 (26 February 1994), pp. 506–7.

Farrakhan's running for black American leadership has thus been crucially founded upon a persistent praxis of running against—and running down—established African-American political leaders. The effective exercise of spatial leadership by Farrakhan has depended upon his successful exploitation of intrablack cleavages at both elite and mass levels, and his retention of a novel political identity and distinctive outsider locus among current national black American political actors. It is however, ironic that in partially compromising that

novelty through his increasing participation in national politics, Farrakhan has made his political influence subject to its own (albeit limited) internal constraints.

INFLUENCE IN ISOLATION

As chapter five argued, while they have contributed to perpetuating
the national prominence and to sustaining the name recognition of
the NoI's leader, the American mass media did not create the Farrakhan phenomenon. It has been the Black Muslim minister's ability to
secure increasing popular black support without resorting to conventional methods of media manipulation—by steadily amassing direct
links with poorer black urban communities and engaging in a long-
running campaign to increase his elite and mass African-American
prestige—that has distinguished Farrakhan's steady rise to national
attention. Media coverage can of course assist an individual's campaign by amplifying his activism and disseminating his message. To
the extent that television viewers and newspaper readers are more
than passive receptors, however, the grounds for a positive predispo-
sition must typically be in place already for any media-filtered message to achieve significant mass resonance. Rather than create
Farrakhan, media coverage has served at best to animate preexisting
attitudes among African-Americans that were already favorable to
selective features of both the Black Muslim messenger and to parts of
the multifaceted message that he propounds.

In Farrakhan's instance, the positive reception of his message
has substantially been a function of the poverty of conditions—material, spiritual, and psychological—of many members of his putative
African-American audience. Farrakhan's popular black influence,
however, also depends in large part upon his continued political isolation and clear distance from the cadre of established national black
American political leadership. Reflecting widespread elite concern
about the minister's sharp and disrespectful criticisms of his fellow
African-Americans, Charles Rangel argued after the Million Man
March that Farrakhan would not intermittently "go off on the deep
end" in attacking parts of the black community if the minister was
actually seeking a genuine political leadership role.[81] Such a view,
while eminently rational, naively fails to acknowledge the centrality
of such spatial attacks to Farrakhan's overall political project. It is in
his vividly standing apart from conventional American political

procedures and processes—such as running for public office or lobby-ing legislative assemblies—that Farrakhan bases a substantial part of his mass black appeal, and upon which his political legitimacy largely depends. The NoI's leader rests many of his claims and aspirations to national political leadership of African-Americans upon his protest credentials and upon his manifest unwillingness to engage in the horse-trading, deal-making, and log-rolling that are the very essence of many (indeed, most) American politicians' electoral and institu-tional lives.

Therefore, Farrakhan's flirtation with elected politicians and his tentative overtures to other black organizations since 1984 have, paradoxically, partially compromised what had, until that point, represented an entirely novel political niche among national African-American leaders. The most delicate and demanding of political balancing acts is required of Farrakhan, between making only anti-Semitic and paranoid appeals that accord him no leadership creden-tials at all (thereby reducing him to an absurd, Sharptonesque cartoon figure of local notoriety but minimal national political and social con-sequence) and becoming an accepted and familiar part of the national black leadership cadre by tempering his extremist and hateful dis-course (thereby appearing to be no more of a distinctive voice for Afri-can-Americans than conventional black politicians). Much as the increasingly enthusiastic and effective participation over the last two decades of evangelical Christian preachers, such as Jerry Falwell and Pat Robertson, in Republican party politics frequently endangered the base of their popular support among the fundamentalist Christian right, so Farrakhan's political role is fraught with potential dangers for the Black Muslim's organizational and popular African-American bases. The less distinctive and exceptional the message that he pro-pounds (and the less vitriolic, offensive, and provocative the manner in which he publicly does so), the more Farrakhan forfeits his monop-oly upon the niche market of paranoid black American politics.

It is also here that one of the paradoxes of Farrakhan's role and influence—and also of the reactions to him by other black and non-black actors—assumes an especially pronounced political importance. Since his popular black appeal is based extensively—though not exclusively—on his protest credentials, the most logical course for those seeking to reduce that appeal is not, as Rowan and others argue, to censor Farrakhan by denying him the oxygen of national publicity. Rather, the most propitious course is actually to accord him the opportunity—even the responsibility—for implementing effective political, economic, and social change. By properly incorporating him within the national African-American leadership cadre, the strategy offers the opportunity of casting the Black Muslim as merely another conventional American politician. The credibility of his position then rests crucially upon the effective delivery of his many promises, a delivery inevitably complicated and frustrated by the realities of America's plural society and the complex cross-pressures that it exerts upon the governing institutions of the American polity.

Not only does the strategy involve substantial risk for established black American leaders, however—as Bradley found in 1985, as Mfume discovered in prematurely announcing the CBC–NoI Sacred Covenant in 1993, and as many blacks disappointingly found with the World Friendship Tour of 1996—but it also presumes that Farrakhan would actually be willing to compromise his oft-touted independent political credentials by agreeing to participate. Neither eventuality is likely. Having achieved an influential national leadership role through an explicitly unconventional protest route, by stressing and demonstrating the possibilities of private economic initiative, and by vigorously fanning the flames of nationwide political controversy, Farrakhan's desire to risk sacrificing his independence and popularity through being incorporated fully into the ranks of conventional black American political leaders is unlikely to be great.

As Gates compellingly observed, Farrakhan's political identity has been forged upon an uncompromising and unremitting antagonism to the self-image of America. So much of what Farrakhan does is expressly aimed at embellishing and flaunting that antagonistic image for all that it is worth: abusing established public American figures and institutions; attacking the United States as corrupt, degenerate, and doomed; and attaching himself to anti-American despots in Iran, Iraq, and Libya who most Americans understandably loathe and despise. In this respect, Farrakhan is no doubt sincere when he denies desiring entry into any American mainstream; but not so much because that mainstream is tainted and corrupt, more because such entry would inevitably deprive him of the irresponsible leadership role to which he has become so delightfully accustomed and that he has made his peculiar own. For the NoI's leader, giving comfort and solace to the enemy by conciliating with the existing system of oppression would be an utterly unforgivable betrayal of all that he has stood so resolutely for over the past forty years. Farrakhan's express role has consistently been—and remains—that of an unrecalcitrant and unapologetic black gadfly, not a constructive consensus-seeker. The marginal influence accorded any individual politician by public office in the United States has never proven remotely attractive to the NoI's leader. The final resting place in modern American history that Farrakhan evidently craves is less that of a repentant healer of the polity's deep societal wounds, and more that of a misunderstood martyr, unjustly crucified upon the cross of its chasmic racial divide.

SUMMARY

Farrakhan's growing appeal among African-Americans over recent years has its roots in the inter- and intra-racial fissures that remain deeply (if not intractably) embedded in American society in the 1990s. Widespread disillusionment with, and pronounced antipathy toward, white Americans explains much of the popular black appeal of the NoI's leader and accounts for the limited harm that Farrakhan's esoteric theological and conspiratorial claims inflict upon his mass impact. Farrakhan's biblical analogies of America as Babylon are largely tangential and superfluous to his broad appeal, but the belief that American society is fundamentally racist remains widely held by African-Americans. Events such as the King beating in 1992, the Fuhrman revelations in the Simpson trial of 1995, and the spate of black church attacks in 1995–96 confirmed for many black Americans their underlying skeptical beliefs about white Americans, the federal government, and the political and criminal justice systems—all familiar targets of Farrakhan's righteous fury and contempt.

Farrakhan undoubtedly has emerged as an uncompromising and aggressively articulate expression of the intense anger and deep frustration felt by the millions of black Americans desperate to halt and reverse the declining conditions of their individual lives and collective communities. Farrakhan represents a vicariously soothing funnel into which black resentments, fears, and bitterness toward white America can be poured, there to be cathartically replenished. Nonetheless, antiwhite sentiment represents a necessary, but by no means a sufficient, condition of the recent success of the Farrakhan phenomenon. Farrakhan's popular black appeal also rests crucially upon factors specific to African-Americans alone: the existence of strongly negative self-images and stereotypes; the high incidence among blacks of conservative and traditionalist social attitudes, values, and

beliefs; the partial and imperfect reflection of those conservative convictions by established African-American political leaders in representative governmental institutions; and the material actions and
accomplishments of the NoI in many deprived urban black communities across the United States. In running for black leadership by running against and running down black leaders, Farrakhan attacks not
only white, but also black, Americans. This combination of attacks
accords the minister the exceptional role and the unique leadership
niche that he occupies in American politics.

The slight prospect of Farrakhan's full and enduring incorporation into mainstream national black leadership also provides an acute
strategic political dilemma for both black and nonblack American politicians in terms of their relations with the NoI's leader and his organization. At once too extreme to be readily and wholly accepted into the
national black leadership mainstream and too popular among black
Americans to be either ignored entirely or marginalized successfully,
the threat that the emergent Farrakhan phenomenon poses to the
established national African-American political leadership cohort in
the United States is simultaneously substantial and difficult to
counter effectively and enduringly. It is this threat, and the Farrakhan
phenomenon's broader social and political significance in contemporary America, that we address in the concluding chapter.

NOTES TO CHAPTER 6

1. Quoted in Thomas, "Black Radical Taunts U.S. Jews," p. 7.
2. Gates, "The Charmer," p. 131.
3. E. J. Dionne Jr., *Why Americans Hate Politics* (New York: Simon and Schuster, 1991), pp. 336–37.
4. William Schneider, "The Black Vote and a Powell Candidacy," *National Journal* 27, no. 44 (28 October 1995), p. 2690.
5. See "Black Politics (2): Incivility," *The Economist*, 15 June 1996, p. 55. The article was in relation to Mayor Marion Barry's criticisms of the efforts of the control board, appointed by the 104th Congress, to balance the Washington D.C. budget.
6. Reed, "All for One."
7. Harold Cruse, *The Crisis of the Negro Intellectual* (New York: Quill, 1984), p. 157.
8. See Rovere, *Senator Joe McCarthy* (New York: Harper and Row, 1973).

9. Michael Cox, *U.S. Foreign Policy After the Cold War: Superpower without a Mission?* (Chatham, N.J.: RIAA, 1995).

10. See William Chafe, *The Unfinished Journey: America Since World War Two*, 2nd ed. (New York: Oxford University Press, 1991).

11. Lipset and Raab, *The Politics of Unreason*, p. 428.

12. "American Survey," *The Economist*, 3 March 1990.

13. See: Wilson, *The Declining Significance of Race* and *The Truly Disadvantaged*; and James Jennings, ed., *Race, Politics, and Economic Development* (New York: Verso, 1992).

14. See also: *The State of Black America 1994* (New York: National Urban League, 1994); and Hacker, *Two Nations*.

15. Claudette E. Bennett, *The Black Population in the United States: March 1994 and 1993*, U.S. Bureau of the Census, Current Population Reports, P20–480 (Washington, D.C.: U.S. Government Printing Office, 1995), p. 24.

16. Bennett, *The Black Population in the United States*, pp. 17–19.

17. See Stanfield, "Black Frustration," p. 1166.

18. Lipset and Raab, *The Politics of Unreason*, p. 509.

19. Clarence Lusane and Dennis Desmond, *Pipe Dream Blues: Racism and the War on Drugs* (Boston, Mass.: South End Press, 1991).

20. Quoted in Wright, "Fighting the Drug War."

21. See Seymour Martin Lipset, "Blacks and Jews: How Much Bias?," *Public Opinion*, July-August 1987.

22. See Morris and Rubin, "The Turbulent Friendship"; and Marable, "In the Business of Prophet Making."

23. See, for example, Sheila S. Walker, "The Black-Jewish Paradox: Ambivalence of U.S. Race Feeling," *Patterns of Prejudice*, 7, no. 3 (1973): 19–24.

24. See Kaufman, *Broken Alliance*; and the essay by Taylor Branch, "The Uncivil War: Blacks and Jews," *Esquire*, May 1989.

25. Lincoln, *The Black Muslims*, p. 271.

26. Lipset and Raab, *The Politics of Unreason*, p. 429.

27. Quoted in Barnes, "Farrakhan Frenzy."

28. See Reed, "All for One."

29. See: Nancee Lyons, "Muslim Guard Service Grows," *Emerge*, February 1993, p. 9; and Tate, *From Protest to Politics*, p. 161.

30. Baldwin, *The Fire Next Time*, p. 72.

31. See the opinion polls in: "The New Politics of Race," *Newsweek*, 6 May 1991, pp. 22–31; and Ron Faucheux, "Affirmative Reaction," *Campaigns and Elections*, April 1995, pp. 5, 45–46.

32. See Carmines and Stimson, *Issue Evolution*.

33. Stanley B. Greenberg, *Report on Democratic Defection* (Washington, D.C.: The Analysis Group) 15 April 1985, pp. 13–18.

34. It is especially noteworthy, in this regard, that analyses of American election results increasingly contain breakdowns of party identification and voting behavior categorized according to race. Black and white patterns are treated as almost entirely separate analytic foci. See, for example, Paul R. Abramson, John H. Aldrich, and David W. Rohde, *Change and Continuity in the 1992 Elections* (Washington, D.C.: Congressional Quarterly Press, 1995).

35. Sniderman and Piazza, *The Scar of Race*.

36. See the poll evidence in *The Washington Post National Weekly Edition*, 11–17 May 1992, p. 10.

37. Klein, "The threat of tribalism, p. 28."

38. The poll was based on telephone interviews with 1047 New Yorkers (484 whites and 408 blacks; persons with no opinions were excluded from the analysis). See *The New York Times*, 29 October 1990, Sec. A.

39. Reagan's launching of his 1980 presidential campaign at Neshoba County Fair, Philadelphia, near the site of the brutal murder of three civil rights workers in 1964, was a barely concealed nod in the direction of racial conservatives. With his espousal of the merits of states' rights, the traditional southern white defense for segregation during the 1950s and 1960s, the choice of venue was powerfully symbolic to both white and black Americans, in and outside the South.

40. Robert Singh, "The Rise and Fall of Legislative Service Organisations in the United States Congress," *Journal of Legislative Studies* 2, no. 2 (Summer 1996): 79–102.

41. Quoted in "Black Politics: No Sanctuary," *The Economist*, 15 June 1996, p. 55.

42. Faucheux, "Affirmative Reaction," p. 45.

43. Ferguson's actions won praise from Farrakhan's former national spokesperson, Khalid Muhammad, who claimed in a speech at Howard University that he "loved" Ferguson. According to Muhammad, "God spoke to Ferguson and said, 'Catch the train, Colin, catch the train.'" See Wendy Melillo and Hamil R. Harris, "Dissent Raised as Ex-Farrakhan Aide Returns to Howard," *The Washington Post*, 20 April 1994, p. B1.

44. One critic, for example, described the Taylor tome as "classic racism in a new form, a Protocols of the Elders of Africa written for a White suburban audience." See Mark Naison, "Jared Taylor's America: Black Man's Heaven, White Man's Hell," *Reconstruction* 2, no. 3 (1994): 64–66, at 66.

45. According to a *Time/CNN* poll in October 1995, 65 percent of whites believed that race relations in America would eventually improve, compared with only 44 percent of black Americans. While 56 percent of African-Americans did not think that discrimination against them would ever diminish, only 27 percent of whites agreed. See Richard Lacayo, "A Critical Mass," *Time*, 30 October 1995, pp. 34–35.

46. Hacker, *Two Nations*, p. 200.

47. See the discussion of "Negative Characterizations of Blacks," in Sniderman and Piazza, *The Scar of Race*, pp. 38–46.

48. Reed, "All for One."

49. In 1994, 73.8 percent of African-American women had at least a high school graduate education, compared with 71.7 percent of black men. Thirteen percent of black women and 12.8 percent of black men held a bachelor's degree or more. See Bennett, *The Black Population in the United States*, p. 10. Just over 7 million African-American women, compared to approximately 6.9 million men, were in the civilian labor force (p. 1).

50. In terms of the total number of African-Americans employed, black women made up 63.8 percent of all professional, 55.0 percent of all managerial, and 62.6 percent of all technical positions, compared with just 27.6 percent of blue collar ones, in 1990. See Hacker, *Two Nations*, p. 115.

51. See Arthur J. Norton and Louisa F. Miller, *Marriage, Divorce and Remarriage in the 1990s* (Washington, D.C.: U.S. Government Printing Office, 1992), Bureau of the Census, Current Population Reports, Series P23, No. 180, p. 4.

52. The lack of employment opportunities for African-American males in metropolitan centers is documented and discussed at length by Wilson in *The Truly Disadvantaged*.

53. Quoted in Don Terry, "In the End, Farrakhan Has His Day in the Sun," *The New York Times*, 17 October 1995, p. A19.

54. See "Minister Farrakhan Speaks," *The Phil Donahue Show*, 13 and 15 March 1990.

55. Indeed, the continued sensitivity of racial issues was made especially clear by the intense conflict that surrounded the publication in 1994 of the controversial book on race and intelligence, *The Bell Curve*.

56. Gallup poll cited by Martin Kilson, "Problems of Black Politics: Some Progress, Many Difficulties," *Dissent*, Fall 1989, p. 527.

57. Julianne Malveaux, "Black America's Abortion Ambivalence," *Emerge*, February 1993, pp. 33–34.

58. A detailed discussion of current African-American social and economic beliefs is contained in Lawrence Sigelman and Susan Welch, *Black Americans' View of Racial Inequality* (Cambridge, Mass.: Cambridge University Press, 1991).

59. Adam Meyerson, "Manna 2 Society: The Growing Conservatism of Black America," *Policy Review* 68 (1994), p. 5.

60. American Enterprise Institute poll, quoted in Kilson, "Problems of Black Politics," p. 527.

61. Carol M. Swain, *Black Faces, Black Interests: The Representation of African Americans in Congress* (Cambridge, Mass.: Harvard University Press, 1993), p. 11.

62. See the collection of essays in Joe Wood, ed., *Malcolm X: In Our Own Image* (New York: Anchor Books, 1994).

63. Quoted in Reed, "All for One."

64. The three most influential academic works in this respect are: David Mayhew, *Congress: The Electoral Connection* (New Haven: Yale University Press, 1974); Richard Fenno, *Home Style: House Members in Their Districts* (Boston: Little, Brown and Company, 1978); and Morris Fiorina, *Congress: Keystone of the Washington Establishment*, 2nd ed. (New Haven: Yale University Press, 1989).

65. Michael Foley, *The Rise of the British Presidency* (Manchester: Manchester University Press, 1993).

66. Reed, "All for One."

67. Farrakhan, *Independent Black Leadership in America*, p. 39.

68. Quoted in Williams, "Hiding from This Rage."

69. Excerpt from a Farrakhan speech at Cobal Hall, Detroit, Michigan, 8 February 1985. Cited in Gaber, "Lamb of God or Demagogue?," p. 111.

70. See "Farrakhan: Jackson has 'slave mentality'," *The Boston Globe*, 15 August 1988, p. 10.

71. Quoted in White, Thomas, and Salemy, "Farrakhan Defends World Tour."

72. Quoted in Nicoll, "Black Pride on the March Again."

73. See, for example, his addresses: "Disappointment in Leadership," delivered at Muhammad Temple No. 27, Los Angeles, California, 27 May 1987; and "The Need for Leadership: When Did It Begin?," delivered at Chicago, Illinois, 21 June 1987.

74. See: Walters, *Black Presidential Politics*; and Walters "Strategy for 1976: A Black Political Party," *Black Scholar* 7, no. 2 (1975): 8–19; and Chuck Stone, "Black Politics: Third Force, Third Party or Third-Class Influence?," *Black Scholar* 1, no. 2 (1969): 8–13.

75. Among a voluminous literature on American political parties, perhaps the most elegant and comprehensive analysis is provided in Leon E. Epstein, *Political Parties in the American Mold* (Madison: University of Wisconsin Press, 1986).

76. Walters, *Black Presidential Politics*. Aside from the profound inelegance of the term, the content of Walters's argument is not particularly persuasive. The dichotomy of independence and dependence is a largely artificial conceptual device, which hinges upon a notion of political independence that is asserted but never fully or adequately defined. Precisely what constitutes independence in a system that is inextricably fused by institutional structures that compel associative and coalitional forms of political behavior by individuals and collective groups alike, is difficult to establish.

77. Manning Marable, "Race, Identity, and Political Culture," p. 300.

78. Robert G. Newby, "The 'Naive' and the 'Unwashed': The Challenge of the Jackson Campaign at the Democratic Convention," in Barker and Walters, *Jesse Jackson's 1984 Presidential Campaign*, pp. 160–177, at 170.

79. See the account of Raphael J. Sonenshein, "Biracial Coalition Politics in Los Angeles," in Rufus P. Browning, Dale Rogers Marshall, and David H. Tabb, *Racial Politics in American Cities* (New York: Longman, 1990), pp. 33–48, at 45.

80. For a D.C. comparison, see Brian Kelly and Harry Jaffee, "The Farrakhan Fiasco," *Regardies*, (January 1990), pp. 47–55.

81. See Michael A. Fletcher and Dan Balz, "Farrakhan Seeks Wider Role: Some Black Leaders Are Conciliatory, Others Cautious," *The Washington Post*, 18 October 1995, p. A12.

7

Toward an American Apartheid: Farrakhan and Black Leadership in the 1990s

You are going to have to live with me. To some, I'm a nightmare. But to others, I'm a dream come true.

Louis Farrakhan, 1995[1]

Should Americans be concerned by the recent rise of Louis Farrakhan? Should they endeavor to counter him and the Nation of Islam (NoI) and, if so, how? Such questions have informed the plentiful public and private discussions of the minister and his organization that have occurred both before and since the Million Man March. Most American critics, however, have responded with notably sanguine and subdued assessments of the scale and seriousness of the threat that Farrakhan represents to American racial comity. Their clear and concerted repudiation of his views notwithstanding, the fissiparous dangers that the Farrakhan phenomenon poses to the national fabric of American social relations have been conventionally interpreted as being so slight as to be barely worth either prolonged or animated consideration; as straining that otherwise robust fabric, perhaps, but not as causing anything remotely resembling its unraveling or eventual decomposition.

Such phlegmatic sagacity is founded upon a confidence about the American polity's fundamental resilience, and its effective resistance to forces of fragmentation, that is historically well-rooted. After all, as the Oxford political scientist, Desmond King, has rightly observed, "The United States has a remarkable capacity, demonstrated by its history, to absorb and transcend social and political problems."[2] Few political extremists have ever managed to constitute more than passing and

289

minor irritants to the American body politic; few societal conflicts have been so enduring as to be unamenable to resolution; and still fewer social problems have animated a pervasive sense of their complete intractability. Such historic precedents must surely augur well for the many critics and opponents of Farrakhan today, and should also instill among seekers of racial comity in the United States a reasonably well-grounded optimism and informed confidence: that the burden of proof for those who discern in the "American Dilemma" a problem that defies full or enduring resolution resides more firmly and heavily upon their pessimistic side of skepticism and doubt.

At a minimum, however, the Farrakhan phenomenon represents a clear, rich, and timely warning to Americans of undeniable political importance. The oft-touted African-American rationale for dealing with the NoI's leader—of ignoring the fireman's background in the scorching face of a rapidly burning national home—in itself implicitly concedes that Farrakhan's political beliefs, paranoid appeals, and popular black impact are at once exceptional, contentious, and deeply disturbing to many American citizens. That Farrakhan attracts such extensive and antipathetic public and media attention currently—and frequently evokes the most extreme and vituperative of critical reactions—by virtue of his distinctive role, uncompromising message, and aggressive approach in contemporary American politics is transparent enough to even the most inattentive of observers. That many elements of Farrakhan's paranoid and reactionary message should resonate so strongly among African-Americans is powerfully indicative of the grievously strained and mutually suspicious relations of America's races in the 1990s. And that thousands of African-Americans should even contemplate seeking an appropriate solution to their desperate plight in Farrakhan (much less actually finding one) is a stunning and tragically eloquent indictment of the parlous social and economic environment that many black citizens continue to endure in the United States.

For Farrakhan to have become a genuine player within the national African-American leadership cadre is hence, without doubt, a legitimate cause for widespread concern among Americans of all races. The NoI leader's seemingly unerring facility to be accorded such extensive (albeit intermittent) media attention and to cause such recurrent bouts of nationwide public anxiety, anger, and distress is testimony both to his shrewdly demagogic political skills and tactics and to the unusual constellation of social and political forces propelling his outspoken message across America. The rivers of ink that have been spilled on discussing, denouncing, and defending Farrakhan—a charismatic and intelligent man whose delusions of personal grandeur and visions of all-encompassing conspiracies entertain few apparent bounds or doubts—represent a peculiar homage to a curious American public figure whose many eccentricities and contradictions have more helped than hindered his steady national political ascendancy. Farrakhan's prophetic convictions may rightly be ridiculed and his eclectic doctrinal beliefs roundly repudiated, but no thoughtful American can any longer dismiss the deeply resonant and disharmonic chords that the minister has clearly struck among black Americans at large.

Nonetheless, the distinctive features of the Farrakhan phenomenon also reveal a more fundamental and important fact about current national black American leadership in the United States more broadly, namely, its advanced incorporation within mainstream American politics. Although frequently overlooked, national black American political leadership in the 1990s reveals the pluralistic features that have traditionally been common to conventional American politics more generally: fragmentation, differentiation, competition, dissensus, and the overarching need to forge majority coalitions in order to achieve desired public policy goals. The modernization of national black leadership, in so far as this entails its exhibiting characteristics more familiar than exceptional in American politics more broadly, has reached an unprecedentedly mature mark and a seemingly entrenched level. Farrakhan, then, represents paradoxically both a confirmation and an indirect product of the very success, rather than the failure, of the aspirations of civil rights era activists to black political empowerment.

In this respect, although it is undeniably politically significant that national black American political, religious, and civic leaders have thus far failed collectively to condemn Farrakhan, it remains of markedly less political importance than their near-universal and persistent refusal to embrace him—a dogged and determined refusal that even the Million Man March failed fundamentally to alter. While that commendable and consistent reluctance remains intact, as it surely must, Farrakhan and the NoI pose no consequential threat to white Americans. They remain a nagging irritation and a grievous offense to many, a gnawing annoyance and an ugly political curiosity to most, certainly. Neither Farrakhan nor his unconventional organization, however, ought to preoccupy white American and Jewish attentions

unduly. Farrakhan's impact on public policy in America has been minimal. Despite the march and the new political legitimacy that it
undoubtedly conferred upon Farrakhan, his NoI has not won legions
of new African-American recruits; its leader has not obtained elite
black agreement with his reactionary public philosophy and its avowedly separatist racial goals; nor has Farrakhan's extremely unorthodox Islamic creed secured anything remotely approximating mass
adherents among black Americans at large. The palpable scar that the
Farrakhan phenomenon has left upon the American body politic is a
relatively minor one, and an unfortunate political abrasion the ultimate indelibility of which remains in doubt. Not only are the many
obstacles to his further advance strong, but Farrakhan is also, fundamentally, the symptom, not the cause, of the twin current crises of
black American communities and national African-American political
leadership.

Rather, it is the multifarious grounds of the Farrakhan phenomenon that demonstrably represent the more entrenched, formidable, and
dangerous threats to the racial and ethnic fabric of American social life
as the end of the twentieth century approaches. And it is to the several
pillars upon which the shaky yet resilient edifice of Farrakhan's
politics of organized hate is constructed that Americans must closely
and assiduously attend, if that repellent and reprehensible form of politics is to be convincingly challenged and ultimately overcome: the
continuing, disproportionate social and economic maladies of black
Americans; the perpetuation of prejudice, discrimination, and negative
stereotypes of blacks among both white and African-Americans; and,
not least, the national dialogue about race in America that occurs substantially in private and in isolation, all of which assist the advance of
an impending epoch in which black and white Americans know each
other as fellow citizens only in the most shallow and superficial of
fashions, vicariously and involuntarily, from the books they read, the
films they watch, the music to which they listen, and the multicultural
courses for which they are required to register—not from personal contact and uncoerced experience.

For the increasingly pervasive culture of group separation in the
United States that Farrakhan enthusiastically celebrates and promotes
is also one that is increasingly sustained by civics texts and sanctified
in American universities. It is also, moreover, a culture that can serve
as the midwife to a taciturn child of racial ignorance, the catalyst of an
American public discourse about race in which the principal actors—

in city centers, college campuses, and civic groups alike—are frequently accustomed to talking at and across, rather than to, each other. And it is upon the lack of meaningful, candid, and, above all, empathetic dialogue about race that Farrakhan's poisonous and pernicious appeals to mutual racial fear, ignorance, and hostility partially rest.

Neither white nor black Americans bear the exclusive responsibility for the growth of an American public life whose distinguishing feature is the degree to which contemporary race relations are animated by deep mutual suspicion and a starkly intense animosity. Until both African-American and nonblack politicians, however, achieve a substantial material improvement in the everyday lives of most black citizens in the United States, the several grounds of the Farrakhan phenomenon will stay abundantly fertile for the destructive seeds of civic discord that the minister so widely and eagerly scatters. No matter how sincere and deeply held are the convictions of those public figures and politicians that subscribe to a genuinely multicultural public philosophy, that contemporary mantra has instead, in its present form, given rise to a series of effectively monocultural American enclaves. Although, in sharp contrast to the old South African regime, the process has neither express legal sanction nor an explicit public rationale, the United States is assuredly moving toward a twenty-first century society in which black and white Americans lead wholly separate lives, inhabit markedly dissimilar worlds (both physically and culturally), and regard each other with increasing dismay, suspicion, and hostility as aliens and strangers in the same land: a veritable American apartheid.

THE TALISMAN OF THE PAST

In heralding, and in large part hastening, the impending arrival of that ignoble and parlous adversarial state, Farrakhan's abiding apostolic role has been one that has rightly been accorded increasingly fulsome critical attention in America. For Farrakhan has undoubtedly emerged as the most charismatic, shrewd, and successful leader that the NoI has enjoyed in its entire institutional existence thus far. In pioneering the resurgence of the revived and fundamentalist NoI, Farrakhan has represented an especially innovative and determinedly bold leader, not least in his carefully guiding the organization's gradual (though still only partial and faltering) entry into the national American political arena.

Nonetheless, for all his impressively effective strategic and tactical innovations, and his unprecedentedly unremitting self-promotion, Farrakhan's leadership also evinces important continuities with Elijah's NoI. In particular, Farrakhan's invocations of an apparently prosperous future of racial separatism for black Americans are based in large part upon a clear summoning of, and an abiding return to, the past. In style, rhetoric, message, and even personal appearance, Farrakhan explicitly recalls and revives the legacy of Malcolm X during his NoI period. In analysis, Farrakhan's explanations for contemporary black American socioeconomic ills powerfully echo those of the Black Muslims in the pre–civil rights era (and, before them, those of Booker T. Washington and Marcus Garvey). In prescriptions, Farrakhan seeks to reformulate the black nationalist and separatist agenda of the early-middle years of the twentieth century for the fin de siècle. And in his outsider, spatial leadership stratagem, Farrakhan evokes the "prepolitical," protest era of mass black American agitation (albeit with a venom toward other black leaders with which the internal clashes of the desegregation movement brook no comparison). The Million Man March on Washington represented Farrakhan's most audacious attempt to revive and, in the process, successfully to surpass the triumphant direct action mobilization efforts of the civil rights movement during the 1960s—an innovative political initiative in the context of the 1990s, but one that purposefully recalled earlier periods of mass black action and one, moreover, whose principal function of drawing a vivid contrast with other contemporary black leaders would have no doubt made Elijah Muhammad particularly proud.

In sum, Farrakhan represents a reactionary American figure par excellence, not only in his profoundly conservative (indeed, unabashedly repressive) worldview, but also in the sense that he adheres to a core conviction that "the past was better than the present and that society should be turned completely around."[3] Separation of the races, internal black unity based upon a presumed—almost metaphysical—commonality of African-American interests, and the vigorous reinstitution of conservative, traditionalist cultural values together represent the only possible paths to a full and virtuous reinvigoration of black Americans (whether in the United States itself or abroad in a new African homeland, under Farrakhan's benevolent dictatorship). Farrakhan's authoritarian prescriptions and paranoid prophecies are thus truly constitutive of a peculiar, "back to the future" conception of collective African-American welfare and black empowerment. A

mythical, idealized past (albeit in a somewhat different guise), however, is one that many thousands of white Americans are also apt to
find especially comforting and congenial in the disconcerting midst of
profound socioeconomic change and pervasive uncertainty about the
future. Few Americans reject the largely inchoate, but instinctively
appealing, incantations of "family values" and homilies to "community," whatever their race or religion. Indeed, one of the few features
that links together Farrakhan, Newt Gingrich, and Hillary Rodham
Clinton is the often trite platitudes and disturbingly vacuous paeans to
family and community that so frequently punctuate their various
speeches and publications.

The minister's reactionary strategy, however, is also one that is
designed to serve Farrakhan's personal political objectives. In both
evoking and invoking the past, Farrakhan necessarily, and clearly,
draws the attention of African Americans at large (as well as that of
nonblacks) to the present configuration and limited influence of the
national black political leadership cohort. Notwithstanding his barely
concealed public aspirations to join—indeed, to assume the supreme
or preeminent leadership position within—its elite ranks, Farrakhan's
express presence outside the conventional constellation of elective
national black political leaders has served a dual function for the NoI
leader: as a fundamental bulwark of his individual political authority,
and as a transparent indication of the inadequate structure, Pyrrhic
achievements, and deeply entrenched internal fissures of the existing
leadership cadre of African-Americans. As the symbolic black American talisman of the past, Farrakhan thus forges a potent popular political appeal for the present, in the face of which his established
national black leadership colleagues are apt to muster only a tremu-
lous, uncertain, and vacillating response.

The political irony in this respect is indeed a very powerful one.
For in the aftermath of the brutal assassinations of Malcolm X and
Martin Luther King Jr. in the 1960s, national black American politicians invariably sought to stress the pressing political imperative of
developing collective leadership mechanisms. Reliance upon a single,
heroic, concrete leadership figure as some form of exceptional and
especially enlightened savior for black Americans collectively was
subject to a near-universal rejection, in favor of a more abstract and
diffuse set of discrete, electorally accountable career politicians. As
then CBC chairman Parren Mitchell (D-MD) put it in 1977, African
Americans could no longer afford the tragically expensive "luxury"

of a single black leader—titular or otherwise—in the post–civil rights era.[4]

The persistence, however, of pronounced socioeconomic inequalities and the deep malaise of many black communities during a period in which African-American politics has become regularized along the lines of dominant American politics have increasingly seemed to attest only to the practical inadequacy of that very notion. The dramatic emergence of Jesse Jackson in the 1980s, and later Farrakhan in the 1990s, has in part answered a desire among many black Americans—and also among whites seeking to simplify increasingly complex and pluralistic collective black leadership structures—to vest their hopes and aspirations instead in a single, readily identifiable black leadership figure, an incontrovertible "race fighter" capable of dealing directly and effectively with white power-brokers. The old paternalistic white question of "what do your people want?" is assuredly more easily posed when addressed to an individual black leader. Indeed, one of the more curious ironies of Farrakhan's rise, in this regard, is that it lends that very staid and patronizing question renewed salience and vigor for many whites, by obscuring not only the pronounced pluralism of modern black political structures but also the marked heterogeneity of black Americans' policy priorities and preferences at the mass level.

However acute that irony appears, though, it is one that is most definitely not lost upon the leader of the NoI. In fact, it has powerfully informed Farrakhan's strategic political calculus for well over a decade now, in making unmistakably clear the vivid and substantial contrast between himself and other national black political leaders. Like the overwhelming majority of their nonblack counterparts, African-American leaders currently emphasize electoral mobilization at the expense, though not the complete exclusion, of protest or extrasystemic political tactics. Those tactics that a generation earlier had been at the very heart of the landmark movement for black freedom (sit-ins, boycotts, teach-ins, selective buying campaigns, strikes, civil disobedience, and popular demonstrations of all kinds) have subsequently become minimized by, and have steadily emerged as marginal to, the increasingly dominant behavioral framework of current national black political life in the United States.

Farrakhan therefore seeks to cast himself in a distinctive contemporary political light by establishing a symbolic political link to the historic legacies of major African-American activists of the past, such as King, Malcolm, Paul Robeson, Fannie Lou Hamer, and A. Philip Randolph, all of whom were decidedly influential and respected figures in national black politics, yet none of whom were elected public officials nor drew their considerable political authority expressly from the electoral arena. Farrakhan would no doubt agree with the forceful assessment of Manning Marable, that current black American politicians have forgotten the past's lessons and tactics, and instead invest too heavily in a systemic political process that was never really designed either to articulate black grievances effectively or to address their demands fully.[5] But it is, nonetheless, to this apparent crisis of national African-American leadership that Farrakhan opportunistically addresses many of his public lectures and bases much of his own popular political appeal.

Of course, it is at minimum mildly surprising that precisely at the time that black political representation is at its height in federal, state, and local government, national black political leadership is widely held (far beyond Farrakhan) to be in such an acute state of crisis. Although the periodic issuance of such critical charges has been a relatively familiar feature of academic and journalistic discourse about national black politics in the United States for the last two decades now, the current crop of scathingly negative assessments possess a strong and compelling resonance in historical terms, in large measure precisely because of the successful incorporation of black Americans into mainstream political processes. The argument that national-level African-American politics has moved "from protest to politics" is now sufficiently well-established as to be unremarkable, and almost staid, in character. Indeed, U.S. political scientists have extensively documented the marked degree to which many contemporary black politicians resemble white political entrepreneurs in their organizational bases, campaign styles, and institutional behavior.

The rich resonance of interpretations of a black American leadership crisis is not, however, entirely perverse as the twenty-first century approaches, at least when the socioeconomic fortunes of African-Americans collectively are considered. For most social groups in the United States, the achievement of government office and representation in legislative assemblies has, after all, either resulted in or coincided with significant improvements in their social and economic conditions. Black Americans historically not only suffered far more grievously from slavery, legally sanctioned and heinously enforced segregation, and informal discrimination and prejudice than did other

Americans, but the difficult and immensely costly struggle to secure their basic civil and political rights has also occupied many painful decades. African-Americans have only been included in American politics and society as full citizens for a marked minority of the nation's history. The relative lack of progress for black Americans collectively—and the deterioration in day-to-day living conditions that many have experienced in both relative and absolute terms—therefore assumes a particularly pronounced, profound, and puzzling problem when juxtaposed with their growing political empowerment in the post–civil rights era.

Thus, the formal inclusion of black Americans as full citizens in the U.S. political system since 1965 has been accompanied not by universal material improvements, but instead by the continued exclusion of millions of African-Americans from the type of economic prosperity, security, and social well-being that is taken virtually for granted by most American citizens. At the same time, and especially since the early 1990s, black elective office-holding has attained proportions almost commensurate with the percentage of African-Americans in the U.S. population as a whole. The traditional explanation offered by many social scientists for the overrepresentation of African-Americans in the section of U.S. society conventionally classified as poor, namely, their underrepresentation in democratic governmental institutions, therefore no longer appears so persuasive. Moreover, with federal, state, and local public policies that are geared specifically to assist black Americans having been on the statute books for almost three decades now (such as affirmative action and minority set-aside programs), and with the arrival in America since 1965 of other racial and ethnic groups who have also faced deep prejudice (but nonetheless achieved remarkably impressive levels of economic affluence and educational attainment), the persistence of grievous and disproportionate African-American deprivation represents an entirely exceptional state that demands explanation. And, as we have seen earlier in this book, the NoI's leader has many strikingly distinctive, extremely elaborate, and logically related explanations for black Americans' contemporary fortunes readily at hand.

As Farrakhan is well aware, the contemporary crisis of national African-American leadership has thus emerged not from a period of sullen and rapid retreat, but rather from a process of substantial political advancement, that is, the near-complete achievement of "fair" minority representation in government offices and legislative assemblies.

The passage of the 1965 Voting Rights Act, its subsequent amendment in 1970, 1975, and 1982, combined with the Supreme Court's *Thornburgh v. Gingles* (1986) decision, together served powerfully to expand the number of black American politicians elected to representative assemblies at both state and federal levels. That expansion nonetheless advanced the focus of black aspirations to the delivery of material, distributive benefits and to the enactment of effective policy changes to improve directly the lives of most African-Americans nationwide. These substantive benefits, thus far, for many African-American communities have been either few, inadequate, or nonexistent. For inner-city black Americans, especially, the social and economic problems have been exacerbated by the diminishing populations of central city areas and, in consequence, the steeply declining congressional representation and contracting tax bases of the (increasingly black) governing city regimes.[6] And it is this fundamental and acute dilemma that lies at the very heart of the current leadership problems facing African-Americans occupying positions in urban government offices and representing metropolitan districts in Congress: the jarring juxtaposition of increasing political empowerment and persistent material deprivation.

That acute dilemma is also seriously compounded by the relative lack of feasible electoral, party, and policy options that are available to mainstream national black American politicians in the U.S. political system. Collective black electoral independence is as much a political chimera for African-Americans as it is for all other social groups in the United States. The logic of the single-member plurality American electoral system strongly encourages competition between political parties to assume a two-party character. Third parties and third candidates at the presidential level invariably fare notoriously badly in such a majoritarian system (much as they do in the U.K.'s parliamentary, but plurality, system). Only those parties and candidates with a well-defined issue appeal and a geographically concentrated base of substantial electoral support enjoy the prospect of some success in national American elections. Black Americans, dispersed across the nation and in no state representing anything near a majority of the voting age population, simply cannot afford the false luxury of separate, third-party efforts, of "refusing to compromise" with the remainder of the U.S. electorate. Although it certainly cannot guarantee their effective delivery, only a politics of cross-racial coalition-building offers the genuine prospect of African-Americans securing substantial concessions in the form of policy outputs by the state; a politics of electoral separatism is ultimately self-defeating, for black Americans as much as—indeed, crucially, more than—for any other social group.

In this regard, although regularly promoted by some black politicians and commentators as a viable method of advancing black Americans' policy priorities and preferences to material effect, the electoral prospects for a third black political party in the United States are not at all impressive. An independent black political party or independent African-American presidential candidate would be unable to call upon a sufficiently concentrated demographic base of electoral support to secure either legislative seats in Congress or electoral college votes; would be highly unlikely to win the unanimous political endorsement of black elected officials; would probably not manage to attract anything resembling a unanimous black popular vote; and would inevitably be subject to the compelling charge of black votes being "wasted" in the particular cause. (This is notwithstanding the likely prospect of an antiblack reaction or backlash among nonblack voters nationwide.) The inherent logic of such a black party or individual candidacy would ultimately replicate on a national scale that of the third-party black candidate, Charles Evers, in the Senate contest in Mississippi in 1978: in splitting the most anticonservative political forces and thereby allowing the more conservative, Republican candidate (then Thad Cochran) to emerge electorally victorious.[7] Political independence in U.S. elections represents a fundamentally doomed and delusory design for genuine black progress.

In electoral and party terms, then, the vast majority of black elected officials in America are, and will in all probability remain, firmly but uncomfortably wedded to the Democratic party, the home of racial liberalism since 1964. Even with the Democrats as the majority party in Congress, however, the policy concessions that African-American officeholders have been able to achieve for blacks nationwide have been relatively modest (though certainly not insignificant). As a numerical minority of a minority legislative party—as occurred in the 104th Congress after the dramatic Republican sweep in the 1994 congressional mid-term elections—such policy concessions would invariably be more meager still. The strategic political options available to black elected officials and voters seeking a greater attentiveness by national policy makers in the United States to the grievous conditions and disproportionate problems facing many African-American communities are thus exceedingly few, weak, and unattractive.[8]

It is partly for this reason that Farrakhan has increasingly been able to pose such ample and acute strategic and tactical difficulties for established national black political and civic leaders during the 1990s. For nonelected black activists such as Farrakhan, the plentiful seeds of frustration, resentment, and anger that years of benign neglect have sown among many African-Americans offer a potentially rich, though exceedingly bitter, political crop for strident racial militancy and reactionary extremism to reap. The issuance of viscerally extreme indictments and nonnegotiable demands; the outspoken conspiratorial claims of deliberate, malign neglect by whites, government, and Jews alike; and the aggressively populist proselytizing in favor of simplistic political solutions to persistently grave and complex socioeconomic problems—the false fanaticist panaceas that Farrakhan offers of racial separation, cultural disengagement, and economic and social retrenchment—together attract much media attention and win the NoI leader significant popular support and sympathy among African-Americans. They consistently avoid, however, the most fundamental and pressing issues of how a deprived minority in the United States, whose policy preferences on matters concerning the role of government in ensuring the citizenry's collective economic welfare are simply not shared by the vast majority of Americans, can best utilize its limited economic muscle, social resources, and political capital in order to secure substantive and enduring advances for its members. The rotten political harvest that Farrakhan has personally gathered in from a politics of organized racial hatred fundamentally lacks any semblance of either a coherent public program or a plausible bargaining strategy by which to realize material gains for the putative objects of his nationwide activism.

Lest that damning failure occasion an indulgent complacency among observers of Farrakhan's peculiar national progress, however, it is worth emphasizing that the dilemma of achieving effective political influence for a racial minority is not one that is solely confined to black elected officials and other African-American elites. For, as 1992's L.A. riots so vividly and devastatingly demonstrated to the entire nation, the tinderbox of latent racial tension and animosity in America that has been so inexorably crafted over three turbulent centuries of conflict still requires only a few potent sparks to ignite. The resulting explosions may have left the destructive economic and social debris scattered primarily among the already-strained urban communities of the African-American underprivileged themselves; but the social and political wounds remain visibly and deeply etched upon the American body politic more broadly. The apprehensions of white Americans prior to the Simpson verdict and the Million Man March, for example, were sufficiently palpable as virtually to clear the downtown areas of L.A. and D.C., respectively, in two days in October 1995.

While African-Americans cannot see clear and substantial benefits in the form of material policy outputs from their elected cadre of officials, the hollow and false blandishments of unelected extremist figures promising a better future by returning to a mythical past of collective order and group autonomy will therefore doubtless remain tenaciously attractive. The starkly brutal racial animus that informs such prescriptions will also continue to render white reservations and suspicions of their African-American compatriots ever more broad, deep, and fearful. And it is in these respects that Farrakhan, an undistinguished but exceptionally dedicated architect of black pride and white fear alike, stands as the clearest contemporary counterpoint to and confirmation of the "Americanization" of the national black leadership elite that has occurred since 1965.

THE AMERICANIZATION OF BLACK LEADERSHIP: THE DIMENSIONS OF INCORPORATION

The move of black American politics into the national mainstream has often been taken for granted by critics of U.S. politics, yet has rarely been appropriately or fully disaggregated. In discussing this notion, it is important to stress immediately that black and white politics have not yet reached a state of full parity. Most notable, whereas black Americans across the United States remain conspicuously willing to vote for white candidates in American elections, whites generally display a pronounced reluctance to endorse black candidates for elective office, at federal and state levels in particular. Much of this bifurcation in the incidence of cross-racial voting is of course explicable in terms of traditional liberal-conservative ideological divisions rather than race per se. Ideology, however, explains only part of the elective racial dichotomy. With black candidates in statewide (and federal) contests, as Sonenshein argues, "even when race is not an overt campaign issue, it is deeply embedded in the election."[9] The transformation that has been wrought so dramatically in American racial politics since 1965 has clearly not yet encompassed the achievement of a truly race-neutral U.S. polity.

Black American politics, however, has itself become Americanized over these years: that is, it has come to evince the same characteristics and core traits of mainstream American politics more generally. In this respect, the Farrakhan phenomenon serves as a very useful window upon the five central features of national black political leadership in the 1990s: fragmentation, differentiation, dissensus, competition, and incorporation. The responses of national black political elites to Farrakhan—and their commendably protracted resistance to his spatial leadership appeals—has both reflected and rested upon the advanced incorporation of African-American leadership into conventional political structures and dominant modes of U.S. political behavior more generally. For the NoI's leader, that incorporation serves as both an enticing opportunity and a significant constraint. The former, in that it affords Farrakhan a novel niche as an unelected, outsider, protest-style activist, able to appeal to African-Americans on the basis of forging a collective solidarity and unity in the face of great racial adversity. The latter, in that Farrakhan's prophetic project necessarily founders upon the pluralistic dimensions of the African-American community and its national black leadership cadre. Although he can claim his damaging and pernicious place therein and continue to court its many well-respected and responsible members, the preeminent and commanding position to which Farrakhan aspires among national black leaders is also one to which he remains denied.

The fragmentation of black leadership has accompanied the exponential growth in the number of black elected officials since 1965 and has occurred along both vertical and horizontal dimensions. Divisions now exist not only between different African-American groups at the federal and state levels but also within them. To the traditional civil rights organizations such as the NAACP, SCLC, and NUL have been added new and substantially expanded umbrella and peak groups such as the Leadership Conference on Civil Rights; national black organizations representing elected African-American officials (such as the CBC, National Conference of Mayors); organized interest lobbies for minority enterprises and corporations (such as the Black Business Council); research institutes specializing in African-American political, economic, and social affairs (such as the Washington,

D.C.–based Joint Center for Political and Economic Studies); and accomplished individual black political entrepreneurs (such as Jackson, Wilder, Mfume, and Schmoke).

Such leadership heterogeneity was also apparent at the 1995 CBC legislative weekend, the annual national gathering of black American political and social elites. The event was not only the largest ever for the caucus in terms of numbers, but also its most diverse in terms of attendees. The CBC itself encompassed an unprecedentedly large and diverse membership in terms of region, gender, partisanship, seniority, generation, and urban-rural cleavages. The previous year, Mfume, chairman during the 103rd Congress, had been moved publicly to state that the organization could no longer operate on the principle of unanimity—a belated recognition of a long-established reality.

Leadership fragmentation also reflects a growing process of differentiation among black Americans. This intrablack differentiation process has occurred along both economic and territorial cleavages, with a growing African-American middle class increasingly located outside the central city in suburban or near-suburban residential areas. As chapter six argued, Farrakhan has sought to exploit this development, to the extent that the economic foundations of the NoI's public program (such as it is) coincide with the economic agenda of the growing African-American petit bourgeoisie. However bizarre, distasteful, and objectionable his theological convictions, anti-Semitism, and the noneconomic dimensions of the NoI's program, Farrakhan's ringing endorsement of private and individualistic principles of economic behavior resonates powerfully among black American elites.

Farrakhan's exploitation of such cross-pressures within the black community is also linked to the development of national black political leadership dissensus. These problems of dissensus have centered primarily upon the pressing questions of both political objectives and strategies. In relation to the former, confidence in both the possibility and the desirability of achieving an integrated U.S. society has been waning dramatically among black Americans at large since the late 1980s. Skepticism over the Democratic party's commitment to black American priorities has become widespread at a mass level among African-Americans, as well as among many national black political elites. Moreover, according to the Black Politics Study, support for an independent black American political party and other forms of self-segregation and black nationalism had reached an all-time high among African Americans by the early 1990s. Fully half of all black Americans surveyed supported the idea of an independent black political party.

Against this background, established black political and civic leaders have confronted powerful strategic incentives to adopt accommodationist tactics toward those African-American activists (including, most notably, Farrakhan and the NoI) who consistently eschew the politics of moderation, conciliation, and interracial coalition-building in favor of militancy, nonnegotiable demands, and separatist racial extremism. The marked political dissensus surrounding Farrakhan provides telling and important indicators of his current role and influence. At its simplest, for other national black political actors, Farrakhan is simultaneously too influential to ignore completely and too controversial to embrace fully. The responses of many national black political and social elites to the NoI and its leader, consequently, appear to some observers as an astonishingly unimpressive and ineffective melange of inconsistency, equivocation, and uncertainty. The termination of the CBC–NoI Sacred Covenant, the intra- and extra-CBC divisions on rebuking Khalid Muhammad's viciously anti-Semitic and homophobic Kean College diatribe, and the appearance of leading and well-respected national African-American politicians on public platforms with Farrakhan all reveal the very acute difficulties facing established national black civil and political leaders in seeking an effective and enduring rapprochement with the Black Muslim leader.

Such dissensus has, moreover, reflected and reinforced the existence of growing competition among national black political elites in the United States. Although present to a limited extent for many decades previously, intrablack competitive pressures have increasingly assumed three especially dominant forms in the 1990s: electoral, financial, and policy. Each arena of competition testifies to an African-American political leadership cadre that manifests characteristics that powerfully resemble those of nonblack elite politics. Each, moreover, affords Farrakhan further political opportunities to embellish his self-proclaimed status as the most indefatigable, articulate, and dedicated defender of authentic mass black American interests.

Electoral competition among black Americans now occurs both within and between the two major political parties. Reform of the Voting Rights Act has caused unprecedented numbers of black American candidates to win election to federal and state legislatures. Increasing numbers of black congressional incumbents have confronted general and primary election challenges and several were defeated in both the 1992 and 1994 election cycles. Moreover, black partisan identification has also begun to shift perceptibly. While black Americans still identify overwhelmingly with the Democratic party, unanimous black support has begun to crumble. White gubernatorial candidates in Illinois and Ohio in 1994, for example, captured over 30 percent of the African-American vote. Increasing numbers of black Republicans have also contested and won congressional and state legislative elections, the two most notable being Gary Franks (R-CT), the first black Republican elected to the House since the New Deal, and J. C. Watts (R-OKL). Both admittedly represented majority-white districts, but their careers demonstrate—at a minimum—the increasing willingness of aspirant black American politicians to identify and align with the Republican party. Indeed, of sixty-two African-American candidates for Congress in 1994, fully twenty-four were Republicans. Even the candidacy of Alan Keyes for the Republican party's 1996 presidential nomination, though doomed from the very outset, represented an important symbolic breakthrough in black American penetration of the GOP's elite political circles, while Colin Powell's joining the party has provided the Republican party with its most nationally prominent and well-respected black member this century, in what may well come to be seen by future American historians as a landmark political event. The sixty-year lock of the Democrats upon black politicians' career aspirations and mass African-American electoral loyalties remains decidedly strong, but it is no longer free from serious, shrewd, and increasing challenge.

The financial dimension of intrablack competition has centered on the need of individuals and organizations to attract sufficient funds to achieve and maintain economic viability—a requirement compounded by the relative lack of available resources among black American communities. For established organizations such as the NAACP, for example, the need to acquire new members in order to operate effectively is fundamental. In the NAACP's case, this need served as an extremely powerful incentive to Ben Chavis to adopt a more aggressive black nationalist stance in 1993–94. Indeed, the acute financial crisis of the nation's leading historic civil rights organization over 1993–96 served as a stark and powerful reminder of the changing dynamics—political, generational, social, and ideological—of national black American politics in the 1990s.[10]

Policy competition has also developed between rival black American organizations to develop appropriate policy proposals and programs, capable of successful legislative passage and effective implementation, to address black Americans' social and economic concerns. Even within black progressive ranks, skeptical voices have been raised over established liberal public policy and juridical totems, such as racial quotas in education and employment and affirmative gerrymandering. In addition, though, the growth of a significant cadre of both conservative (Sowell, Loury, Williams) and revisionist liberal African-American intellectuals (Steele, Carter, Wilson), skeptical of existing public programs such as affirmative action and minority business set-asides, has strongly increased the competitive character of policy entrepreneurship among national black elites. Although the extent and material mass significance of the intrablack elite dissensus has been widely called into question, the very fact of its existing and provoking a vigorous response—if not quite a dialogue—between the distinct contemporary and historic intellectual tendencies in African-American critical thought is a development of cardinal political importance. [11]

The four preceding emergent features of current national black political leadership, however, also indicate the fifth and, incontestably, the most important dimension of contemporary national black American politics in the United States: incorporation. As the Million Man March demonstrated so vividly, the responses of many African-American elites to the NoI leader have assuredly lacked either clear direction or notable conviction. Those reactions have certainly alternated, at times oscillating rapidly, between accommodationist impulses and exclusionary political strategies. In the process, though, these very responses have served to indicate the marked extent to which national black American political leadership in the United States has been powerfully regularized and incorporated into, and now exhibits the same fundamental features as, American politics more generally: fragmentation, differentiation, dissensus, competition along several dimensions, and the overriding strategic imperative to compromise, conciliate, and cooperate in order to overcome institutional divisions and societal conflict in order to achieve desired policy and political goals.

Whether it is given the essentially neutral appellation of "entering the mainstream" or instead is pejoratively termed "co-optation," the extent and importance of this incorporative development is of critical political significance—and is sometimes lost amidst the often vehement demands made by nonblack observers for Farrakhan to be denounced in the clearest terms possible by his African-American compatriots. For some critics of Farrakhan, the most perplexing and infuriating aspect of the NoI leader's recent public prominence has been the ignominious failure of many national black politicians to condemn him. The 1984 controversy over the particular case of Jesse Jackson has been broadened subsequently to include a vast range of black American politicians across the United States, for whom the crucial litmus test of winning or maintaining political and other forms of support—particularly, but by no means exclusively, from whites and American Jews—has been their complete repudiation of Farrakhan and his methods, beliefs, and style. As Morris and Rubin have observed, many Jewish Americans, especially, fear that in failing to admonish Farrakhan for his anti-Semitic comments, those pernicious beliefs will receive an indirect public sanction from black leaders, and thereby gain greater popularity and legitimacy among African-Americans at large, than would otherwise be the case. That fear is one that many white and black Americans also share and one, moreover, that elite and mass African American support for Farrakhan-orchestrated initiatives such as the Million Man March does nothing at all to dispel.

In the context of black political incorporation, however, the continued and pronounced reluctance of many African-American politicians to associate with Farrakhan, despite the electoral and reputational profit that such action would in many instances evidently yield, is much more important than their failure to condemn him unequivocally and unanimously. The process of black political incorporation in the United States, which commenced with the passage of the civil and voting rights legislation of 1964 and 1965, respectively, has reaped thousands of electoral rewards for African-Americans. The subsequent three decades have been distinguished by a gradual evolution of black American participation in conventional methods of seeking, achieving, and maintaining political power. The victories in 1989 of Dinkins in the New York City mayoral campaign and Wilder in the gubernatorial election in Virginia represented the most nationally noteworthy manifestations of increasing black electoral success, but across the entire U.S. black candidates for elective office had made substantial strides forward by the beginning of the 1990s.

Yet, in their immediate aftermath, the incidence of popular and scholarly discussions of the putative death of black American politics was also notable. For many of those most closely involved in the struggle to secure black civil and political rights, and subsequently to achieve public office and effect policy change, the notion of the demise of a distinctive black politics was as inaccurate as it was wholly irrelevant to achieving meaningful black empowerment. Rather, by the 1990s, many of the core political goals of the civil rights struggle had, after long and costly struggle, been realized. Not only were the ranks of black voters and elected officials substantially swelled after 1965, but proposals once widely viewed as naively ambitious—if not wildly eccentric—became mainstream public policy items: affirmative action programs, Aid to Families with Dependent Children, food stamps, racial redistricting, and minority set-asides. To the extent that a movement succeeds in achieving its objectives, then, its death is to be expected and desired; its life would otherwise testify to a continued exclusion and an incomplete achievement.

It is, nonetheless, true that the very success of the civil rights movement during the 1960s rendered it something of a victim of its own remarkable achievements. Similarly, the expansion of the cadre of black public officeholders in America over the last two decades has rendered national black American politicians peculiarly vulnerable to preincorporative era protest appeals. Precisely by virtue of its success, then, the process of political modernization has left open a significant vacuum for protest appeals to garner popular African-American support. And, since 1984, that vacuum has been increasingly filled—assiduously, vigorously, and extremely effectively—by the shrewd, enthusiastic, and indefatigable leader of the NoI.

As an outsider figure, one untainted by Washington politics and its richly negative public connotations in contemporary America, Farrakhan has aggressively exploited his wholly distinctive black leadership niche to disconcerting national effect. Although only one of the explanations for its success, it was the nonelected, outsider character of Farrakhan's leadership status that proved absolutely vital in mobilizing black Americans to come to the nation's capital in October 1995. Unlike other elected and nonelected black leaders, however, Farrakhan has forged a popular African-American base through exploiting the profoundly negative features associated with, and the substantial divisions within, the black community in the United States. Farrakhan's recent popularity is parasitic not only upon the disproportionate persistence of grievous economic and social maladies among many black communities and the ongoing failure—if not the inability—of their political representatives (both black and white) in federal, state, and local governments to secure their amelioration. It is also heavily reliant upon the deeply negative evaluations of African-Americans harbored by many black and white Americans alike.

That Farrakhan is increasingly treated by national black American political elites as a legitimate and important voice on behalf of a sizeable constituency is therefore a profoundly eloquent testimony both to the transformation of the NoI under his leadership and to the current Americanization of established black political and civic leadership elites in general. As Martin Kilson has persuasively argued, the increasing diversification of black Americans' attitudes, voting patterns, candidates, and policy concerns Americanizes the black political profile in a fashion imitative of the Americanization of Jewish Americans that occurred during the 1970s. For Kilson, this process provides an opportunity for black and white Americans to link their political fortunes in combination, and for what he terms a "transethnic imperative" increasingly to inform black life in general, and its politics in particular. The goal of that imperative is to interlink the leadership of black and white sociopolitical institutions in common cause. Thus, much as during earlier periods in American history, white ethnics such as the Irish penetrating WASP-dominated positions from the 1890s to the 1930s, or Jews penetrating WASP and Irish-dominated milieus from the 1930s onward, so politics remains the most appropriate and immediately available sphere for transethnic penetration by black Americans.[12]

In this context, rather than viewing Farrakhan as further evidence of the continuing racial organicism and essentialism widely attributed to black American politics (as Adolph Reed argues), it is hence more accurate instead to view the minister's relations with national black political and religious elites as testimony to the deracialization and class analyses favored by Kilson, Wilson, and others. Although the racial dimension of Farrakhan's appeal has of course been critical to his national ascendancy, it is the intraracial differentiation of African-Americans in the 1990s—and its associated representation, partial representation, and misrepresentation by national black elites—that informs the political boundaries in which the Farrakhan phenomenon has occurred. No one political actor can fill the mythic role of a national black spokesperson, as if African-Americans actually agree upon all political and social issues, and Farrakhan does not fully bridge—much less reconcile—the many important differences between, and divisions among, African-Americans; but his composite mass appeal is sufficiently diffuse to accord him an exceptional national leadership niche that no other black politician has managed (and relatively few have even sought) to achieve. In this respect, however, Farrakhan's political rise and influence indicate not so much a return to the politics of protest by African-Americans than the clear ascendancy—incomplete but overwhelming—of conventional politics among black Americans in the 1990s.

THE END OF PROTEST AND THE FARRAKHAN PHENOMENON

The mass black popularity of Farrakhan during the 1990s is partially the product, but is also wholly symptomatic, of the deeply entrenched racial divisions and fissures in the United States that have been painfully hewn over many turbulent decades. It is also indicative of the profound tactical and strategic political dilemmas confronting many national black politicians in the post–civil rights era. The long-awaited achievement of formal civil and political equality for black Americans has not realized subsequently the type of marked improvement in African-American social and economic welfare that most Americans—black and nonblack alike—hoped to witness as possible, and that many envisioned as probable. The bright prospect of collective material advancement once harbored by black leaders has gradually dissipated into a deep skepticism among African-Americans at both elite and mass levels about both the possibility and the probability of genuine improvement for literally millions of African-Americans.

The gradual but inexorable evolution of national black American politics from protest to politics is therefore one that has left many black Americans at large confused, puzzled, and angry about their continued exclusion from the social and geographical mobility, and the accompanying economic security, affluence, and prosperity, that so many Americans of all races continue to enjoy, almost as a matter of course or birthright. Even during an age of relative economic decline and increased interdependence for the United States as a whole, the disproportionate locus of African-Americans among the poor, the jobless, the malnourished, the disease-ridden, the victims of homicide, and the jailed is one that continues starkly to differentiate black from white America. In consequence, progress—that notion that remains so central to U.S. political culture, popular belief, and arguably to American national identity itself—continues to stand as a partial, uncertain, and distant prospect for many African-Americans as the twentieth century draws to its close.

That apparent distance provides much of the fuel for Farrakhan's venomous vehicle of black American paranoid and reactionary politics. Farrakhan's success is ultimately the story of a shrewd black opportunist who has zealously capitalized upon America's continuing failure to deal with its serious and abiding racial problems; in this sense, at least, the minister cannot be seen as an unfortunate aberration in American history. As the aggressive and articulate apostle of an impending American apartheid, Farrakhan addresses, amplifies, and aggravates the existing racial division of America. Not just whites and Jews, but Koreans, Palestinian Arabs, and homosexuals have all merited inclusion in Farrakhan's far-reaching compass of bigotry, contempt, and scapegoating. The racial and ethnic tensions contaminating America that his political opportunism exploits with such vulgarly ostentatious relish, however, existed long before the minister was even conceived and, equally, loom as a deeply divisive and precipitously polarizing prospect long after Farrakhan's pernicious political opportunism finally fades away. And that most unedifying prospect is immeasurably more disconcerting and in need of candid and concerted challenge than the crude political posturing, jet-setting antics, and verbally offensive pyrotechnics of Farrakhan currently.

In this respect, constantly isolating Farrakhan for denunciation is a reaction that, no matter how understandable, legitimate, and defensible, serves mainly to elevate the stature of the messenger at the expense of the broader forces upon which the message relies for its mass resonance. The reactionary and paranoid appeals of the NoI's leader depend for their contemporary popularity among African-Americans principally upon the continued economic and social devastation of many black communities across the United States and upon Farrakhan's very effective exploitation of crosscutting political, economic, and social cleavages among blacks nationwide. The underlying social and economic causes of fear, distrust, and resentment will also, in the absence of their effective amelioration, continue to form a potentially powerful popular basis for Farrakhan's demagoguery among African-Americans. Although Farrakhan has undeniably profited greatly from these conditions, however, it would be entirely wrong to view him as a somehow aberrant, unique, or exceptional phenomenon. As Richard Hofstadter cautioned over a quarter-century ago, the paranoid style in American politics is, unfortunately, peculiarly apt to recur in different guises over time. There are other Farrakhans, it seems certain, who will assuredly assume the same ignominious national mantle of organized hatred by capitalizing on the deprivation, disadvantage, and despair of millions of black Americans, should they continue apace.

If the tragic and woeful conditions that have given rise to the minister's political successes merit attention, conceding that there are many causes of Farrakhan's approval and support nonetheless cannot exempt the leader of the NoI from legitimate and extensive criticism. For Farrakhan represents the most starkly brutal and unequivocal repudiation of the commendable liberal principles of diversity, tolerance, and pluralism of all modern national African-American public figures in the United States. Preaching racial reconciliation, Farrakhan practices a politics of polarization and division; proselytizing for racial comity, he advances mutual racial animus; proclaiming his boundless humanitarian love, he readily capitalizes upon the basest sentiments of ignorance, fear, and hatred. Farrakhan's antipolitics is one of negation, condemnation, and malice: a vociferous, unequivocal and comprehensive rejection of the traditional American doctrine, "e pluribus unum." No tentative olive branches offered to Jewish and white Americans can obscure the opprobrious venom that has been so eagerly heaped by Farrakhan, for almost all of his adult life, upon those many nemeses against whom he and his God take offense. No amount of good works that his organization accomplishes in inner cities can disguise premeditated racist demagoguery behind a saintly mask of beneficent justice. No amount of peremptory preaching for racial harmony can hide a public praxis forged disgracefully upon hatred and hypocrisy. Were the tone in which America's race relations discussed in national public life less shrill and adversarial, no doubt many more national figures of all racial, ethnic, and religious shades would concede publicly that Farrakhan writes checks of racial comity that draw upon a long-bankrupt account of the deepest intolerance and insensitivity.

Furthermore, Farrakhan has had opportunities in abundance, in America and elsewhere, to disavow his ubiquitous expressions of racial malice and division. If those plentiful expressions have always been wholly unnecessary to instill racial pride, self-dignity, and individual responsibility among African-Americans—as they most clearly have been and so remain—the minister could perhaps still achieve a position of note by clearly and sincerely repudiating them. Why, then, does Farrakhan compromise a potentially positive historic legacy by engaging in vitriolic expressions of the grossest animosity and bigotry? Why must Farrakhan continually devalue the laudable project of revitalizing downtrodden communities and despairing African-American individuals by invoking an entirely extraneous litany of the most ignoble, base, and repellent prejudice?

The resolution of those vexing questions can only reside in the unfortunate but unmistakable fact—one that the briefest investigation of Farrakhan's voluminous speeches and writings confirms beyond reasonable doubt—that such deep animus is at once integral to the Bilalian faith, inextricable from the NoI's worldview, and completely inseparable from Farrakhan's personal political project. Carefully coded distinctions between despising whites and hating the mind-set of white supremacy are no more persuasive now than were southern white segregationists' claims in the 1950s that they never had a race problem until outside activists came down to Dixie to stir up trouble among their otherwise placid and pliant blacks. The rhetorical subtleties that put a woman's base rather than place in the home, similarly, do not render the NoI's patriarchal belief system any less sexist, rigid, and demeaning to women. It is upon this undistinguished legacy of prejudice, paranoia, and reaction that Farrakhan forfeits a broader public admiration, endorsement, and multiracial support. For black Americans, especially, Farrakhan represents less the light at the end of the tunnel of oppression than the blinding headlamps of the oncoming train.

The appropriate response to the leader of the NoI is therefore one that entails recognizing the Farrakhan phenomenon for what it essentially is: a virulently bigoted, paranoid, and authoritarian expression of mass disillusion not only with white America, but also with African-Americans as well. Defenders of Louis Farrakhan labor under the most heavy burden of legitimizing the prejudice and reaction with which his public discourse is so replete; whereas his many critics, adversaries, and denunciators must correspondingly attend to more than the particular political figure in their condemnatory remarks if they are to witness the full atrophy of the Farrakhan phenomenon. For however repulsive and ridiculous much of the content of Farrakhan's sermonizing and paranoid pontificating most certainly is, some of the minister's views clearly jibe with the attitudes and beliefs of thousands, perhaps even millions, of African-Americans. Bereft of acknowledging the desperate plight of many blacks and the collapsing infrastructure of many black communities, impulsive insults and contemptibly dismissive, self-righteous, and disparaging rebukes are unlikely to dissuade African-Americans at large of the merits of Farrakhan's dubious case. They can instead serve to exacerbate the visceral bases of Farrakhan's appeal by seeming to confirm the very allegations and accusations that he levels at the putative enemies of black America, rendering the NoI's leader more a modern-day black martyr to prejudiced attacks than a political monster who promotes bigoted inter- and intra-racial animus. If Farrakhan is genuinely viewed by thousands of African-Americans as a messianic figure and the Million Man March is similarly seen sincerely as a miraculous and millennial event, those views partially derive from the frequently condemnatory, derisive, and unduly defamatory reactions of whites.

Ultimately, the Farrakhan phenomenon represents both an expression and a function of the abiding American dilemma of race. Its political fate thus far reveals the pronounced extent to which black and white Americans in the United States continue to retain sharply divided conceptions of what it means actually to be an American citizen in the 1990s. Despite the substantial political, economic, and social advances made by black Americans over recent decades, the many sharp fissures in American society and politics centered around race remain deeply entrenched and especially controversial at the close of the twentieth century. Though it occupies no place in either the creedal values or the great promise of American democracy, racial and ethnic bigotry represents an ugly but unmistakably influential and prominent part of America's political history. It remains the province of responsible citizens, critics, and politicians alike to render both those original values and the immense, but imperfectly realized, promise of American democracy a reality if the avowed status of the United States as a truly liberal, pluralist, and inclusive political regime is finally to be achieved. To that admirable end, it is not only the particular paranoid perorations of a Farrakhan and the siren calls of a barren racial separatism that should be implacably resisted and strongly challenged (although they most certainly should). It is also to the root causes of those deep fissures based upon race that the fullest political attention and the most extensive, enlightened, and empathetic public candor must be devoted if the Farrakhan phenomenon— and its related current expressions and future successors—is ever likely to fade.

NOTES TO CHAPTER 7

1. Quoted in Fletcher and Balz, "Farrakhan Seeks Wider Role," p. A1.
2. King, *Separate and Unequal*, p. viii.
3. Sargent, *Extremism in America*, p. 3.
4. Quoted in Alan Ehrenhalt, "Black Caucus: A Wary Carter Ally," *Congressional Quarterly Weekly Report*, 21 May 1977, p. 969.
5. Marable, "Race, Identity and Political Culture," p. 297.
6. See Demetrios Caraley, "Washington Abandons the Cities," *Political Science Quarterly* 107, no. 1 (1992): 1–30.
7. See Lamis, *The Two-Party South*, pp. 45–61.
8. The issue bases of the firm locus of African-Americans within the Democratic fold is also well-documented in Byron Shafer and William Claggett, *The Two Majorities* (Baltimore, Md: Johns Hopkins, 1994).
9. Raphael J. Sonenshein, "Can Black Candidates Win Statewide Elections?," *Political Science Quarterly* 105, no. 2 (1990): 219–40, at 241.
10. For some of the acute ethical and political problems that the need for funds generates, see Novak, "Conservatives and Corporations Plug Into Black Power."
11. The most prominent exponent of the view that affirmative gerrymandering in a single-member, plurality electoral system is inadequate in realizing political equality for black Americans is Lani Guinier. See the collection of her essays, *The Tyranny of the Majority*. Shelby Steele's views are best encapsulated in *The Content of Our Character* (New York: St. Martin's Press, 1990).
12. Kilson, "Problems of Black Politics," p. 528.

Bibliography

Abilla, Walter D., *The Black Muslims in America: an introduction to the theory of commitment* (Kampala: East African Literature Bureau, 1977).

Abramson, Paul R., John H. Aldrich, and David W. Rohde, *Change and Continuity in the 1988 Elections* (Washington, D.C.: Congressional Quarterly Press, 1990).

————, *Change and Continuity in the 1992 Elections* (Washington, D.C.: Congressional Quarterly Press, 1995).

Adams, John G., *Without Precedent: the Story of the Death of McCarthyism* (New York: Norton, 1983).

Adams, Lorraine, "Nation of Islam: A Dream Past Due," *The Washington Post*, 1 September 1996, pp. A1, A28–29; 2 September 1996, pp. A1, A8.

Ali, Amir M., *Islam or Farrakhanism?* (Chicago: Institute of Islamic Information and Education, 1991).

Alkalimat, Abdul and Doug Gills, *Harold Washington and the Crisis of Black Power in Chicago* (Chicago: Twenty-First Century Books, 1989).

Allen, R. E., ed., *The Concise Oxford Dictionary of Current English*, 8th ed. (Oxford: Clarendon Press, 1990).

Altman, Dennis, *AIDS and the New Puritanism* (London: Pluto Press, 1986).

Badger, Anthony, *The New Deal: the Depression Years, 1933–1940* (New York: Hill and Wang, 1989).

Bakst, Jerome H., ed., "Louis Farrakhan: An Update," *Anti-Defamation League Facts* 30, Spring 1985 (New York: Anti-Defamation League, 1985).

Baldwin, James, *The Fire Next Time* (New York: Dell, 1963).

Barboza, Steven, *American Jihad: Islam after Malcolm X* (New York: Doubleday, 1994).

Barker, Lucius J., and Ronald W. Walters, eds. *Jesse Jackson's 1984 Presidential Campaign: Challenge and Change in American Politics* (Chicago: University of Illinois Press, 1989).

Barnes, Fred, "Farrakhan Frenzy: What's a Black Politician to Do?" *New Republic*, 28 October 1985: 13–15.

Barone, Michael, *Our Country: The Shaping of America from Roosevelt to Reagan* (New York: The Free Press, 1990).

Bayley, Edwin R., *Joe McCarthy and the Press* (Madison: University of Wisconsin Press, 1981).

Bell, Derrick, *And We Are Not Saved: The Elusive Quest for Racial Justice* (New York: Basic Books, 1979).

Bennett, Claudette E., *The Black Population in the United States: March 1994 and 1993*, U.S. Bureau of the Census, Current Population Reports, P20–480 (Washington, D.C.: U.S. Government Printing Office, 1995).

Benz, Ernst, "Der Schwarze Islam," *Zeitschrift fur Religion und Geistesgeschichte* 19 (2) 1967: 97–113.

Berger, Morroe, "The Black Muslims," *Horizon* 6 (1) 1964: 49–65.

Betz, Hans-Georg, *Radical Right-Wing Populism in Western Europe* (Basingstoke: Macmillan, 1994).

Beynon, Erdman D., "The Voodoo Cult Among Negro Migrants in Detroit," *American Journal of Sociology* 43 (July 1937–May 1938): 894–907.

Bibb, Leon Douglas, "A Note on the Black Muslims: They Preach Black to be the Ideal," *Negro History Bulletin* 28 (6) 1965: 132–33.

Black, Earl and Merle Black, *Politics and Society in the South* (Cambridge, Mass.: Harvard University Press, 1987).

———, *The Vital South: How Presidents Are Elected* (Cambridge, Mass.: Harvard University Press, 1992).

Black, Edwin, "Farrakhan and the Jews," *Midstream* 32 (August-September 1986): 3–6.

Blackstock, Nelson, *Cointelpro: The FBI's Secret War on Political Freedom*, 3rd ed. (New York: Pathfinder Press, 1995).

Blake, J. Herman, "Black Nationalism," in *Annals of the American Academy of Political and Social Science* 382 (1969): 15–25.

Bolce, Louis, Gerald D. De Maio, and Douglas Muzzio, "Blacks and the Republican Party: The 20 Percent Solution," *Political Science Quarterly* 107 (1) 1992: 63–79.

———, "The 1992 Republican 'Tent': No Blacks Walked In," *Political Science Quarterly* 108 (2) 1993: 255–70.

Bone, James, "Prophet of Hate," *The London Times (Magazine)*, 3 February 1996: 26–30.

Bontemps, Arna, and Jack Conroy, *They Seek a City* (Garden City, N.Y.: Doubleday, 1945).

———, *Anyplace But Here* (New York: Hill and Wang, 1966).

Bositis, David, *The Congressional Black Caucus in the 103rd Congress* (Washington, D.C.: Joint Center for Political and Economic Studies, 1994).

Brackman, Harold D., *Ministry of Lies: The Truth Behind the Nation of Islam's "The Secret Relationship between Blacks and Jews"* (New York: Four Walls Eight Windows, 1994).

Branch, Taylor, *Parting the Waters: America in the King Years, 1954–1963* (New York: Simon and Schuster, 1988).

———, "The Uncivil War: Blacks and Jews," *Esquire*, May 1989.

Breger, Marshall J., "Discriminating in Favor of Farrakhan," *The Wall Street Journal*, 24 July 1995: A12.

Breitman, George, ed., *Malcolm X Speaks: Selected Speeches and Statements* (New York: Grove Press, 1965).

———, ed., *The Last Year of Malcolm X* (New York: Pathfinder Press, 1967).

———, ed., *By Any Means Necessary: Speeches, Interviews and a Letter by Malcolm X* (New York: Pathfinder Press, 1970).

———, ed., *Leon Trotsky on Black Nationalism and Self-Determination* (New York: Pathfinder Press, 1978).

Breitman, George, Herman Porter, and Baxter Smith, *The Assassination of Malcolm X* (New York; Pathfinder Press, 1976).

Broder, David, "Farrakhan reminder that U.S. still has its own racial problems," *The Atlanta Journal*, 18 September 1985: A15.

Brodie, Ian, "Muslim Racism Sparks Uproar," *The London Times*, 4 February 1994: 12.

Browning, Rufus P., Dale Rogers Marshall, and David H. Tabb, *Racial Politics in American Cities* (New York: Longman, 1990).

Bruce, Steve, *The Rise and Fall of the New Christian Right, 1978–1988* (Oxford: Clarendon Press, 1988).

Bryce, James, *The American Commonwealth* (New York: Macmillan, 1888).

Bull, Chris, "Farrakhan Under Fire," *The Advocate*, 8 March 1994, p. 25.

Butler, David and Austin Ranney, eds., *Electioneering: A Comparative Study of Continuity and Change* (Oxford: Clarendon Press, 1992).

Caldwell, Wallace E., "Black Muslims Behind Bars," *Religious Studies* 34 (4) 1966: 185–204.

———, "A Survey of Attitudes Towards Black Muslims in Prison," *Journal of Human Relations* 16 (2) 1968: 220–38.

Caraley, Demetrios, "Washington Abandons the Cities," *Political Science Quarterly*, 107 (1) 1992: 1–30.

Carmines, Edward G. and James A. Stimson, *Issue Evolution: Race and the Transformation of American Politics* (Princeton, N.J.: Princeton University Press, 1989).

Carter, Stephen L., *The Confirmation Mess: Cleaning Up the Federal Appointments Process* (New York: Basic Books, 1994).

Chafe, William, *The Unfinished Journey: America Since World War Two*, 2nd ed. (New York: Oxford University Press, 1991).

Cheles, Luciano, Ronnie Ferguson, and Michael Vaughan, eds., *Neo-Fascism in Europe* (New York: Longman, 1991).

Chong, Dennis, *Collective Action and the Civil Rights Movement* (Chicago: University of Chicago Press, 1991).

Clay, William L., *Just Permanent Interests: Black Americans in Congress, 1870–1991* (New York: Amsitad Press, 1992).

Cohen, Richard E., "Farrakhan and Anti-Semitism," *Torrington (CT) Register-Criterion*, 28 July 1985, p. 15.

———, "Hatred Covenant," *The Washington Post*, 15 October 1993, p. 25.

———, "At Nuremberg-on-Potomac, A Chanting of Jews, Jews," *International Herald Tribune*, 3 March 1994, p. 7.

———, "Farrakhan Too," *The Washington Post*, 16 May 1995, p. A17.

———, "Marching behind Farrakhan," *The Washington Post*, 19 September 1995, p. A18.

Colton, Elizabeth O., *The Jackson Phenomenon: The Man, the Power, the Message* (New York: Doubleday, 1989).

Cone, James H., *Martin and Malcolm and America* (London: HarperCollins, 1991).

Cook, Gareth G., "Race: Feeding the Fire," *U.S. News and World Report*, 7 February 1994, p. 12.

Cox, Michael, *U.S. Foreign Policy After the Cold War: Superpower Without a Mission?* (Chatham, N.J.: RIAA, 1995).

Craig, Barbara Hinkson, and David M. O'Brien, *Abortion and American Politics* (Chatham, N.J.: Chatham House, 1993).

Crick, Michael, *Militant* (London: Faber and Faber, 1984).

Cronon, Edmund David, *Black Moses: The Story of Marcus Garvey and the Universal Negro Improvement Association* (Madison: University of Wisconsin Press, 1962).

Cruse, Harold, *The Crisis of the Negro Intellectual* (New York: Quill, 1984).

————, *Plural But Equal: A Critical Study of Blacks and Minorities in America's Plural Society* (New York: Quill, 1987).

Curry, George, "Farrakhan, Jesse, and Jews," *Emerge*, 5, July-August 1994, p. 28

————, "Unity in the Community: Can Ben Chavis Pull It Off?" *Emerge*, 5 September 1994, p. 28

Curry, Richard Orr, *Conspiracy: The Fear of Subversion in American History* (New York: Holt, Rinehart, and Winston, 1972).

Cushmeer, Bernard, *This Is the One: Messenger Elijah Muhammad—You Need Not Look for Another* (Phoenix, Ariz.: Truth Publications, 1970).

Davis, David Brion (ed.), *The Fear of Conspiracy: Images of Un-American Subversion from the Revolution to the Present Day* (Ithaca, N.Y.: Cornell University Press, 1971).

Davis, John F., "Farrakhan Speaks," *Village Voice*, 29 22 May 1984: 15–18, 20.

DeCaro, Louis, *On the Side of My People: A Religious Life of Malcolm X* (New York: New York University Press, 1996).

De Tocqueville, Alexis, *Democracy in America* (New York: Vintage Books, 1945).

Dent, Gina, ed., *Black Popular Culture* (Seattle: Bay Press, 1992).

Dionne, E. J., *Why Americans Hate Politics* (New York: Simon and Schuster, 1991).

————, "So Many Could Have Been There," *The Washington Post*, 17 October 1995, p. A17.

Duke, Lynne, "Farrakhan Defends Clinton, Asks Critics to 'Get to Know Me Better'," *The Washington Post*, 5 May 1993, p. A22.

————, "Congressional Black Caucus and Nation of Islam Agree on Alliance," *The Washington Post*, 17 September 1993, p. A3.

————, "At the Core of the Nation of Islam: Confrontation," *The Washington Post*, 21 March 1994, p. A1.

Edelman, Murray, *The Symbolic Uses of Politics* (Urbana: University of Illinois Press, 1964).

Edsall, Thomas Byrne, and Mary D. Edsall, *Chain Reaction: The Impact of Race, Rights, and Taxes on American Politics* (New York: W. W. Norton, 1991).

Ehrenhalt, Alan, "Black Caucus: A Wary Carter Ally," *Congressional Quarterly Weekly Report*, 21 May 1977, p. 969.

Eisenstein, Zillah, *Hatreds: Racialized and Sexualized* (London: Routledge, 1996).

Epstein, Leon E., *Political Parties in the American Mold* (Madison: University of Wisconsin Press, 1986).

Esolen, Gary, "More Than a Pretty Face: David Duke's Use of Television as a Political Tool," in *The Emergence of David Duke and the Politics of Race*, ed. Douglas Rose (Chapel Hill: University of North Carolina Press, 1992), pp. 136–55.

Essien-Udom, E. U., *Black Nationalism: A Search for an Identity in America* (Chicago: University of Chicago Press, 1971).

Eure, Joseph D. and Richard M. Jerome, *Back Where We Belong: Selected Speeches by Minister Louis Farrakhan* (Philadelphia, PA: PC International Press, 1989).

Evanier, David, *The Anti-Semitism of Black Demagogues and Extremists* (New York: Anti-Defamation League, 1992).

Farber, M. A., "In the Name of the Father," *Vanity Fair* 58, June 1995, pp. 52–60.

Farrakhan, Louis, *Seven Speeches by Minister Louis Farrakhan* (New York: Ministry Class, Muhammad's Temple No. 7, 1974).

———, "I Am an Alarm Clock," *Black Scholar*, January-February 1979, pp. 12–14.

———, "Farrakhan on Jesse Jackson: A Warning to Black Leaders, A Warning to Black People," *Essence*, February 1984, pp. 30–34.

———, *The Honorable Louis Farrakhan: a minister for progress; the complete historic interview with Michael Hardy and William Pleasant from The National Alliance* (New York: Practice Press, 1985).

———, *Independent Black Leadership in America: Minister Louis Farrakhan, Dr. Leonara Fulani, Reverend Al Sharpton* (New York: Castillo International, 1990).

———, *A Torchlight for America* (Chicago: FCN Publishing, 1993).

———, "Excerpts of Interview," *The Washington Post*, 1 March 1990, pp. A16–17.

———, "Nation of Islam Offers True Liberation for Muslim Women," *The Final Call*, 24 August 1992, p. 28.

Faucheux, Ron, "Affirmative Reaction," *Campaigns and Elections*, April 1995, pp. 5, 45–46.

Fenno, Richard, *Home Style: House Members in Their Districts* (Boston: Little, Brown and Company, 1978).

Fineman, Howard, and Vern E. Smith, "An Angry 'Charmer'," *Newsweek*, 30 October 1995, pp. 42–46.

Fiorina, Morris, *Congress: Keystone of the Washington Establishment*, 2nd ed. (New Haven: Yale University Press, 1989).

Fitzgerald, Mark, "Farrakhan Denounces Critical Stories," *Editor and Publisher*, 8 April 1995, p. 11.

Fletcher, Martin, "Anti-Semitic Gibes Mar Million Man March," *The London Times*, 16 October 1995, p. 10.

———, "Prophet of Hatred Becomes Voice of Black America," *The London Times*, 18 October 1995, p. 11.

Fletcher, Martin, and Tom Rhodes, "Washington Mass Rally Rekindles Black Pride," *The London Times*, 17 October 1995, p. 11

Fletcher, Michael A. and Dan Balz, "Farrakhan Seeks Wider Role: Some Black Leaders are Conciliatory, Others Cautious," *The Washington Post*, 18 October 1995, pp. A1, A12.

Fletcher, Michael A., and Hamil R. Harris, "Farrakhan Announces Voter Drive," *The Washington Post*, 19 October 1995, p. A3.

Foley, Michael, *American Political Ideas* (Manchester: Manchester University Press, 1991).

——, *The Rise of the British Presidency* (Manchester: Manchester University Press, 1993).

Fried, Richard M., *Men Against McCarthy* (New York: Columbia University Press, 1976).

——, *Nightmare in Red: the McCarthy Era in Perspective* (New York: Oxford University Press, 1991).

Friendly, Michael, *Malcolm X: the Assassination* (New York: Carroll and Graf, 1992).

Gaber, Julia E., "Lamb of God or Demagogue? A Burkean Cluster Analysis of the Selected Speeches of Minister Louis Farrakhan" (unpublished Ph.D. thesis, Bowling Green State University, 1986).

Gaines, William and David Jackson, "Profit and Promises," *Chicago Tribune*, 12 March 1995, sec. 1., pp. 1, 16–17; 13 March sec 1., pp. 1, 10; 14 March, sec. 1, pp. 1, 10; 15 March sec. 1, pp. 1, 10.

Gaiter, Dorothy J., "Civil Unrest," *The Wall Street Journal*, 10 June 1994, p. A1.

Gallen, David, *The Malcolm X Reader* (New York: Carroll and Graf, 1994).

Gardell, Mattias, *Countdown to Armageddon: Louis Farrakhan and the Nation of Islam* (London: Hurst, 1996).

Garrow, David J., *Bearing the Cross: Martin Luther King, Jr. and the Southern Christian Leadership Conference* (London: Jonathan Cape, 1988).

Garvey, Amy-Jacques, *Philosophy and Opinions of Marcus Garvey* (New York: Universal Publishing House, 1923).

Gates Jr., Henry Louis, "A Reporter at Large: The Charmer," *The New Yorker*, 29 April–6 May 1996, pp. 116–31.

Gelb, Adam, "Farrakhan Calls U.S. Constitution Racist," *Atlanta Journal and Atlanta Constitution*, 13 September 1987, p. E24.

Gerth, Hans and C. Wright Mills, *From Max Weber: Essays in Sociology* (London: Routledge, 1991).

Gladwell, Malcolm, "Farrakhan Seeks End of Rift with Shabazz; Apologizes for Hurt but Denies Involvement in Malcolm X Death," *The Washington Post*, 8 May 1995, p. A1.

Goldman, Peter, *The Death and Life of Malcolm X*, 2nd ed. (Urbana: University of Illinois Press, 1979)

Gooding-Williams, Robert, ed., *Reading Rodney King/Reading Urban Uprising* (New York: Routledge, 1993).

Graber, Dorothy, ed., *Mass Media and American Politics* (Washington, D.C.: Congressional Quarterly Press, 1993).

Greenberg, Stanley B., *Report on Democratic Defection* (Washington, D.C.: The Analysis Group, 1985).

Griffith, Robert, *The Politics of Fear: Joseph McCarthy and the Senate* (Rochelle Park, N.J.: Hayden Book Company, 1970).

Guinier, Lani, *The Tyranny of the Majority: Fundamental Fairness in Representative Democracy* (New York: The Free Press, 1994).

Gurwitt, Rob, "A Quest for a Breakthrough," *Congressional Quarterly Weekly Report*, 25 October 1986, pp. 2645–46.

Hacker, Andrew, *Two Nations: Black and White, Separate, Hostile, Unequal* (New York: Ballantine Books, 1992).

Hainsworth, Paul, ed., *The Extreme Right in Europe and the USA* (London: Pinter, 1992).

Hamby, Alonzo L., *Liberalism and Its Challengers: FDR to Reagan* (New York: Oxford University Press, 1985).

Hamilton, Alexander, James Madison and John Jay, *The Federalist Papers*, with introduction by Isaac Kramnick (Harmondsworth, England: Penguin, 1987), No. 10.

Hamilton, Charles V., *The Black Preacher in America* (New York: William Morrow and Co., 1972).

———, *The Black Experience in American Politics* (New York: Putnam, 1973).

Harlan, Louis R., *Booker T. Washington: The Making of a Black Leader, 1865–1901* (New York: Oxford University Press, 1972).

———, *Booker T. Washington: The Wizard of Tuskegee, 1901–1915* (New York: Oxford University Press, 1983).

Harper, Frederick, "The Influence of Malcolm X on Black Militancy," *Journal of Black Studies* 1 (4) 1971: 387–402.

Harris, Hamil R., "March of Black Men Is Planned in District; Farrakhan Seeks a Turnout of 1 Million," *The Washington Post*, 19 July 1995, p. B1.

Hartz, Louis, *The Liberal Tradition in America* (New York: Harcourt, Brace, and World, 1955).

Hazlett, Thomas W., "The Wrath of Farrakhan," *Reason* 26, May 1994, p. 66.

Henry, Charles P., *Culture and African American Politics* (Bloomington: Indiana University Press, 1990).

Henry, William A., "Pride and Prejudice," *Time*, February 26, 1994, pp. 21–27.

Hentoff, Nat, "Black Bigotry and Free Speech," *The Progressive*, May 1994, pp. 20–21.

———, "A Black Response to Black Bigotry," *The Washington Post*, 23 July 1994, p. A21.

Herbert, Bob, "The Hate Game," *The New York Times*, 9 February 1994, p. A18.

Herrnson, Paul, *Congressional Elections* (Washington, D.C.: Congressional Quarterly Press, 1995).

Higginbotham Jr., A. Leon, "Why I Didn't March," *The Washington Post*, 17 October 1995, p. A17.

Hobsbawm, Eric, *The Age of Extremes: The Short Twentieth Century* (London: Abacus Books, 1995).

Hofstadter, Richard, *The American Political Tradition* (New York: Knopf, 1948).

———, *Anti-intellectualism in American Life* (New York: Knopf, 1963).

———, *The Paranoid Style in American Politics* (Chicago: University of Chicago Press, 1979).

Holland, Bernard, "Sending a Message, Louis Farrakhan Plays Mendelssohn," *The New York Times*, 19 April 1993, p. C11.

Hook, Janet, "Mfume Cuts Renewed Ties to Nation of Islam," *Congressional Quarterly Weekly Report*, 5 February 1994, p. 219.

———, "House Denounces Remarks as 'Racist' Speech," *Congressional Quarterly Weekly Report*, 26 February 1994, p. 458.

Hughes, Robert, *Culture of Complaint: The Fraying of America* (London: Harvill, 1994).

Humphries, Cameron, "The Sacred Covenant," *Diversity and Division*, 3 (3) Spring-Summer 1994.

Huntington, Samuel P., *American Politics: The Promise of Disharmony* (Cambridge, Mass.: Belknap/Harvard University Press, 1981).

Jennings, James, ed., *Race, Politics, and Economic Development* (New York: Verso, 1992).

Johnson, George, *Architects of Fear: Conspiracy Theories and Paranoia in American Politics* (Los Angeles: J. P. Tarcher, 1983).

Jones, Charisse, "Farrakhan-Shabazz Meeting Kindles Hopes," *The New York Times*, 6 May 1995, pp. 16, 23.

Joyce, Faye S., "Farrakhan Warns Press on Jackson," *The New York Times*, 10 April 1984, pp. 1, 7.

Kagay, Michael, "Poll Finds Most Blacks Reject Farrakhan's Ideas as Theirs," *The New York Times*, 5 March 1994, p. 8

Kaplan, H. M., "The Black Muslims and the Negro American's Quest for Communion: A Case Study in the Genesis of Negro Protest Movements," *British Journal of Sociology* 20 (2) 1969: 164–76.

Karenga, Maulana, "Jesse Jackson and the Presidential Campaign: The Invitation and the Oppositions of History," *Black Scholar*, 15 (5) September-October 1984.

Karim, Benjamin, *Remembering Malcolm* (New York: Carroll and Graf, 1992).

Kaufman, Jonathan, *Broken Alliance: The Turbulent Times Between Blacks and Jews in America* (New York: Scribner, 1988).

Kelly, Brian, and Harry, Jaffee, "The Farrakhan Fiasco," *Regardies*, 10, January 1990: 47–55.

Kifner, John, "With Farrakhan Speaking a Chorus of GOP Critics Join In," *The New York Times*, 17 October 1995, p. A18.

Kilson, Martin, "Problems of Black Politics: Some Progress, Many Difficulties," *Dissent*, Fall 1989, pp. 526–34

Kilson, Martin, and Clement Cottingham, "Thinking About Race Relations: How Far Are We Still From Integration?" *Dissent*, Fall 1991, pp. 520–30.

King, Dennis, "The Farrakhan Phenomenon: Ideology, Support, Potential," *Patterns of Prejudice* 20 (1) 1986: 11–22.

King, Desmond S., *Separate and Unequal: Black Americans and the U.S. Federal Government* (Oxford: Oxford University Press, 1995).

King, Peter, "'PC' Handling of Farrakhan Is Wrong," *Newsday* (Nassau Edition), 8 March 1996, p. A47.

Kirman, Joseph M., "The Challenge of the Black Muslims," *Social Education* 27 (7) 1963: 365–68.

Kirscht, J. P. and R. C. Dilleehay, *Dimensions of Authoritarianism: A Review of Research and Theory* (Lexington, Ky.: University of Kentucky Press, 1967).

Klein, Joe, "The Threat of Tribalism," *Newsweek* 123, 14 March 1994, p. 28.

Kotlowitz, Alex, "A Bridge Too Far?" *The New York Times Magazine*, 12 June 1994, pp. 41–43.

Kotzin, Michael C., "Louis Farrakhan's anti-Semitism: A look at the record," *The Christian Century* 111 (1994), pp. 224–25.

Kramer, Michael, "Loud and Clear: Farrakhan's anti-Semitism," *New York Magazine* 18 (41) 21 October 1985.

Krauthammer, Charles, "The 'Validation' of Louis Farrakhan," *The Washington Post*, 20 October 1995, p. A19.

Kurapka, David, "Hate Story: Farrakhan's Still at It," *New Republic* 198, 30 May 1988, p. 19–21.

Labash, Matt "Inside the March: Farrakhan Is King," *The (Washington, D.C.) Weekly Standard*, 23 October 1995, p. 26–29.

Lacayo, Richard, "A Critical Mass," *Time*, 30 October 1995, pp. 34–35.

Lamis, Alexander P., *The Two-Party South*, 2nd ed. (New York: Oxford University Press, 1990).

Laue, James H., "A Contemporary Revitalization Movement in American Race Relations: The Black Muslims," *Social Forces* 42 (3) 1964: 315–323.

Lawson, Steven F., *In Pursuit of Power* (New York: Columbia University Press, 1985).

Lee, Martha F., *The Nation of Islam: an American millenarian movement* (Lewiston, N.Y.: E. Mellen Press, 1988)

Lemann, Nicholas, *The Promised Land: The Great Black Migration and How It Changed America* (London: Macmillan, 1991).

Lester, Julius, "Blacks, Jews, and Farrakhan," *Dissent* 41 (3) Summer 1994.

Letwin, Shirley R., *The Anatomy of Thatcherism* (London: Fontana, 1992).

Leuchtenberg, William E., "A Klansman Joins the Court: The Appointment of Hugo L. Black," in Leonard Dinnerstein and Kenneth T. Jackson, eds., *American Vistas: 1877 to the Present*, 5th ed (New York: Oxford University Press, 1987), pp. 187–215.

Liben, Paul, "Farrakhan Turns Blind Eye to African Slave Trade," *Human Events* 51 (20) 1995.

Lincoln, C. Eric, *The Black Church in the African American Experience* (Durham, N.C.: Duke University Press, 1990).

———, *The Black Muslims in America* 3rd ed. (Grand Rapids, Mich.: William B. Eerdmans, 1994).

Linzer, Lori, *The Nation of Islam: The Relentless Record of Hate* (New York: Anti-Defamation League, 1995).

Lipset, Seymour Martin, "Blacks and Jews: How Much Bias?" *Public Opinion* July-August 1987.

Lipset, Seymour Martin and Earl Raab, *The Politics of Unreason: Right-Wing Extremism in America, 1790–1977* (Chicago: University of Chicago Press, 1978).

Loury, Glenn C., "One Man's March," *The New Republic*, 6 November 1995, pp. 18–22.

Lusane, Clarence, "Black Political Power in the 1990s," *The Black Scholar*, January/February 1989, pp. 38–42.

————, *African-American Politics at the Crossroads: The Restructuring of Black Leadership and the 1992 Elections* (Boston: South End Press, 1994).

Lusane, Clarence and Dennis Desmond, *Pipe Dream Blues: Racism and the War on Drugs* (Boston: South End Press, 1991).

Lyons, Nancee, "Muslim Guard Service Grows," *Emerge*, February 1993, p. 9

Magida, Arthur J., *Prophet of Rage: A Life of Louis Farrakhan and his Nation* (New York: HarperCollins, 1996).

Malveaux, Julianne, "Black America's Abortion Ambivalence," *Emerge*, February 1993, pp. 33–34.

Mamiya, Lawrence H., and C. Eric Lincoln, "Minister Louis Farrakhan and the Final Call: Schism in the Muslim Movement," in *The Muslim Community in North America*, eds. Earle Waugh, Baha Abu-Laban, and Regular Querishi (Edmonton: University of Alberta Press, 1983), pp. 234–51.

Maolain, C. O., *The Radical Right: A World Dictionary* (Harlow, U.K.: Longman, 1987).

Marable, Manning, *How Capitalism Underdeveloped Black America: Problems in Race, Political Economy, and Society* (Boston: South End Press, 1983).

————, *Race, Reform and Rebellion: The Second Reconstruction in Black America, 1945–1982* (Jackson, Miss.: University of Mississippi Press, 1984).

————, *Black American Politics: From the Washington Marches to Jesse Jackson* (London: Verso, 1985).

————, "In the Business of Prophet Making," *New Statesman*, 13 December 1985, pp. 23–25.

————, "Race, Identity, and Political Culture," in *Black Popular Culture*, ed. Gina Dent (Seattle: Bay Press, 1992), pp. 292–302.

————, *Beyond Black and White: Transforming African-American Politics* (New York: Verso, 1995).

Marsh, Clifton E., *From Black Muslims to Muslims: The Transition from Separatism to Islam, 1930–1980* (London: Scarecrow Press, 1984).

————, *From Black Muslims to Muslims: the resurrection, transformation, and change of the lost-found Nation of Islam in America, 1930–1995*, 2nd ed. (Lanham, Md.: Scarecrow Press, 1996).

Marshall, C. Alan, *The Life and Times of Louis Farrakhan* (New York: Marshall Publications, 1992).

Martin, Ben L., "From Negro to Black to African American: The Power of Names and Naming," *Political Science Quarterly* 106 (1) 1991: 83–107.

Matusow, Allen Joseph, ed., *Joseph R. McCarthy* (Hemel Hempstead: Prentice-Hall, 1970).

Mayhew, David, *Congress: The Electoral Connection* (New Haven: Yale University Press, 1974).

McAdam, Doug, *Political Process and the Development of Black Insurgency, 1930–1970* (Chicago: University of Chicago Press, 1982).

McCall, Nathan, "D.C. Council Votes to Praise Farrakhan's Anti-Drug Work," *The Washington Post*, 25 October 1989, p. A1.

McClain, Paula D. and Joseph Stewart Jr., *"Can We All Get Along?" Racial and Ethnic Minorities in American Politics* (Boulder, Colo.: Westview Press, 1995).

McFadden-Preston, Claudette, "The Rhetoric of Minister Louis Farrakhan: a pluralistic approach" (unpublished Ph.D. thesis, Ohio State University, 1986)

McMillan, Penelope and Cathleen Decker, "Israel is a 'Wicked Hypocrisy'," *Los Angeles Times*, 15 September 1983, p. 1, 3.

McNall, Scott Grant, "The Sect Movement," *Pacific Sociology Review* 6 (2) 1963: 60–64.

Meier, August, Elliot Rudwick, and Francis L. Broderick, eds., *Black Protest Thought in the Twentieth Century*, 2nd ed. (New York: Macmillan, 1971).

Melillo, Wendy and Hamil R. Harris, "Dissent Raised as Ex-Farrakhan Aide Returns to Howard," *The Washington Post*, 20 April, 1994, p. B1.

Merelman, Richard M., *Representing Black Culture: Racial Conflict and Cultural Politics in the United States* (New York: Routledge, 1995).

Merida, Kevin, "Black Caucus Says It Has No Official Working Ties with Nation of Islam," *The Washington Post*, 3 February 1994, p. A16.

———, "Lawmakers Uneasy Over Farrakhan: Black Officials Split on Summit Invitations," *The Washington Post*, 17 June 1994, p. A3.

Mervin, David, "Malcolm X and the Moderation of Black Militancy," *PAIS Papers*, Department of Politics and International Studies, University of Warwick, Coventry, UK, Working Paper no. 107 (April 1992).

Meyerson, Adam, "Manna 2 Society: The Growing Conservatism of Black America," *Policy Review* (68) 1994: 4–6.

Miller, David, ed., *The Blackwell Encyclopaedia of Political Thought* (Oxford: Blackwell, 1991).

Mills, Barbara Kleban, "Predicting Disaster for a Racist America, Louis Farrakhan Envisions an African Homeland for U.S. Blacks," *People* 34 (11) 17 September 1990.

Monroe, Sylvester, "Doing the Right Thing: Muslims Have Become a Welcome Force in Black Neighborhoods," *Time* 135, 16 April 1990, p. 22.

———, "They Suck the Life from You," *Time*, 28 February 1994, p. 24.

———, "The Risky Association," *Time* 143, 27 June 1994, p. 39.

———, "Khalid Abdul Muhammad: Is the Fiery Speaker Undermining the Nation of Islam?" *Emerge* 5, September 1994, p. 42.

———, "The Mirage of Farrakhan," *Time* 144, 30 October 1995, p. 52.

Monteil, Vincent, "La Religion des Black Muslims," *Esprit* 32 (16) 1964: 601–29.

Morganthau, Tom, "Back in the Line of Fire," *Newsweek*, 23 January 1995, p. 20.

Morris, Aldon D., *The Origins of the Civil Rights Movement: Black Communities Organizing for Change* (New York: The Free Press, 1984).

Morris, Lorenzo, ed., *The Social and Political Implications of the 1984 Jesse Jackson Presidential Campaign* (New York: Praeger, 1990).

Morris, Milton D. and Gary E. Rubin, "The Turbulent Friendship: Black–Jewish Relations in the 1990s," in "Interminority Affairs in the U.S.: Pluralism at the Crossroads," ed., Peter Rose, *The Annals of the American Academy of Political and Social Science* 530 (November 1993).

Morrisson, Toni, ed., *Race-ing Justice, En-Gendering Power: Essays on Anita Hill, Clarence Thomas, and the Construction of Social Reality* (London: Chatto and Windus, 1993).

Mudde, Cas, "The War of Words Defining the Extreme Right Party Family," *West European Politics* 19 (2) 1996: 225–48.

Muhammad, Elijah, "The Demands and Beliefs of the Black Muslims in America," *Islamic Review* 52 (10) 1964, pp. 25–27.

——, *Message to the Black Man in America* (Chicago: Muhammad's Temple No. 2, 1965).

——, *How to Eat to Live* (Chicago: Muhammad's Temple No. 2, 1968).

——, *The Fall of America* (Chicago: Muhammad's Temple of Islam No. 2, 1973).

Muhammad, Jabril, *Farrakhan, the Traveller* (Phoenix, Ariz.: PHNX SN and Co., 1985).

Munnion, Christopher, "Farrakhan Tells Whites to Atone for Apartheid," *The London Daily Telegraph*, 29 January 1996, p. 11.

Murray, Charles, *Losing Ground: American Social Policy, 1950–1980* (New York: Basic Books, 1984).

Muwakkil, Salim, "Leaders Lacking in a Black and White World," in *Inside the L.A. Riots: What Really Happened and Why It Will Happen Again* (New York: Institute for Alternative Journalism, 1992), pp. 106–08.

Myrdal, Gunnar, *An American Dilemma: The Negro Problem and Modern Democracy* vols. 1 and 2 (New York: Harper and Row, 1944, 1964).

Naison, Mark, "Jared Taylor's America: Black Man's Heaven, White Man's Hell," *Reconstruction* 2 (3) 1994, pp. 64–66.

Nicoll, Ruaridh, "Black Pride on the March Again," *The Observer*, 1 October 1995, p. 23.

Norton, Arthur J., and Louisa F. Miller, *Marriage, Divorce and Remarriage in the 1990s* (Washington, D.C.: U.S. Government Printing Office, 1992) Bureau of the Census, Current Population Reports, Series P23, no. 180.

Norton, Philip, "Black Nationalism in America: the Significance of the Black Muslim Movement," *Hull Papers in Politics*, University of Hull, no. 31, 1983.

Novak, Viveca, "Conservatives and Corporations Plug Into Black Power," *Business and Society Review* 71 (Fall 1989): 32–39.

Ornstein, Norman and Amy Schenkenberg, "The 1995 Congress: The First Hundred Days and Beyond," *Political Science Quarterly* 110 (2) 1995.

Ovenden, Keith, *Malcolm X: Socialism and Black Nationalism* (London: Bookmarks, 1992).

Pear, Robert, "Despite Praising Farrakhan in 1983, Thomas Denies anti-Semitism," *The New York Times*, 13 July 1991, pp. 1, 7.

Pearl, Peter and Edward Walsh, "Muslims Accuse U.S. of Creating Farrakhan Plot," *The Washington Post*, 14 January 1995, p. A1.

Perry, Bruce, *Malcolm: The Life of a Man Who Changed Black America* (Barrytown, N.Y.: Station Hill, 1991).

Perry, Huey L. and Wayne Parent, *Blacks and the American Political System* (Gainesville: University Press of Florida, 1995).

Phelps, Timothy M. and Helen Winternitz, *Capitol Games: The Inside Story of Clarence Thomas, Anita Hill, and a Supreme Court Nomination* (New York: HarperPerennial, 1993).

Pierce, Paulette, "The Roots of the Rainbow Coalition," *Black Scholar*, March/April 1988: 2–16.

Pinckney, Darryl, "Slouching Towards Washington," *The New York Review of Books*, 21 December 1995, pp. 73–82.

Preston, Michael B., Lenneal S. Henderson, and Paul Puryear, eds., *The New Black Politics* 2nd ed. (New York: Longman, 1987).

Purnick, Joyce, "An Unlikely Matchmaker," *New York Times*, 8 May 1995, pp. B1, B12.

Queenan, Joe, "America's Most Demented; A Startling Scientific Analysis," *The Washington Post*, 30 May 1993, p. C1.

Rae, Nicol C., *Southern Democrats* (New York: Oxford University Press, 1994).

Reed Jr., Adolph, *The Jesse Jackson Phenomenon: The Crisis of Purpose in Afro-American Politics* (New Haven: Yale University Press, 1986).

————, "The Rise of Louis Farrakhan," *The Nation* 252, January 21, 1991, pp. 51–52, 54–56.

————, "All for One and None for All," *The Nation* 252, January 28, 1991, pp. 86–88, 90–92.

————, "Behind the Farrakhan Show," *The Progressive* 58, April 1994, pp. 16–17.

————, "Black Leadership in Crisis," *The Progressive* 58, October 1994, p. 16

Reeves, Thomas C., *The Life and Times of Joe McCarthy: A Biography* (London: Blond and Briggs, 1982).

Rich, Frank, "Bad for the Jews," *The New York Times*, 3 March 1994, p. A17.

Robinson, Cedric J., *Black Marxism: The Making of the Black Radical Tradition* (London: Zed Press, 1983).

Rose, Douglas, ed., *The Emergence of David Duke and the Politics of Race* (Chapel Hill: University of North Carolina Press, 1992).

Rovere, Richard, *Senator Joe McCarthy* (New York: Harper and Row, 1973).

Rowan, Carl, "Antidote to Farrakhan: Ignore Him," *The New York Times*, 25 September 1985, p. 22.

————, "Farrakhan's Poisonous Journey," *The Buffalo News*, 28 February 1996, p. 3B.

Sabato, Larry, *Feeding Frenzy: How Attack Journalism Has Transformed American Politics* (New York: The Free Press, 1993).

Sanson, Michael, "Farrakhan Means Business," *Restaurant Hospitality*, April 1995, pp. 22–23.

Sargent, Lynne Tower, ed., *Extremism in America* (New York: New York University Press, 1995).

Sartori, Giovanni, "Video-Power," *Government and Opposition* 24 (1) (Winter 1989): 39–53.

————, *Comparative Constitutional Engineering: An Inquiry Into Structures, Incentives, and Outcomes* (London: Macmillan, 1994).

Scheim, David E., *The Mafia Killed President Kennedy* (London: W. H. Allen, 1988).

Schlesinger Jr., Arthur M., *The Disuniting of America: Reflections on a Multicultural Society* (New York: Norton, 1992).

Schneider, William, "The Black Vote and a Powell Candidacy," *National Journal*, 27 (44) 28 October 1995, p. 2690.

Shafer, Byron E., *Bifurcated Politics* (Cambridge, Mass.: Harvard University Press, 1988).

Shafer, Byron and William Claggett, *The Two Majorities* (Baltimore, Md.: Johns Hopkins, 1994).

Shaikh, Farzana, ed., *Islam and Islamic Groups: A World-Wide Reference Guide* (Harlow, U.K.: Longman, 1992).

Shipp, E. R., "Candidacy of Jackson Highlights Split Among Black Muslims," *The New York Times*, 27 February 1984, p. 10.

Shore, Paul, "Farrakhan and the Filling of the Mythic Gap," *The Humanist*, July-August 1994, pp. 4–6.

Sigelman, Lawrence and Susan Welch, *Black Americans' View of Racial Inequality* (Cambridge, Mass.: Cambridge University Press, 1991).

Singh, Robert, "The Congressional Black Caucus in the United States Congress, 1971–1990," *Parliaments, Estates and Representation*, 14 (1) June 1994: 65–91.

———, "The Rise and Fall of Legislative Service Organisations in the United States Congress," *Journal of Legislative Studies* 2 (2) Summer 1996: 79–102.

Smith, Robert, "Black Power and the Transformation From Protest to Politics," *Political Science Quarterly* 96 (3) 1981: 431–43.

Smith, Tom W., "Changing Racial Labels: From 'Colored' to 'Negro' to 'African American'," *Public Opinion Quarterly* 56 (4) Winter 1992: 496–515.

Sniderman, Paul, Philip Tetlock, and Edward G. Carmines, eds., *Prejudice, Politics, and the American Dilemma* (Stanford: Stanford University Press, 1993).

Sniderman, Paul M., and Thomas Piazza, *The Scar of Race* (Cambridge, Mass.: Harvard University Press, 1993).

Sonenshein, Raphael J., "Can Black Candidates Win Statewide Elections?" *Political Science Quarterly* 105 (2) 1990: 219–41.

Southgate, Minoo, "Slavery Ignored," *National Review*, 23 October 1995, pp. 26–27.

Sowell, Thomas, *The Economics and Politics of Race* (New York: Morrow, 1983).

———, *Civil Rights: Rhetoric or Reality?* (New York: Quill, 1984).

Spitzer, Robert J., *The Politics of Gun Control* (Chatham, N.J.: Chatham House, 1995).

Stanfield, Rochelle, "Black Frustration," *National Journal*, 16 May 1992, pp. 1162–66.

Steele, Shelby, *The Content of Our Character* (New York: St. Martin's Press, 1990).

Stern, Kenneth S., *Farrakhan and Jews in the 1990s* (New York: Institute of Human Relations, 1994).

Stevens, William K., "The Muslims Keep the Lid on Drugs in Capital: The Dealers Simply Move to Another Area," *The New York Times*, 26 September 1988, p. 8.

Stodghill, Ron, "Farrakhan's Three-Year Plan," *Business Week,* 13 March 1995, p. 40.

Stone, Chuck, "Black Politics: Third Force, Third Party or Third-Class Influence?," *Black Scholar* 1 (2) 1969: 8–13.

Suall, Erwin, "Look Who's In Farrakhan's Corner," *ADL Bulletin,* 42 (10) December 1985.

Sullivan, Andrew, "Call to Harm: the Hateful Oratory of Minister Farrakhan," *The New Republic* 203, 23 (1990), pp. 13–15.

Swain, Carol M., *Black Faces, Black Interests: the Representation of African Americans in Congress* (Cambridge, Mass.: Harvard University Press, 1993).

Tate, Katherine, *From Protest to Politics: The New Black Voters in American Elections* (Cambridge, Mass.: Harvard University Press, 1993).

Terry, Don, "Shabazz Case: A Gain for Farrakhan," *The New York Times,* 3 May 1995, pp. A15, B8.

———, "In the End, Farrakhan Has His Day in the Sun," *The New York Times,* 17 October 1995, p. A19.

Thomas, Christopher, "The Man Who Haunts Jesse Jackson," *The London Times,* 8 August 1984, p. 6.

———, "Idol Who Strikes Terror into Whites," *The London Times,* 26 March 1985, p. 5.

———, "Black Radical Taunts U.S. Jews with 'God's Oven' Gibe," *The London Times,* 10 October 1985, p. 7.

T'Shaka, Oba, *The Political Legacy of Malcolm X* (Chicago: Third World Press, 1983).

Turque, Bill, Vern E. Smith, and John McCormick, "Playing a Different Tune: Louis Farrakhan Is Trying to Reach Out to the White Mainstream," *Newsweek* 121, 28 June 1993, p. 30.

Tyler, Lawrence L., "The Protestant Ethic Among the Black Muslims," *Phylon,* 27 (1) 1966: 5–14.

Van Deburg, William L., *New Day in Babylon: The Black Power Movement and American Culture, 1965–1975* (Chicago: University of Chicago Press, 1992).

Vincent, Theodore G., *Black Power and the Garvey Movement* (San Francisco: University of California Press, 1972).

Walker, Martin, "America's Great Divide Widens," *The Guardian* 2, September 1995, p. 25.

Walker, Sheila S., "The Black–Jewish Paradox: Ambivalence of U.S. Race Feeling," *Patterns of Prejudice* 7 (3) 1973: 19–24.

Wallace, Mike and Louis Lomax, "The Hate that Hate Produced," Newsbeat, WNTA-TV, 10 July 1959.

Walsh, Edward, "Farrakhan Says U.S. Concocted Plot Charge," *The Washington Post,* 18 January 1995, p. A3.

Walsh, Kenneth T., "The New Drug Vigilantes," *U.S. & World Report,* 9 May 1988, p. 20.

Walters, Ronald W., "Strategy for 1976: A Black Political Party," *Black Scholar* 7 (2) 1975: 8–19.

———, *Black Presidential Politics in America: A Strategic Approach* (New York: State University of New York Press, 1988).

———, "The American Crisis of Credibility and the 1988 Jesse Jackson Campaign," *Black Scholar* 20 (2) March/April 1988: 31–44.

Walton, Hanes, *Invisible Politics: Black Political Behavior* (New York: State University of New York Press, 1985).

Washington, James Melvin, "Jesse Jackson and the Symbolic Politics of Black Christendom," *Annals of the American Academy of Political and Social Science*, 480, July 1985: 89–105.

Watson, Denton L., "Chavis's NAACP: Embracing Farrakhan," *The Washington Post*, 29 June 1994, p. A23.

Weisbord, Robert, *Genocide? Birth Control and the Black American* (Westport: Greenwood Press, 1975).

Weiss, Nancy, *Farewell to the Party of Lincoln: Black Politics in the Age of FDR* (Princeton: Princeton University Press, 1983).

West, Cornel, *Race Matters* (Boston: Beacon Press, 1993).

———, "Learning to Talk of Race," in *Reading Rodney King/Reading Urban Uprising*, ed. Robert Gooding-Williams (New York: Routledge, 1993), pp. 255–60

Whalen, Charles and Barbara Whalen, *The Longest Debate: A Legislative History of the 1964 Civil Rights Act* (New York: New American Library, 1985).

Wheen, Francis, "Voice of Islam," *The Guardian*, 8 November 1995, Sec. 2, p. 7.

White, Byron, Jerry Thomas, and Shirley Salemy, "Farrakhan Defends World Tour," *Chicago Tribune*, 26 February 1996, p. 1.

White, John, *Black Leadership in America: From Booker T. Washington to Jesse Jackson*, 2nd ed. (London: Longman, 1990).

White, R. X., "Minister Ava Muhammad: An Inspiration for Black Women," *The Final Call*, 27 January 1992, p. 17

Wilentz, Sean, "Backward March," *The New Republic*, 6 November 1995, pp. 16–18.

Williams, Juan, *Eyes on the Prize: America's Civil Rights Years, 1954–1965* (New York: Viking-Penguin, 1987)

———, "The Farrakhan Paralysis: How the Demagogues of the Disenfranchised Are Silencing Black Leaders," *The Washington Post*, 13 February 1994, p. C2.

———, "Hiding from this Rage Is Harmful," *International Herald Tribune*, 18 February 1994, p. 7.

———, "President Colin Powell?" *Reconstruction* 2 (3) 1994, pp. 67–78.

Williams, Walter, *The State Against Blacks* (New York: McGraw-Hill, 1982).

Wills, Garry, "The Militias," *The New York Review of Books*, 10 August 1995, pp. 50–55.

Wilson, William Julius, *The Declining Significance of Race* (New York: McGraw-Hill, 1978).

———, *The Truly Disadvantaged: The Inner City, the Underclass, and Public Policy* (Chicago: University of Chicago Press, 1987).

————, "The Underclass: Issues, Perspectives, and Public Policy," in "The Ghetto Underclass: Social Science Perspectives," *Annals of the American Academy of Political and Social Science* 501 (January 1989).

Wines, Michael, "Farrakhan Is Bitterly Denounced by House Black Caucus Member," *The New York Times*, 5 February 1994, pp. 1, 7.

Wright, Lynda, "Farrakhan's Mission: Fighting the Drug War—His Way,"*Newsweek*, 19 March 1990, p. 25.

Wright, Stuart A., *Armageddon at Waco: Critical Perspectives on the Branch Davidian Conflict* (Chicago: University of Chicago Press, 1995).

Wolfenstein, Eugene Victor, *The Victims of Democracy: Malcolm X and the Black Revolution* (London: Free Association Books, 1989).

Wood, Joe, ed., *Malcolm X: In Our Own Image* (New York: Anchor Books, 1994).

X, Malcolm, and Alex Haley, *The Autobiography of Malcolm X* (New York: Penguin Books, 1968).

Index